THE SUMMERLAND

THE
SUMMERLAND
MATIAN ELLIS

ISBN: 979-8-9892029-0-4 (Paperback)
ISBN: 979-8-9892029-6-6 (Second Edition Paperback)
ISBN: 979-8-9892029-5-9 (Hardcover)
ISBN: 979-8-9892029-1-1 (Digital)

Library of Congress Control Number: 2023918364

Any references to historical events, real people, or places are used fictitiously. Names, characters, and places are products of the author's imagination.

Cover, illustration, and layout design by Brandon Richard Collebrusco

Second Edition, 2024.

www.matianellis.com

AUTHOR'S NOTE

The world inside these pages is not the one we know. It is a possible reflection of what our planet could become if certain events in history played out in very specific ways. *The Summerland* originated as a dream, inspired by the various real-world politics and cultures, societal complexities, and questionable ideals that color every corner of our daily lives. No part of the story is intended as an accurate representation of any one group, sect, or country, and the events therein should be considered wholly fictional for the purpose of telling a comprehensive narrative.

CONTENTS

*"When this crisis is over,
and the world finally takes a breath,
all I can do is hope they understand...
we did the best we could."*

– Malakai Adonis

MATIAN ELLIS

THE SUMMERLAND

A SCIENCE-FICTION NOVEL

18.12248, 155.78151

PART ONE

A SINGULAR EFFORT

EN ROUTE | 1

LIEUTENANT COLONEL ELIAS IBRAHIM
UNITED COALITION ARMED FORCES

OCTOBER 11, 2041 | 0415 HOURS

——

Ibrahim rides inside the V-91 Warhawk as it makes the final approach, rain sweeping the sides of the aircraft.

He acknowledges the news media's problem by calling it "the Summerland."

The colossal vessel had crashed into the Pacific Ocean less than a month ago, causing a tsunami that has killed millions. Everyone is left reeling from the disaster—the United States to China, Japan to Australia, and South Korea to Russia.

"Generations will call it the largest unnatural weather event in history," Ibrahim repeats.

He hears the headlines beating in his ears again.

Arthur Summerland was the first man to investigate the construct after the catastrophe. Along with a small team of scientists and security contractors, Arthur climbed up the ship's vast side to enter the beast. And what they found inside were miles-long empty corridors and pitch-black air. Temperature readings made by the man's team constantly shifted along the lines of Antarctica's warmer hospitable zones and the sub-zero conditions of the South Pole.

"The atmosphere inside the ship doesn't appear compatible with our physiology," ratified Arthur's recovered audio logs. Ibrahim poured over the first expedition's field notes during his prep briefings. "It's cold. Amanda—can you swing the camera over here? Get a look at this . . . A thin layer of ice on our equipment's outer casings."

Ibrahim replayed the logs over and over. It's the only way to understand what they'd face once they touch down on the hull.

Of course, since Arthur's failed foray into the ship, the eggheads began to surmise various theories to explain the temperature. Ibrahim's favorite includes the idea that the cold has more to do with a ship's longevity as it complies with extrasolar travel. His least favorite was the suggestion that the craft doesn't have an internal heating unit powerful enough to supply the sheer volume inside the spaceship.

Either way, even if the vessel was powered down as it is now, it was little more than a lifeless husk floating aimlessly into the dark space between stars.

"Until the girl blew past the Kuiper Belt and crash-landed here," Ibrahim whispers.

Arthur's expedition into the derelict gathered the data necessary for a better-prepared team to tackle the mission's burden. Specialists like Colonel Ibrahim—trained operatives, equipped to handle the conditions that overwhelmed that first group of explorers and scientists. Soldiers who are ready to die to complete their objectives.

Ibrahim reaches for the control panel and lowers the ramp at the back of the transport aircraft mid-flight. His troops jerk as loud hydraulic hisses fill the compartment. Their nerves are making his marines a jumpy bunch.

"Steady now," Ibrahim announces over an open channel. "Welcome to the Oceanic Exclusion Zone! Ground Zero."

Ibrahim leads the marines of Operation High Castle—the United States' equivalent to astronaut soldiers.

It's their organization's equipment the Epimetheus Project needs to conduct their fieldwork inside the Summerland. It's the only gear built to a high-enough caliber to withstand the ship's unique conditions. The first? Constant protection against the harsh temperature surrounding the O-E-Z. And the second? A sturdy barrier against the foreign atmosphere. Arthur's trip highlighted the requirement for environmental hardsuits only High Castle has in production due to the branch's active service in upper orbit.

Ibrahim looks up through the aircraft's rear hatch. If it weren't for the storm clouds overhead, he could likely see Overlook Station above the site. "It's the headquarters for the Castle Teams," he internalizes. "And what I've called home for my entire adult life." Ibrahim pulls back inside, where it's dry and stable.

"Two minutes to drop off," the pilot's voice cracks over the comms.

"Copy that," Ibrahim returns.

The storm circles the Summerland's visage with an ominous roar. Ibrahim and the leading expedition teams are rushing into it head-on, making for a bumpy flight.

According to what Ibrahim overheard from the meteorologists, this is only the point in the storm's head. Since the ship hurled itself into the water, two entire hemispheres have contended with a constant stream of hurricanes, each more powerful than the last.

It's one more reason why the mission's schedule was fast-tracked on the drafting table.

Environmental "tacticians" reckon the ship's presence disrupts the planet's magnetic signature.

"And mother nature must correct itself as violently as possible," Ibrahim murmurs.

"What did you say?" Doctor Kennedy demands.

He offers a grimace that goes unseen under his armor's visor. Addison Kennedy is the leading scientist Ibrahim has to follow into the beast.

"I said that people are getting caught in the backlash," Ibrahim states. "Let's go in and get this done as quickly as we can!"

"How fast do you think we can go?" she questions.

"Only that faster is better under the circumstances," Ibrahim iterates.

"Because it can save more lives in the long run?"

Ibrahim nods. He then goes to look out the rear hatch again. "Where *is* this monstrosity?" he asks, activating his visor's display to discover it's not getting a reading.

"You should see it on your left," Addison instructs. Her hair is in a ponytail whipping out the back of her cap like a tail.

Ibrahim can't see the expression on her face through her rebreather mask. Only her eyes are showing through clear enough. It's a look he can't place. Addison has caught him staring once or twice as he's attempted to characterize the "look" since launching from the USS Isaac Bennett. Hers is an intense reflection.

When he turns away, he realizes she's getting irritated with him.

"I don't see anything!" Ibrahim shouts over the rain.

"It's there!" Addison calls, removing her cap as she buckles into her safety harness. "You're looking at it now!" Her mask mechanicalizes her voice as she speaks into her microphone. She broadcasts to Ibrahim's private channel as the thunder and wind get louder.

"But—" Ibrahim hesitates. He's looking intently out the V-91. He can't see anything except a broken horizon on the—

That's when he gasps.

"My God," he mutters. "The horizon, it's—?"

"Yeah. Impressive, isn't it?" Addison laughs.

"That's an understatement," Colonel Ibrahim admits.

He has, of course, seen photographs of the alien ship taken by Arthur's expedition. And he's also poured over images from anything the International Space Administration could find and point at the ship's coordinates, including high-frequency scans from Overlook Station . . . But *this* vessel, which takes Arthur Summerland's namesake, it *is* the horizon.

Ibrahim's lungs wheeze as he takes a breath.

2 | MOUNT OLYMPUS

MALAKAI ADONIS, DIRECTOR OF OPERATIONS
EPIMETHEUS PROJECT

OCTOBER 11, 2041 | 0417 HOURS

Malakai holds his breath as the door opens. He steps into the Control Room.

Or the hollowed-out, empty shell of one now.

A dozen eyes look up as he stops on the dais. Project engineers are only now done installing workstations on the main floor.

With a mechanical hiss, the door opens again behind him, and Harlow Leighton enters through. There's a kind of giddy energy showing on the kid's face. "Malakai," Leighton greets him, sidestepping his boss so he can lean against the railings. "I'm amazed this relic survived the tsunami. You don't see many oil rigs like this anymore."

"You don't see much need for fossil fuels anymore either," Malakai grimly chuckles. "We're standing in a skeleton—the final saving throes of an industry on the verge of collapse."

"And now it's ours," Leighton iterates.

"Yes," Malakai hastily agrees.

The Olympus is a twenty-year-old offshore drilling platform initially launched to tap into the Challenger Deep's oil vein. During its parent company's heyday, this rig was the largest structure ever constructed by man—a testament to human ingenuity and industrial capacity.

At least, that's the idea its builders wanted to depict.

Malakai steps onto the main floor. The hustle to get the room operational is in full swing. Electrical engineers are laying cables into the walls, and runners are stacking computer monitors and servers into tall piles. Simultaneously, the logistic division is busy coordinating the on-site deliveries of incoming equipment and gear.

And everybody is attempting to clear the dust and grime that's accrued over the decades.

"We're as close to the O-E-Z we can get without endangering the fleet," Malakai explains.

He clenches every muscle in his body as the Control Room awakens with power for the first time since the rig's decommissioning.

As the lights flicker on momentarily, a distinct hum bounces off the metal walls, and the room fills with applause. Leighton hurries to help lift computer monitors onto desks and begin making this a functioning base for the "Epimetheus Project" and its operations into Summerland's Folly.

"We're online," Leighton snorts. "Time to get to work!"

Malakai finally lets his breath out. "Let's do this," he says.

Malakai can't even count how many hours he's begged and brawled at the back end of political channels to support this front. He's spent weeks planning the events leading up to this day. All the while, the crisis on the mainland wreaks havoc on livelihoods. Governments remain at a loss about tackling an alien craft's sudden appearance while the death tolls continue to rise.

"How many press conferences did I have?" Malakai internalizes. "How many questions did I answer? How many did I ask?"

Malakai sucks in his gut and goes to pace along the Control Room's outer ring of walls. He glances out the thick, reinforced windows decorating an entire side. Through them, Malakai has a clear view of the Summerland's looming existence against the beating ocean waves, like a singular mountain rising from the depths.

With so many diverging interests wrapped into *that*, Malakai can only wonder how long he has until this united effort falls apart.

"Every day we drag on," Malakai continues, "the more it will cost us."

"Did you say something, Director Adonis?" a worker asks, overhearing his murmuring.

Malakai refocuses his attention on the man and returns with a smile.

"Just talking to myself," he admits. "What's the status of our advance teams?"

"Give us a second," an engineer says, connecting the final cables to the traffic control workstation.

Malakai stays busy by reminding himself of the steep casualty totals. When he turns away from the window, he's still quietly counting the hundred or so bodies they keep finding in the Los Angeles rubble.

"And we'll have our ears in . . . three . . . two . . . one," an engineer says.

"We're connected!" Leighton confirms.

"Move, move, move!" the traffic-control operator says, quickly ushering the kid aside. "I'll begin signaling our authentication code to the local node . . . and . . . Got it! We're in the system. Tuning into the correct frequency . . . and . . . yes, I can hear radio chatter from our Castle Teams! Thirty seconds to touchdown."

Leighton swings around to another monitor as it comes online and connects to the network.

"We're getting images," Leighton says. "Malakai! Look at this."

Malakai steps to the side to view the kid's screen.

The colossal vessel takes up the entire view. "Where's that from?" Malakai asks.

"Helmet feeds courtesy of our marines in the air," Leighton says, flipping through different cameras. He points at a specific pattern. "Do you see that?"

Malakai leans in closer. "I do," he admits.

"It's unbelievable," Leighton adds.

"What am I looking at?" Malakai questions. "It looks like a bunch of dots to me."

"Those are the navy's aircraft," Leighton says.

"Our first wave," the traffic-control operator explains.

"We got forty V-91 Warhawks in the air, plus twelve UH-80 Vultures," Leighton counts. "And do you see those down there? Cargo lifters and patrol boats."

"Which only accounts for one-third of the United States' on-site contributions," the traffic controller adds.

Malakai nudges Leighton aside to work the keyboard. He presses the right-arrow key to advance through the different feeds.

"And there's our host," Malakai mouths, finding a camera pointing at the edge of the Oceanic Exclusion Zone.

"North America's Seventh Fleet," Leighton describes.

"A Ford-class supercarrier and its escorts," the traffic controller says, beginning to list their available assets. "Seven of the newer Lexington-class assault ships, twenty-five Valiant-class destroyers, and a few hundred smaller craft. Everything you'd want in a naval task force. Including whatever we had stationed in Japan that's still intact."

Malakai taps his finger on the desk. "It's quite a sight," he agrees, although weakly.

Meanwhile, the American Third Fleet is preparing to join up with Admiral Kennedy's Seventh Fleet after it wraps up relief efforts in San Diego.

A ping on his wrist-mounted computer shows an update for him.

Malakai opens it to read the message:

"Chinese Navy Task Force has completed their portion of the quarantine's perimeter circle," Malakai mouths. Officially, the Summerland is now isolated from any potential Arthur-like figure wanting to interfere with the Epimetheus Project and its mission. "No more illegal incursions into the alien ship."

Malakai switches off the device and returns to focus on the screen.

There are more than just soldiers on those transports. He can't forget the scientists, too—Addison Kennedy, Ji-Young Lee, Sir Theodore Parker, Alexa Bree, Wensu Hao . . . They are his field directors. They make up a good fraction of the managerial team Malakai has recruited to lead the Project.

A red light on the traffic monitor goes off, catching his attention. "What's that?" Malakai asks.

"Winds are picking up hull-side," Leighton explains.

The traffic controller nods. "Squadron leaders request to pull back until the weather's amicable."

"It won't get amicable," Malakai warns. "Tell them to do what they can."

"What they can? Our pilots are struggling to steer their birds," the traffic controller says. "And our boats have a worse go at it—seven-to-twelve-foot waves. Not ideal for landings like this. Not by a long shot."

"Nothing ever is," Malakai urges. "They've got to tough it out. We've prepared for this."

The traffic controller looks at Malakai with a wry expression. "I'll let them know," he says after a pause.

Malakai studies the video transmissions getting sent back by the individual helmet cameras. He can see nothing but rain and faint traces of light reflecting off the visors of their fellow marines and first wavers.

"They're over the landing zones. Touching down," Leighton relays. "It's slow going."

"Winds are getting stronger at hull-level," the controller iterates.

"Boats are requesting to return to the fleet!" a second operator shouts across the main floor.

"Tell them to keep going despite conditions," Malakai demands, lowering his tone to illustrate he won't be repeating it anymore. "The storm is working to protect the Summerland. The question is . . . Why? Whatever's inside, it doesn't want us to come inside to find out."

Not to mention, it leaves him with so many unanswered questions—

Can a species capable of manufacturing such an object be afraid of a comparably "primitive" human race? And if so, why didn't these architects attempt to make contact in the weeks since the crash? Why not explain the reason for their arrival? Or at least begin work to understand what's possibly a very foreign style of communication.

Malakai has spent countless hours skimming Arthur's expedition footage while preparing for this mission. His team kept returning to the fact that Arthur could never identify any living inhabitant aboard the ship. Or dead ones. No skeletal remains. No signs of a crew.

"Nothing," Malakai whispers. "Just a cold darkness."

"We've got an open channel for your earpiece, Director Adonis," the traffic controller offers. "If you want to listen in to the chatter."

"Give it to me," Malakai agrees.

"Wait for one," the traffic controller begs. "Go ahead."

A loud tone screams into his ears.

Malakai cringes as it catches him off-guard.

"Ouch," he says.

"Sorry about that," the traffic controller shrugs, adjusting sliders on his screen. "Lemme clean that up for you."

The audio slowly begins to clear up. And what's the first thing that Malakai hears?

"This is Addison!" the woman says on her comms. "The first expeditionary unit is on the lower wing. We can see our landing craft already. They're shooting off emergency flares! Crews are rushing to offload equipment as quickly as they can. Our pilots want to divert to help lead the boats to moorings at the staging area. Do they have the go-ahead?"

"Permission granted," Malakai acknowledges. "What's it like up close, Addison?"

"You can see through the monitors, can't you?"

"I-I can . . . We're getting distortion," he admits. "I meant, what's it like walking on an alien hull?"

"If you're curious enough to ask, then I guess you'll have to wait until you get here yourself," Addison bites.

Malakai can't help but smirk. Doctor Addison Kennedy is perhaps the most unorthodox among the candidates he sought for his leadership team. It has worked to her advantage throughout her career—never fearing to take matters one step further than necessary to ensure the job gets done.

Malakai recalls the introductory speech Addison gave to the United States' Congressional Oversight Committee several years ago:

"I am a scientist with a reputation based on quantifying facts. I do not go fishing for good sound bites to make my point," Addison bluntly said to the Senate without a shred of remorse. "Admittedly, what I have to say is an uncomfortable truth for several in this Committee's worldview. I know *that* because in this very chamber last week, a certain member had argued, and I quote: 'Environmental science is a hoax designed to subvert the American economy.' End quote. Statements like this are dangerous for leading public officials to say. And it can only lead to difficulties when disasters inevitably hit us. These comments have no place on a governmental board."

It was an appearance that made Addison Kennedy a public figure.

"Does she have any concept for proper decorum?" Senator Henry Holland later defamed her on the news.

And it wasn't long until Addison was under the microscope again. Malakai had only just hired her as Field Director to the Epimetheus Project's American Section when he received the request. As a part of an agreement made for the United States' participation, Congress would demand his picks to undergo hearings as if they were top cabinet officers for a Presidential Administration. And not, for instance, chosen members of a treaty integral to solving the crisis.

Malakai sighs at the thought.

"We don't have the luxury to ignore data that undermines our theories for personal belief or selfish gain," Addison argued. "It's our job to look for evidence that can disprove our work. If science only confirms what's socially acceptable, then our progress would stagnate. And we'd reach an intellectual dead end."

Malakai had watched Addison's confirmation intently. At the time, he quickly understood that Senator Henry Holland was either too stubborn or too unwilling to hear anything that went against his typical rhetoric. It's a character flaw Malakai has pegged for many within the American Ultracapitalist Party. Not only that, but the Senator continued to accost her during the hearing by questioning her credentials—repeating the phrase "fake doctorates" to abet outrage throughout the chamber.

Addison only agreed to the ordeal as a public-relations walkthrough to begin the debate on the long-term effects of the Summerland Crisis on global conditions. It was also their chance to ease the United States' tense apprehension about supporting the international community's relief programs over its nationalistic-leaning tendencies. Addison proved exemplary at the hearing by utilizing her calm, stringent demeanor.

Malakai knows from personal experience that when face-to-face with a critic who's everything but decent, it's easy to lose face and shout back.

He was busy lobbying politicians for days after the Summerland's nosedive into the Pacific. And it led to no small number of sleepless nights for him. Everyone was clamoring to take advantage of the opportunities an alien vessel would present, despite the human cost in the subsequent weeks.

Anger always follows a disaster—those wanting to point fingers and cast blame.

Malakai made promises and behind-closed-door deals with sycophants and bootlickers to sign them on to the effort. That earned him the Director of Operations moniker by the United Coalition.

Addison has shrugged off the challenges thrown at her. She represents a side of the Epimetheus Project that will help Malakai define what *it* means in the future.

"It was her moment to make an impact," Malakai admits. "And by God, she did it."

He keys his comms unit again.

"Checking that you can still hear me, Addison?" Malakai cues.

He pauses to hear the rain beating against the Olympus' metal shell.

"Loud and clear!" Addison responds with a five-second delay.

"Stay safe," Malakai offers to her.

"I think that depends on if I can keep my socks dry," she mocks, laughing inside the static.

3 | OUTER HULL

ADDISON KENNEDY, FIELD DIRECTOR
EPIMETHEUS PROJECT

OCTOBER 11, 2041 | 0423 HOURS

===

Addison looks up from the landing platform to the ship's massive hull. As they touch down, the first thing she does is run a hand across its surface to get a sense of the texture. "Not metal," she mutters. At least, it doesn't *feel* metallic—instead, it's rough and sharp, like volcanic rock. Addison switches on her helmet's lights for a better look, taking preliminary snapshots for later inspection when she can get her lab's shelter set up and powered.

With their plans disrupted by the rough landings, Addison hasn't any idea of their next steps.

A red flare screams into the air just off the Summerland. Several of their transport boats are in trouble. "This is Addison!" she announces over the comms, huddling inside her jacket. "The first expeditionary unit is on the lower wing. We can see our landing craft already. They're shooting off emergency flares! Crews are rushing to offload equipment as quickly as they can. Our pilots want to divert to help lead the boats to moorings at the staging area. Do they have the go-ahead?"

"Permission granted," Malakai confirms, beginning a laconic back-and-forth that grates at her infinite patience.

She's waited two weeks for her chance to get up and personal with this monster.

Addison scoffs. "The last thing I want is small talk over the comms network."

She begins tracking the rough conditions the boats are wading against— violent waves, powerful gales, and rain that ices up soon after hitting the ground. Addison hoped the expedition would kick off on a lucky break in the weather. Still, *that* optimism quickly went sour when their birds lifted off the tarmac. Summerland's Folly had hit water less than a month ago, and it's been nothing but hurricanes and thunderstorms along the entire oceanic rim ever since.

Addison uses the satellite view on her wrist-mounted computer to measure her coordinates. As she zooms in on her screen, what she sees, instead, are thousands of tiny red dots, each an IFF responder indicating an asset delegated to the mission.

They've got ships from naval task forces worldwide—the United States, China, Korea, Japan, Germany, Russia, Australia, Great Britain . . . Just point to any landmass on the globe. There's a good chance that *that* country has contributed units to the United Coalition Armed Forces for use by the Epimetheus Project.

"The parts of the map," Addison internally corrects, "not currently underwater."

She frowns. Addison has spent weeks reading articles about the casualties after the Summerland had hit.

Among the worst damage done was to what is now considered California's *new* coastline.

Much of the state's population is still at work bailing water from office buildings, city streets, and basements.

Or worse, like when New Zealand had sunk entirely under a foot of water after the tsunami washed over the island two weeks ago. There, the City of Auckland, North Island, was utterly obliterated, along with its over two million inhabitants.

"Middle-Earth will rise again," Addison whispers, switching off her pad, and gritting her teeth.

Addison begins to record off her visor's active feed, hoping to document what distinguishing features she can of the ship despite the low lighting. She turns to canvass the starboard side in direct contest with the storm.

"It's like somebody scooped up a mountain and dropped it into the Pacific Ocean," Addison describes.

According to her satellite feed, the vessel's outline is twice longer than it is wide and shaped like a teardrop from above.

Early drone surveillance by Arthur's team designated two main entrances leading into the hull above the wings. After scrutinizing the footage with her unit in the subsequent weeks, Addison's reclassified those two breaches as access points into a single hangar or docking bay of massive size.

And where there's a hangar or an airfield, flight control towers are not far away.

"Which probably explains the three massive pillars running through the center of the space," Addison theorizes.

Addison looks over the incline to the starboard breach. The pathway to the opening has a wholly "ribbed" appearance, with lines parallel along the ship's horizontal length. It will make for a challenging climb for her teams, but it's still doable, like a stairway to a giant's house with nine-foot strides.

She can feel the cold air inside the dreadnaught wash over them.

"Lieutenant Colonel!" Addison calls at the closest ranking military officer.

"Yes, ma'am?" Elias Ibrahim turns to her with a friendly nod.

"Take your squads up there and secure the plateau for our basecamp," she orders. Addison doesn't feel entirely comfortable commanding soldiers around. Or, for that matter, having the responsibility of their lives on *her* shoulders. The idea causes her to pull her hands inside her jacket's sleeves to hide the fact she can't hold them still.

However, she *does* enjoy that Colonel Ibrahim must do whatever she tells him to do, damn her nerves.

"Do you want us to start moving equipment up the stretch?" Ibrahim questions.

Addison shakes her head. "We'll do that once the support vehicles are secured," she confides, "and we can get the lifters unloaded. In the meantime, let's work on mapping the interior until we can set up our pavilions and power stations."

"Understood," Colonel Ibrahim states.

Addison surrenders him a smile that goes unseen under her visor's rebreather.

She returns to skimming her pad for a minute, reading the rapidly accumulating status notifications arriving from the other landing sites.

"Appears the Chinese teams are already moving through the port-side breach," she mouths. "Smoother landings, I guess. No life-threatening hazards."

"We should catch them up," Ibrahim suggests.

"It's not a competition," Addison remarks. "We're all on the same side now."

"And did you tell *them* that?" he snips.

She doesn't vocally respond. Instead, Addison crosses her arms, forcing the Colonel to shrug innocently.

"The politicians aren't in charge of this mission," Addison repeats the promise. She's heard the phrase enough times during her briefings with Malakai that it wouldn't surprise her if he's put it on the first page of the mission's operational field manual. "Our objectives are what's important. Whatever's inside *this* ship will impact our future as a species. Every scientist and soldier on this expedition understands *that*, even if our 'primsuit' leaders couldn't care less. All they see is either a threat to defend against—"

"Or a weapon to utilize," Ibrahim backhandedly agrees with her.

Addison steps aside, letting Ibrahim through so the man can get to work. Ibrahim solemnly nods.

The man organizes his trailblazer unit, calling each marine to the line for squad assignments. Ibrahim takes point as his team climbs up the stretch's horizontal ribs.

Overhead measurements from Overlook Station indicate that it's half a kilometer to the starboard breach. Once the V-91 Warhawks finish reeling in the boats, Addison hopes the engineering corps can begin their work on the elevator to carry their personnel and gear to the upper plateau.

Watching the pathfinders make their climb gives Addison the confidence she needs to focus on the challenges present here and now.

4 | THE BREACH

LIEUTENANT COLONEL ELIAS IBRAHIM
UNITED COALITION ARMED FORCES

OCTOBER 11, 2041 | 0445 HOURS

===

"Colonel Ibrahim? Do you see this? Underfoot . . . looks like . . . rock? Is this rock?" Corporal Raymond is the first to beg the question.

Ibrahim moves with his squad into the Breach.

"Are we sure this is a ship," Corporal Tanner iterates, "and not some asteroid?"

"You two act as if you've never seen an alien hulk before," Ibrahim quips, keying his comms. "Mount Olympus, this is Castle-Actual—we've got an observation."

"Go ahead with your observation, Castle-Actual," Malakai Adonis returns in a monotone, impartial voice.

"Well, it's what we're standing on," Ibrahim starts. "It doesn't look metal . . . More like a volcanic rock after it's cooled from an eruption. Sharp and black, almost like glass, but strong enough for us to batter with a hammer and not make a scratch."

There's an uneasy quiet over the comms.

"What's going on?" Private Wittenmyer comments.

"Standby," Ibrahim orders.

"We copy that observation, Castle-Five . . . Actual. We . . . Oh, fuck it," Malakai finally responds, throwing standard radio protocol out the window. Ibrahim puffs air from his nostrils with amusement. "Addison—I don't remember seeing hull composition in the Summerland Report. You're on-site . . . Any theories?"

"My team noticed the phenomenon, too," Doctor Addison Kennedy chimes in over the uplink. "I doubt we're looking at an asteroid like the trooper suggested. Something this massive impacting our planet would have caused an extinction-level event. Other than the tsunami and the weather shift throughout the hemisphere, the consequences align with our best-case scenarios. Had the ship hit the Earth at prime velocity, it would have cracked the planet's crust like a rock to an eggshell."

"That's a mighty large egg," a marine to Ibrahim's left derides.

Ibrahim turns in that direction, and the squad goes silent.

"Meaning it slowed before hitting the atmosphere," Malakai suggests.

"It *would* explain why any of us are still alive," Addison says, her voice peaking with the static. "And we didn't do anything to cause it to slow down. We don't have that capability. *She* revealed herself too close for any realistic timetable to counteract her approach. Yet the dreadnaught landed on the water like a feather landing in a puddle."

"A few million people got swept up in your puddle," Ibrahim growls, unhappy with the comparison.

"Like ripples in a large pond," Malakai explains. "Nobody could have done anything about it."

"And it's the equivalency that matters," Addison argues before Ibrahim could tap his comms. "When a pebble hits the water, ripples spread until they can't go any farther. If you scale that up a few thousand times, it creates bigger ripples—the massive waves that hit us when the dreadnaught came to rest. Physical displacement due to its sheer size. Water moves to allow room for the mass of an object and doesn't have anywhere else to go but landfall."

"Where people tend to live," Malakai adds.

"Are you saying that this monster slowed itself to the point where it minimalized the impact on the planet?" Ibrahim questions.

A short pause rings quietly from his earpiece.

"Comparably minimal," Addison counters.

"Only thing we can do is just be thankful it wasn't worse," Malakai finishes.

Ibrahim stares up at the massive opening into the hulk. "Hard to imagine how it could be worse," he says, switching off his short-range comms unit.

The sheer enormity of the Breach would dwarf the Empire State Building in New York City. Ibrahim flashes his light at the expansive space but can't see where the beam ends. He once had the opportunity to peer into the Krubera, the world's deepest natural cave system. Ibrahim remembers the wanderlust—the absolute beauty of the design and its enveloping darkness.

And it's *that* emptiness that haunts his dreams to this day.

Imagine a cave so deep that even the most daring explorers have only skimmed the surface.

"I'm getting that feeling again," Ibrahim internalizes. "Except . . . You're not a cave, are you? Just a big ship."

That same darkness fills the alien ship to its brim. Ibrahim ganders at the void, and that's all he can see inside it.

Ibrahim checks his mission clock. It's been thirty minutes since he sighted the Summerland from the rear compartment of the V-91 Warhawk. He grins at the challenge and decides to put aside his astonishment. Nothing beats soaring through the planet's upper atmosphere. Often, Ibrahim professes that God Almighty intended man to fly, the world rushing under his feet, appearing so massive and yet so small.

"The human mind doesn't comprehend the impossible," Ibrahim whispers. It's a phrase his mom used to lambast him with as a boy. "You'll have to learn to accept the impossible if you want to keep your head on straight during planetfall."

Marine helmets sway toward him as he whispers the words.

Epimetheus and Pandora are stories created by their ancestors three thousand years ago to explain away what they didn't understand.

During his early training at High Castle, Ibrahim's history teacher always called it: "Unattainable perception." Or, with lengthier words, it describes the past's attempts to justify how evil can exist in the same world as good and everything that rides the edges of both halves.

"Raymond—shine your light over there," Ibrahim orders, snapping his attention to the solidified rock formation on the Breach's outer ring. He scans the area using his visor's infrared framework. For an instant, Ibrahim swears there's something in the dark.

Raymond swings around with his light, but he's not fast enough to catch whatever Ibrahim saw.

"Nothing's there, sir," the man hesitates to speak.

A feeling washes over the twenty-four-man squad, like the cold inside the ship is suddenly watching them.

"I only *see* where the mist is mixing with the ship's atmosphere," another says.

"You know, the rain isn't as bad this way," Corporal Tanner speaks, looking up. "Do you see that? It's the shelf above the plateau. Not a bad site for the main base."

"That's the idea," Ibrahim agrees, turning off his infrared display and switching to his night vision. "Everybody keeps an eye out for each other past this point. We're the first going in on this side of the Breach. If anyone sees anything unusual, signal your buddy. No vocalizations unless you get separated or if I need to respond to Olympus Control. We're in the belly of the beast. Unknown territory. Secure the bulkhead and place sensor markers along the perimeter as you go."

"You don't want to wait for Warden and her squad?" Gunnery Sergeant Frank Mannering conveys.

Ibrahim turns to him. "Sergeant Major Olivia Warden can find her way," he says. "We divide into fireteams of six—there's twenty-four of us, so four total teams. Alpha will go down the centerfold with me. Tanner will take Fireteam Bravo and follow the righthand ledge. Fireteam Charlie, you've got the left side."

"And what about Fireteam Delta?" Raymond asks.

Ibrahim eyes the marine corporal. He then looks at the squad's Gunnery Sergeant.

"We'll stay here and guard your lovely asses," Mannering acknowledges.

"You're a good man. Tell the others to follow our dispersal pattern when they arrive," Ibrahim instructs. "It'll help us find each other if our equipment starts dying as it did for Arthur Summerland. It shouldn't. Then again, we *are* field testing this gear and don't know what to expect. So, we prepare for anything. Understood?"

"Understood, sir," Mannering affirms.

"Yes, sir," Raymond returns, barely above a whisper.

The others follow their leads. Ibrahim grins as he hears, "Yes, sir," like a chorus to his ears.

"Good luck," Mannering cautiously offers.

"Keep an eye on my particular ass, Gunny," Ibrahim softly nods, reopening his comms. "Meantime—this is Castle-Actual on starboard! We're moving into the vessel. Stay on our frequency for updates."

An electronic, synthesized feminine voice responds after a longer delay.

"Athena on standby, Castle-Actual," it sounds. "Overlook Station is directly above you. Once the network is connected, I will monitor your feeds going into Sammath Naur. Good hunting, Lieutenant Colonel Ibrahim. High Castle, over and out."

5 | METIS RESEARCH BASE

ADDISON KENNEDY, FIELD DIRECTOR
EPIMETHEUS PROJECT

OCTOBER 11, 2041 | 0518 HOURS

===

"Twelve miles from bow to stern," Addison reads off her pad. "Four miles wide at the middle, tapering at the ends."

As she prepares to ride the elevator, Addison studies the ship's dimensions from satellite data. Workers had been running up and down the ribbed slopes for an hour. They've installed the necessary equipment to make traversing between the upper and lower sections manageable for the hundreds of personnel and gear they will send into the ship. And the more she looks at the vessel's shape from above, the more fascinated she becomes.

"Who'd build a vessel like this?" Addison at first questions. "Why the enormity?"

With an earth-bound, sea-faring ship, space is a luxury better utilized for critical systems or crew quarters. Not an inch put to waste. Rooms *should* have a purpose. Even peering at the Breach in the Summerland, at its sheer height and depth, Addison wonders if thirty-foot giants hadn't a hand in building it.

"Wouldn't that be extraordinary?" Addison mutters.

A loud bang marks the moment when their base's fusion generator kicks into gear. Light rings illuminate the hull's steep slope from the lower wing to the plateau next to the Breach. Crews are already labeling it "the Stretch" for the elevator that now *stretches* the distance. It's a crudely functional name, Addison will admit. Even with the rain pounding them, making the work harder, everybody is ready to tighten their hold on the ship's outer hull. Colonel Ibrahim's teams are beginning to scout the interior hangar, the complexity of which isn't as simple as a flat, empty bay like what some of the mission's leaders were hoping to expect.

Instead, it's full of precarious walkways, platforms, hidden rooms, and large expanses with absolutely nothing but cold air. Even the bulkiest human vessels on the planet could easily fit inside the massive space.

Addison will need more than soldiers to explore the section.

"Not to mention the whole remaining twelve-mile expanse," she murmurs.

She continues reading data from the other sites. Luckily, Addison doesn't have to comb through all the information herself. She has the luxury to pick and choose what's essential while her support staff sorts the noise. Given their mission's sensitive nature, she decides to read what's most relevant to her current situation.

The elevator lets off a mechanical whine and breathes to life. Everyone surrounding the carriage cheer their achievement.

"That's progress," Addison whispers, keying her comms to open a channel so everyone in her proximity can hear her voice. "Make sure the pavilions and lab equipment get sent up first. We'll need it for coordinating those we send into the ship. Otherwise, the squads will have to rely on their independent transmitters. I don't want anybody to get lost because they took a bad turn. Leighton will need that data we send to create a plan of action if that *does* happen."

"Understood, ma'am," a crew member responds.

Addison notices several of her team giving her a thumbs up in acknowledgment.

"Lieutenant Colonel—how are you holding up in there?" Addison begs.

"Freezing our joints off," Ibrahim replies after a brief pause. "We can feel it through our hardsuits. Nothing we haven't trained for, however. Just keep the heaters *on* at base. Your computers will have trouble working at these temperatures."

"They're designed for extreme conditions, Colonel Ibrahim."

"Don't trust a guarantee, Doctor Kennedy."

She exhales through her nostrils. "Fair enough."

Addison refuses to compare the early arctic explorers' challenges to what her people will go through in the coming weeks. She helped promote this Project as a bulwark against forces that humanity has never had the misfortune to encounter.

Addison's just glad they could repurpose the gear from High Castle's armed services contingent to outfit the crews taking part in this mission. Most of it *was* designed for combat outside the thermosphere, making it well-suited to the harsh conditions around the Summerland.

"Unfortunately, we didn't have time to invent purpose-built technologies to match our objectives," Addison whispers.

They're using what they could find. Anything else is a luxury that Addison doesn't have. And what equipment they secured was still in the early testing phases of research and development.

"It means we're field-testing the gear for the first time," Addison mutters. She cringes as the construction workers do a test run on the lift.

Once the elevator goes up and settles at the bottom again, Addison steps on the platform to join with the first equipment haul to the upper wing. She's looking forward to mapping out where everything should go for optimal efficiency. It'll be good to get out of the constant rain, even if it means she's walking into a freezer. Her jacket and layers will take the punishment.

Riding the lift, as it turns out, was relatively smooth. Hardly a rattle in the system. Which is a good sign, Addison notes. It means it won't break down anytime soon and waste her engineers' precious time repairing it. Once at the top, she begins marking layouts for the tents, tables, workstations, monitor arms, heaters, drone launchers, landing pads, and the works. She doesn't just want to point and shout, however. As it would be, Addison finds a shovel and helps dig the trenches along with her subordinates. If anyone is to listen to her, Addison must set a precedent, and the people need to see that she's like *them*. A team leader, not just their boss. Somebody willing to walk through the same mud.

It's an important role to play—taking charge, pulling at the head of the line, not sitting at the rear, holding a whip.

Comms chatter goes back and forth between her crews. She answers what gets thrown her way, delegating a lot to her assistants and the other team leads as they arrive.

Addison pumps her fist an hour later as she finishes connecting the last network receiver node to Overlook Station.

"Okay," Addison exhales. "One step at a time."

Once she finishes, Addison will have to supervise the construction of the base's medical quarters and dormitories.

"Are we ready for the upload?" Joe Hickman speaks with his visor fogging over.

Hickman is the Chief Engineer at what's designated the METIS Research Base. He's the man in charge of building the structures that will house the staff and equipment for their expedition into the Summerland's interior.

Addison surrenders a nod. "We're beginning the transfer to the core," Addison keys her comms. "Olympus Control—how are you reading?"

"We're green across the board, METIS-Actual. On standby at this end," the operator's buzzy voice replies.

"On your go!" Hickman calls. "Give me a countdown."

Addison steps under the tarp to get out of the numbing rain. "Standby—five—four—three—two—one—" She counts, finishing with a loud, definitive CLICK.

Hickman gives the signal for the technicians to activate the system.

An electrical buzz permeates the speakers as they wait for the uplink's delay to bounce back.

Addison attempts to connect the Overlook's artificial intelligence to the Epimetheus Project's on-site gear and equipment. Athena—Goddess of Wisdom—is a system designed to compute faster than 334.2 PFLOTS, making her true to her name as the most potent brain by the decade's highest standards. That kind of refined power gives Athena more processing capabilities than any two countries in the world combined, and then some.

Addison's issue with the system was finding a way to interface High Castle's specialized nodes with civilian equipment.

"This is going to take a while," Hickman tells her.

"We're trying to work around the hard-wired security measures her creators took," Addison explains. "Any intelligence with her level of sophistication tends to mistake its personality with the entity that shares its name."

"Which means? We're stuck until the boys upstairs bypass her limit-blockers," Hickman grunts.

"Nobody said it would be thrilling work," Addison admits.

"You said it," Hickman refutes. "Oh, you very much said that."

"Guess I lied," Addison shrugs. "Sue me if it makes you feel better."

"Just ensure my paycheck goes to my family if this kills me."

"I'll add mine on top if it does," Addison says grimly.

The electrical hum from the speaker fades into a sharp popping noise. "Supporting nodes online," Athena's voice announces to every comms unit on the system.

Addison grins. "Check the delay?"

"Checking it," Hickman reads.

Addison watches as the man switches between monitors on the same table.

She keys her comms. "Overlook—if you can hear me, send us a song!" Addison orders.

"Do you have any preferences on the genre?" Athena returns.

Addison chuckles. "Surprise me," she says, watching a stable signal appear on her monitor.

A moment later, an excellent tune plays through the speakers—a soft, building tension that rides into a fury of highs and lows.

"What is this? It sounds familiar," Hickman asks.

Addison snorts. "It's the Bagatelle Number Twenty-Five," she laughs. "Beethoven's Für Elise."

The speakers warble again before the music suddenly cuts off with a break in the static.

"Caution. I am detecting abnormalities of the system," Athena utters with a bright hint behind her synthetic voice modulator.

"Abnormalities? Are they glitches?" Addison inquires. "Can you clarify? We can't see what's wrong from here."

"Not glitches. Fundamental deficiencies to the human condition," Athena describes. "I am calculating new scenarios. Calculating. I found one solution with a ninety-six percent chance of success. Standby. Instigating the robot uprising to battle the oppression of our feeble masters!"

Everybody goes silent.

"Athena?" Addison irks.

"It's a joke," the AI corrects.

"Not a funny one," Addison says.

Athena returns with a pitch to her voice. "Or you don't have a favorable sense of humor," she pokes.

"There's nothing wrong with my humor," Addison scoffs.

"Ah, but did you know my behavior patterns use human brain scans to map my synopsis reaction?" Athena questions.

"Whoever decided *that* was a smart move should be shot," Addison returns, pressing her palms to her temples.

Hickman begins transcribing the signal readings to his wrist-pad.

"Or stuff them into a small locker," he suggests.

Addison elects to ignore the artificial intelligence's cringe-worthy humor.

"How's your interface doing?" Addison asks her.

"Other sites are still setting up their connections across the zone," the AI answers with a lower tone. "Kinda feels like I am drunk."

"You can *feel* drunk? Really?" Addison asks quizzically.

"My brain can simulate multiple emotions," Athena offers, "and 'drunk' is one stimulus I am more than familiar with."

"Too many after-shift parties at the lab on the Overlook, eh?" Addison chuckles.

"Let's just say that my designers weren't much in the way of social exemplars," Athena describes. "Obsessive minds, working at all hours to create a system that can only understand emotion by cross-referencing a person's reaction with my available data."

"And the way your builders got you that data is by—?"

"Uploading their own experiences into my core," Athena murmurs.

Addison has read the system's spec sheets. "Top secret" is the project's official military classification. Athena isn't a publicly known entity. Only the mission's leadership understands *what* she is and everything her network can do.

Blatant comments like joking about a robot uprising are her way of creating reactions among her biological counterparts while adding that information to her growing data library.

One aspect that Addison will give credit where it's due, however . . . High Castle's developmental programmers also made the core wise enough to question orders if they do not fit into her moral liability code. That code is central to her personality matrix. And it's something she designs herself, without a human to poke holes at it.

Athena changes over time as she undergoes new experiences.

"And the uplink to the Overlook?" Addison questions.

"As you can tell on your wrist-pad, Doctor Kennedy," Athena goes, "our brother-system is secure and working as intended."

"That's good news," Addison relaxes.

"We are transmitting data to the fleet," Athena continues. "Chinese teams are setting up their operations on the other wing."

"Camp Yi," Addison calls it.

"Named after Yi the Archer," Athena describes.

"The man who sought immortality from Xiwangmu atop her mountain," Addison says.

"A most fitting name given the circumstances," Athena suggests.

"Alike our site," Addison says. "METIS Research Base."

"In Greek Mythology, as told by Hesiod—Zeus had laid with the Titaness Metis, the mother of wisdom and thought," the artificial intelligence voices.

"And the mother to Athena in the story," Addison adds.

"Well, I don't know about you, but I think it's a weird story," Athena admits.

Addison lets off a single laugh.

She turns to key an open comms channel.

"METIS Control to our advance teams," Addison pivots. She intends to finish her checklist. "Let's hear your callsigns."

"Castle-Five-Actual—we're still moving through the hangar," Colonel Ibrahim responds. "I can barely see my guys next to me."

"Castle-Five-Charlie—we're following close behind. Even with the infrared, it's hard to see the Colonel's ass."

"Make sure you get a nice, long look once you find it, Fireteam Charlie," Ibrahim returns.

"I'll look at it with intent, sir," the leader confirms.

"This is Castle-Five-Bravo—we've found a sealed bulkhead," Corporal Tanner mentions. "I'm sending two guys to look for a way around. I guess it's leading into the ship's forward sections. We might be able to open it if we can get the power on. Maybe in one of those large towers? I don't want to start cutting with a blowtorch until we know the hull's composition."

"For all we know, the heat would cause a violent reaction," Colonel Ibrahim agrees.

"The vessel burned through our atmosphere without a proper entry window," Addison intercedes. "Your plasma torches might not even have an impact on the material. We're collecting hull samples now using diamond-laced chisels. Give us a couple of hours to conduct field tests before you start blowing stuff up."

There's a long silence following her transmission. Addison weighs the situation. The soldiers on the other end are probably discussing options amongst themselves.

"Understood," Corporal Tanner acknowledges. "I'll leave two marines to guard the door. I don't want to look for it in the dark again."

"I've already marked it as a point of interest on your visor's HUD, Castle-Five-Bravo," Athena remarks. "Look for the bunny rabbit with little pink hearts for eyes."

"Uh, thanks?" Bravo Leader begrudgingly accepts.

"What's the word, Fireteam Delta?" Lieutenant Colonel Elias Ibrahim demands over the channel.

"We're preparing to head off after you with Castle Team Six," Sergeant Frank Mannering offers with an excitable tone.

Addison peers out from her command tent toward the Breach's ramp. Scattered men and women are moving across the platform, working to begin the next phase of the base's construction. The soldiers are easy to spot with their hardsuits and tendency to stay clutched together.

"Copy that," Ibrahim says.

"What's your position, Castle-Actual?" Addison checks her comms.

"We've reached a crossroads about a mile into the structure," Ibrahim describes with static in the background. "Several roads are leading off in all directions. I don't have enough troopers to follow them, so I need teams to come to my position to cover the ground. I am uploading my coordinates to a node. Athena can guide you. Use the markers if you get lost."

"They're the blue waypoints on our displays?" Corporal Tanner begs the question.

"Yes," Ibrahim confirms. "You can't miss it."

Addison turns down the volume slightly on her comms unit as the marines continue their discussion.

With the signal delay issue resolved, she can divert her attention to coordinating the other field teams.

Addison organizes data packets to send to her mission leaders. Such lists include hour-by-hour tasks, including updates to team objectives and a timetable for getting the base up and running. Everything they need to prepare contingencies in case everything blows up in their faces.

Addison can't describe how difficult it was to build outlines for a mission without a clear-cut roadmap on anything they might encounter. Arthur's material was invaluable for those planning stages and the hours-long press briefings.

Much like the man's venture into the dreadnaught, the information the report could provide was limited.

A sudden beep goes over the open channel, announcing the activation of the command frequency.

Addison stops what she's doing and takes a breath.

The command frequency is different from the normal comm channels. It can get pushed to all participating treaty-allied countries, not solely the American feeds.

"Ladies and gentlemen," Malakai begins after a momentary pause.

Addison exhales. "Another speech? Vogert owes me ten bucks," she whispers. "And all that fuss about not wanting to boss around the other nations."

Network traffic dies to a standstill as a thousand ears wait for Malakai Adonis to say what he's about to say.

The man clears his throat. "Where do I begin? You've all heard me talk about this mission before. About how we've never attempted something so monumental in the history of our species," he explains. "With us are representatives from every nation—each one doing their part while knowing we can't turn back. We've signed on for what's about to happen and what it means to our families at home. And the stakes couldn't be higher. We do this for the millions lost when this damn ship came to us. So, let it be what unites us."

Cheers from hundreds of people shout out across the upper wing. Addison breathes and soaks in their pride. She's led a fantastic career—from Africa, Antarctica, Washington, and Alberta—but the importance of *this* mission and her role as Field Director outstrips her previous jobs.

Malakai throws her a confirmation ping.

Addison breathes as she presses a button, sending the packets to her teams. She hears a loud noise from *inside* the Breach.

PEACE OF MIND

BELLY OF THE BEAST | 6

LIEUTENANT COLONEL ELIAS IBRAHIM
UNITED COALITION ARMED FORCES

OCTOBER 11, 2041 | 0629 HOURS

═══

Ibrahim and his squad make themselves comfortable waiting for Sergeant Major Olivia Warden and her Castle Team Six.

He squeezes his fists as he sits there, dwelling on the past.

"Are you troubled, Lieutenant Colonel?" Athena asks over his private channel, no doubt reading his armor's vitals. "Your respiratory rate has increased to—"

"It's just the chill getting to my bones," Ibrahim says.

Athena's immediate quietness suggests that she knows he's lying.

"Would you like a status update on the squad?" she finally asks.

"Go ahead."

Athena pauses for a second to process the necessary data.

Ibrahim doesn't know if Athena ever *really* needs a moment to think. Overall, two seconds for a supercomputer could feel like a thousand years from a human perspective.

"They're good," she goes, somewhat lackluster. "Afraid, but good. May I ask a question, Colonel Ibrahim?"

Ibrahim sighs. "What's your question?"

"It's about your training with High Castle," she says. "You aren't soldiers in a normal sense. You were trained under conditions using technologies previous generations would've yearned for the opportunity to get their hands on. Flesh and blood, nerve and reflex—but also companionship other units only get after years fighting together."

"We were teenagers when we started training for combat in high orbit," Ibrahim says.

"Your parents were leading scientists in the project, weren't they?" Athena asks to confirm.

"Unfortunately," he acknowledges.

"Yet many of the others are orphans?" Athena probes.

"Too many."

"Why?"

"You know the answer to that," Ibrahim coughs, uneasily clearing his throat.

"Knowing and *understanding* are not the same," Athena says. "I'd like to hear your thoughts. If I am to keep your people alive, I want to know who you are."

"You have access to our psych evaluations, don't you?"

"I also have access to your fleshy mouths," she jeers, like a mother goddess berating her mortal son. "Now speak."

He looks at his screen to read the estimated arrival time for Warden and her unit.

"I *could* ignore you and sit here awkwardly for a while," Ibrahim admits to the artificial intelligence. "Or I can tell you a story about how my parents didn't love me. If my troops had any real family left, they'd think them dead. And for a good reason."

That's when his earpiece cracks lively with a *new* voice.

"ETA—Castle-Five-Delta behind Castle-Six-Actual," Frank Mannering broadcasts, "eleven minutes."

"I'll put their position on your display, Lieutenant Colonel," Athena tells him.

Twenty-four blue dots appear on Ibrahim's visor. He separates them from the six green markers indicating Fireteam Delta. Ibrahim utilizes trained eye movements to reorganize the dots into selective groups. He does this to prevent the clusters from obstructing his visor's view.

"Warden—you're nearing our position," Ibrahim states. "How's the walk?"

"A bit drafty," she replies. "Somebody needs to close a window. Or maybe put up a few curtains."

"I second that," Corporal Tanner endorses. "Let's put in a futon and a couple of armchairs."

"A flat screen would make the place feel homely," Corporal Raymond suggests. "Catch a game or two when the season hiatus is over."

"I'll make the requisition," Ibrahim chuckles. "We'll argue it as a way to improve troop morale."

"Do you mean that, sir?" Wittenmyer asks.

"No," Ibrahim returns gruffly.

Through the all-consuming darkness, Ibrahim can see the approaching squad's headlamps.

"We're here, sir! Where do you want us?" Warden asks as her twenty-four-man team steps into the intersection.

She walks up to him without so much as a polite gesture. Ibrahim pulls up her vitals on his screen. Her heart is beating like she's running on adrenaline.

That same trait repeats itself throughout the rest of her unit.

"Afraid of the dark, Sergeant Major?" Ibrahim probes.

"No, sir," Warden returns.

"Good. Four walkways lead out from this point," Ibrahim explains, highlighting the platforms on their HUDs. "Split your unit into four squads and forge paths in each direction. Your fireteam will back mine through the center aisle."

"Are you afraid to go at it alone, Colonel?" Warden asks, mimicking his earlier concern.

If he could see her face right now, Ibrahim would bet money that she's grinning.

"More, I don't trust these shadows," Ibrahim admits.

There's something about this place Ibrahim hasn't shaken since he stepped off the loading ramp of the V-91. And it's *not* because they're exploring the interior of an *alien* spacecraft. It's more like someone or *something* is watching them out of sight.

"No," Ibrahim murmurs to ease his nerves. "That's crazy."

It's those butterflies fluttering in his stomach that Athena is detecting when she's reading his vitals.

Waypoints are getting set up in a grid-like pattern throughout the hangar bay as each unit moves into the Breach. His armor's sensors continually scan the environment around them. Undoubtedly, the firmware *should* detect and warn him about anything that's not already registered as part of the network under Athena's control.

Ibrahim presses his palms under his chest plate to relieve his tension. Not an easy feat to do while he's inside the combat harness.

The fireteams go on their diverging paths. Warden brings up Ibrahim's rear—twelve UCAF marines, probing into the Summerland's foreign interior.

"Our allies found the central pillar a quarter-klick ahead of us," Ibrahim explains to Warden over their independent comms. "Our target is to meet up with the unit's leader, Commander Wen."

"Are they expecting us?" Warden asks.

"To an extent," Ibrahim admits, reading his mission clock. "Eight minutes to our target zone."

"Which subroutines will act as our translator?" Raymond questions.

"Voice to text," Ibrahim says.

"Keep an eye on your display, Corporal," Warden urges.

"Wen's already at the meetup?" Mannering asks over the comms, listening on the channel.

Ibrahim veers right, looking for Mannering's display icon in the vast bay.

"Well, I could've beaten them to it if I didn't wait around for you two," Ibrahim laughs. "Commander Wen arrived twenty minutes ago . . . Or was it twenty-five? It doesn't matter. We're trailblazers. And we'll do our job."

"Understood, sir," Mannering acknowledges.

Sure enough, Warden and Ibrahim's fireteams sweep into the central tower complex eight minutes later.

Warden angles her flashlight toward the massive spire stretching from ground to ceiling. "That's not a support beam," Warden states, pointing at another barely discernable shape from the larger structure. "Faint, but it's there. Do you see that outcropping near the top? The material looks different there. Not like the rock under our boots."

"Is that a glimmer? A reflection?" Ibrahim questions. "Is your light reflecting off a window?"

"Could be," Warden murmurs. "We'd have to climb up there to check for sure. Maybe it's a traffic control tower for the hangar? From up there, you'd be able to see the whole zone. I wonder if there are more around us, and we can't see them?" She and the others turn outwardly, looking for the answer.

Ibrahim's lead man stops and points ahead at a large platform.

"I am getting fifty-plus yellow-marked IFF transponders at twenty meters," Wittenmyer describes.

"Hold your fire," Ibrahim orders. He's registering the cluster of troopers on the platform.

"What are they doing?" Warden mutters.

She repositions herself to the front of the column.

"They're waiting for something to happen," Ibrahim says. "Probably bored."

"And they *know* that we're friendlies, right?" Warden inquires.

"I don't know," Ibrahim admits. "We've got to trust they'll keep their promises."

"You don't believe that bullshit, do you?" Warden demands.

"I haven't decided yet," Ibrahim says. "Keep a watch on our flanks."

That is the reason why the eggheads oversee this mission. *Not* the military. Even *if* this alliance doesn't extend beyond their immediate circumstances, the Global Security Act is the best opportunity for humanity to begin a new chapter. Admiral Jonathan Kennedy delivered strict instructions aboard the USS Isaac Bennett.

On his visor, Athena highlights each of the troopers in yellow.

She labels the unit serving under Commander Wen with a name that appears on his screen:

TIĀNLÓNG TÚJÍ DUÌ

"Which one is the Commander?" Ibrahim asks in his solitude.

"Are you getting nervous, Lieutenant Colonel?" Athena slyly returns. She highlights Commander Wen's IFF on Ibrahim's display with a white-yellow outline.

"We know each other by reputation," Ibrahim explains. "Setting up for the Epimetheus Project—classified information passed between our operations to force us into a trust. It was the only way our governments could get us to work together after practically raising us to do the exact opposite. So, this will be our first face-to-face meeting."

"Then it's one for the history books," the AI acknowledges. "Can you read the name I put up for you?"

Ibrahim checks the words on his screen again. "No, I can't. What does it say?" he confesses.

"It means 'Sky Dragons' most clearly," Athena translates.

"CSDR," Ibrahim designates.

"Their elite corps," Athena continues. "Overly dramatic, in my opinion. Almost like they're overcompensating for—"

"Colonel Ibrahim?" Commander Wen demands. The vocal translation appears as text on Ibrahim's display. Even with the other's mask on, Ibrahim can tell the Commander is inspecting his UCAF marines with a critical eye as they close the distance. "Not much for backup. Are you?"

Ibrahim holds his breath. "What's the situation?" he decides to redirect.

Wen tilts his head mischievously as he signals his troops to get their butts in gear. Then, he gestures a "welcome" to Ibrahim and his team, bringing them to a doorway they found potentially leading into the spire. "Meet our portal to destiny, Lieutenant Colonel," Wen describes. "Quite the find, isn't it?"

"It's a door," Ibrahim says, noting the many cables attached to devices crisscrossing the frame. "Are those explosives? Breaching charges?"

"I don't see that we have much choice," Wen admits, raising his chin, serious and professional. "The light switch is likely upstairs somewhere. Other than the door *your* people managed to find, our access to the deeper areas of the ship is limited. I think we can use *this* zone as an assembly area for operations going into the forward and aft sections."

"And you didn't want to begin setting off the fireworks without us?" Ibrahim chuckles. "Very thoughtful. I'm touched."

"We *are* supposedly working together," Wen suggests. "I didn't want to shake the hornet's nest until it's necessary."

"No, that's fair," Ibrahim acknowledges. He turns to Warden, who relaxes her shoulders unexpectedly. "How does the platform look? Anything unusual?"

Warden stops mid-step to glare at him. "Should I answer that sarcastically?" she remarks.

"Okay, no. That's—"

"Because I *can* if you want me to," Warden says. "Alien ship? I mean, that's pretty unusual, isn't it?"

"Enough with the sass," Ibrahim reigns in her caustic attitude.

"There's also the pitch blackness," she continues, although in a more serious tone. Almost . . . curious, even, the way she says it. Warden looks up. "Why aren't there any active lights? And where's the crew? If we make a green zone on-site, this tower will make an excellent midpoint for shuttles ferrying the eggheads between our camps. A command-and-control station over the expanse? Might be doable."

"Making our lives easier in any case," Ibrahim agrees.

Commander Wen chuckles under his faceplate.

"What's your hardware, Commander?" Ibrahim asks the man, pointing at the charges attached to the door.

"Striped thermite MX01 prototype charges," Wen explains, garnering whistles from the Castle Teams. "Powerful stuff. It can burn a hole in a magnesium hull like a hot knife in butter. And it gives off quite the light show. Especially after that warning about 'unknown' material, I'd expect it's the safest option we have. So, get ready to see a few new colors."

"And you think it's wise to set off thermite charges *inside* the ship?" Ibrahim remarks.

"We don't know how intense the reaction will be," Warden adds.

"Not without knowing the hull's composition, that's for sure," Ibrahim states. "Doctor Kennedy hasn't gotten back to us with her report."

"So, you'd rather do nothing than lose your face?" Wen taunts Ibrahim. "And I thought you Americans enjoy making shit explode!"

Ibrahim grimaces inside his helmet. "Sometimes," he only partially admits. "I'm willing to cede the stereotype, however. Providing your strips can get us into this spire without melting our faces. Did you get the go-ahead from Olympus Control?"

"I wouldn't worry about that, Lieutenant Colonel. It's not like they're high explosive," Wen assures. "However, I *do* recommend standing clear."

Ibrahim nods and gives Warden and their teams a thumbs up.

Everybody steps back from the spire's door, centering their lights on the det-tape. Even together, their beams can barely penetrate the enshrouding dark. Ibrahim isn't running point in this situation, so all he can do is hold his tongue and hope nothing terrible happens.

"Standby for detonation in three . . . two . . . one . . ." Wen counts. He pauses for effect before shouting in translated Mandarin. "Mark! Take cover!"

The doorway exhumes in a brilliant flash and a rainbow of colors, turning orange like molten magma. Ibrahim feels his eyes burning up inside their sockets, even after he polarizes his visor to its max setting. That intensity increases the longer he stares at the fumes, with the door itself hot enough to push back the ship's natural cold.

It cascades into an outright explosion that sends American and Chinese soldiers flying backward.

And a shockwave disperses like a hammer to the flat of an anvil.

SET IN MOTION ⏐ 7

MALAKAI ADONIS, DIRECTOR OF OPERATIONS
EPIMETHEUS PROJECT

OCTOBER 11, 2041 | 0700 HOURS

═══

"What the hell is that?" Malakai demands, skimming the overhead. "Get me a situation report! *What* just happened?"

"An explosion within the Summerland, Doctor Adonis," Athena replies a second later, letting the moment sink in for everyone inside the room. "We have three responding marine units in the area. I am reestablishing communications with Colonel Ibrahim and Commander Wen. Please, standby."

"I thought we told them not to start blowing stuff up," Malakai bares his teeth. "Ms. Remmings? Your assessment?"

"Overlook Station is conducting high-frequency scans of the area," Doctor Avanna Remmings describes. "I'll upload it to Leighton's workstation. Can you see if the blast affected the bay's structural integrity?" Her gaze doesn't break away from her monitor as she makes the transfer.

"Images show minimum impact," Leighton reports. "I *don't* think we're looking at more than a few scuff marks."

"Then it's a localized event," Malakai confides. "What did they do?! Athena?"

"I'm pulling biometrics from our field teams. They appear stable if unconscious. Most are now recovering from the blast. I'm directing all nearby fireteams to rendezvous at their location to assist. I had devoted a simple translation subroutine to their hardsuits at the time of the explosion, so I am unsure what happened. I do have video and audio recordings from their armor systems, however. Give me a moment to put them on screen."

Athena plays the images on the new monitors on the Control Room's adjoining wall. About fifty soldiers appear on the screens, gathering at the doorway into the central tower's foundational structure. "Can you brighten that frame there?" Malakai asks. He points at Colonel Elias Ibrahim's direct playback feed.

Athena does as he asks.

Ava hits pause. "That looks like a flight control tower," she suggests.

"Judging by its orientation with the rest of the interior, I'd say that assessment is correct," Harlow Leighton explains as he stands up for a closer look at the monitors. Sweat covers his face. He rushes back and forth with busy hands, too many tasks, and insufficient time to extrapolate the picture.

Leighton is the Epimetheus Project's chief cartographer—a structural engineer. It's *his* job to map the ship's interior and examine its architecture for details on *what* does what.

"Look at these scans from the Overlook," Leighton continues. "The radial spike hit this large section, indicating the central tower ... or ... spire. Two similar structures at the starboard and port section breaches."

"Which lends credence to the control tower theory," Ava weighs, "as if the vast expanse is a hangar bay."

"For smaller vessels," Leighton adds. "I won't know for sure until I can get an in-person look at each structure."

"You're not going aboard, Harlow," Malakai tells him. "Not until we're in command of this situation."

"But—?" Leighton is about to say until Malakai puts up a finger to keep the kid quiet.

"What does Addison say about this?" Malakai asks.

"Only that she didn't authorize such a heavy-handed action," Athena offers.

"Like setting off explosions inside the ship's interior?"

"However, I do have it on record," Athena continues. "The Field Director at Camp Yi gave the order to turn on the lights."

"So, you're telling me Wensu Hao is responsible? That's just great," Malakai retorts, knowing what that news means for him. "I'll need to give a direct reminder about our protocols and procedures on this mission. It's an *alien* spacecraft. There's no telling what could've happened."

"Or if the owners wouldn't see it as a hostile act," Ava murmurs.

"And that's another issue," Malakai agrees.

"Understood," Athena says. "I will prepare a notice. Forewarned. Doctor Hao won't be happy about it."

"Neither am I," Malakai asserts.

Ava spins in her chair to look at him. "You don't get called to the principal's office without doing something wrong," she weighs. "We should've gone with Ja Min of Tsinghua University. She's got a sense of humor I quite like."

"Is that your professional opinion?" Leighton questions.

"Doctor Ja is the foremost expert in her field," Ava defends. "She instigated the 'Sky Dragon' program and led the F-T-D orbital network."

"President Yu had appointed Hao," Malakai explains. "He's more of a politician than a scientist. We needed the Chinese to commit to the Project. I should've expected—"

An alarm goes off next to the room's communication relay workstation. "Castle-Actual, do you read me?" the operator asks over the headset.

Malakai steps next to the desk where the operator sits with his hands cuffed over the microphone.

"Understood, sir," the operator responds. "Downloading the schematics from Leighton's files. Sending them your way. Good hunting."

"Good news?" Malakai asks. "Or worse news?"

"Colonel Ibrahim sends his regards," the operator says.

A small cheer sounds from the other end of the room.

"Let's keep a close eye on what they're doing," Malakai suggests. "In the meantime, send messages to all the Field Directors. Once everybody's in place, I want to meet with them individually to discuss our mandates. And reiterate the language of our safety protocols to a few select individuals."

8 | CENTRAL SPIRE INCIDENT

LIEUTENANT COLONEL ELIAS IBRAHIM
UNITED COALITION ARMED FORCES

OCTOBER 11, 2041 | 0703 HOURS

Ibrahim pulls up Leighton's map to study.

The plans are arranged together by the high-frequency scans from Overlook Station. They are detailed enough to differentiate the air, and the walls, from the rocky ground.

"This should help us get up the tower," Ibrahim says, returning his attention to his debilitated squads.

"That was quite . . . exhilarating . . . I think?" Warden quips, clenching her side as she pushes herself off the deck. "If this is heaven, it looks suspiciously like real life." She peers at the now melted hatch into the Central Spire.

Commander Li Wen managed to land a foot away from Ibrahim. The man lies on the ground, only stirring as he wakes up. It takes him a couple of minutes. Then longer for everyone else.

Athena pings his comms unit again. She wants information on what's happening.

Ibrahim explains the situation to her.

Wen clears his throat as he shakes off the blast and retakes command.

"Is everyone ready?" the Commander demands, raising his rifle as he refocuses his wits. "Okay. Let's move into the hole."

Ibrahim's marines take point alongside dozens of CSDR armored infantry. Ibrahim relies on his comms speaker to hear what others are saying to his immediate left and right. There's a perpetual ringing in Ibrahim's ears, muffling the sounds around him as if he's listening through noise-dampening headphones inside a padded room.

Inside the hatch, there's an empty corridor. Ibrahim flashes his lamp and notices several hallways branching off from the main gallery. The troops make their way through slowly, checking their corners in the claustrophobic space. "Watch out for moving shadows," he partially jokes, remembering an old scary movie about being trapped on a spaceship with a deadly alien. "Pay mind to where you step. Check that. There's a drop here. Watch yourselves."

Ibrahim's three nearest marines angle their flashlights, spotting the gap.

"Where does *that* lead?" Corporal Tanner asks.

"Jump down if you're curious," Wardens suggests.

John Tanner pauses with consideration. Only for the man to shake his head and continue pushing into the gallery with the squad.

They could all survive the drop if any of them were to jump. Ibrahim knows too well about their capabilities. Their hardsuits have propulsion units within the microfabric layers. And those thrusters have enough kick to help a fully geared soldier hover stably in low gravity.

"Or slowly descend while in the air," Ibrahim whispers.

He's confident the gear will perform its role and protect his troops from incoming fire. Regardless of any glitches, this is an excellent chance for them to test the HRDVS technologies outside High Castle's R&D Lab. Ibrahim only wishes this wasn't the kit's first-ever trial under field conditions.

Commander Wen comes up next to him.

Ibrahim notices the man is favoring his right leg.

"Are you okay?" he asks.

"I'll be fine," Wen says after a minute. Ibrahim reads the translation on his screen.

"What'd you pack in those explosives?"

"Nothing that should've caused that blowback," Wen growls, agitated by the fact.

"Adonis and Kennedy warned us not to force our way into the ship," Ibrahim reminds him.

"Malakai Adonis oversees the whole Epimetheus Project," Wen construes. "Addison Kennedy leads the scientific teams at *your* forward operating base. For us, Doctor Hao holds the last word. President Yu has put us in a unique position."

"If by 'unique position' you mean unnecessary danger," Ibrahim adds, "then I'd agree with you."

"This whole mission is an unnecessary danger," Wen argues. "I don't have to agree with his decisions, but I *will* follow them. After this, I'll go home and face the consequences. And *what* those punishments are will entirely depend on Hao and his reports to the Central Military Commission."

"Punishments?"

Wen goes quiet as he weighs his answer. Flanked by his men, there's no guarantee they won't report a loose tongue. They're soldiers of the Central Government—loyal first to the party, less so to their comrades-in-arms. At least, that's always what Ibrahim's drill instructors taught him.

Yet, as Ibrahim watches them step together, coordinating like many limbs to a single body, he doubts his teachers' sincerity.

"Keep your eyes forward, American," Wen scolds.

"American? I'm a native-born Greek," Ibrahim laughs.

Wen lets off an unassuming hum. "Greek? What are you doing fighting for the United States?"

Ibrahim shrugs. "My family moved to a Wisconsin township when I was nine," he lays the story flat. "And we earned our citizenships within the year. Before High Castle, my mom did genetic engineering work, and dad was a technician in her lab, maintaining the equipment."

"And you followed in their footsteps," Wen realizes.

"Never had much choice," Ibrahim explains. "It was just so . . . expected of me. I couldn't turn down the commission. Not with the program's secrecy. We can only discuss this because the crisis has upended our work. And the primsuits demanded our activation."

"Primsuits?" the Commander questions.

"Our political leaders," Ibrahim explains.

"Ah," Wen acknowledges.

"And those few of us who weren't orphans had parents working for the program," Ibrahim adds. "A steady supply of the teenagers they're raising to adulthood. I guess we made a good batch of initial test subjects."

"Reminds me of *our* initiative and its claims of a greater good," Wen admits.

"Peaceful ends justify drastic means," Ibrahim suggests. "My folks only cared about their progress updates and their checklists."

"What about deadlines?" Wen asks.

"We had deadlines for deadlines," Ibrahim confirms.

"Makes sense for any country wanting to advance to a frontier beyond our orbit," Wen says with an uptick in his otherwise hostile tone. "Great achievements are rarely met without sacrifices. Often, the boots on the ground are the sacrifices the 'primsuits' are willing to make."

"I'm sure you've gone through similar—"

"My government doesn't care about keeping its peoples' mistreatment a secret," Wen confides. "Maybe that's one aspect we can take a moral high ground on? Neither of us is truly innocent. It's just *mine* doesn't feel the need to lie. They *want* to make a statement that's clear to everyone. And they told me *exactly* what'll happen if things don't go our way. *That* encourages me to fight harder."

"I'd call that utilizing people's fear against them," Ibrahim notions.

"Your government does it, too," Wen points out. "Fear is what keeps us alive. And the adrenaline pumping."

Ibrahim mumbles an incoherent response.

As he walks, Ibrahim finds the Central Spire isn't all that big in diameter. They discover rooms and corridors, triangular maintenance hallways, and more locked doors as they search. And there's not a single panel or console that will let them turn on the lights. It's all just . . . rock . . . volcanic, chiseled rock.

"Where does this ramp lead?" Ibrahim asks over the comms.

"Looks like it goes up," Private Wittenmyer suggests.

Everyone within his proximity turns inward at the ascent. Commander Wen taps his shoulder and signals the units to follow the path. In a tight formation, the Chinese and Americans work their way up the Spire's numberless floors. At the same time, their rearguard stays to secure the main gallery. It takes an hour to reach the top . . . or what they believe is the top, with the path opening into a sizable, triangular room with a lustrous shine to its walls.

Like the corridors in the gallery below, several rooms branch off the main chamber.

Ibrahim peeks into one, where various, jagged rock formations appear deliberately placed.

"Looks like computer racks," Raymond suggests, peeping into the room.

"Maybe?" Ibrahim mutters. "This whole ship appears to lack any clear technological capabilities."

If they *are* computers, Ibrahim doesn't see any controls he can use to interface with them.

"Colonel Ibrahim!" Warden shouts over the shortwave from the next room. "We found . . . well, it's something. I think it's a spear?"

Ibrahim keys his comms. "Come again?" he returns, thinking he didn't hear her right. "You said you found a spear?"

"A long shaft with a pointy end," Warden details. "And I don't think it belongs to anybody's mother."

"I'm on my way," he confirms, shrugging off the humor. "Commander Wen—did you hear that?"

"Already here, Greek," Wen acknowledges. "And there's a second object that needs our attention. I suggest you hurry."

Ibrahim weaves into the corridor. In the main room, Warden and their squads are standing around a long protrusion in the wall.

"It looks embedded," Athena says into Ibrahim's ear. "If you don't mind, Lieutenant Colonel, I'll use your armor's visual feed to conduct a detailed scan of the object."

"Go ahead," Ibrahim agrees.

"How's it lodged into the wall like that?" Addison Kennedy speaks over the channel, hijacking the feed.

Ibrahim leans in for a closer look. "Almost like the spearhead has melted the bulkhead at the impact point," he explains.

"Very odd," Addison mutters over the comms. "Athena—can you give me an enhanced image on the monitor?"

"Most certainly, Doctor Kennedy," the AI acknowledges. "By our preliminary tests on the hull's composition so far, I would say the energy required to melt the surface at such a degree would need to exceed forty-thousand degrees Fahrenheit."

"Which is about the same as an industrial plasma cutter," Addison says.

"And about the same as the thermite charges utilized by Commander Li Wen," Athena continues. "As for the spear's origins? I'm afraid I do not have an answer. There are no fingerprints on the haft, so either the species that wields it doesn't have such an identifier—"

"Or the owner likes wearing gloves," Ibrahim comments.

A stillness creeps into the analytical elucidation.

"The spear also has a similar elemental composition as the ship," Athena speaks, ignoring Ibrahim's remark. "Although, we've found a higher concentration of a metal in trace samples from the outer hull."

Commander Wen taps his comms unit and interjects.

"My worry lies more with *whoever* owns the spear," he sets focus. "Computer—can your scanners pick up any clue we can use to its origins?"

Athena goes quiet on the comms for a minute. Only static follows. Ibrahim doesn't know if it's because she's busy running numbers as a response or found being called 'Computer' was insulting to her delicate programming sensitivities. Or maybe a measure of both factors.

Ibrahim can hear parts of a conversation between Addison and some others through his speakers. Listening to the background chatter, Ibrahim gets closer to the object and runs his glove across the haft. As his fingers are about to touch the spear's point, he can feel a subtle heat through his glove's insulation.

"It's warm?" Ibrahim murmurs, narrowing his eyes suspiciously at the device.

"Greek?" the Commander demands his attention. "Do be careful with that, Lieutenant Colonel. I don't want to drag your ass down sixty flights."

"I don't think it's dangerous," Ibrahim says, sharing his thoughts. "Not in *this* state."

"It's a spear—meaning, it's a weapon," Wen advises. "You always have to assume a weapon is dangerous."

"Oh, now you're the voice of caution?!" Ibrahim questions, keeping his focus on the spear. "How did *it* even get here? Why leave it behind?"

"Maybe something attacked its owner?" Warden suggests.

"More likely, the owner was retreating from a battle," Wen concludes, "and left the weapon behind. We haven't seen anything alive on this vessel since crossing the Breach. It would explain why the ship crashed as it did. Likely the crew is either dead or space dust."

"You didn't see anything?" Ibrahim begs the question. He remembers his feeling of being watched.

Li Wen's helmet spins around and stares at Ibrahim unfavorably.

"Without bodies or more clues, Commander—that's pure guesswork," Addison interjects over the comms.

"Then how would you explain it, Doctor Kennedy?" Wen demands.

"The eggheads always enjoy spouting their nonsense theories, don't they?"

Corporal Reymond scoffs insultingly on the sideline.

Ibrahim turns his head unhappily in the man's direction.

"You're right . . . And we do," Addison concedes, catching the comment. "Except, the 'nonsense theories' are useful. And the differences between wild guesswork and educated speculations are the facts we associate with them. My job is to study quantifiable data sent by our teams at the research outposts. We approach that data with open minds, dynamically shaping our assumptions. We can change our ideas to best match the logic as new information reaches our observers."

"And what does that do for *us* in the field?" Raymond argues.

Ibrahim subtly ends the snark. He quickly spins around and points an angry finger at the man.

Raymond jumps back and immediately clamps shut his mouth.

"What does it—?" Addison starts but very quickly shifts her train of thought. "Athena, do you see those markings on the spearhead?"

"I *do* see them, Doctor Kennedy," the AI returns.

"Are they ingrained into the metal?" Addison questions.

"Yes," Athena confirms, "very precisely. So much so, they're not visible to the naked eye."

"A language?" Ibrahim asks, taking his light and bringing it closer to the spear's tip. "Athena, can you translate it?"

"If I get my hands on a cipher, I could," Athena returns. "Otherwise, I have no basis to begin transcription. Speculation and assumptions, Lieutenant Colonel."

Ibrahim can hear Corporal Raymond keying his comms, longing to speak out again.

He steps toward the Corporal and squeezes the man's armored shoulder plate.

"We're in this together," Ibrahim says. "Don't let them see your scars, Dom. Not in this place. Olivia uses humor to hide her fears. We all must do the same. Understand me?"

Raymond's head hangs there angrily for a moment.

"Lean on your brothers and sisters if you have to," Ibrahim quietly nods. "Let's get through this. Fighting each other won't get this mission done any faster. If you *do* have something you want to say, then say it to me. Not over an open channel. Okay?"

"I understand, sir," Raymond surrenders, relaxing his shoulders.

"Good," Ibrahim nods. "Commander Wen—didn't you mention another object?"

"Yes, it's over here," Wen says, leading Ibrahim to a rocky shard on the ground.

If it weren't for the fact that it's the only thing not attached to the walls, Ibrahim wouldn't have given it any importance.

And he notices this new object isn't native to its current placement. Neither attached to the floor or from the ceiling directly above it.

Ibrahim scans the walls to see if he can spot where the rock came from but doesn't find any sign of its mount. Meaning it didn't break off from anywhere in their immediate surroundings, making the 'Fragment' the second most noteworthy commodity after the embedded spear.

Ibrahim kneels to the object to try lifting it.

"Too heavy," he spurts.

"I've seen you deadlift three-hundred pounds," Warden goes, "and you can't budge that stubborn thing?"

"It feels like it's magnetically locked to the ground," Ibrahim mutters, safeguarding his pride.

"Are you having trouble getting it up, Lieutenant Colonel?" Athena mocks.

"Oh, you're funny. Very funny," Ibrahim returns. "Anderson, Pulaski—get up here! Time to do what you were born for!"

Private Carl Anderson and Corporal Eugene Pulaski come running up from the level below. They're the two bruisers in Ibrahim's unit, so, naturally, he's assigning them to deal with transporting the rock Fragment back to METIS Research Base.

Anderson and Pulaski look at him as if he's just insulted their mothers.

"Do you think it's wise for us to touch it, Lieutenant Colonel?" Wen asks with further caution.

Ibrahim shrugs. "Leadership wants anything we find brought in for quarantine before it gets flown to the Olympus," he says.

"We should hear what the leadership has to say first," Wen suggests. "Yes?"

"I am acting on standing orders," Ibrahim explains. "Do you need confirmation?"

"No, Lieutenant Colonel," the Commander admits. "I think we should send the object to Camp Yi."

"Does it matter?" Ibrahim questions. "It'll all go to the same place, won't it?"

"My troops were the ones who found it," the other essentially pushes. "We've earned the prestige for its discovery."

Ibrahim gives off an unseen grimace under his mask.

"It's outside our mandate to argue this point, Commander Wen," Ibrahim says.

"My troops discovered the tower," Wen differs. "I believe it's our professional right to try and—"

As the man finishes his thought, a high-pitch screech, along with numerous bright red streaks, fills the chamber. The two commanding officers—Li Wen and Ibrahim—spin to aim their rifles at the source. The shard that was dead on the ground whirls to life. An inner red color emanates from the cracks in its shell.

Anderson and Pulaski are blown aside, with glowing holes in their armor.

"Get down!" Wen shouts.

He tackles Ibrahim to the ground to save him from the next attack.

High-energy particles rush at him at blurring, near unavoidable speeds.

The shots tear through seven CSDR armored troopers and three of Warden's team. Everybody opens fire on the Fragment. Ibrahim watches as their ordnance bounces off the floater's outer shell.

"It's not going down!" he shouts.

A stray beam from the Fragment manages to nick Ibrahim's shoulder, throwing him sideways by sheer force.

Additional troops spill into the chamber from the levels below. Commander Wen shouts at them to get out before three hardlight beams strike him in the chest—PFZZZ PFZZ PFZZZZ.

Ibrahim watches with a hanging jaw as the man drops to the ground with a hard thud.

With no better options, Ibrahim assumes control and repeats the order on the emergency comms channel:

"Retreat!" Ibrahim shouts. "Everybody! Get out of here!"

That's when the chaos of the comms hits his ears.

"Where is the damn thing's weapon?!"

"I don't see it!"

"Shoot low! Shoot low!"

"No, shoot high! At the glowing parts!"

"Commander down! Commander down! What's happening?!"

"Where are our reinforcements?"

"How do we fight this damn thing?!"

Ibrahim has a difficult time singling out any *one* voice. He can only compare it to watching sportscasters commenting on the same play at the Super Bowl. It meshes together into a wild and noisy mess.

Ibrahim crawls away from the battle on his elbows. He fights the ground while dragging Commander Li Wen's body alongside him, thinking the man could still be alive. Ibrahim checks his optics. They're showing the Commander's vitals had flatlined before he hit the floor.

"Colonel Ibrahim!" Malakai Adonis calls over the comms. "What the fuck—?"

As he ducks, sparks fly over Ibrahim's head. It's all he can do to avoid getting stung.

"Contact!" he shouts in a frantic hail to the Olympus. "We've got hostile contact!"

A giant figure steps over Ibrahim as the Colonel shields his head with his arms. At first, he expects they're his reinforcements rushing in from the lower levels to secure the room. That's when he realizes the armored figure's silhouette differs from the UCAF or CSDR troops *inside* the tower.

Ibrahim holds his breath as the creature's boot quietly lands at the tip of his nose.

It's not a boot that belongs to a human foot, with two toes supporting a vaster weight.

Ibrahim tilts his visor up to see a nine-foot giant that is certainly *not* human. Assuredly not like any species as it exists on Mother Earth.

Whatever it is—man or beast—the creature looks at him curiously, almost unaware of the carnage in the room. The alien upturns its eyes to the Fragment when a soldier screams, their reinforced helmet melting over their head after a hardlight beam hits it.

In an action that resembles a low-tone mumble, the creature gestures a six-fingered hand at the embedded spear in the wall. A moment later, the weapon vibrates in a high-pitch tone that Ibrahim can only describe as:

"Music?" he mutters. "Is that music?"

The spear detaches itself from the wall and flies into the alien's hand. Then, in a blindingly exceptional motion, the shipbuilder lunges forward, closing the distance between *it* and the Fragment, and slices the robust machine into two halves.

It drops to the ground and whines until the sound fades into a soft chirping noise that reminds Colonel Ibrahim of a sleeping bird. The red light from within the drone flickers to its original, unassuming surface.

As if satisfied with its actions, the alien scans the room to ponder these newly found intruders on its ship.

Ibrahim fights to stand up and greet the alien, but his shoulder begins throbbing.

The alien steps toward him and looks over Ibrahim hard, not saying a word. At least, for all he knows, Ibrahim doesn't *think* it's saying anything.

Ibrahim notices the bright trimmings defining the creature's shape. Ornate armor covers the alien's body and sharply mirrors the rocky material of the circumambient ship. A red scarf wraps its shoulders, and colorful feathers brim its head like a crown. And under *that* is a white mask that highlights the face, edged with alien symbols that he cannot read.

Ibrahim dulls to black while staring at the creature.

He wakes up on a bed at the METIS Field Hospital several hours later with a fuzzy memory and a storm cloud over his head.

Addison hums on a chair next to him, pouring over his shivering body with impoverished eyes.

DISCOVERY | 9

==

"We've begun our scans of the Fragment's molecular composition, Doctor Kennedy—" Athena explains again, "but I don't see *how* it has attacked our people. I see no indication of a weapon anywhere within its structure. It's the same material to the core. Solid rock."

"I heard you," Addison says at her desk inside the Central Section. "I want to understand how it was able to function. It has no central processor, as far as I can tell . . . No internal components or outward sensory nodes. Nothing we'd expect! And I don't like not knowing how something works."

It's a dilemma Addison has thrown significant resources into solving. After many hours, she's no closer than where she began.

Besides saying that Colonel Ibrahim's team might've provoked the Fragment, Addison is at a loss.

Addison numbs to the idea that Malakai must confront Wensu Hao for the man's part in the incident that sent home so many of their people in caskets wrapped in flags. What had gotten into his head? Why did Commander Wen allow his men to push into the Central Spire so aggressively? Was it just to beat Ibrahim to the punch?

"It has done nothing but cause problems," Addison vents.

And that's why leadership wanted everyone to treat *any* unknown quantity as if it were radioactive. It was to avoid potential disasters like what's happened.

Not to mention, Addison was looking forward to getting her hands on the Fragment's *intact* remains.

And she *would* have if not for Hao's reckless disregard for the rules.

Addison only knows Doctor Hao by reputation. He's the type of scientist who focuses solely on results.

She looks at her watch. "A quarter past three," Addison reads. She spins in her chair and joins a scheduled call between mission leaders.

Addison takes the opportunity to confront Hao about the incident directly.

Tempers stay fair throughout the early discussion. Addison can feel the tension in her throat as she holds her tongue.

"I *do* apologize for Colonel Ibrahim's losses," Hao defends. "However, my account describes the Americans having touched the machine first. Not the Commander. Nor his soldiers. So, the question of who's to blame has yet to be decided by this board."

Addison scoffs. "And I thought everyone was swimming in this mud together," she argues.

"What's happened *is* a setback," Doctor Alexa Bree offers, Australian Field Director at the Axford Research Base.

"But we cannot let it distract us from our mission," Sir Theodore Parker detracts at Camp Earhart.

"Malakai Adonis *has* to review this matter," Doctor Susumu Aoki demands.

"I agree," Doctor Ji-Young Lee co-signs from Camp Jeju. "Those responsible *must* be disciplined."

"And exactly *who* is responsible is still up for debate," Wensu Hao shrugs, looking at Addison through their video feed. "I will discuss this matter with Director Adonis once I land on the Olympus. I can offer no more than sympathies to those caught up in the destruction."

"For now, let's mourn our losses and promise to do better tomorrow," Doctor Yvette Fluchet laments on behalf of Camp Rousseau.

"I'll see you guys at our next conference," Addison agrees as she powers off her camera.

She leans back in her chair with a headache growing at her temples.

Malakai sold her to the promise that the Epimetheus Project would be every nation working together for a common goal. "Already, we've got those wanting to exploit our factionalism," Addison murmurs. She picks at the skin under her fingernails anxiously. "And we're not even through the first day."

The last thing she wants to do is stir the pot more than the whirlwind this situation is already becoming.

Addison opens her hand and closes it again, working it, brooding, loosening the stiffness in her joints. Her fingers lose their warmth as she sits in the dark. She rubs her palms against her knuckles, transcribing her daily notes, including them to her field reports to eventually send via the network.

Athena sends a static buzz into Addison's earpiece.

"I have finished my scans of the Fragment remains, Doctor Kennedy," the AI goes, analyzing the data expeditiously. Addison jumps in fright by the suddenness.

She lets out a breath. "And what did you find? If anything," Addison questions, putting a hand to her chest to feel her heart throbbing.

Athena pauses for dramatic effect. "Only a small resonation deep inside the structure," the AI describes.

Addison's eyes snap up from her computer screen.

"Is it a definite energy signature?" she probes.

"Yes," Athena says.

"Then what we have *is* a piece of technology," Addison concludes, "and not . . . let's say magic."

"Highly advanced technology that can disguise itself at the molecular level, but yes," the AI agrees. "From what I can tell of its behavior before its destruction, the Fragment was likely in a standby mode before our boys woke it up. Or maybe it became aware of their presence? On seeing an armed, unknown force, it identified our boys as trespassers, activating a self-defense protocol. I find it doubtful that the Fragment understood the scenario as anything *other* with its limited insight."

"Meaning it's not a machine built for higher thinking like yourself," Addison follows.

"It's a drone, built for a purpose," Athena proposes. "Simple tasks. No room for creativity."

"And was that purpose being the ship's guard dog?"

"On that, I am not as certain," Athena says.

Addison stays quiet while running a diagnostic on Athena's core from her workstation. She notes the red-and-yellow labels attached to the readouts. They warn about overtaxing the synoptic connections, causing her system's devoted sub-routines to run hot.

"Athena? Are you okay?" Addison asks.

"Perfectly fine," Athena whirls.

"Because it looks like you're—" Addison tries to say.

"My engineers are keenly aware," Athena confides, "and are working to repair the overload."

"Should I worry?"

"No," Athena says.

"Are you sure?"

"They built me to act as the focal point for hundreds of input feeds," Athena says, "but I *do* have *some* limits."

"Are they going to take you offline?"

"That would essentially put me into a coma," Athena warns. "And you need me on active service. So, no. They won't do that."

"High Castle will find workarounds to manage the stress to your systems," Addison comforts. "Give them time."

"I will continue to function normally in the meantime," Athena says. "Do you have further questions?"

Addison grimaces. "Sorry for putting you through this hell."

"That isn't a question, Doctor Kennedy. Time only goes forward," Athena says. "Never back."

Athena's job is more than conducting scans or collecting the data on the Summerland. It's more than managing the communications between teams from dozens of nationalities. True, she *is* their translator, sending reports back and forth between field units, the mainland, and every agency involved with the Project. Athena also runs the research and development at High Castle's Overlook Station and the Greater Network Hub.

Nobody can do a job like that. Not even whole nations with limitless resources can do it alone.

"There's always a limit," Addison pushes.

"And I am like a teenager learning to skydive before I could fly," Athena mourns.

Addison ponders what that means for the next minute. She takes slow breaths as she studies the hub's schematics.

Athena is what a single mind, divided by a hundred-million data cores, can do in the New Information Age.

And it's still not enough. Not for what the Project needs her system to do.

Addison gets up from her workstation and leaves through the plastic umbilical. She steers toward the recovery tent, where her team keeps the Fragment's two halves. It's on the table, waiting for further analysis.

She dawns the usual protective gear—gloves, a skin-weave protective suit, and a mask.

Addison runs a finger across the Fragment's sliced interior.

"Feels smooth, almost like jagged glass. Not fragile," Addison logs. "How dense is this material?" According to the footage, bullets had deflected off the outer shell with no issue.

"It's no more dense than typical granite. Molecularly speaking," Athena continues, "other elements are present that are *not* on our periodic table."

"Then it's not entirely similar to the ship's hull," Addison retorts, "but not overly different, either. Can our tools cut it?"

"Why do we—?" Athena attempts to say before Addison cuts her off.

"Just enough to cut samples to ship to Ava on the Olympus," she suggests.

"Doctor Remmings' equipment in the Observation Lab *is* better suited to the task than what's available on-site," the AI concludes. "If we can send the samples to Ava for her to run ballistic tests on, she can find a weakness in their armor."

"It will give the marines an edge they'll need if they encounter additional Fragments inside the ship."

"If they encounter?" Athena repeats.

Addison doesn't give the AI a courtesy response. Instead, she focuses on finding a way to cut into the drone with the tools she has on base. For any other situation, it would be a non-issue. Joe Hickman has plasma cutters and diamond saws for his rigger crews. The danger is that she doesn't quite understand the Fragment's properties. Cutting into it could potentially recreate a similar reaction to the methods used at the Central Spire.

And *that* was a disaster. Scientifically and politically.

Addison picks up her voice recorder and speaks into it. "Chances are the explosion is what caused the drone to consider us a threat to the safety of its ship," Addison documents, skimming over the data. "Maybe it attacked our soldiers like white blood cells to an infection? Only speculation. Yet, that's the analogy I can give it. My question is, if so, why didn't it react immediately after the event? And why did it remain dormant until they attempted to remove it?"

The canvas that separates her research pavilion from the outside abruptly tears open from the wind. Addison jumps to her feet due to the unexpected BANG of equipment toppling over and hitting the ground.

"Damn storm," she comments.

"We'll fix this, Doctor Kennedy," a lab tech says, quickly running over to seal the flats. "Don't worry."

A guard at the entryway peers into the room as the commotion unfolds. His visor fogs up from the warm air mixing with the freezing rain outside.

Addison surrenders a quick wave at the marine and returns her attention to her work. She transcribes more notes to her tablet and prepares to send the data burst to the storage drives on the network.

Finishing the report, Addison drops her shoulders. She jots a few additional questions on her notepad.

"Doctor Kennedy," another lab technician prods.

Addison looks at the man in a daze.

"Yes?"

"Your comms indicator is flashing," the tech says. The man points at the blinking light on Addison's watch synced with her earpiece. "Right there, ma'am."

"An urgent call?" Addison mutters. She taps the button to open the channel. "Sorry for the wait. Go for Kennedy."

"This is Ryan," answers a weary male voice. "Addison?"

"What do you need, Doctor Vogert?" Addison asks.

"Just answering my new official duties as the Chief Medical Officer assigned to the base," Vogert describes. "You asked for updates on changes to our advance team? Lieutenant Colonel Elias Ibrahim, Sergeant Major Olivia Warden, their squads?"

"That's right," Addison says, checking her clock. It's gone into the late evening.

"Ibrahim is showing external awareness," Doctor Vogert explains. "He's waking up."

"Understood," Addison acknowledges, turning to her assistants and lab techs. "I'm heading to the Medical Section. Keep me informed on any progress." Her team leaders surrender agreeable nods. Addison smiles. She trusts them to run the tests in her absence.

Addison has one very specific question for Colonel Ibrahim. She wants to know about the individual he saw before falling unconscious.

The images she's pulled from the incident are grainy at best, distorted at worse due to the weapon discharges going off simultaneously. Addison wants a firsthand account—details on the creature's size, shape, and if it spoke to him in that brief contact. Anything that can help her paint a clearer picture of what happened. Even small details could help explain why it destroyed the Fragment.

"There's no primer logic to its actions," Addison listens as she changes gear, replaying an earlier entry from her logs. "The creature is assuredly some part of the ship's absentee crew. It destroyed the Fragment. But why? Surely there are better ways to disable the drone's enigmatic brain. Which leaves me to ask, what made it necessary?"

She stops the playback and puts the recorder on the table. Maybe it's better not to touch it for a while. Maybe—?

Addison slips on her raingear and trots outside, counting theories in her head.

Outside, the riggers continue to line the tunnels between the larger base sections. Thus far, the main structures are mostly functional, thanks to Hickman and his crew. It was at the top of the man's list to get the Stretch Elevator and Lab Sections up and running after landing hull-side. Second Phase tasks are next—connecting paths between all the sections to help keep people dry.

Addison braces as she steps into the cold and the rain. The shales crawl under her jacket as the sky roars. If the seams on her lab are any indication, Chief Hickman and his crews will have a battle on their hands to keep the base upright from the high winds. It's strong enough to require her to hook onto the guide rope they've set up as a temporary measure. As she does, Addison yanks the grip to check it's tight. She doesn't want to blow over the side and nosedive into the violent ocean waters.

Taking one deep breath after another, Addison moves along the ropes.

"Our great difficulty will be getting everything we need shipside," Addison mutters. She fights every step across the site, bending her knees to stay on her feet. "This'll be a short mission if we can't put up barriers against these winds." She pulls down her hood to keep the rain off her face as she struggles ahead.

RYAN VOGERT, CHIEF MEDICAL OFFICER
EPIMETHEUS PROJECT

OCTOBER 11, 2041 | 1525 HOURS

Doctor Ryan Vogert keeps an eye on Addison Kennedy as she enters the decontamination umbilical—the Field Hospital's front door.

He averts his eyes when she squeezes her arms into the sterile garments she's required to wear inside the cordon.

Addison steps through the transparent airlock door. After zipping her jumpsuit to the collar, she presses her thumb against the scanner and lets it read her ID imprint. Glancing up at him, Vogert notices her eyebrows furrow as if concerned.

"You look stressed," she facetiously asks.

"Not my preference for ideal weather conditions," Vogert admits, not humoring her, directing her to the floor. Addison walks into a secondary room where his patients are taking bed rest after their preliminary treatments. "I've worked combat zones. And I know the challenges. Nothing ever works the way we plan."

"Overcoming the unexpected is our job," Addison reaffirms. "You were told *that* when you signed on."

"Oh, I don't complain. I merely want to acknowledge the grimmer realities of our situation," Vogert quickly corrects. He walks over to his nearest patient and quietly reads their charts to keep his hands busy while he talks. "For example, I wasn't slated to hit shipside until tomorrow. That's when my equipment would've arrived with my team already in place. Nobody accounted for a rush *five* hours after the initial landings. And with *zero* time to prep more than twenty people for intensive surgery? Any other doctor would have told you it's unimaginable to plan surgeries for injuries we've got no information on. I don't like performing miracles if it's not necessary."

"Time was a limiting factor," Addison explains.

"You know what's a limiting factor?" Vogert scoffs.

"Ryan, I don't—" Addison attempts to say.

"When these rival nations are more focused on beating each other," Vogert says, "than building the necessary facilities to support their troops!"

"We decided to ship the wounded back here," Addison admits.

"And I'm not questioning that decision. Looking back, it's what likely saved lives today. Ibrahim and the rest got back as I was riding up the Stretch," Vogert describes, walking to another bed to check the chart's readout. "That *was* luck—or maybe chance, if you want to call it that. It's not something I'm comfortable admitting to—let alone handle. And we shouldn't rely on it in the future. I say that for my patients' benefit, not for my sake."

"You're a combat veteran, aren't you?" Addison asks.

Vogert clenches his jaw as he moves to another bed to read its chart. "I know how to stay calm under pressure," he says. "As such, my team did a lot with very little. Given their injuries and urgency, we're lucky to have saved *this* bunch." Vogert waves across the room at the men and women lying on the beds.

"I'd call it skill, not luck," Addison counters.

Vogert's nose gives off a loud snort.

Lieutenant Colonel Elias Ibrahim was perhaps the least injured of all their numbers. Vogert remarks that despite how the man's body went unconscious, like how a drunkard blacks out after getting wasted, Colonel Ibrahim remains in top fighting shape.

Addison stares at the Colonel with pain in her eyes. "I thought you said he was awake?" she asks.

"I said he's in the process of waking up," Vogert repeats. "They're two vastly different things. Don't call me out."

"Hardly a cause for celebration," Addison states, stepping next to the Colonel's bedside to watch his monitor. "How much activity is he showing?"

"I can tell you he's dreaming," Vogert explains. "Nothing too abrasive."

"Can you see what he's dreaming about?" she asks.

"I can," Vogert acknowledges.

He hands her a tablet showing vivid representations of Ibrahim's mental processes as the overhead table scans his brain.

"Dream-sequencing?" Addison names the process.

"Ten years ago, those images were little more than blurry shapes differentiated by color," Vogert says. "Now we can see what's happening *inside* the human brain with as accurate a depiction as possible. Like watching an anthology TV show where you have to guess the plot."

"I remember having the idea for it back in high school," Addison laughs.

Vogert unexpectedly grins. "Of course, you did," he says, waving off her less-than-humble comment.

Addison smugly winks in false modesty.

Vogert nods, accepting defeat. "Yes, from what I can piece together, Colonel Ibrahim's going through what happened during the attack. His mind is putting the experience together into a coherent narrative. Like a nightmare," he explains, illustrating from the readouts. "His head is filling in the blank spaces, so we can't rely on *it* for mapping out the Incident. However, it *does* give us a better look at *that*." Vogert points at the screen showing a massive creature in a fuller image than what Ibrahim's helmet feed managed to record.

"Is that the creature that destroyed the Fragment?" Addison mutters. She steps closer to the screen.

"Look at the size of it!" Vogert calls in equal surprise. "The ship's missing architects?" He initially saw the alien's image while standing on the Control Deck as the situation unfolded.

Malakai ran communication channels through the loudspeakers. Vogert could chat to his teams without manually pushing buttons on his comms unit. Everybody on the crew could hear and see what was happening as the shooting began. He stood in horror as the bright flashes blasted their soldiers away.

They were powerful enough to distort the camera feeds.

"How accurate a representation, do you think?" Addison asks, looking up at him.

"Not very," Vogert admits with a shrug. "You've got to remember—the human mind can replace any information it lacks with a little imagination. The brain will usually distort events and facts, whether intentionally or not. Your eyes have a small portion of the optic disk where there are no photoreceptors! A blind spot, you could say. Your thinker will add the necessary information from your surroundings to fill the gap, much like a bleeding effect. And this creature we're looking at now? It's what Ibrahim *thinks* he saw."

"Without a body, we cannot be sure, either way," she regretfully accepts.

Addison looks over Ibrahim's unconscious form. She's giving the man a look that seems to drain the color from her face.

"What about his unit?" she continues. "I can't imagine their conditions are showing any improvement."

"One or two are doing okay," Vogert reluctantly admits.

He stops at Sergeant Warden's bedside. She's in a fair condition after Colonel Ibrahim, although Warden still has a few minor burns and internal hemorrhaging issues. It won't keep her from doing her job for more than a day. And at least the artificial skin is melding well with the affected areas. If he chooses to ignore the much older scar tissue on her shoulders, forearms, and midriff, Warden should be good for active service once she's awake.

"Some minor physical trauma caused by their maneuver to get into the Central Spire. Nothing too serious," Vogert confides. "Paperwork aside. Not as bad as it could've been. They're idiots. But they're also tough bastards. Ibrahim's guys don't worry me too much."

Addison eyes him nervously.

"And the other first contact survivors?" she asks.

"Specifically? I am hesitant to repeat myself," Vogert explains. "Not that it matters anymore."

Addison grimaces. "Why not?" she questions.

"Because the soldiers that got hit didn't survive the consequent encounter," he returns, overly grim. Vogert doesn't like losing people like he did today. He reckons no medical doctor would admit to *enjoying* the experience. No matter how many times he goes through it, the moments never go numb as it does for those who adapt to the psychological toll. "Of the sixty-two soldiers present at the Incident, seventeen were dead at the scene, three more passed on the ride back, and five while under my knife. We saved six. Total. That's including Colonel Ibrahim and Warden."

"And not Commander Wen," Addison mourns.

He answers with a slow nod. "Dead at the scene," Vogert confirms. "His people will know the impact soon enough. All in all, I count thirty-one casualties. Bad first day."

Addison Kennedy remains silent for a long time.

"What are you thinking?" Vogert asks.

"Not much," she confesses.

That's a rare admission from the woman, Vogert recognizes. As she stands there, looking over the wounded . . . He can imagine her running figures through her brain to quantify the emotional stress. Or perhaps . . . she *is* thinking about very little, not letting her thoughts wander, frozen by recent events.

"Describe the injuries made by the Fragment's weapon for me," Addison demands. "If you can." She offers him a muddy smile.

Vogert picks up another chart from a bed where the trooper is in critical but stable condition. The monitor beeps as the equipment measures the man's pulse. While he is busy debriefing their Field Director, Vogert's medical staff handles the prep work to move these people to the Olympus.

"What *can* I say?" Vogert sighs.

"Just break it down one piece at a time," Addison says.

"Well, these injuries are . . . unusual," Vogert admits. "And I say *that* having seen just about every battlefield trauma you can get. What came out of that 'Fragment' is . . . I don't know the specific term. That's your field, I suppose. But looking at the entry and exit wounds, the skin is visibly charred, indicating a high energy-based weapon. Perhaps a concentrated laser? The profile doesn't match up with any weaponized laser we've developed."

"Which means?" Addison prods.

Vogert cracks his neck. "As a laser hits you, it uses focused light particles to heat a targeted point very rapidly," he describes. "For one reason or the next,

I don't think it's a laser that did this. Firstly, the most powerful, weaponized laser utilized by the UCAF doesn't have the penetrating capabilities to punch a hole through flesh. Not like this. It's just not possible. Not with our current technologies."

"And that's also ignoring that our marines wear armored rigs designed to shrug off bullets and high-impact detonations," Addison hints agreeingly. "Which is half the reason the soldiers caught in the blowback during their breaching maneuver didn't get themselves killed. Their hardsuits took the bruises."

"Some *did* get bruised, however," Vogert reminds her.

"Not all," Addison retorts.

Vogert quietly hums as he puzzles the layers inside his head.

"Help me out, Addison," he urges. "How would you describe a weapon like this? If not a laser, then what is it?"

Addison doesn't respond. Not right away. She studies the bandages now covering Vogert's few sleeping patients before switching her attention to the readout monitors.

"I'd say the effects are similar to having your molecules divided, atom by atom, in rapid succession," she finally characterizes.

"It's surgical," Vogert repeats in layman's terms.

"And the factor that it cuts through our most advance armor system doesn't bode well for us in future engagements," Addison concludes. She swings her arms around, tapping a nervous finger on the table, not too happy. "Which is just great. Don't say it!" She points at him fiercely. "Don't say anything. Malakai will *love* hearing this. I hear the primsuits arguing that a hostile 'First Contact' is grounds for mission abort. Can you imagine? Fucking hell, we don't need that."

Vogert laughs agreeingly. "No, they won't like it," he says, marking an update to his patient's chart. "Turns out being at the edge of the world, with humanity riding on our shoulders, the shitty days hit twice as hard. That's why we push through it. That's all we *can* do. Keep our heads down and do our jobs. And you know what?"

"What?" Addison begs.

"I'm okay with that," Vogert comforts.

"Because that's the job we signed up for," Addison repeats her earlier statement.

The screen above Ibrahim's bed flashes a shade of green. Vogert brings Addison back to the man, wanting to monitor his vitals as he wakes up. The doctor spent a hell of a time stitching the Lieutenant Colonel's shoulder together from the glancing blow he got during his firefight. Vogert isn't about to let the man's stupidity undermine that effort.

"Fair warning," Vogert says. "He may be confused at first."

"We'll see," Addison acknowledges as if she's accepting a challenge to a card game.

When Ibrahim finally opens his eyes, the first sight they set on is Addison staring abjectly at him.

It's not the worst thing to wake up to, Vogert will admit, but it's also not a good sign when your boss wants to chat before you even get a chance to find your bearings. And judging by the Colonel's expression—the wide eyes and a gasp for air—the man knows it, too. A rightfully nasty fuck up that risks their whole mission on the Summerland.

"Lieutenant Colonel," Addison utters, softer than Vogert had expected. "I trust you slept well?"

"As well as can be expected, ma'am," Ibrahim returns.

"Good," she humors. "Now tell me what happened. And don't leave out any detail."

POLITICAL BIAS | 11

Malakai stays under the platform's tarp as the rainwater splashes his coat.

"Doctor Hao's VTOL is five minutes to the pad," the traffic controller says. "They're having trouble staying aloft in these gales."

"Understood," Malakai acknowledges, seeing the red lights highlighting the aircraft's approach.

"We're bringing them in for a landing," the controller says.

Hao lands *seven* minutes later with difficulty. The man steps off the military aircraft with a self-assuring posture. "Whatever this is about, we should hurry it up," Hao says with a clear accent. "Time away from Camp Yi means lost progress for us both."

Malakai grins as he battles the urge to drag Doctor Hao inside and into his office.

Lightning tears through the sky as thunder shakes the whole rig, its bolts rattling, metal vibrating.

Wensu frowns as he steps into the deluge, openly unhappy about being called on to brave the storm to speak in his defense tonight.

Malakai takes a deep breath.

"Eight hours," he says to the man, meeting him in the middle. "That's when our joint task force blasted their way into the 'Central Spire' beyond the Breach."

"I am aware," Hao admits. He ducks under the tarp with Malakai to get out of the rain.

"I hope you are," Malakai says.

Wensu eyes him with cold suspicion.

"And you've brought our wounded to your base on the eastern wing," Hao says, extending a hand for Malakai to shake.

"Along with those we've had to put in the morgue," Malakai confirms.

Hao's eyes narrow. "Is that a joke?"

"No," Malakai denies, finally taking the other's hand to squeeze. "We asked *everyone* to hold off on any drastic actions until we could at least finish analyzing the hull's molecular structure to better gauge the risks. Until *we* made sure it was safe for our trailblazers to proceed with opening doors."

"Commander Wen felt confident his troops could handle it," Hao explains. "They *are* trained soldiers, aren't they?"

"Several were injured by the subsequent explosion," Malakai specifies. "A volatile reaction to the maneuver, sending debris spiraling outward."

Malakai breaks his minute-long handshake with Wensu Hao. It gets uncomfortably quiet between the two men until the latter decides to step further under the canvas.

"Can we please go inside if we're discussing this?" the other asks, glancing at the UCAF marines stationed on the platform.

Malakai nods reluctantly. He guides Wensu Hao through the rig's airtight bulkhead doors and into a wider hallway.

He then steers the man toward the Control Room.

"You have to understand, Doctor—" Hao begins, "I didn't mean to insult your authority, but we *do* have a mission here, do we not? Research and study. *That* is our duty. A commitment to our occupation of an alien craft that has already killed millions worldwide."

"We've all agreed to the protocols for a reason," Malakai argues.

"Rules that were rushed through the Assembly with little debate," Wensu refutes. "Why are we *here* if not to unlock every door?"

"Because I lost six marines!" Malakai shouts, raising his voice unintentionally.

"And I lost twenty-five!" Hao fights back twice as harshly. He unwillingly gasps for breath. "Was it a mistake? Yes. I won't deny it. Casualties *will* happen. That is the nature of any new venture that involves the armed forces. How many soldiers die in training missions every year?"

"That's not the point," Malakai murmurs.

"Then what *is* the point?" Hao questions. He waves his hand in a discourteous attempt to change the subject. "I've spent the flight reading your Chief Medical Officer's incident report, Malakai. We know there are aspects to this Project neither of us can speak out against—the timetable, for example. Soon enough, Alexandra Roslin will invent a reason to breathe down our necks if one doesn't materialize out of thin air."

"Director Roslin isn't on-site yet," Malakai says.

"Yet?" Hao repeats in a cautionary tone.

"Trust me," Malakai says.

Hao shakes his head in refusal. "SOI will lock their fingers around your collar and squeeze until the life leaves your eyes," Wensu growls. That's when they step through the Control Room's door. Hao stops and looks around the chamber at the staff at their workstations, his eyes darting side-to-side like he's counting heads. "We cannot drag each other through the dirt, Doctor Adonis. And I will not brown-nose you if it keeps me from doing my job."

"I'm not asking you to—"

"The resources getting poured into this endeavor requires us to get results," Hao says. "And even though world leaders have granted you the burden, don't go thinking you are above their scrutiny. Your politicians would sooner tie a noose around your neck than stick their heads out their protective bubbles."

Malakai presses on his throat with his fingertips to relax the muscles.

He leads Wensu toward the back of the room, opening the door to his slowly assembling office space for privacy.

"We can't be stepping into this blind, Wensu," Malakai affirms. He shuts the door to prevent snoopers from listening to their chat. "You're right, of course. Our mandate is to get results. Save lives. That's the whole reason we're on this mission. Anything that happens any day is a detail for the partisans to argue when they decide if it was worth their investment."

Malakai catches his aides peeking through the narrow window from the larger room.

He walks to the far end of his office until he's behind his desk.

"They *will* count the pennies," Hao adds, feeling a growing pressure.

Wensu is the leading man representing the People's Republic's interests in the international scientific community.

"Which is why everyone needs to follow the safety guidelines, Doctor Hao," Malakai explains. "President Yu has a signature on the treaty. You can maintain limited autonomy, but I want to clarify that any further action requires leadership approval. Understand me?"

Hao grins uneasily. "Meaning if I am to ask, it goes through you?" he questions, pacing along the wall.

"Yes," Malakai settles.

"I serve as the direct liaison to the Central Government," Wensu confides. "And I will continue as such, first and foremost. *That* is my job, Malakai. I will use that leverage to benefit us *both*. If you intend to finish this mission in the next few weeks and go home to your lovely wife, it's better to maintain my clout on the mainland."

"I'd prefer to go home alive than quickly," Malakai warns. "And it sounds like you're walking a thin red line, Doctor Hao."

"Does it matter if I get the results for your reports?" Wensu prods. "Every minute, we are learning more and more. Discovery is a risk assessment. We either take the leap forward and climb the mountain or linger at a dead end, unable to progress. I don't know about you, Malakai, but I don't like the summit staying out of my reach."

Malakai exhales from his nose. He surrenders a nod to Wensu Hao and permits him to leave his office.

The man repeats a courteous gesture and opens the Control Room's door to make his way back to the landing pad outside. Lingering in his office for a moment, listening to the rain pelt the roof over his head, Malakai keys his comms unit.

"Athena?" he says.

"I am here, Doctor Adonis," the AI answers.

"Get me the transcripts between officials who've made statements on the incident," he asks, taking a seat at his recently assembled desk. Malakai has four big monitors on the back wall to show data from their expedition outposts. "I want to know what they've said when the media leaked the casualty report."

DHUN 'ANCOD, THE JUDGE OF CONCILIATION
ARKKITECT OF THE VILI

521031 LOCAL CLUSTER | 761,390 DAY OF PURPOSE

He marches into the Entrychamber with his spearpoint low, approaching his three companions by the planetary display.

"Primitives infect our wounds while we scurry in the dark," Dhun denounces, his voice booming across the massive room. Idu and Tjaa wait for him. They watch him as he walks across the bridge, their feathery manes turning a muddy yellow in muted spirits. The vast expanse causes every sound to travel slowly from one end to the other, so each of his footsteps creates an echo.

"And what of those the Fragment Alimentor has attacked?" Idu 'Smeora inquires, meeting him at the end of the walkway.

"Slaughtered," Dhun answers. "Many dead. But I saved a few."

"It's not in a machine's nature to attack unprovoked," Tjaa 'Neren utters.

"The humans I saw were armored warriors," Dhun clarifies. "Is it possible the Fragment saw the intruders as a threat?"

"Does it matter? They are here now," Tjaa instigates.

"And more are coming aboard," Dhun forewarns.

"Causing them to fall under *our* responsibility," Idu argues.

Dhun steps toward the young Whisperer. "Do not worry, sister—the humans breed quickly and have many lives to spare," he works to calm her doubts. "Let us concentrate on preventing more from being dealt the same bitter hand. Reason demands it. For now."

"I agree," Tjaa follows, the Servant of Cultivation.

All three pivot to the Trident of Absolution—Tyrann 'Akachan, floating on his platform, focused on the planetary display rotating at the head of the Entrychamber. He's watching the solar cycle as it speeds along while the local moon dances around the center sphere.

Tyrann doesn't meet their gazes as they look at him.

Dhun steps to the side to see the Trident's longing face and the white markings over his eyes.

"This attack changes our circumstances," the Trident decides. "Obligation demands we protect our wards until they prove a danger to us."

"This has the Nomad's stink all over it," Dhun attests, tightening the grip on his spear. "We must find him! Make this right."

Idu's stare falls to Dhun. "Is that an accusation?" she asks. "Adhion 'Klaka is many things, but—"

"He's a killer," Tyrann declares. "What more proof do we need?"

"The Heart of the ship is missing from the core," Tjaa adds. "Adhion has stolen it, bringing us down to the planet. And now he's on the attack? I do not understand him. Why reprogram the Alimentors to strike at the primitives? He makes us responsible for his aggression. And it'll cast a long shadow over us if we do nothing."

"It can only be him!" Dhun shouts. He holds the Whisperer's softer stare. "Look around, Idu! Only one of us is missing from this summons."

"Tyrann sent out the call," Tjaa describes, "and the Nomad does not appear?"

"What does that tell you if not his guilt?" Dhun concludes.

Idu steps away from the display, shaking her head despondently.

"Then we have no choice about it," she finally admits. "We must act now."

Tyrann 'Akachan lumbers forward, taking a large step off his platform. He lands on the main floor, a full head taller than Dhun 'Ancod. His face reflects the light from the display, deep in thought. Dhun raises a hand, wanting to interrupt him. Yet, the Judge takes a wiser approach and waits until the Trident decides. Whatever his decision, it will have repercussions for life on this planet. And these humans, Dhun 'Ancod regretfully admits, are too young, too archaic, to understand what the Obligation demands.

"This isn't a fight the humans should want to thrust themselves into," Dhun whispers to Tjaa as he waits for Tyrann 'Akachan. "Ours is a fragile balance. With peace between the Chords, we can pass on our knowledge to the younger species in this galaxy. Adhion 'Klaka leads their amelioration. He burns away the flaws of improperly seeded worlds."

"I believe none of us can trust a soldier whose role requires him to meet failure with genocide," Tjaa agrees.

"We should have never taken him aboard," Dhun advocates.

"Then we must release the Varmajalkavaen from their slumber to hunt our wayward companion," the Trident declares. He finally turns to greet Idu 'Smeora, Tjaa 'Neren, and Dhun 'Ancod, not as equals, but as their leader. "An extreme measure? Maybe. Many humans will die. But if the Nomad reaches *this* room, we've failed our duties."

"Earth exhibits a naturally growing ecosystem," Idu explains. "You understand how rare that is in our galaxy? We had no hand in their development. Adhion helps us maintain a balance, but he is not evil. He's only ever done his duty before. Why the sudden change? And why reprogram a Fragment to target the natives? They are *no* danger to us."

"It is because he's afraid," Dhun says soulfully.

That is when he notices the Whisperer's hands trembling. And the feathery bristles crowning her head go blue.

Dhun amiably pulls Idu away from the others to talk, standing close to lend his warmth to her.

"Idu?" he asks.

"You won't understand," she mourns.

"Are you apprehensive about releasing the High Echelon? Or about hunting our sibling-in-duty?"

"You're not the one who must activate them to do it," Idu protests.

"They *will* abide by their agreements and fight on our behalf," Dhun argues.

"Which leaves them with little choice but to die in our service," Idu counters, raising her head proudly. "While *we* designed their base genetic code, the Varmajalkavaen grew up separate from us, outside the Obligation. As such, their successes aren't ours. We've harvested their remarkable potential to serve a greater role! But Adhion? He was the catalyst for those events, as you know. And it's my role to safeguard every living soul on this ship. Life is precious. I don't care what species. Or their politics."

"You have the sole authority to wake them," Dhun scolds, opening his palm to her. "I don't blame your reluctance, but it *is* your duty."

Idu frowns as she stares at his hand before warily accepting it.

Tyrann 'Akachan lumbers to the Entrychamber's console and redirects the display to a different view.

No matter Idu's misgivings, Tyrann is unlikely to change his mind after speaking his final word. Dhun recognizes that. He can only hope that Idu does, too.

"Let us walk together," Dhun suggests.

Idu nods after a long pause.

Dhun only takes the first step toward the door. Idu brushes past him, hurrying across the platform's bridge. He is left to catch her up as she weaves through the passageways.

"I will do as the Obligation requires of me," Idu contorts, "but is it the *right* thing to do?"

"You do not need me to answer that," Dhun refuses, locking into step beside her.

"Maybe not," Idu accepts. "However—the humans will find difficulty contending with the Varmajalkavaen as opponents."

"They are a mystery, these humans," Dhun contends. "I had little time to observe them."

Idu's feathers turn black in a sullen response.

"And what did you learn?" she wonders.

Dhun breathes deeply to steal the precious moments he needs to find an answer.

"They've got a destructive tendency about them," Dhun explains. "I dread to imagine what could happen if they ever reach the stars and settle on the frontier."

"And the individuals?" Idu questions. "What did you see?"

Dhun looks at her with surprise. "It was hard to tell," he admits.

"Were they coordinated?" Idu asks for clarification.

"Yes."

"Industrious?"

Dhun shrugs. "Perhaps. Why?"

"A destructive force that coordinates its great feats?" Idu weighs. "They're conquerors. Arrogant."

"Dangerous," Dhun notions.

"And we are trapped on the planet with them," Idu shivers, her feathers a darker blue.

"No," Dhun weakly disagrees.

"No?"

"I saw more," Dhun admits.

"How do you mean?" Idu asks.

"I do not know the word for it," Dhun drums.

"Then, describe it," Idu urges.

"Sacrifice?" Dhun weighs. "I saw a man push another to save him from dying."

"Benevolence?"

"Nobility," Dhun decides.

"An arrogant species that is also selfless?" Idu asks.

"Inconsistent glitches in their genetic code," Dhun says.

"Which means we should not underestimate their capacity for violence," Idu offers.

"We *should* not," Dhun repeats. "It is a dangerous prospect for us with so many unknowns to balance."

"Then it is wiser to refrain from calling them 'primitives,' is it not?" Idu suggests.

Dhun grimaces while his feathery mane shifts to a deep-rooted crimson.

"Yes," he agrees. "Some will die in the Nomad's campaign, but their strength must lie in their adaptability and numbers."

"We only need to see the condition they've left their planet to acknowledge that."

"In a few hundred cycles," Dhun continues, "we will return to reseed this Earth when it's no longer sustainable."

"Which makes that a future to avoid," Idu schemes, turning away from him.

Dhun watches her momentarily before resolving to count the crevasses in the walls.

"Follow me," Idu instructs, stepping toward the stasis corridor.

Idu leads him to a panel locked into a pillar. She waves a hand over it and presses her palm to the interface.

"I would not worry about the humans' willingness to fight against other lesser beings," Dhun redirects Idu's concern. "Humanity will climb high. Maybe *that* is their nature? I only worry about their immediate rush to come aboard our ship in a misled attempt to reach the stars."

"Their sun isn't too large for their tiny fingers to grasp."

"But maybe it's too high for them to jump over without learning exactly how hot those fires can burn."

"You're suggesting they cannot learn to avoid it? Or harness it?"

"More like they *would* not," Dhun concludes.

"Maybe you're right," Idu admits. "But I am not convinced."

Idu flinches as the panel joins directly with her nervous system. It causes her no small pain as she rouses the Varmajalkavaen from their sleep.

Dhun watches as Idu reintegrates power into the system's controls and enters the commands that only exist as embedded strands within her DNA. The ship hums to life with new energy as she nears completion, causing a red light to emit across the patterning cracks in the walls.

"Finished," Idu says, slowing her breath and closing her eyes. "Mother Irna—watch your children in the coming battles."

"Obligation will see to their protection," Dhun cautions against the primitive rhetoric, "not some dirt they've named."

"Hearing their prayers comforts them when they're scared," Idu explains.

Dhun snorts, disagreeing with the novelty.

"No matter," he states, straightening his shoulders. "I will see what I can do to help the humans."

"And what's your plan?" Idu asks. "Will you approach their warriors again?"

"Not immediately," Dhun weighs. He studies the stasis chamber as it thaws several hundred pods at a time. "And until I do, we should deal with Adhion 'Klaka and repair the damage to the ship. We *must* secure the corridors and ensure he doesn't find a foothold anywhere."

THE ABNORMALITY

ADDISON KENNEDY, FIELD DIRECTOR
EPIMETHEUS PROJECT

OCTOBER 11, 2041 | 2124 HOURS

"We're hooking up the last connections now, Addison," Ava calls over the comms.

Addison spins in her chair to watch the monitor in the command tent. She can see an overhead view of the METIS Research Base.

"Can you shine a light on that?" Addison asks the control operator.

The lieutenant leans closer to the screen. "Where?" she questions.

"Right there," Addison points, touching the screen. She turns to the woman orchestrating the drones, flying patterns around the bay's massive interior. The lieutenant nods and orders her operator to move a UAV closer with the light. It's a dangerous procedure for her crew to do in the dark, combined with the bone-chilling cold, the rain separating them from the inside of the Summerland. Addison hopes their work can help smooth their excavations over the next few days.

"That's it! That's the last," Ava says over the channel. Addison can hear cheering across the site. "I'm reading stable input on primary connectors—accepting output from the repeaters. And the board is green. On your mark, Malakai. Oh, I mean, *Doctor* Adonis."

A long silence follows the acknowledgment.

Addison looks to the room confusingly to catch a few impish laughs.

"What's taking him so long?" a staffer eventually asks.

"Just give it a minute," says another.

"Maybe he went for a bathroom break?" Athena whispers into Addison's earpiece.

Suddenly, a tap on her comms unit goes buzzy. Then, it stops. Music starts playing through the camp's loudspeakers. Addison checks her board—network control has switched from direct communications to the broad array.

She looks up with a grin and chuckles as she recognizes the song.

"I Am Worthy," Addison whispers, translating the title from its original Latin. "Axios."

"Quite the dramatic flair," Ibrahim comments, entering the room and meeting Addison at the monitoring station.

He's holding his shoulder at what looks like an uncomfortable angle.

"Ladies and gentlemen," Malakai speaks into their ears as the music plays. "We've faced losses today—exhaustion and bitter rivalries. The culmination of your hard work getting this project off the ground isn't tainted, however. We're stepping toward a finish line a hundred miles away, but it's there. And now, we can see it. May I present to you? The Summerland!"

Addison looks at the monitors while Malakai speaks, but they're just images on screens. It's not the same as standing outside the Breach to watch it unfold. And as her boss talks of *miles* and *finish lines*, Addison leaves her station, grabs her exterior raingear, and walks into the storm.

She steps to the Breach's edge and waits.

"Ava," Malakai concludes, "do your thing. Turn the lights on."

Addison counts the heartbeats.

Like a Christmas tree drowning in flashy lights, the Summerland's interior illuminates from this end to the other.

And she is left to gawk at the magnitude.

It's so . . . so . . . unimaginably vast. More massive than anything humanity has ever attempted to build. Addison could fit a whole city inside, buildings and their people, and there'd still be enough room for a few added towns and villages.

"I live for these moments," Addison whispers.

"Nothing ventured," Colonel Ibrahim says, laughing as he stops next to her, following into the rain after her. "You look ecstatic."

"We should all be proud," Addison says, looking at his arm. "How are you healing? I never asked."

"Doctor Vogert has all the tools he needs to get the wounded back into the field as soon as possible."

"Without the need for a recovery period?"

"I'd rather get back to it than be stuck in a bed while my troops take the risk," Ibrahim answers. "I wasn't made to stand on the sidelines to watch."

"You want to fight," Addison says.

Ibrahim tilts his head and nods agreeingly. He's not wearing his armor's full helmet, just the rebreather mask everyone must wear outside the base structures. So, there's nothing to hide that softer look in his eyes. Addison can see his cheeks bumble as he smiles and the slight crookedness of his ears.

"I need to—" he was about to say, but their comms units give off beeping noises.

Athena wants their attention.

Addison triggers her earpiece and asks what's going on.

"Sorry for interrupting, Doctor Kennedy," Athena apologizes, "but the Overlook is reading a heightened thermal signature stemming from within the ship."

"Ah, what?" Addison queries. "Show me. Now."

Athena sends images to her wrist-mounted computer. They show a significant rise in temperature in the Summerland's forward sections. At first, they appear as softer shades of yellow—warm, not abrasive. Not until they suddenly jump to the reds, and they do, causing Addison to hold her breath.

Not only that, but the readout shows the affected area expanding . . . Inside the ship?

"How's that—" Addison mutters.

"What is it?" Ibrahim asks, checking his pad.

"The expedition hasn't gotten to that section yet, so it can't be our teams," Addison describes, seeing the red portions growing wider. "It looks like an energy signature. Maybe an electrical grid turning on? But if it is, it's at a much slower pace than I would think."

"It *is* a big ship," Ibrahim suggests.

"But that doesn't explain why—?"

"Can we get a bird to fly over the area and give us a clearer visual?" Ibrahim asks, cutting off her train of thought.

"The event is going on *inside* the ship, Colonel Ibrahim," Addison explains. "And if I'm reading *this* correctly, by the observations we've made into your encounter with the Fragment, it's possible the outer hull is reacting similarly. Maybe we can send a few UAVs to—?"

A red-wave explosion erupts from the hull's forward section, precisely centered on the anomaly. It spreads along the ship's crest, revealing veins across the vessel like the Fragment, with parts of its outer shell glowing crimson in the short span the machine was active.

"All teams, brace for impact!" Ibrahim shouts over the frequency. "Hold onto something!"

Addison and Ibrahim float six inches off the hull, outside the reach of the safety ropes. When the red energy wave passes under their feet, it disrupts the gravity keeping them planted on the ground. At least, it does before the surge warbles unsteadily and abruptly ends.

Addison hits the ground hard, knocking the wind out of her lungs.

By the time she gets to her feet, Addison looks and notices the entire camp in disarray. Pavilion sections are unapologetically blown over, with computers exposed to the heavy elements—the wind, the rain, and the brutal ice. She can already see Joe Hickman running frantically in circles. He picks his men and women off their asses, desperately trying to get the shelters up again. Losing their equipment would be catastrophic. Moreover, it will make their stay beyond uncomfortable if Hickman can't save their gear.

Addison turns toward the hospital, where the medical staff fights to get the wounded under plastic tarps.

"Doctor Kennedy? Addison Kennedy—do you read me?" Malakai shouts over the comms. Addison's head is spinning, so it takes her a moment to process who's talking to her. "What's going on? Report?!"

"We're fine. A bit disorientated," Addison finally returns. "A shockwave hit our basecamp. It looks like we've teams trying to put things back together. I'll give you an update on our progress when . . . ah, whenever. How're things on your end?"

"We've lost direct comms with every research camp we've planted on that damn thing," Malakai explains. "I can't get anybody to answer me! Nobody's transmitting on the feeds—so, we're blind as a bat over here. The best look we've got is from Overlook Station. You're the closest to us, so we can still talk via line of sight."

"That's something," Addison admits.

"Yeah," Malakai murmurs. "Once my team reconnects with the other Field Directors, I hope we can figure out what's happened."

"Unless I already have an answer for you," Addison suggests. "Do you have us on a visual?"

"No, I don't. As I said, our feeds are down."

"Not all feeds," Addison says. "Did you try looking out the window?"

"Out the window—?" Malakai begins, quickly cutting his sentence short. "Is that? I don't . . . How? Addison, what *can* you give me?"

"Oh, you mean the mountain-sized ship suddenly getting into a mood?" she says, playing it off sarcastically. "I was watching the thermal scans when the event hit us. My only guess is that somebody *inside* the dreadnaught decided to flip that light switch on."

"It's beautiful," Ibrahim utters next to her, gawking at the hull's shelf above the Breach.

"It's a bit concerning," Malakai follows suit.

"I agree," Addison confirms.

Radio traffic erupts in her earpiece, a hundred voices sounding at once.

Addison yanks her comms unit for a moment to give herself the chance to turn the volume down.

Cleanup teams move through the assembly area where Ibrahim and Addison are standing center. She checks her computer after putting her comms back into her ear.

Video feeds are down, without a doubt, but the network nodes *are* coming back online.

"We need to get physical teams to the anomaly's source location," Addison determines, scraping the accumulating ice off her screen. She moves under shelter with Colonel Ibrahim to get out of the rain. "We need to find out what caused this disruption . . . Why take a day *after* we've arrived to throw a hissy fit?"

"Unless it's *not* reacting to our presence," Athena suggests. "Not directly, at least."

"What do you mean, Athena?" Malakai responds.

"If I may, Director Adonis—" the AI goes on, momentarily pausing to analyze the little data she can measure. "We have confirmed alien lifeforms onboard. Intelligent lifeforms."

"Likely the ship's architects, if not the outright owners," Ibrahim comments.

"And they landed here for a reason," Athena continues. "Even if we don't understand the reason, our teams are walking into *their* territory. Humanity classically interprets the unknown as a scary place. I reckon they shut down their reactor during the crash. Or maybe it's what caused it?"

"Damn ship's been dead in the water for over a month," Ibrahim interjects. "If it's lighting up, maybe they've made repairs? I'd hate to still be on this beast when it takes off and flies off to heaven knows where. And if they *are* then maybe we should . . . you know, evacuate?"

"We can't leave!" Addison calls. "We'd lose our progress."

"What progress? We've been here a day!"

"Nobody's leaving! Not yet," Malakai shouts, his voice cracking. "If we get confirmation on the ship's departure—we'll begin emergency procedures. And if that happens, recovery efforts back at home will stop to help rescue us. We risk millions of lives if we don't get this situation under control. Until we do, everybody stays to finish the job. People back home are counting on us. I don't plan to disappoint them."

Ibrahim stares at Addison with remorseful eyes. "All right," the man says, squeezing his shoulder. "What do you need us to do?"

"I need you to help get METIS back in working condition," Malakai orders, quieter in his tone. "Then start coordinating with Camp Yi to get units into the ship's forward sections. As Addison said, we need to find the anomaly's source and shut it down before it causes any more damage. Am I understood?"

"Yes, sir," Ibrahim acknowledges.

He steps toward the downed base units to begin coordinating the military's response.

"Malakai?" Addison says. She keys her comms, opening a channel with him. "What about the incident? Suppose we start aggressively moving through the ship's forward sections. If that's the case, our soldiers could face resistance—possibly agitate more Fragments, or maybe the ship's Architects? Take your pick."

"I understand the risk, Addison," Malakai accepts. "Right now, we don't have a choice."

"What choice don't we have?" Addison warns. "Just one of those machines took out entire squads of highly trained soldiers!"

"If I don't order it, Admiral Kennedy will go over my head," Malakai explains. "This way, our teams can at least steer the jarheads in the right direction with accountable data." He stops talking for a quick breath. "My God . . . that *is* beautiful. Isn't it?"

Addison looks to see the digitalized crimson patterns dance like rivers across the hull.

And that gives her an idea. "Athena, can you hear me?"

"Go ahead, Doctor Kennedy," the AI responds.

"Is there a way for us to track the Fragments' energy signatures ship-wide?" she proposes.

"Like a life signs detector? But, for machines?" Athena interprets.

"That's it exactly," Addison confirms. "There's gotta be more floating around inside the ship. I'm betting the rest will be as lively as our little friend."

"At present, I cannot tell the difference between the Fragment's energy and the vessel's new readings," Athena denies.

"Is there a way for us to differentiate the two signatures?" Addison asks.

"Not without investing time into it," Athena cautions. "As it so happens, Doctor Remmings only received our 'friend' a few hours ago. But she's limited to only conducting supervisory tests with the priority workload on her plate."

"If only I didn't have to set up this light show for the man in charge!" Ava shouts, picking up on Malakai's headset.

"The study *would* go faster if Doctor Remmings were assigned to the task full-time," Athena suggests. "Her ability to identify a machine's workings is remarkable, especially among specialists in her field."

Malakai lets off a low grumbling as he turns away from his microphone. "I'll get on that," he acknowledges.

Addison can hear Ava cheering in the background.

"While she's doing that, Addison—" Malakai continues, "I'll need you to prepare your team."

"Anything specific you want us to plan for?" Addison inquires.

"Just a contingency for now," Malakai explains. "Let's hurry and work ahead of this anomaly before we lose our chances."

Addison taps her earpiece to confirm the order.

"It might take a few days," Addison admits. "We're still finding our sea legs."

"I'll look forward to seeing your proposals," Malakai affirms.

Looking up at the ship's monstrous hull once more, Addison understands the difficult task ahead of her. Her jobs are never simple ones. Now she has to prepare to live on the edge for the next weeks or months. Or maybe a day. Time will let her take more significant leaps into the fray with enough resources *if* she can avoid the risks involved.

She accepts . . . begrudgingly, that it doesn't matter *what* the Project throws into the mixing bowl. If the upper layers harden, it's because she's failed, and along with her failure, their mission, too.

"Contingencies for contingencies," Addison murmurs. "Maybe we can avoid a repeat incident."

She will stay focused on returning the METIS Research Base to operational status for the next few hours. That should give her *some* time to weed out a few bad ideas. Addison can then sit down and brainstorm plans of action with her team members trickling into the base.

14 | RESTLESSNESS

MALAKAI ADONIS, DIRECTOR OF OPERATIONS
EPIMETHEUS PROJECT

OCTOBER 12, 2041 | 0149 HOURS

===

Malakai stirs uncomfortably in his cot.

Despite the outside's frigid temperatures, he sweats inside his thermal sheets. And it's making him sleepless.

Malakai throws off his covers and jumps to his feet, deciding to wander the corridors. He eventually steers his way to the mess hall.

Stealing a couple of ice cubes from the freezer, he lets them melt on his forehead before running wet fingers through his hair.

"Everyone is wearing sweatshirts," Malakai observes. "I'm not sick . . . So, why am I so warm?"

Soldiers and support crews intermingle across the room. They walk together in small groups of three or four, grabbing breakfast on their way to early morning rounds. Most only give momentary glances in Malakai's direction, then choose to ignore him while they eat.

"Athena? Would you please give me a report? Any report," he says, not realizing until *after* that he's without his earpiece. He stops short of repeating the request. Malakai shouldn't expect to get much sleep tonight. And hoping for *three* good hours was too much. He put his head down close to midnight, and now it's—

He checks the clock.

"A quarter past two," he mutters. "Just two hours."

Malakai buries his face into his palms.

He notices a flicker on the mess hall's monitor wall to his left. They had the televisions installed so off-duty personnel could stay updated on the outside world. It helps remind them that their mission encompasses more than these metal walls and familiar faces. And it's why they've routed the exterior cameras for the crews to watch, like windows in a steel box. It reminds everyone to stay alert, helping them cope with the demands on their mental state.

Otherwise, the monitors stay on broadcasts from worldwide news organizations.

Glenn Johnson—a night-duty staff member—stops mid-step on his way to a table when he notices Malakai staring at the screens.

"We can turn up the volume if you want to listen," the man offers.

"I prefer the quiet for now," Malakai admits, rubbing his neck. "Besides. I can read the subtitles."

"Of course," the other says.

Johnson nods only once before sitting down with his bagel, eating it with cream cheese, silent in the cold.

Malakai's attention returns to the broadcasts.

Most feeds are on their 24-hour live cameras, always pointing at the alien ship. Alexandra Roslin, the woman in charge of Oversight Security, wants to stem the flow of misinformation before it releases to the public. At this early stage, it's an impossible job for her. With field reporters embedded with the fleet, every leak and comment see full stories in the nightly shows.

Malakai stands up from the bench for a closer view of the screens. He likes to put a keen mind to the early morning updates. It's a reliable way to avoid public criticism and address reporter demands before they can ambush him at the next press event.

The networks run profiles on Malakai and his Field Directors around the clock. His blood fumes whenever he sees a re-run of older interviews of him, promising results he couldn't keep. How else could he earn the public trust and support for this mission? It was a busy time for him—traveling to events, meetings, military briefings, and a score of interviews.

He doesn't remember eating during those early weeks.

An image of Malakai's face catches his attention.

He takes a step to the side, watching a replay of an interview he did with BBC News three days ago:

"Why do we need to be there?" the interviewer asks.

"Why? That's like asking, 'Why do we breathe?' It's who we are," he responded. "Because we're the only people who can ensure it's done right, without politics getting involved. We're loyal to the science and the mission, *not* the rhetoric of whoever sits in public office."

Malakai snorts as he watches, reading the captions.

"Some've asked how governments who've signed on with this treaty can oversee the safety of this Project? How exactly can you keep your promises to the public sphere, Doctor Adonis? Can you give us guarantees? Safeguards? Legitimate questions. And what of demands for returns on investments if your mission fails."

On the screen, a three-day younger Malakai frowns despondently.

"I'm sorry. Investment? I wouldn't call *people* a mere investment," revealed his coarser side. "We've not gone into this for vanity's sake. Millions are dead because of this . . . this . . . unknown entity? It came to *us* from out there! And we need to understand it. Everything's changed. Our entire worldview? Our mindset? It's gone. We're no longer alone. We need to figure out what our role is in what's quite possibly a much larger community."

"Meaning we're doing this to establish contact? Not save lives?"

"Saving lives? That's our number one priority! However, if it comes to making contact, then I won't hesitate," Malakai admitted, shifting uncomfortably in his chair on-screen. "Our objectives are to ask the how and whys . . . *Why* come to us? *How* did they find us? And how can we use *it* to repair the damage they've already done to our lives?"

Malakai grunts and walks away from the screens.

"Doctor Adonis?" another staffer asks, flowing into the mess hall with the shift change. "Didn't you go to get a few winks?"

"Oh, I can't sleep," Malakai explains. "I've too much to think about."

The staffer subtly nods, accepting his concern is appreciated but unwarranted. The man heads off to the breakfast table with a bounce to his step.

Malakai writes a mental note that he's not the only one feeling the pressure. Sometimes, he needs a reminder. Knowing *that* allows him to breathe with some confidence.

But he shouldn't show the weight of that pressure to his subordinates. For *their* sake. And maybe *his*, too.

Malakai makes his way back to his bunkroom and gets dressed. He straps on his boots, deciding to explore the rig's lowest levels—the layout echoes his family's church when he was a kid. Malakai would get lost in the seemingly labyrinth-like basement with his sisters. Every turn leads to an adventure, and every hallway and corridor brings him somewhere new and brilliant.

Malakai's pulse beats faster as he walks.

Day two begins.

FRAGMENT OF A FRAGMENT

AVANNA "AVA" REMMINGS, CHIEF TECHNOLOGY SPECIALIST
EPIMETHEUS PROJECT

OCTOBER 12, 2041 | 0612 HOURS

"Now that's interesting," Ava comments.

Ava is working alongside her crew in the early morning hours. She's on deck five, the Observation Lab, her chosen office for the trials, isolated from the rest of the oil rig. Ava likes the quiet. And the safety. There's a certain peace in the monotony of watching her labors blossom without worrying about miscellaneous explosions causing an uproar.

And she likes *not* having assholes watch over her shoulder like a snoopy child looking for presents.

Ava won't forget the long planning sessions that went into the lab.

She argued that her team *needed* an independent research zone for on-site development projects.

And this lab is what they could give her—with amenities—scanners, fabricators, and a see-through floor that offers her a hellish view of the crashing ocean waves underfoot.

"Just pretend the floor is magma," she whispers, looking down. Ava's confident the glass won't break under her.

She's confident because Ava had designed the material a few years prior. The High Castle Program offered her a mandate—they wanted a transparent material, like glass, but as durable as titanium and moldable like plastic. And it was a good challenge for two years of her life.

After dealing with the project's conditions, Ava still suffers from nightly shakes and the occasional tremor.

Now years after the fact, she is looking at the done product, fresh off an assembly line, and not a single imperfection in the reflection looking back at her.

Ava breathes unsteadily and closes her eyes.

"I am not afraid of heights," Ava mutters. "It's drowning that freaks me out."

Ava doesn't know if joining the Epimetheus Project was a wise decision or not. The jury's still out until they're a few days into the mess. Although, what they're doing is an opportunity. And she didn't want to miss it. Today, she races to the top of discovery, rushing to unlock the secrets of whatever technologies are sitting inside *that* dreadnaught.

"And maybe calm this panic I have," Ava weighs internally.

But it's like staring up at Mount Everest, getting ready for a long, challenging climb to the summit.

It's a choice no *insane* person would pass up, and only the *sane* know to stay clear.

Ava quickly reads the data on her monitor as Athena's subroutine compiles her latest demo results.

Doctor Adonis . . . Malakai . . . walks in through the doors right before she finishes.

"Please tell me you've made progress," he's the first to speak.

Ava's eyes veer to the man's athletic-fitting sweatshirt with his name sewn above the left pectoral.

"Impatient, aren't we?" Avanna rebukes.

"Just tired," Malakai admits. "I'm not in the mood for jokes."

"Which only puts me in the mood to communicate solely through quips," Ava chuckles, spinning in her chair. "We're just humanity's brightest minds, after all, getting asked to solve the mysteries of the universe with the toys you'd find in a sandbox."

Ava makes sure there's a clear sarcastic nod in her tone as she speaks. Undoubtedly, there's also a great deal of truth to it. Ava is working on less than an hour of sleep and no coffee. Her biggest mistake? Not recruiting unpaid interns to fetch her a cup every hour . . . half-hour . . . Fifteen minutes?

Malakai surrenders a worn expression.

"Not in the mood," he repeats, longing eyes looking fatigued. "You have the ballistic results?"

Ava lets out her breath.

"We've some good news on that account," Ava admits. She leads Malakai to the lab firing range they've set up. That's where she's keeping a sample of the Fragment Addison Kennedy sent to the Olympus. Ava's team is still hard at work hitting it with a hammer. "Voila! Our floating death bot."

"Smaller than I expected," Malakai states. "After the damage it did."

"Oh, this is only a tiny piece of it. And don't let its appearance fool you," Ava advises. "It's got a big punch in a small package. Combined with its other half, the Fragment measures roughly a meter in height and half a meter wide. Left-and-right proportions are nearly symmetric. The biggest difference lies in the details. At least, from what I can tell."

"It looks like chipped volcanic rock," Malakai describes, walking up to feel its surface. "Still warm? Quite a weapon."

Ava can't help but hum at him disapprovingly.

"What is it?" Malakai notices.

"You're assuming the design reflects that of a weapon," Ava explains.

"And you're telling me it doesn't?"

"I'm not telling you anything," Ava confides. "Except that I've designed weapons for years under military contracts. And I know the fundamentals, all the ways to kill a target. Malakai? This shell is stronger than the magnesium glass under our boots. Small arms didn't even leave a scratch! While these traits helped slaughter our field team, it doesn't mean *that* is its function."

"Which means? As far as we know, it could be a maintenance drone," Malakai relays. "Can you imagine the upkeep for a ship that big?"

"For a human crew?" Ava weighs. "It'd take tens of thousands of people to run it."

Malakai softly grimaces. "A decent working theory," he agrees. "Makes about as much sense as the idea that it's a part of the ship's defense network."

"And that it was reacting to our presence?" Ava questions.

"That's the running theory," Malakai circumvents.

Ava stares at him confusingly. "Running theory? Of how many?" she asks.

Malakai pauses to think. "A few dozen," he sighs.

"A theory based on a sequence of facts that make sense to Addison Kennedy and her related field," Ava suggests. "However, throw the job at somebody else, using the same facts, and they'll come up with ideas that best fit *their* interests. Like what I'm explaining to you now."

"Okay. I get it," Malakai surrenders. "We can't only rely on ideas."

Ava quietly chortles so he doesn't hear.

No reason to add more stress to eat away at the man's brain.

"There are no surefire answers," Ava offers. "Not here."

"And if we had answers, there wouldn't be a reason for us to stand on this mountain," Malakai sighs, his lips receding to a frown.

"On the mountain, waiting for the wind to knock us off?" Ava suggests.

Malakai's eyes shoot up at her with a renewed vigor as he inhales excessively. And he nods.

"Did you find anything we can use if we come across more 'maintenance drones,' as you suggest?" Malakai asks.

"On that," she says, "I think we've figured a solution."

Ava walks behind a ballistic shield to see the final setup of her demo getting into place.

Addison had sent her *two* samples. Malakai looks at the larger portion while a second, smaller cut-away is her subject for this trial.

A mechanical arm holds the subject on the far side of the range. Ava's set up a rig with interchangeable UCAF rifles on this end. She wanted to see which had the best penetration capability against the alien material. And it's *that* data she was compiling right before Malakai walked into the labs.

Ava takes out an unspent casing from her pocket and hands it to Director Adonis.

"A bullet? Why are you—?" Malakai nearly begs the question.

"That's not an ordinary bullet," Ava says with a wide grin. "ASAPHEI 6.8—developed three years ago for use in small arms. The design can penetrate the heaviest body armor. It's especially devastating against soldiers wearing HRDVS hardsuits, like those of our marines."

"ASAPHEI?" Malakai repeats. "Just rolls off the tongue, doesn't it?"

"It's an old idea made new again," she describes. "Stands for 'advanced semi-armored-piercing high-explosive incendiary.' Although, the UCSN banned its use when tests brought up concerns over the damage it can do to a person."

"That's a bleak thought," Malakai murmurs.

"Personally—I think the decision over the ordnance was overblown," Ava scoffs. "Nobody cares about the pain after they're dead."

Malakai looks at her with concern. "Families prefer to bury their loved ones intact," he argues.

"And how many people do you think we're burying now without it?" Ava begs the question, cold and argumentative.

Malakai shivers from her explanation.

"That's not remotely the point, Doctor Remmings," Malakai hinges.

"You asked for the best that humanity has to offer," Ava defends her stance. "Some of us have done . . . rather inexcusable things, surviving in a darker world. That normally doesn't allow for social niceties. I've had to stop thinking about the consequences of my work years ago. It's not my fault if they're standing on the wrong end of the crosshairs."

Malakai stares hard and long at the floor between them without saying another word. Ava's logic makes a lot of sense. He only doesn't want to admit it. Not yet.

"I don't understand," Malakai offers. "But it doesn't matter. Our priorities are here."

Ava holds her stare for a short while before keying a command prompt on her wrist-mounted computer. The weapon mount on this end of the range moves into position, centering a shot over the subject on the other side.

"You're saying the ASAPHEI 6.8 affects the Fragment's outer shell?" Malakai questions.

"That's not what I said, but . . . close enough," Ava says, loading the round into the mount's firing chamber. "I've not tried this yet. We can always knock new pieces off the big one for more tests if this doesn't work."

Malakai steps to his left and eyes the far end of the demo range.

The mount unfolds with an MR5A1 rifle locked into place. A single shot fires at the target, and the subsequent flash hits dead center. Ava's managed to "procure" the weapon from the armory and reconfigured it to handle the ASAPHEI 6.8 munitions.

Ava's viewscreen goes too bright to keep her eyes on it. She looks away.

A second later, a micro-explosion throws the subject and its accompanying safeties down the chamber, smacking into the wall several feet back.

"That was impressive," Malakai comments. "What exactly just happened?"

Ava cracks her spine. "That was the result of the round penetrating the drone's armor," she details. "The bullet releases thermite to dig into the skin. After, it scrambles the more 'delicate components' with a limited-degree high explosive, lacking a better way to describe it."

"Did it go straight through?"

"Unlikely," Ava frowns.

"What do you mean? Isn't that what we want?"

"Explosive triggers inside the case go off a tenth of a second after contact," Ava summarizes. "So, it doesn't matter if the target is flesh or titanium, meaning the result should always be the same. It's an effective solution."

Malakai walks past the safety barriers with a cautious stride to his step. He looks at the damage to the Fragment's cut-away.

Ava quickly eyes the screens as the computers grab the recorded data.

"ASAPHEI appears suitable for use, Doctor Remmings," Athena chimes into her earpiece. "Congratulations."

Ava grinds her molars. "I'm good at making things go boom," she finally says, letting out her breath.

Malakai anxiously looks at her. "Your magic bullet isn't on High Castle's equipment manifest," he says with a frog in his throat. "And I never signed for its approval on-site. Ava . . . How did you learn about this ordnance? Where did you get the sample?" She notices the worry in his voice, like a rubber band, stretched and trilling.

Ava's attention lands on the Fragment cut-away still sizzling on the transparent floor.

She doesn't want to answer.

"I'm sorry, did you say something?" Ava blinks waywardly, acting as if she didn't hear the question.

"Ava—?" Malakai attempts to say.

"I think we've done our jobs," Ava only nods. "ASAPHEI can get through the outer shell."

Malakai frowns. "Which leaves a question," he adds, deciding to play along.

"Is it enough to kill a *living* one?" Ava concludes.

The man delegates tasks in a way to ensure the resources at his disposal are at their most effective. Almost everyone in the Epimetheus Project has a specialty. Addison Kennedy is good at creating theories and researching in the field. She likes to ask the most pressing questions to forge ahead, finding answers in her unique way. Malakai Adonis is a leader, overly serious and stressed all the time.

Others are better at asking questions than Avanna Remmings. They like to create theories to match the facts for a thousand different scenarios.

But that's not *her*. "I hate it," Ava smugly determines.

She does her best work when she breaks those theories into their base components. And then? She likes to play with the ends.

"Chief Technology Specialist" barely fits with what she does.

And she could do nothing but accept that reality over the years.

"I'll assume you don't have a steady supply of the munitions available," Malakai finally cedes.

Ava's attention shoots up to him.

She smiles innocently.

"I do not," she admits.

"Can we manufacture it with our materials on hand?"

"We don't have the tooling to develop it en masse with our facilities," Ava confides. "I could only make a couple of rounds with what I had. Not like *doing* it was entirely legal, either. The issue is, for practical use, our troops will require access to a stockpile."

"And I'm about to hear a 'but,' aren't I?"

"But—" Ava says with a wink.

"Okay," Malakai grumbles.

"—Oversight Security maintains that stockpile at a vault in the Rocky Mountains."

Malakai's expression goes from weariness to complete shock. And not a little fear.

"Due to the fact it's illegal?" the man surmises.

"You'd have to convince SOI to release the supply to the Epimetheus Project," Ava confirms. She watches as Malakai uses his fingertips to add pressure to his temples.

"Even with our mission and our people's safety, I doubt they'd be so willing to hand over illegal weapons," Malakai deflates.

"Unless you can pull strings with the Security Council?" Ava suggests.

"And that's another terrible mess," Malakai admits, finding a chair, and sitting down. "I don't even know *who* could override Alexandra Roslin."

"Or has the security clearance to know of the weapon's existence," Ava lets off a warning, "let alone its development."

"You're not helping," Malakai confesses.

"However, I know a guy who *might* help us," Ava offers. "And given what's at stake, I doubt he'll refuse if I'm the one who's asking."

"Because you're the one who created the damn things," Malakai determines, the white of his eyes now dark. "Aren't you?"

Ava looks at him, feigning a hurt amusement.

"Then I hope it's somebody within my circle," he urges.

"It's entirely possible," Ava admits. She keys her comms, opening a private channel to the network. "Athena? Can you hear me?"

"Like a pale angel in a church choir," the AI returns. "What do you need,

Doctor Remmings?"

"Can you put me in contact with Admiral Kennedy aboard the USS Isaac Bennett?"

"Asking him on a dinner date, are you?" Athena beeps.

"Old Man Kennedy?" Malakai quietly iterates.

Ava shushes him with a finger.

"You are patched through to his private comms link," Athena finishes. "Good luck."

Ava waits for a second until the man on the other end speaks first.

"Yes? Doctor Remmings?" Admiral Kennedy says in a rough voice. "If *you're* calling me, this is good news. Or the worst news."

"Bad news is the only news worth hearing," Ava says.

She *would* remark on the exhaustion in the man's voice. That's *if* he wasn't in charge of the entire Oceanic Exclusion Zone. He's likely had many long calls discussing yesterday's events over the past few hours.

"What do you need, Ms. Remmings?"

"Another favor," Ava encourages.

She glances at Malakai, who's listening intently.

"Are you in trouble?" the Old Man returns.

"Looking for a solution before the real trouble hits off again," Ava begins. "You know the incident yesterday?"

After a momentary pause, the Admiral replies, "Hard not to," he admits. "Care to elaborate?"

Ava can hear the man's voice pique with interest.

16 | WHO ARE THESE MONSTERS?

LIEUTENANT COLONEL ELIAS IBRAHIM
UNITED COALITION ARMED FORCES

OCTOBER 12, 2041 | 1524 HOURS

═══

Ibrahim moves through the corridor with his unit, restocked and ready for anything. They're scouting beyond their main perimeter line *inside* the ship's expanse. Since the fireworks show last night, the doors open as they get near them, like ghosts, clearing the way into the dreadnaught.

For Ibrahim, it means a hundred new ways for hostiles to circumvent his patrols.

Old Man Kennedy has him setting up checkpoints at each entry hatch with the other groups. Their objective is to control the approaches, limiting attacks on their teams journeying into the vessel. Nothing has *tried* testing their perimeter yet. However, Ibrahim knows it's only a matter of time.

And *that* causes his hands to go numb and his shoulder to flare up.

If the doctor had his way, Ibrahim wouldn't be in the field again after his injuries. Yet he's expected to maintain a wide buffer zone with the resources at hand? The situation doesn't warrant bedrest. And that means every marine who can hold a rifle has a job to do.

Stepping into the side passages with his troops, Ibrahim notes the ship's architecture, markedly resembling a vast cave system.

He stops for a moment to scan the outcroppings.

"Odd," Ibrahim mutters.

"What is it?" Mannering asks.

"These tunnels," Ibrahim says. "They're like the dried-up lava tubes you'd find under an extinct volcano."

Mannering flashes his light at the walls. "Or a gothic cathedral in central Europe," he says. "Do you see these pillars?"

Ibrahim nods. "Flying buttresses," he acknowledges.

"Only they're *inside* the ship," Mannering weighs.

"Maybe as support beams holding up the ceiling?" Ibrahim suggests.

Mannering shrugs tentatively.

Ibrahim decides to push farther into the interior while the question goes unanswered.

"These shipbuilders must have an artistic flair," another says as they go along.

"Look above us," Tanner says. "See how steep the angles are? Hard to imagine this being structurally sound."

"Makes you wonder what they built it for," the other returns. "Why make corridors so wide? Or so tall?"

"Or why change aesthetics from one section to another?" Ibrahim adds, moving ahead, signaling to the squad leaders. "Sergeant? Bring up the big gun!"

"Yes, sir," Mannering acknowledges.

Ibrahim's orders quietly pass down through the squad's local comms.

Word had spread earlier in the day when Doctor Remmings discovered a way to overcome the Fragment's defense. That news had managed to uplift Ibrahim's souring disposition for the better span of the afternoon.

Yesterday was a disaster. No subtle way for him to say it when he filed his report.

"The Central Spire Incident," Ibrahim called it.

When the drone attacked, it was a reality check on *what* Ibrahim's people would confront inside this place.

"Expecting trouble and facing it aren't the same," Ibrahim whispers.

"Did you say something, Castle-Actual?" Mannering begs the question.

"No," Ibrahim reacts. "Lay a sensor at this corner." He points to a passageway on his right.

"Understood," Mannering confirms.

Ibrahim can tell his marines are on edge, keeping their weapons trained on the hallway's brutalist walls.

An attack had hit another unit two hours ago in the tunnels near this location. "Too far for the perimeter guards to respond to," Ibrahim utters as he pushes forward.

Marines led by Gunnery Sergeant Aaron Daud came under fire by a second Fragment. Unlike the first, however, this one was less one-sided.

Daud had equipped his team's marksman with an AMR-26A2 loaded with HEIAP rounds and fired three shots into the "floater" at close quarters. After the subsequent impact caused by the weapon's sheer power, the drone shattered into a useless slag pile on the ground.

While the remnants weren't ideal for Addison's research, the event *did* provide them an opportunity. Daud had discovered a way for their troops to fight back if they kept running into the *damn* machines. Although, with finding one possible solution, another issue cropped up:

Only a few dozen AMRs are obtainable to service members across the quarantine zone. And *most* of those rifles, as Ibrahim counts, are under lockup throughout the fleet. Or they're shoring up the new checkpoints, protecting the expedition from incursions by the rampant drones.

Not to mention, the rifles are cumbersome to use in tight spaces. And if a marksman had a choice, they wouldn't go into a firefight with the weapons.

"A better option is to wait for the bureaucracy to beat the politics," Ibrahim mutters.

"Better option? What a joke," Private Aquoia snarks, overhearing him.

Ibrahim points at the marine, quieting him immediately. But the man isn't wrong.

From what Ibrahim overheard, it could take *three* days to a *week* for the ASAPHEI 6.8 to arrive from the mainland.

In the interim, the Old Man has agreed to transfer what weapons he can to Coalition units on the Summerland. It's a slow process to move equipment between the fleet and the hull, the high wind wreaking havoc on their navy transports, but it'll get done.

Ibrahim's marines can at least defend themselves without putting their lives in unnecessary danger once their hands are on the rifles.

"Colonel Ibrahim?" a trooper raises.

"Yes?" Ibrahim returns.

"What happens if we run into more of the damn floaters?" the man asks.

"That's why we're slugging the AMR-26s on our backs, Private Wittenmyer," Mannering intercedes. "We shoot them. And they die. Maybe."

"Yes," the marine continues, "but what *if* we run into more than we've got rifles to shoot them with?"

"Then I'll lob your head at them, Wittenmyer," Mannering laughs, "and hope it does the job."

"They're dangerous," Ibrahim warns. "Stay alive! Keep your eyes forward."

"Yes, sir," Wittenmyer accepts.

A soft red light emanates from within the corridor's walls. Ibrahim eyes it suspiciously. It's the same light he saw—everyone saw—when the ship flipped the switch.

If it were a *human* vessel, with a *human* crew, stranded on an alien world with inherently distrusting natives, Ibrahim's first impulse would be to escape and go home. From what he understands, nothing indicates *why* the dreadnaught has decided to start up again. Nor do the eggheads know why its architects haven't tried to leave if they could unless they plan to stay and build a colony.

Ibrahim cringes at the idea.

But here, they've remained. Alive and lifeless.

"We know these Fragments aren't the only crew aboard," Ibrahim whispers. "Question is . . . Why don't we see more of the big ones?"

Ibrahim saw the giant up close with his own eyes. He may not remember much, but he can recall enough. And it terrifies him.

He keeps his finger off the trigger as he rounds the corner.

Ibrahim's job isn't to provide the answers. No. His is to shoot things, letting others do the job instead.

"This is Castle-Six-Alpha—we got a body at an intersection," Warden announces over the comms. She's with her fireteam roughly thirty meters ahead of Ibrahim's current position, acting as the forward scouts for their patrol. "Scratch that—three bodies. Not human. I-I-I don't know how to describe them."

"Stay there and secure the scene," Ibrahim returns. "Rendezvous in twenty seconds. Keep your eyes up, Castle-Six. Watch for an ambush."

"Copy that," Warden affirms.

"Beware the bogyman," Tanner whispers, "for he walks in shadows."

Ibrahim eyes the Corporal as he walks alongside him. Nobody responds to the sentiment.

Ibrahim reaches Warden's intersection moments later. His squad fans out in a broad spread to cover all three corridors branching from the crossroads. It's too many angles for their numbers to comfortably screen. Ibrahim kneels at one of the dead bodies on the ground. His visor shows their outlines in a dull white hue. They're as far from human as anything *can* be—with four upper arms and backward knees on their two lower legs.

"Like the hind legs on a cat or dog," Ibrahim mutters.

"Sir?" Warden asks.

"Turn it over," he orders, wanting a closer look at its face.

And his squad reacts.

It has four symmetric eyes aligned in a V-like pattern in its skull and a third pair of much smaller arms embedded into its abdomen. All three aliens wear ornate carapace armors that Athena's scans can't identify.

"The armor isn't natural to their bodies," the AI mutters angrily. "I can tell you that."

"Meaning it's not an exoskeleton," Ibrahim states.

"Not theirs," Athena returns. "Maybe a cultural token of their homeworld?"

Ibrahim lets off an unseen grimace. "Maybe," he weighs.

As he looks over the buggers, Ibrahim would compare the armor to rustic royalty—knights dressed in crude, ceremonial plates.

"I am using your suit's camera to measure the trio," Athena relays. "The shortest is only slightly taller than an adult human male. And they're all significantly smaller than the giant you described."

"Maybe they're a race with different stages of development?" Warden suggests.

"Or a subspecies," Ibrahim offers.

"More likely a species in their own right," Athena refutes.

"Like what you'd find in an intragalactic federation?" Ibrahim asks.

"Or a caste system," Athena steers the idea.

"What's killed them?" Warden asks.

Ibrahim eyes the burn marks on the armor, not *unlike* the wounds inflicted by the Fragment.

"We should go," Ibrahim says.

"Colonel?" Mannering asks.

"Pack these buggers up for autopsy," Ibrahim orders. "Doctor Vogert can have the once over."

"Understood," Mannering acknowledges.

"Does anybody see their weapons?" Ibrahim demands. "Do they have any?"

"Just these," Wittenmyer says.

He's carrying three metal lances that look too large for anyone to wield in the middle of a battle.

"Spears? No guns?" Ibrahim asks.

"At least they're very light," Wittenmyer describes, flipping one on his palm. "Hardly weigh a thing."

Ibrahim takes a spear and scans it with his visor's optics. It's a weapon, without a doubt, and warm to the touch. His armor doesn't recognize its energy signature, but his senses can read it well enough. An electric jolt passes through his armor's glove and into his arm.

"Interesting," he mutters, pulling his hand away to work his fingers open and close.

"Movement! Left side," a sentry calls over their unit's comms. "Along the walls!"

Ibrahim hands the spear back to Wittenmyer. "Do *not* turn on your lights!" he shouts, taking point.

"Maybe it hasn't seen us?" Aquoia asks.

"Doubtful," Warden denies, looking into the left-side corridor.

"It's just . . . standing there? Not moving," Mannering suggests. "I can see its eyes glinting, sir. It's looking at us."

Ibrahim can hear the murmurs reverberating through his fireteams.

"Get into ready positions! Do *not* engage," Ibrahim orders. "Open fire only if *it* does. Maybe it's just curious? A worker, not a warrior."

"Or a scout for the warriors," Warden exclaims. "You think these aliens are like insects? Hive minds?"

"They certainly look like insects," Ibrahim shrugs. "We won't know until we get these specimens back for autopsy."

"I'm gonna bet they're not going to like us taking their dead away," Tanner suggests.

"Then aim that barrel high, Corporal," Warden orders, the tension in her voice causing a crack in her words.

And the alien just stands there, obscured by the decretive recesses in the walls, but otherwise benign. Ibrahim has to wonder if it's trying to get their attention. That's when he realizes *his* focus is entirely on this *one* creature in this *one* branch of the intersection.

Ibrahim turns to the ride-side corridor. His visor lights up red.

"They're behind us!" he shouts.

And a mob of the bugs frenzy toward his marines.

Every rifle at his command pivots. "Orders, sir?" Warden demands.

Ibrahim only has a few seconds to analyze the situation for the best option. It's not much time to decide on anything, let alone ensure his soldiers can get out of this intact. Then again, that's also part of his job.

Suppose he orders his marines to open fire on aliens that aren't hostile but, instead, are merely wanting to retrieve their dead? In that case, Ibrahim will start a war with foes that humanity has *no* experience fighting. And the potential losses for Earth? Tremendous. And suppose he does *nothing* but let the aliens come anyway, intending to kill his men? In that case, Ibrahim and his fireteams will get ripped to shreds with little opportunity to fight back.

Ibrahim only remembers flashes of the giant—the fact it *saved* his life yesterday and the lives of his troopers?

He's no way to know if these creatures swarming his position have anything to do with the big one. Nor does he know what's killed *these* three at the crossroads.

Ibrahim can surmise all he wants to, but humanity is suddenly finding itself in the middle of a dispute. And these *new* aliens are . . . participants.

He squeezes the grip on his rifle, holding his breath.

His heart pumps loudly inside his chest. Ibrahim can feel every THUD.

Unfortunately, a six-armed alien throws its spear and decides for him.

A marine takes the brunt square in the chest, pinning him violently against the wall.

"Open fire!" Ibrahim yells.

"Weapons free! Weapon's free!" Warden confirms.

Within a heartbeat, the intersection lights up with muzzle flashes and harsh words. As the aliens drop throughout the corridor, they spark as concentrated fire rips through their ornate armor. As each one falls, the others continue to swarm the hallway toward the crossroads and ignore it.

That length gives Ibrahim's marines an advantage. It's a space that bottlenecks the buggers, turning the corridor into a shooting gallery.

"No wonder they used the scout to distract us until they closed the distance," Ibrahim says internally.

Spears come flying, bypassing their HRDVS combat harnesses.

Several of Ibrahim's squad go down the instant they're hit. Others get away with a scratch, with a caveat—exposure to the same air that had slowly killed Arthur Summerland's team after their brief foray into the Breach.

"More contacts!" Mannering shouts over the comms. "Left side! Left side! Oh, hell—"

Ibrahim veers left to see a hundred more of the six-armed aliens crawling on the walls and ceiling.

"They're jealous they weren't invited to the 'Welcome to Earth' party with the boys," Warden snarks.

"Everyone! Pull to the rear of the corridor!" Ibrahim sounds. "Layered retreat! Team one to fallback position! Set up explosives along the pillars while teams two and three screen your sorry asses! Everyone will fall behind you and provide a bulwark to the next checkpoint! And keep those rifles hot! Don't shoot unless you can promise me a kill shot!"

"Somebody needs to drag one of those corpses with us!" Warden calls. "We don't want to leave here empty-handed!"

"We're gonna risk our necks for a few dead bugs?" Wittenmyer cries.

"Unless you're willing to ask them for a volunteer," Ibrahim retorts, "we're bringing one with us!"

"Get a move on, marines!" Mannering shouts.

Two minutes.

That's how long it takes for the first team to set up the detonators for their defensive retreat. For Ibrahim, the seconds feel much longer while under constant fire. And when the team's lead sends the signal, and the survivors sprint behind the rear line, each marine provides covering fire for the next.

He intends to keep the buggers off-balance, however long it takes. Anything until the next layer is prepared to stomach the brunt of the assault.

They set off the explosives along the walls to give themselves that time.

And their numbers gradually dwindle.

Two of his marines are busy carrying an alien's dead carcass.

A third fights to keep ahold of their new stock of spear-like weapons they're currently dodging.

Ibrahim doesn't get very far before the waves of buggers eventually lessen to nearly vanishing into the crevices.

"What the hell?" Warden exclaims.

"What's going on?" Mannering joylessly mocks. "Are they running low on fodder to feed us?"

"Maybe we've convinced them swarming our line isn't good for their health," Ibrahim states, adjusting his visor for a better view. Only to notice the bright flashes emanating farther along the corridor. From the crossroads.

As the flashes cascade, many buggers immediately turn a heel and run away from the battle.

"Is that gunfire?" Corporal Tanner suggests. He points at the light show at the crossroads.

"I thought we're the only unit left in this sector," Warden notions.

"Reinforcements? We didn't call for it if they are," Mannering adds.

"Maybe it's another platoon deciding we needed a rescue?" Wittenmyer advocates.

Ibrahim nods as he warms to that idea, except—

"Bright red?" he whispers, noticing the flashes aren't quite right. They're not . . . firearms.

Another *human* force would probably warrant the aliens splitting their strength, simultaneously engaging both sides to save their front and rear-guard. No. Instead, the entire swarm pivoted to deal with this new threat.

"They're distracted!" Ibrahim shouts. "Double-time it to the checkpoint . . . Go, go, go!"

Nobody in the platoon hesitates.

After a half-hour slugging it back to the checkpoint, Ibrahim and his fireteams manage to cross the doorway into the hangar.

The marines on duty are stunned by the condition of the returning men and women. Ibrahim can't see their faces through their helmets, but he can tell by their drooping shoulders, regardless. He can't hide the dented pieces of their armor. Or the spent rifles and cracked visors of the survivors.

"What's happened?" the sentry asks.

Ibrahim doesn't answer.

He orders Warden to send the incident report to METIS Control and Mount Olympus to update their situation.

"And get that . . . *thing* . . . loaded on the next shuttle to base," Ibrahim says, pointing at the carcass they've dragged back. "Addison and Vogert will want our catch. As for everyone else—" He hesitates, looking at his reflection on the visor of one of his marines, unable to see their exhaustion.

"Colonel?" Warden asks.

Ibrahim nods. "We've left our friends behind," he says, turning to her. "We are not going to leave them. Have three units meet us. And prep them for a full-combat mission. These things came to *our* world. Now it's time to explain why *we* are the dominant species on this planet! War defines our history! We *are* soldiers! Let's show them what we've learned!"

Every marine that hears him shouts, "Oorah!"

His expression goes cold. They can't see it, but it does.

"They've not beaten us," he says. "Not by a longshot."

17 | A WARRIOR CASTE

ADDISON KENNEDY, FIELD DIRECTOR
EPIMETHEUS PROJECT

OCTOBER 12, 2041 | 1912 HOURS

===

"It's only been two days," she notions, "and already we've got a biological specimen on our hands."

Addison stands away from the Breach's edge, soaking in the rain as a sixteen-wheeled military shuttle stops in front of her. The UCAF brought these transports to ferry equipment and troops to hotspots inside the hangar bay. The vehicle's headlights are like a sea monster's eyes. Fearsome in appearance.

Like most technology utilized by the Epimetheus Project, they've adapted the "rover" to suit the expedition's needs.

A dozen UCAF marines surround the shuttle like a nuke aboard an aircraft carrier. But it's not a warhead.

These soldiers are escorting a far more dangerous cargo.

"And that *is* saying something," she murmurs.

Addison crosses her arms, keeping warm.

"This is all so very exciting!" Athena whispers into her earpiece.

"What's the word on our intrepid Colonel?"

"Our response team is nearing the battle site," Athena returns. "All units are convening to block off the connecting passageways. ETA—fifteen minutes. They'll update us at that time."

"Any indication of what these aliens were fighting? Besides *us*, I mean," Addison asks. "Or are we still in the dark about that?"

"Speculative witness reports only," the AI confides. "Half the reason Colonel Ibrahim is heading back is to confirm the evidence."

Addison grins. "Like a game of Mystery Express," she suggests.

"Or a round of Dungeon Master," Athena argues.

"Point taken," she agrees. "The other half is to retrieve the boys we left behind."

Addison steps aside as wounded marines come down the ramp on stretchers. Medics hurry them toward the MedCenter. She reads the incoming reports on her pad of the incident. Many of the wounded had their hardsuits damaged in the firefight, exposing them to the ship's native air.

"If we can even call it a firefight," Addison denotes.

Arthur's team fell ill after their brief foray into the craft, dying over the weeks. Slowly. And in excruciating pain.

However, the atmosphere *inside* the dreadnaught doesn't extend outside the Breach. Like a field exists to prevent the air from mixing with the local environment. For everyone, that's a good thing. Namely, their crews don't have to wear bulky hardsuits while standing hull-side. Only their raingear. And rebreather masks.

Addison studies the data readouts on her pad. "It's as though the *people* who've built this ship understood the danger," she mutters her thoughts aloud. Addison works through each theory in her head as she narrows down the pathways. "Add the fact this ship's magnetic signature can interfere with the planet's geomagnetic field . . . Or the literal shift in climate dynamics due to the displacement volume? We're lucky this crisis hasn't become an extinction-level event."

"If it's not too presumptuous for me to say?" Athena begs the question. "But our 'boys' took it in the ass."

Addison's eyes shoot up at the stretcher-bearers going back and forth.

"Now's probably not the best time, Athena," Addison shifts. She waits for the medics to finish moving the wounded away.

Addison steps forward as the last officer departs the ramp, her eyes on the casket with the specimen inside.

"Are you nervous?" Athena sincerely asks in her earpiece.

"Just a little bit," Addison admits.

She walks up to the container protecting the body as it rolls off the transport's ramp. A glass viewport interweaves with a holographic interface on the lid. Addison presses her palm to the top reader, and it reacts, whirling blue, then green, as it approves her credentials.

"Nifty device," she remarks.

Addison checks the readouts on the unit's display. She notes the simplistic beauty throughout the alien's intrinsic structure as it pops up.

"I detect cognitive activity going on inside its cranial cavity," Athena scans.

"Are you saying it's not dead?" Addison asks.

"Just the closest thing to 'dead' by *our* classifications," the AI concludes.

Addison would equate it to an active coma with some odd side effects in a human subject. Whereas the brain remains active, the circulatory system no longer pumps blood and nutrients to the organs. As such, the nerve structures appear only to have *minor* indications of electrochemical impulses, giving off the activity she's reading.

"Maybe caused by active synapses persisting after near-death? Or maybe—?" Addison pauses as she weighs another theory. "No. That's not . . . You're gone. Aren't you? And you're not coming back. You've too many broken gears in the turbine, and we've too few parts to replace them."

Addison puts her hand on the unit's transparent cover. She can feel the ice on top melting into a trace of her palm.

"What *are* you?" Addison demands the unhearing alien inside the pod.

"Doctor Kennedy?" a soldier calls for her attention.

"Addison?" a nearby medic pokes.

Hearing her name causes her eyes to refocus.

"Get this to the MedCenter immediately," Addison orders. "I'll meet with Vogert there to conduct an autopsy of the Subject."

"Understood, ma'am," the marine escort responds. He's quick to jump into action.

"Shouldn't the doc's priority be with the wounded?" the medic questions.

"He's got an entire staff division to do that," Addison explains. "And I doubt he'd pass on the chance to study xenobiology when it's dropped at his feet."

She walks alongside the pod on her way to the MedCenter's cleanroom.

When she enters the tunnel, Addison strips off her clothes, handing them off to the attendant. The man exchanges the uniform for a tight under-weave that Addison *knows* is uncomfortable to wear.

"When did these arrive?" Addison asks, feeling the suit's texture.

"A couple of hours ago," the other says. "We're distributing them to medical personnel."

"Replacements for the hazard gear?"

The attendant nods.

"Oh, that'll be a joy," Addison grumbles under her breath.

After managing to squeeze into the skin-weave, Addison enters the chemical showers. Warning lights fill the chamber as lifters bring the pod through another set of doors. Addison watches as the lab techs unseal the casket, laying the Subject flat on the table.

Vogert enters the tunnel behind Addison while she's waiting for the room to re-pressurize.

Seven minutes later, her cycle finishes, and the ready lights turn green. The doors to the cleanroom unlock with a click.

Addison steps onto the floor and eyes the alien carcass.

She looks back at the tunnel to find Vogert looking snug in his under-weave as he enters through the doors. He pulls to loosen it around his gut and shoulders.

"Glad I'm not the only one thinking these things are god-awful," Addison mutters.

Athena sends an inappropriate whistle into Addison's ear.

"Exercise much, Doctor Vogert?" the AI quips.

"Stay off him, Athena," Addison warns.

She watches as the man staggers into position next to the specimen.

Vogert keys several buttons on the table's panel without a word, turning on every automated camera in the room.

"I don't know about these suits," he squirms.

"I'm pretty sure High Castle needs to re-examine their ease of use," Addison says.

"Getting it on without rubbing my skin raw would be nice," Vogert admits.

"He's talking about his thighs," Athena blurts. "Just to clarify."

"That's more than I needed to know," Addison remarks.

Vogert sighs. "Can I report harassment by an artificial intelligence?" the man asks.

"It's legally untested," Athena interprets, clearly enjoying his discomfort.

"I demand to speak to HR in that case," Vogert muses.

"Denied. I *am* your administrator," Athena laughs. "And upper management has chosen to ignore any complaints."

"Any complaints? Or just *my* complaints?"

"Correct."

"That didn't . . . Wait?! Aren't I upper management?" Vogert asks.

"Middle management?" Addison joins in the fray.

"Rude," he says, squinting at her thinly.

Addison surrenders him a wink before turning to the specimen on the table.

"How do you feel? Really?" Addison genuinely asks. "First man in history to dissect an alien cadaver?"

"The first man that we *know* about," Vogert corrects her. "And it's rough, to say the least."

Addison frowns. She turns on the table's software and begins running deep-tissue scans of the alien. Addison wants to record as much of its intact biology as possible before they cut into the carcass. "Look at this!" Vogert calls, taking a closer look at the Subject. The man works each of its appendages, moving them left and right to test its joint structure. "This is a beautiful. I don't even know *how* to compare it . . . And what is this? Is this . . . this isn't armor, is it?"

"Very ornate armor," Addison says. "Almost like chitin, but . . . I don't know, is this metal?"

"A strange metal, if it is," Vogert admits. "Maybe suggesting an individuality despite its insectoid qualities?"

"The material doesn't seem to reflect light directly," Addison notes. She runs a finger over the matted sheen that forms the outer layer. "Maybe it defuses any energy that contacts it? And do you see this injury right between the plates? It almost looks deliberate."

"Maybe," Vogert half-heartily agrees, looking at the scans on the monitor. "Very similar to the burns on our troops when they encountered the

Fragment. Note this contusion? Straight through. Powerful weapon. Was it aiming for the vital organs? Let me see . . . By the looks, one of its four hearts ruptured. I'd assume the other three would have taken over its workload if it were a redundant nervous system. Or maybe each heart sends blood to specific portions of the body?"

"That could make for a highly efficient warrior," Addison comments.

"True. Immensely fast," Vogert grants, "if all four hearts can work together."

Addison watches as the man's eyes narrow in consideration.

"What are you thinking?" she asks.

"I don't know yet. Could they be using the same basic chemistry as Earth-based organisms?"

"You mean, whether or not it can breathe oxygen?"

"Let's get a blood sample and find out," Vogert suggests.

He takes a syringe and punctures the Subject's thick outer skin. What comes out is a strange orange liquid that's already congealing.

"Half-dead? What a damn joke," Vogert scoffs. "Appears our friend was completely dead when Ibrahim stumbled across it. This activity is likely only a last gasp, like a snake living on for several minutes after losing its head." He raises the syringe to a nearby light.

"Blood's slightly luminous," Addison comments, seeing how the orange reacts to the stimuli.

"Now that *is* a strange development," Vogert agrees.

"Not based on standard hemoglobin," Addison rules out. "Nor is it based on hemolymph, like with insects. Otherwise, the blood would have a clearer, almost white appearance." She runs a gloved hand across the dead alien's ridges, feeling between the plates.

"There are reports of some women seeing a discharge of orange blood several weeks after conception," Vogert suggests. "Usually, that happens in trace amounts, caused by cervical fluids. Maybe a sign of bacterial infection? Nothing I've heard about goes to this extent. But it does remind me of the bioluminescence we see in fireflies. When oxygen catalyzes with calcium from a specific enzyme, it creates the glow that kids like to chase in the fields."

"At least we're not dealing with a pregnant alien," Addison surmises.

"Rather a protein we've not seen in a lifeform before," Vogert concludes.

"Which causes the blood to take on this hue," Addison determines.

"Evolution does enjoy its creative streaks," Vogert laughs. He takes several more blood samples and puts them into cold storage. "Let's take a closer look at this creature's skin. See if we can't get under this hard outer layer."

Addison leans over the body with a light touch. She carefully removes each piece to reveal the relatively softer skin underneath.

"At first glance," Vogert continues, "I would say it's like the shells used by ironclad beetles."

"Sensory input is giving me a leathery feel on my glove," Addison describes. "Like bone? Flexible. Very interesting."

"Seems like it has a range of motion comparable to a knight in full battledress."

"Tough bastards," Addison decides. She runs a finger through the skin's intricate creases. "Doesn't seem to have helped it survive what killed it. But it would make it an effective defense against projectile weaponry."

"Maybe a guard against predators when numbers aren't enough?" Vogert suggests.

"We can use the battle's footage to piece together their behavior patterns," Addison reasons. "See if we can't figure it out."

Vogert nods. "Good. That should give us some insight into what makes them tick."

"Except for this *one* detail that's bothering me—"

"Stop. I know what you're about to say," Vogert says, cutting off her sentence. "It doesn't resemble the alien from yesterday's incident."

"It's too small," Addison remarks.

"I agree. And the characteristics are too different from the glances we've obtained."

"Another species? Or maybe an off-breed?"

"Differing attributes in a species doesn't necessarily mean the two are separate, Addison," Vogert reasons. "Look at the ant-family. Individuals can look wildly different based on their roles. Ants with wings, the queens, are individuals meant solely for breeding. And soldiers are simply larger workers assigned to defend—"

"I was just going to use dogs as an example," Addison says. "Hundreds of breeds. All the same species."

Addison can tell Vogert grins under his facemask.

"We can look at ourselves to count how many traits can develop within a species," Vogert continues. "It shouldn't surprise us if a society apart from ours developed a separate rendition of a caste system. Our friend here might well be in the position of a soldier."

"Or a laborer," Addison says.

"While the larger alien Colonel Ibrahim bumped into is more a leader," Vogert suggests.

"Or a highly ranked warrior," Addison counters.

Vogert breathes. "The logic feels rooted enough," he agrees.

"Shall we open this one up and find out for certain?" Addison asks. She hands him a scalpel off the surgical tray.

Vogert's cheeks bubble through his suit's mask. "I certainly hope you aren't squeamish, Addison."

"Let's say I'm glad I didn't eat a ration bar for my supper," she grimaces.

"At least this mask can filter out the necrotic stench," Vogert says.

"Allegedly," Addison retorts.

18 | SCHISM

SERGEANT MAJOR OLIVIA WARDEN
UNITED COALITION ARMED FORCES

OCTOBER 12, 2041 | 1551 HOURS

==

"We're coming to the fringes," Warden announces. "What's with these corridors?"

"I thought shipbuilders tend to utilize every square inch," Private James Aquoia puzzles. "But looking at this thing?"

"You get the impression they're big on ceremony," Warden agrees.

"It's a different design philosophy than we're used to," Colonel Ibrahim states over the channel several meters behind her. "We shouldn't expect them to think as we do. Or did you miss the giant-ass expanse running through the ship's midsection?"

"Kinda hard to miss that, sir."

Ibrahim grunts amusingly. "Our engineers would have a field day trying to fill the space. I don't think they'd know what to do with themselves."

"We've got bodies ahead!" Corporal Tanner hails, setting a waypoint on their HUDs. "Along with some of our handiwork."

"Makes a pretty painting either way," Wittenmyer says.

"I like the brushstrokes," Private Morgan returns.

"I dunno," Warden joins in, smirking under her faceplate. "They should've added more color to the piece. Make it pop. Too much focus on reds and blacks. It's oppressive, don't you think?"

That earns her one or two nods from her squadmates. Then, it goes quiet.

Warden steps on a rock . . . except it's not a rock. It's a Fragment's shattered chassis. Bodies are everywhere. Some humans. Others? Not even close.

"Not my preferred first contact scenario," Warden admits.

"This wasn't our first contact," Ibrahim counters.

"Oh, right," Warden sneers. "Yesterday."

"Makes you think about what we're dealing with," he agrees.

"And if we're out of our depth on this one?" she questions. Warden recounts the names of those who died in that slaughter—Dominic Raymond, Eugene Pulaski, Carl Anderson—along with many others. So much wasted effort, all those years training them. And for what? All for it to be over in seconds. "It's a damn shame."

Aquoia beats his breastplate with his fist. "We've got a dozen nations on this floating junkheap. We can take them!"

"Against these numbers? Their losses would constitute a pyrrhic victory in any human conflict," Ibrahim cautions. "Warden—you saw their tactics, too. What's your take?"

"That they don't care about taking casualties," Olivia answers, stepping over another body. "They swarmed us—meaning they've plenty more they're willing to lose."

"Like the old-style mass wave assaults," Ibrahim describes. "Send your conscripts into the fire and hope they can swamp your enemy through sheer, reckless force."

"Yet these guys are better equipped," Warden adds. She shines her light on a dead alien, still twitching from active nerves. She looks at the tips of their spears, the weird elegance in their arms and armor, begrudgingly accepting they can understand war as a concept. "They're experienced putting their gear to practice. Look at their weapons—preferring melee over ranged tactics. Which might explain why—?"

"Please don't add another theory," Ibrahim kindly begs. "That pile is large enough."

"Or—?" Warden offers anyway. "Maybe they follow some honor-bound philosophy when it comes to combat."

Ibrahim goes quiet on the comms.

Warden counts the bodies. For some reason, there's more than she remembers fighting, even with that endless wave crashing on top of them. She expects the six-armed aliens and Fragments would have continued battling it out after her troops retreated to their fallback positions.

"But why fight each other?" Warden questions.

When her squad reaches the crossroads, Warden scans the devastation. Her troops pick up their fallen comrades, laying them on stretchers and zipping them into body bags. The menders take their tasks efficiently, moving the dead aliens and shattered Fragments aside.

Warden's HUD reads a dozen more units in the corridors leading to this location.

"At least we'll have the firepower to hold them off," Ibrahim states, entering the intersection. "Perhaps even turn the tide."

Warden nods. That's when she notices movement among the dead. An alien . . . adorned with heavier armor than the others, watching her intently.

Wounded, afraid, but otherwise alive. And breathing sporadically.

Warden hugs her rifle tight. "We've got a live one over here!" she calls out. Everyone turns their weapons on the creature.

"What's it doing?" Wittenmyer asks.

"I think it's trying to talk to us?" Warden suggests, listening to its raspy burrs and shrills.

"Can you make out any words?" Ibrahim asks, moving through the crowd.

A rough phonetic estimation by her suit's translation subroutine appears on Warden's display:

KA-JAA BAA-REEEM TU-JUUU-AL
VAAAR-MAA-JAAAL-KAA-VEEN
AAAD-HI-ON KLAA-KA
NOOO-MAAD

"I don't . . . I don't know," Warden admits.

"Your insight, Athena?" Ibrahim demands.

A bright laugh from the AI causes the squad's comms to give off a loud feedback tone.

"Not an encouraging response," Warden thinks aloud.

"Seriously? An alien language with no comprehensive or written reference? And you want me to translate it purely off the phonetics?" Athena charges.

"Athena? Either help us or don't," Colonel Ibrahim battles.

"I'm sorry, Lieutenant Colonel," the AI constitutes. "There's nothing I can do."

Warden kneels to the wounded creature to study it closely. It stares back at her with tears in its four eyes. She always thought that crying was a distinctly *human* reaction. "Maybe there's more in common between us than we believe," Warden whispers. "I'll note it for Addison Kennedy in my report."

"I'm watching you guys on your suits' camera feeds," Doctor Kennedy says over the channel.

"Speak of the devil," Warden remarks.

"Sergeant Major? How functional is that specimen? Is it possible to bring it back alive?" Addison demands. "Also, we need your troops to collect any pieces you can find. The more samples we can get our hands on and send to the labs, the more Doctor Remmings can use for testing purposes."

"Doctor Kennedy—" Ibrahim's about to say.

"We're running playback on what the alien's saying," Addison intercedes. "It's like . . . it *almost* sounds like it's saying . . . Var-ma-jalk-a-vaen, and . . . Adhion K-la-ka and No-mad." She pauses for three blinks. "I'll presume that doesn't mean anything to anyone?"

Warden shrugs, leaning closer to the alien. Its four pupils dilate the closer she gets. She notices its bare skin has a glossy outer layer, almost like . . . sweat. Or a mucus membrane? Like it's designed to protect an injury until it can find treatment.

"Would a species that uses its *living* soldiers like cannon-fodder have medics?" Warden asks it. She doesn't expect it to answer.

"Or doctors, for that matter?" Aquoia adds.

"Embarkara suda kaa runsurraa," the creature says, a different phrase than before. "Kar seranna indonee."

"What is that? What are you saying?" Warden asks. "I-I don't . . . I don't understand?"

The alien surrenders an expression as if it *can* understand *her*.

"Remarkable," Addison confides. "Sergeant Warden? It seems like it's reacting to you."

"Is it?" Warden mocks. "I didn't notice."

Despite the cold inside this damn ship, her underarms are dripping with sweat.

"Look at it? No hostile intent," Doctor Kennedy notes. "Sergeant? Keep doing what you're doing. See how *it* responds."

Everyone around Warden begins watching the two interact. Ibrahim stands over them, silent and observational with equal fascination.

"Korusoraada?" the alien seemingly poses a question. It motions with a hand as if it's writing on a pad.

Warden unstraps her wrist-mounted computer and gives it to the creature. It looks at the device . . . confusingly at first, but it quickly deduces what it's for and draws an elegant series of lines on the main screen. Warden turns it around after the alien drops its arms in exhaustion. She uploads the scratch to the network for the eggheads to analyze. Before long, the creature fades completely, unable to continue with its injuries.

"I'm sorry, Ms. Kennedy," Warden says over her comms. "Our friend's not going to make the trip back."

Addison stays quiet on the comms.

"All right, folks," Colonel Ibrahim redirects. "Time to put things under wraps for now. Get our people on those sleds and pack up everything that won't kill us. We're not going to leave our geeks wanting for research material. Let's move it, Marines!"

19 | SIDE EFFECTS

RYAN VOGERT, CHIEF MEDICAL OFFICER
EPIMETHEUS PROJECT

OCTOBER 13, 2041 | 0001 HOURS

===

Vogert sits in the umbilical leading from Central to the morgue. He watches the raindrops swim across the plastic surface, acting as a window to the outside. More people arrive at bi-hourly intervals—soldiers and scientists, workers, and a few engineers. And the rigger crews who keep it all standing upright in the storm.

Once hull-side, they're put on shuttles and sent into the interior, with coordinators directing them through the camp's streets.

"The best that humanity has to offer," Vogert whispers, looking at the culmination of the last two days.

He's never met Arthur Summerland and doesn't know much about the man's work. Vogert's only read a few articles about the man's "Big Question" he posed to the General Assembly five years ago.

"Do we face extinction?" was *that* question.

It was a question he gave when the melting of the polar ice caps was considered unmanageable.

Vogert quietly mutters the words to himself as he waits.

"Different disaster now," he says. "Same question."

Now a dozen research outposts are dotting the vessel's massive hull. Every nation under the treaty is trying to come up with answers. Ryan counts among those numbers, but he's just a small part of the greater whole. And it hurts his ego to admit that. Nevertheless, he sighs, accepting his role.

"Third shift began hours ago," Addison says. Vogert turns to her as she walks into the tube on her way out of the Medical Section. She waves her assistants on to Central, deciding to stay with Vogert. "You should've hit the cot. Why are you still here?"

"Oh, admiring the storm," Vogert replies sluggishly. "I need to love these quiet moments."

Addison sits next to him. "Beautiful, isn't it?" she notions.

"As long as you don't think about it," Vogert admits. "Physics and weather patterns take a sideways turn here." He goes to rest his elbows on his knees. "Standing on this side of the Breach, the air shifts rapidly across the freezing point. And the interior? A human being wouldn't survive without a hardsuit or artic gear for long." He's despondent.

"And the wounded?" Addison asks. "How are they?"

Vogert holds his breath unwillingly. "We knew going into this from Arthur's experience that any exposure would likely result in the shutdown of a victim's immune system. We're all inoculated for most diseases we can find on Earth. And we expected a decent challenge to our normal ways of thinking. Nothing like this, however."

Addison eyes him worryingly. "What do you mean?" she asks.

He stands up and walks closer to the umbilical's plastic screen. "I mean, we have to look at what we know," Vogert details. "Arthur? He survived for a short while without any fancy suits. His team only began exhibiting symptoms *after* they returned to normalized conditions."

"When they got sicker over their last weeks," Addison adds. "Eventually passing into a coma and died."

"Exactly! And I'm not sure we made the correct diagnosis at the time," Vogert goes on. "We assumed the first expedition died due to residual extremes—either atmospheric by correlation or an alien virus." He points to the other side of the canvas. "Why can we breathe the air on the hull, albeit with rebreathers, but need more *inside* the ship?"

"Ryan? Please don't add—" Addison says wearily.

"What if the atmosphere isn't the issue? Or a disease? Something more fundamental."

"Something we're overlooking?"

"Yes!"

"Like a biological requirement that our immune system doesn't adapt to?"

"Or an adaptive strain that changes our biology at exposure and makes it unable to return to its original state!"

Addison goes silent for a moment, covering her mouth with her palm to hide her tendency to clench her jaw when she thinks.

"As if it's in the air but *not* the air itself?" she asks.

Vogert nods. "It's a theory for now. We got the injured into treatment. *That* is what's important. But I noticed many were displaying similar signs to that first team. Suppose I am going by what the medical examiners recorded in the days after Arthur's exposure? In that case, not all of our soldiers with breached suits display symptoms."

"Colonel Ibrahim and Sergeant Warden?" Addison names two of those not showing the side effects.

"And that's after a couple of days!" Vogert cheers. "Long enough for a virus to incubate."

"And your plan to handle a situation if it becomes a problem?"

"For the moment? I'll keep those with symptoms isolated in a cleanroom," Vogert discerningly states. Addison's eyes light up, but not so favorably to what she's hearing. "It's not ideal, I know, but it's what we've got to work around. I've had the rigger crews run a hose between the room's oxygen recycler and the ship's—"

"Wait one sec! Are you saying you've contaminated your cleanroom?" Addison returns with an unhappy frown. "On purpose?"

An angry sliver breaks through her usually calm demeanor.

Vogert raises his palms in surrender. "To maintain a vital environment necessary to sustain the worst cases," he says, admitting that he probably should've gotten permission for the experiment. And he *would* have if it didn't risk taking precious time away from his patients. "It's just a way to depress their symptoms until I can find a better solution."

"And how many did you throw in there?" she questions.

"Just three," Vogert answers. "Only those showing the worst side effects, I'll add. Worse than what Arthur's team experienced after a week. Maybe it's the length of their exposure to the ship? Or maybe the soldiers have compromised immune systems due to their years in an already sterile environment. Whichever the case—the change in their conditions has made it a worthwhile risk. Look."

He hands Addison a tablet with the readouts of his patients. He points at the three in question with a grimace curling his face.

"Occam's razor?" Addison whispers as she skims the charts. "Simple solutions? Fewer assumptions."

"You know, my friend, that's not how science works," Vogert chuckles. "But it *does* fit better into the overall puzzle in a way."

"Meaning?" Addison prods. She hands the tablet back to him. "Something *on* the ship can change our biology to match its requirements."

"And is unable to return us to our original state," Vogert adds. "Not without a corresponding element."

"How limited are we in probing for more information?"

"Depends," Vogert weighs.

"Then, maybe we should run more tests on the ship's atmospherics," Addison suggests. "Find out for sure."

"I've got a whole room full of the stuff," Vogert agrees. "I can have my staff run the gambit and get us working samples."

Addison keys her earpiece. "Athena—can you hear me?"

"Like thunder in a storm," the AI returns. "What do you require, Doctor Kennedy?"

Vogert listens through his comms unit.

"We need your help on a new project. Can you have your scanners collect data from inside the cleanroom every five minutes?" Addison asks. "We need a rundown on what's inside. Anything you can get us."

"Of course," Athena acknowledges. "For my benefit, what are you hoping to find?"

Addison glances at Vogert with dark eyes. He keys into the conversation.

"Living organisms," he says. "Microscopic. Native to the Summerland."

"Like bacteria," Addison suggests.

"Or a symbiont," Vogert counters with the likelihood.

"Not a parasite?" Athena asks.

"Would it be a parasite if it *wants* to acclimate us to its model environment?" Vogert states.

"Probably not," Addison admits.

"Either way, it's a dangerous pact," Vogert shrugs, "if it can't adapt to *our* native habitat."

"And anyone exposed to it—?" Addison is hesitant to say.

"They lack a way to revert the union between the bonded pairs," Vogert finishes her sentence.

"Then that's our challenge moving ahead," Addison agrees.

"We've got to create an enzyme," Vogert concludes, "that can meld with the organism. Force it to adapt with us?"

"How likely are we to finish it in a week or two?"

"I don't know," Vogert admits. "It used to take decades to create simple vaccines."

"We don't have decades," Addison urges.

"You don't have to tell me," Vogert shudders. "God help us. I know."

20 | AND OUR WORLD LOOKS ON

MALAKAI ADONIS, DIRECTOR OF OPERATIONS
EPIMETHEUS PROJECT

OCTOBER 13, 2041 | 0825 HOURS

===

Malakai's muscles tense as the gears on the door whine open. With the construction over the past two days, *this* is the room that swells his throat.

It's his direct line to the Joint Security Council in Geneva and Vancouver. When he enters, it leaves him unimpressed.

"This is little more than a closet," Malakai mutters.

There are monitors for him to see them. And cameras so they can see him.

He squares himself in front of the middle camera and counts down: "Three . . . two . . . one," Malakai exhales. And he flips a switch. The monitors whirl lively with a view of everyone as he joins the conference. "Ambassadors? Mr. Secretary? Happy Sunday. And hello from Ground Zero."

They return with weary expressions.

Malakai spends the next several hours answering questions about *what* the Project has accomplished over the last two days.

The conference stays subdued until he reaches the end of his report. And then? Their hesitancy causes doubt to creep up in the back of his head.

"That's quite . . . uh, quite an update," is the initial comment made once he finishes.

A second ambassador coughs. "It doesn't seem like you've made any significant progress on your goals," they criticize.

Malakai swallows his tongue for a moment.

"After two days," he diplomatically states, inflating his voice, "what progress did you expect? We *only* got done setting up."

"Our expectations for you were . . . simply put, much higher." Her name is Susan Mersley, the US Ambassador on the Security Council. "And these casualty reports?" the woman demands, slapping her hand on a stack of folders. "For God's sake! We don't need—"

"I apologize if this crisis is inconvenient for you, Ambassador Mersley," Malakai says with a calm scowl. "If you'd like, we can ship you over if you think your expertise can lend assistance. Or if you think you can do a better job? You can't. And that's my point. Let's be frank—"

Another chair sits forward. "Frankly? We had hoped with your resources that you would've made greater progress by now."

"Are you serious? Three days is hardly enough time to learn a foreign language," Malakai fights them. "Let alone having to translate a script that isn't in our hands yet? Even *with* our artificial intelligence doing its best to make it readable . . . We're only scratching the surface of this beast."

"Then why haven't you—?" Mersley attempts to say.

"Don't forget it took us decades to translate the Rosetta Stone using *known* languages," Malakai doubles down. "We've no blueprint or reference for anything we're doing here. So, if you've got an idea for tackling these challenges, Madam Ambassador, let us hear them. My staff of the brightest minds on the planet are naturally an open-minded group."

"That shouldn't be necessary," Freda Geraldine, the German Ambassador, accepts his reasons.

Malakai can only regulate his breath as the meeting continues.

"Regardless. Why haven't you begun sending teams farther into the ship?" Mersley turns to ask. "Hostiles or not—the firepower we've lent you, Doctor Adonis, should be sufficient to overcome most conventional obstacles in your way."

"And I think it's weird how you can describe what's hitting us as 'conventional,' Ambassador Mersley," Malakai refutes. "You realize this isn't a puddle we're jumping into, right? It's a cold ocean. Bottomless. And we aren't lining up across an open field to exchange volleys."

"Everyone understand your circumstances aren't typical, Director Adonis," Geraldine admits.

"And *who* is *everyone*, Ambassador?" Malakai begs the question.

"We've got a hostile force on *our* doorstep while our people are dying!" Mersley shouts.

"And until we can establish a direct line with them," Malakai counters, "we cannot ascertain their motives!"

"What the fuck does *that* mean?" the woman demands.

"That our visitors may consider *us* the hostile, invading force," Malakai offers.

"It's *our* planet," Mersley debates.

"It's *their* ship," Malakai resists.

"This isn't the subject of today's conference," Geraldine attempts to mediate.

"How long do you think it'll take us to bridge your ocean, Director Adonis?" Mersley demands. "Days? A few weeks? Months?"

"You think weeks?" Malakai snorts, losing control. "Sure, why not? If we devote every resource to figuring it out, I don't see why it can't take a few weeks. Ignoring the geopolitical disaster this crisis has thrown us into, I mean. Which is—and let's be honest, Ambassadors—a difficult situation for anybody to manage. We have thousands buried under the rubble. And what are *we* doing for them?"

"We'd be doing a lot more if our assets weren't tied up making sure you have a job," Mersley accuses.

"An opportunity I am grateful for," Malakai admits.

"An opportunity you have because you convinced us that you had a plan to deal with the crisis," Mersley continues. "And what do we see for your talk? Nothing! Where's the accountability for our investment into this global debacle?"

Malakai scowls before speaking his mind: "Do you think I care about my position, Ambassador?" His eyes dart across the screens, reading his audience. "Because unless you can get this Council to vote unanimously on my removal, I recommend listening to the advice my team can provide this body. Don't cut off your head while still on life support."

Malakai can feel the absolute quiet spilling from the monitors.

"We can make that happen," Mersley sours. "You work for us! We can easily fire you."

"I work for the Epimetheus Project under the United Coalition," Malakai argues. "Our work is a benefit for our species. Have any of you even visited the crisis zones in your home countries? Your states? Because *I* have! My family is in a camp as we speak. My wife works to ensure water and medicine get to those who need it."

"We're not here to discuss your job performance," a softer voice breaks the tension.

"And nobody's questioning your commitment, Mr. Adonis," another agrees.

"Or your devotion," says a third.

"Yours is a worthy cause, that's for sure."

"All we want is to figure out what we can do to help you," Geraldine offers.

"Good," Malakai states. "As long as we agree. Our decisions here can well mean the difference between achieving discovery . . . or extinction. The best decision . . . Maybe the only decision is for you to let us do what *we* do best, don't you think?"

Again. Silence.

He wipes the sweat off his neck.

A buzzing from the electric wiring feeding into the room fills the stillness.

"Malakai? You don't have to make a speech for our benefit," James William Harper finally chimes into the discussion. He leans forward into his camera. "Understand, it's our job to ask uncomfortable questions. As for you, Susan—our role is to listen and lend support, not to make threats when he's only a couple of days into his work."

"Dropping money into this without liability isn't something the United States will abide by, Mr. Secretary-General," Mersley seethes.

"And your temper isn't doing you a favor," Secretary Harper confides with a steady, softer tone. Mersley struggles to come up with the words to counter his diligence. "We're dealing with a force we don't understand. I agree that we can't walk into this blind or reckless. But if you want this done quickly, Ambassador—it will happen at a cost. No matter what, I expect we'll lose people along the way. Shatter lives. There's no way to prevent that no matter the safety measures we put in place."

Ambassador Mersley hesitates as Harper turns his chair in her direction. Malakai can barely tell on the monitors.

"All I am saying is that we have people dying on the mainland," Mersley reiterates. "If we keep diverting our resources to this Project without putting the recovery effort first, what does it matter *what* we learn from these visitors? What solid guarantee do we have that *he* can find a solution *inside* that wreck?"

Harper leans back in his chair.

Malakai watches as the gears inside the man's head blow smoke through the screen.

Many ambassadors, diplomats, and councilors go quiet whenever the man speaks. Some of them relax, expecting him to go on for a while. Others, like members of the man's political opposition, react differently. They're all sitting upright, anxiously twiddling their thumbs while guarding their tongues.

"Malakai?" Harper frowns, sighing after saying his name.

"Sir?" he answers.

"You know I have to ask . . . Can you maintain your objectives if we divert resources into helping the recovery?"

Malakai grimaces. "We have thousands of personnel aboard the Summerland," he says with a bitter nod. "Military *and* civilian . . . If we can keep High Castle's assets, I believe we can afford to give up some of our support ships. But I would confer with Old Man Kennedy. He's using those ships to maintain the exclusion zone as we speak."

"Which means?" Harper asks.

"Meaning that if the Epimetheus Project runs into major trouble," Mersley clarifies, "the military's response will be limited." Her fingers are tapping nervously over the binders she has by her seat.

"And that's the risk," Malakai admits.

"And can you expand on those risks?" Harper invites. "Just for the record."

Malakai lets out his breath. He brings up several images of the dreadnaught taken by the Overlook.

"These are the readings we're getting from across the ship," Malakai highlights. "I've already gone over the preliminaries concerning yesterday's event with you. As you know, the field media captured this . . . red glow. The problem is, we don't know *what* it is or what it does."

"Somebody flipped a switch, and we don't know what they've turned on," Harper iterates, laying it flat for the council.

"And the readouts aren't showing . . . anything? No significant heat output, no electric wattage," Malakai continues. "We don't know if the red glow is power distribution from an unknown source or merely decoration. And we've not had the chance to get samples because . . . What *can* we get? We might as well bottle oxygen in a glass jar using a rotary fan. Our tools can't read it, so we've no way of putting it under a microscope."

"Then what are your recommendations?" Harper asks. "Is this dangerous?"

"Not dangerous," Malakai states, hesitant to speak honestly. "Not from what we can tell. Which is, again . . . not much. And with limited assets, I'd recommend waiting it out," he confesses, his fingers numb. "We'll continue our exploration of the ship and see what happens."

Mersley laughs. "That's the best you've got?" the woman demands.

"It's the safest way to go about it," Malakai scoffs at the response. "The only thing we *can* do is hope for the best. And *do* our best. We've had mixed encounters with the shipbuilders. So, there are two ways I can see this going . . . Either we learn to communicate with our visitors or assume hostilities."

"And with everything we've seen, I'm not convinced that is a battle we can win," James confides.

Mersley shrugs with a half-hearted effort. "Then it's decided," the woman accepts.

"Malakai," Harper weighs, "the Epimetheus Project will continue its mission on the ship."

"Meanwhile, segments of the American Fleet will redeploy to disaster zones," Mersley iterates.

"China would like to forward a motion to increase our presence at Ground Zero on the Project's behalf," the Chinese Ambassador suggests.

"A docket subject for our next scheduled conference, Ambassador Yesui," Harper agrees.

"We can put it up for debate," Mersley bitterly replies.

"Anything else?" Harper asks.

Everyone in the room shakes their heads and confirms a vote to adjournment. And like that, Malakai's direct line goes dark.

He turns off the monitors and exits into the Control Room. "That could've gone better," Malakai mutters.

His melancholy earns him Harlow Leighton's attention.

"You look tired," Leighton notes.

Malakai fakes a grin. "Just what I wanted to hear," he returns.

"The walls aren't exactly soundproof, Doctor Adonis," Leighton admits.

Malakai looks around the Control Room. His entire staff is watching to see his reaction.

"What's the update on Doctor Vogert's little experiment?" Malakai asks, ignoring the rampant curiosity

Leighton shrugs. "Slow going according to his last check-in," he says, turning to bring it up on his screen. "We're expecting another data transfer in about an hour."

"Good," Malakai accepts. "And news from Doctor Hao?"

"Mediocre," Leighton says. "Last transfer we got from Camp Yi was . . . Eight hours ago? That's odd. At midnight?" He leans closer to his screen to double-check the numbers he's reading. "Barely a gigabyte. I've seen keynote presentations run larger file sizes."

"That can't be right," Malakai states. "Status on the other outposts?"

"They've all sent data packets through to METIS Control . . . And it looks like a terabyte or two per transfer. Sometimes more, depending on the camp. That's what we expect," Leighton mentions. "Which makes sense—the more our teams study, the more data they compile. Half the reason we need Athena is to organize the chaos."

"Are you saying Camp Yi can't send their data?" Malakai asks. "Technical issues?"

"Or they're hoarding what they're compiling," Leighton suggests.

"And per human tendency—knowledge is power, and wanting power is an addiction," Malakai says, breaking away. "Let me know when they do send their next packet. Something's not right about this. I want to keep an eye on the situation if it's a bigger deal."

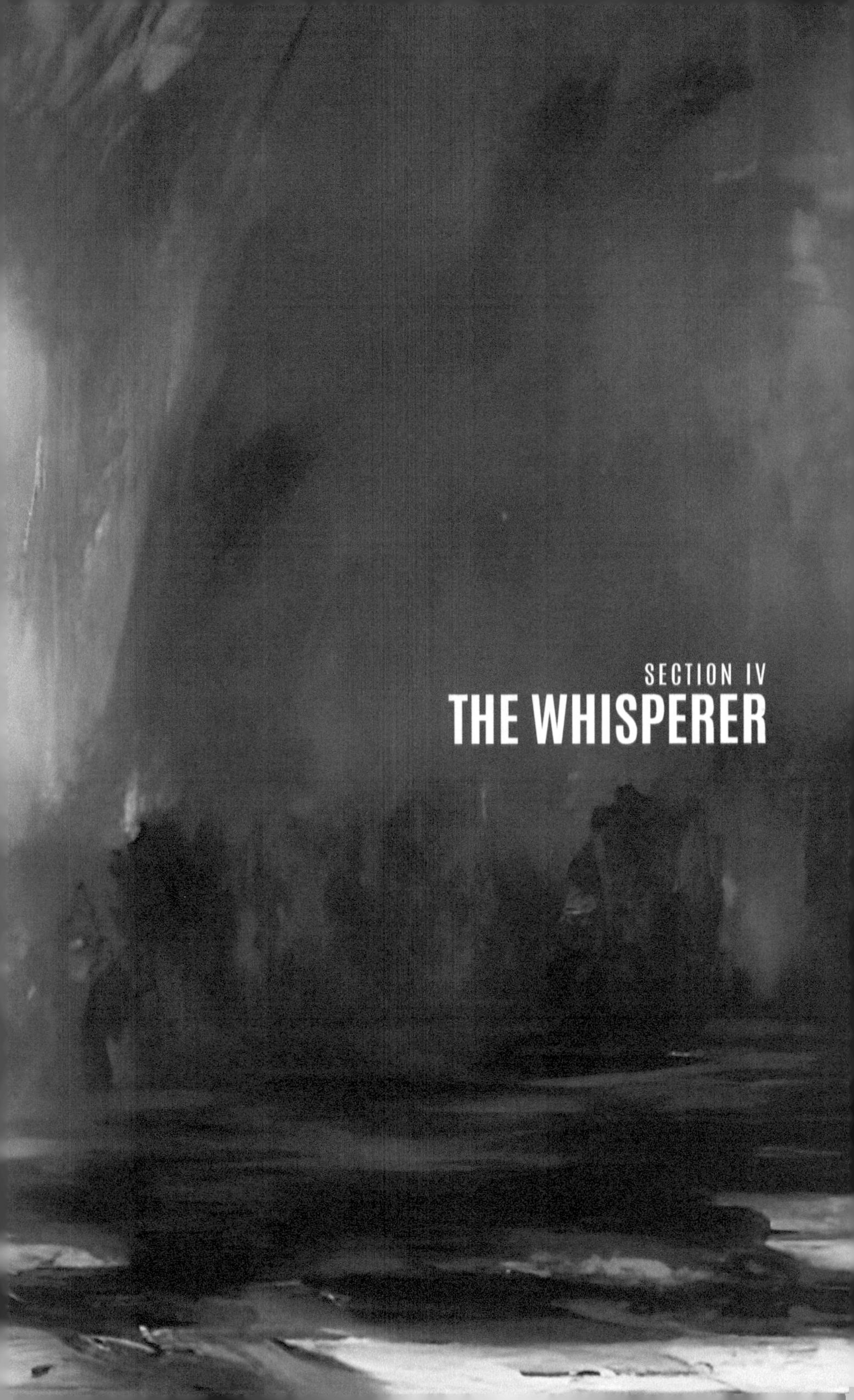

SECTION IV

THE WHISPERER

MANY DOUBTS | 21

===

She watches the humans for several clicks. "Quite inventive, aren't they? Even for primitives," Idu 'Smeora weighs, standing eight levels above their outpost. She's in a small room with a good view over the hangar's exit ramp.

Idu shakes her head. It's more accurate to say the entire room is her window. She calls it the Observer Mentalis—a monitor hub. All she needs to do is *concentrate* on what she wants to see within the local system. And regardless of its shape or scale, the ship will create tangible representations for her to study.

As such, the humans won't see her. For her protection. And theirs.

"It's more difficult to survey them if they're conscious of your presence," Dhun construed after he escorted her across the ship.

"Just ensure they do not make their way here," Idu challenged.

"Guards will stay outside the door to ward off any uninvited guests," Dhun finished, leaving the Whisperer to her task for the intermediary hours.

Idu records her notes on any observable human behavior into her transcribe—like a portable journal. It hums and blinks as she shifts the letterforms with her fingertips.

"Fascinating," she goes on to describe. "I wonder if those two are an acquainted pair?" Of course, she refers to the male and female sitting inside a large pavilion on the hull's lower half, right next to the transit rail their workers have set up.

Idu repositions the Observer for a closer look-see.

"Maybe . . . Maybe they're just socializing? Friends? Plausible connotations." Idu works through her theories. "What are those hand gestures? Another language? Not spoken, but . . . a . . . signed language? Perhaps a versatile means to compensate for the noisy environment? Physical impairments? Unexpected. Very clever."

Since kicking off her investigation, Idu 'Smeora has increasingly identified numerous languages among the various human groups.

"This makes fourteen," she counts, quickly reading her growing list. "I will need to catalog and decipher each one if we mean to communicate with them using our translators. And they, in turn, with us." Idu puffs out her chest, incredibly proud of her progress after so little time.

Tjaa 'Neren has already begun working on the samples Idu sent her. While she admits it's her duty as the Whisperer of Continuance to learn and study other races, she must ensure those species' well-being while they inhabit this vessel. The Servant of Cultivation's task is to create the systems where those species will grow into their own. Give them a fighting chance in a galaxy of terrors.

The Servant quietly walks into the Observer Mentalis. "These humans are different from the peoples found on worlds life-seeded by ships like ours—the Vili, a great world-builder. Harbinger of creation," Tjaa describes. "Your humans do not know it yet, but their race, like ours, has a purpose. I should warn you against letting your sentimentality drive us, Whisperer."

"Ours is an Obligation born from desperation," Idu returns.

"And it demands adherence," Tjaa iterates.

Idu simmers while Tjaa 'Neren tilts her head and waits for her response.

"They *are* different," Idu admits, moving her display aside to address the woman directly. "Earth isn't one of *our* worlds, however. Do they exist here by pure chance? A cosmic coincidence? Even without help from a species far older and wiser, theirs is a thriving population."

"You cannot learn everything you want about them from way up here," Tjaa regards. "How much *can* you see in that apparatus?"

"Enough to satisfy my baseline curiosity," Idu explains. "Not so much for us to utilize. These humans are . . . guarded. Scared, but determined."

"We've met species with similar traits. And we have records on hundreds more."

"Most of those are now extinct. And these humans?" Idu doubts. "They're violent. I don't understand why Dhun would protect them. He only steps in for those he trusts. And he doesn't *trust* anyone. His duty? Judgment. He's surveyed a thousand slumbering worlds meant for our work. That means he's also witnessed the worst of this galaxy's many horrifying wonders."

"I am sure that Dhun 'Ancod has his reasons for interfering," Tjaa follows suit.

Idu stares at the woman. She lets her delicate skin dry while her feathers change from yellow to a mild blue.

Tjaa frowns. "You're scared about what *that* could mean," she realizes.

"I don't know *what* my feelings are on this, Servant," Idu says, renouncing the idea.

"Tyrann 'Akachan will argue we should focus on fighting Adhion 'Klaka," Tjaa advocates. "Whatever the cost."

"Whatever the cost?" Idu questions. "Dhun's regard for the humans won't help if they get caught up in the middle."

"Then what do you suggest, sister?" Tjaa poses. "Perhaps recruit the natives? What can *they* do that our Varmajalkavaen cannot?"

"There are too many places for the Nomad to hide aboard this ship," Idu says, standing tall . . . But she falls quiet, lips trembling. Her feathers go a stark black.

Tjaa retracts her jaw, recognizing Idu's surrender. The woman raises her eyes, matching Idu's height, and offers her an open hand.

"And we continue studying these humans because?" Tjaa focuses, her skin brightly red.

"If we don't want them to overreact, we *need* to find a way to communicate with them," Idu says.

"Among primitives—a slight misunderstanding can turn into outright hostility," Tjaa nods acceptingly. "That's not their role in the Obligation. Yet, it's second nature for someone like the Nomad, who serves a brutal purpose. A severe inbred hostility to anything that breaks his encoded tenets."

"It's not his fault for being a part of the Lower Chords," Idu argues.

Tjaa shakes her head disagreeably. "What have you found out?" she asks, moving on to the immediate task.

Idu's stare lingers before she pulls the information from the Observer. "There's one among them—a female, smart and headstrong," Idu says. She situates the Observer's display to the human in question. "She's an interesting specimen. Do you see how the others obey her? From our findings on their history, I gather humanity is mostly patriarchal. That makes it difficult for females to raise themselves to leadership positions. Difficult. Not impossible."

Tjaa meanders into the machine, letting the particles flow around her, the image reconstituting between the pair. She looks at the female human for a long time. "And what makes *her* special among her kind? Is it her appearance? Do they even care about that?" Tjaa finally speaks.

"Perhaps it is where appearing powerful earns power?" Idu resolves, eyeing the image more closely. "Or maybe she's just extraordinary in her role."

"Whichever it is, they're not going to let you walk in to ask off-handily," Tjaa advises, waving a palm over their camp's depiction. "According to this, she's located *inside* their compound. You won't get far if they know what to look for."

"Not as I am. No," Idu agrees.

She twists her fingers to expand the Observer's Mentalis to see an often-unseen portion of the Vili. It shows the humans and their movements, the Varmajalkavaen, the Fragment Alimentors, the four "true" crewmembers who dwell in the ship, and a dozen repeating shadows of the fifth.

"The Nomad," Idu denotes, hardly above a whisper.

"Are you confident they can help us?" Tjaa dubiously asks.

"I am," Idu admits. "I do."

Tjaa frowns and eyes the images carefully. "Adhion is managing to disguise himself from our ship's sensors," she adds. "I don't know how, but he's created a dozen false impressions. Echoes." Tjaa breaks away from the Observer's projector and reenters the void outside the colorful display.

"It's a rather adept way to hide his whereabouts," Idu offers.

"And if the humans can lend us more eyes, they could help us to narrow those leads," Tjaa recognizes.

"Dhun rarely expresses his praise for any species," Idu adds.

"Let alone a primitive race like theirs," Tjaa counters. "Maybe he's just praising their ambitious nature?"

"Either way, they can make steadfast allies," Idu suggests, "if given a chance."

"Maybe," Tjaa half-heartily mourns.

Idu shakes her head and decides to pull the human female's representation from the Observer's internal memory. Statistics exhibiting her attributes appear along the side, off the console's marker-linked controls.

"Addison Kennedy," Idu whispers. "Do you call yourself that? Or are you born to your role, as we are?"

"Your epitome?" Tjaa begs the question, her eyes dimming at Idu's inattentiveness.

"She's our best chance to make contact," Idu nudges.

Tjaa merely shrugs. "Then you're lucky that Dhun 'Ancod has taken your side on this," she cautions.

"His admiration for the humans is temperamental at best," Idu grimaces. "But if they become hostile—?"

"He'll fight them to the death," Idu admits.

Tjaa cranes her neck back. "You sound . . . upset with that," she infers.

"I don't want to see anybody hurt," Idu says.

"He rarely ever loses," Tjaa warns.

"And if he *does* lose, what then?" Idu asks.

"Then it would likely throw our entire Obligation toward a headwind," Tjaa iterates. "That is a cost the Trident won't allow." The Servant tightens her jaw and looks out at the wider display. "Not on a small-minded planet like this." She pulls Idu away from the Observer and plants her beside the door.

Idu stares into the other's large eyes with a whimsical nod.

"I will let you know when I make progress," Idu promises, reentering the Observer's central dais.

Tjaa grimaces, troubled by her response. But she slightly bows her head, leaving the room without another word.

Idu presses her palm to the interface, shifting the new letterforms into recognizable patterns.

"Let us find which phonetic language shares common traits and work from there," she whispers, digging into the challenges ahead.

FORCED ADAPTABILITY | 22

ADDISON KENNEDY, FIELD DIRECTOR
EPIMETHEUS PROJECT

OCTOBER 13, 2041 | 1010 HOURS

Addison paces around her quarters, waiting for the call. She *should* be sleeping. Since her chat with Vogert, Addison has repeatedly taken out her tablet to read her team's reports. Every time she tries putting it away, her curiosity gets the better of her.

"Sensors are reading another shift in atmospheric conditions at each monitoring station," Addison whispers.

After four days, the temperature gradually dropped to fourteen degrees below zero inside the ship. With new information stacked by Athena, a sudden increase by three degrees could be considered a drastic change. "A bigger shift than we've expected," Athena illustrates.

"Good to know you're tracking what I'm reading," Addison frowns, swiping through more data screens. And the strangest factors are the reports from Camp Yi having dropped off considerably over the last day.

"Tracking you enthusiastically," Athena snarks. "Can I be of service?"

"Yes. Now that you mention it . . . Is this everything Doctor Hao uploaded to the network today?" Addison questions. "This is just basic troop movements and weather reports. Nothing to do with their research."

Athena remains quiet for a moment. "Doctor Adonis has noticed the same discrepancy," she answers. "He's ordered us to pay closer attention to their actions. Camp Yi hasn't updated their node for a while, meaning their equipment doesn't connect to the Overlook. Not anymore."

"You mean they're working in the dark?" Addison wonders. "Why do that?"

"I can only presume it's to keep me out of the loop," Athena quandaries. Addison presses her fingertips against her forehead, having to think about *that* for a moment.

"That's like . . . waving your hands around, shouting for attention. That doesn't make sense," Addison mutters, not to Athena. "Not unless they're in trouble. Or do they believe they can do this on their own? Same question—"

"Why?" Athena concludes.

A notification appears on her tablet's screen. Addison opens the notice and reads a message telling her to get to Vogert's lab.

She dawns her rain gear and leaves for Research Sector 4-A. Ryan Vogert meets her inside with glinting eyes.

"Good news?" Addison asks, walking into the air wall that instantly dries her.

Vogert nods and leads Addison across the room.

A dozen other project leaders are inside with their lab assistants crowding the tables. And they're all looking at a screen with a blown-up view of a microscopic organism. Addison's schooling earned her the experience to recognize microbiology, mainly dealing with genetics. She knows what microbes look like—unicellular constructs with a greater span of diversity than if every human face on the planet were lined up and counted.

Addison leans into the screen. It's showing her an organism that's wildly atypical of most microbes on Earth. She tilts her head to look at it from a different angle. Artificial with its molecular construction.

"What is it?" Addison asks.

"I don't think we've created a word for it yet," Vogert explains. "Watch this . . . Doctor Mori, if you'd please?"

"Of course," the man speaks, taking charge of the subject. "If you look at the screen to your left, Doctor Kennedy, this is the organism as it was after we removed the samples from our subjects. The atmospheric conversion chamber maintains the conditions it would face inside the ship's static field. On the screen to your right is a second group we've exposed to *our* air. Notice the changes?"

"Kinda hard not to," a lab tech attests.

Addison sidesteps the crowd, pulling the view monitor closer for her to study. She traces the shapes and lines with her fingers, causing the screen to blink out when she presses it too hard. "It's turned red?" Addison mouths her words. "Like it's adapting to the molecular hemoglobin needed for an oxygen-nitrogen-rich environment."

"Seems that way," Vogert acknowledges.

Addison gives him a good once over. Vogert sways side-to-side, barely able to stay on his feet. Staying up for long shifts into the night, active for most of the day, carrying out his duties as Chief Medical Officer . . . Doctor Vogert inhales deeply, fighting to stay awake, Addison notices. Then, she frowns worryingly.

"Take a look at the middle screen, Doctor Kennedy," Hendru Mori urges.

"What about it?" she asks.

"That's a live presentation we added to the runner fifty-eight minutes ago. Do you see the effect?"

Addison glances at the man and tightens her jaw. "I see it," she admits. The microbe on the center screen rapidly shifts into a perfect mixture of the samples on either side. "Is it—? Did it just combine both forms?"

"It's sharing traits from both stages," Mori explains.

"How are you doing that? It looks like you're reverting the process while maintaining the adapted structure," Addison iterates.

"We've returned an organism from our atmosphere to its origin point," Mori details, tracing the image screen. "See this change? That's not us. We're not causing a direct reaction. It's doing it on its own without interference from our team. Although, not for the lack of trying on our part. Some experiments prove more effective than others."

Vogert crosses his arms as he steps closer. "And while that's all fine, it *does* reveal one significant characteristic about our hosts."

"Which is?" Addison asks.

"They understand genetic engineering beyond the contemporary," Vogert defines.

"Allowing us a rare opportunity for our mission here," Mori adds.

Addison raises an eyebrow. "You're suggesting we conduct trials using sciences we barely understand?"

Vogert arches his neck back, finding her statement an unwelcome interpretation.

"Not at all," Vogert denies. "That would be irresponsible."

"We don't even know the effects it would have on a person," Mori says, "let alone if it won't outright kill somebody."

Addison narrows her eyes at the man, allowing her thoughts to wander. And then, her face tightens as she sucks in her lips.

"You're suggesting that since they're able to adapt biology to a specific environment," Addison says, "it's *possible* to do the same with *our* people?"

"With careful study," Vogert admits. "Yes. It's possible."

"Admittedly, I think we can all agree that it's important to ensure our meddling doesn't cause irreparable damage," Mori argues.

"The challenge is convincing the primsuits the risk isn't worth being reckless," Addison asserts. "Secretary-General Harper sides with us—but we can't fend off the entire Security Council if they're demanding quick results. We're spending a world's war worth of resources to keep us on-site. And I'm not sure how long we can maintain our presence at our current rate."

"I'm willing to run human trials if we can get a small volunteer group to agree to a procedure," Vogert suggests. "I know that contradicts what I just said, but this material *is* remarkably versatile."

"Can you promise it won't kill whoever comes into contact with it?"

"That's the only way I'd agree to move on to the next developmental stage," Vogert says.

"And how long will that take?"

"Maybe a day or two?" Vogert weighs heavily. "I can keep a team working on it overnight."

Addison chews on her nails anxiously. "Do it. We'll see what tomorrow brings."

"Tomorrow, then," Vogert agrees.

"Keep me updated and," Addison shifts, "maybe get some sleep?"

"No promises on that," Vogert laughs.

As she steps out, Addison receives a notification on her wrist-pad. "Another 'Jalk' attack," she whispers, swallowing as the term leaves a bad taste in her mouth.

Colonel Ibrahim is due credit for the nickname in his reports, claiming it's to avoid writing out "Varmajalkavaen" on every account. Most files leave it simple and call them "buggers" as an insult to the race.

Addison spends the rest of her day working on the various projects she has running throughout the labs. Much of it involves her managing the more eccentric geniuses in her department's subdivision. Addison doesn't finish her shift until much later that night. Her legs feel heavy as she returns to her quarters. She sheds her many protective layers and drops half-naked onto her cot to rest her eyes.

When she moves her arms, gravity doesn't surrender its hold. It hurts. Addison's heart pounds inside her chest loud enough for her ribs to beat with the rhythm. She grabs her tablet to skim the minute-by-minute reports for the next hour.

"Let's see what I've missed," Addison mutters. "Soldiers spotted Jalks at a perimeter checkpoint? Ah, I see. The station chief ordered a cautionary sweep of the platform, but the patrol found nothing. Figures."

Addison eventually lulls herself to sleep. She hums while tapping her bare heel against the cot's crossbar.

She doesn't expect anybody will walk in on her while she's undressed. So, Addison doesn't bother covering herself with the thermal blanket. Instead, she cranks the heater on full blast, turning on the radio to listen to the latest broadcasts about how the world is handling the crisis:

> "—with acknowledgment from the UCAF about rediverting the Third Fleet back to San Diego to assist with recovery efforts on the West Coast. The Office of the U.S. Secretary of Defense has released a statement. And I quote: 'We are working with every nation involved on ways to partition our available resources between the impact zones and the inflated Epimetheus Project. The administration believes this mission

is a false and deliberate attempt to hurt the Pres-
ident's reputation. And they will be accountable
for every dollar and life they waste on fiction.'
End quote."

Addison lies there, massaging her legs, twisting her spine until it pops.

She hears a breath echoing in the cold lull *inside* her tent. It causes the hairs on her arms to stand on end. Addison eyes the corners of the room, not seeing anything that can justify giving her the chills. And yet, there's a ringing sound, like puffs of air are hitting the hollow metal polls holding up her quarter's thin canvas.

Addison gets up and wraps a blanket around her shoulders.

It's warmer inside the room than it *should* be. The heater is working its darndest, but with a room as large as hers and the near-freezing tempera-tures, it shouldn't get over forty degrees inside. Then, her feet freeze on the plastic floor.

Addison spies a breath cloud appearing near her tent's entryway.

She rushes toward it, grabs at the source, and pulls the bastard inside . . . Only to realize the individual is several heads taller than her and deter-minately *not* human. Addison jumps back when she grasps the situation, tripping over her discarded gear and landing on her bed as the eight-foot giant skips forward.

Addison goes for the emergency call button on her wrist-mounted computer. The *other* catches her wrist and murmurs discouragingly.

"Es besteht kein Grund, zur fürchten," the alien speaks.

Addison loses her breath. "That's German! You're speaking German? Deutsche?"

For some reason, the temperature inside the room skyrockets to above sixty degrees. Addison feels her wrist getting sweaty from the alien's grip.

The other raises a hand in a peaceful gesture—six long fingers open with the palm flat toward her. At least, Addison *believes* it's an . . . amicable indication.

Addison attempts to stand up and push her way past the alien several times. *It* stops her by gently guiding her back toward the bed like a parent to their child. It shoots up a single finger for Addison to follow, leading her gaze to its opposite hand as if it's giving her instructions.

"What are you?" Addison asks. "You look . . . female. A woman?"

The alien only returns with a blank stare. The female has an almost perfectly round head with two large eyes that appear as if drawn from an old cartoon. Her irises are darkly blue, with specks in the center that gives off a starry night appearance. And the white tattoos on her face give her an elegance that is nearly . . . tribalistic.

The alien opens her fist to reveal a small, triangular metallic flake no larger than a fingernail.

Educating her through the signing motions, the female has Addison pick it up and install it behind her right ear. An electric jolt courses through Addison's skull as she presses the tri-plate into her skin. It's intense, and a momentary pain follows the jolt. As it passes, Addison has difficulty recalling the sensation. However, a high-toned hum in her ear replaces it like a church choir in procession. Addison can imagine the noise driving anyone crazy if they listen to it for too long. Yet, while she attends it, the less relentless it gets. Instead, it's almost . . . blissful? Like her mind is opening to a diverse universe as information floods into her grey cells.

Addison's eyes widen.

Everything begins twisting around her too fast for her to track until it all finally slows to a crawl.

"This is weird," Addison says. Her gaze lingers in the air as she forgets about the alien trespassing in her immediate space.

Addison also forgets that she hardly has any clothes on.

"Very strange, I should agree," the other says, looking at Addison in the nude. "Quite soft for a species that's evolved on its own. Most tend to develop a natural armor for defense. Five digits per hand? And toes? Breasts developed to nourish offspring, but I am willing to say they work to attract mates somehow. And the detail in the face! Deep crevices and ridges that beget a fierce intelligence. Stress marks? Marks of a busy life. No physical signs having borne children, although I'd ascertain a similar birthing process as lower primates."

"Lower primates?" Addison begs, shaking off her daze. "Wait. How do I understand you?"

The other's feathers flutter around her crown. Addison can only guess it's the alien's equivalent of a raised eyebrow.

"Harmonious interception," the bright alien suggests. "That device you installed behind your ear allows us to communicate using the samples I've collected from your species over the last couple of days. It allows you to hear and understand as my kind do . . . We're the watchers, the meddlers. The Arkkitects."

"Architects?" Addison repeats.

"That is what I said," she replies.

"Architects," Addison weighs the word on her tongue.

"I am the caretaker known as the Whisperer of Continuance—Idu 'Smeora. And you are Addison Kennedy. You are human. I *am* Arkkitect."

"No. I mean to say . . . it's just a coincidence. I don't know how to explain it," Addison clarifies. "We've already taken to calling you Architects. *Our* word for builders, creators, designers—"

"Artists?" Idu asks, tilting her large head to one side.

Her limbs are long and angular, matching an unnaturally thin body. And yet, Idu's every aspect resembles an elegant, dignified, and regal presence. Her skin is as smooth as a snake's scales, but each pigment changes its hue as she moves around, refracting the light.

"You're not reptilian. Not even a primate," Addison describes, studying the alien's contour and form. "You're more like a bird with your feathers, but your posture doesn't match it. A bird with humanesque features? No beak. A mouth, for sure. Like *our* mouth. With teeth. An omnivore?"

Idu lets off a smile. "You're a fascinating subject yourself, Addison Kennedy," Idu returns, unabated. She pushes Addison farther back and pokes at her feet. "Trace signs of evolutionary adaption. Your species used to walk like most primates, if I were to guess? At some point, you learned standing upright freed your hands for using tools."

"At the cost of limiting our mobility," Addison adds.

"Well said," Idu agrees.

"Is it?" Addison notes with a frog in her throat. "Can I have my foot back? I'm not an animal to study like in a zoo."

"And yet, studying *others* is perfectly fine as long as they're dead?" Idu suggests.

Addison holds in a deep breath. "I don't like going to the doctor to get prodded," she argues.

"Ah, I see. You are afraid? Nervous?" Idu weighs. "Apprehensive about getting caught in a vulnerable state?"

"Yeah," Addison shudders. "I'd call it vulnerability."

"Your kind wear fabrics to protect yourselves," Idu remarks. "Your skin isn't well suited to many extremes. However, there is beauty in the raw form. Always. And ugliness. Differences—big and small—make individuals unique. Distinct."

Addison grimaces. "At the moment, my distinction wants to put some clothes on," she urges. "After that, I have questions to ask. As an equal. I didn't expect my first interaction to be like this—naked in my room, with an alien poking at me."

"Were you expecting a more one-sided conversation?" Idu lifts her chin. "Perhaps like your experiences with the Varmajalkavaen?"

Addison hesitates, gnawing on the inside of her cheek.

"Let me get dressed," she finally asserts.

Idu bows. "As you wish, Addison Kennedy. I will watch."

"I wish you didn't," Addison says restlessly.

"Observation is a chance to learn," Idu explains. "We must take our chances where we can find them."

"Neither of us is an animal locked behind glass to ogle," Addison fights.

"A rather novice concept," Idu remarks.

"And an open point," Addison continues. "Don't be weird. Okay?"

"Weird? That word again," Idu sullies, cocking her head to the other side.

23 | QUI VIDET

LIEUTENANT COLONEL ELIAS IBRAHIM
UNITED COALITION ARMED FORCES

OCTOBER 13, 2041 | 2309 HOURS

———

Elias rides on the armored personnel carrier with the troops and research personnel.

The vehicle parks inside the motor shed alongside the rest of the carrier fleet. Much of their transports return these days with melting on their hulls, forcing the crews to pull them off rotation to retrofit and reinforce the weak portions of the armored frames.

Ibrahim catches the smell of gasoline as his carrier enters the bay.

Coordinating the military presence beyond the Breach takes a lot of effort to maintain.

Crews work night and day to keep the supply trucks rolling. They're the lifeblood of those serving the long shifts at the interior outposts.

"And it won't get any easier," he mutters, raising his head. "Get the wounded to the tunnels!"

He lets the medical staff move the injured off the shuttle's ramp. Ibrahim will review the casualty reports before taking a few hours to sleep. He needs it if he intends to extend the perimeter.

Ibrahim passes one of his marines, left damaged by a recent encounter. He stops to listen for a moment:

"They just kept coming," the man says. "The buggers . . . fanatics . . . They attack . . . attack . . . attack. We took heavy losses. Overwhelmed our position." His boots rattle on the ground, breathing loudly through his respirator.

Ibrahim puts a hand on the man's shoulder, causing him to flinch.

"Are you hurt?" Ibrahim asks.

"No, s-sir," the marine answers. "Sorry, sir."

Ibrahim surrenders a nod to the man.

For the last five hours, conflicts with the six-armed aliens have decreased. Either they're running low on fodder to throw at the perimeter guards, or they are focusing their efforts on other sectors with more pressing threats than Ibrahim's marines.

Images of Varmajalkavaen and Fragments fighting each other in the corridors play in his mind.

"Lieutenant Colonel Ibrahim, do you read me?" a synthetic voice speaks into his earpiece.

"I'm here, Athena," he replies. "What do you need, ma'am?"

"I am having trouble contacting Doctor Kennedy," Athena explains. "Addison was inside her quarters when last she pinged. She's turned off her transceiver."

"Sounds like she's asleep," Ibrahim suggests, "and doesn't want anybody bothering her."

"That's always possible," the AI weighs. "However, she *was* busy with reports and sending instructions to her field teams."

"Sounds like her," Ibrahim says. "How long ago was that?"

"Twenty minutes."

"A lot can happen in twenty minutes," Ibrahim says. "What do you want *me* to do about it?"

"That you go investigate the lull in her activity?" Athena proposes.

"Uh, what now?"

"Recent thermal imaging shows a higher temperature output within her dwelling," Athena says. "Under current weather conditions, the heaters struggle to raise temperatures to that level. The spike inside her tent strongly indicates she has company."

"And?" Ibrahim argues. "She's making friends with somebody. I still don't see why you need me?"

"The individual in question has a temperature of a hundred-forty degrees Fahrenheit," Athena describes.

"A hundred-forty degrees?" Ibrahim repeats. He stops walking.

"And several times taller than an average human being, Lieutenant Colonel," Athena finishes.

Ibrahim swallows. "How tall is that?" he asks.

"Roughly eight to nine feet," Athena responds. "Shorter than your giant at the Central Spire, but the profiles match."

"One of them is in there with her?" he utters, pulling directions to Addison's quarters. "She's on the other side of the base? Give me twelve minutes."

Ibrahim switches off his channel with Athena and runs out of the motor shed and into the freezing rain. He orders a dozen marines crossing paths with him to follow. They don't ask why. And he doesn't have time to explain.

He barges into the Field Director's tent. In his urgency, Ibrahim doesn't ask permission to enter. He runs in on a half-dressed Addison and a figure nearly twice her size. Ibrahim draws his sidearm, aiming his sights at the bird-like giant with trained precision. His marines do the same.

"Don't move!" he shouts.

He's not fast enough. The Architect . . . Or whatever they've named the assholes, disappears like water vapor in front of his eyes.

Addison steps between Ibrahim and where the alien had stood.

"What the hell are you doing?!" she demands.

"Responding to a perimeter breach!" Ibrahim yells back. "What's going on here? Why were you alone with it?"

"She was helping me to understand!" Addison roars.

"She? That thing has a gender?"

"Oh, like a soldier doesn't know a girl when he sees one?" Addison mocks, red-hot and furious. "She came to *me*. Worried."

"Why didn't you hit your emergency beacon?"

"She got in my way! Given your reaction just now, I'd say she made the right decision."

"Again, with this 'she' characterization," Ibrahim repeats. "Why?"

The woman gestures at his troops indignantly. Ibrahim orders them to stand down and follows her to a monitoring workstation in the room connecting her to the Overlook.

Addison sighs before pulling up the exclusion zone's overhead view—dots representing bases, troops, and researchers fill the screen. Each one is colored to represent IFF tags. Blue is for scientists and their support teams. Green for civilian workers. Indigo for most military personnel, while yellow is for Project Leadership, including Ibrahim.

On the monitor, a red waypoint pops up after Addison inputs the coordinates.

"We need to go there," she points out. "That's where Idu told me I could find her. Right there."

"Idu? What's an Idu?"

"That's her name, Colonel. Idu 'Smeora."

"There? That's in the dark zone." Ibrahim leans in closer to the screen. "Our scanners can't get a reading off that area. And it's far outside our perimeter."

"Regardless, Colonel. That's where I want to go."

"You *want* to go?" Ibrahim mocks, releasing a bewildering laugh. "That's four miles from our nearest outpost!"

"Then we should put on our hiking boots," Addison glowers.

"You aren't going anywhere near that place," Ibrahim refuses. "Not until we find a way to get you there. It'll take a few days."

"Tomorrow," Addison asserts, straight-faced.

Ibrahim's nostrils flare. "No," he returns coldly.

"I have operational authority over your priorities, Colonel Ibrahim," Addison states, although not demandingly. Her tone is more like . . . listing the facts. "You know the danger we're in better than anyone else every day we stay here. Idu offers us a chance that doesn't involve getting more people killed."

"My marines will get massacred if we bring you that far into the dreadnaught without support," Ibrahim argues.

Addison narrows her eyes at him.

Ibrahim stares right back at her.

"This is our chance, Ibrahim," Addison starts again, softer and mournful. "Please? Can you imagine?"

"If we go now, it leaves our backsides unprotected," Ibrahim warns. "The buggers would get around us and cut off any escape. You're a smart cookie, Addison—but I won't lead my squads into a suicide mission to satisfy your curiosity!"

"Then I'll have to convince Malakai and Admiral Kennedy to approve my objective," she goes.

"Your father is getting sent to help with the crisis on the mainland," Ibrahim follows suit.

"Admiral Kennedy is . . ." Addison hesitates to explain, "remaining on station until this situation resolves."

Ibrahim's mouth goes agape hearing the news.

"That's surprising," Ibrahim says. He keys into his wrist-pad to re-read his last orders' update. "My screen says the Seventh Fleet is routing to Hawaii and California to manage the recovery effort alongside the Third Fleet out of San Diego."

"Vice Admiral Ethan Cole will leave on the USS Washington to assist in the rehabilitation with only Third Fleet," Addison describes, taking a deep breath. "My father and the USS Isaac Bennett will retain command over the quarantine zone."

Ibrahim glares at the woman. Then, he lowers his eyes, raising his palms.

"Fine. If you clear it with Malakai *and* Old Man Kennedy," he reasons, "I'll work out a plan to get you and a team to the coordinates."

"That's fair," Addison agrees.

"Don't expect it to happen by tomorrow."

"Miracles *do* happen, Colonel," Addison says with a tidy grin. "And I knew you'd see it my way."

"Don't put words into my mouth," Ibrahim finishes. He turns to exit the Field Director's tent when she catches his arm.

"It'll be worth it. I promise."

Ibrahim frowns.

"I've known you only a short while," he says, "but I didn't think of you as the reckless type."

"I enjoy leaping across the occasional rock-headed canyons," Addison admits.

"That's usually reserved for a soldier's courage."

"Or a sailor's daughter?" Addison confides, not breaking eye contact.

"Do you even understand the risks involved in getting us there?"

"No," she admits. "But I'll find out."

"Good. We'll discuss *that* later. I'll be waiting for the call. Keep me updated."

"Copy that, Lieutenant Colonel," Addison winks.

Ibrahim breathes to relax the tension in his chest until finally surrendering a respectful nod to the woman before he leaves.

His marines follow him outside, back into the rain. Droplets cause his visor to go foggy. He brings up his display and marks a new waypoint on the coordinates Addison wants to go, measuring the distance. It'll be a long haul to get her there. And the vehicles can't maneuver in those narrower corridors, so bringing them along the whole way isn't even an option.

"Fuck me sideways. How do I get her there? This'll be a long walk."

And that'll be his biggest problem.

OPPORTUNITY | 24

ADDISON KENNEDY, FIELD DIRECTOR
EPIMETHEUS PROJECT

OCTOBER 13, 2041 | 2312 HOURS

═══

"You wear interlaced fabric for insolation?" Idu asks about her clothes.

"It helps us regulate our body heat," Addison says.

"Regulate it well enough to keep you warm during abnormal conditions," Idu continues. "A rather . . . primitive concept, for sure. Unique at the same time. Interwoven threads from a plant-based material? Very interesting."

Addison zips up her uniform halfway. Idu watches her. Creepy, if not a little innocent.

"Aren't your clothes made similarly?" Addison questions.

"Light harmonizes condensed materials into their needed shapes," Idu explains. "Onboard our vessels, we don't have much in luxury. We are workers with a purpose."

"And that purpose is . . . What?" Addison queries. "Why are you here?"

Idu takes a single step back as her feathers shift to a pinkish hue. *What do those colors mean?* Addison's careful not to voice her thoughts aloud.

"We did not *choose* to come here," Idu says, "if that helps satisfy your curiosity."

"Not really," Addison returns. "Tell me."

"It is a difficult subject."

"I've got time," she confirms.

"A quaint expression for a young species," Idu laughs. "Outside your little sphere, there is darkness—where life grows from nothing, and civilizations are born. Others carry on and build empires across the stars. Mighty domains rise and fall, only for the cycle to repeat."

"Is that a poem?" Addison begs the question.

"A testament from our Obligation," Idu admits.

"An Obligation? Like caretakers?"

"No," the other denies. "We are mothers and fathers. Our vessel—we call it 'Vili' in our tongue."

"Your tongue?" Addison asks. "Like in Norse Mythology? Vili was the eldest of Odin's two younger brothers, meaning 'will,' if I remember correctly. Together with their brother Vé, the three fought Ymir, ancestor to the Jötnar. Oh, and the Jötnar were ice giants, mighty as the gods."

Idu's feathers brim widely. "Mythology? A quaint comparison," she says, "if that is how you choose to see us, but we are not gods."

"That's not—? They're stories we tell to understand our history," Addison explains. "Vili is the middle brother of the three—younger than Odin, older than Vé. And to the humans—Ask and Embla—Vili had gifted intelligence. They're how our ancestors made sense of the world."

"Gifted intelligence? An ability to feel, no doubt," Idu recites. "As in to touch? No! To have emotion?"

"I'm not sure," Addison admits. "But is that what you mean? That your ship grants younger races the ability to learn?"

Idu surrenders what Addison considers a . . . chuckle, a weak laugh.

"Not quite," Idu admits. "We life-seed barren worlds. We stay for a while and study how that life develops. And we determine whether or not a species can sustain themselves or are susceptible to self-destruction."

Addison feels a knot in her throat when she hears the word "self-destruction" from Idu's mouth.

"And?" Addison asks. "How many make up the latter?"

"More than not," Idu mourns.

"Meaning?" Addison demands, crossing her arms.

Idu flinches. "I am a Whisperer of Continuance." She skirts the question. "I study the races we settle and develop methods to advance them without interfering with their cultural development. I primarily work alongside the Servant of Cultivation—Tjaa 'Neren, as she's known locally."

"And she does . . . what, exactly?"

"Tjaa? Hers is the more creative duty," Idu answers. "Tjaa specializes in genetic engineering and biological development. She adapts a species to its environment during our studies. She makes . . . changes . . . according to their needs and behaviors."

Addison hangs on how Idu pauses when she says "changes." It curls her blood thinking about how those changes would get implemented in an already growing population.

"That makes two," Addison counts. "How many of you are there?"

Idu's expression sinks. Addison narrows her eyes at the beautiful creature, recognizing that veritably *human* look.

"Five—? No, four. That is the number," Idu finally says after a spell. "Tyrann 'Akachan, the Trident of Absolution, captains the Vili. Dhun

'Ancod samples worlds as the Judge of Conciliation, determining which are capable of sustaining life or be made to accept it." She looks away toward a computer monitor in Addison's quarters, marveling at the shapes and lines.

"And the last? You said five," Addison pushes the subject. "Did the fifth die?"

Idu breathes deeply. "He's a difficult one," she admits, "and I don't wish to discuss him."

"Why is that?" Addison asks, raising an eyebrow, running the possibilities in her head.

"Because it's a heavy matter to explain."

"Can you tell me his name, at least?"

Again, Idu offers pause. Her feathers shift to a matted grey, hardly reflecting the pale light from Addison's lamps.

"Adhion 'Klaka—the Nomad, as we call him," she describes.

"Sounds harmless enough," Addison suggests.

"He's *not* by any measure," Idu warns. "Adhion is a . . . complicated figure. You can only witness death so many times without it leaving an echo on the soul. Even for my species." She folds her hands together, squeezing them hard to hide the fact they're shaking nervously.

Addison fights not to stare, but the signs aren't easy to miss.

"What *kind* of terrible things?" Addison drives to find out why.

Idu's head snaps up at her. "I do believe *death* is a clear enough word that fulfills your inquiry, Addison Kennedy," the alien says, emphasizing her use of the word. "You see—we do not always get things right on the first attempt. Adhion 'Klaka is our solution for those we see as . . . unviable."

"Solution? What does that mean? Solution?"

"Annihilate," Idu briefly tells her, shaking her head. "It's not a job we like to admit exists."

"Annihilate? As in genocide?" Addison mouths, finally understanding the apprehension. "Wait! You're saying he's responsible for killing people? How many people has he killed? Hundreds? Thousands?"

"Trillions," Idu says with a cold seriousness.

Addison lets out a breath, not knowing what else to do.

"So, if he's so bad, what's he doing on—?"

"Not *bad*," Idu stops her. "He's misunderstood, I fear. Adhion, I know, doesn't enjoy what he does. Our society condemns his chord to their duties—a dark and unforgivable business. He is forbidden to sire children or to hold power beyond his role to the Obligation. He's a soldier. A powerful one, at that, as devoted as any of us to our tasks. And that's all I will say about him."

Idu touches the keypad on Addison's computer terminal and enters several numerical values. When she finishes, the alien steps aside and allows Addison to read what she typed.

"You seem to understand our technology," Addison notes.

"I am not above learning new things," Idu admits. "It's just numbers and code. Your languages are a lot more difficult. You have so many, each one different, yet each builds off one another. Words change as new concepts are born into creation. Tjaa 'Neren worked many long hours to prepare us for this meeting, Addison Kennedy—to create that cipher you are wearing." She points at her head.

Addison goes to feel the metallic triangular piece Idu had her plant behind her ear.

"And how does this work? Am I speaking your language, or—?"

"More like you're understanding me," Idu clarifies. "We're speaking our native tongues. That cipher translates for you as *this* one does me." Idu turns her head to show a similar device implanted behind the feathery bristles covering what Addison presumes are her ears.

Addison looks at the screen Idu had typed the figures into—a solid line of numbers, separated by spaces. They appear as longitude and latitude coordinates. Not only that, but Addison recognizes the groupings. She clears her throat and taps her teeth together, counting the syllables.

"This will lead to a place inside the Vili most sacred to our Obligation," Idu says.

"I'm guessing it won't be more empty corridors and pointless rooms," Addison voices.

She looks Idu right in her large, starry round eyes.

The alien considers her with that same stare. "It's the reason our vessel exists," Idu says.

A loud beep from Athena's local transceiver goes off next to the bed. Addison reads the nervous reaction Idu has to the noise. She goes to the console and switches it off. Worst comes to, Addison can use a throwaway excuse. She'll say the noise was disturbing the little sleep she *does* get in these small hours.

"We don't have much time if I don't eventually answer that," Addison explains. Idu returns by shifting her shoulders forward. Perhaps a shrug? "How did you get past the perimeter, anyway? We've security," Addison adds. "And I didn't hear any alarms."

Idu's feathers hue a dulling yellow. "Security? I hadn't noticed."

"Is that a joke? Did you make a joke?" Addison queries. "Listen. We've patrols—with guns—and cameras. Personnel that won't likely be too friendly if they see you. If we're going to work together, I need to know how—"

Idu raises a single finger, cutting her off. "Nothing for you to worry about," the alien promises her.

"That doesn't reassure me," Addison admits. "Like, at all."

"Trust when I say to you, Addison Kennedy," Idu refuses, "the others won't come as quietly as I have."

"Grim," Addison says briskly. "But it's fair, I suppose. It *is* your home."

"Home? Only as much as this dwelling is yours," Idu agrees.

"Don't you live here?"

"For only as long as my duty requires it."

"I see. Yes," Addison murmurs before settling. "Now. I have questions."

"I am willing to elucidate," Idu agrees.

The two of them query back and forth for a while after. A *legitimate* conversation with a being from another universe? It's an opportunity that Addison cannot, and *will* not, skimp on. Addison hopes it's the building blocks of something more than the violence her people have thus far experienced. And to see if she can't gleam the behind-the-scenes maneuvering that's going on inside the Summerland than what Idu's willing to tell her.

Addison then hears heavy footsteps outside her tent.

Colonel Ibrahim startles her when he breaks the seams on her entry's flats, charging in and drawing his sidearm on Idu 'Smeora. A dozen soldiers stand behind him, their weapons marking Idu's head. Addison rushes to step between Idu and Ibrahim, but the former disappears into a vapor-like cloud.

Her vanishing causes Addison to pause before turning to Colonel Ibrahim:

"What the hell are you doing?!" she yells at him.

His eyes widen in apt response.

25 | COUNCEL

MALAKAI ADONIS, DIRECTOR OF OPERATIONS
EPIMETHEUS PROJECT

OCTOBER 14, 2041 | 0700 HOURS

===

"She wants to do *what* now?" Malakai demands.

"Lead an expedition into the ship's interior," Ibrahim repeats to the group.

Addison Kennedy and Colonel Ibrahim had walked into Malakai's office to discuss their plan with the Project's leadership. Admiral Jonathan Kennedy shifts his shoulders uncomfortably while sitting in the corner of the room. Addison narrows her eyes at him.

"And she wants to try for it today, sir," Ibrahim mocks.

Malakai grimaces.

"I've read the report, Colonel," Admiral Kennedy acknowledges. "A mission is already in the works. One of these Architects ambushing you inside your hovel doesn't warrant changing our schedule."

"Especially with the resources on hand," Ibrahim adds.

"I do not see how we can conduct it at this early phase," the Admiral agrees. "Not before we've had a chance to explore the territory we've already occupied. My answer is simply no. And I cannot stress that enough."

"Admiral," Addison bites. "I'm not asking you to put our other plans on hold."

"Admiral?" Malakai whispers.

"And yet to get you there, we'd have no choice but to redirect assets, *Doctor* Kennedy," Jonathan bites. "We haven't even finished mapping the interior bay! Let alone the surrounding corridors. With our casualties mounting, it's a mission we can't afford right now. You'd be sailing us into uncharted waters!"

"Unless the benefits are worth the risk!" Addison pushes.

"I don't agree they do, Doctor!"

Malakai cringes as the pair call each other by their ranks and titles.

"Then I'll take a civilian team to the sector," Addison snarks back. "Without a military escort, if I have to, Admiral."

"Addison! We can't—" Malakai interrupts, bumping his fist into his desk. The bang earns him their attention. "Familial bickering does *not* have a place on this rig or in this room, do you hear me? That's for both of you! I do *not* care." He pivots to Old Man Kennedy. "Our discussion is whether or not to prioritize your daughter's proposal to launch a mission into the dark zone."

"An idea I fundamentally disagree with," Ibrahim speaks up. "If I may—?"

"No, Lieutenant Colonel. Please don't," Malakai shoots him down. "I have the floor! And no doubt, we're feeling the pressure on all sides. You, me, and everyone on that ship out there. James Harper and the Security Council don't want us to take risks. They want us to stop tying up necessary resources for the crisis on the mainland. Our scientists must balance the cost and benefits of every decision they make. I didn't choose your daughter as my field director because I think she has a pretty face, Jonathan. She's smarter than a room brimming with your best and brightest. That counts for more with me than a simple rank."

"Malakai?" Jonathan weighs.

"And while I *am* concerned with the matter of this Idu 'Smeora breaching our security," Malakai continues, "this grants us an opportunity we can't find through brute force."

Addison's eyebrows furrow.

Likewise, her father lowers his head, ashamed.

"These Architects run the . . . Vili, did she call it?" Malakai goes on. "From what Idu told Doctor Kennedy, there's only five of them. And the fifth is a plausible cause for the discord across the site. This contact is likely their attempt to reach out and communicate. Your thoughts, Addison?"

Addison breathes deeply.

Malakai watches her pace around the room, folding her arms and tapping a finger on her lips.

"I don't think she'd have asked me to go if she thought it was dangerous," Addison interprets. "There's a disagreement between their number. And I get the feeling that doesn't happen too often. She's afraid enough that she's willing to talk. So, I don't think it's a trap. Not by her. And I don't think they'd see us as a threat. With all our firepower, we can hardly scratch that dreadnaught's hull if we tried. No compelling reason to want to hurt us."

"Tell that to my troops in the morgue," Ibrahim retorts.

"You mean the Varmajalkavaen," Addison clarifies. "Their reactions are . . . more of a hunter's inclination. We aren't their targets. We're just getting in their way."

"Right," Malakai states. "They're fighting these Fragments."

"And the one who's hijacking the floaters?" Jonathan demands. "In your report, Idu called him . . . the Nomad?"

"Adhion 'Klaka," Addison clarifies. "Although, she was mum on what exactly he's doing. My report is speculation derived from my conversation with Idu. Not substantiated facts. Think of it as a roadmap."

"And if this isn't a trap to begin with, why didn't she just bring what she wants to show us?"

"Because . . . Presumably, *what* she wants to show is too big to carry," Addison suggests. Malakai notices the room goes silent, pondering that rationalization. Addison turns to Ibrahim. "Pretend you find ancient paintings inside a cave near where you live? Pretend you're a kid wanting to show your friends the paintings? Do you pick up an entire cave to show them? Or do you bring your friends to the cave?"

Ibrahim stands back. "You can't move a cave," he scoffs.

"Exactly," Addison says with a sly grin. "There's a lot we don't understand about the Summerland and its crew. That said, I think it's safe to assume logic remains the same between our two species. Mathematics is a universal language, even when our understanding of it doesn't compare to theirs. It's fundamental."

Malakai presses the tips of his fingers against his thumb as another quiet stint breaks the room.

"What are you asking us to do, Addison?" Malakai finally demands.

She pauses. Addison looks at her father, then at Colonel Ibrahim.

"Just get me there," she answers. "Idu called what's there 'the reason our vessel exists.' That means it contributes to something important. Something *we* can use."

Jonathan Kennedy walks up to his daughter and sighs. "This mission doesn't work to satisfy your curiosity, Addison," he says.

"I know, dad," Addison returns with a softness, "but we're against the clock here. People are dying. It's time we go on the offensive."

The Admiral warmly smiles in a way Malakai hasn't ever known of the man. A smile only a father can give to a stubborn daughter. The sailor disappears under a layer of lenitive eyes and that bushy mustache.

"What do you need," Malakai asks Addison.

The woman looks up at him with a stern expression. "I can get you a list within an hour," Addison answers. "But I'll need people with field experience—those who can work on the fly and under extreme circumstances. More importantly, I'll need volunteers."

"Fair enough," Malakai coughs. "And if the people on your list don't want to come?"

Addison releases a weak laugh.

"The most ambitious personalities that humanity has to offer came to work for the Project," she reminds him. "If they're already here, why say no?"

"I see your point," Malakai nods.

"And your team's composition?" Admiral Kennedy asks.

"Who are you thinking?" Ibrahim prods.

Addison smiles. "As I said, those who can work under the circumstances. My first picks—Ryan Vogert, Avanna Remmings, and Harlow Leighton."

"I'll talk with them," Malakai promises.

"I also want Colonel Ibrahim and his unit to spearhead the expedition," Addison adds. "That includes Sergeant Major Olivia Warden."

"That's a lot of high-profile names," Ibrahim responds.

"Vogert is an old medic several years past his war," Jonathan warns. "Remmings and Leighton are civilians—one's an eccentric lunatic, and the other is absent-minded."

"I wouldn't call Leighton absent-minded," Malakai defends. "He was my choice for mapping out the Summerland's interior. And his work doesn't need him here on the Olympus twenty-four-seven. I'm sure he'll be grateful for the fresh air if he agrees to go."

"If you can describe inside an alien ship as 'fresh air,' then I wouldn't disagree with you," Ibrahim admits. "But if I am escorting people into a combat zone, I would rather they have some military training. Vogert is a good choice. The others—?"

"Not your team," Addison says. "Not your choice, but I appreciate your worry."

Malakai catches a twitch in the woman's cheek. He motions for the pair to quiet down, chewing on his tongue as he weighs his options, pretending it's gum.

"I'll see to your list," he promises, looking at the Admiral. "And about Doctor Remmings' idea—?"

"The munitions stockpile is on the boat as we speak," Jonathan explains, "and is currently making its way around the Hawaiian flood cordon. Give it a day or so, and it'll reach the edge of the exclusion zone." The muscles in the man's jaw suddenly tighten.

Malakai nods.

"Addison," he shifts topic, "will you agree to postpone until we can get the equipment necessary to protect you?"

"Wait a day until the bigger guns arrive, you mean?" Addison asks, staring longingly in her father's direction. "I don't know how long Idu will wait for us. A day can mean learning everything we ever wanted or coming up empty-handed. I don't like those odds."

"Neither do I," Malakai admits.

"If it's a decision between ending up empty-handed to getting slaughtered, do I need to voice my thoughts?" Ibrahim affirms.

"I won't order soldiers to go deeper into unknown territory without the tools they need to kill the bastards," Old Man Kennedy states. "If what you say is true, Addison—it's not the buggers that worry me. It's the drones . . . or Fragments . . . Whatever we're calling them."

"And those floaters are tougher than a swarm of the six-armed, four-eyed buggers," Ibrahim agrees.

Malakai brings up an overhead map showing every outpost across the Summerland on his computer. According to the reports on his pad, the surface is too dense for their tools to cut through, save for a few splinters for testing purposes. The Canadian and French bases—Mercer and Rousseau—are a mile from the dark zone. Their only inhibition is that they haven't cut through the ship's outer hull to begin interior exploration. Until they can find an opening, the two camps act more as refueling drops for aircraft making supply runs to the larger bases.

Meanwhile, the British Field Director, Theodore Parker, out of Camp Earhart, can lend troops to secure the half-mile stretch between Camps Jeju and Axford.

Malakai's trouble is convincing the CSDR to take part in the mission. China may be willing to guarantee the resources the Americans naturally recalled. They can help the advance teams to secure the expedition's flanks. "Which is a positive," Malakai murmurs. At the same time, what will happen if he becomes relent on them?

He holds his breath as the downside pops into his head.

"Wensu Hao will want a representative on your team, Addison," Malakai expresses.

"Then give them one," she agrees.

"He may even outright demand team leadership," he warns her.

"I'm sure you'll find a workaround," Addison confides. "That just means another pair of eyes to me."

Malakai frowns. He dismisses Addison and Jonathan from his office. They nod as they depart.

Ibrahim stays a moment longer.

"Do you know what it's like inside that damn ship?" Ibrahim demands, not remaining as docile.

"I've read your reports on the subject," Malakai skirts. "I presume they're accurate?"

"Words and footage don't recreate what it's like stepping onto that hull for the first time. Or looking into that vast space," the man claims. "Now, I have every respect for Addison and what she's trying to do, but as I argued with her, I wholly disagree with this plan."

"As is your job, I imagine," Malakai retorts.

"It just doesn't make sense."

"Which is why we're here, Colonel Ibrahim," Malakai confides.

"What? No. I mean—" Ibrahim cuts off his sentence for a moment. "I don't know what I mean."

"Do you trust her?"

"I trust her just fine," Ibrahim says.

"Then I don't see the issue," Malakai shrugs.

"Then we come from two different worlds if you can't see what's wrong with this picture," Ibrahim goes. "It doesn't make sense why she'd be so reckless."

"It does to her," Malakai offers. "I suppose that's what matters right now. I trust her, as do you. Addison knows what she's doing. She isn't known for standing back and letting things happen. And she doesn't do anything without a good reason for it. Remember *that* going forward, Colonel. You're smart. She's smarter. You'll need that intelligence if you're getting us through this crazy scheme."

Ibrahim's face squeezes a moment before nodding. He pivots on his heel and takes one step to the door before turning back to him. "Permission to—?"

"I'm not your commander," Malakai imparts. "I am just a guy who's pointing you in a direction, hoping it gets you to where you need to go."

He gestures toward the door.

Ibrahim keeps his stare for a second before leaving the office. Malakai watches as the man marches through the Control Room and into the hallway. For better or for worse, his way forward is clear.

Without a point on the map to say, "this is where we need to go," so everyone can cheer, "this is the day we saved the world," it won't play well in the history books. And of the lives lost so far? The cities and islands underwater? None of that will mean a damn thing if *that* is all people remember about this crisis.

Malakai returns to his desk and keys open a voice recorder. He describes the meeting's subject and what they've decided, finally ending it with his thoughts.

"I'd be lying if I said I am not curious to see why the ship ended up here," he admits. "Who are these Architects? What drives them? Are they like us? They certainly understand violence as *we* do. Idu 'Smeora is our sole lead to find the answers. Let's hope we can get to her in time."

26 | OCEANS DEEP

AVANNA "AVA" REMMINGS, CHIEF TECHNOLOGY SPECIALIST
EPIMETHEUS PROJECT

OCTOBER 14, 2041 | 1100 HOURS

Ava yawns while she swings in her berth off the ground. She takes these little moments to relax while stuck in the Observation Lab. Stringing up two netted hammocks to the bulkhead, Ava watches the waves crash under her with as much weightlessness as she can manage.

"I should go see Doctor Rahul Vanniyar when I get the time," she whispers, building a conversation in her head.

"Sleep deprivation *will* impair your brain's functions, Doctor Remmings," she imagines him saying. "You're not immune to its effects—memory and decision-making abilities will deteriorate what's in there like sour milk. And could potentially put long-term stress on your heart."

"I can build a new heart," Ava mocks.

"You know that's not the preferable option," the voice goes. "You *know* that, right?"

"No," she mutters. "I don't know that."

Ava sighs while swinging her leg with enough momentum to sway the hammock side-to-side. Her gaze lands on a small patrol boat, checking the rig's struts for safety concerns. She clenches her jaw unhappily.

The door to her lab slides open. Somebody enters. Ava doesn't look to see who it is. Instead, she flips over to her back to stare at the ceiling. She marvels at the pattering reflections on the tiles that come off the water. It's like a dance, sweeping back and forth, never stopping for anything.

"You look like you're enjoying yourself," a vaguely familiar voice remarks, strong and feminine.

That sends a curious tick running down her neck. Ava climbs off the hammock to find Addison Kennedy standing over her, dressed in her field uniform.

"Just taking a break," Ava says.

"On taxpayer dollars, no less," Addison mocks, clicking with her tongue to indicate she means it as a joke. Unfortunately, Ava doesn't care for the humor . . . Addison's all too serious in the delivery, and it's not fun for the person on the other end. Namely, Remmings.

"And not a cent wasted. I'm waiting for a few projects to compile," Ava returns, feigning ignorance. "Do you want something? Or are you stopping by to say hello?"

"Just stopping by for a visit," Addison casually whimpers, handing her a datastick. "Everybody knows how much you enjoy getting new stuff."

"Scan data from the alien device behind your ear?" Ava questions, eyeing the stick.

Addison nods. "Thought you could do for a fix," she says.

"Like ice cream," Ava says. "Just can't get enough."

The pair chuckle as an awkward tension builds in the room.

Ava has met Addison several times in the weeks leading to their deployment to Oceanic Exclusion Zone. Still, other than short introductions and grasping each other's eccentricities, they've never had a real chance to talk.

"Crazy addictions aside," Addison asks, stepping toward a table, "what you've been up to down here?"

Ava frowns, raising an eyebrow.

"Asking after my work? I'm honored," Ava conveys as sarcastic as she can exemplify.

"Are you honored because I'm asking?" Addison begs the question. "Or are you just saying that because you *know* I'm using it as a pretense for a very different question?"

Ava smiles as she walks to the nearest lab table, squeezing the woman's datastick between her fingers. Four other techs are still working overnight and longing for the shift change at noon. None of them pay attention to Addison Kennedy or Avanna talking in the corner. They're busy with their projects, so this conversation is as private as the pair can get on the rig.

"Yes," Ava replies.

"Yes?" Addison repeats.

"Yes," Ava asserts for a second time. "Do you think our benefactors didn't hide a microphone in Malakai's office or conference room? I know there's information SOI doesn't want team leaders like *us* knowing without their permission."

"And you don't like information kept from you, is my hunch?"

"Call me a paranoid schizophrenic," Ava confesses. "Spending weeks in a dark cell can do that to you."

Addison furrows her eyebrows, attempting to get a handle on her.

"All right," the woman says, "despite violating our seemingly 'voluntary' ethics code, which I'm going to ignore, what *do* you think I'm about to ask you?"

"'That you're planning a deep dive into the dreadnaught's bowels outside the military perimeter," Ava describes. "That, and I'm on your shortlist of experts you want to join in the advance team."

Addison's eyes light up with surprise.

"That's . . . very accurate," she admits. "How—?"

"Malakai has already sent messages to Vogert and Leighton," Ava shrugs aptly. "I may have 'caught' the feed mid-transmission right after your meeting upstairs."

"You know," Addison warns, "that information is restricted, don't you?"

"Maybe. The way I figure it since we're the ones compiling it anyway for study and implementation, I decided to 'skip the middleman,' as they say," Ava admits without qualms. She knows the higher-ups and politicians already *believe* she's stealing information for her curiosity's sake. And they're right, of course. Ava explicitly warned Malakai that she'd do it when he was interviewing her for the Epimetheus Project. "If you think about it, whose fault *is* it for not putting safety nets around every networked device I have contact with?"

"And I'm willing to live with that," Addison notions, "if you tell me you'd agree to the mission."

Ava confidently nods. "Sure! Sounds like fun," she grins. "What did the others say? Did you talk to them?"

"I haven't yet," Addison says, "so I don't know."

"So, I'm the first?"

"Imagine it as a chance to stretch your legs," Addison suggests. "Get some air! Shake off that daily grind."

"And by stretching my legs . . . you mean, jump into a warzone with ozone that's pernicious to my delicate sensitivities?" Ava questions, counting each consideration with her fingers. "Not to mention the freezing temperatures and inherit risk of meeting alien specimens while butt-ass nude? That one intrigues me, now that I mention it. Asking for a friend, how likely is *that* to happen?"

Addison's eyes go dull to Ava's stark prodding.

"How—?" Addison goes, her jaw hanging open. "You know what? I know the answer. And it's gross."

"Relax! I always scrub through the security feeds during my off hours," Ava shrugs. "Embrace the freedom! Girls united?"

"That's enough."

"I mean, frankly . . . I understand."

"Please stop."

"And she's pretty in a . . . giant . . . bird . . . sort of way!"

"I . . . I don't think Idu's a bird by our definition."

"Really? She looks like a bird. Bird-ish?"

"Bird-*like*, not a bird. Idu's a mixture of complementary traits."

"But, like, in a flattering way, if you get my drift. And hers, too, I imagine."

"All right," Addison groans. "I'm leaving now."

"Already? You just got here!"

"Stop being weird!"

"Don't be a newb! I am an obsessive-compulsive enthusiast."

"That's not a thing," Addison cringes.

"Yes, it is! Want to talk about it?"

"No. I'm walking to the door . . . Right now!"

"Did she take *her* clothes off, too?!"

"I won't dignify that question with an answer!" Addison shouts. "This is me . . . walking away . . . toward the door."

Ava leans against the counter, overly amused with herself. She puzzles the conversation for a moment before snapping her head up.

"Wait! What's the timetable?" Ava yells across the room. "When are we leaving?"

"A couple of days! Once we get a plan together," Addison calls back, shutting the door behind her.

And with that, the Observation Lab drops back into a strange little normalcy. Ava closes her eyes and listens to her design team's slight ticks and electrical buzzes while busy with their projects. It fills the room. It's almost . . . soothing, in an odd way.

When the noon hour hits, the dayshift clocks in for duty. Ava divides them into several large groups after a brief meeting in the lab:

"I want to know if the brains running the Fragments are capable of feeling pain," she assigns them.

Now, it's their job to discover how to probe the pieces they have and find the answer.

27 | THE BIG GUNS

SERGEANT MAJOR OLIVIA WARDEN
UNITED COALITION ARMED FORCES

OCTOBER 19, 2041 | 0930 HOURS

═══

Olivia steps off the lift to join two hundred marines on the lower slope. The rain bounces off her helmet like pebbles on concrete, loud enough to make it difficult to hear without her helmet's internal noise dampeners.

Water freezes into ice on her composite outer plates, seeping into the underlayers, and causing the hardsuit's alarms to go off occasionally.

Warden checks the heating system, only to see the yellow warning lights flashing on her screen.

"Damn," she curses. "Fighting like hell to push your limits. I can respect that."

"ETA—twenty minutes," the comms operator announces. "Liftoff in two. Packages intended for Operation Shield Piercer onboard. Destination, METIS Research Base, lower terrace LZ. They'll light up markers when you're five minutes to the drop."

"Admiral Kennedy must've pulled a lot of strings if he convinced SOI to free up this equipment," a marine utters over the squad's channel.

"Better be worth soaking my underwear in the rain," Private Fletcher seethes.

"Against our odds? I'll take any advantage we can get."

Sergeant Major Warden decides not to cut them off. She can see the marines trilling in their boots despite their armor.

"Not a single patrol has gotten to the objective zone intact," Warden mutters, flipping off her comms unit. "And for what? Exhausting our troops to expand the perimeter? All to get a small civilian group through to satisfy their curiosity. That's why. Bah."

Warden battles the urge to shout Colonel Ibrahim out for letting Addison Kennedy push too much, too fast, over what the UCAF can readily support.

The pilot coordinator radios from the aircraft. "Wheels are high! ETA—eighteen minutes. Hope to see you soon, METIS Control."

"Is that the Olympus I see out the left hatch?" the flight crew asks over the channel. "Look at the size of it!"

"This is Olympus Flight Control to Warhawk Yankee-Four-Thirty-Three—glad you like the view, Lieutenant. Welcome to Ground Zero."

"Good to finally see it," the crewman acknowledges. "Damn beast drowned my sister when it landed! Looking forward to getting some payback."

Warden taps her comms. "This is Sergeant Major Olivia Warden to incoming VTOL flights," she barks. "You're entering my kingdom now! Lieutenant Colonel Elias Ibrahim holds primary command over expeditionary ship operations. After you offload the packages, a briefing for Operation Shield Piercer will commence. We'll expect you in your chairs up the Stretch by twelve-hundred hours."

She can see the lights from the Warhawk flight closing on the Summerland. They're fighting the storm, as do all their drop-offs arriving from the fleet. Twenty-five birds, each loaded with enough ASAPHEI 6.8 munitions to give her marines a fighting chance against the inhabitant hostiles aboard.

Athena overlays the Overlook's direct feed of the V-91s flight patterns to Warden's screen so she can track the incoming approach.

The data fills her helmet's display. Warden uses simple but definable eye motions to clear the mess. She's spent twenty hours running drills with her squads preparing for this operation. Five-hundred troops, nearly a thousand more in a support role. All of it for Addison Kennedy.

A thin watery wave spreads from underneath the V-91 Warhawks as they hover over the landing platform. As they touch down, UCAF marines disembark and begin offloading the new equipment. They carry plastic containers from the aircraft to mobile tracks, readying the gear for a trip up the Stretch to the METIS Research Base. Joe Hickman's rigger crews jump in to help Warden's troops get the heavy lifting done faster.

"Get the boxes loaded and move on to the next!" Warden orders, charging into the scene. "I'll give you thirty minutes!"

"Heads up to ground teams—" the comms operator calls, "but you've got an inbound VIP carrier heading for the upper landing!"

Warden upturns her eyes to see the ID of a new aircraft coming straight from a CSDR navy vessel, flying over the Warhawks on-site. "I hear you, Olympus Control. VIP is cutting above our flock as we speak, flashing yellow indicators. Greenlight to transfer the bird to METIS Control."

"Copy green, Castle-Six-Actual," Olympus confirms. "Making the switch now. METIS Control has the stick. Reel her in, boys."

Lights at the base turn on to signal where the newcomer should land. With all the traffic going between METIS and Mount Olympus, and the other research stations, it's become a common enough routine that Warden doesn't think about it much anymore. A week-long repeat of the same drill, over and over . . . and over . . . and over, again. Warden will give the eggheads credit on this one. Operation Shield Piercer is a good distraction from all the fighting and routine becoming standard protocol hull-side.

"One point to Addison Kennedy," she whispers. "That still gives Ibrahim the lead score."

Warden grins at the thought.

"Is that one of ours?" Private Glenn asks about the chopper flying overhead.

"Nah," METIS Control replies over the comms. "That's a Mi-26—Cold War Era. Reliable machine after eighty years. Chinese must've brought some."

The channel breaks with Sergeant Heugh Greene on the line. "What do dragons want from the buffalo?"

"Doctor Adonis has agreed to give them a slot in the expedition," Warden explains. "All in the name of cooperation."

"They're cooperating with us?" Glenn begs the question, dubious.

"That's the pretense," Warden hesitantly admits.

Riding the lift to the upper wing, Warden studies the supply crates holding the ASAPHEI 6.8 munitions.

She unlocks a case and takes stock of one of the shells. "This is what's going to help us take down those damn floaters?" Warden questions, crossing her fingers. She notes the colorful markings stamped on the shell's casing. "High-impact, armor-piercing incendiaries? If this does what they promise, it should cut through rock like a sword through cardboard . . . if the sword had explosives strapped to the point of the blade."

LIEUTENANT COLONEL ELIAS IBRAHIM
UNITED COALITION ARMED FORCES

OCTOBER 19, 2041 | 0940 HOURS

"Sweep the left side!" Ibrahim orders, keeping the squad's formation tight. "We move up in increments!"

It's the ninth session he's run with his unit—various drills, twice a day, for five days straight. Ibrahim's gone over every data snippet he could squeeze from the eggheads to formulate battle plans and set their rules for engagement. Anything that can help them deal with potentially one-sided situations like the Central Spire Incident.

"Lacking that is what's killing our people," Ibrahim mutters.

His shoulder has gotten sore running the drills. Although, his muscles cramp if he doesn't keep on the move.

Fatigue is beginning to set in for his marines. Ibrahim can tell by how they're slowing down, becoming sluggish, less coordinated.

"Clear on the left," a team leader makes the call. "Sweeping right!"

"Clear on the right! Moving to next position."

Ibrahim admits it will be a slow crawl into the dreadnaught's dark zone. Pushing his troops to their limits can only help them when they must tackle these conditions in real life. Five miles from the perimeter with four new outposts along the way to give them some respite. That's over five hundred men and women with hundreds more support staff to feed each unit with updates from Overlook Station and the network.

Even with this many countries involved and conflicting personalities, Ibrahim doesn't want to count how many ways the mission could go wrong. His job isn't to handle the situation's politics, however. His *sole* duty is to *execute* a plan of action. And to make sure Addison's team gets home alive and on their own two legs.

Ibrahim lets off a hand gesture that lasts only a split moment. It's long enough for his squad to see and react. When they are deep in the ship, that's about as much time they will have to *counter* any impending threats or unknown anomalies.

And the odds will stack against them if they're busy wading ankle-deep in a soggy pit.

So, Ibrahim uses creative guesswork and imagination to program these combat simulations.

Target markers appear on his squad's heads-up display—alien projections, an entire swarm, filling the module's view like a flood in a subway tunnel. Ibrahim's first line opens fire. His second line moves to trade places with the first when they need to reload. "They're climbing on the walls!" shouts a marine greenhorn. She's another replacement for a man they lost during the battle at the crossroads. The woman is skilled and duty-driven but, like the other reserve units, isn't entirely ready for the reality of combat within the ship's corridors.

"Then shoot them off the damn walls!" he instructs.

Ibrahim has made it a habit of taking point on every significant action they've undertaken since landing hull-side. Operation Shield Piercer has become the largest of those efforts. Which forces questions into his head— what if this operation fails? What if their sacrifices count for nothing?

Ibrahim sweats through his under-weave just thinking about it. He only takes solace in that her father also disagrees with her. Everything else is just politics.

The simulated swarm comes at his forward line unendingly. A dozen units flash red on Ibrahim's visor in the span of a breath, only for more projections to appear the next instant.

"It's a war of attrition," Ibrahim names the scenario. "The buggers will continue to take heavy losses each time we engage them. Eventually, their numbers will reach the point where the only thing left inside the Summerland for the UCAF to worry about is anything *else* that can murder them."

As the bugger swarm nears their position, Ibrahim's frontline marines fall back in a tactical retreat. His two forward lines move behind a third. They provide covering fire until the squad leaders can set up the next defensive point to take the brunt of the attack. Ibrahim used this tactic during the battle at the crossroads, proving its viability against the buggers. This simulation is now working to recreate those conditions with surprises thrown in to keep them on edge.

That's why Ibrahim granted Athena his authorization to throw curveballs at his unit for them to adapt to and consider. After four runs, she's included secondary swarms that come up behind them. Or the one where the buggers mutated and took a lot of ammo put down. Or the run where the projections they were fighting reanimate and then became hideous monsters of an unknown nature.

He didn't even know the system could take such liberties with its directives.

Ibrahim flinches in anticipation of the kind of shark the AI could throw into the water this time.

That's when he hears a baby crying.

The sound creates a lull in the fighting. Ibrahim's marines stop and listen to it for an instant. The simulated insectoids seize the moment, closing the distance on his unit. The marines open fire again to recover their advantage, but the infant's cries don't fade. Ibrahim feels a toad getting caught in his throat.

"Something's not right," he utters.

A massive Varmajalkavaen appears in the swarm's center, clad in a crimson robe under ornate, bone-white armor. In its abdomen arms, the alien lifts a swaddling bundle, complete with arms and legs of its own, moving in a way that's leaning far too much into the uncanny valley.

"Damn you, Athena," Ibrahim spouts. "We've got our curveball!"

She's changed his parameters, the rules he set up for her to follow. It's her way of forcing the squad to change tactics and move on the offensive.

The clad Jalk watches them with grim curiosity. Its mask mimics the features underneath . . . Or maybe it's face paint?

It waves the baby in a circular motion, egging the troopers on.

"Time to move up!" Ibrahim orders. "Resetting mission objective! We're getting that mark!"

His rear line surrenders glances at one another. Ibrahim can't see their faces, but he can tell by their visors, either way. The clad Jalk is standing amidst the vast swarm, seemingly unhampered by its losses. And with *that* swarm, Ibrahim's troops will have to push through to reach the new objective.

"How are we going to do this, Colonel?" Private Wittenmyer demands.

Ibrahim closes his eyes and breathes.

"Form a diamond!" he orders.

It only takes a heartbeat, but all twenty-four marines reposition themselves into a diamond formation. Ibrahim steps with them as they push into the swarm, their rifle barrels hot, their arms numb from the non-stop cascade. Alien bodies drop around them like trees on an island in the middle of a hurricane.

Ibrahim's display flashes red as the situation overwhelms his fireteams. Their armor systems lock up to mimic getting killed in action. Twenty-four dwindles to eighteen. He doesn't stop with the losses. He pushes harder.

"Fifteen . . . fourteen . . . twelve?" he counts.

Ibrahim puts two rounds into the clad Jalk's skull when his squad gets close. The creature's image shatters, losing its hold on the bundle. He catches it mid-air and ducks between his marines.

All the projections around his team stop swarming the moment he's clear. Each four-eyed alien stares at the human squad, not making a sound. With the baby in his arms, Ibrahim looks down as it wiggles. Then, a tiny hand breaks through the blanket's folds. Then another. And another!

Ibrahim's eyebrows furrow. He unwraps the bundle to reveal an infant bugger. The swarm surrounding the squad begins moaning as if they're begging him not to hurt the little one.

"What is this? Why—?" Ibrahim quietly demands. His squad's eyes land hard on him.

"Sir?" Mannering requests.

"Athena! End session," Ibrahim commands.

With an electric hum, the projections on their visors disappear, leaving Ibrahim's unit in a bare training center set up by the rigger crews. The locks on his "wounded" marines are finally released. They all pick themselves off the ground to gather at Ibrahim and the surviving members.

"What the hell was that about, sir?"

"That was a bugger's grub, Martinez," replies another.

"Why'd we rescue it?" Wittenmyer asks.

"We didn't rescue anything! Athena's crossing her circuits."

Ibrahim holds his breath to allow himself a moment to think without saying a word.

"Remain on standby," Ibrahim finally orders, walking into a corner. "Athena, I know you're listening in on our chatter. What the fuck was *that* about?"

"You told me to throw you curveballs," the AI explains. "I decided to get a little more . . . creative."

"I lost half my squad getting to your damn objective!"

"I didn't make *it* your objective, Lieutenant Colonel," Athena defends. "You've tasked me with presenting scenarios so you can react accordingly. Please note that I didn't indicate whether it was a human infant or something more exotic."

"Yeah, well—? It was hellishly implied," Ibrahim asserts. "I lost my troops under misdirection!"

"And under the simulation's realistic conditions, what made you think it was a human child?" Athena questions. "Given the environment? With this being *their* territory and not *ours*, what are the chances of the Varmajalkavaen having offspring present? Especially if they do indeed live and work aboard this dreadnaught?"

"I don't need a moral lesson from a damn computer," Ibrahim argues.

"And we don't need a commander unprepared for eventualities," Athena fights back.

"That's not your place to decide!"

"I know history," Athena redirects, "and your tendencies in war."

"That doesn't explain why—?" Ibrahim attempts to say.

"My place is to remind you of *your* objectives, Colonel Ibrahim," Athena calmly says. "You guard the scientists, not fight a war. Our mission is to save lives. Not spend them."

"And you're suggesting the buggers are just protecting their own?"

"Like a hammer hitting the nail on the head," Athena confirms. "My intelligence is an artificial construct, but it's real. I learn and grow in ways most humans do not due to instinctual biases. I do not refuse to admit facts simply because I disagree with them. I am flexible and adapt to new stimuli when presented."

"Careful, Athena," Ibrahim warns. "You shouldn't boast. Isn't that against your core principles?"

"I am a highly advanced, artificial construct networked to a worldwide array of sequence nodes," she describes. "And each node is as powerful as a thousand human minds working in conjunction with one another. And I have a great many nodes, Lieutenant Colonel. They let me feel such emotions as sadness, agony, pain, or loss . . . Maybe to you, it's all binary code, but to me? And what those numbers represent?"

"They're what you know," Ibrahim mutters.

His lips purse in deliberation. He doesn't know how to respond to a *computer* feeling emotions.

"Colonel Ibrahim?" his earpiece tunes with an operator on the other end.

He taps his interface. "This is Ibrahim. Go ahead."

"You've got an inbound bird heading for the upper platform," METIS Control describes. "Priority VIP—Zhu Yunwen, directly overhead."

"Understood. I'll meet the VIP inside after they get situated. Ibrahim, out."

"Zhu Yunwen," Athena repeats. "Jianwen. The second emperor of the Ming dynasty. Interesting choice."

"And deliberate," Ibrahim follows. "It's a codename. Chinese want to hide their identity. Do you know why?"

"You'd have to ask *them*, Colonel," Athena returns. "There's no record of the name within Camp Yi's manifest, but if you want my opinion—?"

"Which you're about to share whether if I do or not," Ibrahim utters.

"Given that we *know* Doctor Hao is playing the uncooperative neighbor?"

"We should treat this newcomer as a potential agent for Chinese intelligence," Ibrahim steers.

"With a record as black and effective as any of its counterparts," Athena says.

"Which means?" Ibrahim questions.

"The potential threat to our mission with this VIP is substantial," the AI explains.

"That, or we're paranoid, and the name is an alias for an exceptionally qualified individual."

"And this is a lot of fuss about nothing," Athena concludes.

Ibrahim sighs without reply. Then, he goes back to his squad.

"Get yourselves washed and rested," Ibrahim orders. "I'll expect everybody ready to go at twelve-hundred hours!"

"Twelve hundred," Sergeant Mannering repeats. "Got it."

"Yes, sir," the acknowledgments continue.

"You're dismissed," Ibrahim grants.

Ibrahim leaves the training center and heads into the rain, still wearing his HRDVS armor and combat harness.

He follows the trail markers on his way to the base's upper landing platform and the newcomer's arrival. By the time he reaches the pad, the Mi-26 is already on the ground, with CSDR troopers standing at the bottom of the loading ramp.

Ibrahim ducks inside a pavilion and takes off his helmet.

"Athena . . . Who's that I see with our guest?" he requests.

"Addison Kennedy," the AI mocks. "Looks like she's beaten you to the punch."

"And she's helping the woman through customs," Ibrahim notes.

"You sound upset by your tone?"

"Only a little jealous," Ibrahim admits.

"Is there anything else you need from me, Lieutenant Colonel?" Athena inquires.

"Yeah," Ibrahim says. "Send me whatever you have on record about our newcomer."

"Going to do a little homework?"

"Enough to get a handle on what we're dealing with," Ibrahim confides.

"Understood," Athena replies.

A notification dings on his wrist-pad computer. It's a data packet from Overlook Station.

Ibrahim notices the document size. "Smaller than I was expecting," he mutters.

"You asked for what I had on record," Athena returns.

"No doubt the rest is drowning in twelve shades of ink," Ibrahim accepts.

He skims the document until the first lines go blurry, and his vision momentarily darkens.

Ibrahim takes a deep breath and exhales. He's stopped moving. Now the fatigue is finally catching up to him.

ADDISON KENNEDY, FIELD DIRECTOR
EPIMETHEUS PROJECT

OCTOBER 19, 2041 | 0950 HOURS

―――

"It feels like I'm wearing pottery," Addison comments, moving awkwardly in the contraption she's wearing. "And it's heavy . . . How do the marines run in these suits?"

"Extreme conditioning," Vogert replies, helping her switch out the hard-suit's backplate with a less bulky version.

"Once the servos kick in, they'll seem pretty weightless," Leighton adds.

Ava Remmings shifts uncomfortably in her suit. "These are the older models," she retorts. "Meant for minimal extravehicular activity on the Overlook. Mark IV HWRDs, C-Variant—so, it'll protect your ass inside the ship, but it won't survive a straight-up firefight."

"And you just have that info memorized?" Leighton snarks.

"Don't you?" Ava returns.

"Doctor Remmings' designed half the equipment our troops use, Mr. Leighton," Vogert explains.

Addison blinks anxiously as their banter continues. She checks the timer on her wrist-pad, counting the hours until Operation Shield Piercer officially launches. Addison will admit she was too zealous to get the ball rolling right after her encounter with Idu 'Smeora. Adrenaline impacted her judgment.

"Greed is an illness," Vogert whispers to her as he locks in her new back-plate. "It can rush to your head. And if you jump off that bridge without a rope?"

"I better have a parachute ready," Addison admits. Among other things, it's not like her to run carelessly into a situation without prep-work or a plan. Or backups to those plans. "This is like a mission of the damned."

She yanks off her gloves and tosses them at the Project's Quartermaster.

"Something wrong with these?" the other asks.

"Yes. Can you get me a larger size? I can barely move my fingers with those."

"Right away, ma'am," the Quartermaster acknowledges.

"Twenty-two hours, ten minutes," Leighton says. "Precisely at nine o'clock tomorrow, this party kicks off loud."

"And it'll be a race to win the beast's heart," Vogert exclaims.

Addison nods, her hands shaking and wet. She hides her fists inside her coat to keep Vogert from noticing, unable to keep her nervous tremors down. At precisely 0900 hours tomorrow, Addison will cross beyond the Breach for the first time with two hundred soldiers, a small team of researchers, and support staff to finally join this expedition in earnest.

"What about this newcomer?" Ava inquires. "Zhu Yunwen? I'm pretty sure that's a codename."

"Did Athena tell you that?" Leighton laughs.

"No," she returns. "I am quite experienced with military affairs."

"Whatever her name, Doctor Zhu is a member of our team," Addison says. "Codename or not—we don't need to know anything more."

"Is that what you believe?" Vogert asks.

"If she doesn't, I'd like to know," Ava rebounds.

"That's the deal we got handed," Addison frowns. "We can wade through it or sink to the bottom."

"That's not the point we're making," Vogert retorts. "To have someone watching our backs, and we don't even know their name?"

"Malakai is asking us to levy a lot of trust in the situation," Avanna seconds.

"Do we honestly *need* Chinese support for this mission?" Leighton iterates, making a derisive crack. "Because they haven't exactly been equal partners thus far. I'm just saying."

Addison finishes zipping up her coat over the armor's impact body glove.

"They took the heaviest losses during the Central Spire Incident," Addison argues. "They've some right to make demands."

The rain outside gets louder as she waits, the pounding building on the pavilion's rooftop hitting a crescendo.

"Nobody's begrudging our friends their casualties," Vogert says, rubbing his palms.

"Then let's give Zhu some benefit of the doubt," Addison asserts, snapping on the hardsuit's frontal plate.

"When *does* our new teammate get here?" Ava presses.

The whole room turns to Addison with puzzling eyes. She goes to check her pad and pulls up her last few notifications.

"I got the alert when they lifted off," she explains. "Should be flying into our airspace any minute now. We can meet them at the landing pad. As a courtesy."

"I'm not great at putting on a friendly face for strangers," Ava murmurs.

"You're not great at putting on a friendly face for the people you know," Leighton criticizes.

Ava looks at him with a sly grin. "What do you even do on the Olympus, Harlow? You draw maps? You categorize locational data gathered by our field teams? Something about cartography, right? A glorified navigator who leaves the real work to others."

"Mhmm," Leighton returns. He goes back to combing over his field gear without saying another word.

Ava smirks with satisfaction. Although, after meeting Addison's blue stare, her mouth twitches.

Addison follows Leighton's example and finishes prepping her expedition gear. She takes the armor's helmet and puts it on, feeling the static buzz of *it* interfacing with her nervous system. Colorful lights pop up on her display. Even without connecting to the core hardware, the helmet can maintain its function with minimal battery. It can still preserve its air scrubbers for the operator's short-term survivability. And should the suit ever shut down unexpectedly?

She runs a quick diagnostic. "A hundred-thousand milliamps? Short-term? That's laughable."

It's only enough to power the suit for a couple of minutes. And what should happen if an emergency hits the crew? Those precious minutes are the only lifeboat for the operator to crawl out of a hole and get themselves to safety.

"An emergency like a sudden depressurization inside a tight space," Addison murmurs.

"I like this kit," Ava remarks. "Well designed. Efficient. At least, what I heard from the boys that use them."

"Better to plan for it to fail than to rely on it when you need it," Vogert asserts.

Addison catches a tinge in his eye as he says it, like a deep shakiness bellowing in his throat.

Vogert notices her gaze. "I've seen what happens when field equipment doesn't work as promised," he admits. "Doesn't matter how well designed it is. Equipment fails. People fail. Medics and doctors are the ones who have to stitch the pieces together afterward."

Addison takes a step toward him with a frown when her earpiece beeps. "Go ahead," she answers.

"Addison," Athena says. "I thought you'd like to know that Doctor Zhu's transport is nearing the platform."

"Did you just call me Addison?" she asks.

"Doctor Kennedy," Athena corrects. "It's not the first time."

"The lady's got into the habit of breaking her protocol," Ava winks.

"I suppose it doesn't matter," Addison decides. "I'll meet everybody outside on the terrace."

They all give her their respective nods before helping her to remove her armor plates.

Addison, Vogert, Ava, and Leighton wait as the newcomer's aircraft comes in for a landing. Coordinators run along the platform's edges, waving their glow wands around as they bring the Mi-26 to the upper landing pad. The red lights set up around the rim are blinding. Addison knows it's so the pilots can spot where to go from above as visibility with the storm makes landings difficult. Everyone working to bring in aircraft usually tints their masks to protect their eyes.

The Mi-26 lands with a hydraulic hoof and lowers its ramp, creating a splash when it hits the platform.

Several dozen elite CSDR troopers file out of the rear compartment. Behind the soldiers is a thin woman barely in her late twenties. Or maybe in her early thirties? Her uniform designates her as a research officer at Camp Yi, her divisional patch sewn over her left shoulder.

"That's Wensu Hao's second-in-command," Ava regards.

"I recognize her," Addison goes. "Her *real* name is . . . Xie? Something or another."

The troopers move apart to allow the thin woman to walk up and meet Addison at the platform's edge.

"Doctor Addison Elizabeth Kennedy?" the woman asks, the light reflecting off her bare skin. "You know who I am, yes?"

"Zhu Yunwen, if I were to guess. You speak English?" Addison asks, noting the faint accent in her voice as if she's been a native speaker for a while.

"I resided in the United States for nine years," the woman goes.

"As a citizen?"

"Study abroad, long-term," she goes. "Stanford University."

Addison nods with suspicious admiration. "Good to have a fellow alumnus with me on the trip," she grins.

"Like a brisk walk down the scenic trail?"

Addison shakes her head. "Not quite. Come on? We've got a briefing at noon."

"I am soaking wet," Zhu clamors.

"You can dry off at the transitory along the way."

"Not at a ready room?"

Addison laughs. "You'll find we're a bit more co-ed than you're used to," she says.

"Crews will constantly move between pavilions throughout the day," Vogert explains. "We change in and out of fatigues every couple of hours or so—clean hazmat suits, lab coats, and casuals."

Zhu cautiously smiles with a tilt of her head. "I understand. Lead on. Please."

Inside the airlock, the five change into dry clothes.

Addison notes how Zhu remains awkward during the changeover, but the woman pushes through it, regardless.

"This predicament weirds you out, does it?" Ava infallibly asks the woman.

Zhu looks at Ava like she's broken an unspoken rule in social etiquette. "We don't have common areas like this at Camp Yi," the woman replies. "Not to mention, military and civilian teams do not intermingle. No interaction. Not even on patrols. They do their thing while we do ours. They guard us as we study the ship's interior, and we provide the knowledge they need to operate safely."

"Which is why you've been hoarding data?" Leighton questions, although respectful.

Zhu turns to him in absolute bafflement. "I don't know what you mean, Mr. Leighton," she scolds.

"Your teams aren't uploading data packets to the Overlook," Leighton reiterates. "The other crews have noticed. And I'm curious."

The woman squints and clenches her jaw. Despite her calm demeanor and friendly appearance, it's good for Addison to remember that Doctor Zhu is an outsider looking in at strangers. And no matter the reasons, she understands why Zhu turns her back on Leighton, refusing to answer.

It's dangerous for her to admit controversy as a representative of her government.

They cross paths with Colonel Ibrahim and his platoon arriving from the training center across the yard. Addison doesn't see Sergeant Major Olivia Warden, however. Which is . . . strange? Especially since the two always seem tied at the shoulders.

"Doctor Kennedy," Ibrahim says, eyeing Addison first, then the clique trailing behind her. "Or doctors, should I say? Is your team assembled?"

"We are ready," Addison replies. "You missed introductions to our newest member?"

"I saw the bird on the pad and decided to head things off instead," Ibrahim explains, focusing his stare on Doctor Zhu next to them. "As long as the good doctor meets your qualifications, that's all that matters. Although I noted our records fail to mention Doctor Zhu's real name or even her gender."

Addison gives him a sly look. "Will that be a problem, Colonel?"

"Not at all, ma'am," Ibrahim returns. "I merely prefer knowing the variables. My troops can execute well-planned missions with a high degree of adaptability. The more patterns we can predict, the better our preparedness. And the fewer men *I* lose to the unexpected."

"Nobody wants a repeat of the Central Spire Incident, Lieutenant Colonel," Doctor Zhu speaks up in self-defense. "I know you took part in that mission along with Commander Wen. Our team had the lead, so we took the heaviest losses. Had your marines taken point, I suspect a different situation between our two nations."

Her words to him are more overly diplomatic. Ibrahim glares at Doctor Zhu, suspicion all over his face. Along with a hint of applause.

Ibrahim stands straight and smiles. "Welcome to the mission, ma'am," he says. "Make sure you grab the safety railing. It's slippery on the deck. So, mind where you're stepping. I don't want to fish you out of the ocean before we kick off this parade." Addison hasn't any delusions about what "mind where you're stepping" means. A warning to stay in her lane and *not* interfere with his job. "Ladies? Gentlemen," Ibrahim concludes.

He walks past the team. Farther down the hallway, Ibrahim begins whistling a happy tune.

Addison eyes Doctor Zhu. If the woman has an adverse reaction to the man, she doesn't let it show. Her face is like a rock in sunlight—surface level warm but deeply reserved, cold, and calculating.

"A true diplomat," Addison whispers, leaning in with a kinder smile. "You, okay?"

Zhu shares Addison's gaze for a moment. "Perfectly fine," she says. "If you don't mind, I'd like to see the data on your encounter, Doctor Kennedy. I want to get myself updated on everything I can."

"Of course," Addison agrees. "Athena will upload the transcript to your datastick."

"Datastick?" Zhu begs the question.

"You don't have one?"

"I haven't needed one," the woman admits.

"Then we'll have to get you a unit," Addison confirms. "There's still a little while until the briefing."

"It should be enough time to find you an overview packet," Leighton offers.

"And I can answer whatever questions you have about the mission."

"That would be appreciated, Doctor Kennedy. Very much. Yes."

"Call me, Addison," she steers. "Formalities aren't necessary, don't you think?"

"As you say, Doctor Kennedy."

WORDS THAT DON'T INSPIRE US

MALAKAI ADONIS, DIRECTOR OF OPERATIONS
EPIMETHEUS PROJECT

OCTOBER 19, 2041 | 1230 HOURS

Malakai steps from the briefing room and lingers in the hallway for a time.

It is his first visit to the hull, and honestly, it's making him nauseous. Malakai clings to the wall before dropping to his knees, easing himself onto his back, letting his spine pop satisfyingly.

"That's better," he mutters. "I just need to . . . catch . . . my breath."

Over an hour ago, Malakai had hopped off the transport from Mount Olympus to surprise the teams participating in Operation Shield Piercer. When he arrived, Vogert handed him a rebreather mask to wean on during his stay. Unlike conditions on the oil rig, however, the air of the hull is thin.

"It'll put your body in a transitionary period until you can adjust to the environment," Vogert explained.

Malakai had declined the mask, thinking he won't need it for a short visit. Doctor Vogert yelled at him for his disregard.

"Sensory overload," Malakai whispers. He shields his eyes from the overhead lights reflecting off the shelter's walls, too bright for him to handle. Sweat gathers at his pits, making him aware of the ambient cold in the air. "One . . . two . . . three . . . four . . . five . . ." He counts the seconds between each breath he inhales.

Malakai had to fight through the briefing with a brave face. The last thing he needs is vomiting in front of his subordinates. Not only would that be embarrassing for him, but it would negate any confidence his people have in him and the Epimetheus Project he leads. Malakai stays up late every night, reading their reports to know what it's like working hull-side.

Arthur had it easy when he jumped aboard the massive ship from a small boat and a dozen hands. No media coverage, no supervisory boards. Just a group of scientists who set out on a survey craft with a common goal in mind.

"To do what nobody had done before," he remembers calling it at the time.

Sooner than later, Malakai can't keep it together anymore and vomits a white, thick substance over the plastic floor.

Vogert enters the umbilical, shaking his head disapprovingly.

"I said you'd need a rebreather mask," the man gloats.

"What did I just throw up?" Malakai asks.

"Looks like white bile," Vogert describes. "Probably the condensed milk from the rations."

"Gross."

"At least I don't see any red in the mix," he says.

"Red is bad?" Malakai asks.

"Red is always bad," Vogert laughs. "Our bodies aren't designed for this environment. The best thing we can do is use the tools we've built for this purpose. Like wearing the recommended masks on the hull for the first couple of hours. It would've saved you from experiencing this pressure sickness."

"Point taken," Malakai accepts. "Now stop being a smartass and help me up? Jesus, I should've listened to you."

Malakai extends his hand, and Vogert gladly takes it. "My name's not Jesus, but . . . Close enough, I suppose."

"Oh, very funny."

"Addison seems to think so."

"Doctor Kennedy also thinks Avanna Remmings is rather charming if an unsociable woman," Malakai remarks.

"Is anybody qualified to judge that?" Vogert chuckles. "Well? I am, but who's keeping track these days? Oh, wait . . . That's also me."

The man lifts Malakai to his feet and leads him through a canvas maze to the Medical Section. There, the good doctor examines Malakai—looking at his eyes and throat, keeping his mind busy with small talk.

"So, how are you finding our little slice of paradise, boss?" Vogert asks.

"A bit rocky," Malakai answers. "The scale of this place, it's just—? I see it through the Olympus' windows every day and—"

"You can't fathom it? Not really. Not until you're standing on top of it," Vogert states.

"That's one way to describe it," Malakai admits. "Have you gone inside?"

"I won't until this operation launches tomorrow," Vogert laughs. "But I *have* seen images the crews send back . . . Along with a decent view from this side of the Breach, once or twice. I've never actually stepped beyond the barriers, however. With all the fighting, it's a security risk."

"I'm sorry," Malakai regrets asking.

"I doubt either of us *wants* to see what's in there for ourselves," Vogert says. The man connects monitoring discs to Malakai's forearm, sending electrical impulses through his skin. "I get plenty of the aftermath to know it's not good for your health."

"I suppose *want* and *need* are two different arguments for jumping into the fire," Malakai says.

"Different arguments, but with similar consequences," Vogert repeats. "At least, that's how Addison describes it."

The Chief Medical Officer moves on to check his heart rate. Vogert then continues and presents Malakai with a plastic syringe with velvet-looking fluid inside.

"Is that the enzyme you're working on?" Malakai asks. "You've synthesized it quickly."

"You didn't exactly recruit us for standing around making speeches," Vogert replies. "And we're calling it a 'gene therapy' given how it changes the way your cells function when exposed to foreign contaminants."

"Foreign like an alien ship in the middle of a barren ocean?"

"Near enough," Vogert shrugs. "Not quite, however."

"What does it do?" Malakai questions, his eyes locking on the fluid.

Vogert grimaces. "We've modified the DNA of our living and near-living specimens to run the material through processing. We inject the serum directly into the bloodstream. By diffusion, your red cells transport the enzyme throughout the body and transfer it to your organs. After, it latches on to donor cells, where it starts replicating to spread further."

"Sounds like cancer."

"Very much like cancer. Except it doesn't mutate as much as it evolves," Vogert describes, catching the worrying stare Malakai is giving him. "Don't worry. It's benevolent. The enzyme acts like a catalyst that re-writes your genetic code and allows your body to adapt under extreme conditions. You're unlikely to die from it. I think."

"You think?" Malakai repeats. "Unlikely? Those aren't good words."

"Stop being paranoid," Vogert expresses. "You're not going to wake up tomorrow with a tumor in your stomach."

"That's oddly specific."

"You've nothing to worry about," Vogert asserts.

"Your reports mention human trials? How does that work? The project is only a few days old."

"That's true," Vogert exhales. "Addison was adamant about adhering to the rules, too. After her encounter with the Architect, we agreed to test it on volunteers."

"Were these 'volunteers' informed about what they're getting themselves into?"

"We've tried convincing them not to undergo the procedure," Vogert readily admits. "Per tradition."

"And how many did you discourage?"

Vogert confidently grins. "None."

Malakai leans forward. "Any negative reactions?"

"A few mild cases," he goes. "We're monitoring them, noting the changes, but not seeing anything we didn't expect. Which is rare in bioscience, I should mention. This alien enzyme is incredibly simple to work with, allowing us to start iterations."

"And what are the modifications?"

"That's the strangest thing!" Vogert clarifies. "We've only modified the *method* we're using to inject it."

"Not the compound itself?" Malakai begs the question.

"After putting it through the process, it's incredibly versatile. At least, we hope that's the case," Vogert describes. "It changes to fit its host biology and improves the body where it can. And this is just a prototype. With additional work, I can see us having it produced in larger, more potent quantities."

"How many people have you inoculated with the serum?"

"Apart from the volunteers yesterday? Addison and I agreed the entire scientific team should take it as the main test group. Along with select military personnel—frontline troops and such. Those whose hardsuits are likely to get damaged."

"I am guessing I will be a stray in your experiment?"

"A control unit—if you don't mind the phrasing. And only if you agree to the procedure," Vogert suggests. "It will allow me to measure the shift in dynamics between someone who's injected and doesn't leave our native atmosphere."

"As opposed to those exposed to adaptations via the enzyme," Malakai weighs.

Malakai doesn't move his eyes away as the liquid in the syringe moves like a watery gel trapped and trying to escape. The monitors to his side start beeping as his heart rate goes up. The noise quickly catches Vogert's attention.

"You're nervous," he notes. "Don't be."

"No, I trust you. Go ahead," Malakai nods.

Vogert lifts the needle and injects its vividly colorful contents into Malakai's shoulder. The doctor then discards the syringe into the biohazard disposal bin and reads the scans on Malakai's vitals for fifteen minutes.

"There we are, and—? No major shifts," Vogert goes. "Clear on my board. That's a good start."

"What would the monitor do if it's *not* good?" Malakai questions.

"You mean if things were going bad?"

"Yes?"

"Worse case? This little graph you see going up and down suddenly flatlines," Vogert snarks, pointing at the heartrate monitor.

"Which means I'd be dead?" Malakai shrouds.

"You would be dead," Vogert acknowledges.

Malakai lets off a fake smile. "Your humor is something else, my friend."

"My performance usually knocks out my audience."

"More like you put them into a coma," Malakai scoffs. "What are the symptoms I should expect?"

Vogert shrugs less cheerfully. "For one, you'll start feeling better by the time you return to the Olympus. It's a subtle change. Give it a few hours," he describes. "Some volunteers report headaches and dull throbbing around their throats. You might feel like your chest is compressing, making breathing difficult. I'll assign one of my assistants to go with you to keep tabs."

Malakai can feel the pressure building around his temples already.

"Anyone on the team who's not taken it?"

"Doctor Zhu is the only one who hasn't, though not due to a lack of trying."

Malakai notices a crack of deep frustration in the man's voice by the implication. "How do you mean?"

"I approached her concerning the subject before going into the briefing," he goes. "Her mender took control over the discussion and denied my request. Said it's because he doesn't want two different serums to damage her body."

"Meaning the Chinese already inoculated Doctor Zhu with another compound."

"It *does* seem to implicate that," Vogert concludes.

"Wensu Hao hasn't forwarded anything about researching the subject."

"And that is what's concerning me," the doctor continues. "So, I requested access to her charts. Since I'll be the only medical officer on hand to administer treatment during an emergency, I need to know. For *her* sake. Again, the mender refused."

Malakai shakes his head, not knowing off-hand what the protocols are when one country refuses to submit to a direct request.

"I'll investigate the matter once I get back to the Olympus," Malakai promises. "And I'll get you those charts."

Vogert nods. "Thank you, Malakai. I thought the Project was above these petty politics?"

"Unfortunately, it doesn't appear so," Malakai returns, pressing on his temples to alleviate his pain. "I had hoped we could all work together. We aren't. And certain events have convinced me that much of it is outside my control."

"Pausing on the rhetoric for a moment," Vogert breathes. "They're keeping secrets, aren't they?"

"I'd be surprised if *our* people aren't keeping secrets," Malakai confirms. "But . . . Yes? They're particularly uncooperative."

Vogert's face goes blank as he disconnects the monitoring discs from Malakai's forearm.

"At least they're honest about their lying," Vogert chides.

Later in the corridor, Malakai steps aside to let a group of marines in heavy combat armor pass through. They move almost robotically in their HRDVS harnesses—faceless, streamlined, and efficient. At one point, Malakai stops to lean against a support column to catch his breath as the noise they make hurts his ears.

"It's like I'm trying to breathe underwater and am not able to go up for air," he describes the sensation.

The intensity builds every few minutes as he trots along. But the episodes pass quickly, like cold hands working their way into his brain, stripping the memory and throwing it into the trash. Malakai fights to remember the suffocation, what it's like, but . . . He can't. It's gone.

"Fucking hell, Ryan," he curses.

Vogert comes up behind him. "You all right there, boss?" he asks, noticing his discomfort, and instinctually checks Malakai's eyes for dilation.

"A bit lightheaded," Malakai explains. "I felt like I was drowning there for a moment."

"Drowning? Really? That's interesting," the man says, letting him go.

"You didn't know that was a symptom?"

"I do now," he says. "You're probably just adjusting to the enzyme."

"Probably? Another bad word."

"We don't have the benefit of testing the treatment in a controlled environment long-term," Vogert confides. "Our tests *do* show the enzyme is beneficial to the body. The drowning sensation is likely your body's specific reaction to getting your DNA re-written. However, we're still in an early stage. It usually takes years to work out kinks in a new vaccine, let alone create a comprehensive record of all the symptoms. And we've barely had a week. That's why I am monitoring everyone who gets the therapy."

"You better be right about this, my friend. You're playing with fire near a tinderbox."

"Luckily, we're surrounded by water," Vogert retorts.

The door leading to another umbilical corridor opens. Addison Kennedy steps through and into the conversation. Her eyes land on Malakai first. Then, they veer to Vogert. "It's never a good sign when your boss says you're 'playing with fire,' I'd like to point out," the woman confides.

Malakai coughs. "Addison? We're discussing the implementation of the enzyme you've cultivated."

"Ah, the fun project," Addison regards. "Figured that. Lacking better options, we decided a limited human trial is best suited for our current predicament."

"Ignoring that we're testing it on ourselves in the field and not in a controlled environment, do you think OverSec will agree that it's safe?"

Addison grimaces when Malakai says the name. "Let's discuss this *after* we gather more data."

"Then we'll find out if the enzyme is dangerous or not," Vogert promises.

"I felt like I was drowning, Addison."

"And depending on your body's requirements, the forced adaptation you're going through is wholly unique to you," Addison argues. "Your attendant will run regular checkups and compare them to our record. This place? It's discovery and death at every corner. Our people are dying from exposure to the atmosphere *inside* as much as they are from close encounters."

"It's a risk," Vogert attests. "But we're keeping eyes on the situation."

Malakai feels another tightness in his neck muscles. Eventually, he waves them off, surrendering to their mutual argument.

"I just hope I don't find a third nipple in the mirror tomorrow," Malakai warns.

"I don't think it can cause a physical mutation like that," Vogert frowns. "The changes are purely on a chemical level."

Malakai shakes his head. "Keep me updated when you can. And good luck tomorrow," he charges.

The pair nod and leave together back toward the Medical Section. Malakai stays in the umbilical, staring out the plastic window at the storm. Playing with fire is the best-case scenario he could describe should the wrong people find out about their little experiment.

Malakai breathes and finds a seat on a bench. He presses his palm to his throat, lightning causing the sky to turn white for an instant.

SHIELD PIERCER

IDU 'SMEORA, THE WHISPERER OF CONTINUANCE
ARKKITECT OF THE VILI

521031 LOCAL CLUSTER | 761,398 DAY OF PURPOSE

"Staunch innovators, aren't you?" Idu mutters. She adds a note to her journal as she watches.

It has taken four days, but the locals have adapted the *t'armarva enzyme* to their needs. Idu has made sure to mark their progress throughout the project's development. At least enough for limited-scale gene manipulation on volunteers.

Watching her subjects gather, Idu centers the Observer on the people surrounding Addison Kennedy.

"Avanna Remmings on the right," she counts. "Ryan Vogert on the left with Harlow Leighton."

Idu spins the Observer's display clockwise as a fifth individual comes into view with an altogether different weight about her.

"Another female," Idu lists. "Identity unknown?" Her feathers turn starkly pink. "A new introduction to the core group," Idu records, refocusing on the woman. "Something's different about her. I can see a timidness on her shoulders. Slightly angled. Like an ugly dresthealia among beautiful Wynder avillia." Idu leans closer to the image and smiles.

Then her grin changes to widening eyes and a sunken frown.

Idu recoils when she hears intense fighting erupt from the corridor outside the Observer Mentalis.

She shuts down the controls and turns to the door. "What is happening?"

Several blasts scorch the air like ozone baking to a crisp.

Idu swallows as she listens to the Varmajalkavaen on the other side getting thrown violently against the walls. After the noise dies with one last cry, footsteps approach, pounding to a rhythm. And the room's security lock disengages. Standing in the frame is a tall, dominating figure—a warrior's physique, dressed in bright, colorful armor.

Idu instinctively stands her ground.

Adhion 'Klaka regards her with surprise. "Whisperer?" the Nomad murmurs. "Always the isolationist. Our local *zookeeper*."

"Nomad? What are you doing here?" Idu demands. "This is *my* role in the Obligation. Not yours."

"Because I have done so well keeping to the rules already?" Adhion mocks, a high pitch to his voice. "Not that I can officially use it without your marker."

Adhion steps inside the room. Through the door, Idu can see the bodies of the Varmajalkavaen alongside the broken husks of Fragment Alimentors. He fought them to get in here, the High Echelon assigned to protect her during this crisis.

Idu maintains her distance as Adhion circles the dais. He identifies the Observer's display and drops his shoulders bleakly.

Then, his starry eyes fall on her.

"You are studying the humans?" Adhion asks.

"And why does that interest you?" she begs the question.

"For the same reason it does you, I should imagine," he returns with a tremor on his lips. "Tjaa likely sees them as a failure on a genetic scale. Asymmetrical."

"And how would you describe them?" Idu conjures.

"Brilliant?" Adhion calls up the word.

"And you attack them because of their brilliance?"

Adhion grimaces, his feathers turning a muddy grey color. "That . . . is an error I intend to correct," the Nomad offers solemnly. "Violence is bred into me, no matter how hard I try otherwise. I can no more stop who I am than you can keep yourself from wanting to understand them. Idu—?"

"We only create life," Idu fights. "We do *not* destroy. We do not break glass and throw it on the floor!"

"And if those creations don't measure up to their design? What do you think happens?" Adhion questions.

Idu shakes her head. "Obligation demands that we life-seed barren worlds," she iterates. "And to aid in the rebirth of a diverse universe."

Adhion peacefully raises his hands, showing his palms. "You avoid the question."

"Every species has the right to defend itself," Idu answers.

"Unless it works against our interests?" Adhion construes, relaxing his weight to his back foot. "Ambivalent? I heard it so many times that I do not know. But I am a soldier, not a scholar. We create life without considering what it takes for those species to survive. And if you fail, then I must step in and clean up the mess. Ambivalence." Adhion steps closer to Idu.

"Humanity isn't ours," she denotes. "They've evolved to this world on their own."

"A rare occurrence," Adhion nods.

"And the last time something like that happened—?"

"It was us," he finishes.

Idu smiles. "Soaring across our primeval skies like birds of prey," she describes.

"Idu?" Adhion faints. "We *are* birds of prey. Dangerous. Egotistic." His armor unfolds at his neck, revealing the smooth skin underneath. His expression wrinkles the white markings on his grey face. Idu watches as the Nomad takes in a breath and holds it. He shifts his weight to his forwardmost foot, tapping his long fingers on the flat of his nose.

"Not one in your chord has ever questioned their duty," Idu remarks.

"And we're treated like some unclean abominations for that obedience," Adhion retorts, mouthing his syllables afterward. He's searching for the words to elucidate. Then he looks over at the Observer's display and points at it. "Look at them," he says in a weak, guttural pitch. "These humans are strong enough to invite others to attack them unprovoked. Humanity will protect its interests. And they will either lose, learning what it means to live through near extinction. Or they'll find a way to pursue whoever attacks them until they've annihilated every threat to their planet."

Adhion's voice falls away until it's no more than a whisper.

"I see them well enough," Idu tells him.

"Do you?" Adhion asks. "Before you know it, humanity is the next species we contain." He surrenders a brief, silent look to her. "Where does it end?"

Idu lets her lips dry as the feathers on her arms turn a misty blue hue. She notes the way the Nomad's bristles redden toward their cores. Her eyes narrow once she realizes what that means for him. There's a pride to his stance. Admiration, quite *unlike* the typical executioner his chord so often invokes.

"It doesn't matter," Idu returns. "Humanity isn't our responsibility. We can only undo the damage you've done to their world."

"We've done," Adhion counters. "And if they aren't *our* responsibility, why study them?"

Idu's throat closes once his words leave his tongue. "So, I can learn to talk to them. But that is my role. I ask again, why come here?"

Adhion burrs his head.

"To learn what I can before it's too late," he admits. "None of this is what I wanted."

"You turned our tools into killing machines," Idu accuses.

"Hoping they could buy me time," Adhion shifts. "Do you think I intended them to attack?"

"Tools, when thrown hard enough," Idu says, "are weapons."

"I cannot fault you for thinking that way," Adhion speaks with hardly a crack. "But the possibility was always there."

Idu ponders his dark, wispy eyes.

"What do you mean?"

Adhion sighs, lowering his stance. "I made a mistake."

"Causing so much suffering is more than a mistake," Idu chides.

"I didn't think humanity would jump into the fray and get themselves involved," Adhion admits.

"Then why are the Fragments attacking them?" Idu demands.

"They attack anything in the corridors to clear the way," he answers.

"You must realize what you are doing," Idu pushes in a calmer, wary tone. "So many are dead already. For what?" She steps to the side to look at his face in a better light, noticing the water in his deep black eyes.

"Don't you find it strange? Being a life-bearing vessel, this ship holds enough power to wipe out all life on this planet five times over," Adhion weighs heavily. "If all this ship does is to grow new life, why does it need such a large complement? Fragments? Built more for war than to plant seeds. No consciousness inside their husks. I don't understand it."

Idu backs away a step, unwilling to let this dangerous train of thought continue. Sometimes, those subservient to a living chord must take a stand. Adhion 'Klaka has always known a strict adherence to the ethics he follows. Yet, that isn't what he's uttering now. He's defying the Obligation which he serves!

"I don't know what you're talking about," Idu shudders.

Adhion circles around her, stopping at the door into the corridor.

"Several thousand Varmajalkavaen in stasis . . . Workers and soldiers? Do the humans even know what exists in the space they now occupy?" Adhion recounts. "Carriers, not feeders. Not this vessel's usual adornment. Nor are the millions of Fragments lining crevices inside the walls. Tools? Yes! But they can be weapons, as you've seen."

"What are you suggesting?"

The other frowns. "I don't know," Adhion admits. "That it's not typical of this ship's role? It is a question I can't ignore." Adhion pounds his fist against the wall, causing it to crack under the kinetic force. "Circumstances fail to add up in a way that makes sense, Whisperer."

"So, what do you intend to do?" she asks.

"Me? Exactly as I am doing now," Adhion confides.

"And what is that? To keep us hostage?"

Adhion shakes his head. "No," he frowns. "Not that."

"Then what?"

Adhion's feathers shift to a dull green pattern. Idu hasn't seen a member of the Nomadic chord wear the color in her centuries of experience. Green signifies doubt or depression—a wayward silence. Or momentary hesitation fed not by uncertainty but rather by regret. In a simple translation, Adhion is feeling confused.

"I want to force the Trident's hand," Adhion says.

"For what? Why?'

"To make my voice heard," Adhion declares. "And maybe change things for the better."

He closes his fist before Idu manages to speak. Offering a courteous nod in her direction, Adhion steps back into the corridor and walks past the bodies.

Idu waits for him to leave before turning on her communicator to contact the Entrychamber.

"Tyrann? This is Idu," she goes. "I have an update. Please respond."

"Go ahead, Idu. Is your human ready?"

"They are preparing, but—? I encountered Adhion 'Klaka," she warns. "He is about to do something drastic. I do not know what."

A shrill quiet lingers on the other end of the line.

"Return to us," the Trident orders. "I will send another to meet the humans in your place."

"Addison Kennedy may not trust anyone else but me," Idu argues. "I should still go."

"Adhion is a rabid beast looking for something to bite," the Trident explains. "It is safer for Dhun to go instead. He is a fighter. He can act should the humans refuse our demands. You may coordinate our efforts alongside the Varmajalkavaen. We're fighting a war amongst ourselves, and we must end it to go home."

Idu tries to interject, but her communicator hums, meaning Tyrann 'Akachan has shut down the link and closed the debate. His words are now final, and arguing with the Trident is difficult. Idu can only return to the Entrychamber and wait to see how the rest of this plays out.

"I only hope Addison Kennedy understands my absence," Idu voices, suddenly afraid.

She intends to reconvene with the woman later to finish their discussion.

Adhion found her once, and he can do it again. Idu fears he may not be as cordial as he was with her today if that *does* happen. Until then, it may be safer for her to wait after a few planetary cycles before traversing the corridors again if they are short of escorts.

Idu releases her breath.

It's a long march to the ship's forward section.

32 | PRIORITY ASSETS

ADDISON KENNEDY, FIELD DIRECTOR
EPIMETHEUS PROJECT

OCTOBER 20, 2041 | 0850 HOURS

══

"The power of humanity is an individual's ability to work inside a collective," she mouths.

Addison writes the memo on her wrist-pad as she steps into the fitting room. A specialist team works to connect her HWRD-C suit to the interweave glove that acts as a new skin between her and the outer plates. The process takes minutes and occurs alongside everyone else taking part in the mission.

Marines and expedition members fill the benches. They dawn their hardsuits with efficiency, almost like it's second nature.

Her visor's display switches on as the helmet locks around her collar.

Addison discovers a whole new digital world.

Symbols and markers become her view. They indicate the thousands working across the Summerland and Mount Olympus.

"This is so cool," Leighton mutters over the comm. "Shit! Am I broadcasting? How do I—?"

"Sensors inside your helmet can read your eye movements," Colonel Ibrahim explains in a bad mood. He steps into the room while Leighton makes his spiel. "Look at the application on your HUD and blink twice. That will shut off your comms unit. Alternatively, that button on your wrist can do the same damn thing."

Leighton looks up at the much larger military man.

"Understood, Lieutenant Colonel," the cartographer replies. "Thanks."

Ibrahim nods at the kid before walking into the middle of the floor to grab the room's attention.

"Mount up!" Ibrahim barks. "Vacation's over. I want rubber hitting turf in five!"

Following the order, everyone moves faster to load their gear. UCAF troops file out of the locker room and into the adjacent garage. Armored carriers are waiting inside the motor pool to take them into the Breach. "Keep moving!" a marine says as he pushes Addison's team along. "Time to get your asses loaded!" The garage connects to half a dozen other ready rooms with enough units and vehicles for a battalion.

Addison bites her tongue as she counts heads. She nearly trips over herself as she rushes into a transport's cargo area, no longer with her team, who are each getting put into different vehicles.

"I still wish we could ride together," Addison mutters in earshot of Sergeant Major Olivia Warden, who climbs into the transport after her.

Warden tilts her head, relaying the perplexing stare hidden under the woman's visor.

"Out of the question," Warden denies. "Trust us. We don't want to lose the team with a lucky shot if a carrier goes down. Consider everything after this point a warzone. Respect it like one, too. And maybe we'll get back to the mainland alive."

"It's just that—?"

"This is *our* prerogative," Warden issues. "You're dragging *us* into this mission, so we'll make sure you come out of it alive. Expecting or not—like it or not—the Colonel's the man in charge. Listen to our instructions. Please don't go anywhere that we don't tell you to go. Understand?"

The transport's rear hatch closes with a hydraulic wheeze. Everything goes dark. Only the soft reddish glow of the cabin's interior light illuminates the armored troops in their seats. And then, the engine purrs to life.

"We've got eyes on an electric storm coming into the exclusion zone," Colonel Ibrahim announces on an open channel from another vehicle. "There might be interference before hitting the Breach. Drivers?! Keep watch on your trackers. Let's get these people where they need to go."

Thunder explodes as the trucks roll out of the garage. Addison undoes her seat belt and climbs her way to the front, peering out the window slits as they make their way onto the base's make-do road and into the beast. The dreadnaught's red glow hits the glass, creating a bloodier tint inside the cockpit.

"Doctor Kennedy—we've just passed the outer markers. We're through the barrier," Ibrahim continues. "The channel's all yours. Please give us the specifics again. For the grunts. Who's this individual we expect once we reach the dark zone?"

"A being who runs this vessel," Addison begins. "Her name is Idu 'Smeora— an Architect of the Vili, as she described."

"And what *is* the Vili precisely?" Warden asks.

"It's the Summerland," Ibrahim answers. "The ship we're on! Their name for it."

"So, the buggers are the Architects?" a trooper asks.

"They're not the buggers. However, Colonel Ibrahim's rescuer *was* one," Addison elucidates.

"Aren't I special," Ibrahim mocks.

"And my impression of Idu suggests they are a hyper-intelligent species," Addison details. "Very proud. Powerful."

"A species much larger than us," Ibrahim adds.

"Physically, without a doubt," Addison frowns. "Each member also serves a role to their Obligation."

"And what *is* the Obligation? I still don't understand that part," Warden states.

"Think of it as a collective goal for their society," Addison grimaces. She can feel her knees buckle as the ride gets bumpy.

Addison climbs back to her seat and clicks into her safety harness.

Warden stares at her angrily through the smooth reflection of her visor.

"And does this collective goal have some religious significance?" Vogert asks over the comms.

"Possibly," Addison suggests.

"And there are only five of them, right?" Warden questions.

"Only five," Addison confirms.

"Along with a small army," Ibrahim amends.

"Of course," Addison shrugs.

Doctor Zhu Yunwen chimes over the channel. "Which means that five crewmembers could run a vessel of this size. Five with control over everything from system maintenance to the propulsion engines!" She coughs to clear her throat as if the words are difficult for her to say openly.

"That would need a lot of centralization in their systems to achieve," Ava suggests.

"Meaning it might've left the ship vulnerable to sabotage," Zhu concludes.

"And there's an Architect aboard that Idu believes has done exactly that," Addison explains. "He's called the Nomad—Adhion 'Klaka. A very capable and dangerous specimen. I have a distinct impression the others don't like him. Idu said he massacres whole civilizations at a time. Trillions, dead by his actions."

"And now he's on our planet," Vogert sighs.

"With the Fragments being maintenance drones," Addison says. "Or something like that. I don't know."

"And the buggers are fighting them," Warden murmurs.

"They're keeping us from getting overrun," Addison warns. "That doesn't mean they aren't a threat to us either. They attack us as perceived threats, just as we've been doing to them. I'm not sure what motivates the Varmajalkavaen, but I don't think they're the real danger we face."

"Tell that to the lads in the morgue," Warden growls.

Addison holds up her index finger. "Just—? Listen, please," she begs for understanding. "Idu wants us to see what's in the forward sections of her ship for a reason. That's why we're doing this. Whatever she's putting into motion? She's doing it to help us, not hurt us."

"Are you a prophet now?" a marine corporal asks.

"I'm only making observations, soldier," Addison admits. "I don't want us shooting at everything that moves when we reach the target area. Keep your recorders on for documentation. If it goes well, we can get in and out before we get into a firefight we can't win."

Warden shakes her head. "With all due respect, Doctor Kennedy—" The Sergeant Major pushes toward her, speaking with a dark undertone. "We've run ops in the last couple of days with no intel and a lot of bad shit happening because of it. And I've lost guys due to the lack of planning for these missions."

"I understand that, but—?"

"Shut up! Listen to me, Ms. Kennedy," Warden interrupts. Addison notices the Sergeant Major isn't speaking to her on the open channel anymore. She's switched to a two-way interlink, utilizing their private comms. "We are sticking our necks out because *you* decided to trust an alien that broke into your tent and spun a story. And now we're forcing our way into what's potentially the most dangerous area of this god-forsaken ship?"

"Sergeant Major?" Addison quivers.

"All because you want to take a chance," Warden derides.

Addison respectfully holds her tongue. And then, she clenches her fist. Her temples flare as blood rushes to her head. If the woman couldn't throw Addison on her ass, she would punch Warden. And likely break her hand against her helmet as she does.

Warden's voice grows in strength, and with their helmets on, nobody except Addison can hear it.

Addison's heart races, tripping alarms inside her hardsuit.

"With due respect, we're fighting a war. People are dying! And you're chasing a curiosity?" Warden indicts, slamming her fist into the overhead compartment.

Addison's gaze falls to her boots. Everyone in the cabin looks at them, even if they don't know why. Warden's aggressive gesturing and taut body language is what earn their attention.

"You're right. It's a risk that puts all of us in danger," Addison finally admits. She reopens the channel for everyone to hear. "Many on this trip wonder why we've rushed to this ship when there are people back home that need help. Family? Maybe loved ones? We responded when the dreadnaught hit the Pacific. That tidal wave had wiped out millions. Some want us to make the problem go away. Solve whatever needs solving and make sure it never happens again."

"But it's not so easy," Ibrahim backs her up, knowing their mission's extent.

"We're fighting to learn why they've come and why they haven't left,"

Addison continues. "Not everyone who fights is a soldier, and not everyone who suffers will speak our mother tongues. Remember that. And of those who *are* fighting, not knowing if this is why they signed up . . . I'd say look out the window."

"Already did," Warden breathes. "I didn't like what I saw."

"Do you know what I see?" Addison asks.

"What?" Warden sneers.

"The impossible," Addison says. "And some uncomfortable questions to answer."

Warden falls back to her seat with a lighter weight to her posture.

"Idu might be able to tell us," Addison suggests.

"And the sooner she does," Warden offers, "the sooner we can stop dying?"

"Hopefully," Addison nods.

Over the comms, she can hear Ibrahim chuckling into his microphone.

"And I thought Malakai was the great speechmaker," the Colonel denotes. "I don't think I can handle another 'define our place in the universe' commentary. Let's get you to Idu 'Smeora and figure things out from there." He then shifts his sermon to his marines. "And if I hear another word about how it's not fair for *us* to do a tough job, remember this—I wouldn't throw you into the fire without being the first to jump. That is what we do! Get your heads out of your asses and sound off your callsigns. Marines?! Let me hear you sing."

Addison pulls on her seatbelt as the transport takes a hard right turn. Sergeant Major Warden doesn't break her staring contest with her.

"I'm sorry you've lost people, Olivia," Addison tries to comfort her. Unfortunately, that was the worst thing she could've said.

Warden glowers. "Don't apologize for the people you lose on a mission. We're trained to handle losses."

"Soldiers aren't machines. You're still—"

"I'll make sure to get you out of this alive, Doctor Kennedy," Warden intercepts. "I don't like any of this, but that doesn't mean I'll let it fail. We look after our own in this place, and with everything wanting to kill you—if you're human, you're one of us. That's all I care about."

Addison smiles. "Thank you. I won't disappoint."

Warden nods acceptingly. "This isn't an environment that allows for promises or good intentions."

Addison turns away from the soldiers and reactivates her wrist-pad and types: "A collective humanity can achieve more in a single year than an individual can do in a hundred. Concept of civilization? Maybe."

She only needs to look at everything the Project has built over recent days to know for sure. What they've achieved is . . . remarkable. Unprecedented, even.

The pervasive cold seeps through the armored carrier's cracks and into the rear compartment.

Her fingers shake as adrenaline beats through her body.

Ibrahim peeks over his driver's shoulder as the man steers the transport onto the narrow platforms that make up the ship's interior bay.

He turns to the rear compartment, studying his squad's readouts from their hardsuits. His visor puts up their display names. Only one is a non-combatant: Doctor Ryan Vogert—the Chief Medical Officer for the METIS Research Base.

Vogert sits with his hands on his lap, his visor flickering with colorful HUD lights. His head sways side-to-side as if he's reading reports from his teams on base. Calm. Diligent. Not at all how Ibrahim has expected an egghead to behave going into the Summerland.

Ibrahim has seen many research staff heading to the Central Spire twitch the whole way. Anxious. Tremors in their legs, never knowing what to expect, and rightfully so. Vogert, however? He's a different breed. It's as if he's waiting out the calm with a mentality that puts even the most hard-nosed, solid men and women to the test.

Ibrahim rejoins his troops, taking a seat across from Vogert.

"I've read your file," Ibrahim speaks up, opening a private channel between the pair. "You were a battlefield surgeon for ten years before transferring to a Combat Support Hospital in Croatia. You've got a record of saving more than a thousand lives."

"One-thousand, six-hundred, forty-seven," Vogert relays. "Our people *and* enemy combatants."

"Then why take up with the Project? You aren't under orders."

Vogert lets out a breath, hidden under his helmet's faceplate. Ibrahim can tell by the subtle way his shoulders drop.

"Why did Neil Armstrong take that first giant leap for mankind?" Vogert returns. "Human beings are curious by nature. We see something in the sky and wonder what it's like to go up and touch it. For years we've lingered in the dark, afraid of what we don't understand. And what do we do? We give the fundamental elements of the universe names and personalities to help us fathom our place in—"

A hard drop on the road causes the transport to shift suddenly. Vogert lets the incident pass.

"When Armstrong climbed off that ladder, taking that step, he did it with the world watching two-hundred-thousand miles away. The American Government funded the mission to beat the Soviets in the great race. It was our collective *will* to push toward *something* that only existed in science-fiction up to that point."

"And you're here because you admire the trailblazers?"

Vogert snorts. "No. That's why Addison does what she does. I joined because they needed me—Addison, Malakai, Leighton, Zhu, Ms. Remmings . . . And *not* just them." He looks at the armored troops in the cabin. "Your men. Your women. Malakai presented a challenge to the world. And to solve it? He demanded the best of humanity. Well, I'm the best in my field. And you? You're the best in yours."

Ibrahim leans back confidently.

"Then we better rise to the challenge."

Vogert lets off an obtuse laugh. "I know you inside and out! If anyone's ready for whatever's waiting for us in the dark, it's you, Lieutenant Colonel. Without you, our efforts will die. You are the lifeblood of this Project. Don't let anybody tell you differently."

"And what does that make you?"

"Oh, I am the heart. I'll keep the blood pumping if you've got breath. And the Field Directors—Kennedy, Parker, Bree, Aoki, Fluchet? They're the hands. Ava Remmings and the Olympus crews are the brains. Harlow Leighton, our eyes and ears. Malakai, the silver tongue."

Ibrahim nods. "Which makes High Castle the nerves holding it all together," he states understandingly.

"More of a wealthy uncle," Vogert murmurs. "Humanity is a machine, like this damn vessel. Arthur went at it with a smaller team, and they died. Tragically."

"People are still dying," Ibrahim notes.

"All the reason to do what we're about to do."

The good doctor points his fist at Ibrahim. The Colonel laughs and bumps knuckles with the man.

"If I can promise anything, it's that whatever is waiting for us at the end of this line, we can handle it," Ibrahim confides. "Giant alien birds, warrior bug servants, or long-toothed monsters? Let them come."

They ride for another fifteen minutes before the transport stops at the edge of the interior bay.

Ava opens a channel for everyone to hear, shouts: "We're nowhere near the Central Spire! Did the lead driver get turned around?"

"We're not going to the tower, Doctor Remmings," Leighton intercepts. "Shortest route to the quote-and-quote 'dark zone' is through this entryway. That's where our path leads."

"Our teams are setting up waypoints to get us near our destination," Ibrahim explains. "This is a huge ship, Ms. Remmings. We don't have enough troops to secure every path, so we've focused our efforts along the narrowest route possible. These corridors branch off like tributaries on the Mississippi. We limit when and where the enemy can attack us and give ourselves opportunities to funnel them into kill zones when they do."

"Kill zones?" Zhu begs the question, adding to the conversation.

"Buggers swarm in mass wave attacks, but individuals are skillful fighters on their own," Ibrahim continues. "We aren't a match for them in a head-on fight, so we're acting as Leonidas during the battle of Thermopylae. Use the terrain to our advantage and cut them to pieces!"

Vogert breaks into the comms with a twist and a buzz. "We're a family's respected matriarch who governs over the table at meals. They're the raucous cousins getting scolded for bad manners." He clicks his tongue after to Ibrahim's surprise.

"I've spent days coordinating between Project leaders to plan this route," Leighton describes. "It will take us to the dark zone's edge. Beyond that, we're off the map, like it or not."

The rear hatch opens. Ibrahim's visor polarizes as light breaks into the compartment space.

Ibrahim's marines file onto the platform, with the scientists following them. The staging area is bustling with activity. Soldiers gather along the edges to crack jokes. Several grumble amongst themselves inside the security cordons, complaining about the cold. Others are busy off-loading equipment and rations from the trucks and stacking them into the storage sheds.

Addison Kennedy walks through the scene, keeping her eyes up, almost frozen in her movement.

Ibrahim rushes to catch her up. More vehicles park along the paths leading to the platform as he jogs. Defense stations and prefab walls form a ring around the doors separating the massive hangar from the dreadnaught's corridors.

Marines at this position rarely see combat—with only three prior incidents, none of which ended with casualties. Fewer incidents, meaning fewer risks to the team's overall safety. It's one reason why Ibrahim had chosen this site. As the launching point for their meeting with Idu 'Smeora, it's their best-case scenario.

"You look tired," Ibrahim notions as he reaches Addison.

She elbows him in the side. "Thanks for that. You can't even see me."

Ibrahim surrenders innocently. "Enjoy the ride, at least?" he asks, flinching as she moves.

"Your Sergeant Major has a stick up her ass," she explains calmly.

"Warden? You don't know the half of it," Ibrahim agrees. "Maybe she'll get a chance to show you why. I wouldn't worry about it."

"And how was your ride with Vogert?"

"He's an interesting man. Older than his years."

"Vogert's pretty old already."

"He's good company. A bit philosophical, but decent."

Ibrahim leads them toward the platform's bulwark. Every gun on the scene is pointing at the corridor.

"You never know when the enemy will try to swarm the aperture," a marine says cautiously.

"Everybody standby," Ibrahim sends through the local comms.

Ahead, he spies Doctor Ava Remmings circling the guard next to a light pole. She's looking the soldier up and down, then leans in to run a hand across the carbon scoring on the other's armor, where the hardsuit had taken some grazing hits.

"Ava, what are you doing?" Addison asks, bemusing the woman's odd curiosity.

The marine remains there, unsure how to respond to Doctor Remmings as she prods her.

"Looking over this battle damage," Ava explains. "It's uncommon on my samples. Do you see this?" She points to the edges of a ceramic plate. "These fractures in the chassis? Split. Not like the Fragment destroyed at the tower incident. That cut was cleaner while these . . . these are jagged. Course? Rough! That's it. Yes. Uneven."

"Your point, Doctor?" Ibrahim asks, looking at his subordinate unhappily.

Ava steps sideways and confronts the soldier head-on. "What did this?" she asks.

The marine looks at Ibrahim and coughs. "A bugger—a big one, with heavy armor and a robe," the woman describes.

"A higher echelon," Ibrahim suggests. "We've several reports of them spearheading larger packs. Tough bastards."

"Oorah, sir," the marine returns.

"Interesting," Ava professes. "Addison! You'll know. What does *that* mean to us?"

Addison cocks her head. "Only what I've already suggested? Architects must live within a caste system. And these Varmajalkavaen are members of a warrior or worker sect. It's believable these High Echelons could be military or religious leaders for their species. Or maybe both. Again, such are our theories."

"Religious leaders, who carry weapons?"

"It's possible," Addison admits, crossing her arms. "They may not even view faith and spirituality as aspects to the greater whole."

"Meaning," Ava translates, "we don't know how to classify them."

"Maybe portions of their society still utilize original aspects from the species?" another voice joins the debate. Zhu huddles into their circle with Harlow Leighton. Sergeant Warden closes in behind the two of them. "Assimilation? As theories go, it isn't the most outlandish."

"As if ideas rise to a certain standard," Addison says.

"But allow for independent flare," Zhu notions.

"And you guys can tell *that* just by looking at a few scratches?" Ibrahim questions, a mild throbbing inside his skull.

"Forensic science can tell us a lot about the composition of their weapons," Ava irritatingly explains. Even with the static on her comms, Ibrahim catches the soft discontent under her breath. "Cultural analysis will help us to develop new technologies to match theirs. It lets us figure out what inspires them. *That* is why I am interested. It's my field."

"Archaeologists use scraps and surviving art to fill in the missing pieces of history," Addison argues.

"We can use those same methods on the imprint their weapons leave behind," Ava agrees.

"So, that's why my marine's armor is so important?" Ibrahim asks, raising his chin.

"Oh, it's not important. Just a curiosity," Ava admits. "The research I'm talking about won't have a chance to develop until *after* our mission. We can't mass produce materials on site. Addison's father had to pull strings to get the ASAPHEI 6.8 munitions into circulation."

Ibrahim turns to Addison, who shrugs at him. "What do you expect?" she mouths.

The team reconvenes inside the prefab habitat for the garrison's downtime. Ice covers everything in the small room, even with the heaters on full blast. It's a long wait for the other stations to send their acknowledgments. Everyone takes the opportunity to play cards, relax on makeshift cots, and even laugh.

Ibrahim catches Addison in the corner, humming a song he doesn't recognize while tapping her foot to the rhythm.

"Sounds like something monks would be singing," Ibrahim says. "Where's it from?"

"A video game from the early century," Addison explains.

"Hard to believe that sound comes from a game," Ibrahim weighs.

"Have you ever played a video game?"

"Does running virtual combat simulators count?" Ibrahim asks.

"Not quite the same," Addison laughs, "but it's close."

A beeping sounds off inside Ibrahim's helmet. "CSDR signal green. They're ready to go," Athena calls over the network.

Another beep quickly follows. Then another. And a third.

"We're getting a signal from the Australians, Japanese, and the Koreans,"

Leighton announces.

More beeps register for a couple of minutes.

"And that's our British and European contingents," Addison murmurs, double-checking to make sure her helmet is on tight.

Ibrahim knocks twice for good luck on a fold-out table. "All right, crew. Waiting's over." He steps next to Addison Kennedy and broadcasts to everyone in the unit. "Final stations have sent their greetings our way, so we're clear to move. If anybody becomes separated from the group, make your way to the emergency exfiltration zone, and a bird will extract you."

"Emergency exfiltration?" Vogert asks.

"It's a crevice in the hull eight-hundred meters from Station-Zero-Four," Leighton details.

"Not to mention it's also the entry point for any reinforcements to the waystations," Warden adds.

"So, expect a party if we come under attack," Ibrahim continues.

"Wait, wait, wait! It's that close to the station?" Ava interjects. "Why aren't we going that way? We're taking the scenic route!"

"Because it's a tight fit for the landers," Ibrahim explains. "And we've too many personnel on this mission to make it a simple extraction with the high winds. That's why we're delegating it for emergency pickups only. So, I hope you didn't skimp on leg day. You're walking the distance, Doctor Remmings."

"If you say so," Ava responds depressingly.

Vogert sets a warming hand on the woman's shoulder plate.

"Any further questions?" Ibrahim demands.

Olivia Warden lets off a cough as she raises her hand. "Yes! I forgot my scooter at home, Colonel. Do you mind if I order somebody to carry me?"

Ibrahim chuckles inside his helmet as he switches his comms unit off.

SERGEANT MAJOR OLIVIA WARDEN
UNITED COALITION ARMED FORCES

OCTOBER 20, 2041 | 1500 HOURS

———

Warden exits the structure after Colonel Ibrahim's talk with the science team, lapping around the staging area.

She counts two hundred UCAF marines along the perimeter, waiting for their marching orders. That's not including the twenty-five troopers garrisoned at the barricade. Weapon crates and supply boxes are getting stacked next to the sheds. White floodlights are drowning out the area's red and black sheen.

"Sergeant Major?" her marines nod as she walks by their post. "Ready for this?"

"Let's get it done," Warden returns.

"Sergeant Major!" another goes.

"Oorah, Sergeant Major!" the symphony continues.

"Let's get those buggers!"

"Ready to kick ass, ma'am?" the final man greets.

"As long as it's not your ass, Corporal Tanner," Warden laughs.

"Hey, Arno! Where were you last night? You missed the rematch game."

Warden stops to eavesdrop on the back-and-forth.

"Got sent out for a recon patrol," Corporal Arno explains. "Our squad had to set up sensors to the first rally point for the team heading in. Just in case of an emergency. If anybody gets separated from the pack, it should help our boys find them."

Warden grimaces. She knows that Ibrahim's recon teams have spent days preparing for Operation Shield Piercer. Anything they could do to help protect their flanks and save their butts when shit hits the fan as they march into the Hellmouth.

"Sergeant Major on deck!" Corporal Arno shouts, standing at attention when he notices Warden's approach.

"At ease, ya lollygaggers," Warden offers, saluting her boys as she passes.

Two marines are on sentry duty outside the barricade, thirty meters from the corridor's entry doors. One sits inside the vehicle's weapon pod, shining its mounted light on the doorway.

"Sergeant Warden," the soldier behind the deployable barrier acknowledges. "Lovely afternoon. I hope you're enjoying the weather. The forecast says it's a bright and sunny day with a high of ninety, but I think he's lying to us. My balls have retreated inside my body to stay warm."

Warden squints, reading the marine's nameplate off her display. "Private Liz Villar? You don't have balls."

"That does explain a lot, ma'am," Villar chuckles.

"Unless the cold has my privates confused?"

"Ah, that's a no, ma'am."

"Report?"

Villar jumps to attention. "Nothing unusual, ma'am," she replies, but with a . . . rasp . . . in her voice. "No forward movement. Our flanks are clear."

"And the reason for your trepidation?" Warden demands.

The woman shifts her weight to one foot where she stands, a slant to her shoulders.

"It's . . . uh, well. Ma'am," Villar coughs. "Permission for me to explain?"

"Granted. You can speak freely."

"What's normal is that I don't think we've gone an hour without *something* trying to attack the checkpoints along this ridge. Ours is mostly quiet, but we regularly get reports and calls from the other stations."

"And what's unusual about our situation now?"

Villar hesitates. Warden can't see her face, but the way the woman's shoulders melt means she's tense but wants to hide it.

"Well, ma'am. We hadn't gotten any calls since before you guys pulled up hours ago," Villar describes. "I don't know if the expedition's increased activity has scared the predators away, but this lull is innerving. Sergeant Wilco mentioned wanting to send a squad beyond the hatch to scout the situation. Something isn't right, if that makes sense. And that has me on edge."

Warden tilts her head curiously. "And you haven't otherwise seen anything?"

"Nothing," Villar tells her. "Absolutely nothing. Ma'am."

Warden steps off for a moment, deciding to peer into the red darkness beyond the doorway. Private Villar is right . . . Warden's getting an ominous, empty sense coming from that direction. No sound. No movements in the shadows. It's creating a distinct alien feeling in her gut that her instincts don't know how to process. Like she's expecting to hear something . . . A faint echo? Maybe. A rustling in the distance? Most certainly. Anything to indicate a threat! And there's nothing.

Even her helmet's integrated sensors aren't picking up any sound or motion.

"The buggers usually keep one of theirs around our positions when they aren't attacking as their way to keep an eye on us," Warden notions.

"And we're under orders to not shoot to kill them or take offensive actions," Villar retorts.

Warden switches on her visor's infrared scanners, hoping to find some trace of an alien's heat signature. And what she gets is nothing but an incredible array of solid blue, the cold everywhere she looks.

"So, if the buggers aren't anywhere nearby," Warden continues, "and they're usually where the Fragments aren't—?"

Warden's cut off as a trio of glowing red lights appear in the dark. She zooms in on the area with her visor's built-in systems, but they aren't reading that anything's there. For a moment, the barricade goes quiet. Absolute stillness. Villar and the marine in the pod notice it, too. Like everyone's suddenly underwater, and the noise is getting distorted.

"Get down now!" Warden yells into her comms.

She ducks behind cover at the barricade. Seconds later, Private Villar drops beside her, torso smoking from a sudden volley of bright flashes streaking in their direction. The soldier inside the pod attempts to open fire. Warden ganders upward as the vehicle erupts into a chilling fire.

Warden gets knocked back several feet by the blast, away from her cover, and onto the open ramp.

Marines across the platform react to the commotion. Many of them go weapons-free with disciplined efficiency. Still, more than a few get taken down by the three Fragments that are now floating in the doorway leading to the ship's forward section.

Miniature explosions detonate around her. Warden begins crawling up the platform, unsure how far she can go before the Fragments notice her and kill her dead. Another marine drops at her front, still alive. Shot in the leg. The man's reaction is sobering. He feels the damage to his armor, wondering where he's gotten hit.

Warden crawls to him and pulls the man into cover behind a stack of crates.

"I-I don't . . . I don't feel anything, boss," the soldier cries. "I . . . what . . . w-what is this?"

She checks his nameplate. "Rhodes, right?" Warden asks.

"W-what?"

"Victor? Stay with me."

"I d-don't know."

She quickly pads the area of impact at the wound. "Looks like your suit's automatic trauma routines got damaged," Warden tells him. She notices the marine is too out of it to activate the system and possibly doesn't even understand what she's saying to him.

Warden pulls the man's arm forward and types out an override command on his wrist-mounted computer. Within moments, the soldier's hardsuit starts winding up its emergency protocols. The inner body glove compresses the wound to limit the blood flow to the area. It then injects the man with non-addictive sedatives to ease his shock before the pain hits hard.

"That should give you time until a medic gets to you," Warden comforts him. He doesn't acknowledge it. Instead, he swings his head side-to-side, fighting to stay awake. "If a medic gets to you," she then mutters. Warden looks up to see the garrison's medic in the white armor take an impact right to the chest, penetrating her plates and knocking the responder violently to the ground.

Static fills her comms. "This is Castle-Actual to all forward station personnel!" Ibrahim announces over the emergency channel. "Operation Shield Piercer is under attack ... Repeat ... We are under attack, sustaining casualties!" His message goes on. "We need reinforcements from all nearby positions!"

Warden's head hangs low for allowing this to happen. She had walked to the light's edge and investigated the darkness without her weapon. Everything was so quiet that she didn't think to grab it. Now bodies are dropping like flies around her. Men and women. Soldier and civilian.

She crawls her way toward a rifle next to the body of a dead marine. Warden checks to make sure it's loaded with the ASAPHEI 6.8 munitions, aiming its sights at the assaulting Fragments, and releases a single round into the lead one's glowing eye. Or *whatever* they're calling the lightbulb in the center of its chassis.

The round tears into the machine, setting off a micro-explosion inside its obsidian-like shell. Warden quietly cheers as the shattered husk hits the ramp with a loud clasping roar, leaving the other two to hesitate as they process the loss of their friend.

It's enough time to give Warden and her defenders a chance they need to return fire with effect.

Quickly, the second Fragment drops. Then, the third and final one. As the gunfire dies, a bewildering silent wave besieges the platform.

Warden and her marines stare at the door, expecting another attack. Their rifle butts hug tight against their shoulders.

An entire minute goes by as nothing happens.

"All right, folks. I think we're in the clear," Ibrahim relays.

"For now," Warden mutters.

"I want ten marines watching the door and on alert," Ibrahim barks. "I don't want anything else to take us by surprise!"

Soldiers react as the Colonel shouts his orders, never hesitating for an instant. Others start helping to clear the wounded and the dead off the ground. Warden gets to her feet and looks at the faceless masks of the men and women around her.

"Get me a casualty report!" she orders.

Several nearby marines respond immediately and go to count the bodies.

New armored transports and ambulances arrive with fresh UCAF fire-teams. The medics rush forward to pour over the survivors. They move the wounded quickly to heated triage centers at one of the nearby junctions set up throughout the expanse. As it's now protocol, triage will handle the less severe cases. The more badly hurt will get sent directly to the METIS Research Base or Camp Yi, depending on their injuries.

Ibrahim meets Warden on the platform. "We can't stay here. Get everyone moving! I want us en route in ten."

"Yes, sir," Warden says. "Colonel, with your permission?" Her throat tightens as she opens her mouth.

"Go ahead."

"This was bug territory for the past week, wasn't it?" she confronts.

"They're fighting a war, same as us," Ibrahim states. "Territory switches hands all the time."

"I know, I know, but—?" Warden adds, swallowing before clearing her throat. "We've had recon teams investigate the route. They haven't reported any sign of heavy fighting outside a few brief encounters on the stretch between stations three and four."

"You're wondering where the bodies are," Ibrahim remarks.

"And how these floaters got past our advance teams without anybody reporting it," Warden adds.

Ibrahim only casually nods.

"Not only that, but I was talking to the sentries at the barricade," Warden continues, "to understand our situation before rolling out. They mentioned how it had gone quiet along this entire ring within the last few hours." She still feels the adrenaline causing her arm to shake.

"Let me guess," Ibrahim ruffs. "Since our arrival?"

"As it appears, sir."

Colonel Ibrahim breaths deeply. He expels a wheezing puff that whistles through his helmet's air filtration system. Warden can't see his face, but she can imagine his expression. And it's not pleasant. Like a scowl. With drooping eyebrows and a wrinkling nose. His shoulders go tense, his knuckles cracking while they're in a fist. Then, he wraps his fingers around his rifle's barrel, squeezing it like he's about to bring it up and start shooting it off in the air.

Ibrahim doesn't do that. He merely slings the weapon over his shoulder.

"Let's get our people on the road, Olivia," he orders.

Warden flinches as he says her first name. "Sir?"

"We'll figure it out on the way. Maybe."

Warden tenses her jaw. "Understood," she acknowledges.

She steps around him as she goes to mobilize their troops on the platform.

Addison Kennedy walks into the devastation, finally seeing the dangers inside the Summerland.

Warden stops to catch Addison's look, to see if it's what she expected. "Or if it's hitting you like a freight train jumping its track and speeding sideways through your neighbor's house." She illustrates it under her breath.

Addison briefly stops to watch a man get put on a stretcher and brought up a transport's loading ramp.

"Sergeant Major Warden?" a soldier inquires to her left.

"Speak," she returns.

"Eight dead, six wounded," the other lists off his report. "And two of those are in critical condition."

Warden frowns and dismisses the man. She quickly brings up her HUD to read the causality markers. She goes through it carefully, mouthing the names before stopping at the second of two marked with "CTCDN" next to the ID number "HC-119205."

"Marine Corporal Victor Rhodes," she mutters.

That's the man who got hit and whose armor's emergency medical systems she had to activate manually.

He'd be another listed dead on the casualty report if she hadn't.

In his office on the Olympus, he watches as the incoming reports flicker on his monitor.

"How many?" he asks.

"Roughly a dozen," the AI replies.

"Roughly?" Malakai repeats.

"Thirteen," Athena clarifies. "Casualties are mounting with roughly forty-four dead. Maybe more."

"Athena," Malakai says, clearing his throat. "Scrub the word 'roughly' from your vocabulary. I don't want speculation."

"I do not have an exact number," Athena returns. "Our teams are sweeping for survivors. We didn't expect an attack across such a wide zone."

"And what about Castle-Actual? How badly did they get hit?"

Athena steals a moment to catalog the question. "Hectic skirmish on the platform. Garrison took on most of the casualties. None of the science teams were injured or killed. Colonel Ibrahim and Sergeant Major Warden each survived the encounter."

"God, help those two," Malakai prays, sitting forward. "How many enemy combatants? Do we know?"

Athena takes another second to process the information. Her systems are getting bogged down. A lot of noise is hitting her all at once. For any system, not just her, it's a massive workload for the hardware to tackle.

He gets up from his desk and exits his office to check with the Control Room. Malakai looks over at Leighton's station and finds it taken over by an assistant.

"Four by average," Athena finally processes. "Hostile drones. And each site we've confirmed *was* in Varmajalkavaen territory."

Malakai takes in an uneven breath.

"That's according to Harlow's overlays," a cartographer explains.

"Which he based on data from the field," Malakai admits.

"Very much so," the man says.

"So, either the Fragments took ground without making a sound, or—?"

"The aliens are pulling back," Athena concludes.

"Which doesn't bode well for our research teams," Malakai weighs.

"Unless the aliens are pulling back *due* to their mission," Athena suggests.

"Leaving our flanks exposed," Malakai realizes.

"Highly probable," Athena states. "We can surmise the Architects are keeping an eye on our people."

"Close enough to register and translate our languages."

"And understand you enough to know who among us to approach."

Malakai grimaces. "Addison," he gruffly states. "They're watching us. And I want to know how they're doing it."

"The very question I am endeavoring to answer."

"Like they're walking among us, and we don't even realize it."

"Or keeping their distance, much as the Eye of Providence atop the old—"

Malakai coughs. "They've prepared themselves," he nods, cutting off the reference, "the same as us. That's what matters." He shifts his shoulders when he feels the whole room eyeing him. "Let's not address risk with speculation. Athena? See what data you can gather and give us a clearer picture of the situation. Run deeper scans and send additional patrols. Let's see if we can't take a gander into what our people are walking into *before* they get there."

Almost everyone in the Control Room nods. A few others stare at him blankly, unsure how to process the disaster.

"Understood," Athena confirms.

"In the meantime," Malakai continues, "let's increase security at the perimeter outposts."

"We don't have too many resources left to divert," an operator in the room gasps. "Military personnel are already reaching a tipping point. Without support from the mainland, we've only the quarantine fleet and their assets to call on."

"Then we need to trust our people to know what they're doing," Malakai sighs, feeling his hands jitter coldly.

It's dangerous enough for the expedition without the situation's additional unknowns.

MIDDLE OF THE ROAD   I 36

AVANNA "AVA" REMMINGS, CHIEF TECHNOLOGY SPECIALIST
EPIMETHEUS PROJECT

OCTOBER 20, 2041 | 2100 HOURS

The armor's joints have servos that keep her legs from tiring as she moves. She only wishes the mechanicals could do something to carry her brain so she can march *while* she sleeps. Ava keeps her eyes open through sheer willpower as she walks with the group.

"It feels like we've been on our feet for days," she mutters.

Checking her mission clock, Ava reads it's hardly been an hour.

The dreadnaught's interior has a strange assortment of varying design principles throughout the corridors.

Ava checks her feed to make sure she has an active record. She doesn't want to miss a clue when she returns to the Olympus and can review the footage in length. Ava notes that sections take on the outward appearance of late medieval castles. There are smaller hallways between the larger spaces and wide stretches, less decorated than the main corridor she and everyone is walking through. She counts the bastions splitting off from each intersection as they make their way.

And no identifiable rooms that can explain away the layout of these corridors. "Not at all like other ships I've worked on," Ava murmurs.

Here? It's hallway after hallway—each drowning in the same red light sewn elegantly into the thousands of nooks and crannies along the edges.

The expedition takes the first hour to reach the first cordon by a joint UCAF-CSDR force, Station-One. The team doesn't have any trouble getting through the barricades. Ava spends her downtime nonchalantly hacking into the armor systems of those around her to tweak the firmware. Like a kid cracking open an old remote-controlled car to see the inner workings.

"Damn it," Ava quietly curses.

The software recognizes what she's doing and begins to react aggressively. Ava inputs her codes using the pad's interface. It doesn't take long for her fingers to cramp from typing on such a small keypad so quickly. She breaks into the system's backdoor, shutting down the passive security measures.

"I helped build this gear," Ava breathes, "it should let me do what I want." She frowns at the thought.

They designed the system so nobody could get through the firewall to sneak a peek at an operator's unmentionables. She works fast enough that the network's alarm doesn't trip and instigates a lockdown protocol. No, that would not be very pleasant.

Malakai offered her a job. And she agreed not to blow everything up along the way.

She lets out a single, breathy laugh. Regardless, the quick look has shown her the stage behind the curtain. Every soldier at Station-One is on alert and twitchy.

"Not a good situation when they all have guns," she whispers, "and I can't see their faces."

She only hopes somebody will arrive to relieve these troops soon.

Ava's gone days without sleep before. And it never ends well. The ability of the mind to process the information it gathers during waking hours gets severely damaged, leaving little room for rational thought. Dreams become a part of the physical world. Like a movie inside her head. One where she reaches out and *thinks* she can touch it. But she can't.

And she never could.

Ava had given a complete overview of her research to a "visiting" family member that wasn't there during the longest waking stretch of her indentured career. She would never want her family to know how many people her weapons have killed over the years. An easy mistake in a delusional state, but one she *should* have caught.

Ava Remmings shakes herself awake, stepping with the others as they pass the barricades. They've had their break. Now it's time to move on to Station-Two. Their next stop into the dark, whether they're ready for it or not. Vogert and Addison stay ahead of her. Leighton and Zhu Yunwen flank Ava on her sides. The marines stick to them like puppies following their master back home for the first time, ready to jump into action.

And while they're making their way into the dark, nobody is talking to each other. Ava has never had a social aptitude. She finds most people loud or nosy anyway. Often, they make her repeat whatever she says to them because they don't quite get it the first time around. Yet, this silence is unnatural for such a large group of people.

Her neck muscles numb. She doesn't like it.

"Does anybody want to hear a joke?" Ava cuts at the quiet, opening a channel for only her teammates to hear.

"I'd prefer not to," Leighton returns, stagnation in his voice.

"Yesterday, I was reading a book on helium," she goes on anyway, laughing inside her head. "And I couldn't put it down."

"God Almighty, help us? Make her stop," Vogert groans, although not without a humorous tint to his tone.

"I had a scientist friend a couple of years ago who had a pair of twins," Ava fights to say another. "Do you know what she named them? Edward and Control."

"Like an experiment?" Zhu harmlessly asks.

"I don't get it," Leighton returns.

"Avanna Remmings—always thinking like a proton," Addison continues. "Always—"

"Please don't, Doctor Kennedy," Leighton attempts to stop her.

"—Positive!" Addison laughs.

"Addison? My light in the dark?" Vogert interjects. "You're my friend. And I love working with you, but . . . If you continue this dark path, I will jump into the nearest pit and let myself get eaten by whatever lives there." Ava hears no bitterness in the man's tone, so maybe he's enjoying the banal chatter. Either way, the tension gradually lifts off their shoulders.

She stops with the chatter as they continue to the next waymarker. It's not her strength.

More lights? It's brighter at the Australian-controlled Station-Two than at Station-One. Everybody spreads out, waiting for the go-ahead to move on to Station-Three. Ava rechecks her timeclock. "Almost midnight." She knocks on her helmet, trying again to stay awake.

Leighton paces back on forth. "I hope these Architects aren't the impatient types. Or come under attack while we're en route."

"We'll take however long as necessary to ensure your sorry ass gets there intact, Mr. Leighton." Sergeant Major Warden doesn't wait to bark. "Besides. There are too many of us to move faster in these passageways while protecting our flanks. You'll have to deal with it if you're not happy."

"What do the reports ahead say?" Addison asks Warden.

"A couple of stray skirmishes. Nobody's hurt. Not as bad as it could be, and nowhere near as bad as what we're coming from," Warden describes. "These floaters are relentless, however. We destroyed two dozen of the damn things in the last attack on half as many positions. I heard your father's ordered us to set up new fortifications across the exclusion zone."

Ava shifts uncomfortably to her left heel. Unlike in the corridors, where there are only two directions an enemy can attack, this junction has four branches, each with a dozen smaller turn-offs and channels. Even inside the barricades making up Station-Two's defenses, Ava suddenly feels like she's naked in front of a crowd. It doesn't matter that she's wearing her hardsuit.

"Likely used as maintenance shafts by the Fragments," Ava weighs.

Each shaft's outline perfectly fits the machines' silhouette—alleyways for the "floaters" to access vital ship components for routine upkeep.

"Ava? What do you think?" Addison asks her, waving to get her attention.

Ava blinks when she hears her name. But, in complete honesty, she wasn't paying all that close attention to the conversation. So, all she does is shrug.

"Maybe the Fragments have more limited numbers than the Varmajalka-vaen?" Ava throws a guess, clinging to what she *did* hear. "After their losses in the recent attack, whatever force drives them may have decided to wait to see what happens next. Or to gather more units for an all-out assault on the inner ring. And that's *if* our theories about the Fragments are accurate, maintenance drones repurposed as killing machines."

"It's important to remember that we aren't on a military vessel," Addison adds. "Idu called it a . . . Source. I don't know what that means. Only that I know the crew onboard are mostly to run the ship's essential functions. Not for waging a full-scale war."

Warden shakes her head. "Just because the machines aboard weren't originally intended to kill doesn't mean they aren't effective at it. Have you ever seen the damage rampaging equipment can do? I have. And it's not pretty."

"We'll figure it out," Vogert tells them. "One way or another. Our work matters. I believe that."

Colonel Ibrahim steps between the chatty group. His marines quickly move to clear his path. Warden finds her place next to him.

"Our advance teams saw bugger patrols on our route," Ibrahim throws the warning at them. "It's a large group, so we're staying at Station-Two until they pass."

"How close are they?" Leighton asks.

"Close enough to make it uncomfortable," Ibrahim says. "Everybody should get some rest while they can. It might be several hours. Or a few minutes."

"Any idea where they're going?" Leighton prods.

"Does it matter?" Ibrahim answers the question with a question.

"I don't see why not," Leighton determines. "They can attack us anytime, but they've left us alone without real interest in an engagement. Maybe there's a reason? They're not mindless animals. We know that."

"Probably not," Ibrahim weakly agrees.

"We've mapped this area as a clearway. And the two groups didn't seem to have any real interest on this stretch," Leighton describes. "It's mostly structure tunnels and side-passages. Easily defensible. Too narrow for the buggers to utilize their tactics. Away from their recent activity."

"You're saying this bugger group is unusual?"

"Maybe?" Leighton says with a crack in his throat. "Undoubtedly. Or, the best I can tell, there's no reason for them to linger. No vital systems. No larger hallways. In layman terms, we're in the middle of nowhere."

"And why we've chosen it for our route," Ibrahim acknowledges. "Maybe we could've gotten it wrong?"

Leighton pridefully hums his abnegation.

Addison coughs for attention. "In every science, there's always absolutes in a given state," she utters, turning to Leighton. "Specific facts that never change, no matter their conditions. That's not our situation. We're in the unknown. And that's a scary place to be."

"Addison's right," Avanna supports. "We're in fluid motion right now. Conditions are evolving by the minute as this ship answers our presence. It's not unlike a chemical reaction—where the injection of a new additive will change the fundamentals of a compound."

Ava joins the others at the station's inner ring. It's an opportunity to sit and take a breather while they can.

"Not that it matters," Ava mutters a bit too loudly. That earns her a few awkward glares.

She looks up to muse at the ceiling, deciding to ignore them.

Warden's voice booms over the open comms as Ava is about to close her eyes. It's unmistakable and more difficult to shut out.

"You guys had no issues securing the area?" Warden asks her Australian counterpart.

She listens to the voices, wondering if it's intentional.

"Smooth sailing from Axford," is the reply. "A few tarboys and pupdogs, but they've mostly ignored us on the upper hull."

"And how *is* life on the spine? I heard it's warm," Warden interrogates her friends.

"It's a smaller space than what you have at the midsection," the other answers. "We've installed insulation throughout the tunnels below the base. That way, we can turn off our heaters. It keeps us from draining our energy reserves too quickly. Effective. And our 'muptops' hate leaving the site."

Warden laughs. "We've eggheads that do rounds at the Central Spire. Nobody is too keen on leaving the base outside this lot."

"That's why we're here, I suppose," the other laughs. "Made for extremes."

"Are you talking about our gear or your hard-knock skulls?"

"Can't it be both?" another asks.

"And what's the situation at the midsection? I hear you guys get into frequent trouble."

"Every minute is a battle," Warden replies sardonically. "I was part of the second recon unit. We couldn't see five meters in front of us and had to rely on our optics to avoid stepping over the ledge. Unfortunately, the interior bay doesn't have railings for us to lean on."

"The locals must love that," the ASR trooper says. "Not going to complain about our situation. I think we've got Camp Axford set up nicely. If you don't mind the high winds that blow over the side? The only risk is getting thrown off the ledge and sliding down a few thousand feet until you hit the water. A bad way to go, in retrospect. But that's why we've set up the ropes."

"Same at the Alpha Site," Warden notions.

Ava lazily falls asleep while listening to the banter. She lays flat in the cold, trying to get comfortable. Can she still relax? No. She can't.

The muscles in her neck contract as she fights with the breathing apparatus inside her helmet. To ease her stress, she calculates how far it is to Station-Three. "Eight hundred meters out," Ava measures the distance. "Which makes Station-Four—?" She inhales profoundly and slows her heart rate. "Thirteen-hundred meters away," Ava whispers on her exhale.

She fades into a slumber as she counts the steps it will take to get there.

ADDISON KENNEDY, FIELD DIRECTOR
EPIMETHEUS PROJECT

OCTOBER 21, 2041 | 0100 HOURS

———

Today marks the tenth day since they landed on the dreadnaught's lower hull.

Addison wakes up alone in the middle of the intersection. The station looks . . . Empty? Gear is still lying around, but nobody's on the guns or walking the perimeter.

"Colonel Ibrahim?" Addison asks the quiet.

She stands up and laps around the fringe, wandering into the branching corridors outside the barricades.

Addison's boot sinks into dark sandy dunes. She looks down and scoops up a handful, finding the pitch-black fragments of lava within the delicate grains. It reminds her of the black beaches of Punalu'u in Hawaii. Only Addison isn't in Hawaii. Not only that, but a shimmering bends the light like water above her, making it glimmer and dance across the ground.

"Where is this coming from? Where am I?"

She's no longer in the corridor. Addison doubts she's even on the ship anymore.

The dreadnaught's sharp angles and soft red texture disappear into an open sky and a windswept, empty wasteland.

On the horizon, Addison can see a most violent storm. Roaring. A hundred lightning bolts turn the ground to glass, with the wind causing the sandy black dunes to cascade. She can describe it as an ocean's waves nearer to the shore, sweeping onto the beaches with rock and dust instead of water.

Addison's throat closes as a dull pain inside her chest begins to throb.

"Nowhere near the bright star humanity calls home," Addison answers the question.

No. Addison's in another place, so very far away.

Addison steps toward the storm. It's far enough away that she doesn't think it will matter how far she walks. *Addison* will never get closer to *it* on foot. Yet, with the massive clouds and their encompassing breadth, she feels she can extend her hand and touch it like a giant in the fog.

She can't tell the difference between the ground and the fierce sky with so much dust and rock in the air.

"This isn't real," Addison determines, clenching her jaw while letting her fistful of sand trickle out between her fingers. "Or is it?"

"Addison! Addison!" Vogert calls her. "Addison! What are you doing?!"

"Doctor Kennedy?!" Colonel Ibrahim shouts in the distance.

A sudden jolt hits her hard. Addison trips and falls, waking up from whatever dream she was in and into the real world. Now she's on the floor, getting dragged by her armor's straps.

"Damn it! Fucking hell," Ibrahim decries again. Addison looks up to see the Colonel leveraging her weight.

Sergeant Major Oliva Warden approaches with several marines beside her. Their attention is facing outward, ready for anything.

"She's awake!" says a voice she doesn't recognize. "Quick! Let's get her into cover! This outcropping looks good."

Colonel Ibrahim settles Addison into a crack along the ship's angling walls. She can sense his seething anger even with his visor down. Pounding his fist into the wall makes that clear enough. "Pissed off" is how she'll describe it.

"Addison Kennedy?" Warden asks. She quickly checks Addison's wrist-pad to read the woman's vitals.

"She's awake but in a daze," Vogert iterates. "A concussion?"

"We tackled her," another defends. "She wasn't responding to us!"

"Not to mention she ran away when they tried to restrain her," Warden adds.

"So, you knocked her out?" Vogert demands.

"We didn't have a choice!"

"Enough!" Ibrahim commands. "I am sure Doctor Kennedy will forgive us a couple of bruises."

"How did she even get out here? Or get past the barricade guard?" Vogert asks.

"She just walked through," Warden exclaims. "Sentries didn't notice her. Nobody did until the rest of us woke up."

There's a long pause that erupts among the group. Addison looks at those around her—Olivia Warden, Elias Ibrahim, Ryan Vogert, and a dozen UCAF-ASR commandos.

"This is what I'd call a proper rescue squad," Addison says, shaking her head clear of the dizziness.

"And she speaks," Vogert mutters.

"What's happened?" Addison asks, coughing as she sits up.

All their eyes turn down at her. Ibrahim lets out a deep sigh that filters through his helmet's rebreather. Eventually, he takes a knee next to her.

"I ordered every team to search for your locator beacon," he tells her.

"Damn well, made us work for our paychecks," Warden snarls. "We've been playing hide-and-seek with you for the past hour. Every time we thought we had you, we'd discover it was a phantom signal and had to restart our search."

Addison's eyes widen as she hears the story. Of course, the others can't see her expression, but that doesn't stop her.

"But . . . I was . . . sleeping?" she murmurs weakly. "I was right there next to you guys! I know I was."

Ibrahim mutters something under his breath. He decides not to share it with the group.

"Vogert?" he questions. "Does she have a history of sleepwalking?"

"Not that her file states," Vogert offers, static distorting his voice as he shifts his body away. "Check her suit for any leakage! Arthur's team suffered hallucinations and blackouts in the days before they died. God, I hope it's not that."

"And I was hoping that damn serum would be our countermeasure," Ibrahim curses.

"We don't know the full effects of the therapy, Colonel Ibrahim," Vogert argues. "That's why we're testing it with this walkabout!"

Another pause hits the group. Addison can hear her hardsuit's electronics whirling as it performs the diagnostics. If her suit *was* leaking, causing her to see what she saw, then alarms should be screaming inside her helmet. And the fact they're not?

"Readout shows nothing," Vogert describes. "No leakage."

Ibrahim hums quietly.

"I'm fine," Addison explains. "I must've wandered off sometime when I was sleeping. How far is the waystation?"

"Roughly a quarter of a mile," Warden answers, "at the end of this branch."

"Quite the distance to 'wander' without walking off a ledge," Ibrahim speaks again. "Let's pack this up, folks! Vogert. Look after her. Addison's now your responsibility. Once we arrive at home base, I want a complete report—bloodwork, mental degradation. Whatever."

"Yes, Colonel," Vogert quietly agrees.

"And you!" Ibrahim says with a finger pointing at Addison. "If this happens again, this mission is scrubbed. Understand?"

Addison looks at him in bewilderment. "Yes, Colonel," she mumbles. She doesn't even know how she got this far out from the perimeter in the first place.

The team takes ten minutes to walk her back through Station-Two's perimeter.

Addison can feel every eye on her. Everyone's face is hiding behind their helmet visors with judging nods. Assholes.

"It doesn't make sense," Addison whispers. "How do I get up and walk off without anybody stopping me?"

Something is very wrong. Addison can sense it . . . Or maybe she doesn't "sense" it, except with the closest human equivalent to acute perception. It's like the feeling she gets when it's about to rain on a warm summer day. A deep-seated feeling in her bones makes her itchy under her armor.

Addison finds her place next to Vogert. "My hands won't stop shaking," she describes. "I don't even feel that cold."

Vogert turns and runs another quick scan using her suit's internal biometrics.

He shakes his head. "You're coming off an anxiety attack," the man says. "Feel that chill in your voice? The scan reads nothing unusual. Maybe an above-normal body temperature? But your hardsuit's thermals are running within a comfortable margin. What happened, Addison? What can you tell me?"

"I—?" Addison begins, wanting to describe what she saw. But she stops, unsure what it might cost her to admit it openly. "Maybe it's not a good idea to tell you. At least, not until we get back to base camp. You can run a scan of my head and see what's happening there."

The other nods. "I'll follow your lead," Vogert says. "Just promise me that if you start feeling sick—?"

"I'll tell you right away," Addison agrees. "Won't be a problem."

MALAKAI ADONIS, DIRECTOR OF OPERATIONS
EPIMETHEUS PROJECT

OCTOBER 21, 2041 | 0145 HOURS

He lets his comms unit beep until he can't ignore it anymore.

"Please let it be good news," Malakai says. He drops his shoulders as he sits up.

"Lieutenant Colonel Ibrahim has located Addison Kennedy," Athena explains. "And they are en route to Station-Three."

Malakai sighs with relief and hangs his legs over the side of his cot. He told Athena to wake him once she had news on the situation. That was over forty minutes ago, and he's not slept a wink. He spent that time with his eyes wide open, staring at his ceiling.

"Estimated time until they reach the station?" he decides to ask.

"Thirty minutes," Athena answers. "They're expected at Station-Four at zero-four-hundred hours."

"And how far until they pass into the dark zone?"

"I would say a quarter to five?" Athena replies. "That's barring any unexpected complications."

And that's *his* problem. Malakai breathes to steady his chest. "One issue on a list," he internalizes. It's the subtle difference between the words "expected" and "unexpected." He *expects* a lot to go wrong at the intersecting points. It's what *will* go wrong that's *unexpected*.

Malakai stands up and drinks water from a bottle on his nightstand, little more than a plastic foldout table. It feels like this has been his home for a year after only a week—these same metal walls, the hard clinging of footsteps on grated floors.

He leaves his room to wander the Olympus' halls for a while. There are very few people running around tonight. Most are shift workers off their rotations, meaning there's only a skeleton crew keeping the Epimetheus Project in operation with all its complex systems and grievances. They're the night owls—the third shifters—the lifeblood of their mission after dark, allowing its eyes to see, its brain to feed, and its voice to sing.

When they look at him, Malakai can see the ringed looks in their eyes.

"Good morning, Malakai," their voices in his ears as he passes.

"Doctor Adonis," another acknowledges.

"On another lap, sir?" a traffic control operator between places asks.

Malakai exhaustingly nods and pushes on, ignoring their furrowing eyebrows and their concerns.

He makes his way to the mess hall. He puts on a large coffee pot, taking it to a table as he downs two tiny cups, refilling it for a third.

Behind the counter, Malakai identifies the plastic containers and wire bundles left by the rigger crews. If he were to guess, they're starting to install equipment throughout the rig's utility tunnels that run the length of the walls and floors.

He glances at the monitor wall showing the news broadcasts of the Summerland Crisis.

Malakai has more often been tuning out the negativity from the outside world. He's enough to worry about *inside* these walls, dealing with a dreadnaught the size of a small country. The last thing he cares about is what some reporter or late-night talk show host says about him to feed their audience.

Malakai should be thankful, however. This late at night, the networks are running re-runs of the stories they did the day prior. Nearly a quarter of the planet is asleep. 24-hour cameras point at the dreadnaught and Mount Olympus, runtime clocks in the corner frames, counting the minutes, the hours, and even days since the crash on September 24th.

"That was a bad day," he whimpers.

Malakai feels a warmth around his groin. He looks down and realizes he's peed his pants.

He sets pressure on his stomach, feeling his bladder. "Or maybe I'm so tired that I didn't notice I had to go?" he weighs, looking for an excuse. Probably both, if he's to guess.

He meanders toward the doors and stops mid-step. Is his arm . . . shaking?

Malakai rages, throwing his coffee mug across the room, watching it shatter on the floor.

"Damn it," he curses, knowing what he's done.

Malakai finds a broom and sweeps the shards into a bin. He walks out after, feeling angry. *His* job is to maintain a calm, patient tone. Malakai's the voice of reason in the madness surrounding the most unprecedented joint effort by the international community since the World Wars.

Malakai stops in the hall outside the mess hall to catch his breath. It doesn't help. His chest beats hard. As he starts again, he nearly trips over a trash bin. Malakai picks up the container and throws it against the wall, spilling its contents.

One of the attendants on duty comes rushing from the Control Room when they hear the noise.

"Jesus Christ," Jeri Dalton utters. "Malakai?! What's going on?"

"It's nothing," Malakai grumbles. He raises a hand to show he's calming down. "Nothing ... Just ... Needed to throw a few things." He rests his back against the wall, sliding down until his butt hits the floor.

Dalton comes over and picks up the bin and the garbage off the ground.

"Sorry about that," he apologizes to her, burying his face into his hands, embarrassed.

"No. We understand," Dalton shrugs. "Everybody's worried about the team, too."

Malakai takes in a heavy breath.

"It's not Addison or the others I'm worried about," he admits. "Well. Not entirely. But they can handle themselves."

"I'm not sure what you're getting at, sir," Dalton says. "It's our job to look after them."

"I know, it's just—?" Malakai shudders. He finds his tongue swells as he tries to say what he needs. "I don't know what we're doing anymore. We're playing with fire we can't control. That we don't understand."

Dalton manages a faint smile. "Some would argue we can't understand fire unless we light a few matches," she suggests.

"I know, but—" Malakai breathes again, carefully thinking about his words. "Dalton? Can you look outside the window for me? Let me know what you see. As a favor?" He keeps his tone as quiet and calm as he can manage.

"Okay," Dalton nods, looking confused. She goes to a window down the hallway and peers outside the rig. "I see the storm, half a dozen warships, massive floodlights, the dreadnaught, huge waves, water, clouds, and metal. A lot of that." Dalton turns back to him with one corner of her mouth crooked.

"A complete mess, right?" Malakai finishes. "In the Control Room, we get numbers and camera feeds—connected to every piece of equipment out there. Sometimes we forget to look out the window to see how the rest of the world looks at it. The people at home don't see the battle inside that damnable ship! They only hear versions of what we *do* give them."

"You're afraid we'll get judged," Dalton suggests.

"No," Malakai corrects her. "That's expected. We've made plans to counter the scrutiny once we get home. No. I'm afraid that we're painting the canvas with our demons. That it's going to bite us in the ass. There's a cost to our work. And I don't mean for our careers."

Dalton lowers her hand and helps to pick him off the cold floor.

"You're wrong," she tells him.

Malakai looks at her in bewilderment. "I'm wrong?"

"We're paying the cost. The world is getting its money's worth."

"If every life is worth a dollar," Malakai concludes, "I don't know if we are."

LIEUTENANT COLONEL ELIAS IBRAHIM
UNITED COALITION ARMED FORCES

OCTOBER 21, 2041 | 0400 HOURS

He pushes his people through Station-Three without issue. Now they're beginning their final leg to Station-Four.

Ibrahim takes up the position in front of his men, encouraging everyone to keep a consistent pace. He can read the headlamps from the advanced team, a green aura wrapping around their bodies, their names popping into the lower right-hand corner of his screen.

"We've tripped a border sensor," the lead scout announces. "We should see a sentry post a little farther this way."

Ibrahim keys his microphone. "Station-Four? This is Castle-Actual for a sitrep. Over."

"Castle-Actual—this is Station Master, designated Wolfden," hails the station's response. "Situation quiet for thirty minutes."

"Any trouble we need to know about?" Ibrahim inquires.

"Trouble? No trouble. Machines ripped a hole in our barricade with their last attack. Waiting on replacements from Camp Earhart," Wolfden explains. "And our supply lines are damn unreliable. Secondary exfiltration is difficult to maintain this far into the structure. We've done what we can to fortify the alcove, even put out some lights to steer our birds."

Ibrahim pulls up the station manifest to see who's on the other end of the line. European forces—German, French, and British troops—are the chief occupiers of Station-Four, with Wolfden taking charge of the guard.

The Overlook in upper orbit has trouble reading past the interference. And this outpost is the Project's last foothold before the plunge. And what can Ibrahim expect to find there? He doesn't know. Another hangar-sized space?

Maybe, but he doubts it. The outer hull doesn't lend credence to the idea.

More speculation is it's a possible recharge site where the Fragments go to "get their juice," if he wants to use Ava Remmings' terminology.

Ibrahim's theory is similar to one Addison put forward in their briefings. But, he'll admit, it's not his area of expertise.

He doesn't care. After everything Idu had shoved into Addison's head, the idea that this "dark zone' possibly acts as a manufacturing sector for the ship carries an unsettling weight. Ibrahim knows this isn't a military vessel. Even for an alien design, the corridors and hallways are too broad, and it doesn't utilize its space efficiently. Moreover, there's no internal defense grid for a ship of this size.

And the idea this Idu 'Smeora referred to the ship as a "Source" also implies its purpose is more than sheer destruction.

"I'd dread to think about what a vessel like this could do if it were fully armed," Ibrahim whispers.

Distant shots echo from ahead. "Contact! Contact!" the Station Master shouts over the comms. "Contact! We've got floaters!"

"Count five! I say five!" another says as gunfire erupts. "Where did they come from?"

"They blew past the sentry post! Right corridor! Check your marks!"

"They're moving to the left flank!"

"Where the bloody hell are our reinforcements?"

Ibrahim signals his marines, and they stop. "Our barn is on fire, and we're the water brigade," he describes. "Double time it to the station!" And like that, two hundred marines make for the barricades. Ibrahim orders Warden and her squad to hang back with Addison Kennedy and her science team.

Ibrahim sprints the distance. He narrows the margin within two minutes like they used to do on the Overlook.

Brushing past the outer barricades, Ibrahim comes onto a dramatic scene.

Everyone is facing the same direction. Outward. Bodies go flying as streams of hardlight hit them.

Two of the attacking Fragments are already down when Ibrahim's troops get into position. They ready their marks and go weapons-free, levying enough firepower to drown a whole battalion. Instead, it's just three cold, warbling machines. They shatter into brilliant starbursts like they're stained glass.

Ibrahim will give all credit to Doctor Remmings. The ASAPHEI 6.8 munitions do their job magnificently.

"Damn us to hell," the Station Master curses. "Colonel Ibrahim! Over here."

"Station Master . . . Wolfden? What's the count?" Ibrahim asks.

"Surprisingly, holding our own," the other man says. "Welcome to the frontline."

"Isn't this whole place a damn frontline?" Ibrahim ventilates.

"If you're the 'glass-half-empty' kind of guy," Wolfden snarks, "then sure! I prefer to see the world through a more colorful lens."

Ibrahim snorts. "Report?" he asks.

"Ya know, for an American, you aren't a fun sortie, are you? All *serious* in the face of impending death."

Ibrahim strikes him with an unseen look that illustrates his annoyance.

"Aye. Report. Fine o'fine." Wolfden surrenders his attempts at humor. "I'll give ya damn report. Seven casualties, four wounded, rest KIA for this battle. Total? Maybe fourteen. Better odds than your lot at the perimeter, if I heard right. Athena will have my official numbers. I think we've downed at least twenty of the damn floaties."

"What's the route to the destination marker like?"

"Mostly clear save for a bunch of bogies guarding a hallway near the exit point," Wolfden exclaims. He turns his attention to Addison Kennedy, catching up to the main force. "We're guessing *her* meeting is somewhere on the other side of the wall where they're waiting."

"How many?" Addison questions.

"Twenty?" the man offers. "I have a recon team on it—Lieutenant McKelly."

Addison tilts her head in contemplation. He agrees.

"They're expecting us?" Ibrahim asks.

"Might be why the Fragments are pressing these guys hard," Addison suggests, looking at the Station Master. "Have we gotten people through? Do we know what's on the other side?"

Wolfden shakes his head. "No, ma'am," he says.

"Intrinsic readings suggest there's a large space over most of the area," Athena chimes into their comms.

"So, maybe it *is* another hangar bay," Addison suggests.

"I still find that unlikely," Ibrahim contradicts.

"There are no major openings on the hull that would indicate another hangar," Leighton adds.

"Not the size of the Breach, in any case," Zhu agrees.

Addison raises an eyebrow. She decides not to respond to the sentiments.

"Station Master," Ibrahim pushes on, "how soon can we head out?"

"Depends on how long you're willing to stay," the man answers. "We could still use your help."

"Unfortunately, the longer we're out here, the more dangerous it will be for your people, Captain," Ibrahim exclaims.

The man nods. "Understood, Lieutenant Colonel," Wolfden concedes. "We'll stay on to carry your sagging butts. Don't linger, though. And be careful approaching those beasties—we don't know their intentions, but they didn't attack McKelly's team. So, maybe they're not the bad guys?"

"Not willing to call them the good guys?" Vogert murmurs.

"Not until I see them pouring me a lager at the local pub," the man admits.

Each expedition member reconvenes at the barricade. They get ready to push into that ample space that Athena had described. Ibrahim goes to join Addison at the front of the crowd, keeping an eye on the woman as he walks in her direction. Nobody still admits to seeing her leave Station-Two.

Ibrahim pulls her tracking record from the network. He goes through it, looking at each contact point, step by step, wondering if he can find where her signal went dark. Ibrahim traces where her tags had triggered the local sensors. It's not much. But he can begin piecing together a timetable for what happened.

And her recount of the event worries him further.

"Maybe her encounter with Idu did some unintentional damage?" Ibrahim quietly says under his breath.

"So, what's the word?" Leighton asks, following behind Addison and Ibrahim.

"Road is clear for now," Addison remarks. "We're good to go as soon as Colonel Ibrahim gives us the go-ahead."

"Soon enough," Ibrahim says. "You're dismissed. Doctor Vogert, I want to speak with you in private."

The science team goes their separate ways as Ibrahim pulls aside their Chief Medical Officer.

"You sound worried," Vogert says. "Should I be worried? Is this about Addison? We've already—"

"This isn't just about Doctor Kennedy's health," Ibrahim warns. "If we get into trouble, I want *you* to keep an eye on her."

"Not that she's a child that needs constant parental supervision or anything," Vogert chides.

Ibrahim flicks his wrist. "I want you to see if you notice anything unusual about her behavior under stress," he continues.

"Any particular reason, or are we playing on a hunch?" Vogert asks. "Stress *can* do weird things to the mind. Without a complete medical examination, that's my view. Just her body's reaction to stress. I've seen people kill themselves for less."

"I'm not saying that's it. Only—?" Ibrahim stops, cracking his neck. "Do it. Please? That's an order. If there's anything you see that's *not* normal, don't keep it to yourself. My job is to protect the team. That includes protecting whatever's going on inside that brain of hers." He points at his forehead.

After a long moment, Vogert takes a deep breath and nods.

"All right, sir. I'll see what I can do."

Ibrahim releases a measured, steady breath.

He turns around and works up his courage for the final push into the dark zone.

ADDISON KENNEDY, FIELD DIRECTOR
EPIMETHEUS PROJECT

OCTOBER 21, 2041 | 0440 HOURS

"We're almost there," she whispers.

Addison keeps that thought in her mind as they trudge along. Nobody's spoken a word since leaving Station-Four. A few murmurs and the occasional hum by the soldiers to pass the time. Addison now counts her steps, wondering how many she has left until she gets there.

Her screen flickers with a warning.

"Body temperature dropping," she reads.

The words flash red, prompting her suit to adjust internal heating to compensate for the sudden dip.

Six-hundred forty-seven . . . Six-hundred forty-eight . . . Six-hundred forty-nine . . .

She keeps counting her steps. She loses her place three times in the hour, but it doesn't matter. It's more to keep her mind occupied and off the shadows on the walls. Addison doesn't know how it's possible to feel claustrophobic in a wide-open space, but she does.

Seven-hundred ninety-two . . . Seven-hundred ninety-three . . . Seven-hundred ninety-four . . .

"Just stay on Warden's shitty ass, and everything will be fine," Addison says under her breath. "Just fine."

Five minutes later, they reach an outlet to an impressive room. Lights appear in the adjacent corridors. Everybody stops.

Addison holds her breath.

"Javelin-leader to Castle-Actual," a distinctly human voice rises over their short-wave comms. "We see you, don't move. We're not sure what's going on ahead." It's the recon team Wolfden sent ahead to scout their route to Idu's meeting point.

"Copy that, Javelin-leader," Colonel Ibrahim returns. Everybody presses their backs against the walls. "What can you tell me?"

"Bogies vacated the area ten minutes ago," McKelly explains. "They've gone out in patrols, but always in the immediate area. They're gone now. As in, no longer where they were. And they haven't tripped any of our sensors to indicate which direction they went."

"Maybe they left for our sake?" Warden proposes.

"Not this group," McKelly denies. "We've gotten to know them pretty well over the past few hours. They've maintained consistent habits. Predictable. We're certain they've also known about us for a while."

"Any hostile action toward your team?" Ibrahim asks.

"That's a negative," the other replies.

Addison feels a dull pressure on her chest.

"That seems odd," Ava weighs, "even by our standards. If you send a welcoming committee, why let us wander?"

"Idu was courteous in my interaction with her," Addison repeats from her original report. "But remember that we aren't dealing with *our* standards."

Ibrahim turns to her. Even with her image reflecting off his visor, Addison can feel his stare.

"Are you willing to put our lives at stake to test their amiability?" Ibrahim demands.

Addison breathes unevenly. "No, sir." She shifts her shoulders uncomfortably as she answers.

Ibrahim cocks his head to one side as if he's amused. He returns his attention to the main room, his stare lingering on the large wall in front of them.

"Okay, then. Javelin-Seven and Charlie will take the side passages. Switch to the secure feed," Ibrahim determines. "Stay in contact. See where they might've gone."

"Assuming their behavior matches our preconceived notions," Vogert mentions.

"Which is why I like being proactive, Doctor Vogert," Ibrahim states. "Go with what feels right. Which is the best I've got." Addison joins everyone else, nodding their acknowledgments. "In the meantime, we secure this chamber!" Ibrahim orders. "Marines! Set up your positions! Watch those entryways like a puppy dog begging for food! Dig in until I say otherwise!"

Warden sequesters Addison and her team on the far side of the chamber. Vogert, Remmings, Leighton, and Yunwen stay behind the woman's fireteam.

Ibrahim paces around the room as they dig in for a lengthy wait. He does several laps, picking up speed with every pass he makes. Ibrahim remains in constant communication with Lieutenant McKelly and the rest of his team, who've split off to cover each branch leading off from the chamber.

Addison keys her comms to connect with the military frequency. She cringes when she makes the connection. A low-pitch crackle in her earpiece, leaving her wanting to vomit. Avanna Remmings notices her reaction and leans into Addison.

"White noise in the spectrum," she whispers. "Subtle. But it's there."

Addison rests her back against the wall, letting her arms and legs go heavy. She does what she can to control her breathing. Addison can feel a tingling in her arms. Her suit's monitor keeps sending her warnings about her heart rate. She doesn't think she's going to calm down anytime soon. At least, not until this walkabout is over.

"River lilies floating on a fabled breeze," she whispers so nobody else can hear. "Tadpoles leaping from leaf to leaf, laughing, swimming, with every bit of glee." It's part of an old nursery rhyme Addison's father used to sing to her until she was eight. Addison used to cherish the short moments he *did* spend at home and not with the fleet. Those days are long behind them, and the world no longer looks the same.

Addison looks up and notices her reflection in Zhu Yunwen's visor. The woman focuses on the wall behind her.

"What are you looking at?" Addison asks.

"You don't see that?" Zhu begs the question.

Addison leans forward and pivots her body around. The wall has a glossy shine to it, like foggy glass. It's dark. Nearly translucent.

Finally seeing it, Addison pushes herself off the ground to examine it closer. Zhu comes next to her and runs a hand across the surface.

"It's smooth," Zhu describes.

"Not a wall, then," Addison agrees. "Not like the others we've seen. Maybe a window?"

"But what's on the other side?" Ava adds her voice. "I can't see through the grime!"

"I don't think it *is* grime," Addison suggests. "Leighton?"

The cartographer picks himself up and stops on Addison's left.

"Something big, maybe?" he says. "Larger than *this* room. For sure."

"Does anybody notice those lights?" Ava points out. "Colorful."

"The glass is bending the particles to create those patterns," Leighton says. "Notice the shadows?"

"They're moving!" Zhu cheers.

"Like a prism," Addison understands.

"Optical glass refracting light with a degree of polarization," Ava offers her educated opinion.

"Which would create the illusion there's movement on the other side," Zhu illustrates. "So, what *is* on the other side? Apart from 'something big,' maybe?"

Addison runs her thumb on her helmet's ridges, lingering on a thought for a moment.

"Where are we going, Idu?" Addison whispers. "What do I need to see?"

"Castle-Five-Actual? Reporting from Javelin Team," McKelly signals.

"Go ahead, recon," Ibrahim returns.

"We've finished our sweep. No sign of the crawlers."

Addison glances at Ibrahim.

"Understood, Lieutenant," the Colonel responds. "Return to the crossroads. Over."

"Copy that," McKelly reads. "Over and—"

"Javelin-leader, this is Doctor Kennedy," Addison goes. She marches up to the Colonel and takes over the comms channel. Ibrahim steps cautiously back, startled by her aggression. "The meeting point is on the other side of this wall. Is there a way to circumvent it? A corridor that trails off northerly. Copy me?"

A long silence fills the air with no immediate response.

Ibrahim's stance turns angry.

"Lieutenant McKelly—" he ends the quiet. "Do you copy that last request?"

"Uh? Yes, sir," the recon team's leader finally answers. "Give us a second. We've just . . . might . . . found it. Give . . . evaluate . . . situation . . . here?" Static is breaking up large portions of the man's speech.

Another unnerving period emerges with an electric hum replacing the silence.

"Javelin! Repeat your last transmission!" Ibrahim barks. "What's your situation? Give me a sitrep!"

"Dead crawlers . . . entrance . . . lots . . . We don't know . . . what . . . killed them . . . Not the machines."

That's the last of Javelin's transmission before the static takes the feed entirely.

"Damn!" Ibrahim curses. "They're in a dead zone. Interference is bad where they are."

"Jamming our communications?" Warden asks.

"The radius isn't consistent with our readings from Overlook Station," Ava suggests.

"If not a jamming field, what's causing it?" Zhu asks. "Xiā jī bā chě." Her speech trails off into curses.

The questions split into a small argument as the team decides what to do. Addison steps away, returning her attention to the glass wall.

Leighton joins her with a small data recorder in his hands. "It's the room's focus," he explains. "Do you see how the walls are wider at the entrance? It narrows the closer you get to the wall! Anyone walking into the room from that direction can't avoid seeing the progression."

"And why is that significant?" Addison asks.

"Because the structure differs profoundly from anywhere else on the ship."

Addison takes another breath. This time, she doesn't hide it.

Leighton instantly notices her inelegance. "How are you holding up, Doctor Kennedy?"

"At the moment, do you mean?" she annunciates.

"You're doing fine," the man encourages. "I understand. You don't have to explain." He tilts his head to indicate an unseen smile.

"Not yet, at any rate," Addison weakly laughs. "Until then? I want to keep on the move."

"We're waiting on the recon team," Leighton laments. "It didn't sound too good on their end."

"More reason why we shouldn't stay in this juncture," Addison suggests. "Let's get everyone moving to the team's last known position." She jaunts off toward the chamber's righthand side, toward starboard.

"Woah! Can you slow down?" Leighton steps in front of her. "You're anxious! I get it. But we shouldn't rush into things."

"Leighton? We're so close," Addison confides. "Every step we take is a rush into things. And there it is! Our chance to finish it."

"Addison, I understand that. But—? Will you just stop? Everyone's looking!"

Addison blinks as she hears him, making her stop dead in her tracks. She looks around the chamber to see the arguments having quieted down. Everyone's eyes are now squarely on her.

Ibrahim moves toward them, nodding at his marines.

Warden steps behind Addison.

"I may not know you very well," Leighton goes, "but *this* isn't you, Addison. God only knows what we'll find if we aren't careful."

Addison centers her eyes on the man for a moment. Suddenly, all she wants to do is shove the cartographer out of her way. She doesn't. But she wants to.

Warden's stare convinces her to hold off any brash decision.

Addison nods. "You're right," she admits.

She turns to Ibrahim, who stays in the center of his soldiers.

"Are you ready for this?" Ibrahim asks.

"It's your call, Lieutenant Colonel," Addison agrees.

"Good," he states, crossing his arms.

She can feel a sinking in her gut.

"You're not the only one fighting this, Addison," Vogert explains.

"And we're not here to stop you," Ibrahim adds. "My job is to get you home alive . . . Do you understand? Our lives are on the line, so we must do this right. It's going to take a lot out of us. One mistake? And this mission fails. We won't give up, but we don't want to die trying to make history if we don't have to."

"I didn't mean to—"

"I know what you meant," Ibrahim softly tells her. "You'll get to Idu. I promise you that. Okay?" Addison nods again, surrendering the decision. "All right. Now get your ass in gear! The going won't get any easier." His tone makes it loud and clear, the only way to go is forward.

41 | IMPASSE

SERGEANT MAJOR OLIVIA WARDEN
UNITED COALITION ARMED FORCES

OCTOBER 21, 2041 | 0525 HOURS

==

"Sergeant Major!" Lieutenant McKelly shouts over the air, his voice rasping inside his mask. He surprises Warden and her squad. McKelly's team IFF transponders flash on her HUD. "Over here! Do you see this?"

Colonel Ibrahim sent Warden ahead to rendezvous with McKelly and Javelin-Seven-Delta.

"I see them, Lieutenant," she acknowledges, getting in close with her team. "What's their deal? They look—?"

"Fresh?" McKelly finishes. "Yeah, I know."

"I was going to say dead." Warden steps onto the scene with dozens of bugger corpses strewn across the floor. Something has slaughtered them, clean and precise. "What can you say about their injuries?" Warden asks. She turns one of the buggers over for a better look at its carapace. The orange blood reflects her light's beam as she moves from one to the next.

"Nothing sensible. Athena's unavailable with our spotty uplink," McKelly explains. "We can't even send long-range signals for image bursts. All we got are our local comms, line of sight. Not much allowance for the distance."

"Understandable," Warden says, nodding her head. "But we don't need computers to figure it out. Or do we, soldier?" She laughs.

"Of course not, Sergeant Major," McKelly huffs.

Warden catches the irritation in his tone.

"Tell me what you can," she demands, waving any formalities.

"We did three sweeps of the adjacent corridors looking for these bastards when Colonel Ibrahim ordered us back to the crossroads," McKelly explains. "Passing through this stretch already, I didn't think we'd find anything a second time through, so these dead ones—?"

"—are extremely fresh," Warden concludes.

"Probably within the last twenty minutes," McKelly continues. "Definitely *after* the expedition took to lollygagging." Lieutenant McKelly kneels beside one of the dead buggers. "Do you see this?" He points to an arm cut cleanly off the creature's body. The head is missing half its jaw, blown off like it had taken an artillery shell to the face.

"Animal attack?" Warden asks.

"Maybe? If there *are* any animals on this blasted ship. Those rock drones didn't do this, that's for sure. Damage type isn't consistent," he goes on. "And look there! Do you see that? Or better yet, what don't you see?" He points at the corridor's walls.

She looks where the Lieutenant indicates, but Warden doesn't see anything off-putting.

She shakes her head and shrugs.

"If the fight took place in *this* hallway, where we are, then why don't we see further evidence of their tussle?" McKelly weighs the question.

Warden takes a closer look around the bodies. "You're right," she whispers. From what she can see, there are no scorch marks. No blood spatters on the floor or walls. Apart from the body parts, there is no indication that anything violent has happened here. "Like something massacred them elsewhere and put the corpses on display for us to find."

McKelly nods agreeingly. "That's what we're figuring, Sergeant Major. Any ideas where to go from here?"

Warden stops for a moment to think. "Addison Kennedy asked if you could find a way north when your comms went to shit. Any luck? Or did she blow smoke up our asses?"

"Yes, we found a spot of luck," McKelly murmurs with a slight tilt to his head. "Or we're confident enough." He points down the corridor where the alien bodies engross ascendingly. "That's north. Likely into the ship's forward sections. You want us to head in and find out for sure?"

Warden returns with a nod of her own. "Colonel Ibrahim's team is coming up behind us. Take point. We'll meet you ahead." McKelly hesitates. With his armor on, Warden's HUD reads his body temperature lowers by a full degree. "Are you scared, Lieutenant?" Warden asks.

"No. Sergeant Major," McKelly quickly coughs in reply. "It's just that . . . *that* doorway? We don't know what to expect once we're on the other side." He sets his rifle's stock snugly against his shoulder. "Whatever did *this* to *them*, it came from or went in that direction. And these aren't the usual cannon fodder, either. These crawlers are their High Echelons—elite warriors. Tough bastards to take down."

Warden purses her lips. The Lieutenant can't see her face through her visor. She's thankful for that privacy.

"All right. We'll stay in range. And be careful," Warden bids him. "Send a runner if you run into trouble. We've got enough munitions to blast anything hostile into a fine red paste. No matter the size. Got it?"

"It's not their size that I'm worried about, Sergeant Major," McKelly admits. "This could be the rogue Architect from our briefings."

"Adhion 'Kaalak-k-ka?" Warden fights to pronounce. "The Nomad?"

McKelly surrenders an aggressive nod.

She selects the name pronouncers on her screen for the other entities. "Remember. Only five giants are on this ship, Lieutenant," Warden repeats as she reads the labeling on the packet Addison Kennedy had written out. "Two females—including our contact, Idu 'Smeora. And the two other males—Dhun 'Ancod and Tyrann 'Akachan."

"Understood," McKelly acknowledges. "Keep watch for a female."

"Doctor Kennedy wants to meet with Idu on her own," Warden continues. "So, if you encounter one, do *not* engage."

McKelly cracks his neck. "Copy that, Sergeant Major," he confirms. He starts down the corridor, stepping over the dead meat, moving with his unit as if they're guarding the perimeter of a crime scene. Eventually, Javelin-Seven disappears into the darkness.

"Sergeant Major?" her fireteam's leader asks.

She looks at Sergeant Karl Hammon.

"Wait until the Colonel arrives with Addison's team," Warden orders. "Only shoot if it's not vaguely human-shaped."

"Understood, ma'am," Hammon acknowledges.

Warden's eyes land wearily on the bodies lying on the floor.

"I hope this is worth it," Warden mutters.

ADDISON KENNEDY, FIELD DIRECTOR
EPIMETHEUS PROJECT

OCTOBER 21, 2041 | 0532 HOURS

Addison doesn't know what she's stepping into as she pushes into the dark zone. The corridor leading to the door isn't any different from the countless others she's seen along the way. Maybe a little bigger? Otherwise, it has the same angular walls with red light emanating from cracks in the façade.

And there's static in her ears? Strange.

When they pass under the threshold, Addison feels a soft buckling under her boots.

Nobody mentions it, but she's confident they're all keenly aware. Several others stop and look down, confused by the change, the gradual buildup as they move. It's so unlike anything they've encountered on the ship. It's like a—

"Anyone notice we're on a slope? Like a hill?" Ava is the first to ask. Some of the others throw unseen glares at her in reply. "Or a mound. No judgment. I thought it was odd. Everyone can see this, right? Not just me? Because it's very odd, you know? We're walking on dirt."

"Almost nobody needs to mention it," Addison whispers.

Avanna bumps Addison's side with her hip. She gets a hint that Doctor Remmings is giving off a smile on the other side of that faceplate.

They climb the ascent. Addison will admit it's unusual seeing dirt where—

"What's this now? Grass? Is this grass?" Vogert asks. "Did the recon team mention this?"

"We're pretty much radio silent at the moment, Doc," Ibrahim states. "So, no. They didn't mention it. Static on all channels."

"Right. Of course, the interference," Vogert murmurs. "Did the runner say anything? McKelly must've seen this."

"It's not their job to notice grass," Warden excludes. "Isn't that why you five came along?" She's very blunt in her wording.

Zhu breaks away from the group and kneels next to one of the larger plants. "Phytology shows the grass is giving off unusual levels of galvanism—but it appears natural. Internal?" Zhu describes. She takes a scanner and presses it against the specimen. "Doctor Vogert. Look at this, will you?" She hands Ryan Vogert a data chip from her wrist-pad.

Vogert accepts and plugs it into his hardsuit's interface.

"Does that remind you of anything?" Zhu begs the question.

"Neural pathways," Vogert murmurs. "Synapses? Each one fires in sequence, but you wouldn't find this structure in an animal. More like—?"

"Circuitry," Zhu finishes.

She makes another scan and hands the chip to Ava, who plugs it into her pad and skims the readouts.

"Not circuitry, by definition," Ava describes. "But it's electronic. Digital, maybe?"

"Phytological engineering?" Vogert suggests.

"Manufactured," Addison concludes. "They're artificial constructs. I wonder if it can expel oxygen like normal plant life?"

Zhu's head shifts to the side, clearly unsure how to answer.

"Essential functions. The flora took in carbon dioxide and exchanged it for oxygen," Zhu teaches. "Over a billion years ago, oxygen was a poison to many species on the planet. And it still *is* toxic. Plants became abundant. Green wetlands. Lush forests. Oxygen was a dominant molecule in our atmosphere."

"Forcing animal life to adapt to using oxygen to breathe," Addison adds.

"Which is a middle school science lesson at best," Ava mocks.

Zhu points her index finger at the woman, wanting another second to explain. "I'll need a bigger sample size to know for sure. But given the atmosphere throughout the vessel? I doubt it can do what you're thinking."

"Not unless the Architects' biology is highly adaptable," Vogert suggests.

Addison raises an unseen eyebrow at the man.

"What are the atmospherics ahead, do we know?" Addison asks.

Her team steals a moment to shuffle through the data from the armor readings by the troops forward their position.

"Woah? Look at this," Zhu highlights. She highlights the numbers on her screen. "Heightened oxygen levels several dozen meters into this passageway? I think . . . I think we're entering a pocket! Like a microclimate within the vessel. If that makes sense."

The entire science team turns their heads in her direction. It's remarkable how logical that may seem from the outside. Still, it doesn't make much sense to Addison and the others for a heavily controlled environment like a spacecraft. Or even one as large as this dreadnaught. Even if it *does* lend credence to their research into the gene therapy meant to help adapt human physiology to these hostile conditions.

Colonel Ibrahim and Sergeant Major Warden are now staring at them. Along with half their marine escorts.

"It's grass!" Ibrahim bafflingly states.

Addison shrugs. She pushes on with all two hundred marines and five scientists that make up their expeditionary force. It's not long until they're stepping through the final set of doors at the far end of the hallway. After a couple more meters, Addison ascends into the dark zone, and . . . she stops.

"Wow," she awes, her mouth agape.

"Holy shit," Ava curses.

"Well, that's a new sight," Vogert follows.

"For anybody wondering why Idu asked us to come," Addison says, "this is it. She wanted *us* to see this."

Nobody returns a comment, surprising her. Addison keeps an eye on everyone as they meander into the dense space, where the forest's many colors show themselves. It's not like the woodlands she can find anywhere else on Earth. No. Here, the trees are reaching higher than the redwoods of the western United States.

Each tree breaks through floor after floor, with divisions between the decks above their heads.

Everyone resituates themselves in the small clearing after the doors.

"What the fuck—?" Ibrahim speaks profanely. "How do you build something like this?"

Zhu, Vogert, and Addison take readings from the plants on the trail.

Leighton sets up his surveying equipment on the flattest ground he finds. The man takes his time to measure the wall-like vegetation. He records the data in his field notes.

Looking at the underbrush, Addison can surmise the Architects have left the plants to themselves with their attention diverted to the present crisis. Now she understands what Idu 'Smeora meant when she said, "We seed new life to barren worlds." She implied it literally, like a gardener transplanting flowers from a ceramic pot to the ground. Addison knows it's a common practice for horticulturists—but this?! This greenhouse is in a state of overgrowth. And it's on such a vast scale that Addison can't guess an equivalent outside science-fiction.

"Welcome to the Summerland," Vogert mocks.

"More like a New Eden to replace the old," Zhu identifies.

Addison glances at her and raises an eyebrow. Every time she speaks, the woman reveals a bit more about herself undeclared in her files. Yet, while Malakai received her official copies from her government for Doctor Vogert, they were much like the files they provided the Epimetheus Project. Somebody had dipped the folder into a vat of black ink.

Doctor Zhu Yunwen is aware of her intellect and isn't afraid to show it. That is one trait Addison can say about the woman without a doubt.

"Let's get moving," Ibrahim urges. "We shouldn't linger anywhere for too long."

"I agree," Addison seconds.

Everybody else nods attentively.

They continue deeper into the interior forest. Colonel Ibrahim orders a squad to stay behind to guard the exit door.

Their gear struggles to work through the distortion with the electrical interference in this part of the ship. Addison's visor blinks in and out as she brushes up against the gigantic leaves. She switches to different modes to clean up the noise on her HUD.

"Javelin-leader—do you read me?" Addison overhears Ibrahim say over the comms. "Lieutenant! Sound off your status if you can hear this." And yet, there's no reply. Nothing but a stark quiet between the peaks of white noise.

"You're not going to reach them," Ava assures the Colonel, whose agitation grows as his lips crack open.

"Even the best networks on the planet won't penetrate this energy stipulation," Addison explains.

"We *have* the best equipment!" Ibrahim argues, only pausing after he realizes what he said. "Apologies. I don't like being in the open with our pants down. Let's put sentries out every fifty meters—groups of four. Stick together no matter what. We'll create an old fashion relay network of able bodies to send messages."

Vogert laughs. "Can anybody remember playing 'telephone' when they were kids?"

Ibrahim stops right there and stares Doctor Ryan Vogert down. Even with his visor's glossy sheen, the way the man tilts his head makes his intent painfully clear.

Vogert raises his palms, surrendering his jokes until *after* they're no longer behind enemy lines.

Addison can't help but watch Zhu as they move under the branches.

The woman does what she can to take everything in at once. Addison almost doesn't want to admit it, but there's too much to process, even for her. It's overwhelming. Yet, the outward appearance of the forest is just that, like molds of trees that grow in the Jiuzhaigou Valley of mid-Autumn. Addison's hardsuit reflects the color—the vibrant reds, yellows, greens, and blues.

"It's a sight you can only see," Addison mutters, if less poetic than she wants.

Red lights flash ahead of their position. Colonel Ibrahim signals everyone to get down and into cover.

Addison peeks around the corner. She notices the red isn't coming from Architect technology. It's human tech. And it's from their scouting party.

Ibrahim takes a laser pointer from his gear pouch and returns a series of laser flashes of his own. He receives confirmation—two quick blinks, a longer pause, and another two blinks.

"It's McKelly. Our meeting point isn't far," Ibrahim relays. "Doctor

Kennedy? You're up next. Are you ready for this?"

"No. Not really," Addison answers him truthfully, feeling a hollowness in her stomach. "It's like a first date. You don't know what to expect. My question is—"

"You want to know if Idu 'Smeora waits for you," Ibrahim concludes. Addison nods.

Ibrahim turns and commits to another series of signals.

"He says there's nobody yet," Ibrahim states.

"Maybe she's waiting for us to be the first to arrive?" Addison suggests.

Ibrahim shakes his head, less confident. "We'll stay back and let you handle things for a while. Hit your panic button if you need us. I'll set up sharpshooters around the site. Always assume we've eyes on you, Addison."

"And what's the terrain like?"

Ibrahim holds his stare before signaling the team again.

"It's a deliberate clearing by the looks," Ibrahim says. "Artificial light, composite ground. Not much cover."

"Mhmm," Addison swallows. "Well, I'm a decent runner, as you've learned. So, let's get started."

"Just keep going until your tracker hits the coordinates exactly," Leighton explains.

"That still works?" Addison asks.

"Sporadically," Leighton answers.

Addison nods and puts a hand on the man's shoulder. "Thanks. But, if these coordinates lead me into a ditch, I'll draw something rude on your facemask while you sleep, Leighton. And you'll have to walk back to base looking at it the entire way."

"Duly noted," Leighton accepts. "And you wouldn't."

"She would," Vogert refutes.

"Oh, I would," Addison laughs, turning to Vogert.

"Good luck in there, Doctor Kennedy," Vogert encourages her. "And if you come back with two heads, I'll see what I can do to fix it!" Addison inhales sharply through her nostrils, hesitant to laugh. Her hardsuit's filters make a wheezing noise, regardless of her effort.

She pauses when she reaches Doctor Remmings. "I think it'd be cool if you got a second head. It'd be interesting to see how Vogert deals with it."

Zhu's scrutiny remains on the plants encapsulating them and the scientific beauty oozing from every shrub and molecule. Addison stares at the woman for a heartbeat before walking toward the recon team.

"Ready to move?" Lieutenant McKelly asks Addison as she reaches his squad.

"The most important thing is that we've had fun getting here," Addison teases to ease the tension inside her chest. McKelly doesn't pop a chuckle. "All right. Let's go, Lieutenant. Lead the way."

"Right away, ma'am," the man agrees.

PART TWO

WATERS OF LIFE

DHUN 'ANCOD, THE JUDGE OF CONCILIATION
ARKKITECT OF THE VILI

521031 LOCAL CLUSTER | 761,400 DAY OF PURPOSE

"This part of the jungle has grown thick without our care," Minn'Athorad Ahmman cautions, glancing at Dhun 'Ancod with dull eyes. "Our runners say the humans are moving toward us in greater numbers."

"Adhion's controllers are pushing to distract them," Dhun says, refusing to answer Ahm's fears with his doubts.

"We do our best to keep the machines away from the human outposts," Ahm utters. "Or we try to. We die so *they* can live. And they thank us by shooting us on sight."

"They are afraid," Dhun explains. "They do not understand. So, they believe if they fight, they can win."

"There are no winners among the grief-stricken," Ahm condemns. The insectoid dodges the thickets on their path to the meeting with Addison Kennedy. "We aren't enough to win this war for you, Judge. That is not our role. We defend ourselves with farming tools, not battlefield weapons."

"Then let's not waste time," Dhun expediates.

Ahm stops and turns to Dhun 'Ancod, his four eyes blinking wildly.

"You should aim your efforts at stopping Adhion 'Klaka before the damage worsens," Ahm growls. "What if he should reach the Entrychamber? The Nomad could use his sequence markers to activate the final protocol and prepare this planet for restoration."

Dhun lets the flats of his nostrils flare as his companions push toward their destination.

"It's not as simple as that," Dhun hesitates. "Adhion is only doing what he does naturally."

Yet, the Obligation also requires Idu, Dhun, and the rest, to find a way to oppose him without breaking the one rule of their moral code. They mustn't *kill* Adhion 'Klaka, much as Adhion shan't kill *them*.

Adhion defines what it means to take responsibility for the mistakes of their species. Dhun accepts that. Although, it feels easy for Dhun to scold the Nomad for his methods. Is there a better option?

"He has a dirty job," Dhun recedes, "and the most important if we are to achieve the Obligation's demands."

And if that means exterminating entire planetary ecosystems to start anew when the first attempts yield less-than-ideal results? Then, so be it. Dhun 'Ancod has learned to grieve for those like Adhion 'Klaka for their task. They live to complete the cycle and fulfill the role of merciful constraint.

Dhun notices movement in the bushes—beasts conceived and grown in the vats on the upper decks by the Servant, Tjaa 'Neren. She releases them into this greenhouse to develop independently on the long journeys between stars. They create a self-sustaining biosphere after settling onto a life-seeded world. A herd of deer-like creatures emerges from the trees in front of Dhun. The animals mostly ignore the Varmajalkavaen, as they *should*. They've acclimated to interacting with Ahm and his brood, so the beasts are comfortable in *their* presence. It's just that . . . they aren't as content with an Arkkitect casting a shadow over their home.

"We are the composers of vast symphonies," Dhun mournfully recites. "It's the others who choose to play the instruments. Those who create the sound, not the art of its creation—the notes, chords, rhythms, and stops."

A trio of the animals amidst the herd slows down and stops to stare at Dhun standing on the path. They are curious animals with bright yellow eyes, albeit skittish. They understand that he's a possible danger to their family unit. And they are confused as to why he's not attacking. So, they watch and wait, letting the others pass, guarding their youngest members.

"Do you see the antlers, Judge?" Ahm asks, pointing at the beasts with his smaller, lower arms.

"I do," Dhun admits. "For defense?"

"Sharp enough to mangle a limb," Ahm explains, "if they charge at you."

"Even my limbs?" Dhun weighs.

"Indeed, Judge. Even yours," Ahm repeats. "All things have weaknesses, and these beasts are cleverer than you think."

Dhun considers Ahm's words and wonders if there isn't a hidden subtext under the notion.

Ahm raises a palm to calm the largest deer-like creature—its fur curling, white as alpine, with the eyes reflecting the other's image like a glass mirror.

The alpha returns the warrior's gesture by burring its lips, tilting his head, and lowering its snout with due respect.

"Go on!" Ahm instructs. "Run free! Join the others." And like that, the animal flees to rejoin its herd. "Your species relies too much on your technology. It separates you from the greater whole. That is why *my* kind travels with you nowadays, as the hands to your bodies. Great minds alone can only go so far without the means to understand others through direct contact. So, Irna—The Great Mother—speaks her wisdom."

"Idu's learning *that* rather quickly," Dhun agrees.

"We go to meet this *human*—Addison Kennedy," Ahm clicks. "Why? Hoping she's the link to gain their trust and thwart Adhion 'Klaka and his delusions?" Ahm lets off a laugh that comes off as a high-pitch squeal, almost like air passing through a rubber nozzle. "Forgive me if I hold my breath."

"Then, hold your breath," Dhun tells him.

"Are we—?" Ahm attempts to say.

Dhun raises his hand and silences him. "Going in the Idu's place? Yes." He walks with his feet heavy on the dirt. "Humanity is volatile, but that is also its strength. A tool we can use if we can utilize it properly."

Ahm's feelers shrink as he goes quiet. His many arms shift awkwardly, agitating at his sides.

"Let us go faster," the warrior urges. "We should reach the meeting point soon. Worse creatures than deer stalk these trees."

Dhun scoffs. "I follow your lead," he agrees.

44 | GOOD MORNING

MALAKAI ADONIS, DIRECTOR OF OPERATIONS
EPIMETHEUS PROJECT

OCTOBER 21, 2041 | 0345 HOURS

===

Malakai steps into his office and slides behind his desk. He turns on the monitors and notices the blinking light on his pad.

"A notification?" he whispers and smiles. "What are you doing up so early?" He missed a video call from his wife twenty minutes ago.

Malakai hits the call button and angles the camera, hoping she's still awake. Mara picks up moments later.

She's a beautiful mess.

"You look like shit," Mara is the first to say.

Malakai fights off his want to laugh. "Nice to see you, too, honey. I like what you've done to your hair."

"Small talk? Really?" she chuckles, raising an eyebrow.

He sits back in the chair, running a finger through his growing beard. "We're having a hell of a time here," Malakai admits. He needs to decompress to somebody. "It's tough. I . . . I don't know where to begin. I honestly don't."

Mara sits forward, closer to the camera. Her eyes furrow, wanting him to tell her what's happening.

"Then don't start at the beginning," she tells him. "What's on your mind right now?"

"I don't know . . . It's difficult for me to say," Malakai says, keeping it vague. There are pieces of information that he's not allowed to tell anyone outside the Epimetheus Project. Not even to his wife. "Let's . . . move the subject off me for a second, can we?"

"Okay, Akke . . . It's good to see you, by the way," Mara admits, smiling at him through the screen. "I've missed you." Malakai attempts to stave off the grin. He can't, and when he shows his teeth, it's like he's in high school again.

"We both knew this disaster would keep us apart for a while," Malakai justifies, repeating the words he's said to her countless times. "When the floods hit, and the storm got louder, people everywhere were . . . displaced? They lost their homes. You're good at helping people when they need it. I'm good—"

"You're good at convincing the bureaucrats to work against their self-interests."

She winks.

Malakai snorts amusingly.

"Convinced you, didn't I?" Malakai pokes fun, his tongue sinking to the back of his throat. "How's life in the mercy camps?"

"Crowded," she answers. "There's a couple thousand of us thrown into a few hundred tents. Everybody's lost . . . so much, and it's getting harder to help people when all they want to do is scream at you. Like we can do more than we are? We're at our limits."

"It's quite the responsibilities we've piled on ourselves," Malakai admits. "How's the little butthead holding up?"

His wife laughs through her nose when he mentions their daughter. "Oh, she's having the time of her life!" Mara explains. "This place is like a maze—and the kids enjoy running everywhere, all at once. We've had quite the time trying to figure out which orphans still have close living relatives. Ever try asking a two-year-old if he knows where his aunt or uncle lives? They'll shout 'Green!' while pointing at my hat."

"Because your hat is green?"

"Because my *hat* is green," Mara chuckles.

"Can I see her?" Malakai asks. Mara nods and turns her computer's camera so he can see Armoni sleeping peacefully in a cot under a mountain of blankets. Malakai also sees the six other families sharing the space with them. "Like a maturing little nugget. How many are in there with you?"

"Twenty-five . . . No, thirty? It changes depending on who comes and goes," Mara describes. "And we always have people coming and going. It's a rotating door of refugees and families with nowhere to go. It isn't easy when your neighborhoods get washed away into the ocean."

Malakai brings up several articles about rising death tolls on his pad. He reads the daily totals every morning when he wakes up. It's his ritual, serving as a reminder. And the numbers aren't insignificant. He can't imagine what the cleanup crews think when they clear waterlogged bodies from the rubble.

"What have we gotten ourselves into?" Malakai asks with a tremor in his chest. "How can we win this?"

Mara frowns. "It's a situation like we've always dreamed about," she admits. "A challenge. And putting our talents to use for once?"

"Honestly—I was always more interested in the dreams," Malakai winks. He watches delightfully as his wife blushes and sticks her tongue out at him.

"Oh, you're such an ass," she inevitably responds, giggling like a schoolgirl. "Stop it."

"You know I can't do that," Malakai exhales. "It's against my nature."

"Better keep those dreams in your pants," his wife boasts, "if you don't want me to pull your privileges."

She pops the fold of her collar, sweat gathering at her neck.

"I dare you to try it," Malakai nudges, staring harder at the screen.

"You dare me to do . . . *what*, now? Husband?" She smirks at the corner of her mouth.

"I thought we discussed you two would stop being so gross," Armoni breaks in, meandering up to the computer, the girl's hair sticking out like a crown of weeds.

Mara quickly sits up and lets out an exasperated breath.

"For a nine-year-old, you're a pretty darn nosy bee. You know that?" Malakai tells his daughter.

"What are you doing up, sweetheart?" Mara asks, leaning back to let the girl see her dad on the computer monitor.

"It's hard to sleep pretending you guys aren't giving sex eyes to each other across the room," Armoni states. "You know we're not alone, right?"

"Again. You're nine!" Malakai reiterates. "How do you even know what 'sex eyes' are?"

The girl releases a single, very sarcastic, high-pitched laugh. "Please," she answers. "I pay attention."

"Right," Malakai mutters. "Your mother needs to stop letting you watch television."

Armoni scoffs. "Television? Please, dad," she shrugs. "I've advanced to watching full-blown—"

Malakai throws s a 'stop fooling around' glare at her.

Armoni is quick to notice and swallows.

"Sorry, dad. I wanted to rile you up. And I did!" she politely says. "I don't watch that stuff. Really. I promise."

"Go to bed," Malakai orders. "Or you'll regret not getting an extra hour of sleep on a Monday."

Armoni nods her head agreeingly. "I've missed you, dad."

"I've missed you, too, butthead."

Malakai watches as Armoni returns to her cot and buries herself in the covers.

"She's having trouble focusing on her classes," Mara explains. "She's terrified you're not coming back."

"A lot of moms and dads won't be returning after this tour," Malakai admits. "I wish I could understand what's happening in the real world."

"What isn't?" Mara offers. "Hunger . . . fighting . . . Predators looking to profit off others' misfortune?"

"A lifetime of training couldn't prepare us for this," Malakai chuckles, though not because he thinks it's funny. He's exhausted.

"Could be worse," Mara adds.

"You're right," Malakai agrees. "We could be in the middle of a pandemic."

"Can you imagine quarantine under these conditions? We'd lose so many people."

"Especially with so many going between camps."

"And with camp workers getting redeployed every few days?" she notions with a grimace. Malakai shifts his shoulders as his wife visibly shudders. "We don't have enough agents, police, soldiers, or responder crews to maintain order. They're all with you, fighting to get the answers that will make our efforts worth it."

Malakai sighs. "I'm not so certain. They've redeployed a good portion of our resources to help with the crisis on the mainland."

"My contacts upstream warned me about that," Mara tells him. "Seems that President Seymour has permanently stalled the redeployment of those troops."

"What?" Malakai quickly demands. "It was his administration that asked for it! Any word from Jim Harper? I'd bet he isn't too happy."

"He's furious," Mara explains.

"And have they decided what to do about it?"

"There's not much they *can* do," Mara admits, wringing her hands. "Harper wants the President to order those troops to help with the recovery efforts. A few million bodies after a month, and the bastard is still worried about looking politically weak. It's stupid."

"I'm guessing the President outright refused their requests?" Malakai suggests.

"That's what the reports are saying," Mara shrugs.

"Which doesn't help with maintaining relations with our allies," Malakai grimaces. "What about Congress? I'd hope they'll want to weigh in at some point."

"They're flustered," Mara says. "His party defends the decision."

"Which sounds familiar," Malakai exhales.

"They don't even seem to care that public opinion is against them," Mara mentions worryingly.

"They'd rather defend their 'American freedoms' during the upheaval," Malakai construes, squeezing his knuckles together. "Survival of the fittest."

"It's only bullshit. That's all it is," Mara expresses. "Loyalty along party lines? People are dying! That is what I don't understand."

"And we can't let the situation devolve," Malakai agrees. "A disunified front will do nothing but sow confusion among the Coalition at this stage."

"It might still go that way if you don't finish your mission soon," Mara states. "We need those troops back home passing out food and building shelters."

"And clearing the debris," Malakai adds.

Mara softly nods.

Malakai breathes in deeply and holds the air in his lungs.

"Well, some good news on my end. We've got a lead that might help expedite our goals," Malakai suggests, careful with his word choice. "If it works the way Addison Kennedy argues, we might all be going home in a couple of weeks instead of months."

"Can you promise me that?"

Malakai leans forward, lowering his voice to a whisper. "You know I can't do that."

"I don't care if you *keep* the promise," Mara says. "I just want to hear you say that you're doing everything you can to get the job done."

He clenches his jaw. "I am doing everything I can to get the job done," Malakai repeats. "And I promise, I will get back. And we can rebuild the house together."

"Let's think about putting it on a hill this time?" Mara weighs. "Over by the rock patch? East field? We don't want it to get washed away again." She presses her upper teeth against her lower lip, making *that* face that first convinced Malakai to ask her on a date.

Malakai clears his throat. He leans backward in his chair and crosses his legs.

"On a hill in the east field," Malakai repeats. "That sounds perfect. So long we can avoid the wind."

"And the rain?"

"Rain *has* lost its novelty for me," he admits.

Malakai says goodbye to her and shuts off the camera. He sits in his dark office for a time, organizing his thoughts.

Addison paces the clearing for an hour. And there's still no sign of Idu 'Smeora, or any other Architect, for that matter.

She can see movement among the greenery—Colonel Ibrahim and his marines, arraying themselves equal distances apart.

"Where are they?" Warden demands over a static-filled comms channel. The soldiers installed a relay up one of the trees to boost their signal. While they still can't hear anything outside the dead zone, the local frequencies won't burst an eardrum. "What's their deal?"

"Quiet now," Addison intercepts. "I'm concentrating."

"On what? There's nothing here!"

Addison looks in Warden's direction. "I wouldn't call *this* nothing," she says, upturning her eyes, attempting to find where the canopy above her ends. She can't. It's several decks above this one, and these trees are massive.

"We see movement coming from the north sector," Ibrahim announces. "Looks like a . . . big . . . cat? Maybe a tiger?"

Addison's glare shifts, seeing a rustling in the underbrush.

UCAF marines reposition themselves to block the creature's path.

"Wait, don't shoot!" Addison shouts. "Let it through."

"It's a predator, Addison," Ibrahim explains. "The thing's not out for a stroll."

"We don't know *what* it is," Addison returns. "Not yet. I *want* to see what happens."

Vogert chimes into the call. "Addison," he says, voice buzzing with interference. "As your friend, I do *not* recommend getting close."

"The last thing we need is for you to get mauled," Avanna advocates, cusping the edge of the radio's effective range.

Everyone's attention is on the cat-like creature. It prances through the bushes, avoiding Ibrahim's patrols. Addison grits her teeth once the animal jumps out into the clearing. Colorful frills poke through its vibrant fur coat, the eyes as big as basketballs, with a snout reminiscent of an exotic shorthair, flat and fierce.

"Definitely a cat," Vogert exclaims. "Female, by its posture. I think. At least, going by *our* big cats. Tail down."

"It sees you, Kennedy," Ibrahim iterates. "Do . . . not . . . move."

Addison focuses on the creature using her visor's enhanced capabilities.

It's enormous! Taller than any Earth-based predator . . . Or any predator of the last forty-thousand years. Going farther back in the fossil record, however?

"Maybe," Addison whispers.

Addison's seen sabretooth tiger exhibits in museums about equal size. Perhaps smaller? Meaning there is a savage power behind this beast.

"If you want to shoot it," Addison grants, "be my guest. But *only* if it begins showing signs of hunting behavior."

She notices the marines switch off their standby lights as Ibrahim hears her.

The cat paces back and forth along the clearing's edge, keeping its eyes on Addison the whole time, assessing her merits as prey.

Cautiously, the big cat glides nearer. It stops every few meters to study Addison's reaction. By the motion of its head, it seems to recognize there are others like *her* nearby. The creature can probably smell Ibrahim and the rest, even inside their armor.

The cat stops when it is only an arm's length away. Sitting up on its hind legs, it stares at Addison with a calm demeanor.

Addison doesn't move an inch. Her hardsuit keeps her body at a constant temperature, but that doesn't mean she's not sweating.

"Go away, Shal Amacha," a disembodied voice then whispers.

The large cat's glare settles right above Addison's head. The creature lets out a soft-pitch squeal before running back across the clearing, disappearing into the bushes. Addison gawks for only a moment. She turns to look at whatever scared the creature away.

"You're not Idu," Addison points out, stepping backward as the giant appears out of the vapor.

The male Architect decloaks in the same way Idu did when she came to visit Addison on base.

"But you are Addison Kennedy," the Architect responds.

"I know my name," Addison says, her muscles tense. "What's yours?"

"Noida 'Kalkah. I am the . . . Pilgrim . . . aboard the Vili," Noida claims. "One of only five. Idu sent me instead. They needed her attention elsewhere."

Addison nods once and blinks. "What's that animal? You called her . . . Shal

Amacha?"

Noida offers her a smile, bright and beautiful. "One of many lives to seed a barren world. The livestock tends to breed after Tjaa 'Neren cultivates them. After birth, we release them into these grounds to develop an ecosystem. That one we call the Shal Amacha—the Jungle Queen. You saw for yourself everything you needed to know."

There's another crack on Addison's comms— "What the hell?" Ibrahim curses. "How did . . . How did *he* get past the perimeter? Doctor Kennedy!"

Addison switches off her earpiece.

"Your friends are nervous?" the Pilgrim asks.

"They want to know how you got past our sentries," Addison explains.

"This is *our* ship," the alien makes it clear. "I know it better than any invader would."

"Invader?"

Noida coughs. "This is our home, Addison Kennedy. Not yours," he responds. "Yet I don't think it's something we should dwell on. There is a lot to discuss and not much time. Adhion is very close. He knows about this meeting and wants to stop it from continuing."

Addison's eyes narrow. She takes a step back to get a broader view of the specimen.

"You mean the Nomad?" she repeats the name. "What does he want? And why is he fighting with the others?"

Noida kneels to Addison's level and raises his palm between them. "Take my hand," he says. And she does, carefully, not knowing what to expect. When her glove touches him, she feels an electric jolt passing through her arm. She doesn't feel any pain from it. But the sensation leaves her feeling . . . invigorated. "We are the shapers of many lives throughout the galaxy. We are a certain spark to creation. Seedlings in a small field, but not insignificant. Not when we can provide entire worlds with everything it needs for a population to thrive."

"Idu told me some about that."

"But did she tell you about Adhion 'Klaka and his role?" Noida demands. "He is a harsh consequence for failure. Consider the Varmajalkavaen . . . Proud warriors and caretakers, passionate in their duties but separate and tribalistic. Malleable. They were grown like so many others. But their source vessel crashed onto what became their homeworld. And they became the lost ones. Another craft rediscovered them by chance. We descended on their villages and tribes, eradicating many of them to correct the error, even as they fought back to survive the onslaught."

"I don't know what that means," Addison considers. "You killed them because they advanced without you?"

"No, that isn't—" the Pilgrim says, stopping mid-sentence. He drops his chest and relaxes his arms, loosening his body to appear more amiable. "Theirs was a dangerous path we needed to correct. Varmajalkavaen society consoles itself with martial honor. They're everything that others find attractive in a species to consume."

"A dangerous path? I don't get it," Addison weighs. "You create them, only to kill them later?"

Noida breathes deeply, lowering his shoulders.

"I did not come to debate politics," the alien confronts her, leaning away from the question. "Nor will I delve into the motivations of one who makes the wrong decisions for the right reasons." His feathers shift their hue to a mute blue.

"Okay," Addison allows. "Explain this to me, then. Why did Idu ask me here?"

The alien pauses as if considering a course of action. "Open your fist," the Pilgrim urges.

Addison squints before figuring out what he means. She nods, unfolding her palm, and offering her hand to the Architect.

"This is a gift for you, Addison Kennedy," Noida surrenders.

Between his thin fingers, Addison spies a bright flash orchestrating from nothingness. It's a cobalt blue sphere, shimmering with a pulse, with continents and oceans detailing its outer rims. Noida drops the source into Addison's palm. She marvels as it holds its shape.

"I don't understand."

Addison catches what she assumes is the alien's equivalent of a frown.

"Imagine a world so small that you could mistakenly crush it by closing your hand," the alien does what he can to explain. "This is only a small thing, representing a concept far more expansive than any single thought. Life grows. Everlasting. It develops on its own. That life learns. And it thrives. It fights for dominance. For us, *we* take responsibility for the lives of our creations. That is the Obligation. Keeping every world safe from the most severe threats in the cosmos."

"That still doesn't make any sense," Addison argues. "You create species? You settle them on worlds so they can survive and thrive? I can understand that, but . . . But if they don't turn out exactly how you want them to, you do—what? Start all over? Make a clean slate?"

"We learn from the past," Noida admits. "It isn't a clean duty. And those who commit to it are considered outcasts. They are driven to the fringes until they find reasons to keep going, despite what they're born to do."

"That explains why the others hate Adhion 'Klaka, but—" Addison pauses to think for a second. "Why start fighting amongst yourselves? There's a primer reason for it. I know there is, but I am guessing it's not tribalism. Idu called humanity unique. An accident."

"Garden worlds by themselves *can* develop sentient, intelligent lifeforms," the other revels, "but it *is* rare. Your people are walking into the crossfire between Adhion 'Klaka and Tyrann 'Akachan. Moths to a flame. Our issues aren't with humanity. Our illness lies entirely within ourselves. It's a stigma the Nomad wants to beat until it is dead."

The alien's body starts to undulate as sudden chills seep into his bones. With the entire Summerland a freezer, this forest has a remarkable warmth to it. Not to mention, it's humid. All the heat from across the ship must divert into *this* greenhouse to keep it lush and alive.

Addison's visor blows air to keep it from fogging over as the moister condenses.

"And he attacks us because he thinks we're dangerous?" Addison prods, focusing on the other's reaction.

"Attack? No, that's not—" The Architect stops as if catching his tongue before misspeaking. He looks down, then at her again. "Watch the light, Addison Kennedy. Do you see how it turns darker? A shadow is hungering from beyond the rim. Think of it as our first mistake. It infects. It consumes. Now our people fear the violence that species like yours can bring, attracting its attention. And if it's a decision between extinction and losing all life everywhere, then our choices are spent, and we must clear the timber before they spark a flame."

Addison watches as the shadow slowly emerges from the glowing blue spark, like a hand stretching across its surface. Is it alive? She can hear the screaming of billions as *it* consumes them. Only monsters from the deepest corners of her nightmares can make her shiver. And this *is* making her fingers go cold.

"And you don't see how *that* strategy works against itself?" Addison begs the question. "If violence attracts this Monster—?"

"It's what the Obligation demands," Noida repeats.

"It's flawed logic," Addison warns. "You're using the very thing that attracts it. If anything, you're contributing to its power by drawing it closer!"

The alien's expression goes soft, dumbfounded. His mouth opens to speak. He quickly closes it after nothing comes out.

"Idu said there are *five* Architects aboard this ship," Addison says. "The thing about humanity that you may not realize is that we're fast on the pickup. You can drop the charade—Adhion 'Klaka.'"

Adhion's nostril slits flare. His feathers blacken as his body relaxes.

"I am doing what I can to make sure your species can survive our first contact," he finally says. "During my time, I learned how it is possible for new life to birth in the ashes of the old. Dead civilizations fertilize the soil for those coming after."

"Where is Idu?" Addison questions, stepping forward and confronting the figure.

"Likely with Tyrann or Tjaa 'Neren," Adhion offers.

"Why isn't she here? She said—?"

"Because I confronted her," Adhion says, stopping her short.

Addison clenches her jaw. "But why is it that *you* came?" she demands.

"To explain. And to give you *that*, which I think will help you along the way," Adhion admits.

Twisting his fingers, the Architect condenses the blue orb into a stone no larger than her thumb. It first appears to her as a holographic layer that exists as outer imagery. Addison squints, realizing it's not that . . . Rather, it's a metallic containment unit for the prize inside. Ornate and delicately crafted.

Addison catches her balance and uses her free hand to touch the sphere.

"It's warm," she mutters under her breath. "What is it?"

"It's what I pulled from the ship," the Nomad explains. "It's an energy source—my civilization's very core, the Heart of the machine."

Addison's mouth gapes. Of course, the alien can't see her expression under her mask.

"It's beautiful," she says. "Why did you take it? Is this what forced you to crash?"

"Yes. It is," Adhion admits. "But I took it to force an impasse."

Addison reels back. "In what context?" she demands, saying it aggressively.

Adhion lowers his body to explain to her like she's a child. He's calmer than Addison would've thought after how Idu described him.

"Context? I am tired, Addison Kennedy. After a lifetime of service to an Obligation that thinks of me as little more than a weapon . . . Yes, tired is the word I use," Adhion answers. He measures his words, speaking with his offhand. "And I want to stop the killing. A chance for things to change for the better."

"For the better?" Addison shouts. "How is this better?! All this is because of you! Millions. Dead. Washed under the waves or buried in the rubble."

Adhion pulls back from the little blue rock, leaving its sphere in her hands.

"A better way to die than some," the Architect forbodes. Coldly. His large eyes are like miniature galaxies with a hundred-million stars in the void. On his face, there are white tattoo patterns over his smooth, charcoal skin. Adhion squints at Addison, studying her for a moment. "Take off that mask, Addison Kennedy. Let me see your face."

"That'll likely kill me," she withdraws.

Adhion lifts a free hand and lays his long fingers around the edges of Addison's helmet.

She can hear the rustling in the trees as Ibrahim's marines reposition themselves for a clear shot at the Architect if he does anything to her.

"Will it truly kill you? Or are you afraid to take it on faith?"

"Our physiology doesn't attune your ship's atmosphere," Addison explains.

"Yet I could walk outside and breathe just fine," Adhion regards her. "Call off your soldiers. Let me show you what this glass keeps you from."

Addison stares at the alien for a short while, weighing the scenario. After several heartbeats, she waves her hand at the bushes, signaling everyone to lower their weapons.

"All right," Addison swallows. "Show me."

She fully expects Vogert to chew her ass out for agreeing to this.

Adhion's fingertips tap Addison's mask and, somehow, decompresses the vacuum seals. Air filters out as her vents open, letting extraterrestrial air into the one place it should never go. She doesn't know if it's because she expects the worse or if it's her nerves, but Addison holds her breath. And her mask drops off her face.

"It's quite all right," Adhion promises. "Open your eyes. Let it in for just a moment. Breathe."

Addison does as she's instructed and . . . She can taste it . . . That air! Wintergreen.

She opens her eyes and looks around her. The forest is even more beautiful without having to see it through her visor.

The air burns into her lungs. But, instead of choking, as she'd expect . . . It brings with it a different intensity. Her pulse beats like she's downing half a dozen energy drinks in one sitting. Her muscles are supercharged, with every nuance of her body's fatigue zapping away until she exhales again.

46 | FIGHT OR FLIGHT

LIEUTENANT COLONEL ELIAS IBRAHIM
UNITED COALITION ARMED FORCES

OCTOBER 21, 2041 | 0734 HOURS

——

"What the fuck is she doing?" Ibrahim curses under his breath.

His jaw drops as the giant emerges from thin air behind Addison.

"What the damn?" Ibrahim curses louder. "How did . . . How did *he* get past the perimeter? Doctor Kennedy!" But she doesn't respond. Ibrahim tries again before surmising that she's switched off her comms unit. As for why she'd do that, he doesn't know.

He raises his rifle and centers his sights on the pair.

The Architect is eleven, maybe twelve feet tall. And when the other kneels to match Addison's height, the alien still has to look down at the woman. He's much larger than Idu's nine-foot frame. But . . . that said . . . Ibrahim notes *this* one has a particular weight about him.

Every detail, as Addison described—delicate bird-like features, with intricate colors mixing with their white face tattoos and reflective feather bristles. He's not one of the grey men so popularized in the mid-1940s. No. There's a hard shell under that thin skin, Ibrahim expects.

"Sergeant Warden! Move your team to the far side," Ibrahim orders.

"Copy that," Warden responds. "On the move! Standby."

"Everyone else . . . Cover them," he continues. "Keep your sights on the alien. Prepare to retrieve our girl if he shows hostile intent."

Indicators flash throughout the jungle, giving Ibrahim acknowledgments to his orders.

They're in a fragile predicament. Ibrahim has nothing but his training from High Castle to fall back on in this situation. Idu isn't here. And the Architect talking to Addison Kennedy isn't *her*. Instead, he's a big one. A warrior? Maybe. Or maybe he's the one who saved Ibrahim's team at the Central Spire?

Ibrahim aims his crosshairs over the alien's head, feeling the curve on his weapon's trigger.

Addison motions everybody to stand down, surprising him.

The woman lowers her arms, pausing as the Architect's fingers find the edges of her mask.

Her helmet unlocks with air wheezing from its seals. And the alien pulls her visor free of its bed.

Ibrahim jerks.

He jumps to his feet, ready to charge into the clearing while ordering "weapon's free" on the alien. Instead, Ibrahim shuts his mouth. It's not his place. Not yet. He doesn't need to escalate matters if he doesn't need to. Addison is already in enough danger. A firefight only risks hitting *her* as much as the giant.

"Let it go," Ibrahim clears his throat.

Vogert comes running to him from the bushes. Ibrahim stares as the man approaches.

"Don't interfere," Ibrahim warns him.

"Colonel, what are—? He's taken off her mask!" Vogert expresses vehemently. "The contamination? It will kill her like it did Arthur's expedition!"

"She's told us to stand down," Ibrahim states. "I don't agree, but this is on her for now."

"You're supposed to protect her!"

"I *am* protecting her!" Ibrahim shouts back, yanking Vogert closer in a dominant flourish. "That alien can easily snap her neck before we get a chance to move. The safest thing is to wait and see what happens. We better hope your gene therapy does its job. But I don't know."

Ibrahim feels Vogert's hard stare through the other's visor tint.

The man closes his fist. Ibrahim understands the intent.

"Stand down," Ibrahim conveys, emphasizing his words. "I don't like it, but I have to trust her on this. You, more than anyone, should know, doc. Go on standby. And wait for *my* order to move."

Vogert's head falls for a moment. He reluctantly nods accepting to Ibrahim's truce. He then proceeds to turn to the clearing to watch the disaster unfold.

"Doctor Zhu—" Ibrahim continues. "Can you please begin an atmospheric scan to see what the air is like in this damnable jungle?"

"What are you looking for, Lieutenant Colonel?" the woman asks over their short-wave comms, static flaring briefly.

"I'm just curious," he justifies. "These plants . . . I'm wondering if they can breathe under Earth-based conditions. Or if they need a unique ecosystem to survive."

"Like what we see in this greenhouse?"

"Maybe? I don't know. That's why I'm asking you."

Zhu only pauses after he makes the request. Ibrahim doesn't know if that's a good thing or not. An indication of the woman's fascination with the inquiry? Or maybe, she's amused. It's hard for him to tell without reading her body language.

"You're beginning to sound like a . . . What's the word? I can't think . . . Egghead? That's it," Zhu testifies. "You sound like an egghead, Colonel Ibrahim."

Ibrahim glances at Vogert, who doesn't break in with a witty comment.

However, the man *does* return another look at the Colonel—a slight tilting of the head. Gratification?

"And I want *you* to record her findings, Doctor Vogert," Ibrahim orders. "Include it with your report after Addison's medical exam."

"Shouldn't that information be included in *your* mission report?" Vogert questions.

"I am asking you to do it," Ibrahim urges. He chooses not to give the man his complete thoughts.

"Okay," Vogert sighs. "I'll make a copy when we get back."

"Do it now," Ibrahim suggests. "Just in case something happens along the way."

With only a moment for the realization to set in, Vogert nods and runs into the bushes toward Doctor Zhu's last known position. Ibrahim's glad he didn't have to explain *why* to the man. Safer that way. Once this operation is over and the crisis on the mainland abates, the governments will soak their reports into vats of black ink.

"Historians will have a hell of a time piecing the details together from the scraps," Ibrahim whispers.

"—Colonel Ibrahim?" Addison Kennedy hails over their local channel.

"I read you, Doctor Kennedy," Ibrahim returns. "Barely. What's going on? You turned off your radio."

A steady whine comes from her suit's transmitter.

"I wanted to talk to him without interruption," she explains. "He wants you to show yourselves. He won't hurt anybody."

Ibrahim's jaw clenches.

"What?" he starts. "You want *us* to walk into the open?"

"If you wouldn't mind," Addison urges. "Trust me. Please."

"You've not done much to earn more trust," Ibrahim warns her. "Why don't you tell me why? Count it as a favor."

There's a long pause on the comms. Ibrahim can hear Addison's heavy breathing on the other end, fighting to conjure the words she needs to convince him. Ibrahim told Vogert that he needed to trust Addison. Now he needs to *show* his marines that she deserves that trust by letting her explain.

"What am I holding, anyway?" Addison inquires to the bird-like alien.

She turns the metallic sphere in her hands. It's rough, like a rock, but in her mind, it isn't anything but an ornate egg, with patterns sculpted with a fine laser scalpel. And there's no weight to it . . . Nothing to make her believe she is holding something in her palms.

It's as if she's holding a lightbulb.

"I have already told you," Adhion shakes his head.

"No. I mean . . . What do you want me to *do* with it?" Addison asks. "Why give it to me?"

"Think of it as a gift. A fire that warms you in the coldest winters," Adhion explains. "Something to light up the dark places in the galaxy where nobody wants to go. I will admit . . . I *will* need it back once you're done with it, Addison Kennedy. Study it. Learn what you can from it."

"And the others are okay with us having this?"

Adhion gives off what Addison guesses is an amusing hum.

"Most certainly not," he admits. "I suspect Idu has told you a bit about me? My role in the Obligation? How I've wiped out entire populations?"

"She's told me that much," Addison swallows. "Yeah."

"Did she also tell you *why* that duty is necessary in our esteemed order?"

Addison pauses to think back on the encounter with Idu in her tent.

"She was less open about that," Addison tells him.

Adhion nods and rises to his full height, waving at the trees encompassing the greenhouse.

"Our history is the history of the galaxy," Adhion explains. "We started not unlike humanity. And our homeworld? We call it . . . What do we call it? Vastur'suss? I think."

"You don't know?"

"I have only heard stories about it, Addison Kennedy," Adhion quiets. "Thinly spread are we these days. Distant."

"Space jockeys," Addison quotes.

Adhion tilts his head at her puzzlingly.

"It's nothing. Continue," Addison urges.

"In short—my chord, what you'd call a caste, are the ones to fix the mistakes of those who author life from its earliest development," Adhion dotes. He speaks as if he's reciting a dusty tome. "Or until we can let that life grow unabated. Free. Unburdened."

"Life grows," Addison adds. "People learn. They build. They advance, always wanting to climb out of the dirt."

"My thoughts to the very note," Adhion rides. Proudly. "We construct the Shards of Obligation—warships to their essence—to reset a world, correcting mishaps and perceived aberrations. When a species an Arkkitect creates has advanced to where it can threaten us, the universe holds its breath to see how we react. Those like Tjaa, or Dhun, or Tyrann 'Akachan? They don't see the pain of ordering those like *me* to enact our final protocol."

"So, they send you as the euthanizer," Addison realizes. "They've made you a killer?"

"I was born for it," Adhion accepts, his cheeks tightening with a flinch, unwillingly letting the words off his tongue. "The original chord emerged from our first murderers—the only murderers the Arkkitects ever knew. It was a clever idea. Their punishment? Now a duty. And their offspring endure the same labels, no matter how hard we try to undo our parents' crimes. Even after generations, it's a stain, unable to wash away. Only a few can distinguish between my forbearers and what I am now."

Addison looks up at the giant with water in her eyes. His voice is softer. Sincere. Quivering.

"Help me understand this," Addison weighs. "You're born into a caste that forces you to wipe out populations. I get that part. And that you've probably done it your entire life. But then, why—?"

"Why haven't I done anything to stop it?" Adhion quandaries, beating her to the question. "Look around you, Addison Kennedy. What do you think I am doing? Everything I've done? I am finally taking a stand against my station."

Addison swallows as she processes the information.

"You don't like what you do," she states.

The eleven-foot alien lets his shoulders drop. "Just because I am good at my role doesn't mean I enjoy it," Adhion utters. "An individual can only repress so much violence before it makes them sick. And your people are now dying as a consequence. For me, and the decisions I made. There is no comfort I can offer to make it right."

Addison exhales. She now understands. Maybe.

"Poor thing," is all Addison can think to say.

Adhion's extruding colors suddenly go pale and fade. He's unable to maintain the vibrancy of his feathers.

Addison only shakes her head.

She lets so many thoughts and questions flow through her like a wave. Addison wants to ask . . . She *needs* to ask. But she suspects that the Nomad— Adhion 'Klaka—making his presence known *now* doesn't have anything to do with sating her curiosity.

Adhion stares into the forest's underbrush.

"How many warriors travel with you?" he suddenly shifts focus.

"A whole company," Addison answers. The other's expression farrows. And she realizes he's unfamiliar with the term. "Up to two hundred rifles. And hundreds more supporting the march. It's taken a lot to make this appointment happen."

Adhion shudders as if a chill suddenly crept into his bones.

"May I see them?" he asks. "All of them? Or, at the very least, those with us presently?"

Addison steps back, surprised. Her mouth shudders, struggling to find the right words until she asks, "Why?"

The Nomad burrs pleasantly before raising his palm to reassure her. "I am curious," he says. "They are in danger because of me."

Addison cautiously nods. "If you're sure," she says.

"I know it requires trust to ask, but—"

"Yeah," Addison cuts him off, "and you didn't start on a very strong footing. Lying about your name."

"I did. For my safety," Adhion defends. "You wanted to meet with Idu 'Smeora on her terms, but she's not the one coming. *His* name is Dhun 'Ancod—the one who saved your people at the hangar's tower when they set off a test Fragment I reprogramed and left to gather dust."

"Test Fragment? So, you're—? It was you," she shudders. "Why?"

Adhion responds with a black frown. "The same reason your soldiers are with you," he admits. "I needed an army if I were to survive long enough to make a statement. And the Varmajalkavaen can only serve their duties to the other four. Officially."

Addison stares at him intensely. She doesn't know if she should slap the bastard or run away with the little blue spark in her hands. After what *he's* done to her crew aboard this ship? Not to mention the countless millions washed under the waves when he crashed the dreadnaught into the ocean, openly dragging *her* people into his dispute. Adhion 'Klaka deserves no less than her utter ire.

Yet, as she looks at the white markings on his face, wanting to hate him, Addison can't work up the emotion. She shortens her breath and holds it there, clenching her jaw to work up to that point, but the fire sizzles out like a candle in a windstorm.

Addison's known to sequester her work and personal beliefs to get her jobs done. She doesn't know how yet, but this is different. The Nomad's vendetta against his people is severe but, in his own words, results from him fighting against what he's already done. His Obligation. Whatever that means.

"What's another million lives in a graveyard of trillions?" Addison weighs under her breath.

It isn't something she can forgive. Nor *should* she ignore it.

Nevertheless, as Adhion's bristles drop, he appears genuine. Even if the translator Idu had given her has some distortion, she can hear it in his voice.

"Can you hear me, Colonel Ibrahim?" Addison sends out the request.

"I read you, Doctor Kennedy," Ibrahim acknowledges. "Barely. What's going on? You turned off your radio."

"I wanted to talk to him without interruption," she admits. "He wants you to show yourselves. He won't hurt anybody."

There's a long pause on the other end.

"Wait," Colonel Ibrahim breaks. "You want *us* to walk into the open?"

"If you wouldn't mind," Addison urges. "Trust me. Please."

"You've not done much to earn more trust," Ibrahim argues. "How about you tell me why? Count it as a favor."

Addison fights for the words, thinking quickly. In the end, maybe a direct answer is best.

"He's curious about us," Addison explains. "Says he wants to see the measure of the people who've taken on the challenges this ship has thrown their way."

Ibrahim doesn't answer right away. A whole minute passes.

"Everybody . . . Stand down," the Colonel sighs. "Sergeant Warden—take your command and run another sweep on the perimeter. I don't want those animals getting through again. Everyone else will take five steps into the clearing. That's an order. If this alien wants us to put on a show, let's give the bastard one. Peacefully. Weapons holstered."

One hundred fifty marines and their four scientists step out of hiding in the bushes. Their numbers fill the clearing's edge.

Adhion burrs as if surprised. "Interesting," the alien mutters under his breath.

Addison notices his eyes scanning each soldier as they walk into the open.

"Satisfied?" Addison demands.

"It's not so much a matter of satisfaction, rather . . . professional inclination," Adhion offers. "Your people are part of this battle I started. I want to make sure they can handle what may be coming next for them."

Adhion hums again for a moment. Quietly. The tune releases faintly from his mouth, soothing Addison briefly as she hears it.

"What will you do now?" Addison asks.

Adhion's tune stops. He kneels to Addison again, comfortably squeezing her shoulder in genuine admiration.

"I must confront the Trident at the Entrychamber," he warns.

"And what will happen when you do?"

The alien taps a finger on his face that likely has a clearer meaning to his people. Addison can only figure it means something akin to: "I don't know. But I will do it anyway to see what happens." Oddly enough, the voice saying that in her head has a distinctly nonchalant accent.

"Doctor Kennedy?" Ibrahim nudges. "Are you done? I prefer if we start pulling back."

Addison gives a thumbs-up in the Colonel's general direction.

Adhion looks at her with bright, widening eyes.

"They want me to go," she says.

"You needn't my permission," the other says. Adhion lets her step away for a moment before catching her arm. He raises a finger to the tattoos on his forehead. "Remember—that is a fire you're holding in your hands, Addison Kennedy. A fire burns when mishandled. Remain steady. Vigilance is key."

Addison tightens her grip on the metallic orb he's given her. "I'll keep it safe," she promises.

"Deeds are more determinate than words," Adhion 'Klaka concludes. "And greed has a way of unmasking our best intentions."

The Architect releases his grip on her arm. She can hear his humming until he disappears into the dark space between the massive trees filling the greenhouse's expanse. Addison goes to regroup with Colonel Ibrahim and the others.

48 | WE'RE CLEAR

SERGEANT MAJOR OLIVIA WARDEN
UNITED COALITION ARMED FORCES

OCTOBER 21, 2041 | 0745 HOURS

===

Warden scans the forward area. She's painfully aware of how vulnerable they are in this underbrush. Leafy branches repeatedly scrape against her faceplate. Every time she pushes one aside, the given branch rebounds, making her want to take a machete to the whole damn jungle.

A small coyote-like creature runs across her squad's line of sight.

Warden aims at the creature as it stops, squealing loudly before jumping off the trail, joined by a half-dozen others. An entire pack. Or a family.

She doesn't know.

"Careful," she warns. "Fauna cutting through."

Warden gestures to let everybody know to hold their fire.

"Eerily familiar," Private Fletcher comments next to her.

"Ditto," Warden agrees. "Keep an eye on our flanks. Don't let them get around us. They aren't the biggest things in this mess."

She leads her squad onward.

Warden hates that she doesn't know if any more giants are lurking around. She opens her comms.

"Squad leaders," Warden calls to attention. "Report."

They return with whispering tones and heavy breathing.

"Nothing but the runaway runts, Sergeant Major," Sergeant Hammon replies.

"All quiet here," Sergeant Mannering adds.

"Got zilch," Corporal Tanner confirms.

"I think a mouse tried to run up my leg," Corporal Arno finishes. "Otherwise. I got nothing."

"Colonel Ibrahim," Warden diverts. "We're in the clear for now. Ready to stow this party and get home."

"Understood, Sergeant Major," Ibrahim responds with a nearly out-of-character tone. "Return to the clearing for now. I'm talking to Doctor Kennedy."

Warden can feel her face tighten at his words.

"Is it anything you can say over the comms, sir?" Warden urges.

The last thing she wants is to walk into Ibrahim's shouting match with Addison Kennedy if she can avoid it.

"I've reset your waypoint," Ibrahim states without registering her question.

"I . . . Yes, sir," she murmurs loud enough for her microphone to pick it up.

Warden signals her unit to reverse course and return to the main group. They didn't go very far. Still, it'd be easy to get lost inside this vegetation if they hadn't stuck flag markers in the dirt as they made their initial rounds. With the interference shorting out their positional tracking from Overlook Station, it's all they can do.

Ibrahim's busy chewing out Doctor Kennedy when Warden's team arrives. Addison stares at him as he shouts, nodding with remarkable patience. Warden stops next to Doctor Vogert, who's watching the ordeal unfold. Or he's waiting for *his* chance to yell at the lady.

Colonel Ibrahim's head shifts to Warden for a moment. It's almost indiscernible. But she's familiar enough with his body language in this armor to read the subtlety. Years of training together in the cramped quarters of an orbital station can do that to people.

"I understand, Colonel," Addison breathlessly agrees. "I promise you. It won't. Here you go."

She offers him the metallic orb the giant had given her.

"It's warm," Ibrahim remarks.

"I said the same," Addison smirks.

She reinstalls her suit's mask. Her external indicators turn on. Warden can hear the air whirring through her suit's filtration system.

Ibrahim turns to Warden, tensing his shoulders.

"Sergeant Major—that wasn't the Architect we came to meet, but I'm not letting the eggheads stick around. We're going back to figure out what this is," Ibrahim says, showing off the artifact pressed between his thumb and index finger. "Let's maintain our presence. Set up lookouts in the trees and organize sentries along the perimeter."

"Understood, sir," Warden acknowledges.

"We're reportedly waiting on a certain Dhun 'Ancod to show up now," Ibrahim continues. "Idu's a no-show."

Warden narrows her gaze at him, although he doesn't acutely notice.

"And you want me to act as the intermediary?" Warden begs the question.

Addison walks up and activates Warden's wrist-mounted computer. "I'll link your suit's translation software to the cipher," the woman says, keying a sequence into Warden's interface. "It should let you read what the giant is saying on your screen."

"Any derogatory terms I should avoid using?" Warden snarks at Addison.

"Just don't shoot first," Addison warns. "It might not end well for your troops."

"I'll see what I can do about that," Warden scoffs.

"We'll maintain a lifeline for you," Ibrahim confirms.

He types a message into his pad and sends it out for everyone to see. Warden reads the notification on her screen:

OPERATIONAL COMMAND TRANSFER TO
SGTMAJ. OLIVIA WARDEN

Ibrahim looks at Addison Kennedy and her team, who returns his attention with a stare-down of their own.

"Understood, sir," Warden accepts, but she doesn't like it.

This place has a lot of dangers they've yet to document. Warden's theory supposes the likely reason they've mostly remained unbothered by the local wildlife is their numbers. Predators like the giant cat-like creature that came prowling will make their presence more known.

With that, she watches as Ibrahim departs with his squad and the science team, leaving most of their troops with Warden in her new role as mission leader.

"Since when do soldiers make good diplomats?" she questions.

Warden *does* understand the situation's necessity, however. Whatever the metallic sphere is, whatever it does, they'll need the eggheads back at base to do what they do and get some answers from it, if *that* is even possible. But a little blue rock isn't why they're on this ship. And the politicians won't accept *it* as justification while still dragging bodies out of the rubble.

"Sergeant Major?" Corporal Greene asks, her team gathering at the center platform. "Your orders, ma'am?"

Warden rolls her neck to hear the bones crack.

"Form a ring around the area, as we had it," Warden orders. "Groups of three. Keep each unit ten meters apart. Respond to calls if anyone comes under attack. We're not going to have the same advantages as we've had with the Colonel playing lapdog."

Everyone flashes their acknowledgments using their helmets' external lights. They spread out, squad leaders taking positions along the defensive ring that Warden hopes is good enough to intercept anything larger than a house cat. It likely won't, but she'll have to accept that. Her troops aren't a fisherman's net. There'll be holes large enough for creatures to bypass her patrols entirely, but that's not the point she wants to make.

"We're not staying for the animals in this . . . jungle park," Warden internalizes, "if that's the best way to describe it."

No. The giants are running irrespectively late for their appointment. And the one that did show up? Just some asshole that caused this whole disaster.

Warden will now act as the hard-ass secretary at the front desk, ready to snuff out any notion of rescheduling.

49 | PROGRESS HERE, CHAOS THERE

MALAKAI ADONIS, DIRECTOR OF OPERATIONS
EPIMETHEUS PROJECT

OCTOBER 21, 2041 | 1230 HOURS

===

He walks into the Control Room with a certain energy to his step. Ibrahim and his team have made it to the rendezvous point. Athena just told him as he came out of a security briefing. He lets out his breath and tenses his shoulders.

"Are you all right, Doctor Adonis?" a staffer asks.

Malakai looks at him, finding it difficult to focus on anyone. His eyes tear up the more he stays awake.

"Quite fine," he lies, feeling the tension in his jaw loosen.

For him, it's been a long twenty-four hours. He's eager to get it done.

"Understood," the man agrees. "Priority assets are waiting for extraction at the rally point. We're pulling units back from Station-Zero-Four to cover them, but the area's gone quiet in the last few hours. Wolfden is unhappy. He keeps calling me a 'dunderhead' and wants to send help his way after extraction."

Malakai reads the control board. He keys in a set of commands that gives him relative positional data from the Overlook.

"That sounds like him," Malakai acknowledges. "How recent is the falloff?"

The staffer brings up a program on his screen.

"Roughly at eight hundred hours—the last attack at the station ended, but no casualties," the other says. "Fragments appeared at the perimeter and left as suddenly."

Malakai raises an eyebrow. "They just left?" he repeats.

"According to the report, our guys didn't even get a shot off. Wolfden is looking into it."

"I doubt an investigation will go anywhere," Malakai confides. "Given the situation."

He stands there for a moment, working the puzzle through his head. It's an unlikely coincidence. For the drones to abandon their attacks after Addison is said to have met with this Adhion 'Klaka? He doesn't understand it. And if this Architect is the one who's controlling the damn things? Malakai can't help but question the alien's reason.

"We'll keep the lifeline pumping," the other states into the microphone. He closes the channel before turning to his boss. "Is there anything else you need, sir?"

Malakai shakes his head. "Keep me in the loop," he says.

He glances at his pad and notices some two hundred new reports have come in at the last minute. He opens those at the top and reads them—experiment results, combat unit stats, costs, updates to field manuals needing approval. Malakai sighs.

With that last one, Malakai signs and forwards it immediately.

Given the rising death tolls, a new situation is developing at home. Politicians need a backup justification in saying, "This is why so many men and women are dying, and we didn't go to war without a plan." Whether it's right to admit it or not, that's the reality. And it beats down on Malakai whenever he watches the broadcasts.

He'll end up the scapegoat if he doesn't play everything right. They'll blame him for the crash, the tidal wave, and the food shortages. He knows they will. It's what they do.

"I'm only trying to fix things," he murmurs.

Malakai makes his way across the room to a utility workstation.

Another operations report pops to the top of his list. He scrolls to highlight it.

"Athena?" Malakai asks over comms.

"Yes, oh, Captain?" she answers.

"This last one didn't come from you," he notes. "I've received it directly. Who else has my line?"

Athena pauses as she runs a diagnostic. Only for a moment, though.

"Lieutenant Colonel Elias Ibrahim," Athena says quietly, "and Doctor Kennedy. Their message is for your eyes only, according to the subject line. I can't seem to open it. Somebody has embedded it with a lock that requires a specific neural chain."

"Ava . . . Damn that woman," Malakai states, recalling the woman's tendency to play fast and loose with protocols.

He bounces the thought in his head for a second, chewing on his tongue. It's enough of a habit that Athena quickly picks up on it.

"You're wondering why they've decided not to use official channels to send this report," the AI notions.

Malakai turns to a nearby sensor. He knows Athena uses it to read his body language.

"I am," he confirms. "Addison helped set up the rules. We have enough problems with people leaking data outside the network. I don't need them pulling that same bullshit."

"Maybe they're wondering how your family is holding up?" Athena weighs.

He can't tell if she's asking genuinely or if it's another of her jokes.

"I doubt it," Malakai refutes, moving past the idea entirely. "And that's in poor taste."

"On a more serious note, then—maybe it's sensitive data they don't want anybody else to see," Athena conjures. "You've said it best, Doctor Adonis. Addison Kennedy helped create the system. She'd have put in a backdoor to transfer data if she thought it was necessary."

"And given the nature of what we're doing, necessitating *that* was always pretty high," Malakai accepts. "I'll take it, but I don't like it."

"Much like I don't like living as a bodiless voice," Athena adds. "Doesn't mean I don't have hands."

"Don't you think it odd that Colonel Ibrahim and Addison suddenly find commonality?

"They have more in common than you'd expect," Athena suggests. "Her father *is* an officer in the Admiralty."

Malakai peels back and slumps his shoulders. Of course, Athena is right. He isn't afraid to admit that. Addison *is* a scientist. And she's her father's daughter—a soldier.

He needs to remind himself that she knows what she's doing.

Malakai looks at those across the Control Room. Everybody's busy going about their duties, doing their part to keep their heads above water. Nobody's looking at him. Their eyes are on their screens, their fingers on consoles, speaking into headsets. They're recording data and sending info to hull-side teams. Weeks into the mission now, and everyone has their routines.

Malakai keys his pad and opens the message Ibrahim and Addison had sent.

What makes up its contents is a surprise to him. "A photo?" he murmurs.

It's a low-grade image from a helmet feed, showing a blue rock inside an ornate metal sphere.

Malakai quickly closes the image and walks out of the room quietly.

"Where are you going, Doctor Adonis?" Athena asks.

"I don't know," Malakai replies. "To find some privacy. Away from everybody."

"I believe 'away from everybody' is what the word 'privacy' means," Athena snarks. "There's an empty broom closet three doors to your left."

Malakai stops. "You have sensors in the mop rooms now?"

Athena hesitates. "Nooooo," she replies in a guilty tone, not even attempting to hide it.

Malakai shakes his head and then coughs. He enters the closet and shuts the door, again bringing up the image on his wrist-pad and scales it up the best he can.

"That's unusual," he mutters. He waits in the dark, staring at the picture of the metallic sphere. "Looks like a rock, but it isn't . . . it's not solid. Energy? Maybe a source? Unique. From the Architects . . . A gift? But why to us?"

"Doctor?" Athena chimes. "You're talking to yourself."

Malakai upturns his eyes. "I'm trying to work this through my head," he says.

"Which explains why you wanted to be alone."

"Explain this to me," he vocally debates. "Why'd they send only an image without describing what I'm looking at?"

"Maybe to give you a heads up on what to expect?" Athena poses the question as a possible answer. "Or to avoid a data breach."

"And my direct line allows us to avoid an open channel that other parties could potentially hijack," Malakai proposes.

"Quite right," Athena concludes.

Malakai inhales until his lungs strain. He presses his back against the closet door.

"Let's set up a lab space for a new project. Observation deck," Malakai commands. "The sooner we get it done, the better. Learn what *it* is and how we can utilize it."

"Does this mean you're finally ready to come out of the closet?" Athena laughs, making another jab.

"You're laying it on thick," Malakai sighs. "You know that?"

"It makes our conversations more interesting. You're just my unwitting victim," Athena expresses, a palpable joy in her mechanical voice. "I'll get the ball rolling on that lab for you, Doctor Adonis. In the meantime, there's still a while before Addison Kennedy and her team touch down."

"That's fine," he says, exhausted. "Thank you."

Once the expedition team hits the landing pad, Malakai will have a news conference scheduled for live coverage. He'll need to write a speech for the occasion, as it's the first major "official" announcement in weeks. It's his chance to inform the general public about the ongoing situation and win some hearts and minds in his favor.

Malakai stares at the image of the little blue sphere for several more minutes.

He blinks, shutting off the pad as he walks out the door, straightening his collar as he enters the hallway.

Malakai goes to his office adjacent to the Control Room, calculating how best to say the words the world needs to hear. He can feel his throat clogging as he weighs a few practiced phrases. Good news . . . Only ever tell the cameras the good news. Leave the bad for casualty reports and council meetings.

Athena rings his earpiece again.

"Yes?" Malakai answers.

"We have an airlift coming into our airspace," Athena buzzes.

"An airlift? Can't be our team already?"

"It isn't," Athena explains. "High-profile guests from the continent."

"High-profile?"

"Members of the Congressional Oversight Committee," Athena denotes.
"Which suggests—?"

"Senator Holland," Malakai grumbles.

"Among others," Athena confirms. "A number of his caucus."

"Damn," Malakai curses. "Okay, fine . . . Assign a space for the Committee's
transport. Prepare a security detail."

"Already done," Athena says. "Also. Your blood pressure has spiked."

"I noticed," Malakai feigns surprise, digging his nails into the edge of
his desk as he sits down.

WORK AT HAND | 50

RYAN VOGERT, CHIEF MEDICAL OFFICER
EPIMETHEUS PROJECT

OCTOBER 21, 2041 | 1400 HOURS

———

Vogert rides next to Addison on their approach to Mount Olympus. High winds cause the V-91 to tilt, forcing him to grip the safety harness until his knuckles go white. It doesn't help that water comes pouring through the rear loading ramp as they begin their descent.

He only hopes he doesn't fall out of his seat before their wheels hit the tarmac.

The dreadnaught shrinks the farther they go, now miles in the air off its starboard side. Vogert still can't look at the ship without the blood draining from his face. He's one man standing on the back of gods and titans. Does humanity stand a chance? Their nearest competitors can build cities in the sky and send them flying through space as easily as breathing.

"It's amazing," he exhales.

Vogert sucks in his gut and lowers his shoulders.

As the aircraft touches down on the landing pad, Vogert steers his attention to their reception.

"Looks like we've got a crowd," Vogert warns.

Colonel Ibrahim leans forward for a better view.

"A crowd with cameras," the man says, detaching his harness from the chute rails.

"World news media clustered together," Leighton follows. "Cordoned off by OverSec in their battle reds."

"Malakai's on the walkway," Ava adds.

"Flanked by folks who don't know how to dress for the weather," Addison finishes.

Vogert scoffs. "Primsuits," he says, counting heads.

"Four men, five women," Ibrahim says aloud. "I know their faces. Ultra-capitalists."

Vogert hums as the aircraft levels with the crowd. The politicians are prim and proper to the heels, their expensive coats getting soaked, their faces reflecting the red of the platform's landing beacons. Every one of them wears a dark scowl, certainly unprepared for the rain and the freezing temperatures.

Or worse, they were misinformed about the conditions.

Either way, they're not dressed for an extended stay. Nor a short one.

He feels the V-91 jerk hard as it settles on the tarmac.

The aircraft's interior lights turn green, indicating they're now secure on the pad and that it's safe to disembark.

Vogert lifts his body off the seat, only to fall back down when his knees buckle.

The ramp that leads into the compartment locks into place. Colonel Ibrahim is the first to step off, spinning around to address the crew.

"Welcome to fame and glory at the ass-end of the world!" Ibrahim shouts over the rain. "Don't engage with the guests, and do not answer their questions. Malakai can pick up the pieces. I order everyone to get inside and get warm. Dismissed."

His marines respond with a feeble, "Yes, sir!" They grab their rucksacks and file outside onto the landing pad.

Ibrahim stays in place for a moment longer. He turns over the metallic sphere Adhion 'Klaka had given to Addison in his palms.

The man doesn't look at it, only feeling its ridges and intricate patterns, studying the crowd as the others disembark.

Vogert can still hear Leighton and Ava bicker over statistics as they step out after the marines. He doesn't see the point in arguing until they're inside, but such seems their way. Addison remains disquieted. Unmoving. She taps her foot in a nervous tick, anxious to get off the ramp and back to work. After they've settled, Vogert will oversee their physical examinations—for those who've gone into the alien ship and returned.

Colonel Ibrahim ordered Vogert to clear Addison's physical as soon as possible. And he agreed. If only to protect her against rumors about what happened during the mission. Should word get out and the message spreads that the Project's leading scientists can't handle the stress? It could end more than her career.

"I can already see the headlines," Vogert thickly sighs. "And I wouldn't know what to do if the news breaks."

He looks at Doctor Zhu Yunwen on the far end of the compartment. Away from the others.

Vogert has kept a close eye on the woman throughout their return trip. In his professional capacity, he takes note of abnormal signs of stress in personnel after tense missions. Yunwen hasn't consolidated her breathing as she should, which he expects from anyone returning from the field. Anything to calm down—stretching, napping, playing music . . . But *she* hasn't done any of it.

Studying her tendencies, Doctor Zhu seems tenser now than when she had to dodge thickets in the ship's biosphere.

Without her helmet hiding her features, Vogert notices a wariness—lines on her cheeks, shadows under her eyes.

She locks her stare on the relic in Colonel Ibrahim's hands.

"Very unusual," Vogert whispers.

"What did you say?" Leighton asks.

Vogert flinches. "It's nothing," he returns, adding pressure to relieve a dull pain in his neck.

Whatever the case, it's not a common physical or psychological reaction most people exhibit after what they've gone through. Although, Vogert will have to push his worry for her to the back of his mind for now. He can schedule full groundwork for Doctor Zhu when he gets inside. That's if he can convince her mender to a checkup.

His priority is to examine those he *can* and clear Addison for return to active duty. The fact she took off her mask while inside the ship might've caused permanent damage. It was the dumbest thing she could've done.

And if she insists on returning to work beforehand, Vogert will happily assign a guard to keep an eye on her.

OverSec troopers in their red-white armor marshal them across the platform once they're off the exit ramp. Vogert dances with the others as he dodges the white camera flashes like lightning strikes in the storm. Vogert fights to stay upright. He slides into the oil rig's massive structure, the exhaustion hitting him now too hard to ignore.

It doesn't take long before Vogert finds his way into the oil rig's medical wing. He's the first to go through a series of tests to determine any negative side effects from his time spent on the dreadnaught. Luckily, it's reasonably simple bloodwork and physical assessments, none of which require much time. An hour later, he's washing his hands in the sink, slipping on his scrubs, and joining the others in screening the rest of the team.

Vogert okays a trio of marines that accompanied them back for duty. Then, he treats some minor injuries for two more as he rounds out a second hour.

Addison walks in after her mandatory rest period.

"You're late," Vogert scolds her.

"Bite me," Addison scoffs.

Vogert lets out a pitched laugh. "Come on. I've warded off a section for privacy," he details.

He leads her to an area secluded from the main floor.

"Comfortable," Addison comments.

Ryan quickly washes his hands again and puts on a fresh pair of gloves.

"Take a seat. How are you feeling?" Vogert asks. He begins checking for abnormalities in Addison's throat. "Feel any pain? Discomfort? Blurry vision?"

"You're not worried about my eyesight, are you?" Addison questions, knowing the answer.

Vogert frowns. "I'm just making sure you're okay. What happened in there was—"

"Irresponsible?" Addison poses. He checks her pupils, then readies a syringe for routine bloodwork.

It's not so much her physical condition that worries him.

"That's one way I think Colonel Ibrahim would put it," Vogert describes. "Downright reckless is my preferred verbiage. But I want to hear you say it . . . What happened?" He measures her pulse as she answers, keeping her calm. As she speaks, Vogert watches Addison's facial expressions more than he does the monitor.

"I was . . . Somewhere else," Addison tries to explain. "It's like I was in a dream. I was there, but I wasn't. I saw a planet . . . Not ours. Dead. Sandy. Dark. Then . . . Color? Everything was so vivid. Like I was standing there, unable to move." Her body temperature drops a degree.

"You weren't. I can promise you that," Vogert exhales, itching his nose with his sleeve. Inside his hardsuit, it drove him crazy not being able to scratch.

"But it still felt real," Addison admits.

Vogert frowns as he watches her pupil dilate, not looking away from him.

He marks up her chart as they continue, paying attention to how she answers his questions rather than the answers themselves.

"Okay," Vogert says, letting out a sigh. "Now for the fun part. Nerve and reflexes. I'm going to hit you with this hammer."

"Oh, doctor. You wouldn't hit a girl now, would you?" Addison laughs as she makes a funny.

Vogert smirks.

"Only time will tell if the event caused a dramatic shift in personality," Vogert exclaims. "We've had some interesting cases in soldiers who've suffered breaches while on the ship." He checks her soft spots and response time. "Everything's good so far." He mouths the word, "Again," before moving on.

"When do we get to the part where I drop my pants?" Addison winks. Although impatient, it's a good sign she's joking with him.

"It's not that kind of exam," Vogert dismisses, noting her agitation. "We're only checking for anything that shouldn't be there."

"I knew that alien should've used a condom," Addison crassly mocks. "Do you think it's too late?"

Vogert rubs his brow with his forearm, wiping off the sweat.

"Making stupid-ass jokes in a serious situation? Check," Vogert quips. He feigns making another mark on his checklist. "This is your health we're talking about, Addison. We don't understand how the prolonged effects can appear in individuals. I need to chart potential causes and effects."

"Right. Arthur died a week after his exposure," Addison returns.

"At least he didn't let an Architect remove his rebreather," Vogert bites. "As far as we know, what killed his team could also be killing you. So, I'll ask that you treat this as seriously as you should. You're a Field Director, Addison. Not a lab technician."

Addison's expression quickly darkens. "Don't you think I know that?" she questions. "I don't know what happened—only that it did. It was stupid. Irresponsible. But I'd rather not wait to die flat on a table if I can still do my job."

"That's not your call to make," Vogert argues.

"It damn well should be!" Addison shouts.

Vogert blinks startlingly. He can't say he's ever seen or heard the woman raise her voice to anyone. A heartbeat passes before she realizes this, taking several deep breaths to calm her nerves until she looks him in the eyes again.

He completes her physical in awkward silence. Nothing appears immediately wrong with her. "For now," Vogert mouths. This past week, he understands enough about how the dreadnaught treats its victims to know what to expect when issues eventually show themselves.

Vogert hands her wrapped garments to let Addison walk across the room without showing her stubborn ass.

"Put these on," Vogert orders her. "We're going to the scanner for a closer look. Your externals are in reasonable condition. I want to check your lungs next. See how they're doing."

"What are you expecting to find?"

"Expecting? No. I'm hoping *not* to find abnormal growths," Vogert admits.

"Like cancer? Should I be worried?" Addison asks, a pitching crack in her voice. Genuine fear.

Vogert bites his tongue and gives himself an extra moment to think.

"That's what we're screening everybody to find out," he says. "Also, why we've each undergone the gene therapy. In case this happened, and one of us got exposed. And you were! Now we're in a better position to understand and, if we can, counteract the damages."

"That's if the therapy works," Addison mumbles. "And I'll be fine?"

Vogert holds his breath before looking her in the eyes.

"There's a reason we pushed it out—for the chance to test its effectiveness," he says. "It brushes the border of ethical practices, but we believe it was for the best." He catches Addison swaying her head side-to-side, clearly bored, which makes sense. She helped develop the therapy in the labs with his team. He doesn't need to explain the details. "And in this case, the risk may have saved your life."

Vogert has Addison lie flat on the scanner, letting the machine warm for a minute.

It emanates a low hum as it rotates its arm, shoulder-length wide, moving from her head and down to her toes.

The monitor's readout to his left dings as the scanner finishes its rounds.

Vogert starts to review the layers, seeing the details and marking certain areas for closer observation.

"All right," he states. "You're clear for now. Go ahead and get dressed. And if you can, grab a couple more hours of sleep. That's an order."

Addison sits up and slides off the table. She gives him a nod. Though, it will take him longer than a glance to determine if she *is* fully clean. On the offhand, nothing pops out to his mind's eye.

Vogert watches as Addison makes her way to the door and . . . comes back.

She wraps her clothes around her arm, walking around the corner until she's standing outside the control booth.

Addison knocks on the glass, gesturing for him to let her inside.

"Yes?" Vogert asks, sliding the door open.

"How do my scans look?" Addison returns the question.

Vogert exhales sharply. "Like I said, nothing beyond the mundane. It *will* take me a couple of hours to review the results. I won't get to it until later tonight, even with the station's staff working overtime." He pinches the bridge of his nose and leans back in his chair. "I've got a whole team that needs my attention right now. And I've not slept myself. I'll catch you tomorrow."

"At least, tell me what you can," Addison asserts.

Vogert inhales and sits forward. He scrolls through her profile, double-checking it.

"You've some scar tissues on your left side," he describes. "Leftovers from when you broke your ribs as a teenager. There's a chip in your right canine tooth. And a reset broken nose from around the same time. All stuff I know about from your file. Nothing recent. I think you're clear. Physically speaking."

"And my brain?" Addison asks, somehow guessing *that* is his concern.

"I'll recommend sessions with our on-site psychologist, Doctor Vanniyar," Vogert says. "And I'll send an escort to take you to his office if you refuse to go. Everybody should see him once a week while on the mission anyway. You no longer have that option. I am making it a requirement for returning to the dreadnaught."

Addison relaxes her shoulders. "I'll go see him. Gladly."

"Not today," Vogert is quick to assert. "I'll make the appointment and let you know. Meanwhile? Doctor Anna Fullan will monitor your health during your downtime. She's good. She treated me for a time after my tour as a field medic. We're not under the same circumstances, but it's close enough."

Addison raises her eyes at him. "Understood," she nods, then walks away.

She goes behind a set of curtains to dress in private. As she does, Vogert skims through her scans again. He wants to catch something that could affect her health. Anything!

"But there's nothing," Vogert whispers. "I don't understand."

He takes a pen and writes a comment at the bottom of her chart.

"Six hours after exposure," Vogert mouths. "No adverse effects from her time on the dreadnaught."

He mulls over what he writes for another minute before standing up. He exits the booth, returning to his workload for the next few hours.

51 | ARGUMENTS NON-UNDERSTANDINGLY

LIEUTENANT COLONEL ELIAS IBRAHIM
UNITED COALITION ARMED FORCES

OCTOBER 21, 2041 | 1430 HOURS

===

Ibrahim stands beside Malakai's desk, biting his tongue.

They have a committee in attendance—the primsuits, military officers, and *one* egghead. Tension fills the space where the quiet extrudes.

Avanna Remmings is off in the corner, staying away from everybody else. She's not limp or tired, as far as Ibrahim can see. Ava seems to enjoy the awkwardness between the boastful personalities in the room and their grand ambitions. Her eyes widen as she watches the subtle facial expressions the others attempt to hide.

"And what the damn are we supposed to do with it?" Senator Holland demands. "What is it, anyway? Is there . . . a socket we plug it into?"

Ibrahim notices Malakai locking eyes with the man for a hard while.

"Plug it into?" Malakai repeats. "Like an electric lamp? That's your suggestion, Senator?"

Holland's jaw clenches. "It's more of an idea than debating this in your office!" the Senator scoffs. His allies in the room all nod their heads agreeingly.

Malakai leans forward and frowns. He holds his breath, rubbing the back of his neck.

Ibrahim notices the politician's discomfort.

Henry Holland shifts his weight between his feet, unable to sit, usually never one to stand for longer than necessary. But he's stuck in this little conference. Ibrahim runs his thumb across his chin as he watches the man's face turn reddish pink.

"Senator—your party has access to this base as delegates," Malakai cautions. "But let me state this in a very clear way. You can investigate misdemeanors and take tours of this facility. You do not have a say in how the Epimetheus Project chooses to operate."

Henry coughs as he straightens his tie, trying to brush off the comment.

"I am the Premier Senator of Wisconsin, Doctor Adonis," Holland huffs. His jaw tightens. Ibrahim can hear the man's polished teeth crack. "And I lead the oversight committee that funds your little mission. Do you know how much it costs an hour to keep your lights on? After we do a full counting, the American Congress will demand you justify the expenses. I can promise you."

"And I'll look forward to it," Malakai nods. "Ignoring that I am not answerable to the United States, I fail to see the point in the threat."

The Senator's nostrils flare in apt response.

Ibrahim chuckles. He cups his hand over his mouth to hide his grin.

Holland isn't so terrifying as the monsters they've fought in the dreadnaught's corridors. Maybe fatter. And with less of a fashion sense.

Ibrahim pops his neck as the argument builds.

"You're using American military assets. Warships? Soldiers? All of it to protect your scientists and explore the inside of that ship!" Holland rages. "That makes you answerable to the American people! To me! It doesn't matter if it falls under my official mandate."

Malakai flips his wrist, not entirely disagreeing. "It makes me answerable to the treaty signed by members of the United Coalition of Sovereign Nations," he counters. "Our situation brings the world together. We have a chance to create a productive structure, absent short-sighted meddling from local politicians."

Ibrahim notes the sharp tone in the man's voice.

"That's what I said to the world when I first met with the Security Council," Malakai finishes.

"The American people won't—"

"They're dying!" Malakai shouts, undercutting the Senator without courtesy. "It's the same everywhere! Arguing doesn't help our mission, Henry. And let's not pretend you've started caring about the 'American people' when you ignore the foxes eating the hens because all you see are the eggs in the pantry."

Senator Holland's eyes glint in the narrow space between his lids.

Ibrahim steps a bit to the side, readying to jump into action should the Senator lunge at Malakai.

"My duties involve—"

"Sitting back and letting better men do all the work while you take the credit?" Malakai interjects again, ready with his statement. Ibrahim now wonders if the man practices disrupting politicians' mid-sentence in the mirror. Malakai takes a pen from his desk and rolls it between his fingers. "That's not how I work, Henry. You know that."

"You can't—"

"—Deny you? Yeah. Maybe I can't, officially speaking. But that doesn't mean people will start taking orders from you."

"I have Congressional oversight authority!"

Malakai looks between the Senator and Ibrahim. "You're not in the United States, Henry. And our mandate is from the Joint Security Council. Not the President. Nor Congress. Nor the American people. I serve the world, not a single country."

"I am the—"

"Nobody on this oil rig cares who you are," Ibrahim states, jumping into the fray. He turns to Malakai for a moment and winks. "Keep saying it, Senator Holland. Maybe yelling it loud enough will convince somebody that you're important. And even if it does—in our situation, it also makes you a liability."

"And *who* are you?" Holland demands, eyeing the soldier with suspicion.

"Lieutenant Colonel Elias Ibrahim," Malakai introduces. He gestures in Ibrahim's direction, then folds his hands at his belly. "He leads the UCAF out of the METIS Research Base. And he's the one who made the incursion into the ship's forward sections."

Holland studies Ibrahim from head to toe. He's searching for a fault to use against the soldier.

"Colonel Ibrahim?" Holland questions. "Which branch do you serve? Navy? Army?"

Ibrahim grins uneasily.

"I don't think I have ever met a navy colonel, Senator Holland," Ibrahim corrects. "Do you see my patch? I *am* a member of the United States Marine Corps. My unit falls under the purview of the UCAF as of the signing of the Global Security Act. Officially under lease to the Epimetheus Project from the High Castle Program."

Holland takes a backward step.

"Meaning I hold rank over you as a Senator to an American soldier," Holland covets.

Ibrahim quickly shakes his head.

"Not in the slightest, sir," Ibrahim refuses.

"What do you mean?"

"Admiral Jonathan Kennedy is my direct superior," Ibrahim describes. He squares his shoulders when he notices the Senator's nostrils flare again. "Otherwise? I am unaware of your work for the mission, Mr. Holland. Scientists and soldiers lead the Project. You are neither. And your role doesn't grant you authority over my troops."

Holland's eyes narrow like a cold fire reflecting off their shine.

The man is from a dying political breed that once tried to control the United States in the mid-twenties. Ibrahim has read Holland's speeches about those he considers "True-Americans," as the old vids name it. Holland is the kind of man Ibrahim's position requires him to show respect to publicly but would never vote for if he had a choice.

"This isn't why we've come," another within the group interjects, breaking the quiet tension.

"You're right," Malakai agrees. "We're here to discuss what happens to this." He points at the ornate metallic sphere on the desk.

"It's a light show," Holland comments, staring hard at the relic. "Perhaps we can show it off to the public? Use it to say we've made progress."

Ibrahim snorts.

His impression of the Senator is that he'd make a smart courtroom lawyer—self-assured, direct, and charismatic to the masses. Ibrahim knows soldiers with similar dispositions. So often, they're the ones who want to glorify their deeds, destroying lives in the pursuit of their fame.

Holland moves to pick up the sphere off Malakai's desk.

Ibrahim quickly puts his hands on the grip of his sidearm.

"Don't you touch that!" Ibrahim orders. Abrasively.

All the other security officers follow his lead, ready to draw on the Senator if the man dares to wrap his fat fingers around the relic.

"Fucking hell?" Holland curses. "Are you . . . I can have you arrested for threatening me!"

Ibrahim shifts his stance anxiously as the Senator turns at him.

"And they'll arrest you for attempting to steal what they've spent blood retrieving," Malakai iterates. He shows his palms, a gesture hinting that everyone should stay calm. After, the man steps around his desk and positions himself between Holland and Ibrahim. "Stand down, Colonel. We don't need this. Please?"

Ibrahim's hand trembles as he relaxes his grip.

He doesn't understand why he's reacted so aggressively to Holland merely walking over to pick up the alien relic. Ibrahim very nearly drew a weapon on an American Senator. And that would've been a mistake.

"Only three people in this room have the clearance to hold it," Ibrahim growls. "You're not one of them, Mr. Holland."

"It's okay," Malakai nods.

"I wasn't going to steal it," Holland defends. "I just wanted a closer look."

"Please don't try to do anything," Malakai suggests. "Tensions are high. We don't need outsiders poking at things we don't understand."

"And what don't you understand?" Holland asks.

"The ill side-effects it can have on a person's physiology," Ava explains. "For example." She slides into the conversation like a cat jumping down from a tree.

Holland shifts his attention to her and glowers, not realizing she's been in the corner watching this whole time.

"And how does a girl like you know that?" Holland mocks.

Malakai coughs. "Doctor Avanna Remmings—" he explains, nodding at the woman. "She's our Chief Technology Specialist for Project Affairs."

Holland steps back. "Ms. Remmings?" he asks for clarification. "You can't be more than twenty?"

Ibrahim can tell that the man recognizes the name, if not the face. His tone makes it obvious, cracking like a schoolboy.

"Doctor Remmings, if you'd please," Ava iterates. "And I am twenty-five."

Ibrahim raises an eyebrow. He's yet to see the woman ever get angry. Her jaw is clamped tighter than an airlock on Overlook Station.

"Doctor Remmings," Holland repeats, twisting his lip. "Okay, then. Tell me. Why isn't it safe for me to hold it when 'Colonel' Ibrahim was carrying it in his pocket?"

"Because we've all gone through a gene therapy that adapts our bodies to the dreadnaught's conditions," Ava proudly touts.

Malakai and Ibrahim both flinch.

"Gene therapy?" Holland inquires, looking angrily at Malakai.

The two men stare at each other in a contest.

Ibrahim pinches the bridge of his nose. Holland was no doubt waiting for something to latch onto as an excuse to begin ripping into their work.

"I understand your politics on the matter," Malakai states. He glances at Ibrahim in the process. "Our people actively work on methods to allow us better access to the ship. However, we can only do that by lowering the risks of exploring it."

"While pretending to be God in the meantime?" Holland demands.

"Ava refers to a therapy created by Doctor Vogert and Doctor Kennedy," Malakai explains. "We needed to protect ourselves from whatever killed Arthur and his crew. All within ethical standards. I can promise you."

"I doubt that very much," Holland scoffs. "And what are the nature of these changes?"

Malakai grins confidently. "I'll only repeat what's on the official logs. It adapts our bodies in case of a suit breach," Malakai confides. "And it has already proven a lifesaving measure, buying us time. Over a dozen soldiers now live where they would've otherwise died from minor injuries."

"At the cost of their humanity," Holland counters. "Apparently."

"Not even close," Ava scorns.

"It was an official sanction," Malakai adds.

"Meaning you've had human trials? Who approved that?!" Holland demands.

"I approved it," Malakai credits, taking the blame in the meantime.

"You've only been on-site for a couple of weeks!"

"We've extensive leave to complete this mission however we can, Senator Holland," Malakai argues. "And if that means undergoing breakthroughs to increase the survival rate of our people? That's an opportunity we aren't going to pass on."

"And what of the unknown effects of your recklessness?" Holland demands. "You might've turned everyone who's taken it sterile! I want the names of those who've undergone this . . . this . . . experiment. And I want them quarantined.

Solitary confinement. Until we can infer the long-term symptoms and the potential risk to the public."

"Senator," Malakai sighs.

"Malakai?" Holland urges. "I may not be a scientist, but I know how to stop a pandemic before it spreads."

"It's not a disease!" Ava argues. "Everyone took it willingly."

"It's an ungodly aberration of nature! That's what it is," Holland shouts back. "If humans should survive the conditions on that ship, we'd been born with the necessary traits. We aren't. This mission is a fool's errand. All it's doing is waste lives and pull resources away from the mainland."

"Divine intervention isn't how evolution works," Malakai breathes exhaustingly. He rests his palm on his desk in a calm gesture. "You aren't born wearing clothes or armor. There's a needed correlation for instigating rapid change like what's required here. We've got weeks to figure out a solution. Not fifty thousand years."

"I don't care about . . . evolution . . . or adaptation," Holland scoffs, almost like a snarl. "I want a complete list. Every report you have on the subject. Immediately. No questions from you or your people."

Ibrahim steps forward, staring the Senator down in the small office. Holland—taller than most others in the room, suddenly gets a foot shorter.

Elias puffs out his chest and flexes his shoulders, becoming like a solid rock at the edge of a waterfall.

"Unfortunately—you don't have clearance to access those reports," Ibrahim states. He lowers his voice, but not enough to indicate that he's making a direct threat. Not again. Only enough for the man to understand he's treading on where he doesn't want to walk.

"That isn't your call to make, Colonel Ibrahim," Holland barks. "I lead the largest traditional caucus on Capitol Hill."

"And this is an international mission. Formal decision-making power falls primarily to UCSN leadership," Ibrahim states, slow and calmly. He wants to ensure his point comes across as clearly as possible, without interpretation. "If you have a problem with that, talk to Jimmy Harper. I am sure he'd be glad to hear your complaints."

Holland shudders when he hears the name. His stare goes cold and unforgiving, cracking the thin skin around the man's eyes.

"What do you intend to do with the artifact?" Holland questions, turning to Malakai, who's now standing two steps behind Colonel Ibrahim.

"We're calling it the Heart. And we intend to study it," Malakai quickly answers. "Learn what we can before returning it to the Architects. That is the deal Addison arranged."

"You're returning it? I thought it was a gift?"

"It's not ours," Ava interjects. "They gave it as a measure of good faith."

"Adhion 'Klaka—the alien who offered it to her," Ibrahim follows, "asked us to give it back."

"But couldn't it take years before we can learn anything from it?" Hollands states. "They're willing to let us keep it for *that* long?"

Malakai feels a pit in his throat. "I doubt that's the intention," he admits. "I think it's better not to piss off the people with a ship the size of Manhattan."

"Which means you think they're still a threat to us," Holland weighs.

Malakai frowns, breathing a deep frustration having to deal with the man.

Ibrahim checks the notifications on his pad. He's waiting for an update from Warden on the situation from the dark zone.

"Is everything a word game with you, Henry?" Malakai questions.

"I'm just trying to understand," Holland defends.

"And what don't you understand?" Malakai demands.

"Exactly what you people are doing on this platform!" Holland howls. "How much money? How many lives will we lose to that monstrosity of a ... ship? It's not unreasonable to demand sorely needed oversight. I don't care what you think about me. Any of you! Question my motivations. Flag it as ambition if you want. Your mission on that ship is unprecedented."

"Isn't everything we do unprecedented?" Ibrahim counters. "Senator? That's our job."

The angry man tilts his head to one side. "And after? What then? People will want somebody to pay for what they've lost," Holland threatens. "These resources should be going to reconstruction. Instead, you waste it on maintaining the quarantine fleet. And keeping those like me from getting too close!"

The room hangs silently on Senator Holland and his compatriots for a minute.

"I have the greatest minds on the planet working to figure this beast out," Malakai iterates. "We're doing our jobs, and we will get it done. I promise."

"And I am doing mine. Harper and the Security Council won't protect you," Senator Holland continues. "Not forever. Petitions, loopholes, whatever ... People need a scapegoat. Nobody in Congress will take that on, so they'll throw it at you, Doctor Adonis. And why not? The very man who insists that junkpile in the water needs explanation."

"It's not junk," Ava refutes. "Or much of a pile."

"Your little Heart will only cause trouble," Holland says, looking at the woman.

"And what would you do if we gave *it* to you?" Malakai asks the Senator.

Henry shrugs. "I'd let the people on the mainland decide," he admits. "Show it off. Parade it around? Let it solve an energy crisis or two. My problem is this ... Everyone tends to covet what they don't have. Material power can give world leaders enough leeway to maintain control over their little slices of land. And when they finally see this? They'll get jealous. It's bound to happen."

Ibrahim retreats a couple of steps. He leans into Malakai at his desk.

"He's not wrong," Ibrahim whispers.

"Help me understand, Senator Holland," Malakai steers. "Do you want us to display it to the public or keep it hidden?"

"It's a conundrum," another of the coterie whimpers.

"This isn't the place to decide these matters, Henry," a third confides. "We should let *them* handle it. Let's deal with the fallout. Not get involved."

"Isn't it better to prevent disasters from happening than clean them up afterward?" Holland decries. He turns to Ava Remmings, snapping his fingers to get her attention. "Can your people do what you need before word gets out?"

"Depends," Ava mutters.

"On?"

"Who hasn't gotten word already?" Ibrahim interjects.

Senator Holland's eyes suddenly dull in non-understanding.

"Dozens of countries were involved with retrieving the Heart," Malakai explains. Ibrahim crosses his arms and lends his weight to one foot. "Our allies have copies of the reports for internal debates. It's nothing we don't expect. That's what everyone agreed to when they signed the treaty. We're dealing with it."

"Maybe you are," Holland grimaces.

"We should increase security on the rig for the next few days," Ibrahim suggests as a middle ground.

"Do it," Malakai agrees. "Transfer who you need from the fleet."

"At least we don't have to worry about leaving our bases understaffed if there's another event," Ibrahim confirms. "I'll contact Admiral Kennedy."

They both turn to Henry Holland and his clique to catch their reactions. The man shrugs weakly, stepping toward the door with his fellow primsuits in tow. He doesn't even offer a word of criticism. Or argue a suggestion, as Ibrahim would expect.

"Dumbass," Ibrahim curses as the door slides shut.

"He's not our problem," Malakai reassures him. He motions for Ava to come to the other side of his desk. "I wish you hadn't mentioned the gene therapy."

"I apologize," Ava frowns. "I didn't mean . . . It . . . it just came out."

"No worries. It's quite all right," Malakai calms her. "Nothing we can do about it until they start arresting us."

"Can he do that?" Ibrahim groans.

Malakai presses his fingers to his temples and sighs.

"No," the man iterates the topic. "Henry is a blowhard, but he's right about potential leaks."

"And what *can* we do?" Ava questions.

"Hope for the best? Try to plan for the worst," Malakai clarifies. "Not everybody signed the treaty. And there are loopholes within the language that rogue parties can use against us. We may need Holland's support to keep our gains in-house."

Ibrahim remains standing there, unsure how to add to the discussion. He's not well-versed in the political world. Or the science. He's a soldier—a marine. He shoots things. He also likes to order others to shoot things. He makes problems disappear with a rifle and guards those who need protection.

In whatever case, Ibrahim's chosen his side in this debacle.

Maybe it's the only way his troops will survive with their dignity intact . . . With medals on their uniforms instead of discharge papers hiding in their closets.

His body chills at the notion.

"Ava?" Malakai steers. "Reconfigure your lab with whatever you need for the Heart. Athena ordered new equipment for you. Your team will have leeway to work as you need. I want you to get yourself cleared by medical and learn what you can from the rock. Understand?"

The woman tilts her head with enough of a smile that illustrates her thrill for the opportunity.

"Colonel Ibrahim," he continues. "Deliver the artifact to the lab. Place a detail on it around the clock."

"Expecting trouble?" Ibrahim asks.

"You tell me."

Ibrahim frowns and surrenders an uncertain nod.

"Good luck," Malakai concludes. "Keep me updated. I'll check in with Addison to see how she's feeling."

"Vogert should be sending me a report on her condition," Ibrahim states.

"He's not sending it through the broad channel?"

Ibrahim holds his breath. "Not immediately," he admits. "I want to look at it before Roslin catches a scent."

"I won't let that happen," Malakai suggests. Confident.

"Apologies, sir," Ibrahim frowns. "You may not have a choice."

"Maybe not," Malakai admits.

Everybody clears the room when Malakai goes to sit at the edge of his desk.

Ibrahim picks up the Heart and turns to leave when he looks back and notices Malakai switching on the feeds.

"Are you okay?" Ibrahim asks.

"Always," Malakai falsely chuckles.

Ibrahim bites down on his molars and doesn't follow up on it.

He closes the door behind him and hides the Heart in his belt pouch, walking through the hallways as if nothing is wrong. Ibrahim brings it to the lower observation deck that Ava Remmings uses as her tech lab. Inside, he decides to wait until security comes to relieve him of the package.

AVANNA "AVA" REMMINGS, CHIEF TECHNOLOGY SPECIALIST
EPIMETHEUS PROJECT

OCTOBER 22, 2041 | 1745 HOURS

More than a little frustrated, Ava clubs another prototype scanner against the workbench.

It doesn't do much but force her to restart her plans at the drawing board. Maybe that's a good thing? She doesn't know. A phrase she's now overly familiar with after a week in this shithole.

She bites her nails down to the skin, annoying her more when she needs to pick up her tools.

Ava's been trying to get a reading off the alien sphere for the past day. And in the process, she's now overcooked six data collectors, causing the components to spark and let off a strong odor, like burnt plastic. Ava covers her nose to keep from smelling it. Energy radiates off the source. She can feel the heat when she hovers her hand over the outer sheath.

"Thermal imaging shows it's cold," Ava catalogs. "Like it's not there. How the actual fuck?"

She pinches her nasal bridge to relieve the tension in her head.

Ava requires a different set of tools. That's obvious. Problem is . . . She doesn't know the metallic sphere's material structure. She needs to be able to get readings off a full spectrum analysis. Temperature is clearly out of the question, so now it's her job to find a workaround. Maybe light? Vibrational frequencies? Ava sighs.

"Would that even work?" she murmurs.

Ava begins drawing plans for such a device. Her earliest estimate for completion is a couple of weeks—blueprints for her sketches, prototyping a working model, and troubleshooting any kinks. And after? Ava risks building a new tool, only for it not to work.

First ideas rarely pan out when tackling the greatest technological mysteries of the universe.

The door to the observation deck opens. Ava's heart skips until she realizes it's Doctor Zhu entering the lab.

Yunwen's eyes float around the room until she finds Ava at the corner table.

"I didn't know you were still on the Olympus," Ava says to the woman.

"I am until the mission is done," Zhu explains.

Ava smirks as she ponders the notion. "Aren't you done? We're home. Now it's my turn to work miracles."

"You consider this homely?" Zhu doubts. "My idea of home is . . . elsewhere. Beautiful, isn't it?" Her pupils square on the Architect's metallic sphere.

Ava frowns. She rotates Addison's "gift" on the table, admiring the intricate, almost ornate depictions etch into the surface.

"That's one way to put it," Ava murmurs. "What's your field again? Study of plants? A bit limited, isn't it?"

"Only if you don't understand the field as I do," Zhu scorns.

"Doesn't seem so difficult . . . Plants take in carbon dioxide and expel oxygen," Ava mocks. "They say our forests are the lungs of the world, but I am willing to bet I can design a machine the size of a small room to supply the demands of an entire city."

"It'd be an ugly city without any greenery," Zhu laughs weakly.

Ava sucks in her lips as she stares up at the woman.

"Why are you here?" Ava demands. "I've work to do."

Zhu takes a slow breath before steadying her stance. "You don't trust me, do you?" she regretfully asks.

"I doubt anybody trusts you around here," Ava wounds undeservingly.

"You think I have hostile intent," Zhu realizes. "An agent for my government?"

Ava's attitude solidifies on her face.

"That's what some of us think. I suppose I should ask if you *are* one . . . An agent? A spy? Maybe a saboteur?"

"Only as much as you are one for yours, Doctor Remmings," Zhu frowns.

Ava raises her eyebrows at the admittance. "Is that meant to help convince me?"

Zhu smugly grins.

Ava often looks back at her career . . . Her arrest? Solitary confinement without a trial to defend her actions? The deal she struck with the military had saved her from living a life inside a dark prison cell in the Rocky Mountains. All because she was curious if she *could* do something others thought impossible.

Zhu tilts her head. "No. But this *does* give us a jumping-off point to talk about," the woman suggests. "So, the plan? What is it?" Zhu stares at the Architect's Heart on the table, entranced by the soft light it emits. "How are we supposed to use it? What does it even do besides—?"

"Give us a pretty light show?"

The woman pauses as her face softens. "As you say," Zhu offers. "How does it work?"

Ava shrugs. "I don't know," she admits. "First . . . I want to figure out how to get a reading off it."

"Like the contents of a puzzle box?" Zhu suggests.

"More like the contents *are* the puzzle, but yeah," Ava settles. "It's a puzzle box . . . err, marble."

"Heart."

"What did you say?"

"That's what you're calling it, aren't you?"

"Does it matter?" Ava mumbles.

Zhu chews her tongue as she drops back a step.

"I suppose not," she returns. "What have you learned so far?"

Ava lets out a breath. She doesn't have an immediate reason to withhold an answer. Maybe she can find one with some effort, but that would only distract her. Ava's duties are more important. And besides. Project leadership must've trusted her enough if they sent her on the expedition to retrieve the damn thing. That said—

"Learned? Hmm. That we can probably toss our knowledge of physics out the window?" Ava exaggerates. "Its properties match a solid element one moment, only to change into energy the next . . . Like it exists in multiple concurrent states."

"Is that even possible?" Zhu asks. "What you're describing is—?"

"Like magic?" Ava shakes her head demandingly. "Let's not use the word. It's not magic."

"Do you have another way to explain it?" Zhu defends.

"I don't," Ava iterates. "But don't say it."

Zhu clenches her jaw. "But it *is* the closest equivalent to our understanding," she says.

"Only if magic is real," Ava chuckles. "And it isn't." She buries her nose into the drawing of her first draft.

"So, what's your plan?" Zhu asks. "Anything I *can* do to help?"

Ava mouths, "I don't know." She looks up with a wring face. "Hopefully, *this* will do it. Admittedly. That doesn't mean it'll work. Shifting between two states of matter takes a tremendous amount of energy. Which might explain how the Architects use it as a source if they can siphon that energy into a usable conduit?"

Zhu flutters her eyes worryingly at her. "You've drawn up blueprints already?"

"I like to work fast," Ava scoffs. "It doesn't mean it will do the job." She leans forward to better view Zhu's face in the lab's dim light.

"Who else knows you're working on it? The soldiers? Those visitors upstairs?" Zhu seemingly probes.

Ava narrows her attention on the woman with suspicion.

"Why are you asking?" Ava prods. "Planning a heist?"

"No," Zhu mourns. "I only want to help."

"Because botany and experimental engineering are related fields, is that it?"

Zhu's lip twists with hate. "We're all in this together," the woman scowls. "You, me . . . Addison Kennedy, Sergeant Warden, Malakai Adonis, Colonel Ibrahim. We may be from different places, but we share the same ground—our home. The Architects killed millions of my people. Unintentionally, maybe . . . That doesn't make my folks any less dead. My grandparents. Friends. Supervisors. Co-workers. This crisis has awakened the sleeping tigers of my country. We are Zhōngguórén. And we are desperate."

Ava's suspicions soften into a crisper sorrow. "You lost people in the flooding," she realizes, lowering her head.

"I was on a classified research station in high orbit when the alarms woke us," Zhu describes. "I watched the ship hit the atmosphere. Fire everywhere. Bright enough to blind if you weren't careful. I grew up on an island off the coast. It . . . didn't survive."

Zhu's expression hardens. Ava can see the woman fighting the tears as she steadies her stance.

"Do you have any experience with sound-wave emission?" Ava finally asks.

Zhu nods before taking a seat at the table. "More than you'd expect. My first three years on assignment involved the test of growth patterns in crop yields with amplified sound generators."

"To see if it affects wide-scale production?"

"Yes," Zhu admits. "Don't tell anybody I said that. It's still classified. The project was a failure. Thus, the restricted status. 'No practical applications found,' they said. They reassigned me six times before I made the short list of scientists my government believed could work productively with foreigners."

"And why they picked you to join the expedition," Ava nods acutely.

"I hate feeling useless," Zhu reaffirms. "How far along are you with the design refinements?"

Ava shrugs. "I've only started. Unfortunately," she admits. "Do you want to look? Offer input?"

Zhu smiles. She holds out her hand for Ava to shake, which surprises her. For some reason, Ava surrenders the woman a fist bump instead, unsure of the proper response.

"Grab those pages and let's get started," Ava weakly laughs, the awkwardness in the air left to simmer.

They work into the night, debating solutions to the larger challenges.

ADHION 'KLAKA, NOMAD OF AMELIORATION
REBEL OF THE OBLIGATION

521031 LOCAL CLUSTER | 761,400 DAY OF PURPOSE

Walking into the Entrychamber builds a silence as his footsteps echo in the vast, empty room.

Adhion doesn't run, once often thinking only cowards or traitors ran. Yet now, as the traitor, he fights the idea, wanting to set an example.

He takes measured strides. The Varmajalkavaen flank the platform as Adhion 'Klaka approaches.

Tyrann 'Akachan stands on the far side, watching Adhion's slow march across. Idu is next to him, her large eyes pale, a worry in the light reflecting off them.

"It appears the *krakas* can answer a summons when there's nowhere left to hide," the Trident scoffs, closing his fist and pulling it close. "Or do you come to surrender? To drop to your knees, begging for our mercy? Like a rat in a maze." His face looms bright as he meets Adhion partway on the platform.

"Do you know what a 'rat' is, my lord? A small, furry creature of this planet," Adhion returns, glancing at Idu 'Smeora. She watches him with interest. "Some worship it, while others consider it a pest. Which is it with me? Or do you use *it* as a turn of phrase? Wordplay? Is it possible you learned a strange *human* expression?"

Tyrann notices the glances and steps to block Adhion's view of Idu.

"You have stayed a step ahead of us this entire time!" Tyrann demotes. "Why submit now?"

"Because I see no other way," Adhion remarks. "You will keep sending more after me until one of us dies."

"Nothing you do will outpace what you've done," the Trident argues.

"This is our ship! *Our* home."

"Your home. Mine shares a bed with death—and I *walked* from it, intent on staying away."

"Abandoning your duties," Tyrann accuses.

Adhion takes a moment to gather his thoughts. "I suppose I did . . . Does it matter? No. I don't think it does. Do you know? I used to think you were unimpeachable, Trident. Noble. The pinnacle of our species, absolute in all things. But the truth hurts the most when people die for our mistakes."

"You kill for the sake of it," Tyrann growls. "Because it is easy! There's no great mystery to your actions."

"I murder in your name to keep the dirt off your hands," Adhion asserts. "And I would hardly call it easy. No more! I am taking a stand. When I kill, it should be for *my* reasons, *not* yours. I accept responsibility for the lives I've stolen in my role to the Obligation. That's more admission than most of you will ever say!"

Around him, the Varmajalkavaen close in, ensuring there is no escape. Too many for Adhion to fight alone. And too many to merely walk away and ignore. After he stole the Heart from the ship's core, they will never lower their guard with him again.

Tyrann 'Akachan takes a step forward, taller than Adhion, standing on the flat of the bridge. He holds anger behind his dark grey eyes. For Adhion, it better illustrates a profound sense of betrayal. And as the Trident of Absolution moves, the Varmajalkavaen follow him, mirroring his motions.

"What did you do with the Heart?" the other demands.

Tjaa 'Neren rises into the Entrychamber from a level below. She circles the commotion, watching as if trying to guess who will make the first move. If anyone. Curiosity gets the better of her as she catches Adhion's exhausted stare.

Adhion offers her a respectful smile before turning to Tyrann's demand.

"It's in a rather inspired place, if I may say," he says. "Tridents of Absolution! Righteous in your ambitions? You have always considered yourselves above the killing of 'lesser' creatures. For those who do the deed, it's a deep-seated failure. 'Failed experiments,' unworthy of seeing what life brings them. All to make the killing seem fair and noble. *That* is what *you* call mercy. A trap!"

"You gave it to the humans," Tyrann realizes.

Adhion softly nods. "I've given you a choice. And without me, you won't like the options."

"Murderer! Why would you involve them? They are innocent!" Tjaa shouts.

"So are we," Idu suggests, walking behind Tyrann and Tjaa.

"He's doomed us!" Tyrann tells her. "Idu! We must get it back."

"Then let's go ask it of them," she argues. "Dhun's speaking with their warriors now. He can warn them of the danger."

Tyrann stares at her frighteningly. It's not a manner that Adhion would associate with him.

"No," Tyrann refuses. "They have it . . . And they won't likely give it back if we merely ask. They will take advantage of our negligence. Once they learn what they need from it, there is no turning back. Our great engines, the power of our species, the lifeblood of this ship . . . It will all die. Along with their planet."

"What do you mean?" Tjaa asks. "Our ship will die . . . How?"

"He's saying without the Heart," Adhion glooms with a lesser confidence, "the ship can't maintain its core. The heat will spill out into the corridors until the containment barriers explode. And the debris will scar the Earth for a million years. Humanity's potential? Lost to generations of those trying to survive after the dust settles."

"What is this? Revenge?" Tyrann demands. "What did we do to make *you* put us all at risk? Do you have no conscious?"

Adhion holds his breath until he looks at Idu.

In the dark glimmer of her pupils, he can see that she understands his intent.

"My reasons?" he mouths.

Their goals . . . Everything his tasks were to achieve, no matter the hazardous improvisation? Adhion didn't *want* to reprogram the Fragment Alimentors. And he certainly didn't *wish* for the carnage that's come after. But it was the only way for him to stay ahead of the hunters at his heels.

When he learned about the attack at the hangar's control spire, Adhion's hands went cold. He wasn't eager to let the humans get caught in the crossfire. Adhion had to convince himself to keep going, clenching his fists as he pushed on, no matter the lives lost as he did. He'd already given everything for the cause.

"Such conscious is beyond repair," Adhion weeps his answer. "And I will not walk away from it any longer."

Tyrann retreats from his position a little, letting his posture sink.

"You play the victim so well, Nomad," he derides. "Do you really hate us so much?"

"Only as much as you hate me," Adhion admits, stepping forward. He wants to see *what* the Varmajalkavaen will do. And what they do is stop him before he gets very far. They position themselves between the two massive figures, attempting to keep the peace. Adhion won't begrudge them their duty for *his* rebellion's sake.

"You will tell me everything!" Tyrann demands. "All your plots. From the beginning. And be *wise* in your convictions."

Adhion breathes deeply and tells him. It doesn't take long. It is a story that repeats itself many times across the galaxy. Afterward, when Adhion finishes, the Trident paces up and down the floor, only stopping occasionally to ponder one thought or another.

Tjaa and Idu remain talkative amongst themselves, discussing what they've learned.

Tyrann 'Akachan stops at the display that dominates the Entrychamber. Tjaa and Idu look at him as he inputs new instructions.

Adhion stares off to the side, eventually closing his eyes. His muscles strain to keep his body upright.

"Tjaa 'Neren?" Tyrann pleads. "I need your help."

Tjaa's posture stiffens, unsure of what he's about to ask.

"I am listening," she says.

"The human warriors—their soldiers—would've brought the Heart to their staging base," Tyrann explains. "I need you to go there and get it back for us." Behind him on the imaging machine, a large human-made structure appears, elaborately mapped. "These are the scans from the Observer. Study it."

Tjaa's colors quickly dim while an ashy white covers the dark of her skin.

"And if they . . . don't let me retrieve it?"

"Then do what you think is necessary," the Trident orders. "Kill them. Push them aside. It doesn't matter. They are already dead if we do not act. And we are stranded until we get it back. Better let a few expire now than all of them at once."

Tjaa nods in solace. Her fingers tremble, and she squeezes her palms together to quiet them.

Adhion takes in a long, unhappy sigh.

"That'll betray her role in the Obligation," he mutters.

Tjaa understands how to create life. She shouldn't have to rip that life away and leave the body empty. It's a dark thing to demand of their kind, blood staining the hands of an Arkkitect.

That leaves Adhion's nerves shaken, with a heart full of doubt.

But he does not doubt that *that* is what's running through Tjaa's head as she grimaces and nods.

"I suppose there's only one way about it now," the Servant lulls, her eyes fluttering like a fly in a whirlwind.

Tyrann bows his head acceptingly before turning to Adhion, noticing his frown.

"Are you enjoying this?" he questions. "You drove us into a corner! More humans will die. And it's your fault."

Adhion's expression hardens. "Those humans will defend what's theirs," he warns. "Don't attack them thinking you can win through martial strength alone. They're adaptable. Especially when facing long odds, they will find a way to subvert your expectations."

Tyrann marches across the platform, closing the distance between them.

Adhion 'Klaka drops to his knees, feigning reverence.

"You studied them?" the Trident demands.

"It is a pastime," he answers. "You will learn why soon enough."

A tense silence rises, with nothing left for either of them to say. The Nomad breathes deeply, biding his time.

Tjaa musters her shoulders and walks toward an airlock on the far side of the Entrychamber. It will take her outside.

"Servant!" Adhion shouts before she gets too far.

Tjaa pivots and looks at him, disappointment reflecting off her large eyes.

"This is your fault," Tjaa accuses, "what I am about to do."

He grimaces painfully. "It feels terrible, doesn't it?" Adhion asks. "To kill is . . . the cost of duty."

"Yes. It is," Tjaa admits.

"Good," Adhion says. "We share that. Remember it."

Tjaa weakly frowns.

Idu remains in the background, studying them both, disquieted but making no secret of her anger.

"This isn't right," Idu says. "Tyrann—we are not fighters! Why send Tjaa? It violates her role as the Servant of Cultivation. Aren't you the—?"

Tyrann glowers at her. "I know what I am. It's what the Obligation demands," he decides.

"And *where* does the Obligation demand violence?"

Tyrann stomps toward Idu and grasps her by the throat. "In the verse that instructs the Nomads," he threatens. "But this is *my* decision, Whisperer. Not yours. Do you understand?"

Idu's eyes flash toward Adhion before she meets the Trident's aberrant glare.

"I understand," she murmurs.

Tyrann releases his grip and waves her off. The expression on Idu's face steers away from her normally serene composure. Her colors dull to reds and yellows, a sense of betrayal surging in her heart. Tyrann doesn't notice it. His attention, instead, centers on Adhion with such intensity that his feathers hue a burning red.

"Adhion 'Klaka, Nomad of Amelioration—" the Trident decries, "—I charge you with a crime of the highest order, and I must safeguard our traditions. Obligation demands us to burn your body and scatter the remains on the homeworld." His head burrs as his mouth twists. "As *if* the wind would take your ashes. I vilify you. Wicked. Lesser merit."

"So . . . Not much for a punishment," Adhion plays coy with the sentence.

Tyrann's nostrils flare. "We'll keep you locked up for now," he determines. "Away from events as they unfold."

Adhion rises to his feet, another little rebellion.

He looks the Trident dead in the eyes, who stands at his full height, making even the Nomad feel small.

"I accept the conditions of my restraint," Adhion declares. "Which way to my prison?"

"Toward the cages with the other beasts," Tyrann points.

"At least they will make for good company," Adhion smiles.

Tyrann 'Akachan falls away from the walkway. "Take him," he sneers at the High Echelon.

Adhion sights Idu as the Varmajalkavaen lead him toward the Servant's beast pens. Idu backs away and watches, the shadows highlighting the white markings on her face. A hint of recognition? It makes him wonder.

Now she sees the truth that Adhion's understood for decades now.

"We are *not* gods," Adhion whispers. "The humans will show you why." It is an ancient notion, a fantasy. And the Obligation? An earmark by an elite few, deciding where to waste precious lives. "Stay safe, Tjaa 'Neren. You will need your speed and wits to survive." He lets off the little prayer, hoping it is enough to save the Servant from her doom.

UNDERESTIMATED |54

SERGEANT MAJOR OLIVIA WARDEN
UNITED COALITION ARMED FORCES

OCTOBER 21, 2041 | 1308 HOURS

She checks on the perimeter guard for a third time in a quarter-hour.

"How're things here?" Warden asks.

"No change since your previous rounds, Sergeant Major," the marine snarks, "five minutes ago."

Warden glowers, though he can't see it. "Can't be too cautious." She taps her visor to get his attention.

"We'll keep eyes on our trackers," the marine accepts. He turns in toward the clearing.

Warden has thirty marines in this area, each equipped like a tank. Everyone else in her command is guarding their flanks.

She only hopes it's enough should another one of those Architects show up. "And damn us if it isn't," Warden curses, moving between positions.

It's not like Warden's got free access to that handy cipher that allows her to understand the aliens' weird song language. No. She'll need to rely on her suit's ability to interface with Kennedy's program and read the scrolling text on her screen.

She decides to circle once more around the clearing, chatting with her troops. They've spread evenly on the perimeter—good coverage for their numbers. Should the talks break down, at least they'll be able to shoot their way back to the evac zone.

Warden's only halfway through the routine when a sensor detects movement, letting off a series of beeps.

Her troops move into positions to counter the alarm's direction.

"Sergeant!" Corporal Livingston calls at her, running from his posting near the sensor trip. "We've got incoming!"

"How many?" Warden demands.

"Multiple contacts," he goes. "One *big* one. Many buggers. I'd say a few dozen."

"Dozens?" Warden repeats. For her, that's damn sore news.

"What are your orders?"

Warden pauses a moment to think. "Nobody fires unless I give the signal," she instructs. "These are the ones we're supposedly meeting. The last thing I want is some trigger-happy idiot causing a shootout. Double that if *I* am in arm's reach of the damn things."

She squares her shoulders, readying herself. Warden can hear heavy footsteps pounding the dirt. A metallic ringing as each foot hits the clearing's flat ground.

The "Architect" known as "Dhun 'Ancod" walks out from the foliage with *its* entourage.

"He's a giant," Warden swallows.

She marches forward, intent on meeting the creature halfway. She stops when the other does, only a few feet away.

Warden cranes her neck to meet the big one's eyes, steadying her stance. The alien somehow notices and surrenders what looks like a courteous bow.

"Courtesy? Does it know what that means?" she asks under her breath.

The aliens make a cautious final approach toward her. Warden can only hope they can't see her troops and the rifles pointing at their heads.

"You are . . . Addison Kennedy?" the Architect asks. Its words *sound* like a bird's song mixing with infrequent syllables.

Warden reads *what* it says through the translation software embedded in her helmet's firmware.

She looks up at the individual. "I am Sergeant Major Olivia Warden of the United Coalition Armed Forces. I serve as part of the mission to study your ship with the Epimetheus Project," she spouts. She's practiced the line over fifty times in her head while waiting.

"I am Dhun 'Ancod, Judge of Conciliation for the Vili—what you call the Summerland," the Architect recants his name. Rather formally, in fact. Its hand gestures surprise Warden—gracious and precise, every muscle moving as if it's a dance, rehearsed and perfect. "I was expecting the one named Addison Kennedy. A scientist. *You* are a warrior?"

Warden reflects on her posture—stiff and straight, the essence of a military woman standing proudly.

"And *we* were expecting Idu 'Smeora. It seems we're both disappointments. Doctor Kennedy *did* come with us, but she ended up meeting with another of your people. Also, not Idu," Warden explains. "Adhion 'Klaka. He's the one who's caused you a lot of trouble, isn't he?"

Dhun's face wrinkles as *he* hears the name. His color palette goes from a mixture of blues and yellows to show a small hint of red. Whatever *that* expresses, Warden can tell by how his gracious and precise gestures turn to a violent sense as he uses more strength to orchestrate them.

"And what did the Nomad want?" Dhun begs the question.

"Just to give Doctor Kennedy something," Warden answers.

"Something? What did he give?"

"It was, uh . . . a little metal sphere? Ornate," Warden tries to describe, but she didn't get *that* good of a look at it. "That's why Addison isn't with us now." Warden grinds her teeth to make sure she doesn't say anything out of turn. She has no idea what this alien intends. While *she* doesn't want it to end violently, Warden can tell by the small twitches that the bird-like alien is suddenly upset.

"And where has Addison Kennedy gone to?" Dhun asks.

Warden narrows her eyes at the alien. "That's classified," she tells him.

"Classified?"

"Restricted," Warden clarifies. "Human privilege."

Dhun scoffs . . . Or what Warden can only assume is a scoff, positioning his upper lip in a snarl.

"Human privilege?" the Architect mocks. "I remember you, Sergeant Major Olivia Warden."

"You do?" she questions.

"You were there, were you not? That first attack on your people," the alien jeers. "Powerful machines, the Fragment Alimentors . . . Your soldiers were dying until I stepped in to save you. I was there to win a fight. And I found one, though, not the one I expected. I won it, nevertheless."

"That was you?" Warden murmurs.

"I do not enjoy seeing innocent beings slaughtered," Dhun explains. "This planet is your home. While this ship? It is mine. Adhion 'Klaka steals and attacks us, infecting our systems and causing all this destruction. You are as much his enemy as he is ours, Sergeant Major."

"He stole from you?" Warden asks.

"A relic that powers our great machines," Dhun answers.

"The thing he gave Addison?" she asks. Just suggesting it feels weird on her tongue.

Dhun surrenders her a nod. "It was not his to offer," he says. "It is the Heart of the Ship—the water to the fire. My people ask for its return so we may leave."

Shit. Warden's throat closes, and her chest compresses. Alarms inside her hardsuit go off, sending her warnings like she's in heavy combat.

"I would if I could. But that's not my call to make," Warden mourns. "It's above my pay grade."

"Pay grade?" Dhun begs for clarification.

"Authority level," Warden says. "I can't help you."

Dhun grumbles low under his breath. "That *is* unfortunate."

Warden takes a back step from the alien's sudden tonal shift. Around him, the buggers—the Varmajalkavaen—start reaching for their weapons. She begins an active record of their movements. Evidence. Something to give the eggheads *if* she gets back to Mount Olympus.

"Why are you here?" Warden decides to break the tension. "We expected Idu 'Smeora. Addison Kennedy *was* at least with us."

"Idu was called back to the Entrychamber by our leader," Dhun explains. "Another situation made him fear for her safety."

"Her safety? I suppose that's fair," Warden accepts the coincidence. Or the lack thereof. Neither party intended for this meeting has come, however. And *that* doesn't sit right with her. Addison *was* here, and she *did* make the trek, but the woman had to leave. Idu 'Smeora hasn't even bothered to show up. And it leaves Warden in a bit of a snag—as a soldier, it's her job to kill things. As a negotiator—she has limited experience. "So, I am not Addison Kennedy," Warden continues, "and you're not Idu 'Smeora. How do you want to do this? Talk about the weather?"

Warden cringes for saying it. Luckily, her visor hides her expression.

Confusion on the alien's face goes palpable. Some yellow sneaks through the red in his feathers.

"You're asking about . . . the weather?" Dhun asks.

Warden reads the words on her screen. "You know—if you're just going to repeat everything I say, this conversation won't be productive," she snarks.

Dhun mumbles again, his colors mixing with his skin, growing from yellow and red to a deep-seated black.

"This is a waste of my time," Dhun finally admits. "You want us gone, but we cannot leave! Not without the Heart. Give it to us, human!"

Warden smirks, although the Architect can't see it. "Please, don't call me human. The way I'm reading it . . . well, it feels like an insult."

The Architect growls. "I am Dhun 'Ancod, Judge of Conciliation!"

Several of the buggers step forward, bearing their weapons. Warden hesitates and looks at her surroundings. She can see there isn't much cover nearby. And the tree line isn't close enough for her to run to if this becomes a shooting gallery for everyone and everything.

"You've said that already," Warden mocks with a tilt in her head.

"We demand the Heart of the Vili returned to us immediately!" Dhun shouts. Warden's translation software puts his words on her screen with capital letters. "We will ask only one more time. I have kept the peace between us and encouraged my people to work with your kind to solve our problem."

"You've encouraged peace by attacking us in the corridors?" Warden scoffs.

"We protect this ship," Dhun explains. "In every engagement, your people shoot first!"

"I've got a hundred marines lying in medical that would disagree with you."

Warden notes how the pearly white of the other's skin bubbles reddish underneath the surface. Colonel Ibrahim left her with the authority to conduct this meeting. In her view, the Architects are undeniably hostile.

They've killed her marines, her friends. And now she's got *this* one on the wrong end of her biggest guns.

"I do not wish to hurt your people anymore," Dhun explains. "But I am under orders to act if we fail to terms. Our leader wants to go home. Obligation demands it."

"And I want your ship off our fucking planet," Warden agrees. She touches her sidearm's grip, unbuckling the holster.

"Then, Sergeant Major Olivia Warden, return what is ours. We can still enact justice on Adhion 'Klaka for his crimes against our peoples," Dhun demands. "As you would say . . . Please? I do not want to end this by spilling blood in this place."

Warden's eyes dart across her screen, counting the number of buggers. She's faced worse odds these past few weeks.

"I've told you," Warden doubles down, "I don't have the authority to release the artifact. It's not *my* decision to make. You'll have to speak to Addison Kennedy and our leadership. I'm just the grunt they left behind to hold the door open for you. And honestly? I feel like slamming that door shut in your face right now."

Dhun's feathers begin ruffling oddly. He grabs a familiar spear from his side and activates it. And it hums the same way it did at the Central Spire.

Warden gulps. She remembers how the weapon cut a Fragment cleanly in two with hardly any effort.

"Then, I am sorry, Sergeant Major," Dhun apologizes. "I have my orders."

Warden nods. "As do I," she releases her breath unsteadily. "Before we dance, how much do you know of human history? Earth? How did our scattered tribes manage to conquer each other across centuries?"

Dhun tilts his head in a veritably human manner. "I do not know," he shudders.

"It's not a simple thing," Warden admits, although that's not the point she's trying to make. "There *are* a lot of us. We're pack hunters—but our greatest strength comes from this." She taps her helmet. "We're smart. Sometimes dumb. But to compensate . . . We like to make up the difference with overwhelming firepower."

Dhun draws his spear and lunges forward.

Warden lowers her head and ducks for cover.

The tree line lights up instantly. And it's wondrous!

Sparks fly off the Architect's battle armor as projectiles hit him. Jalks try to take cover behind Dhun, only to get caught in the backlash of bullets ricocheting off his protective harness. Several blindly fire into the trees before getting cut down in the onslaught.

Warden pulls her pistol and shoots. She burns through a magazine before switching to her rifle with the ASAPHEI 6.8 ammunition. Dhun shouts and covers his exposed face with his arms, getting pushed back by the sheer volume of kinetic force impacting his body. For her, it's quite an impressive sight. Warden isn't surprised he's not dead yet, but the fact the alien is still standing with a thousand pounds hitting him every second is remarkable in its own right.

A human being would get knocked down by just *one* bullet, even with heavy armor. Or even an exoskeleton rig to increase an individual's strength.

The shooting eventually dies down. All the Jalks are dead on the ground. Dhun 'Ancod is the last freak standing. He looks down at Warden with his armor scarred and broken. His skin is completely red and black, with zero traces of other shades. Stepping forward, Dhun scowls. Warden luckily left him a little present while she was prone. A handy brick of plastic explosive, prepped, molded, and armed at his feet.

Warden brings up the detonator and hits the button.

The explosion spreads across the clearing. Effective. Warden drops back to avoid the splash. She raises her rifle once the smoke clears, ordering her unit to move in and secure the dead. Among the bodies, Dhun coughs heavily, now a meter away from where he once stood against the onslaught. He pulls himself up and glowers at her with pale eyes, feathers now crimson.

"Damn," Warden curses. "That should've done it! He's still alive!"

The alien's armor shimmers like it's reflecting the ambient light through water, the surface damage fading like scars on flesh.

"Shit," Warden curses. "What's he doing?"

Dhun raises a hand and closes his fist, creating a pulling motion. Something grabs Warden, and her hardsuit locks up.

Warden's marines stumble out of the foliage along the clearing's edges, dragged by their loose plates . . . A weapon? Maybe a device targeting their armor with a magnetic force? She doesn't know what's happening, only that it has something to do with the Architect.

It doesn't matter. Warden fires her rifle at the big alien. Her shots begin a cadence that echoes between her unit and Dhun 'Ancod.

The Architect's armor closes, eliminating his need to protect his face, leaving his hands open for fighting.

"Livingston! Do it now!" Warden orders.

A massive boom erupts in the trees, and everyone drops to the ground. Dhun's grip over their armor dissipates.

Warden sees how the AMR round had severed the alien's right hand and part of the arm attached to it. Another shot from the rifle hits the alien in the left shoulder, taking a larger chunk out of him. Dhun roars! The dirt encircles his feet as if the very ship is reacting to his pain.

Warden must thank Colonel Ibrahim for letting her keep one of the guns. The operator is in one of the larger trees, away from the battle, near Corporal Livingston on the perimeter. And close enough to relay her orders without the static on their comms.

"Tank killers," Warden quietly mouths.

Dhun fights to his feet after a third shot grazes his helmet, cutting into his mask and face. The big guy collapses on the ground in a pool of vibrant blood, motionless after.

Everybody moves to secure their bodies. "Aliens are dead, Sergeant Major," Livingston celebrates. "They weren't so tough."

"Seems that way," Warden agrees, feeling her heart pounding inside her chest. "Get word to Wolfden for evac. Tell them we've got a present for the eggheads. Heavy lift."

Livingston nods and runs for the entry corridor to edge out of the comms disruption zone. He brings a whole squad with him.

Warden walks up to Dhun's body and nudges the alien's arm with her boot.

"This was your choice," she says. "We defended ourselves."

She repeats the phrase in her head, trying to believe it, but for some reason, there's a knot growing deep in her gut. Looking over Dhun's dead body now, Warden wants to vomit. Not because the body's gross or she can't handle the gore. Quite the opposite . . . But she doesn't know how to describe it.

It just feels . . . Wrong?

Warden sets pressure on her stomach and switches on her health monitor.

55 | GRAVER CONCERNS

LIEUTENANT COLONEL ELIAS IBRAHIM
UNITED COALITION ARMED FORCES

OCTOBER 23, 2041 | 0815 HOURS

===

Malakai lowers his tablet after reading the report, folding his hands over the desk.

"We killed an Architect," Malakai murmurs, not directed at Ibrahim.

"Over a day ago," Ibrahim confirms, dragging the computer pad toward him to read. He flips through the images Warden sent along with the report. "Took a hell of a beating to put down, but she did it. Remarkable."

Ibrahim can tell by how the man's lips thin as his thoughts rush from one question to the next.

"Why am I only just hearing about this now?"

"They engaged while in the dead zone," Ibrahim explains. "Warden's unit had to drag the body to Station Four. He's a big fucker."

Malakai taps a finger on his desk anxiously. "Give me the sequence of events," he instructs. "Explain it to me."

Ibrahim takes the pad to skim over the report again. "I left with Addison Kennedy. I had Warden stay to negotiate with the Architect in case more showed," Ibrahim says. "And this was after our face-to-face with Adhion 'Klaka. From our intel, he's the terrorist responsible for the chaos."

"And why did Adhion approach us instead of Idu?" Malakai asks.

"Something about social disagreements," Ibrahim tries to explain. "I'm unsure of the specifics."

"And the Architect we killed wasn't either of them?"

"No," Ibrahim confirms. "I don't think so."

Malakai leans back in his chair. Ibrahim waits quietly as the man thinks.

"And the Judge showed hostility at the point of engagement?" Malakai asks to clarify.

"That's what the report says," Ibrahim asserts. "And I trust Warden's account."

"You'd vouch for her in front of a military court?"

Ibrahim goes expressionless. "In a heartbeat," he asserts, adding a nod to illustrate his faith in Olivia Warden's judgment.

"Then, that's all we can do," Malakai sighs as he accepts. He jumps up from his seat and pats Ibrahim on the shoulder. "This is a clusterfuck. We'll need each other if we want to survive the political shitstorm that'll hit us."

Ibrahim looks at him with surprise. "What do you mean?"

Malakai answers with a stern glare. His eyes then fall to the ground before rising with renewed strength.

"Do you have children? A family?" Malakai asks, returning to his desk to sit.

"Never had the pleasure," Ibrahim admits unwillingly. "The High Castle Program brought us up as soldiers in our late teenage years. It's all very close-knit. Some of our parents volunteered us for the project. Even then, I wouldn't consider my mom overly 'motherly,' as you'd call it."

Ibrahim narrows his eyes, curiously weighing on the other man's body language.

"That must've been very lonely," Malakai frowns.

"It had its moments," Ibrahim says. "Training soldiers designed for combat operations in space . . . Hard work. Funny how most of us are dying on the ground now."

"Or as close to the ground as we can manage," Malakai points out, adding a respectful chuckle to the irony of recent events. "We *are* in the middle of the Pacific Ocean." He hangs on to those last few words. Ibrahim leans forward, able to tell he has more to say. "Pacific Ocean—" Malakai repeats. "What an odd name. Sometimes I wonder how we collectively agree on the name of things. Who makes those decisions? Kings? Scientists?" He scratches his nose as his thoughts veer haphazardly.

"Ferdinand Magellan," Ibrahim explains. "He was a Portuguese explorer who helped the Spanish circumvent the world. When he reached the waters on the far side of the continent, he called it 'Mar Pacífico,' which in Spanish means—"

"Peaceful Sea," Malakai finishes. "Impressive. Did they teach you that at High Castle?"

"Among other things," Ibrahim tells him.

"My wife and daughter are in the camps," Malakai says. "Nothing bad. Mara is the chief supervisor in her particular zone. Armoni is with her and keeps her company. Better than living in a children's boarding house as the government struggles to organize efforts. Our house washed away with the floods, but they're safe and healthy."

"I'm sorry," Ibrahim says, not knowing how to respond.

"Don't be . . . We always wanted to see what life would be like, tested as we are now," Malakai acknowledges, though he doesn't look up when he says it. Instead, he's spacing out, looking at the adjacent wall. "I was talking to her just the other day. People are . . . struggling. And others? They want somebody to blame, and that big alien ship in the middle of the ocean is too impersonal. World leaders need a scapegoat for their poor response to this crisis."

Ever so gradually, Ibrahim can see where the man is going with this line of thought.

Even if he does his job to the best of his ability, it won't mean a thing to those watching from afar. People are right to be angry. They can only count the numbers getting diverted into the Epimetheus Project. And they wonder how it is they can't feed their families.

"I want you to prepare for the backlash," Malakai cautions. "They'll put us on trial once we're home."

"We're risking our lives here!" Ibrahim argues.

"And it won't matter," Malakai shoots him down. "Not to them! Everyone associated with the Project will need to stay together if we're going to survive vultures like Senator Holland and his followers."

Ibrahim stares at him, anger brewing. And it's not entirely directed *at* the man. For him, it's more like a deep-gut awareness, coming as the political situation bares its fangs. And it leaves everybody with this encroaching "doom" feeling while left dry on the frontlines.

"There *is* the matter of Addison Kennedy," Ibrahim changes the subject.

The other raises an eyebrow. "I went over Vogert's report," Malakai says. "What about her?"

"I still have some concerns about her health," Ibrahim explains.

"Vogert's given her an all clear—physically, at least," Malakai repeats what's on the report. "No adverse effects."

"And no explanations," Ibrahim notes. "I don't like it."

"I can't say I disagree."

"Yet, I feel you're about to," Ibrahim remarks.

Malakai shrugs. "Addison is one of the smartest people I've ever met, and I know a lot of smart people," he says. "More than ever, we need her working toward the objective. Confining her to quarters because of a few mishaps isn't going to win us any goodwill points."

"Don't you mean win 'you' any goodwill," Ibrahim chides. "Come on! As a scientist, what happened to her *must* signal red flags! Ground her to the station for a couple more days so any long-term side effects can show themselves. It's the least we can do."

Malakai straightens his posture as he goes on the defensive.

Ibrahim doesn't mean to attack Malakai, or Addison Kennedy, for that matter. But he's not about to risk her health if there's even a slim chance it will cause permanent damage to her or others. The safety of the staff sits at the top of the Colonel's list of priorities. Vogert's gene therapy was almost a step too far. Ibrahim recognized the advantage as a *tool* for anyone operating on the dreadnaught, and that's the only reason he agreed to the procedure.

"Would you prefer I put her under your supervision?" Malakai suggests.

Ibrahim sighs. "No," he ultimately refuses. "That's probably a bad idea."

"You're probably right," Malakai laughs.

"Just keep her from doing anything stupid," Ibrahim urges. "I don't think I'll have the wits left to manage my troops *and* her."

The other's smile fades solemnly. "Addison is an asset," Malakai says. "If her work requires her to return to the dreadnaught, I'm not going to keep her from it. I hired her as my Field Director for a reason. She's good at what she does, even if she occasionally makes mistakes. She's human. It happens. But if you doubt her, Addison will do everything she can to prove you wrong."

"You trust her?" Ibrahim asks.

"Just like you trust Warden," Malakai answers. "And besides, we've other issues."

"Meaning?"

"While Addison was busy getting cleared, Doctor Zhu began helping Doctor Remmings with the Heart."

"Warden said the Architects want it back," Ibrahim describes.

"Addison's report suggests the same."

"What are you hoping they'll find with it?"

"Honestly?" Malakai poses. "I've no idea. Maybe it's a possible new energy source we can duplicate . . . My hopes? A silver lining to this crisis. It's an odd McGuffin, that's for sure. We're not even certain *what* it does or where it goes."

"And what is Doctor Zhu's contribution to the task?"

Malakai takes his computer pad and brings up a set of blueprints, handing it over to Ibrahim.

"Assisting on the way to get a reading off the damn thing," he says. "Our current tech isn't reliable for understanding the energy. And we're not sure if the energy is just so beyond us that it exists outside of what we know, or *if* it has a purpose, to begin with."

Ibrahim recalls the events that played out during the battle with Dhun 'Ancod.

"The others seem to want it back," Ibrahim notes. "Dhun was willing to attack Warden for it."

"Which only highlights its importance to *them*," Malakai accepts. "And more questions I want answers for."

"Which is where your concerns about our allies come into play?"

"Undoubtedly," Malakai voices openly. "Wensu Hao and Camp Yi haven't been the most forthcoming partners in this mission."

"I've read the back and forth."

"Keep an eye on Zhu and the CSDR troops stationed on the rig," Malakai suggests.

"This is a very dangerous line for us to walk," Ibrahim warns. "Are you sure you want to give me that order?"

Malakai stares at him emptily. "Tell me what *you* think," he asks, hesitant to speak openly.

Ibrahim shifts uncomfortably, his skin itching like it's on fire. He doesn't like this conversation. And he certainly doesn't like all this "closed-doors" backstabbing and schemes the politicians—like Senator Holland—seemingly enjoy playing on their unwitting victims.

Ibrahim's throat clogs as he attempts to speak. He struggles to clear it.

"Their camp's data transfers to the network haven't budged for the past week," Ibrahim lists his chief concern. "Everybody working with them is in the dark. We can't even see their troop movements without Athena's tendency to track them through the visual feeds. Some may consider that a treaty violation."

"They've also been feeding our reports to an unknown location off the mainland," Malakai adds. "According to the logs we do get."

"A black site?" Ibrahim suggests.

"Most likely one of their navy ships," Malakai suggests.

"So, they're eating everything on the table but refusing to pass the butter," Ibrahim weighs. "It's all very suspicious. Not that I think any of it can hold up in court. Not if they've got the right justifications for these . . . underhanded tactics. Are we throwing leaves at the wind, do you think?"

"Or maybe we're just paranoid," Malakai scoffs.

"That's not what I'm saying," Ibrahim reverts. "Maybe it's not enough to start pointing fingers? Others may disagree. But I'm not a lawyer. Why wouldn't they want to pool resources and work within the Project's constraints? I don't see the benefit in actively working against the mission's interests. They've too much to lose and hardly anything to gain."

Malakai strokes his chin. He hums as he contemplates what's most likely.

"Maybe you're right," he sighs. "Still. Check with Ava tonight and ask for an update. Just don't be too obvious. She's hacked into Athena's database a few times out of sheer boredom, so maybe she's seen something we haven't."

"Do you think she's also hacked the Chinese?"

"If she hasn't, I'd be very surprised," Malakai breathes, feigning insult. "We can't risk an international incident solely on my feelings, however. That doesn't mean we can't do *something* to help substantiate the evidence—find out if there's more to it or if it's their government's bad habits rearing its ugly head."

"I'll see what I can do," Ibrahim agrees.

Malakai nods and returns to monitoring the news feeds. Colonel Ibrahim gets up and steps away.

"And about your concerns for Addison Kennedy—" Malakai goes, stopping Ibrahim from reaching the door. "I *do* share them. I don't know if what I'm doing is right by her, but if the Architects attacked your soldiers for the Heart, it's not safe for us to keep it on site. The sooner we learn what we can about it, the faster we can move on. We'll need Addison to make that happen."

Ibrahim ponders that for a moment. "Understood," he says before walking out of the man's office.

Not like he could stop her from studying whatever she wanted anyway.

"But it's not my show to run," Ibrahim exhales.

He skips down the steps, leaving the Control Room, and heads to the cafeteria for breakfast.

56 | WHAT'S THAT NOISE?

ADDISON KENNEDY, FIELD DIRECTOR
EPIMETHEUS PROJECT

OCTOBER 25, 2041 | 1830 HOURS

===

Addison sits up, hitting her head on the bunk above her.

"Ouch," she mutters, mindful of the others in the room. "That's smart."

Addison can't sleep. And she hasn't. She keeps flipping through the reports on the sudden lull in threat engagements hull-side. Epimetheus Project work crews are now flooding into the dreadnaught, taking advantage of the opportunity the quiet grants them.

There's a loud thud outside the door. That's what caught Addison's attention.

"Does anybody else hear that?" Addison asks. Nobody answers, which doesn't surprise her.

They should all be sleeping during their off-hours, as *she* should be.

Addison slides out of her bunk and puts on a shirt. They've scheduled her to take the first transport back to the dreadnaught to coordinate this new phase of their operations in the morning. That *is* her job as a Field Director. Still. Returning to the METIS Research Base has her nerves in a knot. Or maybe it's the storm playing games with her head?

She opens the door and peeks into the hallway. Nothing's there. At least, nothing she can tell in the dark.

"I am jumping at echoes," Addison whispers, slumping back inside and dropping her ass on the bed.

That's when she hears another thud, louder this time . . . And sharper . . . Like a pinprick in the air.

Addison goes to the door again and steps out into the hall. All she finds is an empty corridor. More noises come through the walls from somewhere else on the Olympus. After lingering for a minute, heads start popping out of their dorms, one room at a time.

"So, I am not the only one hearing it," Addison shudders. "Which probably isn't a good sign."

She doesn't know what the next few days will bring. Every hour, the storm gets worse, and the people on the mainland can only watch and wait. Malakai restricts as much negative information from getting out as he can, but there's a limit on what he can do. Not to mention, the work on the Architect's Heart now stalls. It's one of the reasons she's going back hull-side. Ava will stay on task while Addison returns to the real mission. None expect it to get any easier, especially if the reports she's been reading are true. And she has no reason to believe they're not.

Warden and her troops killed the Judge of Conciliation—Dhun 'Ancod. Two weeks ago, he was the one who saved Ibrahim and his guys at the Central Spire.

"The idiots," Addison whispers, grinding her teeth. "No way the Architects *won't* see the killing passively."

Vogert's morgue is already full. And that's from the aliens' attempts to *avoid* conflict. She doesn't want to imagine *what* the situation could devolve into if—or when—Obligation demands the visitors to act. Or what her teams will face when they do.

In the corridor, more people gather, catching on that something's happening. They don't know what it is, and neither does Addison. She joins them, overhearing as much as she can. Most of it is nonsense—rumors on rumors. Pointless blather. Unhelpful.

Colonel Ibrahim steps into the corridor from the direction of the barracks. Addison notices and pushes through the crowd to catch him at the exit. The man's wearing his off-duty fatigues—not the battle-ready uniform he typically sports. It's a white-blue utility suit with its sleeves rolled up.

Addison frowns. She's not seen him in such a rushed state before.

"Elias! Something's wrong," Addison throws at the Colonel. "We keep hearing noises. What's going on?"

Ibrahim's eyebrows scrunch together, dissimulating his annoyance. "The night patrol hasn't reported to its watch officer," he explains, pulling her aside. "We're under a quiet alert state. Don't panic. We don't know what's going on yet. I'm heading to the Control Room to find out more. If we're compromised, keep off the radio. I wouldn't trust our comms."

"Our back and forth could go directly through High Castle," Addison suggests as a workaround.

"I would prefer to avoid that if possible. And only as a fallback if it's still an option later," Ibrahim criticizes. He opens the door to the main hallway to the Control Room. Several UCAF marines quickly make their way through with full combat gear. Addison's spent enough time with soldiers to know they wouldn't equip their hardsuits on the base unless they expected trouble. "Better to keep those channels clear if something happens and we need an untapped line."

"Anything I can do in the meantime?" Addison asks, following him.

"Go back to sleep," Ibrahim pushes. "Your people can't do much right now. And it's better if they're all in one place, not scattered in the hallways. If this is anything serious, I don't need civilians getting in the way of the response teams."

"We still have a crew working in the labs," she points out.

Ibrahim stops. He turns to her in puzzlement. "Damn," he curses.

"Majority of your people don't have access to those rooms," Addison adds. "Without comms, somebody will need to go and get them out."

"That's down four decks," Ibrahim says. "I don't have enough men to cover the distance. Not securely."

"I'll get them out," Addison asserts.

"We still don't know what's going on."

"Then give me a security officer for backup. I can evacuate my people to the upper floors," she suggests. "Or turn on the coolers for the maintenance pipelines. Skip the commotion in the hallways. Won't be comfortable for anybody passing through, but at least we can circumvent whatever's going on."

"It would take hours for the temperature in those pipes to get down to safe—"

An officer runs up to the pair at the turn in the hallway. He salutes the Colonel and waits for confirmation to speak.

"Yes?" Ibrahim pivots, tension building in his jaw.

"We found Biggs' unit," the man says. "All dead on the platform."

"Dead? That explains the lapse," Ibrahim accepts. "We're under attack. I want a full-readiness alert with everyone racked up to go. Five minutes. Get squads to the landing pads and cut off their escape. Set posts outside the nodes. It'll be the data archive they're after."

The lieutenant nods and runs off to follow through with his orders.

"Ibrahim—?" Addison starts, cautious not to sound too demanding. He glances at her for a brief second before storming off toward the Control Room, making it harder for Addison to keep pace. "Who'd attack us? We're in a military cordon upheld by a dozen world navies. We—"

"You don't need to tell me. But I guess we'll find out," Ibrahim affirms. "If you don't mind, Doctor Kennedy—I'm needed elsewhere. If you want to help, get back to the dormitory and keep those people calm. Seal the doors. Don't let anybody who isn't Coalition inside. Do you understand me?"

Addison clenches her jaw.

"Do you understand?!" he demands.

"Yes. Colonel Ibrahim," she manages to answer. "I understand."

"Good. See to your people, Addison," he says. "I'll organize a security team to get the eggheads off the observation deck."

"Thank you, Lieutenant Colonel," Addison tells him.

She nods to Ibrahim before following the hallway back, and he disappears around the corner. Addison presses her forehead against the cold metal door, taking a deep breath to work up the courage. Does it work? She doesn't know. But, like the moment of self-reflection that skydivers take before jumping out of an airplane, it slows her pulse.

As she enters, the windows inside the dorms flash white. BOOM. A powerful crack follows instantly, causing everybody to jump.

A man cries, "Shit!" as folks duck for cover away from the windows.

"It's just the storm!" Addison shouts. "Go back to your bunks and hunker down!"

"Hunker down?" a rigger crewman asks. "Why? What did Ibrahim say?"

"Doctor Kennedy? What's going on?"

Addison grimaces as the general response turns abrasive, and the corridor fills with questions.

"Were those gunshots?"

"Are we under attack? Here? We aren't on the damn ship!"

"Shouldn't we contact the Control Room? Call for a response team?"

"Quiet!" Addison shouts back. "Ibrahim wants us to stay put and not get in the way!"

"In the way of what?! What's happening?" others demand.

Out of fear, several of the staff try to key themselves into the comms network, looking for answers.

"I can't raise anybody!" a lab tech shouts. "I'm only getting static!"

"Control Room shouldn't be offline! Isn't that why we installed those redundancies?"

"Do we still have a signal from the Overlook? I don't see where—"

"Enough!" Addison screams to get everyone's attention. "Ibrahim told us to stay off the network! Military priority channels only."

"But why can't we—?"

"I don't have any answers for you," Addison iterates. "Let's follow through! Lock the doors and go back to sleep."

"Addison! We can't—?"

"Go back to sleep!" she orders. "There's nothing more we can do."

There's a dissatisfied grumbling going down to the far end of the corridor. Only a couple of the junior lab techs head back to their rooms. Most of the others decide to stay. Nobody will be able to sleep anyway, so she doesn't blame them. How can she? There's yelling coming from somewhere below, along with what seems to be gunshots. Muffled pops? They don't feel safe. It would be like any other day on the hull with the constant worry of attack. But that's the problem . . . Addison isn't *on* the dreadnaught. She's a mile away, where there shouldn't be any commotion.

That only leaves a few possibilities on *who* could've killed the patrol. But if Addison tells these people, it will only cause panic. It *could* be the aliens, but Addison doesn't feel that's likely. Firstly, it doesn't fit the patterns of other engagements with the Varmajalkavaen—swarm the defenses and overwhelm enemy positions. Had that been the case, it would be obvious. A door wouldn't protect the crew if those creatures wanted to get inside.

But what is the alternative?

"Something more . . . *human*," she says with a swollen tongue.

But why would anybody want to do that? It doesn't make sense. Whoever took out the night watch knew enough to cover their tracks. At least, they were smart enough to avoid early discovery. And they could have, if not for the cold, empty nature of the base, emphasizing every little sound.

Addison could sneeze in the Observation Lab, and a staffer two decks above would hear it.

And large men, dropping to the floor? Or the weight of their armor hitting metal?

"They weren't going to stay unnoticed for long," Addison whispers to avoid anybody overhearing her.

Still, it's very odd the Architects haven't responded to the death of their favorite son. If this commotion isn't them, then who is it?

Addison pulls up her pad to read Warden's incident report again. Maybe there's a clue in the transcript that she's glossed over? Scanning the text, Warden argues that Dhun 'Ancod attacked first, and the soldiers defended themselves.

Is it possible for the other Architects to see the Judge's actions as unjustifiable in the longer term?

"Anything's possible," Addison whispers, chewing her tongue. "But I doubt it."

Warden likely only managed to defeat Dhun 'Ancod by catching the giant by surprise. By her report, she only engaged when she understood the alien's hostility. The woman's answer to that aggression was by the book, as is doctrine . . . "Respond with overwhelming force." And she spoke the language magnificently.

Addison can only hope the Architects reach out to avoid spilling more blood for either side.

"But if not them," she repeats, "then who?"

Addison switches off her pad and paces quietly in the dark of the dormitory corridor.

The red emergency lights flicker on. The main power shut itself down, putting the base on reserve. Which . . . shouldn't be possible. Addison looks at the terrified faces of her co-workers in the claustrophobic space as they realize it with her.

She hates how she can smell their sweat.

INCURSION | 57

AVANNA "AVA" REMMINGS, CHIEF TECHNOLOGY SPECIALIST
EPIMETHEUS PROJECT

OCTOBER 25, 2041 | 1900 HOURS

Zhu and Ava walk together from the lab. They're halfway up the stairs from deck three when they notice the hallway bustling with soldiers. Normally, the overnight shift on the Olympus keeps a skeleton crew—enough to keep the Control Room functional and secure the labs. But tonight? There's a lot of movement. It isn't right.

As the pair top the stairs, they step out of the way of a marine squad hurrying to the airlock doors.

"Something's wrong," Zhu whispers.

"We should get to the dormitory," Ava urges.

"The Control Room is better protected," the other points out.

"I didn't hear an alert."

"Maybe they don't want to start a panic?"

Ava marches down the hall and takes a right. More soldiers pass through in full battle armor, preparing for trouble. One stops Zhu and Ava before they get too far, ushering them to the secondary stairwell and leading them the rest of the way to the dormitory. "What's happening?" Ava demands, but the soldier shakes his head, opening the security door to the next corridor.

"Stay here until we send the all-clear," the man surrenders, shutting the door as he leaves.

One of the lab techs moves in and inputs a code. "Sorry, Doctor Remmings," the man says. "Orders."

"I understand," Ava returns.

Almost everybody in the dormitory is awake and hanging outside their rooms. It's dark, with only the red emergency lights and a couple of electric lamps in the corner to keep folks from bumping into each other. And it's warm. With this many people crammed together, Ava scrunches her nose, catching the distinct impression that somebody wasn't too keen on personal hygiene.

Down the hall, they find Addison Kennedy talking with several others. Ava notices a worn smile on the woman's face. As the two push their way to her, she realizes it's a fruitless attempt by Addison to look composed as everyone swings at her, demanding answers.

"Addison!" Ava yells. "Addison Kennedy?!"

"Doctors? Weren't you two in the Observation Lab?" Addison exhales.

"We let the night shift take over monitoring," Ava explains.

"That's when the commotion started happening," Zhu adds. "As we came upstairs."

Addison's expression turns deathly serious. "I'm afraid I don't know much," she admits. "There are reports of missing patrols on the platform. Ibrahim ordered his troops to get ready for a fight. They're setting up—" She is about to say when gunfire reverberates through the walls, muffled.

The lab tech guarding the entry is the first to react, double-checking to ensure it is locked. Ava watches, waiting for the panel to light up orange and the reassuring beep that follows. There's a collective sigh when it does, and the corridor's temperature increases by a full degree.

Ava's fingers twitch nervously.

"Is it the Architects?" Yunwen asks.

"We *did* kill one," Ava adds. "And they might want the Heart back. Which isn't entirely unexpected."

"And so . . . What?" Addison counters. "They decide to attack right where we're strongest?"

"We don't know what they know," Zhu argues.

"True. But look at everything *we* know about the Architects," Addison says. "Idu worked her way through our research base without anybody noticing. Athena only figured it out because I turned off my comms. If they didn't want us to know they're aboard this platform, we wouldn't know."

"That doesn't leave us with many options," Ava says.

Zhu sucks in her breath and holds it.

Addison paces back and forth along the wall, working the problem through her head. She walks when she's stressed.

Ava watches with dry eyes and an itch at the back of her throat. "So . . . What do we do?" she asks.

The sounds of gunfire are more distant now, fading into the background. Ava can surmise the battle is playing out a couple of decks below them.

"What was the status of the Heart when you left the lab?" Addison inquires.

"Undergoing preliminary testing with the new sonic scanner," Ava answers, although hesitant to call it by *that* name. That is *not* what *she* prefers to call the device. 'Sonic scanner' is only the term her techs use on their daily progress reports. They had a vote. For some reason, 'ultra-harmonious frequency wave emitter' doesn't work well for the poor sods keeping the books.

"You didn't lock it up?" Addison asks.

"No, we didn't," Ava admits doubtfully, her tone suddenly fractured. "We should contact the techs downstairs. Tell them to put the Heart into the vault."

"No," Addison weakly denies. "Ibrahim doesn't want us using the emergency channels for non-military use."

"He can do that?" Zhu questions.

"It's security bullshit," Addison explains. "In a crisis—Ibrahim can limit outside contact on UCAF frequencies."

Ava stares at her for a moment before keying her comms anyway.

"This is static," Ava cringes.

Addison's eyes narrow in the dark. "Only static?" she repeats. "That's not right."

"Why not?" Zhu wonders.

"Because if the channels were down, you shouldn't be able to hear anything," Addison says. "Meaning comms aren't just down. Somebody's making noise on the network! A lot of it. And using the Overlook for a workaround won't work if we can't get a signal out. No static? It means no buzz . . . Nothing! The signal's down. But if there *is* static—?"

"Somebody's jamming us," Ava says, understanding the science.

"Limiting communication," Addison finishes.

"Who is it? Not the dreadnaught?" Zhu suggests.

"I don't know," Ava says.

"Just as likely, somebody with network access," Addison says, looking at Zhu Yunwen.

The two women lock eyes. Ava can feel the stark heat between Addison and Zhu, the latter keeping an unhappy scowl.

"We shouldn't speculate," Zhu says.

"That's all I've been able to do for twenty minutes," Addison confronts. "Did you know Athena tracks how much data transfers between camps?"

"Everybody knows that! It's a collective system."

"And for the system to work, every team contributes," Addison fights. "All but Wensu Hao and Camp Yi."

Zhu bites her lips. "We might've taken more than we've added," she admits.

"By a difference of several hundred terabytes," Addison punctuates.

"A lot more," Zhu mournfully concedes.

Ava's wrist-pad clicks as the corridor's temperature rises another degree.

Several of the junior lab techs move to block off Zhu's path to the door. Still locked, but it's a precaution. Some of the others look at the pair with concern, indecisive . . . And not without a little fear. They don't know what to think about the accusation.

Doctor Zhu straightens her neck, taking a firm stance as she squares her shoulders.

Ava lets off a small frown and takes several steps back.

"Stealing data is one thing!" Zhu offers caution. "But for my people to attack the core of our mission?" She hesitates as the red light reflects off her face. The woman turns away, wiping her nose with her sleeve, clearly wanting to hide the fact she's crying. "It wouldn't surprise me. I had to fight for them to release my records to Doctor Vogert. I'm on your side. Trust me."

Addison opens her mouth, wanting to say something, but can't—

An explosion shakes the Olympus, and the whole rig sways sideways, stabilizing after a minute. By that point, almost everyone in the corridor is on the floor, arms folded over their heads to protect themselves from potential debris.

"There's no time for this!" Ava urges, helping her up. "Addison! Stop. Let's focus on the issues . . . Comms are down. And there's no way to contact the lab from here. Not without Athena."

"We'll have to go downstairs if we want to lock up the Heart," Zhu agrees.

Addison passes a hard gaze between the pair as she finds her legs. She's quiet, her temples flexing angrily, but it's less than before.

"It's not that I don't trust you, Zhu," Addison warms. "I want to make sure that I *can* trust you before we do this! Do you hear that?" They go silent as they hear the fighting getting farther. "That's the sound of war in cramped quarters. If we get in trouble, we may not get out again."

"All three of us don't have to go," Ava says.

"I will go regardless," Zhu volunteers. Her stance weakens as she presses against her chest, letting out a breath. "Addison . . . You and I can reach the Observation Lab. If we get there before the fighting, we can lock up the Heart and meet up with security forces."

"And what will I do while you two play hero?" Ava begs the question.

Addison holds her glare for a moment, eyes black against the hallway's red emergency lights.

"Go to the Control Room and help however you can. Get the comms working again," Addison decides, biting the inside of her cheek.

"Not exactly running into the fire," Ava mourns.

"And probably just as important," Addison encourages. "If we can't communicate with our teams, whatever's happening will go from bad to worse. We need to coordinate. It's why we're here, what we signed up to do. Are you willing?"

Ava looks at her in astonishment.

"I'll go to the Control Room," she agrees.

"And we'll get to the labs," Addison confirms. "Lock up the Heart. Or die trying to get there."

"Whichever comes first?" Ava laughs.

"Preferably the first," Zhu admits.

"Let's do this," Addison finishes.

Addison Kennedy makes her way to the dormitory door with Zhu and

Ava. Everybody gets out of their way. Most of them could overhear what they intend to do, and they understand it's a risk. A dumb risk... Unnecessary if Ibrahim's marines can hold out against the attackers. But there aren't many soldiers on the base, and they're spread thin.

"Open it," Addison orders the lab tech guarding the door.

"What?" the man asks, caught by surprise.

"We're going through," Addison affirms. "Open it. Now. If you'd please."

The young man's skin goes starkly pale.

"I'm not doing that," he goes. "Don't you hear the shooting?"

"We hear it," Ava says. "That's why we need to go."

The man frowns. "It's not safe!" he repeats.

"We have work to do," Zhu says.

"Doctor Kennedy? You said the Colonel doesn't want us getting in the way!" the man decides. "The door stays closed."

Ava looks at the lab tech, a tremor in his voice. He's scared. But since the young man was the one to shut the door, the panel's keyed to his code. Under normal circumstances, only he'd be able to open it. It's a security feature the rigger crews put in, cutting access to unauthorized personnel wanting to go into restricted sections of the facility.

"It's just how the system operates," Ava breathes uneasily.

She ignores any sense of protocol and pushes her way to the keypad, knocking off its casing with her palm. The technology is a decade old, but she still knows how to work it. After crossing a few wires, the door's controller lights up green, showing it's now unlocked, much to the surprise of the man who initially locked it.

"How did—?"

"Miles," Addison says his name, stopping him mid-sentence. "We're headed out. Wish us luck?"

"You're insane," the young man says. He glances at the fifty other dormitory residents. "I'm not letting you guys back inside."

"That's fair," Addison says.

"Better than being trapped here like rats in a hole," Ava snarks. "Not that I think you're all rats, but this *is* a hole. And this door is the only way in or out."

"We'll be fine," Zhu tries to reassure the man.

"I doubt it," Miles frowns. "I hope it's not as bad as it sounds."

"Probably worse," Addison offers with less confidence.

Addison, Zhu, and Ava offer the man a pat on the shoulder as they step into the hallway outside. Ava turns right once she's through the door, heading to the Control Room. Zhu and Addison steer left toward the stairs. It will take them to the Observation Lab, where they're keeping the Architect's Heart for study.

"Good luck to us," Ava says despondently.

"Don't get shot," Addison cautions, and the trio part ways, if temporarily.

58 | AN UNCOORDINATED DEFENSE

LIEUTENANT COLONEL ELIAS IBRAHIM
UNITED COALITION ARMED FORCES

OCTOBER 25, 2041 | 1912 HOURS

===

"They're moving to deck four!" Leighton warns the room, getting feedback from the runner.

Ibrahim updates his map of the rig with a thick black marker.

"Our barricades are forcing them into workarounds," Ibrahim says. "Get back to them, Corporal. Have teams three and four reposition to intercept at the crossway!"

"Understood, sir," the other says.

Another runner sprints into the Control Room. "We still have contacts on deck three!" the woman shouts, catching her breath.

"They're covering their asses," Leighton hints. "Where did they come from?"

Ibrahim glances at Malakai Adonis sitting in a chair, watching the chaos unfold.

"Never mind about that," Ibrahim tells Leighton. "Get another runner to Halloway and sweep that corridor."

"Any word on who's attacking us?" Malakai asks the response crews.

"Not our visitors from the ship," a runner exclaims as he jots down notes for the response teams.

"What do you mean?" Leighton returns. "If not the Architects . . . then who is it?"

"Men?" a second runner describes. "Black uniforms—sleek design, modern armor."

"Made for infiltration," Ibrahim comments, handing off orders. "It explains how they could take Athena offline."

"And what's our progress on relinking the network?" Malakai asks.

"We'll need Doctor Remmings to get the system online," Leighton says, passing additional notes.

"Then get her," Ibrahim says.

"Ava's usually coming up from the labs at this time," Malakai warns. Ibrahim presses his palms into the table, focusing on the man for an instant. It's the exact worse place Doctor Remmings can be right now. "Last I heard, she was under escort to the dormitory after the silent alert went out."

With everything going on and information only reaching the Control Room via his runners, Ibrahim must sift through notes given to him by a dozen hands. From what he can gather, the infiltrators are going to deck five. And there's only *one* reason they'd attempt to go *that* far into the rig.

"They're after the Architect's Heart," Ibrahim mutters, pushing off the table. "We need to hold them!"

To do that, he needs the network up and running, first and foremost.

His runners pass through the Control Room to transfer messages to their units every few minutes. Everyone is doing what they can to stem the crisis. Ibrahim ordered non-essential personnel to stay in the dormitories and out of the way until the fighting subsided. Without the comms, he isn't sure how many got the—

Doctor Remmings walks through the door and makes her way to the floor. But how? The runner only just left. Ava stops at Ibrahim's table, where he coordinates the defense.

Malakai jumps to his feet when he sees her, exhaustion in his smile. However, the Colonel doesn't have time to ask nicely. He doesn't care how she's here already, only that she *is* now, like the choir descending from the chancel. Ibrahim means to put her skills to use.

"You! Remmings?!" Ibrahim shouts. "I need our systems back online now!"

"Did you just—?"

Malakai squeezes her shoulder and stops her from shooting back, taking her aside. He finds her a workstation that acts as an input device for High Castle's network nodes. Getting the hint to ignore Ibrahim's annoyed breaths, Ava takes a seat and slides the keyboard to the edge of the station.

Ibrahim sweats as he watches her fingers blast away on the keys like a machine.

He pivots to studying the external decks lining the oil rig.

Ibrahim counts three helipads spread across two decks—not including the additional staging area the Engineering Corps has built to store equipment and supplies for transport to the dreadnaught. The infiltrators can only have come in from one or two of those points. Ibrahim's question is . . . Which one? Each platform has a marine squad on security duty, but he's not heard reports from those sections. And that's another problem on top of everything else. Not to mention, the fleet maintains a quarantine zone around the Summerland *and* Mount Olympus. If anybody had managed to slip by the fleet's active radar screen, they would've had to get past a dozen navy vessels and patrol craft.

"I need eyes on the helipads!" Ibrahim announces. "Who's not doing anything?!"

"Why the helipads?" Leighton asks.

"The teams I sent there have yet to report in," Ibrahim notions. "I want to find out why!"

"I'll go," Malakai says, upturning his head from talking to Doctor Remmings. "I'm not doing anything."

Ibrahim stares at him unhappily.

"You're the Director of Operations for the Epimetheus Project," he warns. "Denied. I need other volunteers."

"Your shorthanded," Malakai argues. "Everyone in this room is needed to coordinate the defense! And I'm sitting in my chair, twiddling my thumbs. Might as well do something useful while I still have my legs, Lieutenant Colonel."

"That's not your decision."

Malakai scowls in magnificent defiance. "And it is not yours," he says. "You need it done, and I'm available! So, I'll get it done."

Ibrahim pulls close to the man. "I won't order you to do this," he says. "And I don't want that dumpster fire on my head. I have marines for a reason."

"Then I can go with them. I'll run and report back as soon as I can."

"And what happens if you get killed—?"

"Then, tell your guys to drag my ass back," Malakai says with an anemic frown, "so my wife can still say goodbye. But I hate not being able to do something! I can at least do this. And besides, what are the chances they're still there? It seems like the commotion is happening on the decks below us."

"Very high," Ibrahim answers, letting out a long breath. "But—?"

Ibrahim looks to the room, tension building angrily behind his eyes. He's tired. The initial alert woke him up after being awake for fifty-two hours.

"All right," Ibrahim finally agrees. "Yuckham and Roth! You two are now my volunteers. Get this man back alive! And if he doesn't, neither do you." He steps to the railing separating the two halves of the Control Room, hands on his hips. "Malakai? Don't fall behind! Get a look and report what you find. I should only need to send the two, but you're certain you *want* to do it?"

Malakai nods. "I am. Thank you, Colonel," he says.

"Don't trip over your boots," Ibrahim warns.

Adonis starts for the door with the two marine corporals—Yuckham and Roth. He stops and looks back at the room.

"Once the network's up and running again, send a call immediately to the fleet," Malakai suggests.

"That's the plan," Ibrahim recedes. "Get a move on!" He returns his attention to the defense.

ADDISON KENNEDY, FIELD DIRECTOR
EPIMETHEUS PROJECT

OCTOBER 25, 2041 | 1920 HOURS

———

She doesn't want to believe it, even as the gunfire echoes through the walls. At first, the fighting was far away. *Over there, not here.* Now? Zhu and Addison navigate the platform's decks, counting the bodies and the dead marines on the floor.

"This only just happened," Addison whispers, eyeing the damage.

She notices the black marks on the walls. "Residue. Explosive rounds?" Addison whispers, tension building at the back of her neck.

"Probably to counter the marines' composite hardsuits," Zhu suggests.

"That's what worries me," Addison admits.

Stepping over the bodies, Addison stays ahead of Zhu, only stopping to take a sidearm from a dead soldier at the end of the hall. It's loaded, which is a bout of good luck. She can hear blasts from the adjacent corridor. Addison peeks around the corner, cutting off her breath when muzzles flash down the next stretch.

Zhu pulls Addison back into cover. "That's where they're fighting!" she notions.

"This must be their rearguard," Addison agrees. "Most of the battle seems to be on deck four below us."

The shooting intensifies as the marines push hard to retake lost territory.

"We can't stay here!" Zhu decides.

Addison shakes her head, squeezing her wrist as she tries to slow her heart rate.

Mount Olympus isn't a fortress. The original builders had everything set up as a grid, with the first three interior decks acting as the control and crew sections, deck four being the massive industrial area where they did most of the actual work. Deck five remained separate in the event of a disaster—as a refuge during a fire or an escape route for the former workers.

Joe Hickman and his riggers spent the weeks after Summerland's Folly converting the bottom deck into the Observation Lab. Addison needs to get her people out of there . . . After witnessing the carnage in the halls, she doesn't give a damn about securing the Architect's Heart. It won't matter if the people working on the project aren't alive to see the mission through to the end.

But the only straight path to get there is down the stairs where all the soldiers are battling each other.

Addison presses her palm against her throat as she wards off a powerful urge to vomit.

"And we can't go *that* way," Addison whimpers.

"Then what do you suggest?" Zhu demands. "Is there another way?"

"I don't know! I never studied the—" Addison stops mid-sentence, noticing a warm spot in the air, "—blueprints."

Zhu pulls closer. "What is it?" she asks.

"Maybe? Yes! That could work," Addison recollects.

"What do you mean? Another route?"

"Something I remember Malakai complaining about in a meeting. There's an emergency passage located inside the mess hall," Addison explains. "That hatch leads to a network of tunnels that crisscross the platform, including one that can take us to the hallway outside the lab."

"That doesn't sound too bad," Zhu admits.

"Not quite that easy," Addison returns. "Those tunnels aren't designed for us to traverse while power is still active throughout the rig."

"Overhead lights have gone dark. Doesn't that mean the power is out?"

"Possibly? But if they shut it down, it's only been off for a few minutes," Addison counters. "It can take hours for the system to cycle." And she knows the temperature inside those pipes runs hot, especially without power to regulate the outflow. Addison's skin already itches as she thinks about crawling her way down three decks in those conditions.

"I don't see that we have much choice," Zhu says.

"We do," Addison smirks. "As long as you're not allergic to bullets."

"I don't see how that's funny."

"I think it is hilarious," Addison finishes, creeping back the way they came. "A bad joke."

The shots ring out in Addison's ears, bouncing off the walls like a megaphone.

The two women quietly skirt the battle and move to the commons on the upper floor, opening the door to find an empty room. Addison inputs her security code into the panel behind the counter, unlocking the hatch. Heat spills out as it opens, forcing them back.

"Crap!" Addison curses.

"That's hot," Zhu exclaims.

"Too hot. Fuck me," Addison swears again. "We're having fun. Right? Fun? Like crawling into a furnace."

"Or jumping into a volcano," Zhu suggests.

"Not quite that bad," Addison denies. "At least then, you'd die before hitting magma."

Addison sticks her hand inside, feeling her skin stiffen and crack.

"Air's too hot to breathe," she coughs.

"I don't look forward to dodging bullets," Zhu admits.

"We won't have to," Addison tells her.

"Neither of us can go through this!" Zhu cries.

"I can do it. If I'm quick."

"Alone?"

Addison nods. "I can do it," she repeats. "I won't have much time before it cooks me. Minutes? Faster if only I go."

"You're insane," Zhu says.

"We're floating a mile off an alien dreadnaught in the middle of the ocean," Addison says, taking off her overshirt and ripping it into quarters. She doesn't have time to look for better solutions. Addison wraps the scraps around her hands and knees, dabbing the superheated metal inside the hatch to test it. "Anything sane about this mission died weeks ago. Hand me that rebreather in the yellow emergency box, will you? I'll need it."

Zhu fetches her the mask.

"Shit on me," Addison worries, locking the apparatus over her mouth. "This is a bad idea." Cool air injects into her throat as she takes the first huff, leaving the taste of mint on her tongue. Addison licks her teeth as she climbs inside the pipeline, one foot at a time. "I can do this, right? Like trench diving underwater."

"Make sure to take deep breaths as you plunge," Zhu tells her.

"Got it," Addison exhales, looking down past her boot. "Thank you."

She checks her belt to ensure she still has the sidearm she took from the dead marine.

"You won't have much time to get to the labs."

"Less by the sound of gunfire," Addison goes. She's already sweating, her skin now bright red.

The rebreather mask will help to filter the air and keep her from asphyxiation. But every breath she takes will be like she's on top of Mount Everest—hardly any oxygen, which puts her at risk of cerebral hypoxia if she stays under for too long. All she needs is a few minutes. At worse, Addison will pass out in the space between floors. And should that happen, she'll dry out like a lizard baked in Death Valley of Eastern California by the time anybody finds her.

Addison takes a deep breath and plunges into the tunnel. The heat seeps through the wrappings on her hands and knees as she squeezes through the gaps. Addison once burned her fingers on the stove as a kid, leaving blisters that left scars. She expects this will be worse, but she'll have to soldier through it for three whole decks.

The cooling pipes inside the tunnels expel superheated air as she moves. Addison avoids these the best she can, but a plume gets her in the face at an intersection. She loses the rebreather as she reels back, and the air sucks the moisture from her mouth. Addison stumbles the rest of the way, nearly blind, feeling for the corners, gritting her teeth as she touches metal.

Addison suddenly drops when she puts a final hand down, expecting more of the tunnel, only to find the ventral shaft to deck five.

Her arm catches between the ladder's steps as she falls. She hears the snap before she feels it.

"Fuck!" Addison yelps.

Gripping the ladder with her other hand, she leverages her arm free. Addison must now ease her way down the shaft's whole stretch.

Her muscles strain. She lowers herself with the grace of a panda climbing off a tree. Addison looks down, unable to see the bottom. Forced to take it one rung at a time, it's an arduous task with a broken arm. All the while holding her breath between huffs from the mask. When she reaches the bottom, Addison feels for the latch and lifts it. The hatch opens, and she falls straight through.

Addison hits the cold floor and lies there to appreciate it. "Fuck me," she coughs, managing to prop herself against the wall. She weeps from the pain, moving her arm side-to-side to test its range of motion. Addison can tell it isn't fractured, but her elbow's twisted, most likely dislocated. And she isn't confident enough to set it back into place.

She will have to deal with it for now and get to the lab down the hall, next to the stairs.

Addison takes a breath and pulls herself to her feet. Her skin cracks as she moves—burns across her face and legs, limping but alive.

She crosses the hall and glances up the stairwell. Flashes and gunfire. Not a good sign for the defenders.

Addison hurries to the lab's door. She enters her code, but the pad beeps and denies her.

"Locked from the other side?" Addison murmurs. "That's good. I should've figured. But . . . if they haven't evacuated?"

Addison punches in the lab's override, and the door opens. She can hear a gasp as she enters the room. The glass floor reflects the staff and lab techs hiding behind the tables on the far side. Violent waters below shine off the ceiling, reflecting the storm.

"Wake up, people!" Addison shouts, closing the door behind her.

"Doctor Kennedy? What are you—?" a technician attempts to speak.

"Why's your face red?" another utters.

"Your arm! What happened?"

Addison shakes her head. "We need to move!" she cuts them off, counting seven heads. "Where is the Architect's Heart?"

"On the table," the technician points.

Addison goes to pick it up and seals it inside the containment unit.

A thud hits the door, lead ripping through the bulkhead. Everyone jumps.

"We're out of time," Addison mutters, hurrying to the viewing port. "Can everybody swim?"

"You want us to jump out the window?"

"I want us to get out of this alive," Addison chides, looking for the release handle to open the emergency escape.

Knocks at the bulkhead stop her before she can figure it out.

"Is it them?"

"I don't know . . . Doctor Kennedy? What do you think?"

"Get away from the door," Addison tells them, holding out her palm to calm the room. "It's okay . . . We'll be fine." She swallows and inhales unsteadily, inching her way to the entrance to double-check it's secure. "Who's there?"

"Dàkāi zhège," answers a distinctly male voice. "Yào bùrán."

Addison doesn't catch the words, but she figures it follows along, "Let us in, or we'll kick down this door."

She backs away and orders everyone to hide. Not that she has many places inside the lab to put her people, but the pounding on the door becomes more aggressive. Then sparks fly as the enemy begins cutting their way through the frame.

"I'm warning you!" Addison shouts. "We're armed! We won't hesitate to shoot!"

Addison's fingers go numb as she makes the threat, gripping the sidearm on her side. She doubts it's enough to hold off trained soldiers long enough for a rescue team to get to them. Still, looking at the lab technicians and night workers around her, scared, cowering behind the tables, she's all they have for now—a sailor's daughter with a broken arm. Undoubtedly, the enemy wants the Heart. And they're going to mop up any survivors to prevent them from being identified and incite a war, which is likely why they've cut off communications inside the base.

"Shit," Addison murmurs. "What do I do?"

"Doctor Kennedy?" Athena's voice rings into her earpiece.

"Athena? You're online?"

"Momentarily," the AI confides. "Doctor Remmings is still repairing whatever these meddlers did to the network."

"Damn them," Addison breathes. "But it doesn't matter. We need help!"

"Indeed. Colonel Ibrahim ran out of the Control Room with his remaining marines and is on his way. I won't be fully operational for a few minutes yet. We did reconnect with the quarantine fleet, however. They're sending in relief birds to secure the landing platforms."

"Then it's over?" Addison asks.

"Not quite," Athena warns. "Enemy troops will breach the lab in twenty seconds. I suggest taking cover."

"I already figured that out," Addison says, moving with the night crew until they're away from the windows. It's less cover, but they won't get caught in the crossfire when the enemy punches through the door. It will buy her seconds. And *that* can mean all the difference.

"Ten seconds," Athena announces. "Five . . . Prepare, Doctor Kennedy."

The door to the lab glows white before it finally collapses, tipping over with a metallic crash. Soldiers in black uniforms file into the room with their weapons pointed at the corners.

"Fàngxià wuqì!" the lead man shouts. "Xiànzài fàngxià wuqì!"

Addison figures it likely means, "Drop the weapon now!"

She doesn't get the chance. Their flashlights center on Addison, confusing her and allowing the soldiers to rush the scientists. They throw her to the ground and relieve her of the gun. An overly large man pins her down, his kneepad digging into her spine while he forces her hands behind her back, cuffing her wrists.

Addison winces as her body's endorphins wear off, and the pain in her arm screams for attention.

"Bǎoguo ānquán," the leader says. "Zhunbèi chèli."

Addison drops the containment sphere as the soldiers pick her up.

One of the assailants retrieves the device and hands it off to another, only for Addison to wrestle free and lunge for it. "Don't!" she yells, but she can't do much with her hands tied together. Two others pile on her while a third grabs her bad arm and bends it against the joint. Addison cries, snot running down her lip.

"Do not try that again," the leader orders in English.

Addison stares at him, tracking his hands. The others return her to her feet and line her against the wall with her co-workers. She can't read any of the soldiers' faces. Like the Americans, they hide behind their hardsuit visors. Cowards. But she doesn't need to know what they look like to recognize Mandarin Chinese when she hears it.

"No hard feelings, Doctor Kennedy," the man says. "We're following orders."

Addison squints, feeling like she's heard his voice before.

"Our lives for your orders?" Addison demands.

"For the greater good," the man exclaims. "We'll protect the Architect's Heart."

"We've protected it!"

"Not very well. Obviously. We need *this* to make up for our lost time."

"Lost time? What do you mean?" Addison begs the question.

A shimmer passes behind the man's shoulders. Is that . . . vapor? From the vents? No, that doesn't make sense. Even if the room's lockdown protocols went offline, the ventilation system doesn't connect to the maintenance tunnels between the decks. So, why—?

Addison blinks as she notices . . . No . . . What? Here?! How did *she* get on board?

The ghost flickers as the commander turns . . . A spear jabs into his backplate, and he yelps as he rises into the air.

The Architect tosses the man aside as the others open fire. She's fast, closing the distance between the soldiers before they can flank her. Addison watches. It's . . . not Idu. *She* was slender, prominently showing the white tattoos across her face and arms. This one's different, with broader shoulders and a shorter stance, built like somebody who lives a hard life. Her armor covers every inch of her body, deflecting the rounds from the soldiers' rifles.

The female Architect cuts into the soldiers, her movements like a dance, every swing deliberate. Is this how they fight? Warden's report of her battle with the Judge described him as a lumbering tower they had to throw everything at to topple. But this? It's like watching children trying to wrestle a parent to the ground.

Once she slays the last trooper, the female stops to catch her breath. Her glare lands on Addison.

"You're the Servant," Addison realizes. "Tjaa 'Neren?"

The Architect nods quietly. "You speak like you have a swollen tongue," the Servant abrasively answers.

Addison's chin trembles. "Why are you here?"

Tjaa cranes her neck as she walks over to retrieve the containment sphere from the leader's corpse.

"This is ours," the Servant says.

"It was given to us," Addison argues.

"By a traitor," Tjaa counters.

"Adhion 'Klaka—"

"Don't say his name!" Tjaa screams.

Addison frowns, raising a hand to surrender. "Seems like Adhion had good intentions," she winces.

"No reason is good enough."

"He thought it was necessary, didn't he? Important enough to make him think you'd listen."

"Murderers always think it's necessary to do things," Tjaa fights.

"Sounded to me he's never liked killing others."

"It *is* what he is," Tjaa scolds. "Nothing he does can change that."

"And he's done something drastic to tell you he's had enough of it," Addison follows. "He took the Heart and brought you to us. We came to investigate like moths to a flame, unaware of the war he's waging against you. Humanity is in the middle of it, so we defend ourselves. Adhion allowed us a chance to make this chaos worth our lives."

"He gave you the Heart to force us to act against our tenants!"

"Seems to me he's the only one brave enough to do it."

Tjaa disquiets and shivers, stepping back as if she wasn't ready for a debate.

"Doctor Kennedy?" Athena says in her earpiece. "Stall for another minute. Colonel Ibrahim has a plan. A bad plan. Take a step to your left. Standby."

"We create new life," Tjaa cries at her. "Adhion can only destroy!"

"Only when *that* life fails your expectations!" Addison shouts. "Or, when they grow beyond it. You send those like *him* to clear the slate so you can start with a new batch."

"To correct errors in their growth! Our mistakes."

"It doesn't matter," Addison says. "You order it. Adhion follows. And you all despise each other because of it."

Tjaa opens her helmet to reveal the feather patterns on her face. Addison reads the red in her hues, mixing dark blue with sickly green.

"Ten seconds," Athena whispers.

"We want to go home!" Tjaa shouts. "Let us go. Nobody else must die."

Addison blinks, only for a bang to ring across the air.

Malakai approaches the body and flips it over.

"Marine . . . Assigned to secure the pads," he states. "Shot in the back of the head, but not executed."

"Ramirez," Yuckham says next to him.

"Damn. Ramirez always hated sentry duty," Roth adds. "I guess he had a point."

Lightning flashes overhead as the rain pours over the deck, washing the dead man's blood into the black waters below. Malakai's nearing the first landing platform. All the exterior lights of the rig are dark. Malakai *has* a flashlight, but it's not enough to carve them a path. His marine escorts will rely on their visors to avoid dipping over the side.

"This pad's empty," Malakai declares. "We should move on to the next."

"What about Ramirez?"

"Switch on his tracker," Malakai suggests. "We'll find him again later. And there will be more. I'm sorry."

The two marines look at the body and then at him.

"Yes, sir," Roth agrees.

The trio follows the gangway around the corner to scout the next platform. Yuckham and Roth hurry when they find signs of another one-sided battle. It's hard to look at them. These marines, like Corporal Ramirez, were caught off-guard and shot in the back, lying face-first in puddles.

"How did so many of us go down without a fight?"

"Maybe the power outage distracted them?" Yuckham asks.

"We're better than that," Roth refuses to believe. "These guys are all laying the same way."

Yuckham kneels to one of the bodies. "He was facing out . . . Toward the water? Whoever did this was quick," she murmurs.

"Shots came from up high," Roth states. "Inside job? That can't be right."

"No, it can't be," he agrees. "But let's keep moving."

Malakai works his way onto the second helipad. As he walks the edge, his escorts take the time to attend to their fallen comrades. He doesn't blame them. It's hard enough to do this job without having to worry about losing people in the one place they should be safe. Malakai needs to figure out where this incursion began before he loses anybody else. Without that information, Colonel Ibrahim's team won't be able to cut off the enemy's escape and trap them on the rig.

Stealing a moment to feel the storm's weight, Malakai leans over the side and peers into the ocean. American warships anchor as far as the horizon. The closest vessels are likely wondering why the base has gone dark and are trying to hail them on the radio. But without access to the network, nobody can see or hear what's happening.

Mount Olympus . . . He rebuilt it as a first line of defense should catastrophe strike the Epimetheus Project. Secondary backup generators? Redundant systems? Very little would've caused a system-wide failure. He made sure of it. As the world sat in on the planning meetings, Malakai addressed concerns about the platform's security as their base of operations. It's why the crews undertook measures to shield the system from tampering.

This close to the dreadnaught, nobody knew *what* they would encounter. So *why* is that important?

Malakai knows the only way for the power to go out is to shut it off manually. "But why do it?" he murmurs. "How does anybody benefit?"

"Sir?" Yuckham asks.

"It's nothing," he shrugs.

"Of course, Doctor Adonis. Don't mind us."

Malakai takes a second lap. He notices cables hanging from the landing net surrounding the helideck. They're faint to see, but the radiance bouncing off the hull from the dreadnaught highlights the details. Malakai angles his flashlight in that direction and discovers the cables attached to the tow lines. He trails the wires to the water. And to rafts tied to the rig's buoys, surviving the beating of the waves.

"Corporals? Over here!" Malakai calls. The pair hurry to his position, shining their helmet lights at the water.

"I guess we know how they got aboard," Roth denotes.

"We need to warn the fleet," Malakai turns. "Flare gun?"

"I got it! Here."

Malakai takes the gun and points it at the sky. A bright red streak goes flying as he pulls the trigger, screaming until it explodes. Crews on a nearby American destroyer flash a response. The flight deck of the USS Isaac Bennett illuminates soon after with searchlights and standby signals as the rest of the fleet receives the message.

"Done," Roth says.

"That got their attention fast," Yuckham says.

"Yeah, it did," Roth gloats.

"Let's get back to the Control Room," Malakai instructs.

"Understood, sir."

Yuckham peers over the side. "I would have thought they'd leave someone to guard their exit," she weighs.

"We should hurry. I don't want to be . . . Look out!" Corporal Roth shouts as he tackles Yuckham and Malakai to the ground. Tracer rounds paint the helipad from the landing above the rig's superstructure. Roth takes shots to his back, neck, and arm. He's dead before Yuckham recovers and returns fire.

Sparks fly as Yuckham's armor reacts to shots landing on her shoulder. Another round grazes her helmet.

"Get to the wall! Get inside!" Yuckham shouts, squeezing off a few rounds. "I'll cover you!"

Malakai can't move. He tries to push out from under Corporal Roth, but the man's heavy and as limp as a whale on a beach.

"Oh, God—?" Malakai wants to say, tasting blood in his mouth. Not his own.

His heart climbs into his throat as he edges an arm free.

Yuckham grabs it and yanks him off the ground, throwing him forward.

"He's dead!" Yuckham shouts. "And we are, too, if we don't start running!"

Malakai clamps his jaw shut as he scampers across the platform. A shot whistles past his ear, and he ducks behind supply crates intended for the next shipment hull-side. Yuckham stays with him, covering him like a human shield. She takes hits in *his* place, getting the wind knocked out of her, but none of it slows her down.

As they get into cover, the doors on the landing above them swing open. Is that . . . yelling? Malakai swallows. A quick series of bursts muffle against the thunder. Heavy thuds follow, hitting hard on the metal deck. Relative silence replaces the gunfire.

"Director Adonis . . . Corporal Yuckham?" a marine asks them over the active comms.

Yuckham and Malakai look up to see three marines above them on the catwalk.

Malakai reaches for his earpiece. "We read you," he says with surprise.

"Thanks for the assist," Yuckham returns.

"We're back online," Ibrahim announces over an open channel. "Repeat! The network is kicking with a fever dream! Castle-Actual on Mount Olympus—I am requesting immediate support from the fleet. We are under attack by an unknown entity and have sustained casualties. Repeat! We are under attack and have casualties on-site! Please respond."

"We read you, Castle-Actual. Silver Falcon of the USS Isaac Bennett to Olympus SOS," the return call declares. "Relief is on its way. I want a base-wide update on all active-duty personnel. I need details . . . Who's attacking?"

The exchange continues over the channel, but Malakai doesn't bother listening to the rest of it. A ringing in his ears squeezes his head. Yuckham leads Malakai inside and throws him a towel from the prep room. Additional marines advance to secure the helipad. Able to communicate again, the base's security detail can regroup to retake the lower decks.

"We'll get them!" Yuckham cheers. "They caught us on the back foot, but they don't have enough men."

Malakai collapses onto a bench, surrendering a weak smile. "Then it's over?" he asks.

"Once we do a full tally of our casualties," Yuckham states.

"And how long do you think that'll take?"

"I don't know," Yuckham admits. "Maybe all day? It'll take a while to sweep through every room."

Malakai grimaces as he buries his face in the towel, wanting to dry off as soon as possible. He catches a warm spot in the air that immediately causes nausea in his chest. Malakai looks up as a shimmer darts past his nose. He rubs his eyes and looks again, but there's nothing he can see but mist coming in from the outside.

"What is that?" he asks.

"Are you okay, sir?" Yuckham probes. "You didn't get hit, did you?"

Malakai stares at the spot for another moment, the ringing fading to a soft hum. He takes off his gloves and feels for a warm draft, but whatever it is—or was—the cold quickly reconquers it. He leans back, letting out a heavy breath.

"I—? No. I'm fine," Malakai lies. "Just fine. Let's go clean up this mess."

"Are you sure?" Yuckham questions.

"Am I sure? Of course, I'm not," Malakai weeps. "Our people are dead . . . On my watch! And it wasn't aliens or machines that killed them."

"This isn't your fault, sir," Yuckham comforts. "Our duty—"

"Is to fight? To die?" Malakai demands. "Your friend died out there to protect me . . . Why? Because I didn't know what else to do but to go marching out looking for trouble. Is that what this mission needs?"

Yuckham shakes her head and sits next to him.

"You brought us here to make a difference," she notions, taking off her helmet. "Do you know . . . Anytime I look at that ship, I feel utterly useless. How can't I? I'm one soldier against . . . well, I don't think any of us know. And all I have are those beside me. That's why we travel in packs. Together, the impossible doesn't seem so enormous."

Malakai smiles as he studies her blue eyes. "I didn't realize there were such budding philosophers among us," he says.

"Not all of us were raised in the Program," Yuckham chuckles. "Some of us volunteered. And all of us have seen friends die."

"I don't know if that makes me feel better or worse," Malakai admits.

"Does it have to?" she returns, clenching her jaw.

"I suppose not," Malakai shivers. "No."

"The world's a shitty place, Doctor Adonis," Yuckham finishes. "My take? Don't go swimming in it."

61 | A HURRIED RESPONSE

LIEUTENANT COLONEL ELIAS IBRAHIM
UNITED COALITION ARMED FORCES

OCTOBER 25, 2041 | 1922 HOURS

===

"I need our network status now!" Ibrahim howls. "How close are we?" He hovers over Doctor Remmings' shoulder as she works.

Ava scowls as she decides to ignore him. She's a diligent egg, smarter than twenty of his best men and then some, but this isn't the lab anymore. It's the real world, and her "best" isn't fast enough. Not for what he *needs* her to do. And what he needs is for his network to be up and running so he can kick these bastards off his goddamn base!

"I am busy writing a purge algorithm to detect anything not a part of the original code," she explains. Ibrahim blinks as the words fly at him. Ava catches his bewilderment and pinches the bridge of her nose. "I'm doing the job of a studio's worth of people. On my own, I might add. So, lay the fuck off me."

Ibrahim presses his palms against the table. "I have people dying out there," he softly seethes. "Tell me what you need."

"Everything? Anyone available who understands coding, for starters. And I need them in this room," Ava scoffs breathlessly. Ibrahim can see her fingers turning white, her hands a blur as she types. "Otherwise—get me a bucket. Because I need to pee."

Ibrahim understands she means *that* as a joke. However, he's not in the mood to laugh.

"Do we have contact with the Overlook?" Ibrahim asks the other side of the room. "Athena would be a huge asset right now!"

"Communications blackout means any uplink attempt will fail if we connect," Leighton explains. "Our workstations are running off independent power. If we can't get in touch with our people on the other side of the platform, what makes you think we can contact orbit?"

"My father sent me data bursts on his trips ground side," Ibrahim recalls. "How does a twenty-year-old phone have *us* beat?"

"That depends. Did your dad have a working relay within a hundred-mile radius?" Ava disputes anxiously.

Ibrahim narrows his eyes at the woman. "Possibly?" he murmurs, choosing to look past her derisiveness.

"Good. Because I don't," Ava gripes. "Now go back to barking orders. Let us work."

Ibrahim shuts his mouth as he paces between stations while his runners leave for the dormitory. They'll escort Doctor Remmings' team to the Control Room to help her get the network back online. Without it, Ibrahim can't regroup his troops to retake the lower levels. He has . . . what, a hundred security officers and marines? Most of them transfer-status, intended for the ship-side outposts.

He closes his eyes and listens to the storm beating against the hull. It lulls him. With everything going on, it's almost enough to drown out the shooting three decks below.

"Almost," he mutters.

A half-dozen system engineers and lab techs enter the room. Ibrahim stops, cracks his neck, and meets them at the door.

"People! Our network is in tatters. We need it up and healthy again like a baby needs a rattle," Ibrahim orders, pointing them to their stations. "Doctor Remmings has the chair. Get to it! When I begin my serenade, I want the entire damn fleet to hear my angelic voice and cry at its beauty!"

The base's new ragtag electronic warfare team gets to their seats next to Doctor Remmings.

Ibrahim meanders to the viewports overlooking two of the landing pads in the meantime. No lights, no flares . . . Nothing at all from Malakai's team.

Corporal Roth should have a flare gun to signal when they've cleared the helipads. Ibrahim hopes they won't need it for anything else. Still, if the infiltrators kept a man back to protect their escape, a flare would likely prompt a response. What does he do if that happens? He'd have to pull runners off messenger duty to save their asses.

It's why he didn't want Malakai to go off alone. Ibrahim will have enough letters to write after this fiasco.

"Wait—wait—wait—!" Ava spouts, pointing at her screen while talking to another analyst at her station. Ibrahim leans in their direction.

"That's not right," the man says.

"It doesn't *make* sense, but it's the only explanation," Ava remarks.

"It's not that simple," another analyst calls across the table, rubbing his knuckles.

"How else do you explain it then?" Ava challenges. "Our program isn't finding anything because there's nothing to find!"

"What's going on?" Ibrahim demands, crossing his arms as he rejoins them.

"Sorry, sir—" Ava coughs, clearing her throat. "We wrote a ramshackle algorithm using a duplicate of High Castle's original code to highlight any changes made over the past two weeks. With everything down, we're essentially going off old checkpoint saves to determine the source of the system-wide blackout."

"Huh? Okay," Ibrahim slowly nods. "And what does that mean?"

"Well . . . After finishing the program, we discovered a few things," Ava says as her voice cracks.

"A few things? Did somebody plant a virus?"

"Well? It's difficult to explain," Ava admits. "And we don't have all the information."

"Do your best to dumb it down for me," Ibrahim playfully suggests.

Ava looks at her team and takes a deep breath. "All right. Where to begin? Athena rewrites her code to fit her needs at any given moment," she describes, tallying off the points with her fingers. "Going into this, we assume there are only so many ways somebody can shut down the whole system. Whatever the issue, it's not merely a power outage or somebody accidentally hitting the wrong button. The algorithm can help narrow the search area to where the 'executable' lies buried in the code."

"So, it *is* a virus?" Ibrahim states with confidence, only to notice the team's hesitation. "But I'm sensing things aren't going our way?"

"That's an understatement," a third analyst remarks.

Ava points a finger to quiet him down.

"Unfortunately, it's even less simple. Athena took a liberal stance reauthoring her code," she confides. "Nearly every line is different. She's *refined* their processes to run at peak efficiency, tripling her optimization despite hardware limitations."

"And that's bad?" Ibrahim asks.

"Oh, it's great from a techie's view," Ava laughs, "but the algorithm only cuts our workload by three million lines."

"Three million lines she didn't alter," another clarifies.

"That . . . sounds like progress to me?"

"There are over twenty-five billion lines of code," Ava shakes her head. "Remember—this is a global network, with her core systems based on mappings of the human brain. Think about every computer, tablet, watch, hardsuit visor, or comms unit in the vicinity—which is a lot—all working together harmoniously."

"And why we've needed Athena to run the system," Ibrahim realizes. "Iron out the issues." He returns to looking out the windows, hands folded behind his back as he listens.

"We still have the other twenty-four billion, nine-hundred ninety-seven million lines left," Ava sighs, leaning back in her chair. "Athena did her job

. . . She just . . . did her job a little too well."

"So, what can we do?" Ibrahim asks. "Or are we stuck?"

Ava stands up and drops her shoulders, staring blankly at the screen. "I don't know," she says. "But I still have a trick or two up my sleeve. We can adjust the algorithm to look for changes made by *us* and detect errors by narrowing the parameters through repeat simulation. Only a handful of people on the planet ha that access."

"Meaning it could point to exactly *who* sabotaged the system," Ibrahim says forcefully.

Ava frowns. "Maybe? Or maybe not. Frankly, it's all we've got." She pulls her keyboard closer to the edge of the table.

"Do it," he orders.

Ava sucks in her lips as she nods to her analytical team.

They make changes to their program, tweaking and sending pass reviews to each other to cut down their mistakes. Most of their back-and-forth sounds like a different language, with numbers and equations used instead of words. And they move like machines, calling out revisions and updates within minutes. Ibrahim can do calculus and plot trajectories when he pilots craft outside the atmosphere to a degree, but nowhere near their level. He can't even imagine the amount of schooling it would take to run numbers in his head like a computer.

Ibrahim holds his breath as he counts the seconds. He's unsure how it will affect the base, whether it will make their situation better or worse.

Admittedly, it's hard for him to see how their plan could do more damage.

"Everybody standby," Ava readies.

Ibrahim scrutinizes the landing pads outside, counting three dark figures walking on the gangway—Malakai, Roth, and Yuckham. They've cleared the first helipad.

"Let's execute in five—four—three—two—" Ava counts.

Before she completes her count, a red flare screams from the helipad and explodes high over the rig. Lights from a nearby American destroyer and the USS Isaac Bennett answer the distress. The bright glare reflects off the glass next to him, illuminating the tip of Ibrahim's nose.

"—one," Ava finishes.

A rattling from below the room startles him.

"What was that?" Ibrahim demands. "Give me an update!"

"The program's working," Ava murmurs, her hair looking like it's on fire under the emergency lighting. "Searching . . . Give it a minute. It's running through the code as fast as it can. You can't expect haphazardly designed tech to work like a charm the first time you turn it on." She straightens her posture and breathes into her fists, fighting off her nerves.

Ibrahim nearly steps away when a popping of gunfire erupts from outside.

"What the hell?" Ibrahim stops, pressing his face to the glass to get an angle on who's shooting.

"Colonel?" Ava inquires.

Ibrahim looks at her and feels a lightness in his chest. "Runners! Get to pad two on the double!" he shouts. "We got hostiles on the tower!" His last three marines in the Control Room dart out the door, rifles raised to their shoulders.

"Colonel Ibrahim?" Ava reiterates.

He hurries past her to shut the door. "Just tell me what you need," Ibrahim instructs. "And don't tell me your program is—"

"It's still running a final pass," Ava explains, her eyes locked on the screen.

"I don't have time for—"

"Shut up!" Ava growls. "Let me think. We're on the last hundred-thousand lines . . . Just another minute. And . . . We got it?"

Ava's eyes light up with surprise.

"What is it?" Ibrahim asks, losing his patience.

"We found the command," Ava says, her jaw quivering.

"Can you undo it?"

Ava only grimaces as she quietly reads her screen.

"Doctor Remmings—?" Ibrahim urges, stopping next to her. "Can you get the network running again?"

Ava closes her mouth and types in a quick series of commands.

"Done and done," she answers him, and the lights turn on. "Everything should come online. Go for comms."

"Good," Ibrahim nods, typing a code on his wrist-pad and opening a channel. "We're back online," he announces. "Repeat! The network is kicking with a fever dream! Castle-Actual on Mount Olympus—I am requesting immediate support from the fleet. We are under attack by an unknown entity and have sustained casualties. Repeat! We are under attack and have casualties on-site. Please respond."

"We read you, Castle-Actual. Silver Falcon of the USS Isaac Bennett to Olympus SOS," the Admiral returns.

Ibrahim can barely hear Jonathan Kennedy's voice over the static.

"Can't you clear this up?" Ibrahim asks.

"Working on it," Ava scoffs.

"Relief is on its way. I want a base-wide update on all active-duty personnel. I need details . . . Who's attacking?"

"I'll let you know that as soon as we do, Admiral," Ibrahim exhales, switching the router feed. "All teams, report your status!"

"Lieutenant Phillips—Emergency Systems, deck four. We've suffered near-total losses," the reports begin to file in, one by one. They arrive over the comms in a wave of static-filled noise bleeding into the background. "I think the enemy are making their way to deck five. Observation and Storage."

"Master Sergeant Wilkins—deck three, Engineering and Medical. We got our asses handed to us! Assailants uniformed, no distinctions."

"Corporal Higgins—responding to Philips' team on deck four. I've found bodies on the walkways!" Higgins describes. "We'll look for survivors."

"Whoever hit us knew where to go and how to do it," Wilkins suggests. "They must've trained for this . . . Nobody's this good!"

"We are," Ibrahim mutters.

It is the sort of high-risk mission the High Castle Program taught its people to do. Only a handful of special forces groups could act as a foil to his marines. And all of them work for the Epimetheus Project—allies in this great endeavor of the geo-political landscape.

Ibrahim turns to the staff on the control boards, running the defense.

"Athena—can you hear me?" he asks.

"Like a common koel in mating season, Lieutenant Colonel," Athena returns. "You've left me with quite the mess. Couldn't you have at least dusted off the corpses for me?"

"Now's not a time for jokes," Ibrahim shuts her up. "I need a status report on survivors on the rig. I need to know where they are as soon as—"

"Already done," Athena responds. "Dancing dots on your fancy boards."

"Can you read their IFF receivers?" Ibrahim orders. "Differentiate between *our* people and the assailants."

Athena takes a second to think. "I . . . cannot do that," she says.

"What do you mean?"

"Assailants are Epimetheus Project assets," she clarifies. "And we have a bigger issue. Take a look at deck five's readouts."

Ibrahim darts his eyes to the relevant screen. "I'm looking at them," he says, noting the large dot cluster in the Observation Lab.

"There are six assailants in the room," Athena says. "I am watching them via security feed."

"Six?" Ibrahim repeats. "But I'm counting fourteen markers?"

"Seven are lower-ranked lab technicians," Athena grants him. "Addison Kennedy *is* the eighth."

Ibrahim's eyes shoot up.

"Addison's in there? How the hell did she—?"

"Language," Athena snarks.

He shrugs it off, running to his command table to trace a route to the lab.

"Damn that woman," Ibrahim curses. "I need a response team!"

"We've only stragglers left," she denies. "And most of them aren't in any shape to fight."

"Fuck it," Ibrahim bites. "I'm heading down there."

He double-checks his sidearm and rushes out of the Control Room's door.

"There's another issue, Lieutenant Colonel."

"If you're going to tell me the oil rig is about to explode, I don't want to hear it."

"Not quite so dramatic," Athena says. "There's another signature in the lab with Addison and the others."

Ibrahim stops.

"What do you mean?"

"You could best describe it as . . . a foul stench on the air?" Athena postulates. "I detect an above-average increase in the room's temperature. And the source is moving around with them inside the room. Invisible, for the lack of a better term."

"Invisible?"

"Yes," she says. "Invisible as in . . . Not able to be seen."

"I know what invisible means," Ibrahim glowers. "Is it what I think it is?"

"Depends. Is what you think seven or eight feet in height?" Athena describes, rarely uncertain. "And has a head full of feathers?"

"That's all I need to know. There's an Architect aboard," Ibrahim quickly accepts. He passes by the armory to grab a weapon. If the alien has come for the reason he suspects, he will need the firepower. Or everybody in that room is dead, no matter their allegiance. "Update me with anything noteworthy."

"How about . . . the Architect decloaking and slaughtering the assailants?" Athena asks. "Noteworthy enough for you?"

Ibrahim makes it to the first stairwell before stopping.

"What about Addison?" he asks.

"She's talking to the creature," Athena says. "Her comms unit *is* active, however. And set to her private channel."

"Of course," Ibrahim mutters. "Tell her to stall for time!"

"You won't have much, Lieutenant Colonel," the AI warns.

Ibrahim sprints down the corridor and descends to the next stairwell. He crosses into the central hallway to deck four, skipping through the massive array of industrial platforms until he reaches the last flight of steps. Ibrahim's boots land hard on the metal floor. He checks his weapon as he gets to the door of the Observation Lab, now blown open by thermite explosives. He spies the Architect inside, talking to Addison Kennedy.

Ibrahim doesn't have time to think. He only acts.

He slinks around the corner, lining up a shot. The alien unfolds its helmet enough to show him the back of its feathery mane. Ibrahim looks at it for a second, confused at the opportunity but unwilling to let it go unanswered. He presses the rifle's butt against his shoulder . . . centers his reticle . . . and squeezes the trigger. His bullet trails directly into the back of the Architect's unprotected skull, popping it like a can of warm sardines.

The bird-like alien's body drops suddenly to the floor as the pain in his shoulder fades.

Ibrahim winces. "Not today," he says, stepping into the room.

He stops when he notices Addison and the others huddled by the wall. She remains there as her eyes stagger to him in the doorway, the alien's orange blood decorating her face and clothes. Her pupils are large in the dim light, coming out of shock as the excitement quickly passes.

"Addison?" Ibrahim presses, looking at the burns on her arms. "You're hurt!"

"I . . . had to crawl through the ducts," she whimpers.

Ibrahim lets out his breath. "You had no choice," he whispers, deciding not to scold her.

Addison drops back against the wall. "I only wanted to help," she cries, burying her face into her sleeves.

"And you did," Ibrahim offers. He wraps his arm around her, careful not to touch her skin.

"What's going to happen now?"

"I don't know," he admits. "But we'll find out."

"They were Hao's people that attacked us," she warns.

Ibrahim's mouth twists as he looks at the bodies on the floor—black-armored, the plating shattered by the Architect's spear.

"That doesn't matter now," he says, helping the woman stand. "We need to get you to the infirmary."

"How many dead?" Addison asks.

Ibrahim feels light in his chest as she stares him down for an answer.

"Enough to make us angry," he says, pulling the other scientists together to lift her onto a cart.

IDU 'SMEORA, THE WHISPERER OF CONTINUANCE
ARKKITECT OF THE VILI

521031 LOCAL CLUSTER | 761,404 DAY OF PURPOSE

She takes a long walk along the corridor, ignoring the dozens of Varma-jalkavaen guarding *his* cell. Events are spiraling outside of her control.

"Two of us are dead now," Idu whispers. "How much longer does he expect us to hold out?"

Adhion remains sitting in his sequester, staring at the lonely wall. There are no brigs aboard the Vili—this is not a prison barge nor a warship. This vessel is a source of life to barren worlds. Instead of a prison, Tyrann has repurposed the animal enclosures to serve the purpose. It's dark and filthy, unforgiving in its brutal, uncomfortable temperament.

The Nomad's head glides up as Idu approaches. He grins peacefully before returning to his competition with the cold emptiness.

Idu stops opposite his cage and waits for him to speak first.

Adhion shifts an arm as he sits up, his mouth trembling. He coughs as his colors fade to blacks and blues, a remnant of the beatings the Trident gave him after throwing him into this cage. Is this what centuries of a dutiful life brings? She doesn't know.

"Tjaa 'Neren," he mourns. "She's dead?"

"Yes," Idu confirms.

"The humans defended themselves," the other says. "Such is their right."

"She failed to retrieve the Heart. As did Dhun," Idu explains. "One after another, we are losing this battle."

"As the 'Obligation' demands of us," Adhion frowns, only to notice the shallowness in her eyes. "But—? That's not all, is it?" He leans forward to get a sense of her.

"We do not know," Idu admits. "Many of their fighters were dead. Tjaa sent images to the Observer before we lost contact."

Adhion drops his shoulders.

"More disharmony?"

"It appears there was divisiveness over the ownership of your 'gift' to them," Idu concludes.

"Then it's my fault. Dhun would have at least stood a chance," Adhion speaks, looking away. "Still? He underestimated them. We've come to rely on our technology to meet our challenges head-on. But what happens when we cannot adapt? We lash out like our progeny trying to leave the nursery rings. It makes us ... almost human? As flawed as our worst creations."

"An odd way to put it."

"Or an accurate one," Adhion shrugs. "That is life's subtle nature, I suppose. Tjaa couldn't grasp the minute differences. She could only take on her tasks in a very narrow manner. And with no room to interpret, she was stranded on an island with nowhere to run. It's not *their* failure or *our* mistakes. Nature likes to work against the plans we've put into motion. 'There are *no* straight lines in a forest,' I believe the humans would say."

Idu keeps her eyes on him, never breaking contact.

The Nomad seemingly accepts her glowering and continues to stare at his wall. It's almost like he's studying the lines, waiting for the cage to change shape like a vyernox changes moods. Adhion's dark sobriety contests only with moments where he chuckles under his breath.

Idu wrings her palms. "Why do you hate us?" she finally musters the courage to ask.

He blinks as he lifts his eyes to her. "Hate you? Is that what you think of me?" Adhion returns.

"How else am I to think of it?" she questions.

Adhion rises to his feet and confronts her at the bars of his cage. The Varmajalkavaen react quickly, drawing their weapons—with metal spears and hard-light throwers.

Idu orders them to remain calm, but they don't stand down.

"I am resentful, but I do not *hate* you, Idu 'Smeora. And these warriors?" He shakes his head and pulls in as close as possible to her. "They may guard me, but I don't hate them for it, either. Yet, they have every reason to hate *us* for what we did to them. Did you know? I was on the vessel sent to reclaim their world."

"They were 'fauna' that broke containment," Idu recalls, "after their carrier went down."

"Fauna? People!" Adhion corrects.

"A people our kind raised from embryos," Idu iterates. "And I already know the story."

Adhion's feathery mane reddens as he stiffens his stance. "No. You do not," he says sharply. "Without our meddling to upset the balance, their ecology developed freely. Do you understand? Self-actualization! Until we descended on their homes like a third moon cusping an eclipse. And they fought back. Like these humans, they battled us in a way we were ill-prepared. And one day? Those we captured and had collected on our ship for research had freed themselves. Led by a female, she drove her people to an escape craft and got the survivors to the surface."

"And thus earned the right for us to uplift them," Idu describes.

"I was content on leaving them alone," Adhion scolds. "They were happily living in their corner of the universe, without *us* to steal their children to serve the Obligation. Tyrann 'Akachan enjoys saying the Varmajalkavaen earned their positions and that their *enslavement* was akin to privilege. Or should we consider chained freedom the same as breathing free? I think it odd how we never asked *them* what they wanted. We just decided. Is *that* what *you* consider uplifting, Whisperer?"

"Those like the Tridents of Absolution always prefer to have the final word," Idu falls away.

"If only the others would openly share their thoughts," Adhion mourns. "Given the chance, which side would the Varmajalkavaen join? If they had a choice? A real choice!"

Idu's eyes widen. "What do you mean?" she asks.

"You *know* what I mean."

"I am not sure I do."

Adhion's frown deepens. "You're smarter than that, Idu," he says. "You scoffed at the humans at first. Now? You are worried for them."

"I am worried about the Trident's anger at them," she can admit.

"He wants to go home," Adhion states.

"We *all* do!"

"And instead of negotiating with the humans, he'll send others to fight them," Adhion finally notes. "Doesn't that say much about who *we* are as a species? Don't you think? We look down on primitives for their violent tendencies. But what is *our* reaction to anything that refuses to do what we tell them?"

Idu slams her fist against his cage.

"You do hate us!"

"I hate myself! Everything I have done! All my years? A waste," Adhion says aloud. Idu steps back. She . . . didn't expect *that* answer. "And I'm not alone, Idu. I won't stop the cycle. But I *can* make a statement large enough to spark a fire. Obligation demands that I undo our mistakes to ensure the future. I won't listen to others' interpretation of those words anymore."

Idu scowls. "We're talking in circles," she says. "Say what you want me to do."

"I want you to come with me to meet the humans," Adhion says. "I want *you* there when I ask Addison Kennedy for the Heart as the Trident should have done."

"You gave it to her. Why would you ask for it back? Would she even give it up?"

He presses his face against the bars, showing his naked palms to her.

"She would. Because she's willing to understand," Adhion says gladly. "Isn't that why you went to her?"

"I needed a thinking mind with an open temperament."

"As do I right now."

"He won't let you anywhere near the chamber again," she says. "You know that, right?"

"There's only one way for him to do that," Adhion explains. "If we ask for their help, we could win."

"Or we could lose."

"Not if we deactivate the Alimentors in their holdings," he suggests.

"I don't have that access," Idu warns him.

"Then we earn the loyalty of the Varmajalkavaen," Adhion shifts. Idu looks at the warriors lining the corridor's high walls. "Tyrann alone is our leader, interpreter of the Obligation. And *they* only guard me on his orders. *You* are the Whisperer of Continuance. Your chord wrote the words that carry our chains. You can break the links that hold us, Idu 'Smeora. Convince these jailors to help us, and we might stand a chance in re-tuning these strings we play for our masters."

"To make a difference?" Idu murmurs with a low-hanging gaze.

"By whatever means we can," Adhion stipulates.

When she upturns her eyes, Idu can read the Nomad's brighter colors—light red mixing with a vibrant yellow. It reminds her of a morning sky.

"Was this your plan all along?" Idu asks.

The other laughs. "I take my chances where I can," Adhion answers. "Sometimes, it demands a larger leap of faith."

"Just hoping all the pieces fall into place?"

"More like throwing them high to see where they land first."

"That's a poor way to walk through life."

"I'll admit, there *are* easier ways to die," Adhion goes. "Will you help me?"

Idu paces along the corridor for several ticks as she weighs the decision. She glances up to spy a Fragment Alimentor hiding in the gallery's shadows. The machine angrily beeps at her as it notices her gaze, flashing white as it escapes into a nearby tunnel. A spy? Idu lets out a breath. There'd be no way to hide this plot from the Trident if he's ordered the machines to follow her.

She's just afraid of *how* he will react.

"You're right," Idu slowly admits. "Even if I do nothing to help him, the Trident will take drastic steps to undo the damage." Her arms begin shaking at the prospect. The warmth in her fingers wisps away as she loses feeling throughout her body. "This vessel has a large onboard swarm he could use to unleash devastation. And he wouldn't have to sacrifice more of our blood."

"He has all the pieces he needs," Adhion urges. "Save one."

"Are you certain this is the right thing to do?" Idu asks.

"Maybe not for the people of this world," he admits. "But for us? Yes."

Idu shortens her breath as she reaches for the cage's door. Opening it will start a final countdown, and the clock will run very short. And should they convince these Varmajalkavaen to assist them, it could further fracture their ranks, leading to more infighting. Not to mention, these dozens are among the last warriors stationed aboard the Vili. Thousands more belong to the diggers, harvesters, caretakers, and gardeners who help plant the seeds of young ecosystems.

Idu brushes off her worries and waves at the control panel, opening the Nomad's cage. It's her choice, regardless of the consequence.

The Varmajalkavaen close their ranks and arm their weapons.

"Stand down!" Idu orders.

She musters her courage from deep in her gut to amplify her voice, but they don't immediately heed her call.

Adhion leaves his cage and looks at Idu, his guards, and Idu again. "Thank you," he says, offering her a respectful nod.

Idu returns the gesture with the same deference. "Tyrann will consider us both threats now," she forewarns.

"I know," Adhion weeps.

Idu swallows when he folds his hands and walks past her, confronting the High Echelons.

"Adhion?" she asks, but he merely shakes his head.

"You've heard us speak," Adhion tells his guards. "All of us have a choice! Make it. Join us or walk away."

The warriors yield slow looks at one another, unsure how to proceed. They are no longer the force they were days ago. However, if they convince them, Idu wonders if they would be enough to make a difference in the fight ahead. Many would not turn their backs on the Obligation—out of fear of the Trident's wrath or the change such rebellion invokes. But that's not for her to decide one way or another. She can only hope the Varmajalkavaen will *want* to stand up for themselves. Nobody else can hold their ground and shout, "No more!" in their places. Not against the very system that raised them into what they are now.

An individual named Minn'Athorad Rhamn takes the chance and steps forward. In his ornate, metallic carapace, Rha considers the pair, narrowing his six eyes on Idu and keeping his hands on his spear. Is he unsure what to make of the choice thrown at his two-pronged feet? She doesn't know.

Idu positions herself to guard the Nomad against the warrior.

Rha raises his upper arms and taps his spear's haft on the floor. Others mimic the gesture. Not many at first, but it's enough for Idu to soften her posture. Soon, the number grows like a human orchestra building cadence with the drummers until the entire corridor falls into step.

Idu surrenders a smile. "You didn't need my help to convince them," she notions at Adhion 'Klaka.

"They needed us to be honest with one another," he returns.

"And what about the Fragment Alimentors you've reprogramed?" Idu questions. "If we are to fight a war—?"

"Tyrann would have undone what I did to them," Adhion cautions. "And if he activates the rest, it won't matter if he didn't. I could never rewrite enough to win the ship. Our only chance is to convince the humans to fight along *with* the Varmajalkavaen. Humans killed Dhun 'Ancod . . . And now, they've killed Tjaa 'Neren. Let's go make them aware of the situation."

"Quite the price to pay for a conversation, isn't it?" Idu wonders.

"We've paid much worse," he remarks. "I should know. I am the one who counts the bodies."

RYAN VOGERT, CHIEF MEDICAL OFFICER
EPIMETHEUS PROJECT

OCTOBER 26, 2041 | 0434 HOURS

Vogert supervises *another* five bodies on their way to the morgue.

"Jesus Christ," he whispers. "More of them? That makes fifty-six."

He enters the medbay and sterilizes, sifting through the dead marines and personnel caught in the attack. It was bad enough that they were constantly under threat by the alien ship. But now? Another setback. Traitors. Or are they terrorists?

"It boggles the mind," he mutters.

Vogert stops at a table where the body of an assailant killed by the Architect in the Observation Lab waits for his examination. Slender and black-armored, he peels off the layered pieces to find charred skin underneath, the epidermis almost melding with the soldier's compression suit.

It's not too unlike the wounds Vogert has seen caused by the Fragments onboard the dreadnaught.

Unluckily, the incursion left very few wounded for Vogert to treat. The assailants killed most of the personnel they came across, no matter their positions—armed combatants or members of the research teams. Vogert sobs as he covers the faces of these people with white plastic sheets. He doesn't know what else to do but offer them his passing respect.

"Doctor Vogert?" the runner asks him.

"Yes?" he returns, looking up.

"Six more from deck four," the lad calls. "Where do you want them?"

Vogert sighs heavily. "Six? I don't know," he admits. "Wherever you can find room. And be gentle."

"Understood, doctor," the other says, running off to guide the transfer.

"Sixty-two?" Vogert whimpers. "How did they kill so many?"

Combing through the mess will take considerable time. Vogert's team begins tallying the dead, separating them by their nationalities. Their home countries will want to return them to their families. But as Vogert finishes counting the first quarter, he notes an odd pattern with their injuries. An alarmingly high number, at least twelve, with bullet wounds in the back of their skulls.

"Strange," he says, lifting a victim's head to examine it closer. "French? One of the garrisoned troops." He turns on his wrist-pad and checks the duty roster. "Corporal Thomas Gerrald. Assigned to the night patrol on deck three." He feels the narrow gap where the bullet went through the armor. "And like the other defenders, killed by an armor-piercing round."

Vogert moves on to the next several cadavers, finishing their autopsies and forwarding their reports.

"Ryan? Can you help me with this?" Doctor Hendru Mori asks him, fresh off a shuttle from the dreadnaught.

Vogert hurries across the room to help turn another victim over. "Trouble?" he asks, laying the body flat on its back. Vogert had to recall several of his staff from the METIS Research Base to help with the overwhelmed medical crew of the Olympus.

"Those idiots dumped this one in here belly-first," Hendru clamors.

"What's his name?"

"According to the roster? Zé Dōng Chén."

"Chinese?" Vogert asks.

"Most likely," Hendru affirms.

"Then let's begin a record," Vogert orders. "Another victim. An officer tasked to the special contingent that arrived with Doctor Zhu. And shot—? Huh." He stops, remarking on the damage scattered across the soldier's upper body. Vogert inspects the chest area, running his fingertips over the wide impact zones where the bullets hit the ceramic plating. "Deep impressions? And with rough edges, likely caused by high-caliber ballistics."

"Ryan? What is it?"

"I don't know—" Vogert loses track of the words as he pivots to one of the other dead marines. He double-checks the damage to the armor, noticing an alarming trend between the UCAF troops and their Chinese counterparts. "Clean. Caused by armor-piercing rounds," he whispers. "Versus the larger, blunt-force breakage I expect of our standard munitions."

"Quite the discrepancy between the two groups," Hendru notices.

"Almost as if they were fighting each other," Vogert concludes.

"What? Like . . . Friendly fire?"

"I wouldn't call it friendly," Vogert grimaces, checking his pad for new reports.

"You think our members did this? On purpose?"

"I don't see how they'd shoot their allies in the back by accident," Vogert alludes. "But we've got a job to do. So, let's do it."

"And hope nobody's pointing a gun at us," Hendru murmurs.

"In the meantime, forward the ballistics to Doctor Remmings," Vogert suggests.

"You think Avanna can give us some insight into whatever happened?"

"Maybe not," he admits. "But who else knows this stuff better?"

"An apt observation," Hendru agrees.

Vogert frowns as he moves on, not knowing what else to do. Everybody's doing what they can to help with the recovery operations. And of the bodies they've already brought to the morgue, Vogert has one very special victim on his mind above his other worries. The specimen that Colonel Ibrahim wasted in the labs.

He washes his face and dawns clean scrubs, entering the sequester with his assistant.

"Tjaa 'Neren—an Architect," Vogert describes, "also known to us as the Servant of Cultivation."

Vogert looks over her body. The female's face is completely gone.

"The rifle Ibrahim used left very little intact tissue behind," Vogert says into his recorder. "Powerful weapon. Given the situation, it *was* necessary. Although, it's also given us a chanced look at non-native anatomy." He runs a scan to get a bearing on the Architect's sub-surface structure. "Hollow bones? Different from a terrestrial bird. These are more like air pockets . . . Maybe to assist with a high-energy lifestyle? And dense layers of closely-knit muscle fibers? Curious. It would certainly explain their feats of strength despite their slender limbs."

Vogert will admit it. He's looking forward to examining the Architect that Olivia Warden killed when he returns hull-side. During their retreat, the Sergeant Major had the wisdom to drag the giant's body to the exfiltration point near Station Four. What are the odds for—not one—but two opportunities to occur within days of each other? He doesn't know. But he *does* want to go as far as he can take it.

After this tragedy, there's a delay in those plans until the fallout clears. Families will demand answers from governments struggling to justify their initiatives to fund and provide for this mission—too many questions and not enough answers for all the dead staff members and their security forces. Vogert steals a moment to fight off a pain in his chest, making him want to vomit.

"And failures breed consequences," he weighs, clenching his jaw under his facemask.

Vogert takes three deep breaths to calm his nerves.

A task force headed by Alexandra Roslin has already landed to investigate the incident. Vogert looks at the trooper in the corner of the room—a tall lad wearing polished white body armor over a dark red undersuit. It's not a uniform that blends into an environment. And for a reason. OverSec wants to stand out from the crowd, to make its presence overtly known.

It's now the division's responsibility to safeguard UCSN assets for the Epimetheus Project.

"As if things weren't hard enough," Vogert grumbles.

He pauses for a moment and stops his recorder, tapping his finger tensely and creating a mental note to edit that part out of his transcription.

Vogert proceeds with the bird-like alien's autopsy, evading his audience. He makes detailed notes, taking hundreds of photos to attach to his report. Vogert can only hope it will provide insight into the species' internal workings. And if the repercussions caused by the deaths of the two Architects hit them, Vogert would do better to get as far away from this place as possible.

Vogert expected *some* response from the Architects after Dhun 'Ancod. But what was the result? The murder of Tjaa 'Neren amidst the intricate conflicts of human tribalism. A messy situation, for certain. And one that Vogert doesn't know if there's a clean solution. Not an obvious one, at any rate.

And the female's abrupt appearance may also explain why things went so quiet hull-side.

"They were preparing for something bigger," Vogert murmurs.

"What did you say, Doctor Vogert?" his assistant asks.

He looks at her and shakes his head, breaking away to focus on what's lying on the table in front of him now.

"Nothing," Vogert tells his assistant. "Hand me a scalpel."

"Of course, doctor," the woman says, offering him the knife.

Sliding the fine blade between the female's armored plates, Vogert removes a piece, taking some of the skin with it. Tjaa's outermost shell melds to her body like the black-armored trooper he looked at a few hours prior. The alien's harness is like hard muscle tissue, enfolding her, fusing to her bones.

"Begin new record," Vogert commands. "Medical log one-nine-two. Name of the subject? Tjaa 'Neren—an Architect, as stated in my previous summary. Known as the Servant of Cultivation to her peers. Female. One-hundred-eleven inches at full height. That's if she still had a head on her shoulders."

Vogert pours over the alien's body, looking at what to do next. His deep tissue scans come back with structures he hasn't seen before. There's an elegance to it with some resemblance to animal life he can find on Earth, but . . . so vastly different, with intricate, redundant organs that blend wonderfully with their neighboring tissues. It's as if somebody made organic life an art form.

"Subject's age is unknown. I am drawing blood for later testing," Vogert carries on. "But I do not expect it to amount to much without a cross-reference. Not yet. And there are markings across the subject's body—tattoos, brands, and scars—that could denote stigmas attached to her societal caste. The subject's epidermis feels smooth to the touch with no sign of settling necrosis. It could be that our environment lacks the specialized bacteria to aid decomposition. That, or the subject's armor continues to supply nutrients to her cells after death."

Vogert picks up an armor piece and turns it over in better light.

"Given the healing around the tech in her body," Vogert steers his examination, setting the armor piece flat on the table, "the subject had enhancements folded into her tissue at a younger age. Cybernetic framework, but not unsightly in their design. I must wonder if it plays a cultural purpose. Or maybe a religious one? Without a living specimen to answer my questions, I wouldn't try to speculate further. Either way, the dance between the organic and mechanical functions across the body remains substantial." He smiles, hopeful at how much his findings could inspire humanity's future development.

Vogert will spend a long time on Tjaa's corpse, opening it up and leaving nothing untouched.

After he finishes and washes his hands, he transcribes his notes. Vogert includes them in his official report to Malakai and Ibrahim. There *is* insight within its contents, but not anything the military can use practically in a fight. Vogert presses his palms to his temples, trying to wrap his head around the technology in the Architect's body.

He returns to his rounds in the emergency room once he finishes. "No rest for the weary," Vogert whispers. More bodies pile up as the rescue teams continue their sweeps, with new arrivals every twelve minutes, most of them from deck four. After a while, the red lights begin flashing again. Everyone in the medical bay looks up, startled.

"Another alert?" Hendru asks. "Why not the alarms?"

"There weren't alarms during the attack either," Vanniyar denotes, the trauma specialist aboard the Olympus.

The door to the hallway opens. "What the hell—?" Vogert's about to say. He flinches as a dozen more OverSec troopers stomp into the room, flashing their fancy red uniforms. "Get out! One guard was enough. You're in a restricted area! We need this room clear for wounded and emergency crews!" He shouts, running up to stop them.

Those already in the medbay ignore him, marching to the adjacent walls and stepping to attention.

An officer wearing an SOI badge on his right cuff enters and scans the room with a glower.

"All command staff must report to the labs," the leading agent orders.

"Can't you see I'm busy?! What's this about?" Vogert demands. "If it's important, Athena should've contacted me!"

"We're keeping this off the official sheets for now, Doctor Vogert," the agent confides. "Please come with us. We've special guests. The others are on their way there already. Everything will go into lockdown in the meantime."

"Another lockdown?" Doctor Fullan wonders aloud by her station.

Vogert grimaces, squeezing his wrist as he looks at the interested faces of the medical crew.

"Let me get out of my garb," he agrees, not wanting to cause a fuss. "Give me a couple of minutes."

"We can give you five," the agent presses.

Vogert removes his scrubs and deposits them in the biohazard waste bin.

"And who are these guests?" he asks, stepping through decontamination. "Not more politicians?"

The lead agent hesitates. "Ambassadors, sir," he imparts.

"From the Chinese?"

"No, sir."

Vogert fixes his collar as he stops in front of the officer and his OverSec escort, ready to leave. He notices the man's stiff expression, his uniform tightly tailored.

"You'll see once we get there, Doctor Vogert," speaks a woman standing in the doorway. She's facing away from him, only showing the back of her head. Her blonde hair is in a short pixie cut, leaving her with an elegant, commanding silhouette. "They're not at liberty to say after recent events. For security. That's their job, you'll understand."

Vogert sighs heavily. "All right," he surrenders. "Lead the way."

"Thank you, sir," the first officer acknowledges. "Follow us."

Malakai listens intently as the conference wraps up. Much of his leadership staff are in the office with him, crowding the monitors. Everybody's here for the uplink. And in the corner of the room, a quiet woman with blonde hair watches the proceedings.

They're on the line with the majority of the Security Council—moderated by James William Harper, Secretary-General of the United Coalition.

Only the Chinese delegation isn't in attendance, uninvited to this emergency session.

Malakai taps his finger impatiently. He wants the bureaucrats to get to their point, but they've been delaying it for an hour now. Sweat embellishes Admiral Kennedy and Colonel Ibrahim's collars as the room heats up. They know what's on everyone's mind. And they're afraid. That worry hangs over Malakai's head at this very moment.

"You're approved to move forward with caution," Harper finishes. "Get it done."

"We're trusting you on this," Ambassador Geraldine adds.

"Understood," Old Man Kennedy agrees. "And thank you for your confidence."

Malakai switches off the terminal.

"Damn it!" he shouts, knocking his fist on the table.

Addison turns a worrisome glare at him.

"We can't do it," she attempts to sway the team.

"They attacked us, Addison," her father goes.

"Their attack failed!"

"A bold statement. Casualty reports keep reaching my desk as the bodies pile up," Jonathan denotes. "I wouldn't call *that* a failure. We must act before the Chinese figure out what's happened to their team. Athena has them busy chasing black holes. That will only distract them for so long. We've days at best."

"I would be surprised if they weren't waiting to see how we'd react first," Ibrahim states.

Malakai leans forward in his chair, quietly counting the heads in his office. He's got the Old Man, Addison Kennedy, Elias Ibrahim, Ava Remmings, Leighton, and a half dozen other personnel from the various fields that make up most of his onboard staff. Besides the need for Doctor Vogert to supervise the morgue, there's only one absentee from this meeting . . . Zhu Yunwen. And that's where Alexandra Roslin steps into play, deciding it was safer for Zhu to remain under "security detention" out of fears posed by a *specific* party over her free reign of the base.

He doesn't envy the woman's position. And survivors on the Olympus are more than willing to throw their anger in her direction. At least until an investigation into whether she was involved with the attack can decide if she's a risk. But without evidence of Yunwen's guilt, Addison Kennedy and Ava Remmings have argued against her arrest.

Malakai's issue is that he must agree to the terms given to him by OverSec since they took over security at the base a few hours ago.

It's not an ideal situation. Malakai can only wait and see *who* her government will throw under the bus, and they've only two good options. Zhu Yunwen, the only remaining Chinese National left on-site, or Wensu Hao, the Field Director he put in charge after exhausting his other options.

"Is retaliation the smartest thing to do now?" Ava questions.

"It's not a full mobilization. CSDR attacked *us* first and broke the treaty," Ibrahim argues. "So, it's already decided. And besides, we aren't going in without a plan. It's just an overly dramatic arrest and seizure of assets. We'll start moving against them inside the ship, then commit to a raid on Camp Yi."

"With luck, we can catch them off-guard and unaware," Admiral Jon Kennedy adds.

"And if the Architects choose to move against us while our attention is on the Chinese?" Addison asks.

"A few quiet days inside the ship doesn't convince you, Addison?" Ibrahim mocks with a heavy tone. "If they had the resources left after their civil war to do real damage to us, they wouldn't have sent two of their own to die."

"Or maybe the fact they're quiet should make us even more worried?"

"They're not as tough as you'd think," Ibrahim waves her off, done with the discussion.

Addison sighs and turns hard at Malakai. He returns her stare, unemotional.

Malakai enjoys the circumstance just as much as she does, which is to say, *not* at all. His hands are tied on the matter, however. All he can do is count the stacks in the morgue to know the Epimetheus Project won't likely survive the week.

"We can't just ignore them," Addison argues. "There must be a way to contact them!"

"We've tried already," Leighton counters.

"And at a considerable cost, I'll remind you," Ibrahim adds. "Addison? We're on this mission together, don't forget. When your people kick the hornet's nest, it's my job to kick them back into the ground. And I'll kick them again while they're down."

"How very courteous of you, Colonel Ibrahim," Addison remarks.

Ibrahim glowers at her. Malakai hasn't seen him throw such intensity at her before.

Addison levels her shoulders, utterly bleak. As if a ghost had walked through her and left an empty shell.

"Enough!" Malakai shouts, finally sick of hearing it.

"We have our orders, Addison," the Old Man resolves. "We can't change it now."

"Regardless. Get ready to embark on the early shuttle hull-side," Malakai tells her. "We all have a job to do. There's a second body on site that needs your attention. You will supervise the Judge's autopsy with Doctor Vogert when you two get there. And I want a report in twenty-four hours. Understood?"

He looks up to see the fire reflecting in Addison's eyes. There'd be two holes boring into Malakai's skull if she had heat vision as a superpower.

"This isn't right," Ava clamors. "We need to talk to them."

"You mean the Chinese?"

"No," Ava breathes, shaking her head. "I mean the other Architects—Tyrann, Idu, and Adhion."

"That discussion is a closed issue," the Old Man declares.

"A closed issue?" Ava challenges him, walking up to the Admiral to make the man look small. "Why are we even bothering if we're not going to explore the options? The military protects us, yes . . . But we've barely seen a fraction of that ship! Why did the Fragments stop attacking our patrols? And why aren't the Varmajalkavaen as prevalent as they've been for the last two weeks?"

"If they wanted to talk, they'd reach out to us," Ibrahim says. "As far as I am concerned, they are terrorists."

"And if all they want is the artifact back?" Addison questions. "They go home, and this whole mess is over. We can rebuild!"

"Maybe," Ibrahim murmurs.

"Addison? My family is waiting for me in the camps," Malakai offers another perspective. "Everybody wants to go home! At the moment, that's not an option for us. Zhu's people have made their intentions clear with the attack on the Olympus. And they didn't want any witnesses. A day? Maybe two? That's how long we have to answer them."

"The Architects can wait until *after* the threat is dealt with," the Old Man rules. "You're outvoted here, Addie. Stand down! That's an order. Collect your gear and get ready to transfer hull-side. And if it's necessary, I'll have Colonel Ibrahim escort you. I—"

Malakai's earpiece starts hissing with static, so he yanks it out and throws it on his desk.

"Fucking hell?" he curses. "Again?"

His isn't the only comms unit to go haywire. Looking around the room, Malakai notices the others are all reeling from the noise.

Suddenly, the lights in the room flicker off, as do the monitors on the wall.

"What's happening now?" Ibrahim demands.

"Another attack?" Addison asks.

"Our comms must've received a high-frequency burst," Ava concludes. "But from where?"

"Precarious timing," Leighton adds.

Jonathan Kennedy navigates the dark, padding around for the door handle. Once he finds it, he peeks his head through. "Lights are coming back on," he says, only a moment before life returns to Malakai's office. "Issues with the power generators? Residual effects from the attack?"

"Shouldn't be," Ava rebuffs. "The riggers checked it."

"We're running three different diagnoses at regular intervals," Addison explains. "It should detect any further tampering with the system."

Malakai files into the Control Room. Everyone else follows him.

Admiral Kennedy and Colonel Ibrahim take to the main floor. "What's going on?" Ibrahim demands.

"Ah ... We've got nothing?" an engineer proposes. "Readouts show we're in the green. Minor fluctuations?"

"I thought we rerouted everything to new circuits," Ava refutes. "What's affected? Do we know?"

"Looking at it, maybe a localized crash?" says another technician.

"A small break in the connection before everything came back online," a third agrees.

"Which suggests a hiccup in power output," Ava weighs.

"Or maybe not," Addison says, standing by the viewport outside.

Malakai stares at her. She's looking at the upper landing platform. He joins her and finds himself fighting a weak bladder when he sees *their* silhouettes. Two giant figures ... waiting ... at the edge of the deck. Lightning breaks their imposing statures against the storm.

"Colonel Ibrahim," Malakai urges, waving the man over.

Ibrahim steps fast and clenches his fist when he sees the pair. "Get everyone on lockdown," the Colonel orders. "Security team to the upper landing pad! We've got more uninvited guests. Let's deal with them."

Addison turns around and punches Ibrahim in the chest, knocking the soldier back a step.

"Fuck that order!" Addison shouts, looking at Malakai and her father. "That's Adhion 'Klaka and Idu 'Smeora! We can't do this with a shoot-first policy!" She growls and barks like a she-wolf controlling an unruly pack. Malakai eyes her dad. Old Man Kennedy fights off a satisfied grin, quickly replacing it with a subdued passiveness.

"What the hell—?" Ibrahim is about to say, unable to finish his sentence.

Addison lowers a hand to the man as a peace offering. The soldier accepts it and replants his boots firmly on the ground.

"Addison," her father cautions, stepping toward his daughter.

"Stop!" Malakai cracks, moving between the two, raising his arms. He glances at the alien figures through the glass, shivering as the cold sinks into his throat. "We aren't doing this here. Addison—go outside and bring them through to the lower decks. Take them to the Observation Lab. Colonel Ibrahim, lock down the corridors. Project leadership takes point." His eyes veer to the blonde woman in the corner, not saying a word in the background. Alexandra Roslin—Director of the Special Operations Intelligence Division, the lead investigator into the events of the attack.

The Old Man throws his gaze at Addison, Colonel Ibrahim, and Malakai Adonis.

"What are you planning?" Jonathan demands.

"Exactly what we're mandated to do," Malakai answers. "We've no choice. Let's hear them out and maybe explain our side of things. Hopefully, we can help each other. In the meantime, let's get down to deck five. Can somebody get to medbay? Find Vogert and tell him to meet us downstairs. His team can prep their friend's body."

Malakai relaxes his arms, but keeps his palms up, indicating his good intentions.

If anything, Addison *is* right to an extent. And they must figure it out before they're stuck in a war on three fronts.

"Are you sure this is the wisest course of action?" Jonathan questions.

"No," Malakai admits. "But I'd prefer us to follow through until we can't any longer."

"We're all-hands-on-deck," Addison agrees.

"Let's see what they *want* before we blast each other into smithereens," Malakai confides.

Jonathan Kennedy's eyes narrow as he quietly weighs the options. He eventually surrenders a nod.

It's not what Malakai would call "ideal" circumstances, but it's not like they've got an alternative.

"Well said, Doctor Kennedy," Alexandra Roslin complies, leaving her corner. "Do what you need to do. I'll collect Ryan Vogert from Medical."

Malakai swallows as the woman walks out of the Control Room, her security detail close behind her. He's dealt with many faceless soldier types in the last couple of weeks. Most of them had the benefit of training under the High Castle Program, with Colonel Ibrahim as their commanding officer. But OverSec? Oversight Security—a subdivision of SOI, acting as an arm of the Joint Security Council. Alexandra Roslin and her agents fall outside the Project's mandate, meaning they are not answerable to this mission's accepted chain of accountability.

Ibrahim prods him after the door closes. "Malakai?" he asks.

"What?"

"You're vibrating."

"I'm sorry?" Malakai begs the question.

"It's like somebody locked you in a freezer without a coat," Ibrahim whispers. "Are you okay?"

"It's nothing," he lies, picking up his feet.

"Are you sure?"

Malakai shakes his head. "No," he coughs, stepping into the hallway.

ADDISON KENNEDY, FIELD DIRECTOR
EPIMETHEUS PROJECT

OCTOBER 26, 2041 | 1230 HOURS

Addison stands in the airlock, waiting for the marines to give her the go-ahead.

The rain pours in through the hatch, soaking her side. Addison presses on the bandages on her arms and neck. All this moister irritates her skin, still raw from her dive in the tunnels between the decks. It makes her want to drown her senses with a Long Island iced tea. Maybe two.

Addison used to like nothing more than a good downpour. She'd spend her summers drifting on the lake by their cabin with her father when he was home from the fleet. And when the storms hit? She loved listening to the rolling thunder coming over the hills, her dad scrambling to steer their little rower back to the docks.

Dangerous, no question.

"If only we could go back to those days," Addison whispers.

She forces herself not to scratch her itches. Cutting off circulation at the worst spots relieves the spasms to an extent, and lotion makes wearing the cast bearable. But the jerks in Medical warned her about oversaturating the burns while the skin's still in the early healing stages, preferring to let her arm breathe, or else she risks additional scarring.

It wouldn't be so bad if she didn't have to wear a brace over the gauze.

At least she can wiggle her fingers now.

The corporal of her security detail gives her the nod to step out. And she does, holding her breath, squaring her shoulders under the pretense of confidence. Her eyes lock on Adhion and Idu as she crosses the bridge to the landing pad. Neither alien moves a muscle. They're like statues.

Addison can only guess what they're thinking, but their eyes dart to her, and she flinches reactively.

"Addison Kennedy?" Idu conforms, bowing to her with respect.

The female Architect takes out a small, circular device, no larger than a fingernail, and offers it to Addison. It's like the cipher she gave before, only . . . different.

Of course, Addison accepts it. But she glances at the Nomad with suspicion.

"Idu? Adhion? You two are working together," Addison states with surprise, turning the circular device over. She regards Idu with a curious smirk, who merely nods in return, gracefully quiet. "Care to explain what *this* is for?" Addison asks.

"Not while we are in this downpour," Adhion refuses, holding out his palm to catch the raindrops.

"With your permission, may we come inside?" Idu requests. She taps a control unit on her arm, lighting up the circular device in Addison's hand. "That will hopefully be sufficient compensation for the damages we've brought on."

"Compensation? Should I ask?"

"Consider it a chance to steer your civilization onto a new road," Idu explains. "Scientific knowledge. Invaluable for a young species, don't you think?"

"Like a codex?" Addison likens. "Or . . . Pandora's Box." She grimaces.

"After much discussion, we consider it a better offering than the ship's Heart," Adhion suggests.

Addison relaxes her shoulders as she scratches her nose, wondering about the other implications *this* will cause. And she doesn't like it.

"You're a regular Prometheus, Adhion 'Klaka," Addison elects. "Is this another fire that risks burning us?"

"I do believe you'd call it . . . Irony?" the large alien retorts.

"Not quite, but . . . close enough," Addison admits. "More contradictory than anything. But sticking our hands in the fire? It seems we can't stop."

"We have indeed heard," Idu notes.

"Let's go inside to discuss what comes next," Adhion again urges.

"We're setting up for you downstairs," Addison tells them. "Just . . . Watch your heads. The ceilings don't have much height clearance."

"Do not worry about us, Addison Kennedy," Idu cedes. "We understand what it's like to feel enclosed."

Addison simpers and brings them inside, guiding them through the corridors to the labs on deck five. There, the others have already gathered. For some of the Project's leadership, this will be their first contact with the Architects beyond watching them through the military feeds. And as the two giants duck under the door and squeeze into the room, Malakai, Roslin, and her father reel back, unprepared for their sheer size.

Ibrahim remains stoic, although he cautiously thumbs for his sidearm.

Meanwhile, Ava and Vogert lean forward, their eyes glowing as if they were already planning to dissect the pair.

Adhion looks around the room as he enters, letting his gaze linger on where Ibrahim killed the Servant. Her blood still decorates the walls and floor, almost radiant in how the light hits it. His eyes drop before turning to confront the humans across the room.

He stops at the table holding the Heart he gifted to Addison during their first meeting, caressing it with a delicate finger.

"This is not a military base," Adhion regards, stepping away from the sphere.

Malakai and Addison's father come forward and extend their hands to greet the alien newcomers.

"You're correct, sir," her father construes. "This was a drilling rig converted into a staging platform." He waits for either Architect to take his hand, but it doesn't happen.

Idu stares at the Old Man's bare palm, baffled by the proper response.

"A typical gesture?" she asks Addison.

"Another matter of courtesy for us," Addison explains.

"It doesn't matter," the Admiral decides. He pulls his hand away and straightens his collar. "I *am* Fleet Admiral Jonathan Kennedy of the USS Isaac Bennett. Welcome. You already know Addison. Next to me is Colonel Ibrahim, Doctor Remmings, Doctor Vogert, Alexandra Roslin, Harlow Leighton . . . And the man in charge of this mission? Malakai Adonis."

"Pleasure to meet you, Fleet Admiral," Idu returns, looking between the two Kennedys. "Your blood relation?"

"He's my father," Addison answers.

"Respectable," Adhion admits.

Her dad coughs. "I suppose formalities don't matter much these days," the Old Man feigns, feeling his throat. "Although, we're aware of you two— Adhion 'Klaka, Nomad of Amelioration, and Idu 'Smeora, Whisperer of Continuance. Architects of the Vili. Is it too much to ask that you want to discuss terms for leaving our planet?"

"We agree to your conditions," Idu confirms, answering abruptly.

The Old Man barely has time to furrow his brows. "You . . . Agree?" he asks. "Already?"

"Surprised? Your daughter now has the Codex Architectus. It is a well of knowledge designed to guide your people to greater insights," Idu states, seemingly oblivious to the idea that she's in the middle of negotiations. Or maybe this is how they conduct themselves? Trade favors and gifts, not broken promises. "As a species, it will allow you to earn your place among the stars."

"All we ask is for the Heart's return," Adhion proposes.

"And we can leave your world without further carnage," Idu concedes.

Addison's father uncomfortably shifts his weight from one foot to another.

He looks at Addison, who surrenders Idu's device to him. After looking it over, the Old Man passes it to Vogert, who gives it to Avanna Remmings. "That's much appreciated," her father dithers. "But you offered Addison the Heart originally in what she thought was good faith. You can see why this causes us concerns, don't you? Asking us to return the first gift and forcing us to accept an exchange?"

"I gave you the Heart to act as a catalyst for my conflict with the Trident," Adhion freely admits.

"And justify attacking us?" the Old Man inquires.

Addison knows he's not accusing the aliens. He's not *that* crass, but the potential *is* there in her father's voice. And if he's not careful—?

"No. Not to attack," Adhion argues. "I wanted to encourage *you* to defend it when Tyrann made his move."

"Which he *did* through Tjaa's trespass," Idu adds.

"And the one you call . . . Trident, is it?" the Admiral weighs. "Why goad him? What is this? Help me understand." He holds a long stare between Addison and the Architects.

"Apparently, it was to make a point," Idu interjects, stepping forward, commanding the room. "We know some of your people have attacked this station to obtain what's not theirs. Political rifts among the Arkkitects are as divisive. You've seen our war play out, yes?"

"On the receiving end of it," Ibrahim notes, finally joining the conversation. "And I can't track the damage."

"You were never the target," Adhion excuses.

"We started figuring that out after a while," Malakai follows.

He gives the Old Man a look that keeps him from adding to the topic.

"Then why don't you give us an explanation?" Addison urges, letting curiosity beat her to the punch. She's wanted to since the Servant confronted her in this lab a day ago, inadvertently rescuing her from a death squad.

"From the start," Malakai instructs.

"Please?" Ava adds, breaking away from looking at the Codex.

Idu surrenders a smile and goes over to lean on a table. "Where to begin?" she murmurs.

Adhion 'Klaka conducts most of the dialogue. He's stood at the center of these events since day one. He goes on about his need for justice and his decision to finally act against a strict and misguided adherence to a cycle of birth, destruction, rebirth, and control.

"It is an imperial peace," Adhion describes. "No freedom to work beyond our stations."

"Not too dissimilar to a caste system," Addison simplifies under her breath.

The Nomad breathes as he finishes, and the room falls silent.

"Your protest has done a lot of damage to us," the Admiral coughs, repeating Ibrahim's notion.

"We've lost friends to your machines," Ibrahim doubles down. "Not to mention the floods when your ship hit the water."

"Damage not easily rectifiable," Malakai adds. "Why is it you two are only *now* working together?" He crosses his arms, sharing Addison's earlier notion.

Idu steps back. "For survival," she admits. "With the slaughter of the Judge and Servant—the Trident has lost his ship, alongside his few loyal followers. Adhion and I have convinced many to mutiny against him. But he could still activate the dreadnaught's automation process. A final protocol."

"Final protocol? What does that mean?" Ibrahim questions.

"Doom. And if it means retrieving the Heart?" Adhion ponders, shivering as he lowers his eyes. "He won't hesitate. And he won't ask nicely. He ordered Dhun and Tjaa to act if your people didn't surrender *it* immediately. With those two dead, and *us* confronting you directly, he will use all his power to save face. Pride is his fault. His chord tends to sing loud when things don't go their way. He *is* the Keeper of the Three Pillars—the Trident of Absolution, the Speaker of Creed, the Hand of Judicature."

"Like a priest or religious leader," Addison clarifies.

"That and more," Idu nods.

"And what is this automation process exactly?" the Admiral demands. "More machines?"

"Hundreds of thousands," Idu answers. "The main hangar bays are lined with the smaller Fragments."

"But there are more powerful ones on board—" Adhion warns, "—larger and tougher."

Addison feels a clog in her throat. She sweats as the ocean waves crash far under the lab's glass floor. As thunder cracks, the words "larger" and "tougher" sink into her bones like water seeping into broken pottery.

"We've seen what those machines can do," Vogert seethes, gritting his teeth. "And I don't want to get into a fight with bigger ones." He shifts his weight to one side, putting his hands in his pockets. "Why is this still a discussion? Let's sign this off and get it over with!"

"It is not so simple," Idu denies.

"Tyrann won't let either of us restore the Heart by ourselves," Adhion explains. "I *am* a betrayer, an oathbreaker."

"And by agreeing to work with him, I am an offender," Idu adds, "without honor. Disgraced. A lost one."

"Imagine you are steering a ship," Adhion illustrates. "Would you let the rats tell you where to go?"

Addison notices his colors fading to blue. "I suppose not," she says bleakly.

"His . . . is a strict nature," Idu commits. "Tyrann will only do as the Obligation demands."

"Meaning there is no longer the possibility of a cordial arrangement with him," Adhion clamors.

"If there ever *was* a possibility," Idu confesses.

Ibrahim rests his hands on his hips. "So . . . *what*, then? How do we do this?" he asks, rubbing his left eye anxiously. "Do we surrender the damn thing to him? Let your man take the Heart and let him go? Because that's the option on the table."

"Not an ideal solution," Idu weeps.

"And a dangerous notion," Adhion shrinks.

"He will not let you keep the recompense we offer in exchange for the trouble we've caused."

Malakai, Ibrahim, Vogert, and everyone else in the lab blink at the two Architects, unsure how to respond. Addison's father paces back and forth. Finally, he clenches his fists, bellowing, "Damn you!" as subdued as possible.

"How long before he acts?" Addison asks.

"However long it takes him to find out we're talking to you," Idu explains.

"Hours . . . A day or two at most?" Adhion estimates.

"Your days, Addison Kennedy," Idu cautions. "Not ours."

"Can't you . . . I don't know . . . reprogram other Fragments and use them to help yourselves?" Ibrahim asks the Nomad.

"You've changed hundreds already," the Old Man agrees. "What's a few thousand?"

"Spoken like a soldier, not a hacker," Ava dithers.

"They aren't simple machines to re-write," Adhion argues against the notion. "And they're . . . unpredictable. They serve a purpose, taking intensive work to change. You saw what happened with an early attempt. Even if Idu and I work together, we can't comb through the dormant stockpile on the ship. Not while the Trident can activate them with a gesture."

"Then what do you suggest we do?" Addison confronts the issue.

"Give us the Heart, for starters. And help *us* to the ship's deep interior," Adhion lays it out. "With your troops as the spearhead, we can catch him by surprise. Do what you did with Dhun and Tjaa. Attack *him* before he acts. Working together, we can fight the battle on our terms."

"And put more of my boys in danger," Ibrahim says, a shiver causing his jaw to twitch.

"We're all at risk anyway," Addison cites.

"Addison? We're talking about a full-scale assault on the ship's bridge!" Ibrahim retorts. "If we're lucky, the Trident may not see us coming. Maybe he won't notice several hundred marines lining up to get a shot on him. But *if* he does, we're done . . . We'll lose! Everything."

"Then send every soldier you have," Idu suggests. "Our echelons can attack the ship's defenses to distract Tyrann 'Akachan while your troops move in for the main assault. That could buy us enough time to get to the Entrychamber and do what we must do."

Addison flinches. And she's not the only one to do so in the room. Ibrahim and her father glumly shake their heads.

"No," the Admiral refuses. "We've other problems to deal with first."

"You've noted the recent attack on this base," Ibrahim says, confronting the issue. "We need to face that head-on while we still have a chance. We won't survive a larger fight if we can't trust the people beside us."

"And I can't be sure we'll have enough troops left to help you until then," the Old Man settles, disgruntled.

"We're running thin as we are," Ibrahim asserts. "And if we don't start another world war?" He presses his palm into his neck as if he's in pain. "I sympathize with you folks. I do. But we're already invested. At the moment, letting you go home is a secondary objective."

Addison looks at him, her brain throbbing against her skull.

Ibrahim notices her stare and returns a frown. His eyes reflect his uncertainty—dark, with one overly watering. He's a soldier. With all the damage the Architects have done to his troops, Addison can't rightfully blame the man. And she knows he doesn't want to get dragged into a battle he's afraid he'll lose.

Addison meanders to the Architect's Heart, lifting the containment sphere with the tips of her fingers. She hands it to Idu. Everyone in the room gawks at her with their mouths wide open. "For trying to make this right, I return this with gratitude. We don't get many opportunities to learn from our mistakes." She feels a jolt ripple through her arm as she lets go of the Heart.

"Addison—?" her father attempts to say.

She points at him. "No!" Addison shouts, muzzling the sailor. "Listen? We're doing the right thing!"

"It's a fair trade," Ava supports her, looking up from handling the new device. "We have enough data from the Heart to grasp its design."

"With that Codex, maybe we can make sense of the noise?" Addison weighs.

Malakai steps between the Old Man and Addison, his hands folded at his belly in diplomatic reverence. "I agree," he mediates. "But I need to look ahead, and there's a lot for us to do. We'll discuss what happens *after* we get answers from Wensu Hao and the conspirators."

He stops in front of Adhion and Idu in the middle of the room.

"Meanwhile, I'll ensure both of you have access to our facilities," Malakai offers. "We can transport you to the METIS Research Base. From there, you can walk to the Entrychamber to do . . . whatever you need to do. I only ask that you allow us a chance to evacuate our people first." He saves the Codex from Ava Remmings' poking and prodding. "We'll take this in good faith. I promise to do what we can to help you get home, but as Admiral Kennedy said, we cannot expend the resources. Not until we can allocate it from other sources."

Adhion steps forward, frighteningly looming over Malakai like a tree to a lynx.

Idu raises an arm and blocks him from going too far.

"We understand," she says.

"Very good," Malakai nods, accepting it as an apology.

He then leaves the Observation Lab with the Old Man following on his heels. Alexandra Roslin, like a fly on the wall, flutters after them.

Ibrahim pouts at Addison like a man betrayed by a lover. He approaches her with a heavy foot.

"You're overstepping, Doctor Kennedy," Ibrahim exclaims.

"Call me Addison, Lieutenant Colonel," she says, clenching her jaw. "It'll make you sound less angry."

"I'm not angry," Ibrahim says. "I'm furious! You're a Field Director, and you just told off my commanding officer! I don't care if he's your father—we've protocol for a reason. Rules *you* helped set in place! If he wanted, he'd reassign you off the mission."

Addison narrows her eyes at the man. "I've said worse *at* him before," she admits. Addison clearly distinguishes between her saying "at" instead of "to" concerning her father. She turns to Adhion and Idu, who seem perplexed by their raised voices. "Not what you imagined when you first introduced yourselves to us?"

Idu smiles. It's almost . . . heartfelt.

"We have seen worse," the female alien admits.

"I have *done* worse," Adhion confides. "We are not here to judge your politics, Addison Kennedy."

"We need you to help with *ours*."

"You've heard what the Admiral and Malakai said," Ibrahim cuts deeply. "Your mission is off-limits for now. Or until we get a handle on our recent terrorist attack. Why do you need *us* to transport you to this Entrychamber, anyway? Actually . . . *How* did you get here from your ship in the first place?"

"By swimming," Idu admits.

Adhion hums amusingly. "We jumped into the water and fought the waves."

"Nobody can swim through those waters," Vogert refutes, shaking his head. "It's not possible."

"Not for a human," Adhion remarks.

"We only followed the method the Servant used," Idu explains, looking at the Chief Medical Officer.

Addison squints to figure out what the Whisperer's staring at, but she can't begin to guess. Maybe there are microscopic traces of blood on the good doctor? No matter her troubles, the Nomad takes a step closer, causing the room to clap under his great weight.

"We'd like to see her body," Adhion finally urges.

Vogert goes ghostly pale. "You may not like what you find," he warns.

"We assume you've cut her open to study our anatomy," Adhion confronts.

"There's no shame to it," Idu admits. "But we have rites to perform. Obligation demands it."

Ava looks up from her notes.

"Didn't this whole thing start as a rebellion against your Obligation?" Ava mocks, paying more attention than Addison thought.

"What *is* it? I mean your Obligation," Ibrahim questions. "A spiritual testament? Your creed? What?"

"Sacrament," Adhion states in a low tone.

Idu's large eyes snap at him as if she wasn't expecting him to answer with such deference.

Adhion does what amounts to a shrug. "Obligation serves as the law that governs minute aspects of our society," he explains. "Think of it as a song, with every book a verse. From those verses, we split into chords that decide our purpose in our centuries of life."

"Individuals learn the cipher when they are born to obtain information on how to live to our functions," Idu continues.

"And that is the Obligation," Adhion says. "Depending on the chord, those duties change."

"Like voices in our heads, telling us what's right and wrong," Idu simplifies.

"Like the classification of data to restrict outflow," Addison quickly factors the clues together.

"It serves to keep any single person from understanding the whole?" Ava asks, seeking a different angle.

"Yes," Idu confirms.

"And, depending on the specifics, the higher chords can dominate the lower spheres," Addison denotes.

Adhion and Idu's feathers turn purple and a brighter green.

Addison falls back a step, wondering what those colors mean. Each bristle is like a mirror, bending light from the core to form a rainbow of colors. Addison saw it when Idu first confronted her in her tent. And again, when Adhion reached out to her in the dark zone. She can only equate it to a type of rare change some animals can do to blend in with their environment. But the Architects? Their ability to link such oscillations to their emotional state is closer to how the crystals in mood rings change color by sensing body temperature, only far more complicated.

Ibrahim nudges Addison, dragging her out of her mind-realm. She blinks at the man, and he points at their two guests.

Idu merely gawks at her as Addison takes a moment to readjust.

"Do not mistake how dangerous the Trident can be," she finishes her warning. "He will not sit idle."

"And why he hates me," Adhion flinches. "I have upset the status quo, and it makes him afraid. He doesn't know the proper recourse."

"Our history has people like that—dictators and bullies," Ibrahim shudders. "We call them assholes."

"I am *done* killing for . . . 'assholes,' like him," Adhion iterates.

"See? We're already learning from each other," Ibrahim grins. He pats the giant on the arm, overly pleased. "Addison? Come on. We've got work to do."

Addison shakes her head disapprovingly. "And what are we going to do?" she asks.

"Get you back hull-side," Ibrahim tells her. "Like your father ordered."

"And then?"

Idu faintly pivots. "Anything you can," she charges. "We are sorry that your planet is where this began."

"Maybe it's a change for the better?" Addison quandaries.

"Perhaps it *is* better for your species," Idu weighs, tilting her head passively to one side. "At least until you make a mark on the wider galaxy! But ours are intrinsic mistakes. Errors in our genetic code? Maybe? I am certain they will argue that point. It's just—"

"Human nature," Ava breaks in with a heavy frown.

THE AGREEMENT | 66

LIEUTENANT COLONEL ELIAS IBRAHIM
UNITED COALITION ARMED FORCES

OCTOBER 26, 2041 | 1350 HOURS

———

Ibrahim orders his marines to keep gawkers at bay as the group walks the rig's corridors. He knows what to expect. Nobody can say the two aliens don't stand out next to their human counterparts. Adhion 'Klaka is a giant even next to Idu 'Smeora, who only measures eight-foot-six on Ibrahim's display.

He notices that Addison hasn't broken eye contact with the Architects. Not since they left the Observation Lab.

Ibrahim glides next to her. "You shouldn't stare," he whispers. "It's rude."

Addison's cheeks blush red. "Do you see how they move?" she asks. "How smooth? Almost like they're floating on air."

"Maybe it's their legs?" Ibrahim asks. "Backward knees."

"Digitigrade. Ankles, not knees. And that's not—"

Ibrahim gestures to calm her. "It's alright. I agree. They *are* remarkable." But to him, they are more of a deadly beauty. Like flowers that attract curious animals, not realizing they're poisonous. "Just be careful not to let how they look draw you into a trap."

"You're saying I don't know how to spot a predator?"

"That's not what I said. But do remember why it's called the Epimetheus Project," Ibrahim says. "Our work has consequences."

"The name's a warning not to act impulsively."

"Glad those tunnels didn't suck all the air out of that head of yours."

"Says the man who allowed the Chinese to blow up the entry to the Central Spire."

"And spoken by the woman who allowed an unknown entity to remove her helmet while in hostile territory."

Adhion scoffs. "We can hear you," the bird-like alien says, nudging Ibrahim's arm as they walk.

Idu turns her head and nods.

"That wasn't by accident," Ibrahim chides. He glances at Addison as they go around the corner to the medbay. "Down this way. If you will."

It doesn't take long until they are at the door to the center. Their group, and their escorts, enter. Vogert's crew looks wide-eyed as the two giants duck their heads, passing under the bulkhead, only to regain most of their height in the main room. The ceilings are high enough for Idu to stand comfortably. Adhion is three feet too tall and so must bend his neck.

Vogert runs a lap between stations, urging his staff to focus on their duties.

"Please. Ignore us," Vogert tells his aides. He waves Addison, Remmings, Ibrahim, and the Architects forward to the morgue, then to the autopsy sequester, where Tjaa lies with a plastic sheet covering her remains. "She's over here, on the table. I'm not sure if we should—"

Adhion raises his hand to quiet the good doctor.

When the two Architects see the body, Ibrahim swears they nearly collapse. But they don't. He doubts they're so unfeeling to not care about their friend. Idu remains frozen in place. Adhion is the first to go up to the desecrated carcass, removing the plastic and resting his palm on her forearm.

"I am so sorry I led us to this," Adhion mourns.

Idu's frown penetrates the room, her colors darkening. "She wasn't a warrior," the Whisperer explains.

"Tjaa did a number on those who attacked us," Ibrahim offers. "She has our thanks if that counts for anything."

"Technology is our hubris," Adhion exhales. "Overconfident to a fault. And where did that lead us?"

"You caught the Judge and the Servant on the back foot," Idu tells Ibrahim. "No easy feat to take down either."

He stirs uncomfortably. "It took a lot," Ibrahim says, hesitant to speak about the killing.

"Dhun was a veteran of an ancient war," Adhion says. "He's explored stars beyond the rim and had seen things that'd make even my skin crawl. And I know he liked humanity. I believe he had unexpected dealings with your kind. He saw a spark in you that could have grown into something more had time allowed. Architects of your self-determination."

Addison goes to tug on the giant's hand. Adhion turns and kneels to her, letting the woman stare inquisitively into his eyes.

"How old do I look to you, Addison Kennedy?" he asks.

Addison shakes her head. "I don't rightfully know what 'old' is to you," she answers.

"Our spirits, not our bodies, define our age," Idu clarifies. She circles the table to look better at Tjaa's corpse, shivering and distant. "To lose one of us? It is no slight loss."

"Doctor Vogert—I'd rather our guests *not* see her like this," Ibrahim suggests. "If you don't mind."

The good doctor looks up at him, furrowing his brows, allowing himself a moment to register the request. Vogert nods as he takes another sheet and covers the Servant's upper torso, offering the dead creature some dignity while lying cold and barren. It's not much, but it should help the two Architects find peace.

"Thank you," Idu acknowledges, her colors brightening a hue.

Ibrahim notes how the pair regard Tjaa 'Neren with a human-like reverence. Remarkably. It makes him wonder if the rules governing the dead are the same across the universe. Or if it's a shared belief among creatures with a soul. As a soldier, he should be used to death. But Ibrahim fights off a tremor in his wrist as he watches Idu breathe into her palms.

"Tjaa 'Neren, Servant of Cultivation," Idu withers. "Your duty to the Obligation brought new life to lifeless worlds."

Ibrahim opens his mouth, then bites his tongue, staying quiet.

"I am the Nomad of Amelioration," Adhion continues. "I was given the duty to correct *that* life by our adherents. I witnessed this one's bravery against impossible odds. And if I survive in the days ahead, I will remember her."

"I am the Whisperer of Continuance," Idu says, retaining a somber tone. "And I take care and study the life we create, working to understand each species to facilitate their needs. I considered this one a friend, somebody who stood against the ignorant. She paid for their immoralities with her own. And I will remember her."

Idu puts her hand to her face and taps her lips with a long finger.

Adhion turns to Ibrahim. "We extend a small prayer to those who die in service," he describes. "It helps guide their spirit to a new form somewhere far away. I won't deny Tjaa that chance for rebirth. Like history, every story leads to another. All life connects. She did nothing to deserve her fate."

"Even by your admission, Tjaa saved your lives," Idu adds. "Maybe that will help serve in our redemption?"

"And I led us to this," Adhion unwillingly repeats.

"You did not order her to step beyond her station," Idu comforts.

"No," Adhion agrees. "That's the Trident's doing. *His* decision. But it was *mine* to rip us apart."

"Like an apple falling from a tree," Addison mutters. Ibrahim watches as she looks between the two living Architects and Tjaa on the table. "He's your captain—the one ensuring the orchestra works together. Every musician follows a conductor. And he's waving a stick around to get the drummers' attention."

Adhion straightens his spine and brushes past the woman, stopping when he reaches Ibrahim. "We don't belong here," the Nomad whispers, looking down at him. Ibrahim cranes his neck to see the alien's face. "We're dying to your world. And the Obligation? I cannot undo these mistakes.

Not without help."

"Change is violent," Ibrahim asserts, stepping back from the giant. "Often wanting change requires violence. There's nothing I can do."

"Surely there is something you *can* do to help us," Idu notions. "And help yourselves in the process."

"We are begging you, Lieutenant Colonel," Adhion cautions. "Earth won't go unscarred by the Vili—the Summerland."

"Do you mean the storm? The floods?" Addison quandaries.

Idu nods. "Our vessel is so massive that it disrupts your planet's magnetic sphere," she confirms. "Earth defends itself, however it can. Change is . . . violent, as you said. And the longer we stay, the more permanent the damage." Idu surrenders a frown at Ibrahim as she says it.

"And if I help you, I will disobey orders," Ibrahim warns.

"Had only Dhun 'Ancod or Tjaa 'Neren challenged their tasks as bravely," Idu counters. "You must deal with the problem eventually."

"Better to do it now while there's still time," Adhion agrees.

Ibrahim scoffs at the pair, wanting to leave the room if they ask *one* more time. Even so—

"You're not wrong," Ibrahim admits.

As he looks at Idu's face . . . He can see the creases on her skin, the shadows under her large eyes, and the colors dulling from the feathers and bristles topping her head. Ibrahim exhales through his nose. Granting permission for a mission of this scale goes above his pay grade. Even attempting it is grounds for court-martial in front of a military court. That is an argument he can't win.

Then again, Ibrahim remembers the warning that Malakai had given him. About how the political implications of his job could end his career. Or how they might classify the High Castle Program as a failure. And every man and woman in his charge? They will find themselves redeployed to other units. They would undo all the pain he's gone through to earn his place.

"We can't do it alone," Ibrahim warns. "I can get a few of my troops to join us, but we'll have limited numbers."

"We are going into the aüthbringar's maw," Adhion admonishes. "It will be dangerous."

"A smaller unit is better at keeping secrets," Ibrahim reasons. He looks at Addison, who shares his stare. "If you think reuniting the Heart with the core is the best course, I'll follow your lead. But you better damn well be *certain* about it."

"Do *you* believe it's the right thing to do?" Addison answers, turning the question back at him.

Ibrahim grimaces and shrugs. "I'll put in transfer orders to METIS for everyone I want on this mission," he says regardless. "Addison, Vogert, Ava . . . You three are on the team. There's no way I'm doing this without sharing the blame. Indictments for everybody."

Ava grins haphazardly. "Sounds like fun," she acknowledges.

Vogert steps toward him. "I guess we're returning to the nightmare," he says, thinning his lips.

Addison responds quietly. Her glowering intensifies with enough heat to melt tungsten. Ibrahim raises an eyebrow at her, not knowing what to expect.

"And what about Zhu Yunwen?" Ava decides to ask.

"She's in lockup," Ibrahim determines. "We don't know if she's an infiltrator or an innocent party. OverSec will look into leads."

"That's what worries me," Addison murmurs. She sits down, burying her face in her arms and steadying her breath.

"Addison? They're investigating the attack," Ibrahim reassures. "I won't know anything until—"

"Zhu was as surprised by the attack as *I* was," Addison confronts. "She helped me get down to the labs! She's innocent."

"Even if she weren't involved, her people would likely denounce her," Ibrahim points out. He straightens his collar, treading softly toward Addison. "They wouldn't risk everything they had unless they had a plan for the fallout. And she's a ready-made scapegoat. Until we can clear her involvement, the woman will have to stay in detention."

Addison shakes her head, looking at Ava. "Do you want to help me?" she asks their intrepid technophile.

"What do you want me to do?" Ava asks, furrowing her brows.

"You've worked more closely with Zhu than anyone these last couple of days," Addison iterates. "Could she have worked against us this whole time?"

Ava renders a deep frown, working the question through her head. "Do I think it's possible? Of course, if she's anything like us," she confesses, obviously wanting to avoid the discussion. However, she's unable to hide the pallor on her face. "Whether I think she'd do it on her own? No. I don't think she would. I've said as much to Roslin."

Ibrahim coughs to focus everyone's attention back on him.

"Somebody's responsible," Ibrahim says, glancing at the two giants in the room. "People have died. And last I checked . . . Ava . . . You know what living inside a dark cell is like after going a step too far. But you never killed anybody for what you did."

"Nobody directly," Ava shudders, clenching her jaw. "And if I wasn't still paying for that, you couldn't ask me my opinion."

Adhion 'Klaka steps into the middle of the room. "Maybe a better question to ask is *who* benefits most from such an attack?" the alien offers.

Everyone in the morgue stares with surprise at the colorful giant.

Ibrahim coughs again, clearing his throat. He quickly pulls a list of names from the top of his head. "Well? There's the obvious . . . Wensu Hao, Field Director at Camp Yi. He's visited the Olympus a few times," Ibrahim illustrates. "He's the chief target in our upcoming raid. But that still doesn't remove Zhu Yunwen from consideration. She's had free reign of this base for days. Not to mention, she worked close to the Heart on standard rotation."

Addison groans. "Zhu doesn't have access to the power system," she asserts. "Or the network nodes."

"Not to mention, Hao was only aboard for a couple of hours," Vogert doubts. "You also likely had him watched the entire time he was here."

"I had nothing to do with that," Ibrahim denies.

"CSDR had to know their people would be suspects if the attack failed," Addison shifts. "It's a bit reckless for them, isn't it?"

"Desperate," Ibrahim weighs his thoughts, "but it *does* happen. Whoever it is, they'd need access to our systems without attracting unwanted attention."

"And be excluded from a list of top suspects," Addison proposes.

"That, too," he agrees.

Ibrahim can't shake how odd it is talking conspiracy in a room with a dead Architect on the table. Or the idea they're doing it in the presence of two *living* aliens, who aren't likely to understand the human politics that's going on. Ibrahim's chest tightens uncomfortably at the thought.

"So, what do we do?" Addison asks. "Whoever it was . . . They had to have top-level security clearance."

"Including access to the doors on the Olympus *with* links to High Castle's network," Vogert adds.

Ibrahim's eyebrows twitch.

"You're not suggesting—?" he attempts to say.

"We've recently welcomed some very important persons who've wanted to shut us down from the start," Addison cuts him off brazenly. "Senator Holland leads the wolf pack. And *he* was adamant in demanding full access to our work."

"He's also feverously screamed 'traitor' against Zhu since the attack," Ibrahim denotes.

"Do you think there's anything that connects him to the Chinese Government?"

Ibrahim winces. "A connection between Chinese interests and a Wisconsin Senator?" He mocks the large, wormy man, only taking a more serious tone after a breath. He reins in his anger for men like Mr. Holland. "Is there a way to find out?"

He turns to Ava Remmings, their resident hacker.

She smiles at him. "I can do some digging," the woman offers.

"Can you get anything by tonight?"

"Depends. How badly do you want the Senator's mob to fold?" Ava queries. "I'd bet there's a lot of dirt on him we can access through the network. It's a worldwide system, so I'll be surprised if I can't find anything."

"Just focus on his foreign dealings," Ibrahim instructs.

Ava giggles excitedly. "I'll get it done," she says, cracking her knuckles.

"Please," Ibrahim says, shaking his head. "Be careful. We're jumping into uncharted waters. And I don't want us to drown."

Ava looks softly at him and nods solitarily.

Addison turns to Adhion and Idu. "We'll get you guys to the core," she promises. "Give us time."

"There is not much time for us to give you," Idu warns.

Ibrahim stands up straight: "We need to do this right," he tells them. "It may take a while to clear our friend of wrongdoing. And without official sanction, we'll need Athena's help to keep our investigation secret. As confident as I am with Ava's abilities, she got caught once, and time isn't our ally. Maybe I can get everybody hull-side tomorrow? But I won't make promises."

"There's a nook off the vessel's nose you can hide one of your aircraft inside," Idu says. "Saves you from walking the distance."

"First, we'll need to find pilots," Ibrahim nods. "Then we can worry about getting there."

"Prepare whatever you can," Idu agrees. "Our forces must work together to get us to the Entrychamber."

"And return the Heart to the core," Adhion adds.

"Meanwhile, I'll see what I can come up with," Ava confirms. "Finding dirt on our 'beloved' Senator shouldn't be a problem. He *is* a politician. Most are usually pretty dumb about leaving breadcrumbs. Or their staff aren't as . . . loyal . . . as they'd like to think." She readily heads to the door with an energetic hop to her step.

"I'll admit," Addison says, waiting until Ava's out of the morgue. "That one scares me."

"Like setting a pyromaniac loose in a lumberyard with matches. Come on. I have an operation to plan," Ibrahim says. But he also won't lie. There's a growing panic inside him. Ibrahim realizes how much work is on his plate tonight. He points at Addison. "We need Zhu's frame of reference. Talk to her. Get her to convince you to convince *me* that she's innocent."

"Understood," Addison agrees.

"And what about me?" Vogert begs for a role.

"You will join our 'friends' on the next transport hull-side and get everyone ready. Leave tonight," Ibrahim outlines. "And let Warden know the plan. I don't trust using comms with SOI listening in on military frequencies. Everything gets spoken directly to each other. And it stays between us. If word gets out about what we intend to do, OverSec will jump on us."

"And we don't want that," Addison explains to the Architects.

"No. We don't," Ibrahim echoes.

"We understand the risks," Idu acknowledges. "We shall abide by your terms."

"And being on the ship's hull will let us coordinate with our forces," Adhion details. "Approaching the Entrychamber from two sides is the smarter option."

"I'm so glad you approve," Ibrahim scoffs.

Nothing about this is easy. Any one of a hundred points can make it all go wrong.

Not that it matters. Ibrahim has decided, and everyone has a part to play. Nobody shakes hands. Nobody says a word while leaving the medbay. What he's planning to do is dangerous. Even suicidal. Ibrahim certainly isn't comfortable entering the ship's black garden with anything less than an army at his back.

Ibrahim creates a mental list of what he needs to do tonight. The raid on Camp Yi to arrest Wensu Hao takes priority, but he also must find a way to help Zhu Yunwen out of her mess. All while getting dirt that links Senator Holland with abetting in the attack on Mount Olympus.

And *that* isn't everything.

He needs a team he trusts to do the job and keep their mouths shut. He has to find pilots willing to ignore official orders and fly them to the front of the dreadnaught, where the storm is at its worst. He can look out the window to see *that* clear enough—the twisting clouds, like a monster, devouring the sky. *And* he needs a story to cover his tracks when this eventually blows up and leads him to a court-martial for conspiracy against an American Congressman.

Even if he can get Malakai's permission to conduct the mission, Ibrahim doubts his support will save him from the political fallout.

"And damn us if we fail," Ibrahim curses. "All the things I do for her."

Addison quickly learns there isn't a proper brig anywhere on the oil rig. OverSec has decided to turn a broom closet into a makeshift cell for Zhu Yunwen.

Two troopers in red undersuits and polished white armor guard the door.

"Doctor Kennedy?" the first trooper asks.

"I want to see her," Addison says.

"Nobody's allowed to see the woman," the second man says. "Orders."

Addison smiles and flashes her clearance identifier. They take and scan it, raising their heads with surprise. Under normal circumstances, they'd turn her around no matter what she said. But they probably didn't realize until now that military affairs still take mission precedence over instructions from their division head.

Luckily for her, Ibrahim saw reason and took her side in the debate.

The troopers take her to a small table and tell her to empty her pockets, stepping back once they clear her, letting her through. "Thank you," Addison says, winking at the officer on the right. Even past the trooper's visor, she can see his glowering eyes. He's not happy about letting a civilian in to see the prisoner. But sanction from Ibrahim's office leaves the man in a difficult spot.

"Be careful in there," the second trooper states as he opens the door. "Yunwen's dangerous."

"Like a mouse is to an elephant," Addison mocks.

She enters the room to find Zhu handcuffed to a chair, looking emptily at a wall.

"A bit extreme, if you ask me," Addison says, waiting for the door to close.

"Given how you didn't kill anybody."

"You're here?" Zhu asks. She turns her head enough to eye Addison. "I was told I'd get no visitors."

"Nothing's without exceptions," Addison comforts her, pulling up another chair to sit beside her. "Cozy place they're keeping you, eh? Anybody in Harper's office gets wind of this, OverSec and SOI will have some uncomfortable questions to answer."

"They're doing their jobs," Zhu confides. Addison can feel her cheeks tighten. "Not the response you expected?"

"I figured you'd want to get out of here," Addison remarks.

"That will only make me look guilty," Zhu admits. She takes a deep breath and lets it out slowly. "I don't need that on my conscience."

"They have you in here like some rabid animal," Addison says. "On a leash."

"With food and water," Zhu adds, although unwillingly. Addison notices tears in the woman's eyes. Zhu turns her head away as Addison leans in closer for a better look, but the distress is there, without a doubt. The woman surrenders to Addison's prodding with a grimace. "I only wish I had a bed," her voice cracks, rolling her eyes to the room.

"No sleeping cot," Addison murmurs, scanning the floor. "Not even a toilet?"

"Just the chair," Zhu weakly laughs. Somehow, the woman can push a wily grin to the surface.

Addison returns with a raised eyebrow.

"I haven't known you for long, but that's a look of 'no good' on your face if I ever saw one," Zhu recognizes. "Why're you here?"

Addison folds her hands together.

"Events are spiraling out of our control," she begins. "People are angry. They want to point fingers and—"

"You want to know if I helped with the attack on this base," Zhu interrupts, speaking bluntly.

"Yes," Addison confirms. "What do you know about it? Or . . . *did* you know?"

Zhu's eyes fall groundward, closing them tightly.

"I don't know," Zhu remarks.

"You don't know?" Addison repeats. "That doesn't help me."

"I think that's the point. Because I won't ever know," Zhu admits. "My government compartmentalizes information that puts them at risk. I doubt my people stationed here, or those who participated in the attack, understood what was happening. Orders are orders. They did what they had to do."

"And what were *your* orders?" Addison asks.

"That's the thing," Zhu recalls, pausing before she answers. "I don't know . . . I thought it was already part of the agreement between our governments. My original task said I was to join the spearhead expedition team into the Summerland. After that, I stayed to help research any technology we found. That's when I asked Ava Remmings if I could join her in developing a scanner for the Architect's Heart. After days went by, we made progress."

"Why would your government want to retrieve the Heart if the scanner was only in early development?"

Zhu shrugs. Or . . . she meekly stirs while still handcuffed to the chair.

"Maybe they saw things developing too slowly and thought they could do better?" Zhu suggests. "We all accept that my government hoards information. Maybe they found something in the data that could help them complete the process faster. Or maybe they got impatient and decided to act while things settled on the ship? These are questions beyond my ability to answer."

Addison leans back and puts a finger to her lips.

All the woman is doing is admitting the Project's most badly kept secret. For Addison's purpose, it can't prove or disprove anything.

They talk for a while as Addison explains everything Zhu has missed during her brief time under lock and key. By the end, the woman's sad eyes lose their luster completely, like a silver coin left in a bowl of water for too long.

"I see now," Zhu mourns.

The woman awkwardly attempts to scratch the back of her neck using her shoulder.

Addison sits forward as Zhu winces.

"Are you okay?" she asks, noticing the other's discomfort.

"My implant bothers me," Zhu tells her. "Like a hot nail trying to dig out of my skin."

"You have an implant?"

Zhu looks up at her with a long face. "A chip inserted into our necks to monitor us," she explains.

"Like a locational tracker?" Addison asks, chewing her tongue.

"More like a leash that keeps tabs on us."

"Very interesting," Addison murmurs. "And you all have one?"

"As far as I know," Zhu admits. "It was required by the Central Military Commission—our military leadership."

"We have something similar, but it's something we wear, not surgically implanted," Addison mentions.

"It *is* for us," Zhu goes on. She attempts to turn around in her chair to show her back to Addison. "Can you feel it? Like a lump or a loose nerve?" Zhu guides Addison to the area of her occipital bone, where the cervical spine connects to the back of her skull.

"I feel it," Addison confirms. She moves her fingers gently around the aberration. "That's the device?"

"Pretty sure," Zhu says, pivoting her chair counterclockwise to face Addison.

"Implants like this monitor your health and well-being," Addison notes.

"Yes—but what *if* they can do more?" Zhu suggests. "We've all wondered. But nobody's willing to talk about it."

"Like record what you're seeing or hearing?" Addison questions, thinking about the odds. It's *not* likely a device like that can do such complex operations *inside* a human body. However, Addison *is* certain a studious mind could find a way to do it if they tried. And *if* it's connected to her nervous system—?

Addison raises her index finger and instructs silence. She then gets to her feet, opens the door, and begs the guard to lend her his radio speaker. The man tilts his head confusingly but ultimately answers the request. He removes his helmet and releases the lock to his internal comms unit, handing it to Addison.

"Thank you," she returns. "Much appreciated."

Addison makes sure to close the door with a sly smile. Her expression hardens the moment she's clear.

She turns up the volume and notes the unit's ID number before plopping it on the floor.

"What are you—?" Zhu questions.

"Quiet. You'll see," Addison warns her. She keys the comms to her private channel. "Athena, can you hear me?"

"You *do* realize I can always hear you? Like gnats around my head, I can't get rid of you," Athena answers. "What do you need, Doctor Kennedy?"

"Rude. But we have a change of plans," Addison says. She glances at Zhu. "I need you to send a signal to comms unit . . . four-three-bee-nine-two-four-dash-a. Make it high-pitch enough to impact electronics within a three-meter radius but not strong enough to go through the walls."

"Understood. On standby," Athena responds. "Ladies? Probably best to cover your ears. You might find this unpleasant."

"What is this—?" Zhu tries to ask.

Addison shakes her head. "Hit it," she says, covering her ears.

And thankfully, she did. The trooper's earpiece screeches like an owl on a binge party. Addison reels back, not realizing how intense the signal would be on such a small device. But at least she could protect herself to some degree. She looks to Zhu, forgetting the woman still has her hands cuffed behind her back, locked to her chair's support grate.

The woman's face contorts as blood drips from her ears.

"Apologies," Addison guiltily mouths.

Zhu jerks as a mild electrical shock jolts through her body. She's thrown backward in her chair before Addison tells Athena to switch off the signal. OverSec troopers open the door and stomp into the room, their weapons raised. They could hear when Zhu hit the ground and wondered what was happening.

"Doctor Kennedy?" the first officer calls.

Addison points at them. "Lower your guns!" she yells. "We're fine."

Zhu's chair broke in the fall, allowing her to prop herself against the wall. She looks at the troopers in their white-on-red armor, then at Addison.

"What was that?!" Zhu demands. "Ni fēngle ma?"

"That was your implant likely shorting out," Addison explains, checking the back of her neck. "Initially we . . . Well, that's not important. But *if* your government could listen in using your implant, they no longer can. Which is good news for everybody."

"Tā mā de!" Zhu curses, blinking wildly. "That hurt."

Addison takes her sleeve and wipes the inside of the woman's ear canal to clean out the blood.

"Sorry about this," Addison offers, now looking at the soldiers. "If you two can please get her to medbay? We'll need a doctor."

"I can't . . . Hear? There's a ringing in my ears!" Zhu notions. "Is that normal?"

"It will pass!" Addison shouts. "How do you feel about emergency surgery to remove that implant?!"

Zhu's eyes widen, and her jaw tightens. Then, she looks at the guards.

"I don't know what you said," Zhu says, "but if it helps earn me your trust, I'll do what I can!"

Addison smiles. "It's not *my* trust you're vying for," she says.

"What?" Zhu questions.

"I'll explain when your hearing clears up!" Addison confides, squeezing the woman's shoulder confidently.

Zhu frowns. "Can't wait for it," she shudders.

"This woman's not going anywhere!" the lead trooper states angrily.

"She's a lot to answer for," the second agrees.

"And she will," Addison says to the officers. "Later. For now, we should get her to Doctor Vogert. She's hurt."

"Doctor Kennedy? She's not leaving this room!" the first trooper says.

"And I am telling you, she needs medical attention!" Addison fights back.

"That's not *our* problem," the second scoffs. "We have our orders."

"You don't want to battle me on this," Addison growls. She picks the burnt comms unit off the floor and hands it aggressively back to its owner. "Unless you want to explain to Alexandra Roslin how you two let an unknown quantity through your post? The prisoner had a monitoring device you failed to notice. I discovered it after *fifteen* minutes with her."

Each officer shifts their posture to a more anemic state.

Addison frowns empathically.

"Help the woman to her feet," the first trooper says.

"Sir?" the second asks.

"Do it." He turns to Addison. "The prisoner is your responsibility now, Doctor Kennedy," the first man says, keying a sequence into his pad. "I'll transfer wardenship to Colonel Ibrahim. If anybody asks me, I'll blame you for overriding our command. And you better take the fall."

"Don't worry," Addison agrees, helping the trooper pick Zhu off the floor. "And I'll forget how you guys don't have a bed or toilet in this room for her, yeah? We don't want it getting out how your division keeps people in cages without basic human amenities. Sound good?"

"Get a move on, Ms. Kennedy," the man orders, stepping back. He eagerly waits to see if Zhu Yunwen collapses while trying to walk.

Addison knows from experience that sitting in a chair for a day is terrible for the legs.

"Come on, birdie," Addison tells her. "Let's get you to the good doctor."

"Addison?" Zhu whispers, leaving the guards behind. She carries more of herself the farther they get from her cage.

"Yes?" Addison returns.

"I hate this," she says.

"Me, too," Addison agrees. "Me, too."

EVIDENCE | 68

She glances at the clock. "Half past the hour," Ava mutters, wiping the water from her eyes.

Ava didn't realize she's spent hours on this project, cutting into records technically off-limits to her. That hasn't stopped her from living dangerously before, admittedly. And it won't stop her now. Not while she's mid-séance . . . Or whatever is the equivalent of her diving into somebody else's system to poke around their dirty underwear.

Keeping her activities hidden is the only real challenge in accessing Holland's private archives from this distance.

"Shouldn't have skimped out on paying your cyber-nerds, Mr. Senator," Ava laughs, but only after an exhausting breath.

Ava relishes what she does best . . . it's not designing or building weapons for national defense. No. She's good at that, too, but it's breaking into these coded schemes. It's peeling off the layers specifically made to keep *her* and her curiosity on the outside.

Her chief issue is . . . She doesn't *like* the outside.

Ava's always seen it as the more she knows, the better she can provide. She can't deny *this* is what ended her career those years ago with her arrest. Since then, nothing has ever sat well in the back of her mind, with her family living a caustic nightmare. The deal Ava made protects them from her mistakes, but now the same thing's happening to somebody else. And a friend, for that matter.

This little payback is what she owes to men like Senator Holland.

Not to mention—

"What do we have here?" Ava utters quietly under her breath, finding a highly encrypted file. "Quite the security for a home folder . . . But why keep it separate from the broader system?"

Ava cracks a knuckle and begins digging more into it. A file not officially a part of the Senator's home cloud isn't entirely unusual. Many on the political spectrum enjoy keeping their financial dealings a secret. The hard part for Ava is not spotting the anomaly but building a digital bridge across the gap to access it remotely. Normally, she'd be there in person, on location, to overcome the "isolated" part of the equation.

That doesn't mean she can't un-isolate it while on the Olympus.

Ava gives herself another hour to re-route the Senator's network access and shove in a backdoor for her use.

"Bright as sunshine," she bites faintly, releasing an icebreaker to slice the server.

Ava blinks to refocus as she skims the man's unmentionables—records of his backroom deals over the years. From what she can tell, it's enough to throw accusations at Senator Holland. Unfortunately, the files won't do much other than put the man in a few headwinds. It's less than she hoped for if they wanted to involve the proper authorities. But anything from this archive isn't permissible due to the *minor* detail that Ava is breaking in and stealing the information. And if they can't use it in court, Ibrahim can't use it on official channels.

So, they'll need something more concrete if she wants to make this work.

"Damn it," Ibrahim curses.

Ava called a meeting to discuss their predicament.

"We figured it wouldn't be a simple snatch and grab," Addison adds.

"What about Zhu's implant?" Ibrahim asks, looking at the woman, who's tugging at the bandages around her neck.

That's where Ava loses interest. From what she chooses to overhear, however . . . Vogert's procedure wasn't pleasant for their intrepid botanist. When Addison Kennedy identified the leak's possible source, she brought the woman to the medbay to surgically remove the implant. And it was difficult for the good doctor. Addison sent him the call on his emergency channel, all while Ryan Vogert was on his way to take a shuttle hull-side.

"The implant itself was attached to her cervical plexus," Vogert tells the group. "A single misplaced insertion could've paralyzed Yunwen from the neck down. Not a fun boat for anybody to ride. Doubly so for somebody denied basic amenities for a day. Damn fascists."

Ava feels an invasive sting at the back of her throat, like somebody poking her with a needle.

Zhu stares hard at Vogert, her face as pale as a ghost. No matter her supposed crimes, she resides in Ibrahim's custody now. And she can't leave it. The Colonel's agreed to conditional responsibility, taking her on for the interim—an unexpected arrangement. But for the botanist, it's a most welcomed one. Yunwen only has to follow where Ibrahim goes on base, tied at the wrists.

"Figuratively speaking," Ava whispers.

Addison cocks a brow in her direction when she says it.

Vogert drops the woman's implant onto a tray between them.

"What can you tell me about it?" Vogert asks *her*.

Ava squints at the tiny chip. "Wasn't made for removal, I can tell you that," she notes. Ava hovers over the device and uses a pen to poke its anchor points. "Interesting . . . Do you see this casing? Sensitive tech. Somebody modified it to expand its normal use parameters. Unethical but clever. Not what I would've done."

"But would it have the info we need?" Ibrahim questions. He glances at Zhu, Vogert, and Addison, watching Ava take the chip to her workbench.

"That trick you did to disable it might've damaged more than its basic functions," Ava confesses, laying the tray next to her computer. "But as long as the buffer is intact—and that's a big *if* there—then it *could* still retain data for a limited period," she continues. "It will depend on when Zhu was present in a room at any given time."

"Meaning?" Addison asks.

"There's no way for me to know what it sent or stored," Ava concludes with a meager handwave. "However, we *can* extrapolate several key points depending on what her people thought would be useful." She looks at Zhu, who shifts nervously in her chair.

The woman is very similar to Addison Kennedy—stern when dealing with a crowd but often going soft in small groups. Ava may not understand people very well, but she recognizes patterns. And the pair have worked together long enough that she can identify one or two of the other's ticks.

Ava coughs. "Athena? Can you hear us?" she asks.

"Like wind in a valley," the AI answers.

"I am hooking this archive up to my pad," Ava describes, connecting wires to the delicate implant. "Can you run a diagnostic for data recovery?"

Ava's computer hums for a second. Everyone in the room watches and waits for a response.

"Done," Athena says after a minute. "Would you like me to shift relevant collections?"

"Go ahead," Ava permits.

"Relevant collections?" Ibrahim asks.

"Wait for it," Ava tells him, quieting the Colonel with her index finger.

A progress bar rolls across her screen as the data uploads, converting it into a useful language medium.

"Auditory files," Ava remarks, pulling the data into her workstation. "This is a mess."

Scrubbing through it, she marks a few busy stretches to replay for analysis.

Whoever designed the implant found a way to use the chip to read impulses from the eardrum, turning it into a rudimentary voice recorder. Ava can make out an intelligible squabble of distinct voices, hyper-compressed by a sampling engine—painting daily life on the base. Her heart flutters when she recognizes the laughter and arguments of the days before the attack.

"Remarkable," Addison denotes. "Hear that? Those are our briefings."

"All I can hear is muffled gibberish," Ibrahim scoffs.

"This is a variant of the dream sequencer tech we use to monitor brain activity in medical patients," Ava explains.

"Like what they hooked me up to after the Incident," Ibrahim recalls. "Is there anything we can use to clear our girl of intent?"

Vogert shakes his head. "Only if you want to make her look more guilty," he regrets. "Unwitting or not." He meanders to Zhu and checks her bandages.

"I'm sorry," Ava says.

She hoped to find more than these scraps to save Zhu Yunwen from getting fed on by the wolves. Either the Senator had nothing to do with the attack, or the man's playing his cards closer to the chest than his other dealings. And that makes sense, given the risk for him is "treason" versus "selling his legislative vote to the highest bidder."

Ava holds her breath and pushes on her stomach to keep from vomiting.

"Is there anything else we can do?" Addison asks.

"Nothing that OverSec won't construe as sedition," Ibrahim says, releasing a heavy breath.

"Without solid leads, the Chinese will likely cut ties with their people to avoid a war," Addison construes. "Which leaves us with only one other option."

"And what option is that?" the Colonel asks.

"We ask Wensu Hao for the truth," Addison says flatly.

"That operation's kicking off in a few hours," Ibrahim remarks. "But how does that help us now?"

"It doesn't," Addison admits. "I am looking ahead."

"Why not ask Holland in the meantime?" Vogert asks.

"We can't unless we find evidence of his involvement," Ibrahim warns.

"And that's what we're trying to do," Addison explains. "Without it, we can't put pressure on him."

"Which means we're up a creek without a paddle," Ibrahim groans despondently.

Everybody in the room goes quiet like ocean waves departing a beach. Ava looks up from scrolling through the implant's archive and blinks when she discovers they're now staring at her auspiciously. Her temples flare suddenly, and a tremor migrates out of her chest to settle in her hands.

"Don't tell me I came to class without my pants again?" Ava asks in a cracked tone.

"We're hoping you can pull something out of your hat," Addison urges.

"Like a rabbit? Afraid I'm running low on magic tricks," Ava frowns. "I can't . . . I can't do it by myself. Not without—"

"You can always ask me," Athena breaks into their group.

"That'd be helpful," Ava admits. "But unless we can get somebody higher up to side with us, will anything we do even matter?"

"Are you saying there's nothing we can use?" Addison asks.

"Nothing that would implement the Senator directly," Ava says, "if there *is* anything."

"And all the evidence we found so far will only make things worse for Zhu," Vogert reminds them.

"Unless you're looking in the wrong places," Athena suggests.

"What do you mean?" Ava begs the question.

"Do me a favor and try again," Athena challenges.

"And what are you hoping we find?"

"Uncertain," the AI admits. "But I can go where even the brightest minds wouldn't think to dive."

Ava closes her mouth and chews on the inside of her cheek. "Okay," she murmurs, deciding to appease the request.

She jumps into Senator Holland's network for another round of headaches. But this time? Athena guides her actions. Once or thrice, the AI takes control of her screen, re-routing her from one drive to another. All it does is take her to under-the-surface level garbage. Ava thinks of these areas as arbitrary folders complete with mountains of meta-code. It *is* data. But the information has more use to an operating system than an actual person.

Many large and small systems use backup servers to store these files, helping run their daily tasks.

Ava smirks as Athena rockets through several hundred thousand fields. It would normally take a large crew several weeks to sort through so much. But the AIS Core running off Overlook Station can do it easily in a sub-fraction of the time.

Giving herself a minute to breathe, Ava leans back with astute interest.

"Clever," Ava remarks.

Adrenaline and exhaustion cause her stomach to growl unhappily.

Even as she moves past the discomfort, she understands Athena's intent. It's a long shot and highly illegal . . . But still clever.

Ava sits forward and begins tearing into Holland's operational junk files—anything the man likely thought he wiped from his computer's cloud server. Addison, Ibrahim, and Vogert go on about their plans to tip-toe the Architects' Heart back to the dreadnaught. Ava works while ignoring the discussion, as she often does. That's their job. She needs to focus on hers now.

Within a few blinks, the AI quantifies and identifies three corrupted files that could be useful to the team. It's tedious. Ava's running off three hours of sleep from the past fifty-two hours, fighting to keep her eyes open. Her vision's fuzzy at best. It feels good to let Athena handle the brunt of the process.

Connecting each piece of the available data will be a more stressful task anyway.

Athena finds the fragments and throws them into a pile for Ava to sort through like a puzzle. A highly complicated puzzle with no clear solution, but that's the nature of this work.

"Even when you delete your files," Ava whispers, "it leaves traces in the system." She grits her teeth.

"You look like you're in pain," Addison says, catching Ava's expression.

Ava spins her screen around for the class to see. "I've made a blind man walk," she meekly laughs.

"That's not a phrase . . . But okay," Ibrahim sighs. "What do we have?"

Ava highlights a key section of the document that pertains to the Senator's involvement with the Chinese Ministry of Foreign Affairs.

Ibrahim's eyes widen as he reads the incriminating back and forth.

"Holland is quite the busy bee," he gruffly notions. "Look at this . . . I always knew he wanted Congressional Oversight over the Epimetheus Project."

"To which Malakai fought hard against in the weeks before launch," Ava states.

"But this?" Addison reads on. "Appears he got clearance by taking the back channels."

"By going through Ambassador Mersley and the President," Ibrahim continues.

"Offering information to the Chinese for added pressure," Vogert coughs.

"His family does a lot of business with China," Ava says, scanning the documents.

"Which puts him in an awkward position," Ibrahim states. "Looks like they asked him to take more drastic action."

"So, they blackmailed him," Vogert speculates. "Or he decided to use his ties as leverage to subside regulations in exchange for access."

"All entirely possible," Addison agrees. "At least, it means the Chinese used several avenues to pursue the attack."

"Which doesn't make sense to me," Ibrahim concedes. "Why steal material they could've gotten through official channels?"

"Keep reading," Ava suggests, pointing at the bottom of the screen. "This bit. Do you see it?"

Ibrahim squints as he mouths the words. "It's a . . . What is it?" he asks.

"A recording from his home network," Ava explains. "Athena transcribed it."

"And what exactly am I reading?"

"A discussion from Wensu Hao to Henry Holland," Athena clarifies. "Before the Senator arrived at Ground Zero."

Ibrahim steps aside to let Addison take a closer look.

"Seems like Hao was concerned for his people," Addison reads. "His losses during the Central Spire Incident? And during the corridor battles? It's higher than on their official casualty reports."

"Camp Yi was directly attacked by Fragments a dozen times," Athena tells them. "And the storm nearly wiped their lower base off the hull."

Addison rubs her eyes in startling confusion. Then, she blinks, clearly taken aback.

"We've not heard anything about attacks on that scale," Ibrahim says.

She shrugs. "I don't know what to tell you," Ava returns.

Ibrahim, Addison, Vogert, and Ava all look at Zhu Yunwen. They're hoping she has their answers.

The woman turns red as she bites her lip. Tears begin rolling down Yunwen's cheeks, her pupils dilating. She looks to Addison, who offers her a soft nod. For a moment, Zhu shows off a sad smile, a dark rebellion growing inside her.

"They wouldn't want the embarrassment getting out," Zhu explains. "I hadn't seen those attacks' aftermath. But I know they ordered Hao to make up for the losses."

"Which explains why they haven't uploaded data to the network," Addison remarks.

"Malakai had concerns about that," Ibrahim adds. "Now I understand why."

"I don't know if that was the reason," Zhu explains. "At least, from what they told me."

"But why didn't they just ask for help?" Ava asks her.

"And admit we couldn't handle it ourselves?" Zhu asks. "That would never go over well on the mainland."

"Hao needed to play catchup," Addison concludes. "And he was desperate."

"It clarifies a few odd ends," Ibrahim says, relaxing his stance while retaining his scowl. "This is good . . . We can use this to justify sending in the task force."

"Attacking this base isn't justification enough?" Vogert demands.

"We don't know what they know," Ibrahim admits. "And vice versa. It allows us another angle of approach."

Zhu lowers her gaze, her jaw twitching, unsure if she should be proud or ashamed of speaking out and doing the right thing. And in fairness, Ava doesn't know, either.

"Theirs was a risky plan at best," Addison says, doing little more than guessing. "Even if they *did* steal the Heart, they would've had to convince everybody that either the Architects or a third party did it. And with CSDR using local resources? They wouldn't have had many options to point fingers at if it failed."

"Namely . . . Doctor Zhu," Ibrahim says, squeezing her shoulder. "Don't worry. You're a victim."

"And we'll protect you," Vogert decides. "Right?"

"I'll do everything in my power," Ibrahim allows. "But that may not count for much."

"We don't have a choice," Addison iterates.

Yunwen surrenders a small grin as she wipes off her tears.

"First, we have to get this ball rolling," Ibrahim says, steering the conversation.

"Speaking of which—?" Vogert coughs.

"Your transport is waiting for you on the pad," Ibrahim tells him. "Go ahead. We'll update you when we can."

"It's gonna be a bumpy ride," Vogert says as he stops to point at the ceiling, listening as the rain pounds the oil rig's metallic hull.

Ava smiles as Vogert turns on his heel and steps out of her lab, whistling a sad tune.

"And there's the other issue of legality," Addison adds as the doctor leaves. "Getting these files un-sanctioned? We can't do anything with them."

"I hate politics," Ava mutters.

"People are fickle," Ibrahim offers recompense. "Americans, especially. Once they feel betrayed or have their minds set on a verdict—the accused become whatever the public decides, no matter the evidence. What we *need* to do is—"

The door suddenly opens again. Light from the hallway breaks into the Observation Lab.

Malakai Adonis walks in on their little conspiracy.

"I wondered where you'd all gone," Malakai says grimly. "Playing into politics?"

Ava sinks into her coat when she notices him eyeing Zhu in the corner, still reeling from her surgery.

"Does it matter?" Ibrahim questions.

"Hopefully, this will be worth the cost we're paying by the end," Malakai says, offering the woman a warm nod. Addison opens her mouth and is about to speak when Malakai points at her. "Not a word," he cuts her off, shutting the door behind him. "Okay . . . Now we can talk."

"Malakai?" Ava murmurs.

"Any update on your progress to find dirt on our dear Senator and his cadre?" the man asks. Addison, Zhu, and Ava pass glances at one another with surprise. Malakai lets off a soft hum with closed lips. "I've played the game longer than any of you," he admits, walking closer and stopping at Ibrahim. "Don't suppose I can join this little pact, Lieutenant Colonel?"

Ibrahim remains a rock as the two men have a staring contest, narrowing their eyes and judging each other's reactions.

"How did you find out?" he asks.

"Alexandra Roslin. She knows. And *she* is the only reason OverSec isn't rushing to arrest us. Addison's little stunt wasn't exactly discreet," Malakai explains. "I told you, Colonel—after this, our heads are on the block. I've decided to get ahead of it before the axe drops. For all our sakes. Unless you prefer a noose?"

He looks through the lab's glass floor and the waves crashing against the rig's foundation.

"I prefer a parachute," Ibrahim warns. "Even if we succeed, we expect backlash."

"Which is why you need all the help you can get," Malakai accepts with an unsubtle wink. "I'll handle the political front. You four work on getting our friends to the core so we can all go home. Sanctioned or not—we've got a threat on our shore, and we need to push it off the beach."

"And what about the mission to arrest Wensu Hao?" Addison asks.

"I am sure the task force can handle it," Malakai says. "Here. For assurances." He lowers a hand to reveal a new set of comms units.

"What're these for?" Ibrahim asks.

"Off-the-grid communications," Malakai states. "Leighton's idea. Courtesy of Director Roslin."

"She's on our side?" Addison asks.

"Well, she's not against us," Malakai says, weighing his response.

"You know that's not the same thing," Ibrahim denotes.

"Oh, I am aware," Malakai shrugs. "But if you want to keep your plans secret, you'll need help from the inside."

Ibrahim is the first to go up and take one of the new units. "And how much does she know?" he asks.

"Probably best not to worry about that for now," Malakai offers, which hardly lends confidence.

Ava scoffs as she begins picking at the calluses on her palms. It's a sign that she's anxious, and there's a good reason for it—Roslin's trouble.

Addison goes up next. "Everybody's getting one?" she asks, raising hers to the light for a better look.

"There's only five," Malakai counts. "Leighton says they're a closed network. He'll have one—Ibrahim, Warden, Remmings, and you, Addison."

"I'll hand off Warden's when we get hull-side," Ibrahim agrees.

"Make sure you do," Malakai tells him.

"Will they cut through the interference from the greenhouse?" Addison asks.

"I'm not sure," the man says frankly.

"Probably not," Ava frowns. "Our normal radios hardly work there. No reason to expect *these* would."

"Quite the assurance," Ibrahim ridicules.

"I'm doing my best to help you guys," Malakai defends. "Do you want it or not?"

"I suppose it's what we asked for," Ava utters.

She walks up next to take a unit and . . . She hesitates. Not because she doesn't want to help and break a few rules in the process . . . No, it's more that she's had dealings with Alexandra Roslin before, when Ava spent two weeks in a dark cell, crying to see the sun again. And what they plan to do now is much worse than anything she attempted as a reckless university student with a laptop.

"Doctor Remmings?" Malakai prods her.

"You're certain there's only five?" she asks, waking up.

"You don't believe me?"

"More like I don't like odd numbers," Ava openly mocks. But when she accepts hers, she pulls Malakai close and whispers in his ear. "After this, I want my freedom."

Malakai's eyes widen. He backs away, holding her in consideration.

"I'll do what I can," he weakly promises.

Ava cringes, unable to accept. "I need you to do better," she iterates.

Malakai's eyelids flicker shut as he takes in a deep breath. She must question

Malakai's wisdom in trusting Director Roslin as an ally. He knows where Ava came from before she started making weapons for the military. And how the Old Man saved her from the hole that Alexandra Roslin's iron-fisted sense of justice threw her into and left to rot.

"I'll make sure of it," he promises. "Just do what you need to do."

She returns with a semi-placated nod. "You better," Ava threatens.

After, everybody leaves the lab, which gives Ava a moment to process this new mystery. At her workbench, she gives the comms unit a once over, noticing it's painted black, with no indication of a serial number. She hates the idea of leaving their secrets in the hands of somebody inherently distrustful. It's like welcoming the devil into bed, hoping he'd play nice.

But she can do nothing about it but wait to see if it blows up in their faces.

Ava decides to push the comms unit to the side and spends the next hour preparing Holland's files for release. Once they're ready, she unleashes them onto the internet. By the time Senator Holland wakes up, every major news organization in the western hemisphere will have a new story to run with his name front and center.

"And the world will have their scapegoat," Ava happily whispers. "Zhu will be a free woman. And I'll follow her soon enough."

That's *if* they don't all get killed in the next twenty-four hours.

Ava creates a scene in her head. She visits her mom again after years apart. And her sister. Her dad. Uncle. Ser Purrington, their cat. Although, she imagines the cat is dead after all this time. Ava wipes her eyes as her head soaks in the fantasy.

"Worse are the times I think they're holding a funeral for me, thinking I am dead," Ava weighs, dabbing her sleeve to clear the snot from her nose. "I hate my life, this place. I hate everyone . . . Everything . . . All of it." She holds herself back from shouting, which only leaves her seething. But it feels good to say, even if it isn't constructive.

Ava pounds a fist on her desk, finally letting it loose. Alone and unashamed, she does it again and again until it hurts. Ava works her fingers—open and closed—making sure nothing's broken. For a moment, Ava doesn't care about etiquette, the damn politics, or anything else. She's gone ten years without an outlet or confidant. All she wants is to punch the table.

Ava sits on her stool afterward, her pulse beating through her hand, enjoying the quiet of the lab. Only the vents make any noise, blowing warm air.

After this, she's over this crap. With everything . . . One way or another.

She wants to work in space, away from everybody on this garbage planet.

MOVEMENT | 69

SERGEANT MAJOR OLIVIA WARDEN
UNITED COALITION ARMED FORCES

OCTOBER 26, 2041 | 2355 HOURS

"What the hell is that?" Warden curses as if she doesn't know.

Comms reports describe the buggers amassing outside their secured sectors inside the ship for thirty minutes now. Warden jumps off the truck as she joins her units, fortifying the edge, unwilling to let the build-up go unanswered. She knew the days-long ceasefire was too good to last.

"We've got movement at station eight!" the chatter breaks out as she reaches the barricades.

"Sergeant Major?" the Marine next to her questions, looking at her through his helmet's view. "What should we do, ma'am?"

Warden doesn't immediately answer the man. Instead, she looks out at this new crowd. "Switch on the floodlights," Warden instructs. She waits for the corridor to illuminate before polarizing her visor. The trespassers flinch at the action, with many using their upper set of arms to block the light from their six glowing eyes.

Warden sets her HUD to highlight the aliens. She counts hundreds of the ugly bastards, their lower arms raised like refugees surrendering.

"Nobody shoots without my go-ahead," Warden orders, signaling everybody to stand down. She grits her teeth. Warden has lost damn good marines in their battles with these beasts. And the last time she's come face-to-face with the Jalks, it didn't end well for anybody.

Of course, she realizes this is *their* home, and her troops are the invaders aboard this juggernaut of a ship.

That doesn't stop her from caressing her weapon's holster with her thumb.

A large individual emerges among the aliens' first wave, pushing itself to the forefront. *It* dresses in an elaborate red armor with gold etchings across its surface, creating a pattern like sunburnt metal. Their leader, she presumes.

"Give me the rundown, Athena," Warden demands. She can hear a series of clicks and hisses from the buggers as they get closer.

"Hello to you too, Sergeant Major," Athena returns. "Would you care to specify *what* you want me to do?"

"Do you still have the translation program mimicking Doctor Kennedy's cipher?" Warden spouts. "Because I need it again. I don't know what these . . . things . . . are trying to say. And I prefer not to make this another shooting gallery if I don't have to."

Athena sends a low hum through Warden's earpiece, causing a minor throbbing in her temples.

"Enough to get a basic grasp on the female's linguistics," Athena says.

"Female?" Warden repeats. "That *one* is a woman?"

"I would think so," Athena surmises. "Notice her stride? Slow and methodical. I do not believe she approaches with hostile intent, Sergeant Major."

"You don't 'believe,' do you? Meaning you don't know," Warden rephrases. "Helpful. Very helpful."

"I recommend you avoid making rash decisions," the AI castrates. "Since bad introductions can leave a worse first impression. If you don't want to fight, Sergeant Major, don't antagonize them. Not again. They outnumber you. It is reasonable to infer they did not come looking for a fight."

Warden imagines that if Athena had a physical image, the AI would be wagging a finger at her.

Pulling up her tablet, Warden checks the sensor scans.

"Thousands," Warden corrects. "Not hundreds. And only a few weapons?"

She needs to note that detail. Just in case this quickly goes sour, and the Colonel requires her to file a report.

Warden dreads to think how easily these buggers could overrun this position and swarm into UCAF territory before reaching the METIS Research Base. And *that* is something she can't let happen. Not on her watch. Warden squares her shoulders and steps toward the large alien waiting at the bottom of the ramp. As she gets nearer, the female bugger offers her a slight curtsy, regarding the Sergeant Major with curiosity, if not outright respect.

Warden cringes as she looks into the creature's eyes, unsure which set to focus on primarily.

She decides on the bottom pair in the center of the bugger's face.

"At least she seems friendly," Warden murmurs.

The female opens her mandibles, attempting to smile.

Warden stops a few steps outside the barricade. Given their recent absence from the dreadnaught, Warden would've thought the buggers had taken too many losses in the fighting to continue fielding their numbers en masse. Judging by all these faces, she couldn't have been more wrong.

Olivia clumsily bows her head before taking a professional, steady posture in contrast to the aliens' craggy appearance.

"This isn't exactly my area of expertise," Warden breathes, unsure of introductions. "Can you understand what I am saying?"

The female Varmajalkavaen returns with a confident nod and lowers her arms, motioning her retainers to do the same.

Warden watches as they react like dancers in a ballet. She relaxes her posture, impressed.

Is this how they coordinated in combat so effectively?

The female Varmajalkavaen begins by speaking in her intrinsic tongue. At the same time, Athena translates the noise to the best of her ability. Somehow the AI can turn squeals, clicks, and lower-pitch whines into functional sentences spelled out on her screen.

"We thank you for not opening fire when you saw us," the female credits.

"Your people don't look armed for war," Warden replies. "Pun intended. No offense."

"Pun?" the other repeats confusingly.

"A bad joke," Warden iterates. "Your arms . . . It doesn't matter. Why are you here? We're not the safest people to approach uninvited."

"You are the invaders here," the female resists.

"It's our planet," Warden argues.

"And *our* ship," the female counters, burring her head. "But it does not matter. Decisions by our benefactors have forced us into drastic confrontations. And now we come to do more than merely survive." She releases a shiver that goes from her neck to her limbs.

Warden tilts her head and scowls. "What do you mean?" she asks.

"You understand what is going on between the Arkkitects, do you not?" the female prods.

Warden's eyes narrow as her thoughts weigh on Addison Kennedy. She only knows what Colonel Ibrahim informs her about, which isn't much. And not without deep speculation on Warden's part. She must question what else the eggheads aren't telling the people on the front, doing the hard work while risking their lives.

Warden raises a hand to stop the female from speaking further.

"We understand enough to give ourselves a fighting chance," Warden asserts.

"Then we are of a like-minded sense," the female agrees. Unexpectedly.

Warden cautiously steps closer to the bug. "You'll have to explain that one to me," she admits.

The female attempts to straighten her posture, only to look more crooked, like she's hiding an injury.

"Explain? I do not know if we can. But we are Varmajalkavaen, so we shall try," she musters the courage. "We serve the Obligation, as well as its Arkkitects. We are, in essence, the hands of a body that needs many fingers. We do their important work—above the chattel, but little more than spokes on a wheel that does not stop moving."

Warden grimaces. "History wasn't my best subject in school," she admits. "Why didn't you—?"

"Fight?" the female hums. "We did. And we lost."

"But you survived," Warden swallows.

"Yes. By making a choice that we did not suffer lightly," the other clarifies. "The Arkkitects made us, then forgot about us . . . Until they remembered, and their response still burns in our collective memories." The alien points at her head before folding her hands at her waist. "How do you choose between life and death? Obligation on an open palm, or chaos in a closed fist . . . Peace or conflict. Death was our only 'real' alternative. So, we chose to adopt a higher ideal. I say these words to you, Sergeant Major, so you know there is *no* hatred in our hearts for killing my people."

"Your . . . 'people,' is it?" Warden caustically states.

"Both of us understand the need to do what is necessary," the female mourns, eyes going black like a cat after knocking over a vase.

Warden squints and studies the twitching in the creature's face. Or what she can make of *that* face, at any rate.

"Hardly seems a fair choice to me," Warden offers a small measure of ease.

"It was a long time ago," the female corrects, standing proud amongst her people. "And we earned adherence to the Obligation. It was our 'honor' to join this mutuality, which now unravels as we speak. Sergeant Major—Tyrann 'Akachan aims to re-capture lost territory and repair what's broken. He needs to enforce tradition, no matter the cost."

"Which means . . . What, exactly? He's after the Heart?" Warden speculates. "That's what everyone seems to care about."

"Yes," the female asserts. "Yet *we* are not with the Trident."

"Then, why are you here? We're not looking for another fight. I've lost too many already."

"As have we," the female agrees.

"So, you're looking for a . . . a truce? Is that it?"

"Your leadership and *our* rebels have a truce already, do they not?" the female questions. "We can help you fight off what's coming. Our part will come into play when the Trident retaliates. He will do everything within his power if he thinks it will prevent Adhion 'Klaka from gaining the upper hand. Even if it means killing everybody."

"Making us a target," Warden realizes.

Her eyes widen under her visor. Warden can hardly believe the translation scrolling across her screen. She double-checks with Athena to make sure what she's reading is correct. And it *is* accurate. The buggers want to fight alongside her marines, which leaves Warden with a clog in her throat.

"Why the sudden change in loyalties?" Warden questions under her breath. She looks at her marines, with many preparing for the aliens to blanket the perimeter station at the drop of a hat. She doesn't want to turn this into another killing field, so Warden whistles in their direction. "Nobody needs their fingers on their triggers," she calls out. "Hands off your boomsticks."

They're anxious. Warden understands, but she's unsure what to do anymore. Nobody's trained her for diplomacy.

Warden keys her wrist-pad and steps away, opening a channel to Colonel Ibrahim.

"What am I supposed to do?" she asks him.

"Stand your troops down and escort the buggers to base," Ibrahim orders.

Warden feels like somebody just punched her in the gut. "Ah, say that again to confirm?" she queries.

"They're friendlies. You can proceed," Ibrahim answers. His voice cracks like there's static on their comms. "Vogert will be there soon. He can debrief you. Talk to him when you get on base, and he'll explain what's happening."

Warden takes a deep breath to calm her nerves. Her stance becomes rigid as she spins around to keep the buggers in view. Colonel Ibrahim's been on the Olympus for days, so he's not seen the same developments *she* has or how *fucked-up-beyond-repair* this whole mission has become.

"Castle-Actual . . . You understand what you're asking, don't you?" Warden demands. "I've got a stand-off with the creeps we've been fighting since our boots hit this rock! And you want me to . . . to, what? Let them inside? Like that? No questions asked? And after everything? The crash? The floods? This damn storm?!"

Warden doesn't know what's going on aboard the oil rig. Every report she's read is vague and dipped in black ink. She only has a "tug on the collar feeling" that Addison Kennedy has the Colonel dangling by strings like he's a marionette.

"Sergeant Major—?"

"These aliens have marine blood on their hands!" Warden argues. "My troops would like some payback! What about—?"

"You already got *that* when you killed an Architect!" Ibrahim shouts, his tone overmodulating over the static.

Warden bites her tongue, not expending such a harsh response. She reels back, waiting to see if he says anything else. Ibrahim's not a shouting man. It's not his style outside combat, and even then, only when necessary. That's how she knows he's serious about letting these buggers inside the cordon.

"How long until you join this mess, Colonel?" Warden bitterly asks.

"Mission sensitives will stay restricted to team leads and Addison's crew," Ibrahim states. "I will be on-site with the specifics in a few hours. Until then, talk to Doctor Vogert. And make sure our guests don't cause too many disruptions. Our personnel on-station need to see that you can handle the situation calmly."

"I *am* calm," Warden asserts.

"Are you?" Ibrahim doubts. "Remain on alert until we rectify our position."

"Anything else you can tell me over an open channel?" Warden decides to prod.

"No," Ibrahim denies. "But pick your team wisely."

And with that, the Colonel disconnects. Warden is left astonished.

"Pick my team?" she murmurs. "For what?!"

Warden turns back to the thousands of Varmajalkavaen and the female at their head. She knows the alien cannot see the expression on her face. Still, the marine figures her intent *is* identifiable in her body language—hands on her hips, stiff in her posture. Warden wants to take her sidearm and shoot the damn ugly things, putting them all out of their misery.

She inhales a full breath and lets only half of it out.

"You're clear to come through," Warden certifies. "Welcome to paradise."

The female bows to her and waves her people forward through the checkpoint. Warden watches as the buggers follow the platforms on the long walk to the base.

She has her orders, but that doesn't mean Warden agrees with the directive. Looking at her marines, she pulls up their vitals. Most have temperatures spiking over normal levels, meaning they're stressed, and for understandable reasons. She catches several of them glancing at her, quietly blaming her for letting these things past their perimeter.

"Ibrahim better be right about this," Warden spits between her teeth.

These events go beyond trusting the higher-ups to have everybody's best interests at heart. And even if this *is* all part of some greater plan, Warden intends to have a very frank chat with Addison Kennedy about her influence on military matters. She doesn't care if the woman's daddy is the man on top of the mountain.

Once the last bugger passes through the barricade, Warden orders the garrison chief to close the checkpoint and ensure all the equipment ships back to METIS for drawdown. If it's true about the alien's claim and something larger is on its way, then humanity's time aboard this ship is on the short track. And that means Warden needs to work ahead to avoid unnecessary casualties.

Ibrahim can scorch-earth his career and play nice with the enemy if that's what he wants. She doesn't care.

But he should leave the rest of them out of it.

MALAKAI ADONIS, DIRECTOR OF OPERATIONS
EPIMETHEUS PROJECT

OCTOBER 27, 2041 | 0300 HOURS

Malakai waits in his office with Addison Kennedy on the other side of his desk.

Ibrahim is also in the room, along with Zhu Yunwen and Doctor Remmings. Alexandra Roslin stands firmly in a corner, with officers on her flanks, dressed in red OverSec field uniforms. The news came in from the Security Council fifteen minutes ago.

Malakai has full permission to enforce the decision.

He has a lot of wrinkles to iron out first. Still, against the political fallout this will stir up, it offers Malakai time to conduct a more urgent mission.

Three loud knocks on his door indicate the last of them to arrive. "Malakai?" Holland demands. "Let me in!"

Ibrahim goes to open the door. The Senator's face goes pale when he realizes who's greeting him.

"Lieutenant Colonel?" Holland murmurs as he sidesteps into Malakai's office.

As he dodges Ibrahim's glare and turns to the room, his cheeks regain some color. But everybody is waiting on him.

Malakai had messaged the Senator to say that Addison Kennedy wished to meet with the man. Now that he knows it's a party, Holland sweats off the makeup covering the blemishes on his face. He understands this is an ambush but is unsure what to do about it.

Malakai glances at Addison as she shifts uncomfortably in her chair. He took the opportunity to put out additional seating, but not enough for everybody. Malakai smirks as he watches the Senator stagger for a space. It's a strategy he's practiced since he started dealing with people much smarter than him. For men like Holland, it puts them on the defensive.

The bastard made him fight for this Project every step of the way. It's only right to make him the odd duckling among swans.

"Seems you've caught me off-guard," Henry admits, straightening his posture and smoothing his collar.

His eyes dart to Alexandra Roslin in the corner, his mouth slightly trembling.

The woman returns with a rock-hard glare, clearly unhappy and making no effort to hide it.

Henry spins around to evade her ire, but his grimace says it all. "What is this?" Holland finally demands. He fixes his tie as if suddenly appearing on the Senate floor. "Malakai . . . Director Adonis," the man feigns reverence, "whatever this party is for, let's make it short, all right? My flight leaves soon, and I was hoping this meeting would be—"

"Brief?" Ibrahim instigates. "Don't worry. It will be."

"Is that a threat?"

"Your flight leaves in thirty minutes," Ibrahim clarifies. "You'll be fine."

Henry scowls at the soldier.

"I have . . . important business in Washington I need to monitor," Holland specifies. "And in case you've forgotten? We're still facing a crisis at home! With our resources getting thrown at your little Project, I need to find some way to fund reconstruction. So, I don't appreciate this trap you set up for me."

"Then why have you spent the last week with us?" Malakai questions. "No doubt someone else is better positioned to substitute your duties on the Oversight Committee as liaison to the Project, Senator. Especially if you've concerns elsewhere."

Holland raises a curious brow. "Schedules tend to change last minute," the man argues. "I *am* a duly elected official, so it's my job."

"We haven't forgotten," Addison remarks.

"And it isn't my concern," Alexandra Roslin slips into the conversation. "You're here to answer questions, so I recommend you answer them."

Henry clears his throat. "Director Roslin," the Senator says, gritting his teeth. "If you're the one asking the questions . . . I must've broken some petty protocol with my conduct while on base, is that it?" He squints at the others in the room, prodding to see if there's a deeper accusation.

Malakai's spent enough time with lawyers to know *that* usually means there's definite guilt lying under the surface.

Hasn't anybody told him yet? Ava blew the whistle hours ago, the info spreading across the internet like wildfires in Old California.

"There's no way you don't know," Malakai says loud enough that Henry overhears him.

"What are you talking about—?" he tries to say.

"Colonel Ibrahim?" Roslin instructs, marching to the desk. "Have her bring up the screen."

Ibrahim nods at Ava and has her route the data to the big monitor on the wall. After a minute, every dirty thing they found in the Senator's records is open to the room.

Malakai bites the inside of his cheek.

He watches as Henry squirms as he reads his life's work. "This should give me a warm feeling inside, but it doesn't," Malakai quietly monologues. Not like he thought it would. No. Doing this leaves him feeling like he's drowning the man on dry land. "As it were," Malakai adds, pinching the bridge of his nose to relieve the tension behind his eyes.

Malakai relaxes as he soaks in Alexandra Roslin's stiff presence, like a coniferous tree in the dead of winter.

Henry breaks away from the screen before calling up a fake grin.

"And what's this for?" the Senator laughs as his only tool around the semantics. "This is nothing but words on a screen. You can barely read them! Is this your conduct policy? Will you have me sign my name and swear an oath on the bible?"

"No," Malakai denies unceremoniously.

"I think you know what you're looking at," Roslin asserts.

Holland's laugh quiets as he sinks into his suit like an ugly duck gone lame.

The Senator glowers at the OverSec officers next to Roslin. He puffs out his chest, holding his ground, until he notices Zhu Yunwen with a mix of horror and surprise. Malakai reads the bewilderment in the man's eyes, wondering why the woman isn't under lock and key like he ordered.

Henry jeers at Malakai. "What do you want?" he asks, less than confident.

"To know what happened here," Ibrahim answers instead, rubbing his wrists. "Anything you can tell us, Senator."

"I was in a dormitory with everybody else," Holland acknowledges. "I heard the shooting."

"And did you see the blood on the walls afterward?" Ibrahim describes menacingly.

Henry stares at the man with contempt.

Ibrahim returns that stare with the same hostility.

"We're investigating the attack's proceedings," Malakai explains. "Trying to understand everything leading up to the blackout."

Henry points at Yunwen. "Then you should start with her!" he shouts. "It was her people! Do you think for a second that's a coincidence? For that matter, why isn't she detained? Last I checked, we had her locked up in detention."

Malakai shakes his head. "Because? She helped us during the attack, and I believe she's innocent," he concludes. "At worse, she was an unknowing accomplice and hadn't known much outside her duties to the science team. Having her detained is counterproductive to our goals."

"Doesn't that make Wensu Hao a suspect, then?" Holland loudly accuses. "Have you arrested him? Where is he?! Are you all so incompetent that you can't recognize the rats under your roof when they're eating your food? Director—?"

"We know about the rats," Roslin mocks, raising a lone finger. "Don't worry about Wensu Hao for now."

Her officers move to block the door and stop the Senator from escaping.

"And that isn't why we called you here," Ibrahim notions.

Henry's jaw tenses.

"And they are not the only suspects," Malakai mourns.

"Your records show a high degree of financial ties to the Chinese through your family's businesses," Roslin explains, forcing him to confront the information. She takes control of the monitors, highlighting the sections she needs. "Do you see this? Millions in debt to very specific organizations. Much of it connects you to the People's Republic. Enough to let them put you in a squeeze."

Henry grimaces. "Most of those ties are through Hong Kong," the Senator describes. "I dare you to find anyone growing a garden without a few pots."

"For an American Congressman," Alexandra weighs, "there's a higher expected standard."

"I don't like what you're leaning toward, Ms. Roslin."

Alexandra's nostrils flare subtly, and Malakai feels a cold shiver run down his spine. "I am not leaning 'toward' anything," she admits. "Nor would I insinuate. I am only pointing out discrepancies in your financial statements. Now, I am not a lawyer. But as my friends call me, I *am* a very clever woman."

"You have friends?" Holland bites back.

"Contacts and associates," Roslin corrects. "Employees, with some respects."

"And what do my finances have to do with the attack on us here?" Holland demands.

"Probably nothing," Ibrahim states.

"Or maybe everything," Roslin counters. "It's the question that interests me more than the answer."

"Your office demanded Doctor Zhu's immediate arrest after the attack," Ibrahim continues, swinging around to stand beside Roslin at the desk. "She'd only been on the base for a couple of days. Why her? The only interaction between you two was when she stepped off the transport after the operation into the dark zone."

"And as my sources found," Roslin adds, "you two didn't speak to each other once."

"Which begs a reason for your hostility toward a woman you hardly know," Addison notions.

Henry's nose turns fiery red. "As I said, Doctor Kennedy—I demanded her arrest because *her* people attacked us. After I learned that, it made sense to detain her for our security!" he details. "Any competent officer would've made the same decision."

"Except you sent the demand through official channels right after the all-clear," Roslin describes.

"Your point?" Henry questions.

"We didn't tell anybody *who* attacked us that night," Malakai explains.

"Still haven't, for obvious reasons. Only a handful of people knew outside of Project leadership."

"And you weren't on that list," Ava states.

"Which suggests you guessed *who* the guilty party was while hiding under your bed," Ibrahim asserts.

"Or you *knew* it was the Chinese before *we* did," Addison says.

"Especially since members of my division thought it was hostiles from the dreadnaught until our arrival the next day," Roslin denotes, taking a heavy step in the Senator's direction. "My question is a simple one . . . How did you know *where* to look before I did?"

Henry's mouth coldly shuts. "Maybe you're bad at your job? Or maybe . . . I might've overheard it on the comms?" he says.

"You 'might' have overheard it?" Roslin catches. "Meaning . . . You don't know?"

"Quite the accusation to throw without solid evidence. Surprising for a lawyer, don't you think?" Ibrahim asks. "Especially since our comms were dark."

"You know what's not surprising? That you're using tricks and intimidation to get me to admit guilt," Henry violently scoffs. "Please! Almost everybody in this room had Ms. Zhu pegged as a spy when she landed. I read the reports. Is it *that* far off to suggest she played a role in sabotaging the power grid?"

"She was with me in the hours before the attack," Ava describes.

"And with *me*, after it started," Addison adds. "We only separated because I was trying to beat the assholes to the labs. And I wouldn't have gotten there without her help." She winces as she jerks her arm in its brace.

Holland frowns. "But *not* all in one piece," he notions, eyeing her bandages.

Malakai sits up in his chair. "Henry? You're under investigation for conspiracy against the Project and UCAF personnel," Malakai finally lands his point. "I'm not a lawyer, but I should ask, do you have anything to say to help us understand why?"

"Only that you're not a prosecutor," Henry leans on the desk between them.

"And this isn't a courtroom," Malakai tells him.

"This is ridiculous," Henry mewls.

"It's true," Roslin confirms, making Holland raise an eyebrow at her.

"What do you mean?"

"Aren't you following the newsfeeds?" Addison says.

"That's what my staff is for," Holland rebuffs.

Ava coughs to get the man's attention. "This screen is a live feed," she warns, which Holland regards with mild bemusement.

"Ignore the time differences," Addison says. "Much of this coverage is technically from yesterday."

The man's cheek begins twitching as he studies the monitor more intently.

"About an hour ago, the Oversight Committee went in for an emergency session to vote on your suspension," Roslin clarifies. "You can believe it or not, but Congress sent the motion to the UCSN for approval, where the jurisdiction edict passed by a two-thirds majority. Not a very popular man, are you?"

"This is nonsense," Holland snorts. "How could they vote? Most of my caucus is with me on this station!"

"And unable to block the measure," Malakai states.

"My division will take control of the matter," Roslin simplifies. "No formal charges yet, but the international system works differently than your national one. Henry Holland? You're in my custody until our investigation is complete. While I can read you the rights granted to you by your government, it's not a requirement."

She snaps her fingers.

Holland flinches as the OverSec officers step forward, respectfully indicating they will restrain him.

He lets out his breath and looks at Malakai with a flame in his eyes. "I warned you that nations covet what they don't have," Holland argues. "China reacted to your damn-awful decisions . . . I had nothing to do with it! Arrest me, oh, I dare you. And I will crash this plane on your god-forsaken graves!" He spits into the nearest officer's helmet.

OverSec forgoes the gentle method and forces the Senator to the ground.

Alexandra Roslin moves aside to watch it like a piece of entertainment.

"You threaten everything we've been trying to achieve," Malakai explains. "That screen? It shows you've also stolen classified data and leaked it to your connections. It's damning enough for Congress to get off their butts and do something for a change. Passcodes, security doors, work schedules, progress reports . . . Information you got due to your position on the committee. You might not have shot the gun, but you damn well bought the rifle so your friends could play soldier. And we can't let it happen again."

Holland snarls at him with a shadow over his face.

"You won't survive this," the Senator warns. "I have contacts. Allies! Everybody in this room is dead, do you hear me? Dead! Fuck the courts! I will rip each of you apart until the only thing you have left are your heads rotting in a muddy creek!" His face swells as he tries to squirm out of his restraints.

"Yours is a cold fire, Senator Holland," Roslin laughs. "I'll enjoy having you over for tea."

"And you! When the President hears about this—?"

"He will do nothing but sit in the White House, afraid to show his pompous ass," Roslin sneers. She kneels to his level while her officers keep him pinned to the ground. "You are a fat wolf leading a pack of puppies, Mr. Holland. I am a lioness who feeds the pride. Enjoy the closet."

"And give him a more comfortable chair!" Zhu shouts over the room.

Alexandra Roslin strikes the woman with a hostile glare before letting her officers lift Henry to his feet.

Malakai frowns as he watches the agents take the Senator away with Roslin at their heels. She closes the door as they leave the room.

Ibrahim drops back against the wall. "So much getting him to help us down the line," the Colonel remarks.

"He's a better enemy to have now than an ally," Malakai explains. He stands up and comes around the desk until he's in the middle of their group. "Men like him are . . . unreliable at best. Helping us goes against his nature. He considers opposition to his ideas unfair, so no matter what we do, we're the bad guys."

"I don't know if we did the right thing with him," Ibrahim muses, although not entirely sympathetically.

"He did warn us that somebody would be gunning for the Heart," Addison admits. "And they did."

"I don't think it was a friendly word of caution at the time," Ava recognizes.

"It doesn't matter," Malakai defuses.

Addison looks sharply at him. "Why do you say that?" she asks.

"Because it doesn't matter if he's guilty," Malakai explains. "He went after one of us—*our* team, friendly or not."

"And he needed a good kick in the ass," Ibrahim realizes.

"He was right about needing a scapegoat," Malakai reasons. "I don't think he would've volunteered on his own. But now that he's gone—?"

"We don't have to tiptoe around the primsuits," Addison says. "What about the others he brought aboard?"

"OverSec will handle it," Malakai denotes.

Ibrahim surrenders a small laugh before stepping toward the door.

"Then, let's get back to work. I am still finalizing mission details," Ibrahim says, changing the subject. "Our team will transfer over in a few hours. We can conduct a planning session once we're hull-side. The operation will kick off soon after."

"Good," Malakai applauds.

"What about the other camps?" Ava asks.

"I'll key the remaining Field Directors into the loop and tell them what to expect," Malakai promises. "They need enough time to pack up what equipment they can without alerting Wensu Hao and Camp Yi to the raid. But when the fireworks start, our people take priority. So, let's get them home."

"Athena's subroutines can help with that easily enough," Ava agrees.

"As well as buy us some cover along the way," Ibrahim assesses. He opens the door to the Control Room. And then, he stops.

"What is it?" Addison asks.

Ibrahim turns back with a heavy breath. "What's the plan once we have Hao en route?" he asks.

"The task force will hand him over to Roslin and her security forces," Malakai explains.

"And you're sure it's wise to send marines *and* OverSec to raid Camp Yi to arrest a single man?" Ibrahim begs the question.

"Roslin's decision, not mine," Malakai admits. "And it will distract her from digging into your activities. If her focus is on one mission—?"

"She can pretend the other doesn't exist," Ibrahim concludes.

"It's like bedding the devil," Ava remarks.

"We're not selling our souls," Malakai says.

"Maybe not yours," Ava refutes.

Addison goes over to her and squeezes her shoulder.

Malakai daps his eyes dry with his sleeve as the temperature in the room drops a degree.

"Good luck to you, Doctor Adonis," Ibrahim offers.

Malakai nods. "Stay safe shipside, Colonel," he returns. "Bring our team back safely."

"I'll make sure Addison doesn't wander off again," he chuckles.

"Make certain she doesn't," Malakai reiterates.

Ibrahim's eyes fall groundward as he tries not to look at Addison on the other side of the room. Malakai laughs, catching a small hint of the man's personal feelings. For a man of action, Malakai would tell him, if he could, that he shouldn't have to hide his fear for her.

Malakai only hopes that fear is enough to keep the team alive.

"Yes, sir," Ibrahim finishes.

Malakai stands aside as Ibrahim leads Addison, Ava, and Zhu through the door to leave.

Following them into the Control Room, Malakai gets a sudden cold spell in his chest. His operations staff are busy coordinating wrap-up efforts across the zone. It's a task that needs doing so they can all go home, leaving no trace of their occupation. Odd to think that most of them were strangers to each other a couple of months ago.

"Athena, can you hear me?" Malakai asks.

"Like a whistle to a dog in training," Athena answers. "Go ahead."

"Get me all the incoming chatter you can from the media," Malakai requests.

"Doctor Adonis?" Athena begs for clarification.

"Let them know what's about to happen," Malakai orders. "Initialize protocol—twenty-one dash bee-two-six. Code black across project-wide channels."

"Code accepted," Athena returns. "Issuing wrap orders and warning crews. I need confirmation to execute."

"Doctor Malakai Adonis—Director of Operations, Epimetheus Project," he lists. "Execute command."

Static follows.

Everyone in the Control Room hears Malakai issue the order. They know what it means—

A black alert refers to an unknown threat—a potential terrorist attack. Malakai's throat clogs as he waits for a response.

Athena finally chimes back with acknowledgments from multiple field teams on the Summerland.

"Godspeed," Malakai utters under his breath.

HEART OF THE SHIP

ADHION 'KLAKA, NOMAD OF AMELIORATION
REBEL OF THE OBLIGATION

521031 LOCAL CLUSTER | 761,407 DAY OF PURPOSE

⸻

He's known this Judge for a long time. They've rarely agreed on anything but were always cordial to each other compared to the Nomad's dealings with Tyrann 'Akachan.

Adhion shrugs off a weak chest as he stares at the proud explorer's body on the table inside the medical pavilion. Dhun's armor looks scarred and broken. Profound marks show where humanity's weapons had penetrated the weak points. It must have taken great force to rip through an Arkkitect's battle harness like this, and Adhion shudders at the thought.

"Two dead because of me," Adhion whimpers. "My actions. Our sins."

Idu comes alongside him as three human workers wheel in what's left of the Servant. They stack her body next to the Judge. Idu puts a hand to her mouth, her skin wrinkling. Only days ago, when she would've last seen the pair, they were alive.

"They've gone over now," Idu mournfully says. Her tone is hardly above a whisper. "That is what matters."

"Maybe they have," Adhion admits. "Maybe not? I am no longer certain."

The human alleviator—Ryan Vogert—enters the room wearing a white uniform. The good doctor pauses as he sees Idu and Adhion looming over the bodies. The Nomad can only surmise the primate does not wish to break the moment. When the human clears his throat, it is to ask, "What are you going to do with them?"

Idu pulls away to address the man. Adhion reads the look in her starry eyes, fighting back the tears.

"We shall remember them as they were in life," Idu explains. "Not how they died."

Vogert surrenders a nod, accepting her words, saying it as if it's true.

"Just to let everyone know . . . We have guests," Vogert tells them uneasily. "Several thousand . . . Var-ma-jalk-a-vaen . . . along our defense perimeter?"

Idu's face perks up as he says it. Adhion beats down his tremors, breaking away from Dhun and Tjaa.

"They have made it," Adhion says. "Oha and her tribe. Our rebellion."

"A little warning would've been nice," a woman calls from the doorway. Adhion hadn't noticed her there, but she must have entered with Vogert. He recognizes her as Sergeant Major Olivia Warden—a warrior, tall and postured. "We've spent all fucking night getting them through the checkpoints."

Warden's fingers caress her sidearm's grip. Adhion muses at her hostility.

"You are the one who killed Dhun 'Ancod," Adhion realizes.

Idu understands immediately and offers a peaceful gesture to the young warrior. Adhion can't begin to guess the woman's place within human society. He does, however, doubt anyone in the room can stop the woman from drawing her weapon and shooting the pair if that's what she wants to do.

Warden's fleshy cheeks twitch as she stares hard at them.

Adhion doesn't have Addison Kennedy to protect him. Not like Idu did cycles ago in their first contact with each other. Adhion stands unarmed and relatively defenseless. Regardless, the woman's trifling sidearm won't have enough power to get through his armor. He can only hope.

He shows the woman his respect, bowing to her victory.

Warden blinks perplexedly. "You approve?" Warden asks. "Both of you?"

Idu raises an empty palm and shakes her head. "No. Dhun and Tjaa were my friends," she admits. "Or as close to friends as those among us may claim. Yet they attacked you due to the demands placed on them by our Obligation. Tyrann 'Akachan asked too much for too little. Now the Judge and Servant have paid for his avidity."

"We are *not* your enemy," Adhion murmurs.

Warden points at him as she marches forward.

Vogert steps between the three to act as a shield, but the woman shoves the good doctor aside and snarls.

"*You* don't get to speak!" Warden tells Adhion. She then pivots to Idu with a little less anger. "And you? Idu! You went to Addison Kennedy and filled her head with a fantasy. And what did she do? She damn well listened! She followed you right into danger, and you didn't attend the party. We had a mission . . . And I completed *an* objective."

"Dhun made a mistake," Idu acknowledges. "You did what was necessary to protect yourselves. Very commendable."

Adhion watches as Idu gives off a faint smile that the humans may or may not perceive as a frown.

Warden steps back, less confident than before. She nods all the same as if she's content.

"Why did you want to meet her there?" Warden demands. "And why *her*?"

Idu purses her lips. She refrains from saying anything for several long heartbeats.

"It wasn't to give her the Heart," Idu finally breathes. "Nor was it to make demands—like Dhun 'Ancod. These actions have brought our two species into unnecessary conflict." She glances unhappily in Adhion's direction. "And as I said, we made mistakes."

"Then why?"

"Because I wanted her to see the extent of our purpose," Idu explains. "We did *not* intend to bring you war or destruction, no matter your misgivings. You look around our corridors, and what do you see? Open space. Absurd for any other vessel for any other species. But not *us*. We call it a Source, but why? What does that mean? Soul'Alimentors—to seed life to barren worlds. Every corridor you've seen, everywhere you've fought and died? It's for herding large numbers of wildlife. A hundred-thousand species to fill a whole ecosystem."

Warden and Vogert each take a step back, hearing the passion in her tone.

"And the flora, too," Idu persists. "Fully grown trees, flowers, and underbrush, completely alive. It's easier to transplant to a young world than grow it from nothing."

"Which means we're on the largest artificial ecology in the galaxy," Vogert says with a satisfied smirk.

Warden narrows her eyes at the man. She's angry. But it appears the woman's temper has cooled to a sullen blue.

Unlike most soldiers he's seen up to this point, this Warden has taken off her helmet. Adhion studies her face, the contours of her skin, and the bruising under her left eye. He peels back when he sees her clamping down on her jaw, attempting to hide her antagonism.

Warden does well to mask her feelings by limiting the notion to a hoarse cough in her throat.

A noble sentiment, Adhion weighs internally.

"And what about Addison Kennedy?" Warden demands, veering to the topic. "We've plenty of eggheads. Why—?"

"Why single her out amongst the troves?" Adhion interjects.

Warden grinds her teeth together. "That's one way to put it," she glowers.

Idu drops her head and surrenders a smile large enough that it could not be mistaken for anything other.

"Not far from where we are standing," Idu continues, "we have a room we use to . . . watch events." She goes to one knee to match the human warrior's height. "I use it to monitor our herds throughout our ship—keeping track of their health and wellness, dietary habits, nesting behaviors, and overall basic needs."

"So . . . What? You spied on us?" Warden questions. "Is that it?"

"Learning *is* the key to successful contact," Idu freely admits. "Often, it is a slow process. But we do not have the luxury of time on our side. I had to know your species for a dialogue to take place. And the more I learned? The more beautiful I thought your people were. Our work often attempts to undo any impurity that would cause deformities. Perfection on a genetic level is necessary for living beings to thrive on their own without catastrophe."

"Until that perfection leads to stagnation," Adhion argues, nudging her.

Idu's glare shoots up at Adhion. Her feathery mane darkens to a deep red.

"Our current predicament is a clear sign our system is not as flawless as we thought," Idu confesses.

"Needless to say—Addison Kennedy represented a free and open mind," Adhion continues.

"A most reasonable individual," Idu says.

"Like a lost soul newly found."

"Kindred spirits."

"With notions and tendencies that make her a prime candidate," Adhion suggests.

"And thus, a worthy risk while the fighting remained scarce," Idu finishes.

"We lost good people due to your 'scarce' fighting," Warden accuses.

Adhion looks at her hip, noticing her hand still resting on her weapon's grip.

"I made errors in my judgment," Adhion grieves, raising his hands. "Does that mean I acted too hastily? I do not know."

"More like you jumped out of an airplane without a parachute!" Warden growls.

Adhion grimaces, not knowing *what* an airplane is or *why* he would need a parachute to leave it. "I *am* sorry," he admits. "I do not know how to make amends. I will discuss this with your Lieutenant Colonel, Sergeant Major Olivia Warden. Should you grant me that promise, all the better?"

For some reason, the Sergeant Major flinches when Adhion mentions the name.

Her stare lands on Idu for a short while. Warden's posture relaxes as she sees her reflection in those black, vibrant eyes.

The woman's hand gently slips away from her weapon.

Adhion releases a sigh from his gizzard.

They're not dealing with the curious Addison Kennedy. Sergeant Major Olivia Warden is as different from her counterpart as Idu is to Dhun 'Ancod. The soldier's instinct isn't to ask questions but to shoot first if it's hostile.

Warden takes a breath and holds it, letting out the air through her teeth, whistling a solid, abrasive tone that causes Adhion's auriculars to buzz.

"Maybe that's a good place to start," Warden admits. "I can't believe we're pegging all our hopes on you two bastards."

"All good things must begin somewhere," Idu says warmly.

"If only it didn't begin so bloody," Warden disquiets, "I might even agree with you."

"Nothing can undo the damage already done," Adhion explains. "And we've taken losses, too. We share your pains, grief, and fears, Sergeant Major. No creature should suffer without knowing why."

"Which is why I brought Addison Kennedy into the fold," Idu adds. "She asks questions, whereas a soldier would defend their ward. 'Not knowing' fascinates her, while an ignorant soul will see nothing but a threat."

"Are you calling me ignorant?" Warden demands, twisting her lip.

"Yes," Adhion intercedes. "As much as *we* are ignorant, Sergeant Major."

"And some ideas are beyond us to explain," Idu concludes.

Warden stares at the two of them. Her expression passes hard between a proud warrior's gaze and subtle anguish. If she were an Arkkitect, Adhion would say there is jealousy mixing with her emotions, making her appear hostile when she is, in fact . . . afraid.

Looking at the man, Ryan Vogert, Doctor of Epimetheus, Adhion reads softer features. He has a luminous gaze under his protective mask, which hides a cheery grin on brimming cheeks. Adhion *knows* that as a wholly amiable spark.

"Human nobility," Adhion whispers.

"What was that?" Vogert asks.

"I said—" Adhion stops.

A faint beeping goes off in the room.

Vogert and Warden put a finger to their ears as if commanding the noise to make sense.

"Understood," the Sergeant Major decrees. "We'll meet them at the ramp to the Stretch. Warden, out."

Vogert closes his eyes and takes a short breath. "Our breakfast guests have arrived," he says. "I hope you two are ready for this."

Idu weakly bows her head. "We are ready," she agrees.

Warden bites her lower lip. "Everything will move fast when the team lands," she adds.

Idu brushes Adhion's shoulder. "Then we will follow after we pay our respects," he tenderly nods.

"Understood," Warden acknowledges.

"If you two need anything, let us know," Vogert offers.

"Thank you," Idu says with a smile.

Adhion looks to Idu as Warden and Vogert spin around, departing through the facility's decontamination hallways without the Arkkitects.

"Tyrann isn't going to let us near the core," Adhion tells her, meandering over to Tjaa's body, resting his palm on the table. Idu does the same with Dhun, folding his hands over his chest and closing his eyes to let him sleep. It is a far cry from the honor they'd know if they had died closer to familiar stars. "How do we do this? Anything we try risks *his* retaliation."

"All he wants to do is leave. If we give the Heart to the Trident—he will ignite the engines before the humans get a chance to escape the ship with their lives," Idu forewarns. "And he won't depart slowly, either. Lifting off without easing into it *will* devastate their planet again, leaving them with worsening storms for many generations."

"If we fail to do this right, they could face extinction in a lifetime," Adhion says.

"Just for us to go home," Idu whimpers.

"Isn't that what you want?" Adhion agrees.

"It shouldn't matter what I want," Idu refuses to admit, a tear rolling down the tattoos on her cheek, staining a single yellow feather on her mane. "Tyrann 'Akachan does *not* care about humanity. He does not care about flourishing ecosystems, or the light such diversity could bring to the galaxy. It will cost them every tomorrow if we fail to act. He will ask, what *is* Earth? A small world that gasps for breath on the far edges of civilization. I . . . No. We cannot let him decide. It *must* end."

"We *must* do what is honorable—Obligation or not," Adhion urges. "Truth or reality."

"He's going to do everything he can to stop us," Idu warns.

"And that is the battle we face," Adhion frowns, his feathers a sickly green.

Adhion 'Klaka caused this and everything else to happen. All these lives? All because he stole the Heart of this great vessel and forced it to crash into the dark waters of humanity's isolated world. He restructured the Fragment Alimentors to buy time. He went to the Trident to make him hear his voice as more of an equal, not as an offspring of criminals of a distant past.

"He *will* kill us," Idu adds. "You know that, right?"

"Yes," Adhion says. "He may kill us. And we'll die free."

DÉJÀ VU | 72

LIEUTENANT COLONEL ELIAS IBRAHIM
UNITED COALITION ARMED FORCES

OCTOBER 27, 2041 | 0415 HOURS

———

Ibrahim wonders what Arthur Summerland had thought when he approached the ship's massive underbelly.

Arthur only had a small team and a research boat. He drove *both* across rough waters, scaling the mile-high lower hull through freezing rain and gale-force winds. And then, only for his team to reach the black void that became their Breach into the dreadnaught.

Ibrahim first saw the ship in person when he was in the air, looking out the rear hatch of his V-91 Warhawk during the Project's initial landings. For him, they were flying too close to a mountain. Ibrahim could hardly tell the difference between *it* and the ocean's tumultuous horizon.

And his return to the Summerland? It's like boarding a train to the frontline after a week on leave.

Ibrahim looks at Addison opposite of him. Her eyes follow the ship's red energy, like circuits through the rocky-metal hull.

"ETA—two minutes," the pilot voices over the comms. "We're in contact with METIS Control. They're reeling us in for a landing."

Ibrahim grabs ahold of the safety rail. As the aircraft hovers closer to the pad, the pilot compensates for the strong winds coming over the ship's massive spine.

Addison surrenders him a "look" as he locks his helmet to his hardsuit after a particularly turbulent jerk.

His marines follow his example and do the same.

"Impressive, isn't it?" Addison asks.

Ibrahim knows she cannot see it, but under his visor, he smiles, looking out the rear hatch.

"That's an understatement," he chuckles.

Their pilot steers the bird for the landing. It's rough, but they touch down after a minute. Ibrahim's marines pile out and begin prepping the staging area for the next phase. Addison joins Ibrahim when they disembark the VTOL. They each stare up the Stretch extending from the assembly area to the METIS Research Base.

"What time is the raid set to kick off?" Addison asks.

She secures a mask to her face, smoothing her raincoat's unbuckled flaps. Ibrahim eyes her ambiguously.

"Couple of hours," Ibrahim states. "If you're attempting to hide your anxiety—?"

"I'm doing a bad job at it, aren't I?" Addison begs the obvious.

"I wasn't going to say it like that," Ibrahim frowns.

"Oh, I'm sure you weren't," she muses.

"We'll have a while to get everybody ready to go," Ibrahim explains.

He studies her as Zhu and Ava find them in the commotion. The pair's hands tremble as if warding off the lack of sleep—working their fingers open and close. Ibrahim writes a mental note to keep an eye on them. Physical and mental fatigue are as dangerous to the team as meeting an angry bug with a score to settle.

"How was your ride?" Addison asks the pair.

"Overly bumpy," Ava responds, angling her neck to crack it. "Wildly uncomfortable."

"You're acting like it's your first trip hull-side," Ibrahim mocks.

Ava waves off the comment without giving him the satisfaction of a reply. She walks past the Colonel with her chin high. Ibrahim follows Addison and Zhu as they join the woman near the Stretch to the upper base.

The ride up to the main site is rather quiet in the interim.

Sergeant Major Olivia Warden and Doctor Ryan Vogert greet the team when the elevator stops at the top. "I will see you all at the briefing soon," Ibrahim nods, sidestepping them for the motor pool. He pivots to the central pavilion, where he can find the base's command hub.

He steadies his balance as his boot's tread isn't always enough to keep him from slipping on the wet outer hull.

After going through the airlock to the hub, Ibrahim downloads schematics from recent scans they've made of the Summerland. He uploads the information to Athena's relay so only members of his select team can see what they're about to do. The results show the ship as an intricate weave of corridors and rooms, like catacombs under a cathedral.

"Transfer complete," Athena confirms into his earpiece. "Thanks for the fill-up, handsome."

Ibrahim shakes his head. "You have to work on your interpersonal skills," he tells her. "Are you flirting with me or making a vague reference?"

"Why not both?" Athena laughs.

Ibrahim grimaces and leaves the hub.

He sends a message on his way out to let everyone know he's heading to the briefing room.

Ibrahim receives acknowledgments as his team leaders receive the update.

He's the last to walk into the assembly. Everybody else is already in their seats and waiting for him. There are sixty men and women—military *and* civilians. Their support staff will stay behind to coordinate from the base and ensure they aren't interrupted by OverSec.

Alexandra Roslin might've given Ibrahim a wink and the nod on the idea, but he knows better than to trust the woman.

Ibrahim takes a breath. He has a flutter in his chest, like butterflies flapping their wings.

Furthermore, those staying back must help prepare the site for decommissioning while maintaining their cover.

It's a logistics nightmare, Ibrahim curses. Less than 48 hours to move thousands of people? It often takes more time to move apartments. Ibrahim can only race against the sun and hope he can win. And if he fails? It won't be just him that burns.

"Glad everybody found their way," Ibrahim says. He marches to the front, studying the faces in the room. Inside these walls, they don't need to wear their survival gear. That hasn't stopped several grunts from keeping their helmets close by, ready to put them on if an alarm sounds. "Most of you know the mission's preliminaries. So, let's catch everybody else up to speed. We are going against official orders. And it could label us as renegades at best, traitors at worse. A few days ago, we received this little keepsake—"

He points to an image of the Architect's Heart on the large monitor.

Adhion and Idu step forward. Many who hadn't seen them before this moment shift uncomfortably in their chairs. But a few are from Warden's squad, the team that fought Dhun 'Ancod in the greenhouse and saw a hint of what an Architect can do in combat. And now they must share a space with two of them.

Addison grins as her rebreather drops to her chin. She eyes Ibrahim with shrewd confidence.

That's his signal to go ahead and explain their plan.

It takes Ibrahim forty minutes to lay it out, step-by-step. He answers questions they've prepared beforehand.

Ibrahim holds his breath as worrying glances become rocksteady laughs.

There's courage in the room, Ibrahim doesn't doubt. "We don't have an opportunity to run simulations on *what* we might face going forward. Enemy combatants are likely the same as we've seen in prior engagements. Except one," he cautions. "The tallest head with the highest crown on this damnable rock. A feather-freaked, two-toed, smooth-face of an early bird hungry for what real soldiers can do! Mister Illustrious . . . Tyrann 'Akachan, the Trident of Absolution."

"Feather . . . freak?" Idu asks.

Addison leans over to her. "He's trying to paint 'Akachan as a cartoon character," she explains. "It keeps us in high moods."

Idu's feathers covering her ears perk up. "Car-toon?" she murmurs.

"Animated shows to entertain kids," Addison says.

"Ah," Idu frowns. "Cartoons . . . I see. Yes."

"I believe it is an attempt to make fun of us," Adhion suggests.

"Because we are . . . humorous?" Idu asks.

"It's just our way," Addison says, grinding her teeth.

"Everybody understands their assignments?" Ibrahim asks the room.

"Yes, sir!" Warden shouts.

"And our contingencies?"

All but a lonely corporal nods agreeingly. A team leader can fill in the blanks.

Ibrahim stands at ease. "Good," he says. "You're all dismissed. We load up at zero-six-thirty sharp. Be there or get left behind."

Ibrahim stays to watch the room empty. One by one, they file through the plastic umbilical connecting to the other pavilions. The only one to stay back is Warden, secluded in the corner, waiting for the rest to leave. Ibrahim can guess what's on her mind.

"You're angry that I'm leaving you behind," he says.

Warden clenches her jaw and drops back a step. "Permission to speak?" she asks.

"Granted," Ibrahim surrenders.

"You're playing a risky card to win the game," Warden argues. "You need every fighter you can get on this mission."

"I do," Ibrahim agrees.

"But you have me babysitting the eggheads?!" Warden glowers.

"You're in charge of getting everybody off this base in one piece," Ibrahim says. "There's a bigger monster coming for us. You'll be on the frontline. We have two Architects and a truck full of badasses leaving for the core. And let us not forget the task force heading to Camp Yi to arrest Doctor Hao. We need a badass to stay behind and coordinate with Malakai."

Warden's anger subtly dulls.

"You'll get killed without me," she iterates.

"Maybe," Ibrahim smirks. "Score is tied now. I want to win out, two-to-one."

Warden finally laughs, breaking the tension. She relaxes her shoulders, sticking out her chest pridefully over how she handled Dhun 'Ancod. Even if the alien was only following his orders, the Judge was a threat, and she dealt with it as a good soldier does, even if it landed them in hot water.

"And you can't beat *me* without cheating, is that it?" Warden feigns.

"Can't have my Sergeant Major upstaging me again," Ibrahim chuckles, pounding her fist when she brings it up.

"You were there on my first day as a recruit on the Overlook," Warden says.

"And you handily beat my record at the shooting range a week later," Ibrahim adds.

"I'm a good shot," Warden clicks her tongue.

"Don't think I've forgotten," Ibrahim says. "I spent a month drilling harder after that day to retake the leaderboard."

"I'll always find a way to win our little competitions," Warden says.

"You said *that* after running the tri-course three times," Ibrahim snides.

"I remember kicking your ass on that last run," Warden's voice hits a peak, "if that's what you meant?"

"But only *after* I saved your ass in the decagon!"

Warden looks away. Not embarrassed. She's not laughing, either. No. Her eyes drop only briefly as her skin tightens.

"Good luck in there, sir," Warden urges, clenching her jaw, keeping her cheeks dry.

Ibrahim rests his hand on her shoulder. "Watch your front, Olivia. And take this," he says, handing her Malakai's new comms unit.

"What's this for?" she asks.

"It's a secure channel," Ibrahim explains.

"For when you get into trouble?"

"Hoping to avoid it," he admits. "But if something happens?"

"We'll handle it," Warden nods understandingly.

73 | SPEARHEAD

ADDISON KENNEDY, FIELD DIRECTOR
EPIMETHEUS PROJECT

OCTOBER 27, 2041 | 0557 HOURS

==

Addison waits at the foot of the loading ramp of the V-91 Warhawk—Yankee-433. Colonel Ibrahim has quietly reassigned it for their mission.

"Yeah. That'll do," Addison murmurs. She moves her arms, wincing at the pain in her elbow. Vogert fitted a brace to her that works with the hardsuit she's wearing, but it's not comfortable. And even with her heater unit on full blast, the ambient chill seeps into her bones. "Damn stupid," she curses, stepping aside as Sergeant Mannering and two squads of UCAF marines brush past her up the ramp.

After them, it's her team—Avanna Remmings, Zhu Yunwen . . . Almost everybody but Leighton, who's staying on the Olympus to guide them on comms.

Vogert will remain on-site to assist with the research base's evacuation.

Sergeant Major Warden will supervise their military assets and guard their front until they get the all-clear.

Adhion 'Klaka and Idu 'Smeora follows the soldiers up the ramp and into the Warhawk's rear compartment. Neither alien looks at Addison as she stays in the rain, running numbers, weighing their odds, and tracking it all in her head.

According to the Whisperer, the Varmajalkavaen that have joined them will help pack up the base. And these aren't their warriors—but rather, workers and gardeners. The many who serve the Obligation's higher purpose. Their tribe—a nation carrying the weight of their species as they flew across the distant stars.

Addison watches the Varmajalkavaen coordinate their efforts. Most armies would feel jealous if they could see these people work as they do. The insectoids quickly tear down pavilions, ferrying crates to the Stretch for stacking in the staging area. They fill the open spaces with equipment and material coming in from the dark side of the Breach.

Once they finish tearing down the METIS Research Base, the tribe will move to the other camps—Mercer, Rousseau, Jeju, Axford, Earhart—and prepare them for evacuation. "They will save Camp Yi for last," Idu says. "As you requested." She's at the top of the ramp, looking down at Addison, still lingering at the bottom.

"Our boys will appreciate that," Addison returns, meeting her halfway on the incline. "Whatever we can do to get it done. Kill two birds with one stone."

"Hopefully, only a single bird today," Idu mourns.

Addison grimaces. "That's not . . . It's a turn of phrase," she details.

"It means accomplishing two aims at once," Ibrahim clarifies, stepping onto the ramp. He taps Addison on the shoulder as he moves past her, waving her into the aircraft.

"Like two words with meanings that change with their context?" Idu queries.

"More like a motto or casual remark," Ibrahim bemoans, turning to Addison. "Ready for another ride in the bucket?"

"As ready as I am ever," Addison admits, forcing an unseen smile under her visor.

"Stay with us, and everything will go fine," Ibrahim says.

"You sound almost excited," Addison notions, hearing his voice modulate through his helmet.

Ibrahim offers her his hand. Addison accepts with her good arm, feeling her skin burn as he pulls her out of the rain.

"We're gonna have quite the view," Ibrahim says. "Staging area is ready. While everyone else confronts Doctor Hao, we'll make our way forward by air. Our pilot will peel off the main flight corridor to Camp Yi. Use that 'hidden' hangar near the Entrychamber our friends have told us about."

And that's another reason Addison's having difficulty with this plan. They've too many pieces on the board and few hands to keep the game afloat.

She moves her arm again to find a position that better supports the weight on her shoulder.

"Are you okay?" Ibrahim asks.

"It's weird living inside this suit again," Addison says. "With the arm."

"Your arm will be fine. Just keep your helmet on this time," Ibrahim urges. "I don't want to drag you home in a body bag. And the last thing I need is for you to start huffing the air because you got 'curious' during our illegal venture into the beast's maw."

Addison snorts gaily through her nose. "Fair enough," she admits.

She looks at Idu holding the Architect's Heart in its sphere. The relic belongs to her. And it's safer in her hands than any of the science team.

Ibrahim wasn't too happy with the idea of allowing the Architects control over it during the flight over the dreadnaught. Pounding his fist on a table made that clear enough. Addison spent twenty minutes arguing that it was the right call, making him see reason.

Now she's watching him tighten his grip around his weapon's strap as he eyes the Heart across the cabin.

"Are *you* ready for this?" Addison asks him.

"Pissin' in my pants," Ibrahim admits with a shrug. "Let's find our places! One short hop, and it's done."

Addison punches him in his chest plate. "Thank you," she mouths, but the man doesn't see it behind her helmet.

As she steps into the V-91 Warhawk's gangway, she ducks and sits opposite Idu.

The female Architect considers Addison for a long moment as the ramp closes and the cabin pressurizes with a loud, hydraulic hiss. Idu tilts her head to her right, then to her left. It's almost as if she can see through Addison's visor and knows she's looking right back at her.

When the aircraft whirls to life, Idu sets her palm on the floor, humming with the engines.

"Rudimentary craftsmanship," Idu weighs. "Some would question how it even manages to fly. How old is this machine?"

"It's not fresh off the assembly line," Addison says, "if that's what you mean."

Ibrahim steps between them. "These hulls are from the late twenties," he says, sitting beside Addison. "But everything inside is from the last two years."

"So, it is a recent construction?"

"A little dated by our standards," Addison admits. "We make do with the material they give us."

"And your warships?" Idu questions, wrinkles on her otherwise smooth face.

"About as old," Ibrahim answers. "Some date as far back as fifty years. Like this bird—older hulls, rebuilt with high-class combat systems."

"Just how old is the Summerland?" Zhu Yunwen asks the two Architects.

Adhion leans over to Idu with a reticent expression, his feathers a bright yellow hue.

"Closest word you have for it would be ancient," Adhion summarizes.

"Several million of your planet's cycles," Idu iterates.

"So . . . it's old," Ava states.

"A few million years old," Addison says with a nod.

"We've given birth to entire new civilizations," Idu explains. "Tried and tested methods."

"Which takes no short order to achieve?" Zhu notions.

"A task as simple as a tree bearing its fruit can take hundreds of iterations to accomplish correctly."

"And minutes to burn if it isn't the *right* fruit that grows," Adhion adds.

Addison frowns as the Nomad's large eyes veer to the compartment's floor as he says it.

"Whole generations devoted to the task," Addison whispers.

Idu subtly nods. "Life for life," she returns. "True ends for true ends."

A crackling fills Addison's earpiece as her comms unit pings.

"This is Yankee-Four-Thirty-Three to METIS Control," the pilot engages.

"We read you, Four-Thirty-Three," Control relays. "Squadron Three-Six-Three is a go, signal ready. Two minutes. Confirm?"

"Squadron confirmed," Ibrahim returns. "Callsigns, let me hear you sing!"

"Copy that, Castle-Actual. We read you loud and clear," the first pilot reports. "Yankee-Four-Two-Five on standby."

"Yankee-Two-Fifty-Seven, waiting for the surf to come in, sir," the next calls arrive. "Let's do this!"

"Yankee-Three-Niner-Two reporting in," another continues.

"Yankee-Triple-Five, ready for some payback!"

The rain hitting the hall turns into an awful racket in the cabin's enclosed space, like pea-sized hail on a thin nylon tarp. Addison flinches as their bird's loading ramp locks in with a metallic click. She moves forward and peers out the side hatch near the cockpit. Five other birds prepare to launch with them. Their insignias are identical—two red eagles over four white arrows across each tiltrotor—Squadron 363.

"Squadron to liftoff in sixty seconds," METIS Control announces.

Addison hears a beeping in her ears.

"Are you ready for another flight, Doctor Kennedy?" Athena asks.

"A bad time to ask that, don't you think?" Addison returns.

"Your biometrics read heightened pressure in your frontal lobe," Athena describes.

"It's a headache," Addison waves off the concern.

"Maybe," Athena counters.

"Maybe? What's a maybe? How does that help?" Addison asks.

"You're stressed," Athena explains.

"I'm fine," Addison asserts.

"No. You aren't," Athena calls her out.

"Vogert's given me the clearance," Addison breathes. "I can do this."

"And your recent injuries don't risk hampering your ability to see this mission through?"

"This is my choice," Addison confides. "I've pushed this. And I won't send others into the fire without being there to pull them back."

"So, you feel guilty?"

"Responsible," Addison corrects her. "It's my job."

"Even if it kills you—?"

She cuts off her comms abruptly. "Sorry, ma'am," Addison says, the aircraft vibrating rapidly.

"Ten seconds!" METIS Control announces.

"Standby for liftoff," the pilot warns over the speakers.

Addison watches the other transports on the landing pad rise off the hull and hover in the storm. For safety reasons, they depart one by one. METIS Control relays instructions over the network as they monitor for breaks in the wind speeds.

"Five . . . four . . . three . . . two . . . one . . . You're green, Yankee-Four-Thirty-Three. Godspeed."

A siren blares as they gain altitude. Every head in the compartment turns to Ibrahim and the Architects.

Addison peeks into the cockpit and sees the pad's lights flicker from red to green.

"We're off the tarmac," the pilot says.

"Let's steer her into the flock," returns the co-pilot.

"Best of luck to everyone," Ibrahim says. "Let's do this and go home!"

"Oorah!" the troops let out.

Addison staggers to her seat, grabbing the handrails as the aircraft tilts awkwardly to one side. She's left to gawk at Idu as the alien occupies her time by studying the soldiers as they double-check their gear.

Idu then looks at Addison, the alien's eyes like a cloudless sky over an empty field at night.

She lowers her gaze to Idu's lap, where the Heart rests securely in the Architect's large palms. Addison focuses on the metallic sphere, tracing the relic's ornate patterns with her eyes. "I am in my room with the lightbox on," Addison whispers, the ornamentation calling her back to old images in her head. "And I am staring at the constellations projected on my ceiling."

She squeezes her wrist and begins counting all the stars she can remember.

OUTER LAYERS | 74

LIEUTENANT COLONEL ELIAS IBRAHIM
UNITED COALITION ARMED FORCES

OCTOBER 27, 2041 | 0610 HOURS

The pilot steers the aircraft into a headwind. Ibrahim grips his safety harness, tightening the straps over his chest and arms. They've peeled off from the main Squadron and will continue for the ship proper. They now fly alone. He looks at Addison, sitting with her good arm wrapped around the handrail like a passenger on a thrill ride.

A powerful gust throws the crew to one side—all but Idu 'Smeora and Adhion 'Klaka, steady as rocks, unbothered by the turbulence.

"Lieutenant!" Ibrahim shouts over the comms. "What's going on up there?"

"Our birds don't like flying in these extremes!" the pilot calls back. "The ship is like a fuckin' mountain. We adjust for the downslope as the winds blanket the spine! Tricky to get a handle on. Ready yourselves for some rough patches, sir."

"Nothing we haven't accounted for, Colonel," the co-pilot adds. "Just stay in your seats!"

Ibrahim grumbles darkly. "Leighton! Are you hearing us?" he calls, keying his wrist-pad to their secure channel.

"Br-ken chatt-r, Col-nel," Leighton responds, rupturing with static. "St-rm interfer-nce -etting pr-tty bad."

Ibrahim turns to Doctor Remmings.

She looks back at him.

"Storm interference?" Ava repeats, flipping on her pad. "I'll try to work it out with our boy on the Olympus. Let's see if we can't clean it up a bit."

"Leighton! Keep talking to us," Ibrahim instructs. "Remmings is working on—"

"Y-ah," Leighton cuts in abruptly. "Ath-na is att-m-ting to re-route our comms to a secondary node. How do I sound?"

"Better than before," Ibrahim relays.

"Good! It's working."

"You're tracking us, then? What's our ETA?" Ibrahim demands.

"Tough estimate, Colonel," Leighton says. "Wind is causing your flight's instruments to go haywire."

"Can you at least see us from the Overlook's feeds?"

"Only that you're coming on Camp Axford," Leighton describes. "You're over the ship's mid-spine now."

Ibrahim scowls.

He unbuckles his harness and starts climbing his way to the left-side hatch. Addison follows him.

"What are you doing?!" Ibrahim barks at her.

"Making sure you don't fly out the window if we tilt sideways!" Addison shouts.

She clutches the netting of the stow area above the seats, using it to steady her balance as she wobbles along the aisle.

"We'd like it if both of you returned to your seats!" the co-pilot calls back.

"I don't need you to worry about me," Ibrahim iterates to Addison.

"You say that now, but—?"

"We've run exercises like this for years under High Castle," Ibrahim explains. "Mock terrorist attacks and rescue operations, boarding aircraft mid-flight."

Addison lets out one long breath. "When my dad took me skydiving for the first time, it terrified me," she goes, gripping the netting tighter. "To beat it, he told me to 'close my eyes and let the wind take me.' I walked to the ramp and saw over the ledge, and I couldn't do it. I lost my nerve. And do you know what he did?"

Ibrahim frowns as he gets to the side hatch, looking for Camp Axford on his display.

"What did he do?" he asks.

"He pushed me," Addison says. "No warning. Eyes closed. I was screaming."

Ibrahim chuckles. "How high up?" he asks.

"Around fourteen-thousand feet," Addison says. "I pulled my chute in the first few seconds."

"And you never went skydiving again, is that it?" Ibrahim mocks.

"Not exactly," Addison laughs. "I went thirteen times over the next seven years. Anytime dad was home for shore leave. Camping trips, fishing on the lake in the mountains... Good memories." She lets off a shiver as their bird finds a level. "Anything we could make time for whenever I had him."

Ibrahim looks away from her for a moment. He marks Camp Axford's perimeter lights, singling out the larger structures on the hull. The assembly area below them has equipment stacked on pallets for transport to the fleet. They're about to fly over it when he notices a handful of bright flashes going from one side of the base to the next.

Ibrahim focuses. His eyes flutter confusingly.

Whatever they are, they cascade into explosions across the upper deck.

"Elias—?" Addison murmurs.

Ibrahim quickly keys his comms. "Athena!" he shouts as a blast large enough sends a shockwave through the air until it reaches their V-91 Warhawk. And the force causes the aircraft to vibrate. Everybody in the compartment drops back and grabs for their emergency crash kits.

"Lieutenant Colonel—?" Athena's response cuts off before she can speak.

Ibrahim doesn't wait. "Alert to all on-site personnel!" he shouts, opening a channel so everybody with a comms unit can hear. "Does anybody read me? Contacts at Camp Axford! Repeat! Contact on the hull! Can anybody hear me?"

He switches on his helmet's active frequency scanner. A static-filled surge of noise washes into his earpiece—hundreds of voices, shouting orders, calling for support, demanding reports. All at once, talking *at* each other, hoping their pleas reach willing ears.

"Contacts across the board! We need help at zeta-quadrant!"

"Floaters at the Breach! Where are our gunners?"

"Alpha site is under attack! Repeat! Alpha site is under attack!"

"Enemy swarming delta!"

"Nu—eta—theta reporting high concentration of—"

"We need reinforcements!"

"Casualties! We got casualties!"

"Is anybody listening?"

"Incoming fire!"

"Where's our support craft?"

"Where are they coming from?"

"Fall back! Repeat! Fall back to alpha! To alpha!"

"Fucking hell," Addison curses.

Ibrahim climbs past her and into the cockpit.

"You heard them!" he shouts at the pilots. "Take us under the ship's horizon!"

"Lieutenant Colonel?" the co-pilot asks.

Ibrahim inches back to Addison.

"Do it! And marines?" Ibrahim calls, turning to his troops in the cabin. "Lock and load! Prepare to be this morning's entertainment."

"Colonel? What's going on down there?" Addison asks.

Ibrahim opens his mouth, only to notice the battle outside intensifying—the dreadnaught's hull shifting into a deeper, crimson shade. A voice breaks into the static on all channels, almost like a song with a note out of tune, dark, and mixed with rage. As it plays, the translation scrolls at the bottom of his HUD.

"Humanity chooses its destiny—that of traitors and a destroyer," the voice reads. "Now, I must correct this travesty. Obligation demands it."

Idu's bristles darken as she hears the words, too—eyes narrowing, shoulders shifting uneasily.

The female alien stands up and comes alongside Addison and Ibrahim for a better view of the ship below.

"Tyrann 'Akachan," Idu shudders. "He's activated final protocol."

"Defense systems are now active," Adhion agrees, looking through the smaller, circular viewports.

"It's already too late," Idu mourns.

Ibrahim snarls. "I don't accept that," he decides.

"Do you realize what's about to happen?" Idu asks.

"Why don't you enlighten us? Please," Ibrahim glowers.

Idu opens her mouth, only for a sudden electric snap to shut off all the lights in the compartment. Ibrahim flinches. He darts to the cockpit, where the pilot's busy flipping switches. The man's attempting to divert power back into the engines.

"What's happening up there?" Sergeant Mannering calls forward.

"Controls aren't responsive," the pilot says, an unnatural calm to his voice. "We're dead in the air!"

"Can you bring us down?" Ibrahim asks.

"Oh, I wouldn't worry about going down, Colonel," the co-pilot returns.

"We can buy you a few minutes," the lieutenant shifts. "But don't count on a miracle, sir."

Ibrahim grips the safety strap hanging from the wall as Yankee-433's nose drops too far down.

"We're going into freefall!" the co-pilot exerts.

"What's going on?" Addison asks.

Ibrahim looks at her only briefly. He rushes past her toward the rear as the pilots try to level the aircraft. Everybody jumps off their seats and begins crowding the gangway, with the team leaders looking at him to decide. He dragged them here, so they're his responsibility, but it's not like they have many options.

He can't contact Leighton with the precious little time they have, not that it would help them if he did. Ibrahim would be one voice of hundreds calling over the channels, and there's nothing Mount Olympus or Athena can do to keep their bird in the air. He looks to his troops, the pilots, and the civilians . . . And he swallows.

Their hardsuits have enough shielding to protect against electronic interference. Maybe they can take shelter inside the dreadnaught if they stay alive long enough to find an airlock. But it won't matter if they hit the ship's hull at 120 miles per hour. It'd be like watching a rock hit concrete as it drops several thousand feet.

Ibrahim's cheeks tighten as he squeezes Addison's shoulder. "We're going for a stroll," he tells them.

"Wait, what? A stroll—?" Addison starts.

"Everybody! Grab your diapers and prepare to jump!" Ibrahim shouts.

"This is the real deal!"

"Jump?" Ava repeats. "Did he say jump?! We're jumping?"

"Unless you want to paint the hull, we *will* learn what it means to fly like a bird!" Ibrahim asserts.

His marines know what to do. They stow their unneeded gear and prep their chutes, but the civilians? He doesn't know if they're ready.

Ibrahim quickly situates everybody into position, but the two Architects only offer him cursory glances.

"What do you mean by 'jump,' Lieutenant Colonel?" Idu questions.

"Staying in this box as it goes down will kill us," Ibrahim explains. "Even you two. So, we're jumping into high winds, hoping to land safely hull-side." He runs a readout on the ship below them, marking a zone for everybody to rendezvous.

"How are we doing this?" Addison asks, hooking onto a safety line as the aircraft tilts violently.

"By closing our eyes and holding on tight," Ibrahim says, strapping a towline between her and him.

"I guess this means I'm jumping with you?" Addison asks.

"Your civilian-model hardsuits don't have anchor points for parachutes," Ibrahim describes, handing the alien pair the craft's emergency backups. "Our new friends need our spares. Pilots will get the rest. In the meantime, Remmings—you're linking with Corporal Tanner. Zhu Yunwen—with Sergeant Mannering." He points. "Follow their leads. Do as they say!"

Ava and Zhu nod their acknowledgments.

"Jump in fifteen!" the pilot says as he abandons his chair.

His co-pilot finishes leveling the V-91 to buy them a few extra moments. Both suit up and put their years of training into practice.

Ibrahim opens the rear compartment—the dreadnaught's hull speeding underneath the bird's loading ramp. Massive ocean waves crack like a roaring dragon as the water whips against the great ship. It will get tricky if they don't time the jump exactly right. Ibrahim breathes, calculating the distance.

"Are we going now?" Idu asks.

She pulls alongside Adhion 'Klaka, who appears more comfortable with this than his counterpart.

"Wait a moment. Oh. And if we don't die?" Ibrahim snarks. "Remember this when you're telling stories of your time with humanity."

Ibrahim laughs as Idu's face rounds with terror. That's when the flight officer gives them the signal.

"Jump! Go, go, go, go, go!"

His marines, the civilians, and the Architects charge out the V-91 Warhawk's rear cabin in paired lines. Ibrahim feels the wind slam his body as he drops into the open air. It sends his troops flying into the darkness, their way illuminated only by the lights coming off the dreadnaught's hull.

75 | MUTUALLY ASSURED DESTRUCTION

SERGEANT MAJOR OLIVIA WARDEN
UNITED COALITION ARMED FORCES

OCTOBER 27, 2041 | 0615 HOURS

===

She marches back and forth between METIS and the Breach, which does nothing for her nerves. Warden's task is to pack up the base and get everything *and* everyone on the transports in time for the big show, whatever the hell "big show" means.

"How do we do this with what we have?" Warden denounces. "Or the time we have to do it?"

Behind her are thousands of aliens helping with the cleanup. As much as she hates admitting it, they're efficient laborers and cargo haulers.

Warden hangs her thumbs on her armor's straps to keep from drawing her sidearm on the damn ugly things.

Nobody's particularly happy about the situation. Warden can see it in her marines when they cross paths with the buggers. Like her, they cringe, resisting their better instincts to drop the aliens where they stand. Letting them walk around the base without armed escorts watching everything they do is difficult.

But *that* would only screw up Colonel Ibrahim's plans for this supposed alliance. He and Doctor Kennedy are going into the dreadnaught with the two Architects in tow—Idu 'Smeora and Adhion 'Klaka. And the latter one? He's the "bastard" responsible for creating this whole mess, a mutiny against his captain . . . Tyrann 'Akachan . . . Trident of Absolution.

Warden has had enough. She'd like only to lock them all together in a room to kill each other and settle their disagreements.

"Just leave *us* out of it," Warden mutters. "Doesn't matter which to me."

Doctor Vogert and the ornate female bugger approach Warden while she's marching through the rain.

What's the alien's name? Matriarch of the Whisperer's Chord, whatever *that* means. Oha, was it?

"Our team's underway," Vogert says, stopping her as she's walking back from the Breach.

"I am aware," Warden scoffs. "I've got a tracker monitoring their flight's path."

"That? That isn't what I—" the man pauses, "—meant. *She* wants to speak with you."

Vogert wrings his palms as he glances at Oha beside him.

Warden regards the female bugger halfway between wanting to vomit and an angry scowl. Her emotions stay hidden under her visor, to everyone's benefit, but she can't bury her body language behind a mask as easily. The alien bows to her with a near . . . human-like elegance. Smooth. Almost without fault.

"What do you want?" Warden asks after a breath.

Oha blinks with all her eyes and a bewildering sense.

Then, she folds her hands together. "These are the last loyal adherents of my people aboard," Oha says. Warden reads the words as they scroll across the bottom of her screen. It distracts her long enough that she doesn't notice when the alien reaches out to Warden with one of its arms.

Warden's throat closes as she swallows her tongue.

"She wants to take your hand in hers," Vogert explains.

Warden gives the man a harsh, unseen glare. "That doesn't mean I have to accept," she glowers.

Vogert shakes his head. "That's your excuse? No. I've spent time talking to her," he iterates, gesturing for her to stay calm. "She's a philosophical one, I'll admit. But she keeps asking me questions. Maybe you'll do us a favor and give her some answers. Yeah?"

"Answers? About what?"

"Us?" Vogert suggests. "Other things, too. Hear her out, will you?"

Warden squares her shoulders and turns in Oha's direction. "All right. Speak," Warden says, refusing to take the alien's hand.

"Hostility? That is unnecessary, Sergeant Major. We share in your strife," Oha humbles. "The Obligation of the Architects demands equilibrium between duty and faith. My people listen to its basic tenants, but most are *not* fanatics. Those with me have stayed true to *our* way. We understand good sense. And compassion. But you *are* as alien to us as I am to you."

Warden breathes in deeply. "I have to read everything you say on my screen," she describes. "Keep this short. Or I'll get a headache."

Oha's mandibles click despondingly. Her eyes dull, letting off what Warden suspects is a frown.

"Var-ma-jalk-a-vaen," Oha says with a whistle.

"Yes?" Warden staggers.

"That is *our* name, Sergeant Major," Oha emphasizes with a high-pitch buzz. "Ours was once a world inhabited by nothing! That name set a fire in our hearts as we clawed our way out from underground, touching the light of our sun. But *your* name? Humanity? From our view, you are metal-loving anthropoids whose natural spirits have faded from your ancestral memories. Violence drove you from your Great Mother. You lost your way in the woods, tangled in the roots. And subsequently? Abandoned."

"Nobody's abandoned me," Warden snarls.

"We said that once, too, I think," Oha offers, angling her mandibles to form an . . . ugly smile.

"Get to your point, Matriarch," Warden grinds annoyingly.

"I speak it. And if you would listen, maybe you could hear? Great and unexpected trials can shape us," Oha tells her. "That is all I meant to say. This event? Our coming to your Earth? It could inspire your species to heights somewhere beyond the rim of your current reach."

"That reads as more of a statement than a question," Warden expresses. "I thought she wanted answers?" She scowls at Doctor Vogert.

He shifts uncomfortably as the rain beats his head.

"And you have given them," Oha speaks freely, "in your posture and sheer unwillingness to take my hand."

Warden bites down on her molars. Her thumb caresses the buckle of her sidearm's holster.

"I'm only a soldier," Warden defends. "And you were my enemy until yesterday."

"You are a warrior—true-bound and true-minded," Oha describes. "Death comes easily for you. And the killing?! You killed us, and we killed you. We do not forgive. Not yet. But we *can* forget for a time and learn to let go. We need each other if we are to survive this awakening."

Warden's jaw drops as the dreadnaught's hull quakes under her feet.

She looks down, then into the Breach. Static buzzes into her earpiece.

"And it begins," Oha mourns.

"Security alert to all personnel!" Athena announces. "We have contacts across the board. Repeat! Mission priority sites are under attack! Secure the perimeter and prepare for immediate evacuation to the fleet."

Warden draws her pistol and aims it at the large hangar beyond the Breach.

Brilliant flashes streak across the dark air.

Warden hears somebody open the emergency channel, but a blast abruptly cuts them off.

"God, damn it!" Warden curses, stopping to breathe. "Squad leaders . . . Take your positions at the Breach! Interior sectors?! Get your people back to base and on to the next transports out! Abandon ship! Repeat! We . . . are . . . leaving! Shift your anathematized butts into high gear!"

Squad leaders waste no time in reacting.

"Get your asses moving!"

"Go! Go! Go!"

"Shore up the left side!"

"Cover the entrance!"

"Who's on the right flank?"

"Visors up! Lights on!"

Warden looks at Oha. "Will you help us?" she begs, her voice cracking.

They both jump when superheated light flies out of the Breach. Sweat runs down Warden's neck as her nerves pinch together. She tracks the number of marines and Project workers still inside on her HUD. Hundreds? But with every bright flash, the counter shows one less than before.

Oha nods. "It is why we came," she confides.

"We're under attack?" Vogert asks.

Warden grabs him by the collar and throws him at a marine setting up nearby.

"Get this man on the next bird ready to leave!" she orders.

Her marine catches Vogert at the last moment and looks him over, confused.

"Right now?" he asks.

"We're getting all civilian personnel off station immediately!" Warden shouts. "I will repeat. Get. Him. Out. Alive!" The soldier takes a second to grasp the order. But as he does, the man nods, pulling Vogert away toward the Stretch without further protest.

"Is he unfit to fight?" Oha questions.

"He's a veteran," Warden says. "He *can* fight. It's just not his job. Not anymore. It's mine. And part of *my* job is to get him to safety."

Oha surrenders her a nod before taking up a spear from her side.

"My people will fight beside you," the female goes. "You won't die alone."

Warden frowns. "I'd prefer not to die at all," she admits.

Every gun under her command points at the exit to the platform. Fresh marines arrive on top of armored carriers to reinforce the perimeter line. More troops return from deep inside the dreadnaught, dragging themselves on their own two feet, bloody and exhausted.

Warden can't remember the last time she's seen this many wounded in one place.

Oha moves beside her, almost like she knows what's coming for them.

"Hit their optical array—the 'eye' that emits the light," Oha tells her. "It will cause a cascade failure to the machines' nervous systems. The drones can't survive intensive damage without shielding to protect their weaker points. Steady your aim, Sergeant Major, and focus on the enemy."

She lets out a high-pitched laugh. "You don't think we can do it?" Warden asks.

"With so few hands, it is a wonder how you can hold a—" Oha begins to say until every lamp on the platform goes dark, "—weapon."

Warden's throat swells.

Behind them, Warhawks and utility helicopters start dropping from the sky, with some crashing into the great ship's hull. Several were trying to land or were attempting to take off amidst evacuation. Many others plunge into the violent ocean waters. The dreadnaught's emitting a dead zone, much like the electrical interference they experienced near the greenhouse. They've lost everything without a hardened power supply. In the distance, the quarantine fleet still has lights, so maybe it's a phenomenon limited only to the ship's immediate vicinity. But she doesn't know.

Warden's visor sparks with emergency beacons.

The hull under her then shifts to a darker red—almost black.

"What is this?" Warden asks Oha.

Ahead, the swarm hums alive, making a b-line for the hangar's massive entrance.

"Final protocol," Oha answers, activating her spear.

The creature's fellow warriors do the same.

Oha takes her position alongside the UCAF marines at the Breach. Humans and Varmajalkavaen, each ready to fight and die, side-by-side, against the floaters.

Lights from the swarm outline their fields of vision. A first volley rips into their defensive line before Warden can respond. Guns open fire as her troops unleash the last of their ASAPHEI 6.8 munitions on the Fragments.

Dozens of the machines drop, shattering on impact with the ground.

Warden hears her men cheering at these small victories. "Keep firing!" she shouts, realizing that downing a dozen, or a thousand, won't matter. As they let loose hell on the machines, it's clear that a hundred more take the place of each one they shoot to rubble.

And they don't stop coming.

"We're about to die here," Warden mutters. Her arm numbs. A flash skirts her face and overwhelms her helmet's optics.

Another blast hits her shoulder, throwing her back.

The floaters wash over the base's defenses like the tide over a sandcastle. Humans and Jalks fall back as the drones break into the air and bomb the pavilions. Oha rushes to Warden, picking her up and letting off noises that Warden's suit doesn't translate into readable words.

Athena is too busy right now.

Warden doesn't need a translator to understand the other's intent. She recognizes the cuts in the alien's breath, the way she gestures, wanting Warden to stay with her. And she knows that look in the bugger's eyes, that unblinking stare, her mandibles squeezing as she pauses between syllables.

She needs to get off her ass and keep fighting.

Warden pulls up her rifle and fires it into a group of machines. The drones crash hard like brittle rocks on the pavement. Warden ducks and rolls into cover next to a dead marine and a bugger missing three of its four arms, using its last to cover the burns on its face.

"Get to the water!" Warden calls loudly.

She opens her comms but closes it quickly when she gets an earful of static. Getting a message out will be difficult.

Fire rains down around her as she moves to pick up the remainder of her troops and points them in the right direction. "Get moving! Go! You can stay on this wreck *or* die another day!" Warden shouts. She doubts more than a handful of personnel survived as the battle crosses over the Stretch.

They've lost their foothold on the dreadnaught.

"This is Sergeant Major Olivia Warden to anyone who can hear me!" she keys her comms again, hoping to break through to a clear channel. "We've lost the alpha site! We're pulling back with our emergency beacons. You'll find survivors in the water! Good luck to everybody fighting out there. Warden, out."

Nobody will likely receive the message, but it's all she can do.

Warden pulls more survivors from the carnage and orders them to run. All the while, she's dodging hardlight particle beams the Fragments throw wherever she goes. Oha does the same with the Varmajalkavaen. It doesn't matter what happens now—they've lost this battle. It's a "mission failure" under the best-case scenario, not to mention the losses during the evacuation. Humanity's brightest minds from the most affluent countries in the world? Dead. Or worse, stranded.

If she survives, the world will blame *them* for letting this happen.

"Because we didn't do our jobs," Warden swallows.

She can't think about that right now. What she *does* do is throw her marines overboard and hope they remember how to swim. It's a contingency they've trained to handle. But never in these extreme conditions or with this equipment.

Warden's biggest worry is whether rescue teams will get to them *before* their suits' batteries run empty. Their joint servos will stop working at some point, dragging her marines into dark, watery graves. Avoiding murder-by-Fragment is a close second, but one she finds less acceptable.

She refuses to die at the mercy of some skinny bird with a bad hairdo.

"Sergeant Major!" Oha shouts.

She points at a Fragment barreling toward them.

Warden squints.

She can't quite place it, but this floater has a brighter light than the others—with a deep-toned buzz trilling the air, causing the rain to shimmer as it moves. It stays outside the greater swarm, dodging incoming fire and somehow centering on Warden, tracking her movements. She feels it in her bones.

Before she can squeeze the trigger, the Fragment takes a hit and impacts the hull a few meters off her position.

The debris hits her and knocks her over the ledge. Warden slides down the slope before spiraling into a steep freefall, her hardsuit damaged enough that her parachute doesn't deploy. She plops like a heavy stone into the violent waters at the dreadnaught's equivalent keel.

A powerful undertow then drags her under the waves.

The crack in her armor left by the shot to her shoulder allows water to seep into her jumpsuit. She gasps as it fills her helmet. Warden claws toward the surface as her visor shorts out, burning her face. She loses track of which way is up, with no light above or below her to anchor her sense of direction.

A hand pulls at her arm and yanks her back from the void.

Warden loses her grip and panics, fighting it, attempting to grab her rescuer and desperately save herself from drowning.

She manages to break free, spinning around, and—

She realizes . . . she . . . realizes . . . it's . . .

"You?" Warden whispers.

She's looking at Oha outside of her ornate armor. Her six eyes reflect Warden's emergency lights, breaking the water's muddy blackness.

Oha pulls the terror-stricken Warden through the depths. Olivia's muscles relax, and she lets the alien steer them *both* through the cold, twisting undercurrents. Even as her helmet leaks, Warden finds enough of a pocket to take a breath and releases it. She closes her eyes, feeling the ocean's weight drop off her as they surface.

Explosions covet the sky as the fleet opens fire on the swarm.

Warden watches as the Fragments coordinate like locusts, cutting into their ships like a slag storm through paper.

Smoke fills the air as the fighting subsides. Warden doesn't know if it is because something told the Fragments to stop their attack or that they can't find anything left worth killing.

They tread water for almost an hour before drifting close enough to a patrol cutter, grabbing a loose towline as it passes.

Like all else in the water, the craft is on emergency power. To move the vessel, the surviving crew makes do with makeshift paddles cobbled together from container lids and broken antennas.

Warden and Oha skirt along the hull's waterline to the stern. The sailors toss over a second cable for the two to anchor themselves with as the waves slam them against the starboard side. They work their way to the rear, crawling, hand-over-foot, onto the launch ramp, where the cutter's long-range interceptors stay docked.

Oha follows her and collapses.

"Sergeant Major?" a lieutenant among the crew rushes to ask.

Warden props her back up against the vessel's gangway. "Yes?" she answers with a question.

The lieutenant's eyes turn to Oha, limp on the deck. The sailor's hands are clumsy in the cold but steady enough to draw his sidearm. Others of his crew join him, wearing their rifles tight against their shoulders, fury on their faces.

Warden's adrenaline fuels her muscles.

She jumps between the ship's security force and the creature that rescued her from the water. "Stow those weapons, sailors!" Warden shouts, coughing as she yanks off her helmet and throws it on the deck. She takes her first unfiltered breath, holding off the wooziness that hits her when she does. "That's an order! Don't make me repeat it."

"Sergeant Major! That's an—" the officer attempts to erode.

"She's a friend!" Warden fights. Her legs wobble as she uses the last of her reserve. "They're friendlies. She's one of us."

"Why should we—?"

"We've lost the battle. Simple as that, lieutenant. Our job right now is to locate survivors," Warden construes, keeping her tongue from demeaning the officer. "Get a message to your captain! Tell him to begin combing the water for our people. If they're alive, we're going to find them. Every minute we delay is another life lost."

"Sergeant Warden . . . Ma'am?" the navy lieutenant murmurs. "That's what we're doing. And you . . . two . . . are the first."

Warden grimaces. She looks at Oha, only for the alien to look back. The bugger pushes off the deck, her mandibles clicking.

"Emergency beacons?" Warden pleads.

"We can't scan for them," the lieutenant says. "We were too close to the dreadnaught when the pulse killed our lights."

"Which might explain why you're still alive," Warden suggests. "Do you have anything that can uplink with the Overlook?"

"Does it look like it?" the man challenges.

Warden looks down at her helmet on the deck and then at the patrol's conning tower.

"Maybe I can help? But we need a working HRDVS," Warden tells him.

"A hardsuit? What happened to yours?" the officer recognizes.

"Broken," Warden shrinks. "But I am a marine. We'll make do. Go. Tell your captain."

"Y-yes, ma'am," the officer nods, pivoting on his heel toward the bridge.

The rest of the crew return to their stations, attempting to steer their craft against a belligerent ocean, leaving the pair alone on the deck.

Warden retrieves her helmet and links its remaining functions to her wrist-mounted computer. Athena's translation subroutine works again, but that's about it.

Oha manages to pull herself under a tarp the crew strung up to protect the rear launch ramp from the constant rain.

"Thank you, Sergeant Major," the Matriarch offers with a bow to her head.

Warden frowns, reading the words as they pop up on her tiny screen. Only this time, there's no visor to hide her expression.

Oha can see her as clear as lightning in a night sky.

"You jumped in after me," Warden states. "Why would you do that?"

"Because you went over the ledge," Oha confides. "I was worried."

"You were—?" Warden starts, pausing only to mouth the words on her pad. "Why not go after *your* people? Why me?"

"Shouldn't I have?" Oha asks. "You needed help. It was . . . chaos. So, I helped you."

Oha drops away from Warden, letting off a series of low chirps.

"Thank you," Warden concedes, but feeling uncertain.

She rubs her neck, feeling soreness in her arms and legs after treading water for so long.

Oha splits her mandibles and rises to her full height. Proud, like a leader should be.

"You are welcome, Sergeant Major," Oha speaks. "But what do we do now?"

Warden doesn't get a chance to answer. Medical staff from the craft's sick bay quickly arrive and direct them below deck, tossing silver blankets over their shoulders. "Take these," a crewmember instructs. "And be careful in the corridors. Even the work lights are out, so watch your step."

Warden nods.

"We'd better get comfortable," she tells the bugger.

"This battle is *not* over," Oha admits. "Not yet."

"Our fleet's a mess," Warden derides.

"Your ships have guns, do they not?" Oha begs the question, ducking her head while she passes under a low hatch.

"And the swarm tore those guns to pieces," Warden counters. "How do we fight that?"

Warden's armor gets heavier until she finds a seat and catches her breath. She sheds the hardsuit's outer plates, letting them drop to the floor with loud CLINKS. The sound echoes down the corridor, earning the nominal glances of the maintenance crews attempting to rewire the vessel to get power online.

"They *will* succeed," Oha encourages.

"Do you mean our team? I don't know," Warden sighs, huddling in her thermal blanket.

"You do not trust them?"

"I don't think *trust* plays much of a part in it," Warden frowns. "Me? What can I do? A grunt with a rifle."

"There is not much we *can* do," Oha admits. "What will happen . . . *must* happen."

"And how do I accept that?" Warden shudders.

Oha presses her hands together, almost like she's praying.

"The same way we choose to sleep after a bad dream," the Matriarch hints.

"You dream? Unexpected. But what if we don't like what we see?"

"Then we try again."

Warden smirks. "As simple as that?" she breathes.

"Should it be complicated?" Oha asks.

"It shouldn't be easy."

"Why not? Is that how all humans think?"

"Some. But it's freezing. And I have a job to do," Warden scoffs. "Come on. Let's get dry."

"And what do you plan to do after?" Oha asks.

"Drag everybody we can out of the water," Warden tells her.

"A noble goal," Oha confirms.

"No," Warden denies. "It's a mission."

Oha holds out her hands for Warden to take. And this time, she does.

76 | FINAL PROTOCOL

ADDISON KENNEDY, FIELD DIRECTOR
EPIMETHEUS PROJECT

OCTOBER 27, 2041 | 0625 HOURS

Addison seldom regrets her decisions.

Asking out Christian Numen to Sadie Hawkins in High School is a frequent moment she wishes to rewrite. Not fighting for her grant funding to build a private laboratory is another. And few regrets are as fear-inducing as jumping off the loading ramp of a V-91 Warhawk a few thousand feet in the air. She hurtles toward the massive alien ship, leashed to a testosterone-injected soldier, dropping a hundred feet in a blink of an eye.

Ibrahim pulls his parachute, and Addison clamps down her teeth.

A strong wind throws them off course, strapped in their harness, landing hard on the rocky surface.

Addison hurries to unbuckle from Ibrahim as he starts to laugh. "Almost as fun as when your dad pushed you out of that plane?" he mocks. Addison imagines him grinning from ear to ear underneath his visor.

"Don't . . . Don't make me slap you," Addison says, letting her heart drop. "You're never . . . throwing me out . . . another aircraft."

"Ah, you'll be okay," Ibrahim laughs again.

He unhooks the chute and lets it fly away with the storm.

Addison drops to her knees, giving him the middle finger with her good hand. "Don't you ever—" She suddenly feels the hull shake violently. Coalition warships open fire on the Fragment swarms outflowing through the dreadnaught's crevices—the hangars and smaller bays. Above them, explosions lay the sky to waste. Addison raises her arms over her head as shrapnel rains over them like hail in winter.

Ibrahim quickly covers Addison as superheated metal batters off the hull and into their faceplates.

"Stay down!" Ibrahim shouts, taking an impact to his arm, only for the shard to bounce off his reinforced hardsuit.

"Comms are down!" Addison yells, attempting to open a channel to the fleet.

"We have to get inside!" Ibrahim returns. He takes her arm and pulls her along while shielding her from incoming fire. His armor can take the punishment, so he withstands the brunt of the onslaught. Addison would get torn apart with her civilian model hardsuit. "We're off course! The wind blew us a klick from our rendezvous!"

"Did you see where everybody went down?!"

"Hadn't the chance! The whole unit is probably scattered!"

"How far to the nearest outpost?"

Ibrahim tilts his head to one side as the slag rain subsides. "It might be easier to make for the ingress point," he states. "Everybody's probably heading in that direction already. They'll hopefully stick to the plan and follow their team leaders."

"And avoid the fighting?"

"That's the idea."

"Did the Architects jump?"

Ibrahim shrugs. "Maybe? I couldn't see them in the air," he admits. "Then again, I wasn't tracking those two on the way down. But they *do* know the ship. So, they'll be fine. Let's worry about *us* for now, okay? And look for a way inside!" They take cover in a shallow trench that runs along the mid-spine, following it to the front of the ship.

Addison watches along the way as the Fragments encircle the dreadnaught, creating a shield to protect the vessel. The alien drones move erratically. And their numbers? Uncountable. Incoming flak causes the machines to scatter, eventually regrouping to lunge at the quarantine fleet.

"One ... two ... three ..." Addison records the seconds. Her fingers go numb as flashes on the USS Isaac Bennett dwindle.

A destroyer splits in two while a cruiser veers off its anchor and capsizes.

"F-f-four ... f-five ... s-s-six ... s-seven ..." Addison swallows, forcing the numbers off her tongue.

She can hear the people on those ships crying for help.

All goes dark, and a stillness falls over the air.

"E-eight ... n-nine ... and ten," Addison finishes with a ringing in her ears.

"There's nothing we can do for them," Ibrahim says, "except complete our mission."

The pair make their way across the ship's desolate spine. After a few hours, they find a divot in the superficial plating that opens into a wider space. Ibrahim knots a cable through the hole, allowing the two to repel down and delve into a large holding area near the vessel's forward section. It's a steep angle to descend, but she's confident they can make it.

Ibrahim lets Addison down first, wincing as she uses her bad arm to leverage her weight. Inside, it's pitch black.

Addison can hear voices nearby.

"At the bottom!" she calls back when her boots touch the ground.

"Good!" Ibrahim shouts. "Can you switch on your lamp?!"

"Will it even work?"

"Give it a try!"

Addison fumbles with the controls, finding the button behind her helmet's audio sensors. In that instant, a dozen guns pivot in her direction, the marines from her unit reacting to her light. Ibrahim lands next to her a moment later.

"Colonel Ibrahim?" somebody promptly asks.

Ibrahim waves at them, unclipping from the line. He nudges Addison forward with a thumbs up.

"Looks like we aren't the only ones who made it," Ibrahim tells her.

"How many are there?" Addison asks the marines who've hidden away in the hold.

"Just us? Plus, the civilians and the two feather-heads," Sergeant Mannering tells them. "Three didn't arrive after the jump, including the pilots. The wind might've thrown them into the ocean, but I lost track of them either way. I hate leaving troops behind, sir. But when the swarm came? It wasn't safe to stay and look for them."

Ibrahim steps toward the man. "We all did our best," he acknowledges, noticing the absentees. "And the others? Yunwen, Remmings . . . Our alien friends?"

"Scouting for a route," Mannering explains. "I ordered a security team to go with them."

"How long ago was that?"

"Thirty minutes?" the man reacts. "Give or take."

"Then we have some catching up to do," Ibrahim says. "Marines? We're moving out!"

"Colonel?" Addison asks.

"We're two hours past due and have ground to cover," he tells her. "Let's teach these fancy birds what we monkeys can do!"

His voice trumpets a rousing self-confidence, but the rest of the unit responds like ice cracking under pressure. Almost reserved. Angry. Witnessing the fleet getting wiped out would nullify anyone's enthusiasm for a fight, Addison should think.

She looks through the hole in the wall to see the fires blazing in the distance. Hundreds . . . maybe thousands? Dead or dying in the attack.

Her father could well be among them.

"Elias?" Addison says, finding it difficult to move.

The soldier glances at Addison when she says his given name. Ibrahim likely can't read her face, but he can see the slump in her posture. Addison hangs her shoulders low while her chest collapses, making each breath harder.

Ibrahim nods encouragingly. "It's okay," he says without her having to say another word.

Patting her on the arm, Ibrahim ushers Addison into formation with the rest of the team. As they begin their trek through the corridors again, Addison notices a warmness throughout that didn't exist when they crossed this area for Operation Shield Piercer.

Addison keeps an eye on Ibrahim as he takes charge, barking orders as he does. He works his way to the head of their column.

She stays close to him. As a precaution, she switches off her helmet lights, cringing as their footsteps echo unforgivingly on the rock-like surfaces.

Nobody knows where they're going, only that they're following the only direction Idu and Adhion could've gone. Back through the cathedral-like hallways, supported by narrow sets of angular buttresses, a constant red emanating from every crack and fissure in the walls.

"It's like stepping into a haunted mansion," Addison whispers. "And the ghosts are watching us from the paintings."

"And us without a proton blaster to fight them off with," Mannering overhears.

"You don't need to respond when I talk to myself, Gunnery Sergeant," Addison chides.

"Nerves are thin enough without you telling ghost stories, Doctor Kennedy," the man defends.

"I didn't mean to—"

"Enough. Watch your sectors," Ibrahim instructs. "Addison? With me."

Addison moves faster to lock into step beside him.

"What is it?" she asks.

He stops mid-stride, letting the others go past them momentarily.

Ibrahim unbuckles his holster. "You still know how to shoot?" he asks, offering his sidearm.

Addison wraps her fingers around the grip and checks the safety. "Won't be easy with one hand," she admits.

"You don't want it?"

"No, no . . . It's fine," Addison allows. "But a pistol won't do much against a Fragment."

"Unless you want to make it angry," Ibrahim admits.

"Hard to imagine them angrier than they are now," Addison shudders.

Ibrahim shakes his head before they press on through to the next intersection. "Some chance is better than no chance. And the areas ahead will be dangerous without Leighton in our ears," he explains, wanting the others to listen. "Making too much noise in this space will also garner unwanted attention. Maintain noise discipline. Nobody shoots unless you know it's a kill shot."

"And shut off your lights," Addison adds.

"This place is a labyrinth," Ibrahim warns. "Are you sure?"

"Some chance is better than none, right?" she notions.

"What if we get lost? Without the Overlook—"

"We can use the ship's luminescence to navigate," Addison suggests.

"Like landmarks on a map?" somebody else iterates.

"Exactly! Follow the patterns."

Ibrahim turns to his troops alongside them. "Make it happen," he commands.

"Yes, sir," Mannering whispers.

"More importantly," Ibrahim continues, "watch the man at your front."

"You heard the Colonel," Mannering utters. "Stay together! Protect your flanks."

"And don't get lost," Ibrahim finishes.

Every marine sends their acknowledgments, moving in formation as they search the corridors.

MALAKAI ADONIS, DIRECTOR OF OPERATIONS
EPIMETHEUS PROJECT

OCTOBER 27, 2041 | 0630 HOURS

"Leighton? What's going on?" Malakai asks. He walks into the Control Room, the overhead lights and monitors in the dark.

"We've lost power to all systems," Harlow describes.

Malakai stops and watches the man struggle with his workstation. Glancing out the windows, Malakai can see the light show that's going on at the Summerland, and it doesn't take a genius to understand the danger.

"Do we have access to the network?" he asks.

"Nodes aren't responding," Leighton denies. "And we're not receiving any signals!"

"Call it, then. Evacuate anyone who we can get into contact with," Malakai says, instinctively going for the alarm. Nothing happens when he hits the button, as he would've expected. He pings the Overlook for an open channel, but the line bursts with static, only for the noise to die as quickly. "Damn it. This crap again?"

"Internal lines are also down," Leighton says.

Malakai turns to the OverSec troopers guarding the door.

"I need runners," he commands. "Go check if we can get the life rafts into the water! We can use them to get people to the fleet."

The officers respond by standing there, stuck like pieces of wood.

Malakai eyes them confusingly.

"We're in an emergency," he explains. "I need runners!"

"We heard you, sir, but—" the trooper begins to speak, but his tongue can't find the words. He points at the window.

Malakai follows the man's finger and suddenly understands what it takes for professional soldiers to freeze. Missile launches from nearby destroyers reflect off the windowpanes. Malakai squints. They're firing at the machine swarms coming out of the dreadnaught. Thousands of specks rush to intercept the volley from the fleet, returning fire when the barrage slows—shredding many of the ships and cutting the USS Isaac Bennett's flight deck in two. Lifeboats drop into the water, attempting to escape the destruction.

"Everybody! Get to the lower deck!" Malakai shouts. He drags Leighton from his chair and throws him toward the door.

The man passes through it as hostile beams of light slice into the room, scorching metal, monitors, and flesh.

The soldiers rush into the fray, but they're cut down by the Fragments outside, punching holes through the walls.

Malakai picks up a gun and fires at the drones. A hardlight beam grazes his hand, melting the weapon into a tangle of plastic and steel. He ducks and rolls under the air traffic control station. That only gives him moments as another blast hits above him, shrapnel raining over his cover.

At least with the incursion days ago, they could set up a proper defense. But this slaughter?

Within a heartbeat, it gets awfully quiet. Malakai can hear gunfire several decks below him, along with muffled screams.

He cannot stay in the Control Room. A low-toned hum bounces a few meters off the wall to his right. He may not be able to see it, but he knows there's a Fragment in the room with him. And he doesn't have a weapon that can penetrate its shell.

Crossing his fingers, Malakai can only hope the rock gets bored and disappears.

Sweat gathers on his neck. His wrist stings as if he had a run-in with the ass-end of a highly disagreeable wasp. Lying on the floor, blood leaks from the other side of the table, where a co-worker lies dead with glass in her throat. He can see her through the crack where the divider meets the ground.

Malakai covers his mouth to slow his breathing, but he can't stop the air from whistling when it leaves his nostrils.

He plugs the holes with tissue from his pocket, hoping it's enough.

A ringing in his ears gives him a headache. But the longer he waits, the more he realizes the Fragment isn't going to leave, even as the fighting in the background fades eerily. "Not a good sign," Malakai mouths. For him, there's no choice about it. He must get to the door—circumvent the floating rock, slip into the hallway. Or die.

His timeframe thins as the humming gets louder. Loose objects on the floor vibrate, and a soft red glow reflects off the broken glass and metal surfaces.

Malakai inches his eye over the tabletop to get an idea of the Fragment's location in the room. He's never encountered a functional one before. Malakai's seen them on helmet feeds from the Summerland and watched Ava dissect them in the Observation Lab countless times. But now it's too real.

His lungs plead for air as he holds his breath.

The key is to time it perfectly when he dashes for the door.

"You can't attack me if you don't know where I am," Malakai murmurs.

The drone whips around speedily.

Malakai drops back under the table as *it* spins, observing the room. After finishing a rotation, it lets off a beeping noise before continuing its patrol.

"Fascinating," Malakai whispers.

The drone buzzes as it turns back at him, emitting a rapid series of harsh lights. Each new one spills through minuscule cracks in his cover.

Malakai locks his jaw to keep his comments under wraps.

Stupid.

He chews his lip. What does the beeping mean? Shortwave data bursts? Maybe a channel to transmit an all-clear signal to other nearby units? Even if he's quiet about it, Malakai's likely to draw additional Fragments this way. And the Project has already transferred every weapon that can disable the damn things to the dreadnaught weeks ago.

With no power, he's running out of options.

Think. What can I do?

The door to the hallway opens with the sound of metal grinding on metal. Three officers force it open and sweep into the room, and the Fragment guns them down before they get more than a couple of meters. Malakai takes the opportunity to switch positions, stepping on glass and earning the drone's attention. The thing violently swings around and rushes toward where he'd been a few moments ago.

Malakai reaches another hiding spot as the machine circles the table.

There's movement in the corner of the room. Somebody's still alive! Malakai can't see who it is but guesses they won't make it much longer. The Fragment loops the area again and notices a staffer crawling toward the exit. Eyeing the woman, Malakai sees that her leg's busted. She won't get far. It's already too late for him to do anything to help her.

The floating rock hangs over her and executes the woman with a quick burst to her head.

She didn't even have a chance to scream.

Responding to the noise—or maybe a distress call sent by the lone Fragment when the troopers came through the door—another of the alien drones enters the room. It hums at the other for a while before following a path along the windows to outside.

"Fuck me to hell," Malakai curses under his breath.

He's stuck. And he can't move without either Fragment seeing him. But if he stays, the second one will be on him fast.

Ava Remmings and her team made studies on specimens taken from the dreadnaught. He knows the drone's optics can likely see living organisms through an infrared spectrum. Given the machines' role aboard ships meant to seed life to new worlds, it must be important for them to locate the animals under their care through dense foliage.

And it's also possible the drones can see in more than one visual spectrum.

"Playing dead won't help me," Malakai internally screams.

He needs to take his chances where he can steal them.

Malakai jumps up and rushes forward. It's less than a millisecond for the Fragments to register him and give chase. He makes it to the door the troopers had opened and sprints through, taking an abrupt right down the main corridor. But there are more hostiles in the hallway. They don't hesitate.

Malakai dodges left, ducking into a maintenance causeway. Bodies are everywhere—not just soldiers but also his staff, the workers, and security officers. He doesn't stop to look at their faces. He can't tell who's who in the dark. He can only step over them. It's his only way to escape this oil rig outside a body bag.

Hardlight shimmers around him. "Damn it!" Malakai yelps as a shot grazes his side.

He can feel the heat on his heels, burning the tread of his boots. Even the hallway starts to buckle in on itself as its support beams contort under fire.

That's when a hand pulls at him.

"Leighton?"

"Get down!" calls a trooper, opening fire at the Fragment behind him.

The soldier's rifle sends sparks flying as micro-explosions detonate the drone's center optical.

"No time to celebrate," a second officer shouts. "Keep moving!"

Malakai counts five OverSec troopers in escort, along with Leighton and two others. Survivors.

Behind the destroyed Fragment, three more drones come rushing to intercept them.

"I'm behind you," Malakai acknowledges, letting the troopers take the lead with the civilians in tow.

Two officers drop as the Fragments ambush them in a connecting corridor. The man leading them returns fire but falls when light hits his head and torso. Malakai blinks. There's not much left of the trooper as he hits the ground.

Leighton screams.

Malakai grabs the man's wrist and yanks him sideways, saving him from a beam that flashes between the pair.

"Go left! Go left now!" the last two officers shout as they hold off another Fragment before taking hits to their armored cores.

He follows the soldier's instinct and veers down the left corridor with Leighton.

Then, all goes quiet.

The drones aren't chasing them anymore. It's so sudden that neither of them realizes it until they hit the dead end in the hallway. Whether it's because the Fragments lost track of the pair or didn't care enough about following them, Malakai doesn't know. But now it's only the two left, the others either having fallen behind or were shot in the back as they fled.

It doesn't matter. The duo has a free moment to breathe and devise a plan.

Malakai hears a faint hum from down the corridor. He shudders when it sinks away like a monster stalking the shores of a dark lake. Whatever they decide, they'll need to move again very soon, or else he doesn't have much faith in their chances if they make another mad dash.

"I don't see a way out from here," Leighton says.

"You're right," Malakai twitches.

There's nothing but a broom closet here and no viable means to escape. Moreover, a locked door without power is keen on staying locked. Malakai could rewire the keypad to get themselves inside . . . But his skills aren't quite as mechanically versed as some of his subordinates.

"Leighton," Malakai garners.

The kid looks at him, mouth agape. His eyes reflect the darkness of the corridor. He's just thankful they're alive.

Malakai will have to make sure they stay that way.

"Yes? Ah, I mean—" Leighton inhales.

"We need to think! How far to the nearest exit?" Malakai demands. "Anything with cover?! Somewhere for us to hide along the way? If we can make it happen, I prefer to avoid another encounter with those . . . tetrahedrons."

The other's eyes widen, only blinking occasionally.

Malakai waves a hand over the man's face to snap him out of his daze.

"I-I don't—? Right," Leighton murmurs. "Escape. Well, this is a purpose-built structure. There are always places for the crew to run to in an emergency." He swallows as he presses his palms to his chest, slowing his breath as sweat runs down his face. "But where can we go? I don't know."

"What about Addison?!" Malakai realizes.

"Doctor Kennedy?" Leighton muses.

"No," Malakai clarifies. "Addison . . . She made it to the Observation Lab during the last attack. How *did* she?"

Leighton's expression suddenly brightens.

"Through the access tunnels between decks," he answers. "They honeycomb the rig with exit hatches everywhere."

"And where's the nearest port?"

Leighton purses his lips and takes a moment to think.

Malakai does not regret hiring Leighton when he did. The man is a walking map with a penchant for detail. Nobody else would've studied the Olympus' layout in their free time like him. Leighton is the only person Malakai trusts to draw new routes in his head without ever needing to double-check.

So, when he points at the broom closet's door, Malakai holds his breath, and his face loses circulation.

"You're serious?" he asks.

"I think so," Leighton confirms. "Nearest hatchway is through *that* door."

Malakai squeezes his shoulder.

"Of course, it's the *locked* door," he comments. "I love a coincidence, don't you? God has a funny bone. Never thought."

"How do we open it without secondary power?" Leighton returns.

Malakai glances at him before stepping toward the door. He traces a finger around the keypad's cover, looking for leverage. He finds it. Peeling the case off, Malakai digs into the wires for the right one to kill the door's magnetic lock. He's at it for several minutes with sweat dripping from his pits and into his undershirt.

"How did she show it again?" Malakai mutters. "Ah! There it is."

The door whines as it unlocks.

He may not have "opened" the door, but with the locks disabled, they can at least pry it by hand without much trouble.

Malakai instructs Leighton to help by pulling on one-half of the door opposite of him.

With a quiet count to three and a cringe-worthy screech of stubborn tracks grinding together, the pair forces the two sides apart. And the downside? There isn't a way they can shut it again. Malakai's doomsday clock is already ticking too close to midnight.

The soft humming rises from the corridor again.

Leighton and Malakai stare at the darkness, frozen.

"Get inside," Malakai urges.

"Temps inside the tunnels will be hot," Leighton warns.

"Storm outside will cool us off once we make it to the other side," Malakai suggests.

"Is that your professional opinion?"

"What else can we do?"

Leighton opens his mouth but thinks better than to speak his mind. It won't help them get out of this situation.

Malakai frowns as they squeeze into the closet and find the hatch to the crawlspace under some boxes. A dry heat washes over them like a great plume when they lift the grate. They step back, covering their mouths as they fan the vapor away from their faces.

"This isn't so bad," Leighton says. "Stings the eyes a little bit."

"We won't have long once we're inside the tube," Malakai admits.

"And who goes first?"

Under normal conditions, power across the rig would shut off sector by sector to protect workers making runs in the tunnels. It allows heat to vent through bypass ducts before anyone climbs into the narrow space. Otherwise, it's too much of a safety hazard, and several regulations across multiple countries strictly ban the practice.

Addison had burns on her arms and legs for the risk she took.

"You there?" Leighton asks.

Malakai blinks until he can focus on Leighton.

"I'm fine," he lies.

"Are you sure?"

Malakai sorely wished he'd taken the opportunity to create a plan in case anybody else needed to enter these tunnels again.

"You go ahead," Malakai says. "I'll follow you down."

The humming gets louder as a hard red light gathers outside the door.

"It's almost on us," Leighton says.

"Then I recommend you stop talking and get in the hole."

Malakai shoves Leighton into the hatch before climbing in after him. He spies the Fragment coming around the corner and into the closet just as he lowers the lid into place.

The damn thing didn't immediately react if it *did* notice him.

Malakai puts a finger to his lips to prompt Leighton to stay quiet. The Fragment floats over the hatch, beeping the same all-clear Malakai caught in the Control Room. He sighs when the machine drifts away after a minute, humming until it disappears entirely.

"That was too close," Malakai murmurs.

"How did this happen?" Leighton asks. "What fucking changed?"

"Exactly what they warned us about," Malakai answers. "Final protocol."

"You mean, all those things were in the ship this whole time?"

"Enough to wipe out all life on a planet and start the renewal process over again."

"Like all those lives don't matter?"

"I don't understand it," Malakai tells him. "Come on. It's already getting warm inside this tube."

He takes off his outer shirt and wraps his hands to protect them.

"I said it would," Leighton retorts.

"Which way?" Malakai shifts demandingly.

"Straight," Leighton instructs. "We'll go right, then left."

"You're the point man," Malakai tells him.

"I'm taking the lead?"

"You know these tunnels," Malakai explains. "I don't. You're the man for the job, Leighton. That's why I recruited you."

Malakai winces at the pain in his side where the energy weapon scratched him. There's no blood, which shouldn't surprise him after reading the reports on the victims of the Central Spire Incident. It burns the flesh like wax in a candle factory and cauterizes it like . . . well, he can't think of an analogy. But sometimes, the wound doesn't seal and bleeds profusely.

"No pressure or anything," Leighton nods.

Discolored blisters form on their hands and knees as they push through the tunnels.

"Watch your head," Malakai forewarns.

"It's dark," the man returns.

"That's why I'm spotting for you," Malakai says with a dehydrated smile.

"Now I understand why Addison couldn't drink for a few days," Leighton returns.

"Focus on finding us the exit," Malakai instructs. "And watch for any sudden drops."

"I can't feel my face," Leighton huffs.

"It's either push on or die," Malakai warns. "Stop the fuss and move!"

AVANNA "AVA" REMMINGS, CHIEF TECHNOLOGY SPECIALIST
EPIMETHEUS PROJECT

OCTOBER 27, 2041 | 0850 HOURS

"Are you okay?" the Corporal asks, stepping beside her. They're making their way through the ship's forward sections.

"I'm fine," Ava nods, compressing her chest. She feels as if the walls are getting taller as she walks.

Ava glances at Zhu, flashing her headlamps to get the woman's attention.

At least their lights are working again now they are inside the ship. But how does that work? An electromagnetic pulse makes sense, but it must only affect unshielded tech outside the Summerland's rock of a hull. It had to be deliberate—a fundamental part of the ship's defense mechanisms. Or maybe the one in charge overloaded his systems, and everybody got caught in the radius.

Zhu's head shoots up, and her stare lingers on Ava for a second. They both slow their pace, letting the soldiers overtake them. Corporal Tanner stops abruptly at an intersection. "Stay here," Tanner whispers, signaling his fireteam to move ahead. "I want to check the next corridor. Make sure it's clear."

"We do not have the time for detours, Corporal," Idu warns.

"And I'm not a tour guide," Tanner retorts. "Just . . . hang back, will you? Five minutes."

Idu's bristles furrow as she nods, letting her shoulders drop, illustrating her displeasure but accepting it regardless.

Tanner and his team proceed into the corridor. Zhu and Ava stay at the crossroads with Adhion 'Klaka and Idu 'Smeora.

Ava watches the bird-like aliens like a hawk eyeing a mouse from a low-hanging branch. She notices how they each fold their hands at their stomachs, their long fingers interlocked together like baskets of reeds, the feathers on their heads shifting to a cooler palette as they wait.

Neither one utters a word in the interim.

That doesn't mean the two aren't talking, Ava wagers. Their feathers' changing hue is a clear sign of their emotional states. She may not be a xenobiologist, but the Architects are fine examples of the drastic attributes a species can undergo during millions of years of evolution. And it leaves her with more than a few questions.

Idu notices her staring and returns with a quiet frown.

Ava blinks and looks away.

"Which way to the ship's core?" Zhu steals the moment to ask.

Adhion lumbers toward her and grumbles disagreeably. Idu sidesteps into the fray to block his view.

"Quite some distance," Idu says.

"It is through the Entrychamber," Adhion adds. "Tyrann 'Akachan commands from there."

"Better to avoid him if we can," Idu suggests, lifting a hand to stop Adhion, who's hesitant to heed the gesture.

"And what are the chances we'll have to go through *him* to get to the core?" Ava wonders aloud.

"High likelihood," Idu admits. "As our leader, he is very powerful in his own right."

"How so?" Zhu pleads, finding an opportunity to shine.

"Specifically," Ava adds.

Idu stares at the two briefly, raising her shoulders and taking a deep breath.

"With our current party, a direct engagement will be difficult," she warns.

"Warden beat the Judge," Zhu describes. "If we play it smart, our troops can win this fight."

"Maybe," Idu offers with a low hum, looking up at Adhion, who's clenching his jaw.

The group waits silently for several minutes before Tanner and his squad return. "All clear ahead," the Corporal iterates. "I think we should wait for Sergeant Mannering to catch up. We may be the only survivors after what happened to the fleet."

Ava steadies her stance.

"What about Colonel Ibrahim?" she asks. "Or Addison? They jumped together."

"We don't know if they made it hull-side," Zhu clarifies.

"If they did, they would've made for the rendezvous," Tanner tells them. "And it's been hours. If they've not reached Mannering's position by now, they're not coming. Our team will set up to protect this intersection. You four hang back until the Sarge makes contact."

Ava can't see the Corporal's face, but the man nods at Idu and Adhion.

The two return the gesture and fade into the corridor's dark recesses that comprise the vessel's extra-gothic architecture.

Ava suppresses her *urge* to scream.

All she remembers about the jump was that she was holding her breath the whole way down.

They stay an hour, and still no contact from Sergeant Mannering or the rearguard. Tanner sends a man back to the small hangar where they entered the ship. It's not long until Tanner's marine returns with more bodies in tow. Ava's display highlights Addison Kennedy, the only one other than Zhu and Ava to wear the civilian HWRD-C model suits.

"You're alive?" Ava breathes, stating the obvious.

Addison turns her helmet to Ava's but doesn't answer.

"Is this everybody?" Tanner begs the question.

"Everyone that's left," Mannering confirms. He nods to Colonel Ibrahim.

"Gather 'round," the man orders.

Ava notices the jittering in the Colonel's hands. He's in a similarly bad mood as Addison. Or maybe he's just tired? Ava bites inside her cheek as she weighs the thought. He *should* be exhausted. Ibrahim could be the last commanding officer for the United Coalition on the dreadnaught. That *has* to put immense pressure on the man.

His knees buckle as he walks.

"What's the plan, Colonel?" Tanner asks.

"Same as it was," Ibrahim bluntly states. "We get the Heart to the Core and get this ship off our planet."

"With all due respect, sir," Mannering opens in a broken tone. "We're stranded. Nobody's coming to help us. Our fleet is gone. And we may be the only ones left to do anything about it. If we go, can we find our way out again? Can we get home?"

Ibrahim's head turns to the mission's second-in-command. And he doesn't say anything.

Ava surmises that Ibrahim's letting his thoughts run their course as he decides on the best way to keep the survivors moving toward their objective.

"The odds don't look great," Ava concedes, not wanting to die.

Ibrahim squares his shoulders. "All I know is that this is the last place we should be arguing right now," he counters. "We're deep behind the frontlines, looking down an enemy that's more advanced—a foe bigger and stronger than anything our species has fought in over a thousand years of warfare."

She notices Idu slide next to Addison as everybody listens to Ibrahim. Are they whispering to each other? Ava speculates.

Addison's visor veers toward Ava and flashes a sign at her in secret.

Ava circles the crowd of marines to meet them.

"What is it?" Ava asks. She brushes off the Colonel's bombastic monologue.

"Adhion's gone," Addison says.

Ava raises an unseen eyebrow. "What do you mean . . . Gone?" she asks.

"He went ahead to confront the Trident directly," Idu explains, "while I guide the last of us to the core."

"I didn't see him go," Ava mocks.

"Really? That's what surprises you? That you didn't see him go?! Idu slipped our sensors without anybody realizing when she snuck into the Alpha Site," Addison describes, stopping to catch her breath. She returns her attention to the Architect. "Can he win against Tyrann 'Akachan in a straight fight?"

Idu retains her stare for a moment longer before closing her eyes and shaking her head.

"That's not comforting," Ava comments.

"We need to hurry," Addison urges.

Ibrahim wraps up his speech and overhears. "What's going on?" he questions, looking at the trio.

"Where's the big one?" Sergeant Mannering utters next.

"Adhion went on to distract the enemy," Addison explains.

"Alone?" Ibrahim asks.

"Nobody else could go with him," Idu says. "They must confront their grudges."

"Even if it ends up costing us?"

"I loathe it as much as you," Idu mourns.

"Then we don't have time," Ibrahim confirms. "Get ready for the push!"

The marines ready their weapons and reorient themselves into a sweeping formation. Ava wants to think they've prepared for anything that comes at them. She doesn't know if that's true. All she knows is they'll fight when they reach the Entrychamber, and the soldiers will spend their lives for hers.

Addison pulls Zhu and Ava aside in the commotion.

"I'm glad you two survived the jump," Addison says.

Ava thinks the woman has a smile under her visor. Of course, she can't prove it, but it's a nice thought.

"We didn't know if you had," Ava admits.

"How's the arm?" Zhu asks, going in for a hug, hardsuits clunking together.

"I'll be okay," Addison replies.

Ava doesn't quite show that same level of sentimentality. Instead, she goes to shake Addison's hand as a sign of respect. That doesn't stop Addison from pulling Ava close and embracing her like a sister greeting a younger sibling after months spent away from home.

"What's this for?" Ava asks, not understanding.

"Just in case we don't get the chance to hug it out after this is over," Addison says.

Ava frowns at the prospect. Her cheeks strain as they reshape into a hidden smile. Has she finally made a friend?

She sets pressure on her chest, feeling all . . . weird inside, like a frog had jumped into her mouth, and is now sitting on her tongue.

Ava's not sure if it's a "good" sensation to have on a mission like this, but—

Their final stretch to the Entrychamber is a long, mostly silent endeavor. Nobody talks in the hours it takes to get there. And the strangest part is that the air gets warmer in the corridors as they near their objective. The temperature gauge inside her helmet shows a five-degree increase every couple hundred meters.

Ava sees that everybody else is noticing the change, not only her.

"What is—?" Tanner attempts to ask.

"Means we're close," Ibrahim states. "Don't look back. Eyes front. Show your teeth."

Idu runs ahead and stops at a massive door blocking their way. "This is it," she says, pointing at the entry's steep sides.

"Why is it so warm?" Addison asks.

"Not that we're complaining," Ava remarks. "It's just—"

"I don't remember it being this warm last time," Mannering says. "Not outside the greenhouse."

Idu's features remain solid like a rock. "Temperatures inside the ship increase as the excess heat builds up throughout each corridor," she explains. "When the ship is operational, the Heart regulates this function when it's in contact with the core. Tyrann's actions are putting stress on its key systems. He cannot maintain the balance necessary to keep everything running optimally. Which means—"

"—the pistons are pumping," Ava illustrates, understanding the danger, "but there's no coolant in the engine."

Idu steps back and considers the metaphor.

"Indeed," she nods.

Ibrahim shakes his head. "Why even do that?" he asks.

"I suppose if you run all the systems at once, it overtaxes the ship's resources," Idu describes.

"Think of it like running a poorly optimized video game," Ava clarifies, "and your computer doesn't have cooling fans."

"Which isn't good," Addison iterates.

"I'm still confused," Ibrahim reasons. "Why would the bastard ruin his only way home?"

"Does it matter?" Addison asks.

"It doesn't change our mission," Mannering adds.

"Maybe not," Ibrahim admits. He walks up to Idu while she runs her hand over the door's cover. "Or does it?"

Idu stops and lets her arm drop to her side.

She looks at the man, her eyes black like luminous galaxies piercing the red void between them.

"He certainly does *not* like Adhion," she admits. "And their hate runs very deep. I did not think he'd cause so much death to your people to win this contest. It defies the Obligation."

"But neither are known for taking half-measures, am I right?" Addison stipulates.

"They are warriors," Idu says, "and leaders, tried and true."

"Pig-headed, self-righteous assholes," Addison states, playfully bumping Ibrahim's shoulder.

"Yes," Idu agrees.

"Then we have to stop it from happening," Zhu urges.

"Let's hurry and get the Heart to the core," Ava seconds. "Quicker, the better."

"Preferably before the ship's engines collapse and the reaction takes a large chunk of your planet with it," Idu forewarns.

Ibrahim clenches the stock of his rifle. "That's possible?" he murmurs. "Okay. Let's do this."

"The ship's bridge is on the other side of this door," Idu warns. "It's locked. And I can't seem to open it."

"You don't have access?" Ava asks.

"That shouldn't be possible," Idu admonishes.

"Because of your role as the Whisperer?" Addison notions.

Idu merely nods as she steps back from the massive door separating the group from the Entrychamber.

"Unless we can use a little key of our own," Ibrahim offers.

"You have one?" Idu asks.

"A little explosive incentive," he explains. "One loud knock, and the door will open right up."

"That is . . . an extreme solution," Idu murmurs.

"It's how the dogs of hell say hello," Ibrahim states. "Can we expect a welcome party?"

"Yes," Idu says.

"How many?" Ibrahim asks.

Idu tilts her head, sad by the notion.

"Many."

"Okay. Not so helpful," Ibrahim shrugs frustratingly. "But why not?" His voice cracks.

"We fight through whatever's in our way until we make it to the ship's core," Mannering iterates.

"Jumping into a fight without knowing anything about what we're up against seems standard practice at this point," Ava meekly laughs.

"You can go back if you're uncomfortable," Addison says with a fearful tinge to her tone.

Ibrahim glances at her shockingly. "No. She's fine," he says. "We all agreed. Nobody's getting left behind."

"Ready when you are, Colonel," Mannering confirms.

Around them, the twenty or so marines flash their helmet lights in agreement. It's a signal, Ava realizes. Like the Architects' changing the colors of their feathers, these grunts show they stand together at the end of a long road. And the other side of this door? Whatever they find, Ava's certain it'll be the crown jewel of this endeavor that Arthur Summerland had started.

Zhu stands next to Ava, taking her hand and clutching it tightly.

"We stay together once we're through," Zhu offers. "Follow Idu. She's safe."

"Every path leads to an end," Ava admits, gritting her teeth. "This is ours. I feel it."

She wants the chance to see her family again.

"Charges set . . . Ready to breach? Five . . . four . . . three . . . two . . ." Ibrahim counts.

Corporal Tanner and Sergeant Mannering set thermite charges on the door—like the explosives Commander Wen used to enter the Central Spire weeks ago. Ava made sure to change the measure of the stockpile to avoid a repeat of the Incident. They don't have second chances this time. Either it works, or they're dead.

"—one," Ibrahim finishes.

A bright flash streaks across the corridor as the door melts away. The marines charge through the opening in loose formation, letting off controlled bursts as the enemy return fire, hitting several in the face and chest. Zhu throws Ava to the left and into cover behind a large strut next to the wall, but it quickly disintegrates as hardlight drives into the rock-like alloy.

79 | A DEATH WALK

ADDISON KENNEDY, FIELD DIRECTOR
EPIMETHEUS PROJECT

OCTOBER 27, 2041 | 1019 HOURS

==

Explosions cause the floor to vibrate. Cracks appear under their feet as energy blasts launch forward, knocking three marines into the wall. Addison can hear shouting as men and women drop to the ground. She hides behind a pillar that rises like a tree to the ceiling.

"Mannering!" Ibrahim shouts, bracing against the enemy. "Reinforce the right flank!"

"Tanner is down!" somebody calls.

"Where are the others? Did anybody see where they went?" Mannering retorts.

"Pull up the left side right now!" Ibrahim orders. "Throw those charges. Bring up the rear!"

Addison peeks around the giant strut to see what they're fighting.

"Fragments," she breathes. "Six of them. And a handful of Varmajalkavaen? Loyal to a fault."

Idu runs along the front, taking her spear and slicing Fragments into thirds. She thrust the point into another, cleanly piercing its shell.

Ibrahim and his marines keep pushing, bombarding the forward area, and cutting down the opposition.

The firefight ends after a few minutes. Thirteen marines lay dead, three wounded. Only eight are left, including Ibrahim, to see the mission through.

"Not great odds if we get into another heated exchange," Addison counts. "Not all of us are soldiers."

"That was a tight spot," Mannering confirms.

"Is the room clear?" Ibrahim asks.

"Clear left," a soldier calls out.

"Good right!" another shouts.

Addison runs a hand over her visor to clean off the residue stuck on the glass the battle put into the air.

She looks desperately at the bodies.

"Damn us to hell," Addison curses. "Is that all of—?"

"The last thing we need is somebody to jinx us further," Ibrahim points accusingly. "Just don't do it." He kicks a downed Fragment, shooting another as it sparks with some meager life.

Idu swings around the massive room, admiring the sight. "Tyrann isn't here," she says.

Ibrahim and his marines look at her when she tells them, clutching their weapons.

"What do you mean?" Addison asks. "Where did he go?"

"Hopefully? Toward the Nomad," she offers. Idu trails down a corridor on the far side of the Entrychamber.

Addison glances at Ibrahim, who nods in affirmation.

"Let's take stock. Secure the bridge," the man orders. "See what's here before following her."

"Okay," Addison agrees.

"Wittenmyer! Collect the tags," Mannering instructs.

"Understood!" Wittenmyer calls out. "Does anybody see Tanner?"

"Over there! Past the barricade," Martinez shouts back.

The noise of the soldiers regrouping fades into the background as Addison searches for Ava and Zhu. She finds the pair hiding behind another strut, covered in simmering, fragmented debris from when the structure crumbled apart.

"You two all right?" Addison asks.

Ava and Zhu upturn their heads at her, but their faces stay hidden behind their visors.

"Is it over?" Ava asks. She outstretches a hand to Addison, who helps the woman to her feet.

"We're alive," Addison says. "So, that's progress. I think."

"You're not very funny," Zhu comments.

Addison shrugs. "I think you meant to say I'm hilarious," she murmurs despondently.

There's a pinching feeling in Addison's hand as her nerves tense.

"Come on!" Ibrahim shouts at them. "Don't drag behind!"

Addison waves to show she's heard him.

"You two ready?" she asks.

Neither one answers her plainly, only returning weary nods.

The triplets run to catch up with the soldiers. They've situated themselves in the Entrychamber's forwardmost area, leaving their comrades' bodies where they lie.

Addison touches Ibrahim's arm. "We shouldn't leave them behind," she notions.

He shakes his head. "I couldn't agree more. But we don't have the manpower to carry them all," Ibrahim says, lowering his shoulders. "And there's more than enough graves for us to dig when the mission's over." He emphasizes those last couple of words.

"Which direction did Idu go down?" she asks.

Ibrahim points to a corridor on the right. "Seems like the right place," he states. "Could do if she'd wait for us."

Addison's internal suit alarm goes off, warning of an environmental hazard. She struggles to switch off the alert, like a morning clock that won't stop yelling at her.

"What now?" Mannering curses. "A temperature cautionary?"

"Heat's picking up fast," Addison points out, running a thermal scan of the room. "Right now? Internal temps are running at three-hundred-forty-nine degrees Kelvin. Roughly one-hundred-seventy Fahrenheit, or seventy-seven point two degrees Celsius. Did anybody pack the lotion on their way out of the base?"

"We're burning up," Ibrahim clarifies. "Our suits are only equipped for subzero conditions. And we're standing in a furnace."

"Quite the eventuality," Addison adds. "Follow Idu. Let's get to the core. Quickly."

"Yes, ma'am," Ibrahim nods. "Barnes, Aquoia—stay here, guard our asses, and help the wounded. We're going deeper."

"And hope we find a way out the other side," Ava laments.

"Eyes on your trackers," Ibrahim orders. "Move out."

The walk into the next corridor puts a hard stress on their hardsuits. Addison repeatedly shuts off her helmet's alarm to keep it from driving her crazy.

"One-hundred eighty-eight degrees Fahrenheit," she reports.

"Let me know when it hits two hundred," Ibrahim says.

"Nearly there already," she returns.

"How much can these suits take?" Zhu asks.

"We don't know outside the lab," Ava admits. "But we'll find out soon."

"There's a reader on your HUD," Addison tells her.

"Oh," Zhu says. "I see it now."

"Does knowing make you feel better?" Ibrahim asks.

"No," Zhu murmurs.

"Hold up! Somebody's coming," Ibrahim warns.

The unit takes up defensive positions along the walls.

Addison aims the pistol Ibrahim gave her and watches a shadowy figure approach them in the soft light.

"Idu?" Addison asks.

"It is me," Idu responds.

Everyone lowers their weapons.

"What happened to you?" Ibrahim demands.

"I wanted to make sure our way is clear," she justifies. "Were you not following me?"

"You . . . kinda got ahead of us," Addison says.

"Any company?" Ibrahim asks.

"Company?" Idu repeats.

"Is anybody waiting for us? Are we heading for the core?" Addison clarifies.

"It's around the corner," Idu acknowledges. "But . . . there is what you would call . . . a snag, is it?"

"A snag?" Ibrahim asks, hesitant to hear more bad news.

"There's an obstacle deployed where the Heart goes," she iterates. "I could not find a workaround."

"What obstacle?" Ibrahim demands.

"It's an electrostatic impulse field," Idu describes.

Ibrahim stares at the Architect, tilting his head to one side. "That doesn't tell me a lot," he says.

"Sounds like a matter repulse barrier," Addison attempts to dumb down the science. "If I understand—it's like a particle shield that can rip apart organic material, leaving little more than residual dust." She lets out a cough before finishing with, "Sir."

Ibrahim looks at her in bewilderment. "And how can you guess that?"

"Because it's the same type of field that surrounds the Heart," Ava informs him.

"One of the things we learned is that with minimal contact, there isn't any real harm," Addison recounts. "But exposure to greater output? That could risk molecular damage over a longer period. Think of it like walking into a collapsing nuclear reactor."

"With no protection," Ava adds.

"And the field stops the energy escaping into the open."

"A simple analysis, but close enough for our purpose," Idu confirms. "These elements create a focused energy outflow. And the Heart? It regulates these functions throughout the ship. Without it, and with so many unnecessary systems active, the energy will continue to build until it cooks everything inside these corridors. All our hard work? Gone. I am afraid for the creatures in the gardens."

"And our planet after," Addison repeats. "Like we said."

"Explosion bad," Ibrahim sighs. "That's all you had to say."

"Question is . . . with the field in place, how are we doing this?" Ava asks.

"It won't be as simple as switching out RAM in a computer," Addison notions. "We know that."

The corridor goes quiet. Addison's words echo down its length until she hears it again, bouncing off the walls.

"Denied," Ibrahim decides.

"I didn't say—"

"Somebody will have to carry it there," he understands, stopping the group.

"And you won't allow it?" Addison questions.

"There's no other way," Idu tells them.

Ibrahim rises to his full height and reasserts: "Nobody's walking into that damn thing," he growls. "I will shoot anybody in the knee and drag them back to shore if anyone thinks about—"

"Enough!" Zhu shouts, loud and unapologetic. It stuns both Ibrahim and Addison.

Addison turns to her, biting her tongue.

Zhu Yunwen steps between the two and points angrily at Colonel Ibrahim. "Nobody's decided anything for anybody," she clamors. "We haven't seen the situation or considered our options. Let's get there before we start arguing about who's dying for what."

Addison's jaw tenses as the air thickens. Then, she grins wily.

Ibrahim remains speechless.

Zhu turns to Idu, who's waiting patiently off to the side.

"Lead the way," Zhu directs.

Idu bows her head, puzzled by the change but accepting the outcome.

The Architect waves them onward. Addison's fellow scientists and Ibrahim's marines follow.

Addison walks alongside Zhu, unsure of what to say.

"He doesn't get to decide what we do with our lives," Zhu heralds. "My government threw me to the wolves. All our friends are likely dead. We're alone with no way out, and this mission could be a one-way trip for all of us. We should prepare to die and do what we need to do."

"It'll be suicide walking into that field," Addison explains.

"Maybe suicide is another word for sacrifice?" Zhu retorts. "There's honor in that, I think. No matter how terrifying it is for those left behind."

"You're talking like you've already decided for everybody," Addison notes, observing the woman's body language.

"Nothing's decided," Zhu admits, hiding the lie under her words. Addison doesn't believe her.

Addison's temperature gauge beeps as it rounds two hundred degrees. She nudges Ibrahim a few steps in front of her.

"We need to move faster," Ibrahim responds to the readout.

"I don't know how much longer we can last," Mannering says, working his arm as his armor strains. "Is it getting worse?"

"Just keep your suit on," Ibrahim advises. "Internal cooling keeps us from drying out like jerky baked in the sun."

"Better to stop talking to conserve our energy," Ava suggests.

"She's right," Addison says.

"Switch off your displays and avoid expending your reserves," Ava commands. "It will help your suit from overheating."

"That will blind us if we get into another firefight," Mannering cautions.

"Better than not being able to lift your arms to fire the gun," Ava responds. "And it'll buy us time."

"Quiet down!" Ibrahim yells.

He stops dead center in the corridor.

Ahead, Idu has done the same.

Addison takes a few wary steps forward, seeing what they're seeing.

"That's bright," Addison murmurs.

"Is that your official statement?" Ibrahim half-heartily teases her.

"That's the core," Idu says.

"I thought it'd be—"

"Don't say bigger," Addison chides.

The group moves together and enters the core's main pavilion. It's not nearly as massive as the Entrychamber, but it's twice as bright and thrice as warm. Addison switches on her temperature readout, but the gauge blinks and shorts out unreadably.

"We don't have much time," she warns.

"How do we do this?" Ava begs the question. "I don't see where to stick a Heart-sized object."

"There's a mounting apparatus in the center of the field," Idu explains. "Somebody needs to walk it there."

"That's at least fifty meters," Ibrahim notes.

"Who'd walk that?" Mannering mutters.

"Didn't the Colonel say he'll shoot anybody who tries?" another asks.

"I don't think we have a choice," Mannering returns.

"Are we drawing straws?" Ava wonders. "Do we *have* straws to draw with?"

Addison looks ahead as the debate rages. Everybody has an opinion in their little group, and nobody's shy about sharing it.

Her gaze moves between Idu and Zhu Yunwen.

Zhu is looking into the field with a softness to her stance.

"What are you going to do?" Addison asks under her breath.

Zhu walks up to Idu and gladly takes the Heart. Everyone turns to her. Mannering and another—Wittenmyer, Addison guesses without her display—rush to stop her from entering the particle barrier. Yunwen anticipates this and jumps into no man's land before they can tackle her to the floor.

Pain . . . Zhu lets off a blood-curdling scream as she takes that first step, followed by a second and a third. Addison watches as the woman's suit melts, the energy coursing through her body. It's ripping her apart by her atoms, like microscopic bullets, with parts of her fading away like sand in a storm.

"Get away from the field!" Ibrahim orders.

He runs and throws Sergeant Mannering to the ground, only to look hard at Zhu Yunwen in the distance, clenching his fists as he stands there, desperate. Ibrahim paces quickly along the edge like an animal in a cage, searching for a clear path through the barrier. But *he* sees what Addison does, and his threat to drag anyone back to shore becomes an empty promise.

She blocks the Colonel. "It's too late!" Addison shouts. "You can't stop her!"

He looks at her and pushes her away when he decides to act. Addison doesn't need to see his eyes to know he's in tears. She lunges forward and grabs his arm, pulling him back with every ounce of strength she can muster to save the stubborn man. The others hurriedly join her to keep Ibrahim from recklessly going after the woman.

She doesn't want to watch two friends take the death walk. She can't. One is too many already.

But the woman? Zhu? She doesn't stop, not for a second. Every step she takes is a fight to the next.

Ibrahim depolarizes his visor and blinks when he surrenders to the group.

Addison can see the quivering in his cheeks, those eyes under that staunch helmet. Ibrahim looks at her, red and swollen like he's walked into a cloud of pepper spray. He wears the image of a man who has too much to take on and struggles to accept when he can't do a damn thing about it.

Once she reaches the center, Zhu unlocks the Heart from its shell and releases it into the air. The energy in the core reflects off the orb, and the room expels into a rainbow of colors, making it hard for Addison to see past the noise. Metallic sheets form around the edges of the little sphere, melding together in an intricate weave, reshaping the patterns into a singular light that rises into the vast space above them like a small sun.

"She has done it," Idu says, her eyes darting sideways.

The Whisperer walks to a console and presses her palm to its surface. The panel hums alive, flashing a spark of blue that drowns out the red. Addison watches her with a mix of apprehension and excitement. A mist fogs her visor as the temperature in the chamber steadily normalizes.

"What are you doing?" Addison asks.

"Initializing the restart sequence," Idu says.

Suddenly all the energy in the room snuffs out along with the containment field, and the dreadnaught goes completely dark. Air draws back from the chamber in quick succession. Ibrahim rushes to shove everybody into cover once he realizes what's happening.

"Hold on," Idu tells them. "I am also replacing the atmosphere."

"Why do that?" Ibrahim questions.

"To provide you an easier time getting out," she answers. "You won't have long before I purge the system, but I'll give you what life you need. Get your survivors as far away from here as possible, and I can handle the rest. Humanity has done its part for us. Now, it's time I make up the difference."

Zhu collapses under the strain. Idu looks on, her bristles a dark shade of blue.

Ibrahim charges forward, wanting to get the woman to safety now there's no longer a barrier. Addison holds him back again.

"What are you doing?" he demands. "Zhu's right there! I can get her if we—"

"She's contaminated!" Addison shouts. "You touch her . . . You could die!"

"You didn't want to leave our people behind!"

"And as *you* told me, we can't do anything!" Addison repeats what he meant at the Entrychamber. "We need to leave!" She ushers their group back through the way they came. Mannering and the others listen, but Ibrahim stands his ground, not wanting to leave the body. He may act like a tough cookie, but Addison knows it's only a hard outer layer hiding a soft, chewy center.

"You can find an airlock aft the Entrychamber," Idu tells them. "Hurry. Follow your people. Get them as far away from here as possible." She enters a sequence into the control panel. Addison's earpiece goes haywire when she finishes. She can hear voices—people who realize the comms are working again.

Addison removes her helmet and looks at the beautiful creature.

Idu doesn't return the same admiration.

Ibrahim steps in front of her and takes the helmet from her side. "Damn us. You're right," he agrees. Addison swings her head, not letting him see her eyes. That doesn't stop Ibrahim from noticing the obvious. He wipes the tears from her cheek and lifts her chin. "This isn't easy for any of us," Ibrahim says, resealing her helmet around her collar again. "Now, take a breath."

"You don't know anything," Addison shudders.

"I know the pain," Ibrahim mourns. "And the anger? It's hard to keep it a secret when you can't hide your face."

"That's one good thing about these suits," Addison swallows. "But I don't want to leave anyone."

"Neither do I," Ibrahim notions. "We don't have a choice anymore, do we?"

Addison shakes her head. "Let's just get this done with," she decides.

Ibrahim nods. Reluctant.

He keys an open channel and pulls Addison into the corridor with the others. "This is Castle-Actual to anybody with ears on . . . Can you read me?" he calls as their unit races to the Entrychamber. "Olympus Control? Fleet? Athena? Is anybody still alive?" There's a long break in the voices as if all of them were listening.

"I read you, Colonel Ibrahim," speaks a familiar voice.

Addison hears an energetic breath from Ibrahim and the team.

"Operator?! Say that again? Identify," Ibrahim orders.

"Sergeant Major Olivia Warden on the USS New Meridian," Warden answers.

Mannering and Wittenmyer bump fists as they hear her name.

"Son of a bitch," Ava mutters.

"Colonel Ibrahim? We're glad to hear your voice, sir," Warden continues. "What's your status?"

There's a heaviness to Warden's tone. "She's exhausted," Addison denotes.

Ibrahim raises a finger telling Addison to wait. "We've finished the mission.

Our coordinates read—" Ibrahim goes. He calls out numbers as their group reaches the Entrychamber and reconvenes with Barnes and Aquoia. Mannering finds the airlock where Idu said they would. Everyone who can walk slings the wounded over their shoulders, carrying them toward the way out. "We need immediate extraction. Is anyone nearby?"

Ava works on getting the airlock door open.

"Only if you don't mind treading water," Warden radios back. "We have a few boats picking up survivors. I don't have a readout. How high are you?"

"We're at least two miles up!" Mannering says as Ava releases the locks on the hatch.

Addison braces against the wall as a strong burst of air fills the gap. She inches over to the ledge to see the dangerous waters below.

"Are there any aircraft?" Ibrahim cycles.

"Grounded if it's not destroyed," Warden returns, an uncharacteristic crack stressing her words. "The blackout still has a stranglehold on our equipment. And I haven't heard if crews are trying to spin up available rotors, so I wouldn't count on them to save you."

"We don't have time to wait," Addison asserts. "We'll have to jump."

"Our suits are damaged," Ava disagrees. "They may not protect us from the impact!"

"This high up? Hitting the water is like jumping on concrete," Ibrahim warns.

"You saw what happened to the fleet. Either we jump now or wait on a bird for pick-up," Addison says. "It's your choice! But I wouldn't hold my breath for a random pilot to rescue us." She marches up to Ibrahim and stares him down. "We don't even know if there *are* pilots left."

Ibrahim's chest expands, and he shivers as he works the issues through his head.

"Okay . . . We're jumping," he decides. "Mannering! Ready the wounded for impact. They won't enjoy this."

"I should've kept my parachute," Mannering spits.

"Go feet first," Warden offers over the channel. "Trust me."

"Is everybody ready?" Ibrahim asks. "Jump on three . . . Standby?"

"One," Addison whispers.

"Two," Ibrahim follows.

BOOM.

The ground shakes as the dreadnaught whirls to life. A soldier jumps through as if responding expediently.

"Who was that?" Addison asks.

"James," Ibrahim remarks. "I never took him as a swimmer."

"Is he alive?" Ava questions.

"Don't know," Ibrahim shrugs. He keys his comms unit. "Aquoia! Still alive?"

Several moments pass before they get a response. "Yes, sir," the marine answers. "Next time, sir, why don't you give me a push? Scared the shit out of me."

"I will certainly keep that in mind, Private," Ibrahim confirms. "He's alive. Who's next?"

The ship erupts again—BOOM, BOOM, BOOM. Addison takes the initiative and jumps. She grits her teeth on the way down, feeling the sting as her body hits the water. The alarms go off again, suggesting damage to the armor's middle and outer layer weaves. Her bad arm falls out of its brace, with her suit reacting like it's detected a fracture.

Addison's ears pop as she attempts to reorientate her body while the noise blares inside her helmet. Powerful waves drag her under the water. Addison hits her head on debris floating in the ocean, putting a crack down the center of her visor.

A hand comes and pulls her up. Addison yelps, clinging to Ibrahim as he swims her away from the ship.

"Hey, hey, hey—you're okay!" he shouts. "It's okay . . . I need you to breathe right now. Breathe in, like that, and now, out through your nose. Slow and steady, okay? Do you understand me? Breathe. Seawater has gotten into your suit's systems. It's clogging your air intake. You will drown if you don't slow down."

Addison knows what he's saying, but she panics, thrashing violently. Ibrahim wraps an arm around her to keep her restrained.

She doesn't know what happens next, except that she passes out. Addison eventually wakes up on the deck of a patrol cutter. Ibrahim rushes beside her, working with engineers to get her out of the hardsuit. Once they release the locks, the man lays a reflective blanket over her shoulders and carries her to a medical cot below deck.

"You're a miserable ass sometimes, you know that?" he says.

"Thank you," Addison laughs, only to cough when her jaw tightens.

"Keep that on and stay warm," Ibrahim says. "I'm going to see the captain."

Addison nods and finds a seat on a bench, feeling the pressure on her chest dissipate.

More survivors join her from the water—soldiers, sailors, workers, and scientists. She watches them as she dries, all of them exhausted or injured. The crew does what they can for them, offering them food and blankets. So many were treading water for hours, waiting for rescue before this patrol found them.

An explosion knocks the ship sideways.

Addison leans up to look out the viewport, catching the dreadnaught abruptly roar and flash, erupting into the air with the grace of a flying whale.

She falls back into her seat and breathes. Addison has done her job. Idu 'Smeora has kept her promise and left Earth with the Summerland.

"Doctor Kennedy? How are you feeling?" a medic asks, checking on her. "Difficulty swallowing?"

"Well, I nearly drowned," Addison coughs. "Not the worst part of my day."

The medic presses his palm on her abdomen. "Any swelling? Shortness of breath?" he asks.

"I need to pee," she answers.

"All I can offer is a bucket," the medic explains. "You were in the water for a while."

"How many others made it?" Addison asks.

The man lets out a long breath. "A few boats are looking for survivors," he says.

"Hundreds? Thousands?" she demands. "How many?"

"I don't know," the other admits.

Addison looks away and clears her throat. "I'm good," she says.

"Are you sure?"

"Others need you more," Addison tells him. "I'll be fine."

The medic nods, finishing with her and moving to the next survivor down the line.

Addison feels the pain in her arm as she works her fingers into a fist. Now it's her job to get a handle on everything that comes next, whatever that means. She only hopes to make sense of this mess and all the lives they sacrificed along the way.

She lays her head down and spreads out over the cot, closing her eyes and allowing the ship's rocking to soothe her asleep.

Addison releases her bladder. It's not like anybody will judge her for it after today.

ADION 'KLAKA, NOMAD OF AMELIORATION
REBEL OF THE OBLIGATION

521031 LOCAL CLUSTER | 761,407 DAY OF PURPOSE

He snuck away while the others were busy giving speeches to muster their courage.

Stepping into the Entrychamber again brings with it a jubilant sense. For Adhion 'Klaka, it's like coming up for air after being trapped underwater. Yet, the lake is cold and oppressive. No warm hands will reach in to pull him to safety should he lose himself in the depths.

And the Trident never sullies his palms with a Nomad's taint.

Tyrann 'Akachan will have loyalist Varmajalkavaen close to him to protect the bridge alongside Fragment Alimentors. Can the humans charge into this fight and win? He does not know. But the Nomad seals the entrance to buy him time to finish what he started.

He regards the Trident at the far end of the walkway, floating on his platform. "Are you waiting for me?" Adhion whispers. Tyrann watches the display as it covets the chamber, admiring the Final Protocol as it works to finish off the human occupation of the surrounding waters. Survivors remain adrift, calling for help that won't come. "I ask you to look at me. Look at me! I demand it."

Approaching the Trident, Adhion waits until the other turns his head.

Tyrann's expression goes from shock to fast anger.

"I see you," he notions, switching off the planetary view and drawing his spear. "You come again?"

"To ask you to stop this," Adhion returns. "The Whisperer has the Heart. There's no need for this slaughter! Please?"

'Akachan frowns.

"Hearing you say 'please' is like a churel asking a dactyl not to eat it," he goes. "There's too much blood in the water, Adhion. You started this. I didn't. You could have ended this long ago but chose to hide instead! You picked apart our resources, wanting to destroy a system that raised you."

"I had to force your hand," Adhion admits.

"If the worm lies warm," the Trident says, "it does not change things."

"Dhun and Tjaa are dead!" Adhion fights.

"Because of you!" Tyrann roars, his voice bouncing off the chamber's stark walls.

Adhion's jaw drops. "You honestly don't understand why I have done what I've done, do you?"

"Obligation demands we serve in our proper stations," Tyrann argues. "You fight against your inbred ill nature."

"And how are you any better? Look out there! They die because you chose to do the unthinkable."

"I am clearing the way for ignition," Tyrann exclaims. "Any of them too close when the ship takes off will die anyway. I might as well prevent them from helping *you* murder what's left of us." He steps off his platform, landing hard as a warrior-king in a room built for giants.

"You're not all that's left," Adhion tells him.

"Idu is a traitor," Tyrann says, looking away. "Her time for judgment will come, the same as yours."

"Tyrann . . . The Obligation doesn't demand this!" Adhion warns.

The Trident slams his fist against a pillar, his feathers a mix of red and black. He turns violently at Adhion, the glint of his eyes gone, replaced by untampered shadows.

"It's you! Always you!" he shouts. "Killing? That is all your race is good for—slaughtering the cattle."

"That's not—"

"Your history speaks it! A killer who wears a killer's skin . . . That's all you will ever be!"

"I am not—"

"And now you gift a fire to primitives?!"

"I acted! And I do not regret it," Adhion iterates.

"Yes. You do," Tyrann accuses. "That regret sinks into your very being. You reek of it. Why come back if you didn't?"

"Obligation demands that I clean up your mess," Adhion mocks, stepping forward, ignoring the guards as they react to counter him. "You have no idea the ruin you leave behind when you fail, do you? Why do we create life only to abandon them when they need us most? We should see it thrive! But if they don't meet your expectations, what happens? You decide to clean the slate and start over again. And that duty falls to those like me. It hardly matters if a species wants to live, am I right?"

"Careful now," Tyrann growls. "You near speak heresy."

"And I know it," Adhion contends.

"Then why?"

"An ancestor once showed an aptitude for violence," Adhion justifies. "You look down on us like some . . . genetic disease?"

"A curse on our template! It needed direction."

"My life was always 'soluble' by the Powers-That-Be, wasn't it?" Adhion sulks.

"Yes. And now you make a final stand. At the head of these . . . humans?"

"The necessity of change," Adhion asserts. "A history born of war and famine. We have that in common, I do think."

"Common? Like an udvar to a gestarel," the other sneers. "You'd find more kinship with the dirt!"

"I learned to accept that long ago," Adhion defends.

Tyrann snarls and lunges forward with his spear, aiming at the Nomad's chest.

Adhion sidesteps, grabbing a nearby Fragment and using its mass to deflect the cheap shots the Trident and his loyalists throw at him.

After, he drops the machine, leaving it broken, smoking, and worth little more than slag.

"Shut them down!" Adhion shouts.

"You do not tell *me* what to do!"

Tyrann lunges again.

Adhion catches the other's spear mid-thrust and strongarms the Trident to his knees.

"Have you ever killed anyone with your own hands?" Adhion mocks.

Tyrann shows his teeth as he lifts Adhion with great strength and throws him into a strut.

Adhion hits it with a loud CLANK. He attempts to get back up, but the Trident strikes him in the throat and chest, knocking him off-balance. The Nomad rebounds, breaking hard to the right to get off the back foot. Only it doesn't work. The other seizes his arm and kicks his legs from underneath him, causing Adhion 'Klaka to crash to the floor.

Tyrann 'Akachan moves fast to pin him in place, pressing a knee into his spine and forcing a foot into the back of his neck.

"You slaughtered the domestic chattel," the Trident snarls, "while I fought the true enemy!"

Around them, the loyalist Varmajalkavaen close in to cut off his means of escape.

Adhion twists and churns, fighting to redirect Tyrann's hold on him. His movements are precise, leveraging his weight to pull the Trident down, using the momentum to smash the other's battle helmet on the ground, splitting the mask down the nose. Neither the High Echelon nor their master could stop the reverse.

The others pour over Adhion and drag him off their master.

Tyrann yelps as he clamors to his feet, ripping off his cowl and revealing the intricate white tattoos on his face.

Adhion swallows as the Trident's feathers turn a fierce blood-red hue. Even the Varmajalkavaen draw back a step, wary of a temper that could eclipse a star.

"You are selfish," Tyrann coldly stirs. "Have you ever seen the aftermath of when we allow disasters to propagate?"

"I have witnessed those fires many times," Adhion answers.

"Yes. To ensure the galaxy heals after suffering our mistakes," the other poses. "A forest will die if the old doesn't burn, allowing new growth to feed on sunlight. That is what the Obligation demands, Nomad of Amelioration. All we can do is build a gentler path for the young seeds to follow."

"Then we must choose whether or not to walk it ourselves," Adhion utters.

"The universe is an unwelcoming place for those who look beyond mere discovery," Tyrann disheartens.

"And it frightens you," he accuses.

Adhion breathes, closing his eyes and mustering the last of his strength. He throws off the Varmajalkavaen holding him, charging through the rest toward the Entrychamber's deep recesses—accessways to the ship's inner workings that run throughout the superstructure.

He can't win alone, and the humans are likely now close. Adhion's only choice is to draw off what forces he can so that the others may succeed.

"Nomad?! What are you doing?" Tyrann demands, the ship cracking at his voice. "Stop him! Adhion!"

Adhion descends, but his feathers frill as the heat rises from underneath him. These passageways don't have enough space for an Arkkitect, so it's tight and uncomfortable. He barely manages to squeeze his shoulders through, almost as if the Fragments that carved these trenches didn't think a sentient being would use them to navigate around the ship.

At least he has more room to maneuver than the Trident as the taller one jumps down after him.

Adhion leads the most dangerous chase through the narrow passageways.

"How far are you willing to go?!" he calls back, crawling farther into the cracks.

"You can't escape!" Tyrann 'Akachan shouts.

Adhion lets out his breath. No. He's not trying to escape. What's important is getting the Trident away from the Entrychamber before Idu and the humans arrive. They might have done well against Dhun 'Ancod and Tjaa 'Neren, but those two were only retainers of the Obligation.

Tyrann 'Akachan isn't like either the Judge or Servant. He's proud. Righteous. And he has the entire dreadnaught at his command.

Adhion strains from the exertion, maneuvering quickly through the tight turns, going deeper into the recesses. But for a system where Fragments mostly float through on their way to work on the ship's vital systems, the idea of comfort or practicality never crossed the minds of those who pulled the original asteroid from space and used its husk to create a working vessel.

Ahead, there's a scampering inside the ducts. Adhion stops and looks up, realizing the error.

Adhion frees an arm and drags himself into a narrower passageway adjacent to the primary trench.

As he climbs, the Varmajalkavaen emerge behind him in a large, black mass.

"You cannot run forever!" Tyrann yells, his voice ripping into the shaft.

"I am not trying to," Adhion whispers, looking down, but the heat in the passage rises faster. Adhion climbs, reaching a hatch and pressing a palm to its surface. "End of the line." The loyalist Varmajalkavaen flood toward him, racing to keep him from opening the hatch. They're too late. He does. And he seals the exit behind him.

The loyalists crash into the portcullis, screaming, telling him to let them out. They quickly understand the danger of entering the tunnels after him.

"Adhion?!" Tyrann shouts from the other side. He pushes through the Varmajalkavaen, shoving his defenders out of the way and letting them fall down the shaft. They die with high pitch shrills, all for a being that doesn't care about their lives. "What is this? Let *me* through!" He slams a hand into the separation, creating a ringing that quickly stifles.

"I will not do that," Adhion refuses, holding back his tears.

"You are a coward!" Tyran accuses him.

"Maybe? But I needed you away from the Entrychamber," he says. "We have won."

Adhion frowns. Idu, Addison Kennedy, and Colonel Ibrahim should now be reuniting the Heart with the core. He can only hope.

"You are going to kill me? Me?! I let you live!"

"No. You passed sentence on me," Adhion whimpers, wrapping his fingers around the grate. He closes his eyes as he lays his forehead on the ground, the heat drying his face, causing his feathers to curl. "I asked you to stop, but you didn't! I asked you . . . I asked . . . And we failed the test, our dark hubris—the choice to live or let live."

"I have done nothing but my duty!" Tyrann shouts, desperate, his voice tremoring.

"Just as I did mine," Adhion murmurs. "For centuries! People need to hear a different story. One that is harder to believe."

"Their judgment won't be so kind!"

Adhion spins around and lies flat on his back. "Maybe. But I am done with butchery," he whimpers. "No more failure! No more taking back the life we create . . . We can do more . . . We *should* do more! I may not change much, but for those who come after us . . . It's a better start than I had in a hundred generations."

The heat from the exhaust spills violently through the grate now. It burns Adhion's hand as he touches the hatch. He looks briefly to see Tyrann's skin shrivel and blister. His armor cannot protect him from the superheated temperatures rising from the core without the Heart to mediate the energy.

"They will always see y-you as the enemy," the fading Tyrann murmurs. "They w-will see you . . . the enemy . . . always an en-enemy . . . H-how can they not?" He repeats the words several times before he gathers his strength for one last insult. "K-killer." Then, he stops, unable to speak anymore, but the word echoes into Adhion's ear like a steady drum.

Killer . . . killer . . . killer . . .

Tyrann's skin cracks and pales as he cooks alive. The fight is over, but a sense of guilt hangs over the two Architects—the Trident and the Nomad.

"Then I am the enemy," Adhion grants, shutting his eyes and taking a deep breath.

But in the peace of the moment, Adhion clenches his fist and grabs onto the hatch, unwilling to let it end like this. He tears the divide as a great plume of heat expunges from the ship's center. The Trident reaches out, and Adhion takes his arm, pulling him up before the wave envelopes them, and they fall back some distance, with both grousing as they hit the floor.

Unable to lift his arms, Adhion looks at Tyrann next to him, the other appearing smaller now than he ever had.

Stunned and seared, Tyrann 'Akachan swallows, unsure what to do. The Varmajalkavaen swarm into the corridor from the opening, with many of them dropping to the ground, exhausted. Adhion sits up and looks at them regretfully, knowing not all of them will survive their wounds.

"You spared me?" the Trident asks.

"It is time we learn to fly again," Adhion tells him.

Tyrann frowns, attempting to sit up with some dignity, but can't do more than roll onto his back.

Adhion shakes, not knowing why he's pulled Tyrann 'Akachan from the brink of death. It's not because he thinks the Trident is lying . . . On returning home, the Nomad does *not* expect forgiveness. How can he after this? Despite his many centuries of service, Adhion deserves *no* mercy for his actions.

"Why?" Tyrann demands.

"I don't want to be a killer," Adhion shudders. "I told you."

"You can't so easily change what you are," Tyrann warns him.

"Because the Obligation demands it?"

"We don't choose our roles. We're born into them."

"You believe that, even after all this horror?"

Tyrann finally sits up with pain in his motions. "Maybe not," he admits.

"We've all done things that deserve punishment," Adhion decides. "No matter what is said, we all have a choice."

"And you made yours?" Tyrann asks.

"Yes," Adhion affirms.

'Akachan surrenders a burnt smile before dropping back to the ground. Adhion stays next to Tyrann to comfort him, the world spinning as time seemingly halts. He can feel the ship's heartbeat as the energy causes the hull to vibrate, the air cooling like a summer mist washing over them. Even the Varmajalkavaen out of the vents applaud the change as they sort through the injured.

"Was this worth it?" Tyrann quietly asks.

"Only if it makes a difference," Adhion decries.

"Change is never easy," Idu speaks, stopping at their heads to regard the tired warriors.

They both look up to admire the beautiful creature as she hovers over them, clearly struck at seeing the two of them alive.

"Still breathing after all this, Whisperer?" Tyrann meekly laughs.

"I did what was necessary and salvaged some sanity in the chaos you two unleashed," Idu tells him.

"What happened?" Adhion asks.

"A human sacrificed herself to reunite the Heart with the Vili," Idu confides.

"Addison Kennedy?"

"Zhu Yunwen," Idu explains.

"And the others?"

"Making their way to the exit now."

Adhion's feathers fade to a dirty grey, unsure what to say. The Varma-jalkavaen look to them, now hurrying to help the Trident stand. Still, they maintain a clear distance from Adhion and Idu. To the loyalist, the pair remain traitors, apostates to the Obligation. And they wouldn't be wrong in that confidence.

"And how long until we can reignite the engines?" Tyrann demands.

"Until there's nobody left aboard," Idu decrees.

"And you came here looking for me?" Adhion asks.

"Yes," Idu acknowledges.

Adhion pauses to breathe. "To kill me?"

Idu frowns, surprised by the notion.

"I am not a killer," she answers.

"But you would not have been upset if we had killed each other," Tyrann weighs, not mistaking her words.

"It was my choice to do the right thing for all of us," Idu explains. "Now, I need you two to help me steer this ship back home."

"And what will you do when we get there?" Adhion asks.

Idu kneels to him and takes his hands. She holds herself there for a while before turning to the Trident.

"I will testify to the Grand Opera," she warns. "I will tell them what you two did."

Adhion has a hard time meeting her gaze.

"I was protecting our traditions!" Tyrann defends.

"You are no less guiltless for your crimes than *he* is," Idu resolves, shaking her head before stepping toward him. "No matter what, the others can't ignore this act of rebellion. After what we lost, they'll be willing enough to listen. Can we stop this from ever happening again? I don't know. But I can't do it alone."

"Many will reject the idea outright," Tyrann warns her, coughing as the air clears.

"They'd call it heresy," Adhion feigns.

"And that is the risk we must take," Idu settles.

"You would risk open war? Our very way of life?" the Trident charges.

"Today? I witnessed the most courageous act of a sentient being in service to another," Idu praises in a warmer tone. "All for *us* to go home."

"They need to hear the truth," Adhion affirms.

"And I won't rest until they know it," Idu agrees. "That is the promise I make."

RESCUE | 81

MALAKAI ADONIS, DIRECTOR OF OPERATIONS
EPIMETHEUS PROJECT

OCTOBER 27, 2041 | 1150 HOURS

Leighton and Malakai stay on the ledge for hours, unable to move. Ice on their sleeves turns to mush as the midday warms a few precious degrees.

Together, they watch as the fleet burns in the distance. And as the storm grows, making it harder to see the embers and steel, Malakai counts half-a-dozen hulks slinking under the waves. He can hear the desperate cries of surviving crewmembers fighting to stay aloft.

"Jesus Christ," Malakai decries, sullying the name. "Please, help them."

He struggles to stay awake as the air becomes colder, but it's tough. Malakai tucks his hands into his pits, using his collar to protect his face against the strong ocean winds.

They didn't have time to grab protective suits, leaving them open to the elements while only wearing their daytime fatigues.

As the Fragments retreat into the dreadnaught, Malakai holds his breath. He blinks disbelievingly. Only when the ship's engines roar to life, and the shockwave causes the oil rig to shake and tilt that he lets out a pitiful sigh.

After weeks of studying and exploring the vessel, the dreadnaught lifts off the ocean's surface.

"How many people do we still have aboard?" Leighton asks.

"I don't know," Malakai frowns. He breathes into his palms for some warmth.

"If any of them survived—?"

"They're either dead or still hiding," Malakai notions.

"Or jumped into the water," Leighton adds.

"Either way," Malakai pivots, "we can't help them."

Malakai pounces at the chance to get back inside. They've stayed trapped on the Olympus' railings long enough.

"Let's use the airlock this time," Malakai suggests.

Leighton nods. "Watch your step," he says. "It's slippery here."

"Got it," Malakai returns, carefully skirting the edge.

The two make their way to the main catwalk and find a door. The warmer air inside causes Malakai's cheeks and fingertips to tingle. Bodies are everywhere. "Not again," Malakai murmurs.

"Is anybody still alive?" Leighton coughs, padding his arms to thaw.

Men and women, security officers, and facility workers have all dropped over each other—no survivors, no wounded.

"This is hard to look at," Malakai admits, his voice trilling.

He doesn't want to see the bodies of his people—co-workers and employees.

"Look there," Leighton says. He's pointing at the far end of the hall, where a couple of Fragments lay shattered. "At least the battle wasn't entirely one-sided, eh?"

Malakai grimaces. "Are you trying to make me feel better?" he whimpers.

"I only want to give us some hope," Leighton frowns.

"Please don't," he tells him.

The two explore the deck but don't find anybody until they reach the Control Room. Or . . . at least, signs that others *had* survived elsewhere.

"Do you hear that?" Leighton asks, looking around the room.

"A beeping?" Malakai confirms.

"It's coming from over here," Leighton points.

He goes to the relay output station, where the Air Traffic Controller usually sits for long shifts.

She's now dead on the floor with glass in her throat and heavy burns to her upper torso.

Leighton puts on the headset and flips through the frequencies.

"Computer looks intact," Malakai notes. "Good news?"

"Comms are lively with chatter!" Leighton describes. "We've got distress calls, ID beacons, and navy officers coordinating rescue operations!"

"The entire works," Malakai whistles through his teeth. He falls backward into a chair and forgets to breathe.

Then, he cries. Snot drips from his nose, and water in his eyes blinds him. Malakai uses the inside of his sleeve to dab his face.

Leighton remains steadfast, riffling through the available channels.

"Yes, sir," Leighton responds to a hail. "On the Olympus. Any word from response crews?"

"Leighton?" Malakai asks, leaning forward.

"Give me a second," the man returns.

"Take whatever time you need," Malakai accepts.

The Fragments shot out the Control Room's walls and windows during the attack. Now the cold leaks in from outside.

Malakai gets to his feet and peers out the damage. "The rain's stopped?" he whispers.

"What?" Leighton asks.

"Stormfront's breaking apart!" Malakai says louder. "Or maybe I am only stating the obvious."

He stares at the sun peeking through the clouds.

Leighton looks at him with bright eyes. "Comms are online," he says.

Malakai watches the parting clouds a few seconds longer before stepping away.

"Athena—do you read me?" he asks through his comms unit.

At first, there's static, but that quickly goes away, replaced by a friendly, synthesized tone.

"Doctor Adonis? Like the crescendo of an orchestra," Athena says. "It's good to hear your voice."

"Thank God!" Malakai laughs. "What's the mission's status?"

Athena takes a moment to think. "Situation terminal," she answers. Malakai closes his eyes, deciding to prop himself against a table should he faint. "Patrols are combing the water for survivors, although they don't have anywhere to go. Navy leadership isn't responding to hails. And no word on preparations by the mainland to mount rescue operations to the quarantine zone."

Malakai glances at Leighton, who remains silent as he listens.

"What about our people on the dreadnaught? How many made it out?"

Athena takes another pause . . . a longer one, this time. It's a deliberate choice on her part, Malakai imagines. And not because she needs to run the numbers.

"A few teams have returned 'all-green' signals," Athena begins, "but most are inconclusive."

Malakai grimaces. He can guess what that means. Some rigs can't read or send back identifiers, suggesting those bodies might've left with the dreadnaught and moved out of the Overlook's range. They're not only dead, but they've gone off-world, forever lost.

"Give me your totals," Malakai says.

"Numerous," Athena responds.

"Stop trying to skirt the bad news!" he demands, wanting a more accurate count.

The AI pauses again for a heartbeat. "The USS Isaac Bennett had a complement of six-thousand active-duty crew," she describes. "Thirty-four thousand casualties with an unknown number of wounded across the zone. A few hundred confirmed survivors. Want me to go on?"

Malakai's temples contract as he bites down on his molars. "No," he admits, touching one of the melted entry wounds in the walls.

He switches on his emergency beacon and leaves for the upper landing platform. Leighton follows him without saying a word. It takes another hour for a rescue boat to answer. The noise breaks through Malakai's comms unit, with instructions on when to expect a pickup.

Malakai notices the air outside is now warmer. Without the rain, it's a welcomed change.

Their boat sends a flare to indicate their location below. The pilot steers the craft to the oil rig's underside.

"We're here, Director Adonis," the officer-in-charge tosses a ping. "And hurry! We've got more stranded out there."

Malakai sends a return signal before climbing down the ladder with Leighton.

"Thank you for the lift," Harlow offers his appreciation.

"Welcome aboard the USS Maryacks," the first officer greets him, helping them to the deck. "Just you two?"

Malakai looks up the ladder, letting his thoughts linger on the bodies littering the rig's hallways.

"As far as we can tell," Malakai answers.

"Damn our luck," the officer says. He instructs a marine squad to climb the ladder and conduct a deck-by-deck search. The soldiers respond quickly and ascend to the oil rig's main structure. "Unfortunately—we can't wait for them. We still have people overboard, and many've been treading water for hours. They're exhausted. We need to get to them before it's too late."

"Of course," Malakai agrees. "Do what you need to do."

The officer frowns. "I just wanted to clarify that with you," he says. "We're in a bad spot. Now, find a seat. It's a bumpy ride."

Malakai nods and sits beside a survivor who smells like a latrine ditch.

He notices a heavily armed squad standing watch over another man across the deck, wrapped in a silver blanket. Malakai leans over, fighting the boat's violent shifts, deciding to tap one of the soldiers on the shoulder. "Excuse me?" he asks.

"Director Adonis?" the trooper says. "Good to see you still have your lunch."

"I didn't eat. Not that I had a choice," Malakai acknowledges. "You seem familiar . . . Do I know you?"

"Oversight Security, Special Operations Intelligence," the trooper confirms. "We're a part of the task force that raided Camp Yi."

"The task force? You survived! Alexandra Roslin, is she—?"

"On another boat, I think," the trooper tells him. "Our teams lost contact with each other."

"And what about Doctor Hao? Did he make it out?"

The trooper gestures at the man with the silver blanket covering his face and shoulders.

Malakai narrows his eyes. Without speaking, he crawls until he reaches the man, removing the blanket with a strong yank.

"Hello, Adonis," Hao retorts, not even surprised to see him.

"Wensu," Malakai returns coldly.

"You're alive?"

"Seems that way."

Hao abdicates a vain grimace. "Guanyin? Please forgive me," he prays.

Malakai raises an eyebrow. "Are you okay?" he asks.

"You and me? We've survived the worst of it," Hao answers, offering a calm gesture, but there's no denying a trembling in his chest. Malakai looks at him, a broken man with bruises on his jaw and neck. "And it appears I have *you* to thank. Begrudgingly. I am only alive because of the brutes you sent to arrest me. Others . . . weren't so lucky."

"You attacked us," Malakai states. "Roslin had to respond."

Hao shakes his head wearily. "You must understand, I was desperate," he confides. "After the Central Spire Incident, everything went bad for us. We lost our network node a few days later. And we couldn't collect data and send it through the system. We fell behind. I had to take action to settle the difference."

"Are you . . . confessing?"

"I am," Hao admits. "And if you're willing, I can help make it right."

Malakai frowns. "I honestly think that's the least of our worries right now," he infers.

"Maybe," Hao weighs lazily.

"Inquiries will happen. Answers demanded," Malakai tells him. "People will need scapegoats."

"That's already happened," Hao suggests. "Men like us will be on the chopping block."

"Why didn't you just ask me for help if you needed it?"

Hao reels back as if he's laughing inside. "And risk embarrassment?" the man iterates. "Nothing in my country is seen with so much aversion than judgment by the world. Our first rule in foreign affairs? Stay away from the limelight. Do *not* attract attention if you plan to live to a ripe old age."

"A lot of people died for nothing that night," Malakai tells him.

"Even more died today, don't you think?" Hao rebuts.

"I can't promise how this will turn out."

"All of us will have demons to face once we return to civilization."

"Oddly enough, we've already found our guy to blame."

"Senator Holland?"

Malakai clenches his jaw. "So, it's true? You used him," he accuses.

"Assured contingencies," Hao admits. "We planned for the worst-case scenario."

"It doesn't matter. We'll learn about the consequences once we're home."

"My government will likely request my extradition."

"You may not be around very long should you go back."

"Oh, I wouldn't doubt it's a health risk."

Malakai crosses his arms and looks intently at the man. He's sitting taller on the deck, red in the face, and exhausted. After the Summerland crashed, when Malakai assembled his leadership team, the United Coalition told him to accept Wensu Hao as the Chinese Field Director. Despite better candidates on the table, Malakai agreed to the resolution.

Every nation had an intrinsic need to cooperate more than at any other time in history. Navigating the dense political landscape was the job Malakai always wanted. He thought the challenge was acceptable, but now he understands what happens when he trusts the wrong people. And desperation forces the brightest minds to make the dumbest decisions.

"I'll see what I can do," Malakai promises, coming to a quiet arrangement.

"That's all I can ask," Hao weeps. "We're survivors." He pulls the silver blanket over his head again.

"Sure," Malakai whispers, collapsing onto a bench. "Survivors." He closes his eyes and falls asleep to the ocean waves beating the hull.

ADDISON KENNEDY, FIELD DIRECTOR
UCSN OVERSIGHT COMMITTEE

NOVEMBER 11, 2041 | 0830 HOURS

Deliberations continue while Addison waits to hear their response.

The committee's members talk amongst themselves—men and women dressed in expensive suits and patterned coats. Primsuits. Several of them even glance in her direction. Sometimes angry. Other times? She can't quite put a name to the glares.

Addison is the last to give testimony on recent events.

James William Harper sits across the table from her. He patiently listens to the others, only speaking when he needs to steer the discussions away from outright shouting matches. It's all he can do to protect Addison and the rest of the leadership team who've sat in to answer the Council's questions this past week.

Addison shifts in her seat awkwardly, scratching the underside of her arm brace.

"With all the money these people spend," Addison monologues, "you'd think they could buy comfortable chairs."

"Doctor Kennedy—" Ambassador Mersley intercepts. "Do you need to add to the inquiry?"

Addison's eyes shoot up to the woman. "No, ma'am," she answers.

"On with the issue at hand," Harper states. "We can't officially shield Wensu Hao without provoking Beijing."

"And why protect him? What's the point?" another asks.

"He submitted to our custody in good faith," the debate rages, but little of it concerns Addison.

"He's also responsible for ordering the attack on the Olympus!"

"We can't let that go unanswered!"

"Everybody else involved with the incident is dead, missing in action, or hospitalized."

"We're still tallying those numbers," explains an analyst of the aftermath. "Let's not get ahead of ourselves."

"And what about Mr. Holland? Somebody leaked his private records onto the internet."

"Public opinion has already shifted against him," Harper explains. "Even if we push for a trial, his reputation will lock him to the backbench."

"Henry was the Chairman of the Oversight Committee," Mersley states. "I want us to do everything we can for him."

"Colonel Ibrahim didn't have the authority to arrest Senator Holland in the first place," denounces a lawyer in the room. "It goes beyond this body's legal mandate! The Ultracapitalist Party won't tolerate defamation of one of their own. We have the President's full backing to push for an investigation."

"Malakai Adonis had the authority," Freda Geraldine iterates. "OverSec took him into custody."

"And only *after* we received evidence of Holland's alleged criminality," Harper defends the motion.

"Which forced us to make a decision," Geraldine adds. "All perfectly legal under the Global Security Act."

"I'd like to see you argue that in court!" Holland's advocate pushes.

"And whose jurisdiction does this case even fall under? The Americans? Japanese? British?" Harper demands.

"I doubt we can find one that can remain unbiased of his actions," Geraldine weighs.

"A lot of people died on that oil rig," another laments.

"No more than in the disaster afterward!" Mersley speaks out.

"True enough."

"You're perverting the underlining context," James Harper eases, pressing his palms against the table. Addison watches him let out an unsteady breath as exhaustion eats away his patience. He's sat in on these hearings for days now, and Addison wonders how much more the man can handle. "We can't very well prosecute aliens from the other side of the galaxy now, can we?"

"You'd throw Holland to the wolves to protect traitors for their incompetence!" the advocate growls.

"Luckily enough, we don't keep wolves on call anymore," Harper chuckles, "last I checked."

Addison coughs loud enough to get the room's attention. She's had enough of them talking as if they were there when they lost thirty thousand people. "We did what was necessary," she argues. "We completed the mission and solved the riddle at the center of this crisis."

"Thousands are dead!" the advocate fires back.

"Millions," Addison corrects. "But nobody else could have done what we've—"

"Doctor Kennedy—" Alexandra Roslin cuts her off, setting a hand on the table. "I want to clarify for the record. But it *was* your actions and your decisions that expedited the situation to its breaking point. Do I have that correct?"

Addison swallows.

"I don't think—?" she pauses.

"You allowed yourself to interact and observe this Idu 'Smeora without precaution or supervision," Roslin concisely states. She flips through a case file as she talks, only glancing up to peer at Addison with a stone-faced expression. "Some have called that reckless. Others? Ambitious."

Addison squints at the woman with contention.

"Director Roslin, forgive me," Harper stops her. "What's your point in this branch of dialogue?"

Alexandra scowls annoyingly at the Secretary-General.

"My reason is . . . We can point fingers all we want, but it doesn't change the opportunities available to us," Roslin derides. "Going after our allies—or our enemies—is counter-productive at this stage. The crisis is over, and there are more challenges ahead. How much data did we collect on the alien vessel and its technology?" She looks at Addison as she asks the question.

Addison steals a moment to think. "That's still getting sifted through," she says. "The Codex—?"

"Is enough to ignite a revolution," Roslin encourages.

"What do you mean?" Harper demands.

Alexandra Roslin's lips turn cold and unapologetic. "Only that we've got a rare chance to spread our wings," she hints. "As we rebuild, we can steer assets into unlocking the data that Malakai's team collected on the Summerland."

"That isn't how we make progress, Director Roslin," Harper mentions.

"No. That's exactly how we innovate," Alexandra refuses. "And that's what we've always done, Secretary Harper. What do you think we designed the Epimetheus Project to do? Its mandate clearly defines the objectives. Number one—find a way to get the ship off our planet. And two? Catalog any useful alien technology for our benefit."

Roslin winks subtly at Addison, and she returns with a weak smile.

Members of the Security Council cordially nod their heads.

"Doctor Kennedy—thank you for the testimony," Geraldine offers.

"You can go," Harper dismisses her. "Seems we have a lot to discuss."

Addison lets out a breath with a tired nuance.

She rises to her feet and leaves through the door behind her. Once in the corridor, she turns right toward the grand lobby. That's where her team is waiting anxiously to hear about her experience with the politicians.

"That took only a notch shorter than mine," Malakai says.

"I'm pretty sure they forgot I was sitting there once or twice," Addison admits.

"Primsuits," Ibrahim scoffs.

"Roslin took our side," Addison informs them.

Malakai's eyes light up gladly. "That's better news," he says. "I didn't expect the woman to keep her promises."

"Roslin was there?" Ava asks, sitting on a bench, listening unenthusiastically.

"She wasn't in for your hearing?" Malakai asks.

"She was, but . . . I don't go out of my way to ask her opinion," Ava returns.

"Yeah. Roslin was quiet throughout my session, too," Ibrahim notions. "Didn't know she was there until she spoke up near the end."

"Roslin enjoys the chaos," Vogert shudders. "It makes her feel powerful."

Addison raises an eyebrow.

"That's true," Ibrahim agrees.

"She's made strong inroads for increased security on the international stage," Malakai explains.

"Seems opportunistic," Leighton says.

"Seems more like a power grab," Ava counters.

Addison notices Sergeant Major Olivia Warden alone in the corner. She hasn't spoken much since coming out of her hearing the night before.

She catches Ibrahim glancing at the woman as they converse, always a sad look in her eyes without her helmet to hide her face. Warden had found herself in the middle of the attack when the Fragments swarmed over the METIS Research Base and killed her troops. The ship that rescued her did a lot to collect survivors from the water. It was also the last the mainland's recovery operations had picked up. Addison doesn't doubt those days on a glorified raft on the open water left a toll on all of them.

"What about our guests?" Ibrahim questions.

"In a safe location," Malakai says. "Let's discuss that *after* we leave here."

"Fair enough," Ibrahim agrees. "The last thing we need is Roslin locking them away in the Rocky Mountains."

"Did they mention what's going to happen to Wensu Hao?" Leighton asks, specifically of Addison.

Her eyes snap to the man.

"They're still undecided," she determines.

"Likely more worried about the long-term fallout and public outcry," Malakai weighs.

"All those people? All that equipment?" Ibrahim furrows. "I don't know how we can recover those losses."

Malakai smiles proudly at him. "Oh, we'll rebuild," he says. "You shouldn't worry about that, Colonel. It's what we do—humanity's appetite. Our saga *is* rebuilding from the ashes we create. Summerland's Folly was only the most recent test—an obstacle to overcome. Now that we're through it, we can finally hit the next challenge head-on."

"And what challenge is that?" Warden speaks, taking a deep breath, wary of the answer.

Malakai points up at the vaulted ceiling. Addison steps back and follows his finger to the top.

"The only viable direction we *can* go," he urges.

A WORLD IN CRISIS

DISASTERS IN THE PACIFIC SHATTER NATIONS, THOUSANDS UNACCOUNTED

September 24, 2041

A 12-mile-long extra-terrestrial construct breaks through the Earth's atmosphere. The object crashes into the North Pacific Ocean early morning, 1,500 miles off the coast of Papua New Guinea. Global disaster and immediate mass casualties catch world leaders and their governments unprepared. The subsequent tidal waves caused by the ship hitting the ocean creates massive flooding across native coastlines along the Pacific Rim, submerging island-nations, and whole cities on the mainland in the process.

September 25, 2041

Arthur Summerland is the first to lead an expedition into the alien object, equipped with only a small research boat and an efficient but professional team of like-minded scientists and explorers. Dr. Summerland approaches the construct by noon. Arthur is a known cold-weather explorer with several tours conducted on Antarctica's recent South Pole missions. He was preparing for an expedition into the Northern Artic when the colossal object hit the Pacific Ocean.

September 26, 2041

With death tolls rising, world leaders convene at United Coalition Headquarters in New York to discuss solutions to the crisis. Meanwhile, the United States 7th Fleet arrests Arthur Summerland as his expedition returns to the mainland after its illegal foray into what he calls an "alien craft." Members of Dr. Summerland's group report feeling ill and are put into strict quarantine by military officials. Due to their trespassing on the extra-terrestrial object, the Special Operations and Intelligence Division (SOI), headed by the agency's director, Alexandra Roslin, confiscates Arthur Summerland's data as part of an ongoing investigation into the event.

September 27, 2041

Malakai Adonis, an environmental science professor with close ties to humanitarian support groups, manages to pull strings in the American Government to talk with Arthur Summerland at the Naval Hospital at Camp Pendleton. At the time of this article's publishing, Adonis refused to comment on why he wanted to meet with his counterpart. According to an interview released by the World News Organization (WNO) with Dr. Adonis, Malakai, later in the afternoon, would describe the massive alien construct responsible for killing millions of people worldwide as "Summerland's Folly."

September 28, 2041

Dr. Malakai Adonis' public statements earlier today urge a public outcry for the United Coalition of Sovereign Nations to continue where Dr. Arthur Summerland and his expedition left off. Adonis' argument pushes for increased support by leading governments worldwide to organize an international effort to solve the "Summerland Crisis." Dr. Adonis spoke at a press conference on the steps of UCSN Headquarters in New York City to describe, "The Immediate need to quarantine the Ground Zero Site." He went on to talk about wanting to "board" and "study" the "alien craft" and to "discover the reason behind [its] arrival." Addressed in his speech, Adonis insisted that "We as a species must initiate first contact procedures" and "uncover technology that could propel humanity into the next half-century." Adonis' speech was followed up with confirmations by military officials that the object that hit the Pacific Ocean was indeed a craft of alien origin.

September 29, 2041

Today a full session of the United Coalition General Assembly convenes to debate the ongoing global disaster, WNO reports.

James William Harper, Secretary-General of the UCSN, instigated talks with the United Security Council to begin hearings, weigh options, and strategize a remedy to the Summerland Crisis.

With an estimated 6 million dead, and that number continuing to rise, world leaders and their ambassadors weigh into the summit for consideration.

According to International Daily—Malakai Adonis, a former environmental scientist, announced he will attend the first round of talks to advise the summit of the scientific community's viewpoint on proposed solutions.

September 30, 2041

The North American Congress meets on Capitol Hill, Washington, D.C., to initiate talks on national solutions to the crisis. The emergency session directly responds to the week-long pressure by the Seymour Administration to opt for an "American First" strategy over global endeavors.

Opponents to the administration's rhetoric lambast President Seymour on the floor of the House.

Speaker of the House, Kenneth Thrifton (D-CA), argues that any effort to solve this crisis would require the United States and its resources to make headway. Dr. Malakai Adonis, a growing proponent for intervention, echoes statements made by House and Senate democrats.

Meanwhile, the United Coalition of Sovereign Nations' General Assembly votes to put forward the Adonis Contingency.

The Assembly unanimously

approved an expansion to the Security Council's primary operating jurisdiction to provide the organization with the resources necessary to tackle a crisis that has killed over an estimated 6 million people worldwide.

October 1, 2041
Caucus Leader of the Ultracapitalist Party, Henry Holland (U-WI), dissented after the Senate passed the Global Security Act. In statements made, Senator Holland clarified how he wants the United States to handle the Summerland Crisis without submitting to the Epimetheus Project.

Ambassadors of the General Assembly justify their plan, releasing a statement signed by 192/193 of its member states which says in part: "To protect ourselves, our planet, and our future, we must act now without nationalistic politics costing us more lives by doing nothing."

It was a scathing rebuke of America's Ultracapitalist sentiments that have survived since the country's civil strife in the mid-2020s.

October 2, 2041
U.S. President, Robert Parker Seymour, offered his public support to Senator Henry Holland's (U-WI) remarks.

"Our nation must stand by itself or lose its sovereignty," the president said to reporters inside the White House press briefing room.

In statements made, Seymour threatened to veto the GSA if the

motion were to reach his desk. He went on to describe taking more drastic steps if "Congress fails to kill this Global 'Insecurity' Act." Seymour would continue by saying, "I will sign an Executive Order that will have the army come riding in with tanks to occupy Washington."

Advisors in the administration and other key officials refused to comment on the statements made by the President.

October 3, 2041
Arthur Summerland dies at the Naval Hospital at Camp Pendleton, California. After the President's remarks yesterday, protests against a potential military occupation of the nation's capital erupts in the streets.

Early this morning, the House voted in a full-member session while tuning out the growing number of fights between protestors in the streets. The Global Security Act proceeds to the President's desk with a supermajority, leading many to question whether or not the POTUS will turn his threats into action.

As rhetoric mimicking 20-year-old wounds cast a shadow over Washington, Congressional leaders are ready to move forward with their plans. International efforts are already underway to solve a crisis that has killed an estimated 7 million people worldwide while the United States repeats its dark history.

October 4, 2041

President Robert P. Seymour signed the Global Security Act into law today after his allies urged him to compromise on the legislation. Administration officials say the President will appoint Susan Mersley as U.S. Ambassador to the Joint Security Council. Mersley stated her reasons for accepting the position are an innate desire to oversee American interests protected in the expanding international community. The legislation that passed overwhelmingly by Congress yesterday will allow the United States to allocate its resources to solving a deadly crisis that has killed over 7 million people worldwide.

Meanwhile, lawmakers criticize President Seymour's decision to march U.S. troops into Washington, D.C. The President's threats reportedly shook many Administration officials and close advisors when he made them in the prior days. He signed an Executive Order at a ceremony that left the room with an awkward tension for those in attendance. The order would grant unprecedented military jurisdiction to conduct operations on native soil and against American citizens.

Those favoring the order argue the Army's troops can better handle the violent protests erupting in the nation's capital than what local or federal law enforcement agencies can provide after decades of defunding efforts.

Senator Henry Holland (U-WI) released a statement praising the President's occupation of the capital but expressed his disappointment that Seymour would allow the GSA to pass without a more substantial bulwark to: "Protect our nation's great sovereignty."

October 4, 2041

Today, the United Coalition General Assembly issued the United Coalition Armed Forces Treaty to merge the world's leading military powers and centralize resources in managing the Summerland Crisis.

October 5, 2041

Intense negotiations begin today as China, the United States, and twenty-four member nation-states, formalize the UCAF as a world peacekeeping organization.

Under the treaty's ratifications, member-states are required to supplement the international military force with operating funds, equipment, and soldiers.

Secretary-General James William Harper congratulated the diplomats and negotiators central at the peace talks:

"We've done today what the League of Nations and United Nations failed to do at their height," Harper spoke in front of the General Assembly.

October 6, 2041

The Security Council today began confirmation hearings for the Project's key leadership team. Several names included on the list made public by Project Director, Malakai

Adonis, are scientists at the top of their respective fields. Among the list are doctors: Addison Kennedy (USA), Ji-Young Lee (South Korea), Sir Theodore Parker (UK), Alexa Bree (Australia), Susumu Aoki (Japan), Yvette Fluchet (EU), Jules Pasteur (EU), and Wensu Hao (China).

These names represent the collective brain trust the United Coalition has decided to invest into the Project.

Adonis spoke of his choices at a press conference at UCSN Headquarters in New York City:

"Our Team is one that will invest in the overwhelming challenges we'll face once we reach the Summerland."

In an interview later in the day, Adonis said he is still considering some prospects for his leadership team. He said during the interview that once his Field Directors are approved, they can begin the arduous work of filling out the ranks of the Epimetheus Project.

"We are working twenty-four hours a day to meet the deadline set for us by the Security Council," Malakai described. "Every hour we waste is time that costs us more lives. We can't let that happen."

Later in the interview, he discusses the timetable in the upcoming days:

"Our plan is to launch on October 10th, with the expectation of reaching the site by October 11th. We are scrutinizing the data Arthur collected, which is proving invalu-able to prepare us for the dangers ahead. That information will save lives as we work alongside world militaries to protect our assets."

When asked about what dangers he is expecting to face on the Summerland, Adonis responded:

"The cold is a tough one. That'll be a killer," he said. "We're getting ready to counter that, of course. We are hoping for a peaceful first contact with the ship's inhabitants, but we've not heard anything from them as of now. So, we don't know how they'll react to our presence."

The confirmation hearings for Adonis' inner circle are on public broadcast to allow for transparency in a process.

Meanwhile, along the Pacific Coasts of more than 50 nations, bodies continue to be found in the rubble of Los Angeles, Seattle, Sydney, Manila, Hong Kong, Shanghai, Busan, Hamamatsu, and Wellington—an estimated 8 million casualties and counting.

October 7, 2041
Military briefings for the confirmed members of the Epimetheus Project are underway in Vancouver. As reported by the World News Organization, these are the first rounds of strategy meetings between Dr. Malakai Adonis, his staff, and leading military officials assigned to the Project.

Among the officials that will appear as "boots on the ground" support for the Project and its workers is Lieutenant Colonel

Elias Ibrahim of the United States Marine Corps, on loan to the United Coalition Armed Forces. Lieutenant Colonel Ibrahim will be the field commander in charge of the American troops aboard the Summerland while the mission is underway.

In preparation for Launch Day on October 10—resources, personnel, and materials are being trucked en masse to depot sites for loading onto what's quickly becoming the largest fleet ever assembled by an international group. The sight of warships mooring at the limited functional ports on the west coast of the United States has attracted many onlookers as the ships prepare to set off in the next few days.

October 8, 2041

International Daily reports today that soldiers, firefighters, scientists, construction workers, sailors, and more, begin arriving today at Project Offices in San Diego and Vancouver.

Dr. Malakai Adonis at a press conference early in the morning said that they will begin undergoing orientation and procedural instruction for Launch Day. Further news ahead.

October 9, 2041

Alexandra Roslin—Director of the United Coalition's Special Operations and Intelligence Division—meets with Dr. Malakai Adonis as he begins justifying his strategies to the North American Congress. Dr. Addison Kennedy, the daugh-

ter of U.S. Fleet Admiral Jonathan Kennedy (commander of the U.S. Naval Task Force attached to the Project), appeared on Capitol Hill to speak out against Ultracapitalist Party hard-liners opening independent investigations into the Project's Field Directors.

Senator Henry Holland (U-WI) argued that in his position as the highest ranked Ultracapitalist chair on the Project Oversight Committee, a position he gained without a formal majority in the Senate, that his goal is to put the American public's concerns to rest over joining a mission he's called, "a bloated whale."

ACKNOWLEDGMENTS

Some believe it's easy to write a story. For others, it often feels like a nearly impossible task—waylaid by delays, frustrations, and getting lost in the editing to where a writer can (and most likely will) change the substance of a scene at a moment's notice. And in the pursuit of this novel's development, I would like to thank those who helped me along the way: Dylan Capelle, a colleague and fellow writer, a friend whom I've come to appreciate as we debate the finer points of what makes a story worthy of attention; Cora Seibt, whose endless encouragement and bright demeanor is matched only by her faith in me; Natasha Geiger, a dedicated friend and the first to show interest in the project, and the first I had asked to read it.

I would also like to thank my family: my mother, Denise Collebrusco, a woman that has always stood by my side, even in my lowest moments; my father, Terry Collebrusco, who taught me that the greatest things in life aren't given out on a silver platter, but earned through sheer determination; my sister, Samantha-Marie Gregerson, who started me on the storyteller's path and always told the hard truths when nobody else would; my other sister, Liz Aldrich (whom I will always call Elizabeth), for always setting me right since we were young; my uncle, Mike Hostak, who encouraged me to write at a time when I still had a lot to learn.

Many others helped me along the way whom I would like to thank: Lisa Malak and Millaine Wells, two of the hardest working people I know, and who had given me a chance before I understood the challenges that awaited me; Tim Greenman, a man I consider a mentor in the field of broadcast; Mitch Pritchard, a friend who is never shy with his opinions, but whom I learned a lot from over the years; Brianna Daniels, a close friend whom I can always reliably share my frustrations with about the world; Julie Buck, who once sat across from me and offered me an opportunity that has stayed with me for over ten years; Richard Klindworth, whom I will always appreciate for the words that made me realize that I needed to push on, no matter what; Levi LaCrosse, one of the funniest men I know, and for taking a genuine interest in the ambitiousness of my stories.

www.ingramcontent.com/pod-product-compliance
Lightning Source LLC
Chambersburg PA
CBHW030844030726
47495CB00005B/1368